Orname

4

1909 – 1934

Chris Fogg is a creative producer, writer, director and dramaturg, who has written and directed for the theatre for many years, as well as collaborating artistically with choreographers and contemporary dance companies.

Ornaments of Grace is a chronicle of ten novels. *The Spindle Tree* is the fourth in the sequence.

He has previously written more than thirty works for the stage as well as four collections of poems, stories and essays. These are: *Special Relationships, Northern Songs, Painting by Numbers* and *Dawn Chorus* (with woodcut illustrations by Chris Waters), all published by Mudlark Press.

Several of Chris's poems have appeared in International Psychoanalysis (IP), a US online journal, as well as *in Climate of Opinion*, a selection of verse in response to the work of Sigmund Freud edited by Irene Willis, published by IP in 2017.

Ornaments of Grace

(or *Unhistoric Acts*)

4

Tulip

Vol. 3: The Spindle Tree

by

Chris Fogg

flax**books**

First published 2020
© Chris Fogg 2020

Chris Fogg has asserted his rights under Copyright Designs & Patents Act 1988 to be identified as the author of this book

ISBN Number: 9781698640457

Cover and design by: Kama Glover

Cover Image: Humphrey Chetham's Dream, one of the Manchester Murals by Ford Madox Brown, reprinted by kind permission of Manchester Libraries, Information & Archives

This book is sold subject to the condition that it shall not, by way of trade or otherwise be lent, resold, hired out, or otherwise circulated without the publisher's prior consent in any form of binding or cover other than that in which it is published and without a similar condition, including this condition, being imposed upon the subsequent purchaser.

Printed in Poland by Amazon

Although some of the people featured in this book are real, and several of the events depicted actually happened, *Ornaments of Grace* remains a work of fiction.

For Amanda and Tim

dedicated to the memory

of my parents and grandparents

Ornaments of Grace (*or Unhistoric Acts*) is a sequence of ten novels set in Manchester between 1760 and 2020. Collectively they tell the story of a city in four elements.

The Spindle Tree is the fourth book in the sequence.

The full list of titles is:

1. Pomona (Water)

2. Tulip (Earth)
    Vol 1: Enclave
    Vol 2: Nymphs & Shepherds
    Vol 3: The Spindle Tree
    Vol 4: Return

3. Laurel (Air)
    Vol 1: Kettle
    Vol 2: Victor
    Vol 3: Victrix
    Vol 4: Scuttle

4. Moth (Fire)

Each book can be read independently or as part of the sequence.

"It's always too soon to go home. And it's always too soon to calculate effect... Cause-and-effect assumes that history marches forward, but history is not an army. It is a crab scuttling sideways, a drip of soft water wearing away stone, an earthquake breaking centuries of tension."

Rebecca Solnit: Hope in the Dark
(*Untold Histories, Wild Possibilities*)

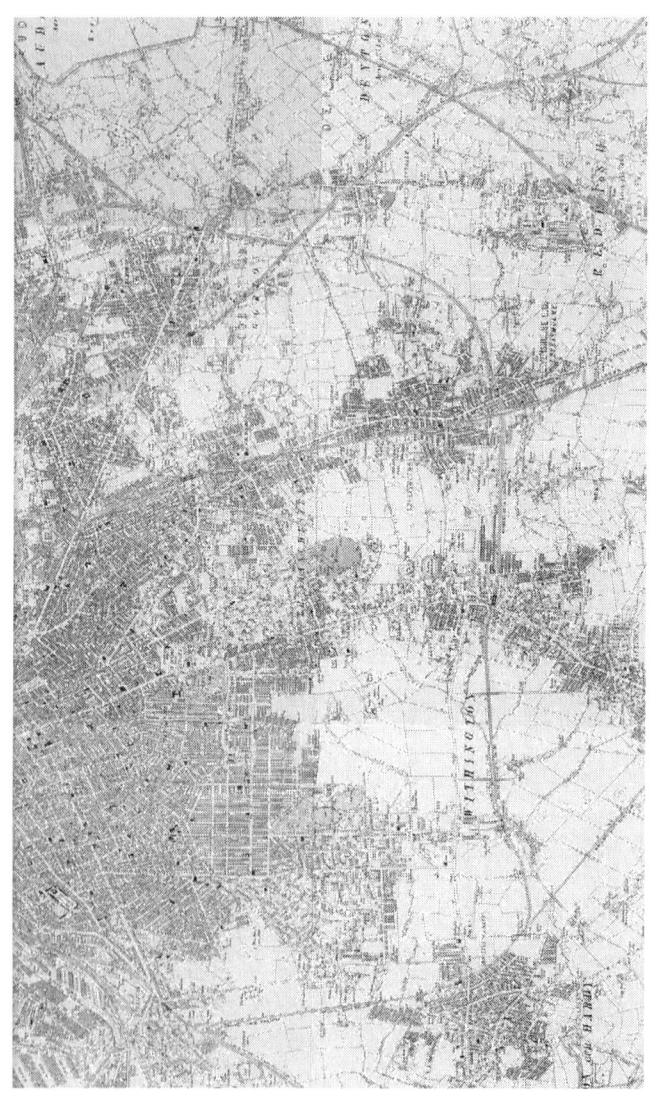

Follow Lily's run along the Nico Ditch
from Audenshaw Reservoir to Chorlton-cum-Hardy

Contents

Chapter 1: 19th May 1911 — 15

Chapter 2: 2nd March 1916 — 53

Chapter 3: 15th June 1919 — 167

Chapter 4: 5th July 1930 — 198

Chapter 5: 25th September 1930 — 477

Chapter 6: 24th April 1932 — 655

Chapter 7: 17th July 1934 — 675

Map: Nico Ditch — facing

Dramatis Personae — 751

Acknowledgements — 766

Biography — 769

Ornaments of Grace

"Wisdom is the principal thing. Therefore get wisdom and within all thy getting get understanding. Exalt her and she shall promote thee. She shall bring thee to honour when thou dost embrace her. She shall give to thine head an ornament of grace. A crown of glory shall she deliver to thee."

Proverbs: 4, verses 7 – 9

written around the domed ceiling of the Great Hall Reading Room
Central Reference Library, St Peter's Square, Manchester

"Fecisti patriam diversis de gentibus unam…"
"From differing peoples you have made one homeland…"

Rutilius Claudius Namatianus:
De Redito Suo, verse 63

"To be hopeful in bad times is not just foolishly romantic. It is based on the fact that human history is a history not only of cruelty, but also of compassion, sacrifice, courage, kindness. What we choose to emphasise in this complex history will determine our lives. If we see only the worst, it destroys our capacity to do something. If we remember those times and places—and there are so many—where people have behaved magnificently, this gives us the energy to act, and at least the possibility of sending this spinning top of a world in a different direction. And if we do act, in however small a way, we don't have to wait for some grand utopian future. The future is an infinite succession of presents, and to live now as we think human beings should live, in defiance of all that is bad around us, is itself a marvellous victory."

Howard Zinn: A Power Governments Cannot Suppress

Tulip (iii)

"You believe
in God for your part? Ay? That He who makes,
Can make good things from ill things, best from worst,
As men plant tulips among dunghills when
They wish them finest...?"

Elizabeth Barrett Browning: Aurora Leigh, Book 2

Earth (iii)

Meanwhile, at social Industry's command,
How quick, how vast an increase! From the germ
Of some poor hamlet, rapidly produced
Here a huge town, continuous and compact,
Hiding the face of earth for leagues."

Wordsworth: The Excursion, Book VIII

1

19th May 1911

Hubert Wright and Annie Warburton married each other twice.

Exactly a year to the day since the appearance of Halley's Comet in the clear night skies above Miles Platting to the east of Manchester's city centre, when Hubert had been so moved by the sheer wonder and spectacle of it that he had sunk to his knees and asked Annie to marry him then and there, and Annie had been so surprised that she had laughed at the sight of him down there on his knees on the cobbled street outside the house where she'd been born and lived all her life, before finally recovering herself sufficiently to say a breathless but delighted "Yes", the first of these two weddings took place.

Hubert was a Quaker and Annie a Methodist. Which were not such poles apart. Both were cut from a similar Non-Conformist cloth, both championed the poor, both fought for the rights of working people, took pains to provide basic education for all children, whatever their circumstances, and both sat outside of the establishment, radical advocates of self-help and self-determinism. But there were also fundamental differences. Quakers rejected the notion of a preacher to officiate between themselves and their God, whereas the minister was the very heartbeat of Methodism, harking back to their early days under John Wesley, whose passion and charisma helped win over so many converts initially. Curiously, however, before the Marriage Act of 1836, Quaker marriages were legal, where Methodist marriages were not, although both were still subject to the Anglican prejudice, which dismissed the Act as the Broomstick Act, under which couples who married outside of the Church of England were disparaged as 'living in sin', or 'under the brush' and, as such, should not be recognised.

For Hubert and Annie the differences were more personal. Hubert had discovered Quakerism for himself. He was a printer. Like his father before him. When he was still a boy, learning the trade, one of his father's jobs had been to print leaflets for the Friends' Meeting House on Mount Street, just off Peter Street, close to Albert Square, in the centre of Manchester.

One day he asked Hubert to deliver these by hand. Hubert knocked on the rather surprising, imposing front door of its gracious, neo-classical façade. The sound of it, the solidity of brass upon wood, gave Hubert a reassuring sense of weight and strength. When nobody answered, he stepped inside and was immediately struck by the calmness and simplicity of its plain, unadorned surroundings, offering a haven from the teeming city streets just beyond its doors. He sat down on one of the wooden benches and looked around. Its high ceilings, its white-washed walls, its tall graceful windows, all lent an atmosphere of lightness and welcome. He felt comfortable, able to pause, and breathe. He sat in easy silence for some minutes before a door opened, and another man entered, acknowledging Hubert with a quiet nod before sitting down himself in a separate space within the room. It took Hubert a while to realise that he was in the place where what he would later learn were called 'meetings' took place. This was after he had made the unfortunate *faux pas* of interrupting this other man's private thoughts by asking him if he was the person to whom he should hand over the leaflets his father had asked him to deliver.

Apologising for the intrusion, Hubert left the man in peace and exited via a different door in search of someone else to ask. Having eventually delivered the leaflets, he made his way back home clutching a different one in his hand, full of information about the activities of the Mount Street Meeting House, which he stopped to read, sitting on a low wall overlooking the Rochdale Canal at Sebastopol Court. He learned that Quakers didn't follow any neat creeds or doctrines, that, although it originally grew out of Christianity, it now incorporated values from other religions too. He discovered that typically meetings began in silence, that out of silence came stillness, and that through stillness a path was opened up to greater wisdom and understanding. Quakers, he read, felt no need for a priest to act as intermediary between themselves and God, and that individuals were encouraged to speak whatever was in their minds, as the spirit moved them, or, if they preferred, simply to stay silent. Hubert found himself drawn towards this notion of egalitarianism, of everybody equal under God, and he responded powerfully to the Quakers' rich tradition of social intervention, how they had campaigned to abolish slavery, how they supported women's suffrage, how they, believing that all human life was of equal worth, were fundamentally against war.

The more he read, the more Hubert found himself instinctively in tune with Quaker values, and as he continued his walk back home along George Leigh Street, to the junction of Poland and Portugal Streets, where his father's printing works were housed in a warehouse on the Crown Industrial Estate, he promised himself to return to the Friends' Meeting House on Mount Street and find out more.

The Friends' Meeting House
Mount Street
Manchester

Living What We Believe

Who Are We?
We are The Religious Society of Friends, sometimes known as Quakers.
We were founded as a Radical Christian Movement in 17th century England.
We come from all walks of life.

How Do We Meet?
We hold Weekly Meetings for Worship when we come together in silence to share our thoughts and experiences, our 'testimonies', as we call them.
We have no paid clergy to lead us.
It is open to anyone who feels sufficiently moved by the spirit to make a spoken contribution.

Who Can Come?
Everyone is welcome at our Meetings for Worship.
Why not join us?
Wednesdays at 6.30pm

Printed by F.G. Wright & Sons

*

Annie lived on Corelli Street, in the heart of the triangle bounded by Hulme Hall Lane, Lord North Street and Clifton Street, in the shadow of the railway viaduct which carried the trains from Oldham to Ashton, in what was known as the Tripe Colony. Hemmed in by the range of mountainous slag heaps from Bradford Colliery on one side, with the iron and steel works on another and the giant Manchester Brick Factory on the third, this was her whole life. Sunlight rarely found its way into Corelli Street, having to negotiate both the high factory walls plus the thick, sulphurous pall of smoke they collectively produced, along with the clouds of brick and coal dust kicked up by the feet of all who lived and worked there, which swirled in plumes and eddies, invading every nook and cranny, crack and crevice of the Colony during the summer, sinking into a verminous sludge of ankle deep mud in the winter.

At fourteen Annie left the rough and tumble but relative security of Nelson Street Elementary School to start work at the Tripe Factory. At half-past five each morning, the knocker-up would stretch his long, padded pole up to the bedroom window at the front of their house and rap three times sharply to rouse the family, although Annie was usually well awake before then. She'd lie shivering in the bed she shared with her sister listening for his footsteps echoing up the cobbled street while the sky was still dark. Then she'd reluctantly scuttle downstairs to where her mother would have heated a kettle for enough water for everyone to wash their faces before leaving the house with a crust of bread to stave off at least a little of the pangs of hunger she always felt. She joined the rest of the working women in the Colony made their slow procession, scarves tied tightly around their bent heads, the long mile along Forge Lane to Howarth Street and Pendlebury's Tripe Factory, the wooden soles of their clogs marching in step like weary soldiers, striking up sparks from the wet cobbles.

Once there they hived off into their various sections, removing their head scarves and tying them around their faces, covering up their noses to mask at least a little of the pungent smells rising up from the enormous steaming copper vats, where the stomach linings of slaughtered cattle would be scraped, boiled and bleached in successive operations in order to be delivered as dressed tripe to the local butchers shops and market stalls. The factory floor was partitioned off into four separate areas where the workers dealt with the linings from the cows' four different stomachs – the *rumen*, from which flat, or blanket tripe was produced; the *reticulum*, from where honeycomb, or pocket tripe was extracted; the *omasum*, from where the book, or bible tripe was taken; and finally the *abomasum*, from which the much prized, highly sought after reed tripe was separated from the surrounding glandular tissue. In another building, the paunch, or hog maw, was cured from the linings of pigs' stomachs; and in a third, the heels and trotters of various animals were ground and processed. From whichever of the linings the tripe was taken, it would be boiled and bleached for up to two days before being finally removed from the huge vats, which would then need to be scrubbed and cleaned, requiring Annie and the other women to climb right inside them, armed with wire brushes.

Annie was part of the team working on the bible tripe, which would be served each day for lunch in Pendlebury's Canteen, the blueprint for the more than a hundred and fifty tripe shops and cafés they set up right across the city. Practically every street, it seemed, had a UCP (short for United Cattle Products) on its corner, and tripe was the standard fare for Annie and all the other families who lived in the Colony. Her mother would ring the changes by serving it raw with vinegar, fried or soused with an egg, boiled in a cheese and onion sauce, or, as an occasional treat, baked with spices as Muggety Pie.

Pendlebury's would organise an annual trip for all their workers the twenty-five miles to Wigan, to Vose & Sons' wood-panelled *Tripe de Luxe* restaurant, now part of the growing UCP empire, with seating for more than three hundred and live entertainment provided by *The Lounge Ladies Orchestra*, who played extracts from Gilbert & Sullivan, Johann Strauss and Franz Lehar, while the members of the Colony tucked into tripe sausages – minced tripe with suet, diced marrow, chopped parsley, eggs and milk, stuffed into sheep's guts and fried – served with boiled cabbage and mashed potatoes.

It was here where Annie first met Hubert. It was the summer of 1909. The trip to Vose's coincided with her eighteenth birthday. Hubert, she would learn later, was twenty.

Hubert had been invited as a guest by Pendlebury's, along with his parents, in gratitude for the printing their firm had been doing for them over the past year, in particular their development of the new trademark UCP design of the red oval label, which was attached to all of their products.

"Buy only where you see the Oval Red Sign," it

announced, underneath the UCP logo and the banner proclaiming it as 'The Sign of Purity and Quality', with an illustration of a smiling housewife holding out a plate piled high with dressed tripe. "Tripe and Cow Heels," it declared, "are delicious served hot or cold."

Annie and her mother found themselves seated at the same table as Hubert and Mr and Mrs Wright, with Annie next to Hubert, and they soon fell into easy conversation. It was rare for Annie to meet anyone from outside the borders of the Tripe Colony, and Hubert, with his stories of visits to different places right across Manchester, seemed enticingly exotic, a notion which would have caused him much amusement, had he known that this was the effect he had caused, for he regarded himself as quite the opposite, something of a recluse in fact, holed up as he frequently was for days inside the Printing Works, not seeing a second of sunlight, viewing the world instead through the lens of his loupe, as he pored over the metal linotype or, in those pieces of work which still necessitated them, the wooden blocks of letters that were Frank's, his father's, which he had inherited from *his* father, Gordon. Nevertheless, to Annie, Hubert represented an expansion of horizons, an imagined life outside the Colony, and she strove to pay him ever closer attention.

At this point *The Ladies Lounge Orchestra* began to play a popular selection of tunes from *Die Fledermaus*, for one of which, *The Laughing Song*, they were joined by the local *soubrette*, Miss Letitia Dring, who delighted the assembled throng with her coquettish rendition.

"*What a curious…*
Ha, ha, ha
Situation…
Ha, ha, ha

What a startling...
Ha, ha, ha
Revelation
Ha, ha, ha, ha, ha, ha, ha, ha..."

Annie and Hubert, along with the entire restaurant, decorously joined in with the sung laughter. This was then followed by a medley of themes from *The Mikado*. Annie watched Hubert contentedly tapping his foot in time with the different tunes, and it was this which gave her the idea.

The grinding work of scraping, boiling and bleaching the tripe at Pendlebury's ten hours a day, six days a week, fifty weeks a year, was already taking its toll, on her hands, her skin, her breathing and her chest. Her mother, not yet forty, looked closer to sixty and, like all the women in the Colony, was worn down to the bone. When Annie caught sight of her mother's reflection in the cracked mirror in the kitchen, she saw a glimpse of what she herself would become in all too short a time, for although each day at the factory dragged, seeming like an age, the years sped by, and she could see her youth disappearing like the dregs of fat draining out of the huge copper vats she tended there.

Her father and brothers endured equally tough lives down the pit at Bradford Colliery. Their childhood games of running up and down the towering slag heaps at the end of their street, then sliding down the tumbling scree afterwards, despite it being strictly forbidden, had given way to the harsher reality of nightly forages after dark to fill what had once been each baby's pram with illegally gathered sacks of coal.

Sundays were their only respite, when they would troop together as a family to the Hulme Hall Lane Methodist Chapel, presided over by the kindly Reverend William Lampton Appleby, who had conducted the wedding of Annie's parents and then proceeded to christen each of their children, Annie included, as they arrived at regular intervals. He understood the hard lives that all the members of his congregation endured, having been a miner himself, and his sermons never failed to stiffen their resolve to face each new week. When Annie said her prayers, which she did every night before going to bed, and asked God to bless her parents and siblings, it was the Reverend Appleby's face she pictured as she did so.

Chapel meant hymns and harvest festivals, Sunday School and Bible stories, Whit Walks and Wakes Weeks, outings to the seaside once a year, bring & buy and jumble sales, picnics in Philips Park, concert parties, whist drives, and the annual Spring Fête.

This year Annie had volunteered to join the Organising Committee. Listening to *The Ladies Lounge Orchestra* playing their selection from *The Mikado*, and watching Hubert's unabashed enjoyment of it, the idea came to her in a flash of inspiration. For next year's fête, they would have a Japanese theme, with a prize for the best costume, and she would suggest they go to Hubert's father's firm to print the posters and the tickets. She smiled and began to tap her own feet in time to Hubert's underneath the table, contriving for her own *petite* left foot to gently collide with Hubert's outsized right. He apologised for his clumsiness, Annie demurely looked down, saying she was sure the fault was hers, Hubert smiled back and resumed his tapping with even more gusto.

Printed by F.G. Wright & Sons

*

Hubert's parents were also Methodists. They attended the Chapel on Eggington Street, over towards Colleyhurst, little more than a mile away from Hulme Hall Lane. Since taking up with the Friends, Hubert had less time to involve himself as fully in the life of the Chapel as his parents, or as he once himself had, but he still attended the weekly Sunday morning service with them as often as he could, so that when he announced after supper one evening, shortly after the trip to Vose's, that he thought he might try the Chapel on Hulme Hall Lane, his parents Frank and Evelyn looked at one another but said nothing, guessing that there was probably a young lady involved.

This new pattern established itself during the autumn of 1909. Hubert continued to attend Chapel on Hulme Hall Lane, where afterwards he would walk with Annie through Philips Park the long way back to her home in the Tripe Colony. Not wishing to upset his parents by his absences from Eggington Street on Sunday mornings, he threw himself into the work of the Methodist Circuit Committee, which met weekly at Central Hall on Oldham Street, for whom his father regularly printed leaflets and other literature, including their monthly newsletters, to organise their various charitable works among the city's poorer districts. In these activities he frequently found himself working with people he recognised from The Meeting House on Mount Street, for the Methodists and the Quakers as often as not combined their resources to support the same aims, especially with regard to the establishment of Ragged Schools for children and Night Schools for adults.

Hubert began attending weekly meetings at Mount Street on Wednesday evenings. The same feelings which he had experienced on that first accidental encounter as a boy more than five years before continued to fill him with peace and calm every time he re-entered that light, airy, silent room. It remained for him an oasis of quiet stillness away from the daily din and clatter which filled his head from waking till sleeping each day. If it were not the incessant noise of the printing presses in the works, or the shouts of the men trying to make themselves heard above the machines' ceaseless pounding, it would be the constant jolt and jostle of the crowds and traffic he had to duck and dive and dodge his way between on his daily rounds to and fro across the city. As soon as he entered the Meeting House and sat himself down on one of its smooth, worn, honey-coloured wooden benches, he would feel the roar and clamour of all the day's demands begin to slip away from him one by one, like the shedding of a skin, so that when he left again, after an hour's peace and solitude, his step would be lighter, his mind clearer, and he would be able once more to take in his surroundings, note the distinctiveness of every road and building, observe the faces, gait and attire of the people he walked among, hear the music in all their different voices, rising up like birdsong, in this growing cosmopolitan city of the world. On evenings such as these, he would frequently take circuitous routes back to the family home on tree-lined Bignor Street, midway between Smedley and Cheetham Hill, just two miles from the Printing Works on Portugal Street, acquainting himself with every street, avenue and courtyard in between.

" *'This island's mine'*," he'd muse contentedly to himself, for he felt a great pleasure in knowing intimately every square inch of his domain, with no desire to spread his wings any further than his work would take him, which, like a bird marking out his territory, he would continue to expand at the same rate as the city itself – unlike Annie, who, he knew, was always looking for what might lie beyond the limits of her restricted horizon, hemmed in by the sunless courts and cellars of the Tripe Colony. She longed to soar, high above the confines of the factory chimneys of mills and foundries, the smokestacks of steel and coal plants, towards some sunlit upper realm, to add her own voice to the growing murmuration competing to be heard.

As he walked back towards home, the sun was setting like spilled printer's ink. Starlings were roosting on the ledges and rooftops. The city was hunkering down for the night. The myriad voices had grown quiet, but still they echoed loud and long in the back of Hubert's brain, urging him on, and he was once again reminded of Caliban, marvelling at the magic of the only world he knew.

"*The isle is full of noises,*
Sounds and sweet airs that give delight and hurt not.
Sometimes a thousand twangling instruments
Will hum about mine ears, and sometime voices
That, if I then had waked after long sleep,
Will make me sleep again. And then, in dreaming,
The clouds methought would open and show riches
Ready to drop upon me that when I waked
I cried to dream again…"

While work and chapel afforded Hubert all his social and financial needs, it was the silent communion he held each week with the Friends at The Meeting House, which provided him with an outlet for these more spiritual needs. They fed his never sated inner life, which teemed with unfulfilled imaginings.

Once, while walking with Annie one Sunday afternoon in Philips Park, he had tried to articulate some of these longings. She had asked him if he enjoyed his work, a question he found surprising, for he had never considered it. Printing was not a job, he explained, but a vocation. Was that because it was a family business, she wanted to know, handed down from father to son? Partly, he responded, but it was more than that, much more, he said. There was something intrinsically important about printing, he claimed, with added emphasis. What do you mean, she asked? The idea that anyone might actually enjoy their work, consider it important, seemed inconceivable to Annie. For herself and her mother at the factory, and her father and brothers at the colliery, work was a continuously deadening toil. Although people liked to talk about the dignity of labour, there was nothing dignified about trying to wash the stench of boiled tripe out of your hair, or watching your father cough up black phlegm from his lungs every night. Hubert tried to select his words carefully. Wouldn't you say, though, he asked, as gently as he could manage, that, bad as that undoubtedly is, it's preferable to having no job at all? She replied that she supposed it was, but that on some days she questioned this. She looked around her, stretching out her arms in the freedom that she always felt when walking in the park. Mustn't it be marvellous, she wondered, pointing to the houses that bordered the boundaries of the park, to live in a house with a garden, one that looked out onto even a single tree? Hubert nodded, saying nothing, thinking with gratitude back to his own house on Bignor Street, with its modest but most agreeable back garden, and the pavements outside lined at regular intervals with gracious sycamore trees.

He steered their talk back to Annie's original question. You asked me what I meant when I said just how much being a printer matters to me, he said. Yes, she answered. He hesitated. Let me try to tell you. Forgive me if what I'm about to say ends up sounding rather strange. This isn't something I've ever shared with anyone before. It's about a dream I had. Oh, said Annie, immediately perking up, I like hearing about dreams. Start right at the beginning and try not to miss anything out. Hubert smiled. Very well, he said. I'll do my best. Here goes…

"Have you ever been to the Town Hall," he began, "to view the Manchester Murals?"

"Yes," said Annie, pleased that she was able to answer in the affirmative. "Mr Appleby took us once on a Sunday School outing."

"Excellent," said Hubert. "Do you recall the one depicting *'The Trial of John Wycliffe'*?"

Annie screwed up her face. "Remind me what it looks like," she said.

"It shows a cleric, John Wycliffe," continued Hubert, "in sack cloth and ashes, standing on a wooden scaffold in 1382, with his arms crossed like this across his chest..." – Hubert demonstrated the pose and Annie nodded – "...while the Bishop of London sits on a throne in his rich, colourful robes and tall mitre on his head, about to pass judgement on him, when a lawyer steps between them, trying to intercede on Wycliffe's behalf."

"What was he supposed to have done?"

"That's just it," said Hubert, warming to his theme. "He'd begun a translation of the Bible from Latin into English, so that ordinary people could read it for themselves, rather than relying on priests appointed by Rome to interpret it all for them. But the authorities were reluctant to let go of their privilege or power, not surprisingly, and so they declared Wycliffe's actions, together with those of his followers, known as the Lollards, to be treasonous, and made him stand trial at St Paul's."

"Why were they called Lollards?"

"Apparently it's from a medieval Dutch word, meaning 'to mutter', for that is what they did. They read aloud from the scriptures in some sort of mumbling unison."

"That could just as well describe what we all sounded like in Bible Class," laughed Annie. "I'm a Lollard," she shouted, whirling around in a circle. "But what's all this got to do with us here in Manchester?"

"Do you mean, why was this scene included in the Manchester Murals?"

"Yes, I suppose so."

"Lots of people have asked that question."

"And how have they been answered?"

"Remember that man in the middle?"

"The lawyer?"

Hubert nodded. "That's meant to represent John of Gaunt."

"I remember him from school. Wasn't he something to do with The Wars of the Roses?"

"Yes. He was also the Earl Palatine of Lancaster and, as such, the King's representative here in Manchester. He defended Wycliffe against all charges, and so, in a sense, the mural depicts an early example of Manchester's Radicalism, taking on the establishment."

"Good old Manchester. What happened?"

"There was an earthquake. It shook the city so hard that the trial was abandoned, with each side claiming it was an omen supporting their own particular point of view. Wycliffe was released and was allowed to carry on with his translation of the Bible."

"I'm glad to hear it. But what's all this got to do with your dream?"

"You asked me to start from the beginning, and not to leave anything out – that's what I'm trying to do."

Annie smiled and spread her hands. "Right." She was enjoying seeing how engaged Hubert had become, how voluble, when normally he was so reserved, so quiet, speaking only in response to specific questions. She felt she was finally getting to see a glimpse of the man who was to be found beneath that polite restraint. To understand a man, she felt, one had to learn about his dreams.

"I don't believe in censorship. I never have. It seems fundamentally wrong to me that somebody else could dictate what I should or shouldn't be allowed to read. We should all be free to read what we like and then make up our own minds about it. Just as we should all be able to believe what we choose, even if that means choosing nothing at all."

"What do you believe in?"

"Freedom."

"Is that all?"

"But it's everything, isn't it?"

Annie opened her mouth to reply but then shut it again. "I don't know things like you do," she said after a pause. "But I do believe that we all have a right to be happy, don't you?"

"Yes," he said, "though what makes one person happy might make somebody else miserable."

"Like tripe," she laughed. "You either love it or hate it."

"I love it," pronounced Hubert, grinning.

"Me too," said Annie. "It's a good job too, for there's nowt else at our house."

Hubert took Annie's hand in his. It was the first time he had done so. Annie considered it, this intertwining of their fingers.

"I know what makes me happy," she said. "Or would do."

Hubert said nothing. Instead he waited for Annie to continue.

"Do you remember learning the Creed when you were in school?" she asked.

He nodded.

Annie began to recite automatically. " *'I believe in God the father, creator of heaven and earth, and in Jesus Christ, his only son, our Lord, who was conceived of the Holy Spirit, born of the Virgin Mary, suffered under Pontius Pilate, was crucified, died and was buried, he descended into hell, and on the third day he rose again from the dead. I believe in the Holy Spirit, the holy catholic church, the communion of saints, the forgiveness of sins, the resurrection of the body, and life everlasting. Amen.'* I said that every day for years," she continued, "like a parrot, my mind completely elsewhere half the time, thinking more about what my best friend Penny

Williams said to Margaret Ness about me fancying Ian Rogers – which I didn't by the way – or whether I'd be made to sit in front of Michael Bell again, who always tried to dip my pigtails into the inkwell, while my lips mumbled these words I didn't understand out loud, like one of your Lollards, and now, though I can still trot them out at the drop of a hat, I'm not sure I believe in any of them any more."

"Then why do you still go to Chapel each week?"

She looked back at him, shocked. "It's what I know," she said, with considerable passion and force. "I've been going there all my life. I was christened there. My parents got married there. The people who go there are our neighbours and friends. They're kind. We look out for each other."

Hubert nodded. Annie searched his face, trying to read his response, but still he said nothing, waiting instead for her to carry on. He liked listening to her talk like this. He doubted whether she had ever voiced such feelings to anyone.

"I liked school," she continued after she had composed herself once more. "Lots of the others didn't. They couldn't wait to leave. Not me. I knew what was waiting down the road. It was life everlasting, alright, day after day at the tripe factory, stretching out for years, like a prison sentence. Just keep your head down, my mother says. I've not looked up for four years. Not till now." She gripped his hand hard. "This is my creed now," she said. "I believe in a better life."

"Yes."

"A better life for me and a better life for my children – if I ever have any, that is." She paused again, looking down at their interlaced fingers. "I'm not clever like you are, Hubert. I've not read as many books or spoken to as many people. But what I want's the same as most folk. A nice house with a nice garden. Enough money to buy food and clothes. A family. A feeling that I'm wanted, needed, doing something useful. Someone to spend my life with, to ease my disappointments, look after me if I'm sick, share a joke with, read to me, tell my dreams to, grow old with. Someone to pass all this on to…"

They had reached the end of the Avenue of Black Poplars. Hubert led Annie away from the path, towards a stand of tall pines. Under the canopy of their spreading branches she leaned back against one of the trunks. He put his arms around her and kissed her.

Some time later Annie whispered, "Tell me your dream, Hubert."

Hubert felt uncertain now how he should proceed. The mood had shifted. That kiss had changed things between them. She had spoken about such strong, personal matters, while his dream, though deeply felt, seemed altogether too vague by comparison. She seemed to want to hear about it, though, and so he tried to fumble his way towards some kind of approximation of what he had felt when first he dreamed it. He'd not in fact tried to put what were just images, ideas, impressions into any sort of words before, and he worried that, once he tried, he might risk losing them altogether, like sand slipping through his fingers.

"Fifty years after Wycliffe's trial," he began tentatively, "a man in Germany invented the first printing press, and although that was almost five hundred years ago, I would still recognise it, for it's not so very different from the ones we use in The Works today. His name was Johannes Guttenberg. He too printed the Bible and, like Wycliffe before him, he wanted as many people to read it as possible. It was translated into many languages and widely distributed right across Europe. But not here in Britain, where it was banned. Then William Caxton introduced a version of Guttenberg's press to England and, for the first time, books no longer had to be copied laboriously by hand onto parchment or vellum, but could be printed on paper and circulated widely. He produced beautiful editions of Chaucer's *Canterbury Tales*, Aesop's *Fables* and *La Morte d'Arthur*. But no Bible, which was still forbidden. That had to wait for another half century before William Tyndale translated it from the original Greek and Hebrew manuscripts into English, what we now know as the King James Bible, copies of which were printed in their thousands by Miles Coverdale. But still the authorities tried to suppress it from falling into the hands of ordinary men and women, and Tyndale was executed."

Annie gasped. "Who knew that printing was such a dangerous profession?"

"It isn't any more – although you still have to take care not to get your fingers trapped between the rollers! But there's still a long way to go. Our thoughts may be free, but we have to be careful when it comes to speech, even more so with the written word, especially if that written word is printed, And even if we do manage to get these thoughts into print, where can people read them? Newspapers open just a tiny window. If we want something more, we need to turn to books. But books are not cheap. They're expensive to print and even more so to buy. Oh, I know we have free public libraries now – Manchester was the first city in England to build them – but they're not on everyone's doorstep…"

"I've never been to one, I don't know where the nearest one is."

"Cheetham Hill or Moss Side."

Annie shrugged and shook her head.

"And of course they can't stock every book that's ever been written. And even if they did, they'd have to cut down every tree there is, just to supply the paper…"

"Oh – I should hate that." She ran her hand along the trunk of the poplar tree they were still standing beside. "A tree is like a book to me. Better in lots of ways. Just imagine all the things they've witnessed, all the birds who've made nests in their branches, all the people who've taken shelter under them. Like we have today." She looked at him coyly from beneath her eyelashes. Hubert took both her hands in his.

"And this is where my dream comes in," he said.

"Tell me."

"I dreamed there was a great, round building, a temple, like the Pantheon in Rome, built here in Manchester, on St Peter's Field, where the church used to be, where the Peterloo Massacre took place, and this building was a library, which contained more than a million books, with mile upon mile of shelves, stacked one on top of the other, running around the perimeter. In the centre was an enormous domed reading room, its ceiling adorned with angels, with painted words issuing out of their mouths, and the words were from the Book of Proverbs, and they said: *'Wisdom is the principal thing. Therefore get wisdom and within all thy getting get understanding. Exalt her and she shall promote thee. She shall bring thee to honour when thou dost embrace her. She shall give to thine head an ornament of grace. A crown of glory shall she deliver to thee.'* And the centre of the ceiling was open to the sky, and the sun shone down through it, illuminating all who sat within. And in my dream, I was one of those sitting there. I looked up towards the sky, and as I did so, I was lifted upwards. I found that I was flying, high above the clouds, and once up there, I saw about me an even greater number of books, all the books that have ever been written in the world, and all the books that have yet to be written. They were as the stars in the firmament, countless and wonderful, stretching out into infinity, and they were all of them free. I simply had to reach my finger, up towards a star, touch it, and at once the contents of that book were delivered unto me. A great comet, a meteor shower of knowledge, raced across the heavens, leaving a trail of light behind it, for ever and ever, life everlasting. Amen..."

Back in their separate homes later that night, Hubert in

Bignor Street and Annie in Corelli Street, each lay awake in their narrow beds, thinking over what they had shared with one other about their innermost, private dreams. Unable to sleep, they got up and looked out of their respective windows into the darkness, which seemed to press upon them like a thick blanket. A single shooting star streaked across the sky, gone in a blink, almost before it had even appeared, as if it had never been. Each dared to hope that the other had witnessed it too.

Hubert found himself musing upon *The Tempest* once more.

"And, like the baseless fabric of this vision,
The cloud-capped towers, the gorgeous palaces,
The solemn temples, the great globe itself,
Yea all which it inherit, shall dissolve
And, like this insubstantial pageant faded,
Leave not a rack behind. We are such stuff
As dreams are made on, and our little life
Is rounded with a sleep…"

Printed by F.G. Wright & Sons

*

The year turned. 1909 gave way to 1910. Through the dark winter days, when, with the exceptions of Sundays, Annie hardly saw daylight from one week to the next, she was sustained by the thought of the Chapel's Spring Fête coming up in May.

Easter was early that year, falling on 27th March. In the weeks that followed Annie took particular note, during her walks with Hubert on Sunday afternoons in Philips Park, of the avenues of cherry trees as they came into blossom. She studied their shapes carefully and embarked upon a mass production of *papier-mâché* versions of the flowers in her back kitchen at home, storing them in piles underneath her bed. Hubert managed to find her a can of petroleum based pink paint, into which she dabbed each separate paper blossom. Hubert also exploited his father's business relationships with Platt Brothers of Oldham, manufacturers of cotton mill machinery, for whom they had done some printing, to loan the Satsuma ware tea set they had on display in their Board room. Platt's had a long-standing relationship with the Toyoda family of Kyushu, through whom they had built up quite a collection of artefacts from the Hashima province, perched on the southern tip of Japan, and they gladly offered the use of these too. Hubert cautiously selected the least valuable, most easily replaceable of these, just in case, posters, ginger jars, a bonsai tree. He also managed to acquire a silk kimono for Annie to wear, with which she was captivated. Through Platt Brothers, Hubert was able to contact Mr Mather, the manager of the Beehive Cotton Mill, in the courtyard outlined by Bengal, Radium, Naval and Jersey Streets, just across the way from the Wright's Printing Works in Ancoats. Mr Mather was a regular customer of Platt's, having bought a jacquard loom from them recently, and he was only too willing to let the Chapel borrow a bolt of cloth printed with Japanese designs, which Annie could see at once, how she might arrange along the length of the main wall of the Chapel Hall, where it would perfectly off-set the various stalls selling cakes and jams and biscuits, which so many of her neighbours had already promised to contribute.

The morning of the Fête dawned bright and clear, and Annie was up early, busying herself with the final preparations. In truth she had hardly slept a wink the night before, such was her excitement, and she was at the Hall as soon as Mr Eames, the caretaker, was unlocking the doors. The Reverend Appleby had decided to dispense with the usual Sunday morning service – which was just as well, for there was so much to do to get the Hall ready before people began to arrive at two o'clock – and to hold a more informal evening service instead, as the Fête came to an end.

When Annie was finally satisfied that everything was ready, she breathed deeply and looked around. The Hall had been completely transformed. With the bolts of cloth, the posters, vases, jars and bonsai tree, not to mention the cherry branches hanging from the ceiling, bedecked with the hundreds of *papier-mâché* pink blossoms she had been making on a near industrial scale for weeks, she could almost imagine she had been whisked far away from the crepuscular gloom of the Tripe Colony to an altogether more exotic land, filled with the light and colour she so ardently craved, even if just for a few hours. She was delighted with the effect they had created. She had discovered new talents she did not know she possessed and was deeply pleased. She hurried back home in order to get herself ready, where she found Hubert waiting for her, outside their front door, with a bunch of yellow chrysanthemums he had managed to persuade old Mr Chadwick to let him pick from one of the greenhouses in Philips Park earlier that morning.

"I thought, perhaps, for your hair?" he said, somewhat tentatively, offering her the small bouquet.

Annie thanked him before stepping inside, promising to see him later that afternoon.

"Have you got your own costume sorted?" she asked before closing the door.

Hubert replied that he hoped she would think so.

CHERRY BLOSSOMS

**Hulme Hall Lane Chapel Annual Spring Fête
On a Japanese Theme**

**Sunday 17th March 1910
Doors Open: 2pm**

Guest of Honour: Miss Agatha Aspinal

**Light Refreshments
Cakes Teas Biscuits
Sale of Home-Baked Produce
Crafts, Stalls, Tombola, Fancy Dress
(Prize for Best Costume)**

**Musical Entertainments
featuring
Popular Local Favourites**

**Proceeds in Aid of Manchester Workhouse
&
Missions Overseas**

Printed by F.G. Wright & Sons

The Reverend Mr William Lampton Appleby warmly welcomed everyone as they arrived, who gazed in wide-eyed wonder at the transformation brought about on their Chapel Hall by the efforts of Annie and her team. Shortly before half-past two he rang a small bell and called for everyone's attention.

"Ladies and gentlemen, boys and girls, welcome to this year's Hulme Hall Lane Chapel's Annual Spring Fête 'on a Japanese theme'. I am sure we are all amazed to find ourselves transported from The Tripe Colony of Miles Platting to the Land of the Rising Sun this afternoon, and we are indeed fortunate that the same sun is shining down on us today, blessing us with such warm and pleasant weather. Who says it always rains in Manchester? I am sure you would all like to join me in thanking everyone who has worked so hard to make this Spring Fête possible, but especially Miss Annie Warburton, whose idea this all has been. Thank you, Annie."

The Hall broke out into spontaneous applause with occasional shouts of "Hear, hear!" Annie, now dressed in her silk *kimono*, acquired for her by Hubert, with her long hair pinned up high with knitting needles and a chrysanthemum tucked behind one ear, blushed appealingly as she acknowledged everybody's thanks.

"And now," continued Reverend Appleby, "it gives me great pleasure to introduce our Guest of Honour, Miss Agatha Aspinal. Miss Agatha was one of the first people to welcome me when I first arrived here, more years ago than either of us care to remember, still wet behind the ears from the seminary, with not much of a clue as to what I was meant to do. The first thing she did was to take me for a walk, introducing me to every single street, not just in the vicinity of our Chapel here at Hulme Hall Lane, but of our sister Chapel at Barmouth Street, where her brother, Neville, was minister for so many years, and who we all now miss so dearly since his recent passing. No doubt some of you have already heard the news that, in honour of his great service to our community, the local Elementary School is to be named after him. I cannot think of anything that would have pleased him more, for children everywhere loved him, as did we all."

Several voices murmured their agreement with the Minister at this point. "Ay," they called. "A great man."

Reverend Appleby raised his hands for quiet before carrying on.

"When Miss Agatha first showed me round our adjoining neighbourhoods, pointing out the various landmarks and places of interest, she kept up quite a pace, I can tell you…"

Small ripples of laughter in recognition spread about the Hall.

"...I tried my best to keep up, but it was no use, and soon I found myself trailing in her wake. 'Time and tide wait for no one, Reverend,' she said. 'You'll soon learn that here.' And of course, she was right. 'Just follow my red umbrella,' she added, raising it with a flourish, before setting off furiously once more. I believe we've all of us had occasion to follow that red umbrella over the years, have we not?"

"I have it still," declared Miss Agatha, an even doughtier, more formidable figure now she was in her seventies, and everybody roared with appreciation as she brandished it playfully towards Mr Appleby.

"I am reminded of a remark my good lady wife made to me shortly after we first met. It was the occasion of a Dinner Dance at The Methodists' Central Hall on Oldham Street. I saw Gladys – Miss Hinckley, as she was then – sitting on the opposite side of the ballroom floor. I plucked up the courage to ask her to dance, only realising too late that I had no idea how to dance at all."

"He still doesn't," called out Gladys to everyone's great amusement.

"But she somehow managed to steer me round without too many mishaps or collisions. 'There,' she said, as the music finished, 'that wasn't so bad, was it? We got round!' Well – that is how I now feel when I look back to my early days here when you were all so kind as to make me feel so very much at home here. I tagged after Miss Agatha as best as I could, so that she could echo those encouraging comments of my wife. 'We got round.' And so, will you please join me in welcoming our special Guest of Honour this afternoon, Miss Agatha Aspinal."

Another huge burst of applause rang out, as Miss Agatha opened and closed her red umbrella.

"Some people say it's bad luck to do this indoors, but phooey I say to that! Stuff and nonsense! If we put our trust in the Lord, we shall be making our own luck. Thank you,

Bill, for those kind words, but as always you spoke rather too many of them."

The assembled crowd laughed in good natured recognition.

"And so I shan't keep you any longer than is absolutely necessary. I know that this is going to be a splendid afternoon, and so please spare whatever you can, for all of the proceeds from today are going to such worthy causes. I now declare *'Cherry Blossoms'*, the Annual Hulme Hall Lane United Methodists' Chapel Spring Fête... open!"

Hubert then took this as his cue to turn on the gramophone, which Annie had put him in charge of, starting with a rousing Strauss Gallop to get things going with a bang, and everyone at once began to spread themselves around the Hall, inspecting the various stalls.

Annie looked about her, surveying the scene. She beamed. The afternoon was already a success.

It finished all too soon. As is so often the way with these things, after the months of planning and preparation, the actual event passed by in a flash, but people would remember it for a long time afterwards, individually declaring particular moments to be their favourites.

The Reverend Appleby gamely offered himself as sacrificial lamb to stand outside in the stocks, much to the open mouthed disbelief of the children, who clamoured to take turns in paying a ha'penny to throw wet sponges at him.

Two of the older ladies from the congregation, with much flapping of home made fans, agreed to join Annie and, accompanied by Miss Agatha on the piano, delighted everyone with their saucy rendition of *Three Little Maids* from *The Mikado*.

> "*Three little maids from school are we*
> *Pert as a schoolgirl well can be*

Filled to the brim with girlish glee
Three little maids from school..."

Young Harold Blundell, in his best Sunday clothes, hair slicked back to within an inch of its life, nervously played *The Flight of the Bumble Bee* on his cornet, watched over with a serious frown by his sister, Esther, who appeared to be playing every single note with him. She drew heartfelt admiration from the other women, the way at only fourteen years old she was managing to look after her grieving father and her five brothers so uncomplainingly. As Harold strained for all his worth on his cornet, a group of younger children, dressed as bees with alternating strips of black and yellow cloth sewn onto old pillow cases, worn as tabards with cushions stuffed inside to lend a more rotund appearance, each wearing an Alice band on their heads with two pieces of wire protruding from it, bobbling on the end of which were two ping pong balls, danced and buzzed around the Hall, hovering around individual members of the audience as if they were flowers from whom they might extract pollen.

Even Hubert had been persuaded to do a turn. Rather stiffly and self-consciously, he stood in the centre and sang, haltingly at first, but gradually growing in conviction, another popular song from *The Mikado*, encouraging the audience to join in with him, which they most happily did.

"A wandering minstrel, I
A thing of shreds and patches
Of ballads, songs and snatches
And dreamy lullaby..."

Annie watched from the side with growing pleasure. He had a most pleasing voice. He looked suddenly vulnerable, younger than he usually did, and she could glimpse the little boy he must have been, quietly studious, always eager to please, to do his duty and his best. Was that how he saw himself, she asked herself? A thing of shreds and patches, an amalgamation of other people's expectations of him, still wandering in search of his true identity? He would be twenty-one later this year, she thought. Would that be a milestone that would see him grow into himself more, she wondered? And as for his dreamy lullaby, well – she had learned something about his dreams, and she knew they would always be the star by which he steered his course. Might she be his travelling companion…?

He looked across to her as he finished his song. She spread her fan in front of her face, smiling at him with her eyes from behind it.

Later that evening, when the fete had finished and everything had been cleared away, Hubert accompanied Annie back to her house on Corelli Street. Annie didn't think she had ever been happier, she in her silk *kimono*, the yellow chrysanthemum still in her hair, her wandering minstrel walking by her side.

"Look," said Hubert suddenly, pointing upwards.

Something resembling a meteor was crossing the night sky.

"What is it?" asked Annie.

"I do believe it's Halley's Comet," he whispered in hushed awe.

Together in silence they watched its long, sweeping arc trace across the heavens, illuminating the whole of Corelli Street in a ghostly, silver glow. They craned their necks to try and catch every last possible ounce of light it cast upon the narrow confines of those cramped and straitened, damp and indigent sunless yards and cellars.

Hubert fell to his knees, clutching Annie's hand and smiled up at her.

"Will you marry me?"

She looked down at him. By rights he should have seemed ridiculous, scrabbling on his knees in the dirt and cobbles in a fancy dress costume. But he didn't. She could see beneath the wandering minstrel, the shreds and patches, to the prince below, throwing off his disguise, returning from his self-imposed exile.

"Yes," she said at once. "I will."

Hubert rose to kiss her, but she put her fan to his lips. "You'll have to ask my father first. Come to tea next Sunday." And with that she bobbed a curtsey, giggled, and skipped into her house with a series of tiny steps, as quickly as her *kimono* would allow her.

*

In all their married life together, Hubert and Annie had just three rows. The first of these concerned their actual wedding, but it was one in which neither of them felt inclined to budge.

Tea with Annie's family went completely well to begin with. Her parents, who of course had seen Hubert several times already at the Chapel, had an inkling from Annie's insistence that every last detail be paid attention to in terms of what they would serve up, even down to her suggestion that they should cut the crusts off the potted meat sandwiches, that a lot was riding on this tea.

"I'm sure he'll take us as he finds us, our Annie," said her father, "so let that be an end to the matter."

As things turned out, it all passed off serenely. Hubert made the best possible start by bringing flowers for Mrs Warburton, a doll for Annie's sister and a tin of marbles for her younger brothers. Mr Warburton liked the fact that, although Hubert's family was clearly a step up from his, they'd done so by dint of their own efforts alone. Hubert was a printer, which, in Annie's father's book, still counted as a trade, as working with your hands, producing something which owed its existence to the skills and sweat of the working man. When the time came for Hubert to ask for Annie's hand, the outcome could not have been more straightforward.

"About time too," said Mr Warburton. "I can't think what's took thee so long. I know she has some queer ideas at times, but she's a good lass at heart."

"I know that," said Hubert, "and as for those queer ideas, I rather like them."

"I should think so," said Annie, who had walked in on them unannounced, "especially since one of them seems to have been my taking rather a surprising shine for you, Hubert."

"Well, as long as our Annie's happy, that's all that matters to me," said Mr Warburton.

"And she is," said Annie, linking her arm through Hubert's.

"That settles it then," concluded her father. "Welcome to the family, lad," and he shook Hubert's hand firmly and warmly, slapping him on the back. "I'll just go and see if Mother needs a hand in the kitchen," he said with a wink, and left the two love birds alone in the front parlour.

It was only when the subject of where the wedding should take place that the mood threatened to sour.

"We shall have to speak to Mr Appleby to book the Chapel," said Mrs Warburton, as she passed round the Lancashire Courting Cake a second time.

"Naturally," agreed Mr Warburton. "I daresay it gets booked up well in advance. We'll speak to him next Sunday, shall we?"

"Will you have another piece, Hubert?" asked Mrs Warburton. "Annie baked it special."

"Mother…"

"Thank you, Mrs Warburton. It's delicious, Annie."

"Of course it is," laughed Mr Warburton. "You're a lucky

man, Hubert."

"Yes, sir."

"What do you think, Hubert?" asked Annie. "About the Chapel, I mean?"

"I'll tell you what he thinks, our Annie," said Mr Warburton before Hubert, his mouth full of Courting Cake, had chance to answer. "He thinks, whatever makes his bride-to-be happy is fine with him, eh Hubert?"

"Of course, Mr Warburton," said Hubert finally, brushing the crumbs from his moth with his handkerchief. "Only I had wondered..." He paused. Everyone was looking at him.

"Yes, Hubert?" said Annie, suddenly serious.

"Nothing. Let's hope the Chapel has a spare Saturday which can suit us all."

Annie regarded Hubert closely.

"And when did you have in mind?" asked Mrs Warburton, pouring everyone fresh cups of tea, as she tried to steer the conversation back to less contentious territory.

"Oh," stammered Hubert, "we haven't had chance to discuss this yet, have we, Annie?"

"Next May," replied Annie, with some finality. "A year to the day after you proposed. That should give Mr Appleby plenty of notice, and enough time for everything that will need to be got ready."

"Well," said Mr Warburton, leaning back in his chair, adding for a second time that afternoon, "that's all settled then. Care for a cigarette, Hubert?"

"Er..."

"He doesn't smoke, Father."

"Doesn't he now?" said Mr Warburton, lighting up one for himself. "Sensible chap." And he laughed, which promptly turned into a cough.

Later in the afternoon, just as Hubert was leaving, Annie

intercepted him on the front step.

"Well," she said, "aren't you going to tell me what all that was about?"

"All what…?"

"Don't you play the innocent with me, Hubert Wright. I saw that look on your face over tea."

"What look?"

"You know very well what look. That look when we were talking about having our wedding at the Chapel."

"Ah. Yes…"

"Well?"

"Well… I just thought…"

"What?"

"I was surprised, that's all. After all you'd said about not really believing any more…"

"I said I had doubts, not that I disbelieved altogether."

"Yes, but I just thought maybe you and I might do something a bit different, strike out on our own, make our own wedding vows."

"With your 'friends' at The Meeting House, I suppose?"

"Well… yes."

"But they're *your* friends, Hubert, not mine."

"They could be your friends too, you know."

"I want a proper wedding, with a minister, not some… Well… is it even legal, a Quaker wedding?"

"You know it is," said Hubert, trying to calm Annie, who was becoming increasingly upset.

"The thing is, Hubert," she said, "I've grown up here. Mr Appleby married my parents and then christened every one of us kids. Including me. He'd be disappointed not to conduct my wedding."

"It's *our* wedding, Annie, not *his*."

"I know, but…"

"Nor is it anyone else's. It's just us. You and me."

"I can't let everybody down, Hubert. They'd think it

47

strange. And anyway, I want everybody there, all our neighbours, all the people I've grown up with, gone to school and Sunday school with, who go to Chapel with us now."

"They could all come to The Meeting House."

"But they wouldn't though, would they? That's the truth of it. And I wouldn't want to get married without everybody there."

"And I wouldn't want to go through with some sort of sham ceremony that neither of us believes in any more."

Hubert declared this with more force than he had intended, and Annie was shocked into silence by it. They both stood there, not looking at one another, almost shaking with emotion. It was Annie who spoke again first.

"I've never heard you raise your voice like that before," she said.

"I'm sorry," he replied. "I shouldn't have. But I meant what I said."

"Yes. I can see. Well that leaves us at something of a cross-roads, doesn't it?" she said.

Hubert was quiet.

Annie lifted her hand to his cheek and gently turned his face to look at her. "What are we going to do then?" she whispered.

"I don't know," he said sadly.

The bell in the recently completed Corpus Christi Basilica, built for the religious order of the Norbertines just a few hundred yards away on Varley Street, began to toll six o'clock. The chimes sounded slow and heavy between them.

"You'd best be on your way," said Annie. "We'll think of something."

Hubert nodded. "Ay. I expect we will."

"Cheer up," she added. "It's not as if you no longer want to get married at all, is it?"

Hubert stopped. "What if we get married twice?" he said suddenly.

Annie looked puzzled.

"What if we get married at The Meeting House, just you and me and a couple of witnesses, and anyone who cares to join us on, say, a Friday evening? Then the next day, the Saturday, we have a traditional wedding at the Chapel?" He looked at her, nervously excited.

"Hubert," she exclaimed, throwing her arms around his neck, "you always were a clever clogs! That's a marvellous idea. And then everyone gets to be happy."

Hubert stepped back from Annie's embrace and then, adopting her father's voice and accent, smiled mischievously. "Is that settled then?" he asked.

"Ay," laughed Annie. "I reckon it is."

Having written their letter to the Clerk of The Meeting House expressing their wish for a Quaker wedding, Hubert and Annie were invited to Mount Street to attend a meeting of the Clearness Committee, at which they were obliged to answer a series of probing questions about the spiritual nature of marriage.

It was the first time that Annie had been inside The Meeting House and, like Hubert had before her, she found herself responding to the calmness of the atmosphere inside, but, unlike Hubert, she found the long silences which punctuated their discussions to be somewhat intimidating.

The Clerk explained to her that Friends marry without fanfare. "Often referred to as the Silent Ceremony," he went on, "a Quaker wedding differs from a more conventional church or chapel wedding in four distinct ways. First there is no priest to officiate. Second, there is no giving away of the bride. Third, a wedding certificate is signed, by the couple getting married and everyone else who is present. Finally, there is a long period of silent worship, during which anyone attending may say something on the couple's behalf."

After having passed through the Clearness Committee, a smaller, less formal Oversight Committee was formed, comprising, in addition to the Clerk, two more Friends, whose task it was to ensure that all the necessary arrangements for the ceremony, including all legal requirements, were taken care of.

On this the 19th day of May, in the year of our Lord 1911, Hubert Wright and Annie Warburton appeared together, and Hubert Wright did, on this solemn and joyous occasion, declare that he took Annie Warburton to be his wife, promising, with Divine assistance, to be unto her a loving and faithful husband; and then, in the same assembly, Annie Warburton did, in like manner, declare that she took Hubert Wright to be her husband, promising, with Divine assistance, to be unto him a loving and faithful wife. And moreover they, Hubert Wright and Annie Warburton, did, as further confirmation thereof, then and there, to this certificate set their hands.

Hubert Wright   Annie Warburton

And we, having been present at the marriage, have as witnesses thereunto set our hands.

Frank Wright   Evelyn Wright   Sam Warburton
Jessica Warburton   Edward Judd (Clerk)

Afterwards, everyone declared themselves satisfied.

"I liked it," pronounced Mr Warburton. "No fuss."

"Very nice," agreed Mrs Warburton, while Mr and Mrs Wright nodded in silent agreement, relieved to have negotiated this first meeting of the in-laws successfully and without mishap.

The following day a smiling Reverend Appleby stood before the packed congregation of Hulme Hall Lane United Methodist Chapel, where every pew was taken, where the men and women of the Tripe Colony sat in excited anticipation in their stiff collars, starched suits and Sunday skirts and blouses, handkerchiefs at the ready, while overheated babies and children cried or fidgeted or scampered up and down beyond the reach of their more than usually lenient parents. Annie's eleven year old brother Jack was given the task of signalling from the Chapel door to Miss Agatha waiting at the harmonium beside the pulpit the moment his sister arrived. As soon as he saw her coming down the path, he raced inside, waved both his hands in the air, Miss Agatha rheumatically started up on Wagner's *Bridal Chorus* from *Lohengrin*, everybody got to their feet, eagerly looking over their shoulders for that first glimpse of Annie walking up the aisle on the arm of her proud and red-faced father.

Reverend Appleby looked down on the nervous, waiting couple, this girl who he'd first baptised as a baby, and who he'd seen every Sunday since for the next twenty-one years, and this serious, thoughtful young man who he'd recently come to know and respect during the last two, and beamed.

"Repeat after me," he said.

Hubert and Annie looked at each other happily.

"I do solemnly declare…"

"I do solemnly declare…"

"… that I know not of any unlawful impediment…"

"… that I know not of any unlawful impediment…"

"… why I, Hubert…"

"… why I, Hubert…"

"… may not be joined in matrimony…"

"… may not be joined in matrimony…"

"… to thee, Annie…"

"… to thee, Annie…"

In the congregation, the babies stopped crying, the children ceased from fidgeting, the ladies made good use of their handkerchiefs, and the men discovered they were developing slight coughs and needed to unobtrusively clear their throats.

"I now pronounce you man and wife."

Miss Agatha burst into Mendlessohn's *Wedding March* from *A Midsummer Night's Dream*, and Hubert and Annie walked back along the aisle, arms linked, wreathed in smiles.

He leaned towards her and whispered in her ear. "Twice blessed," he said.

"Yes," she echoed. "Twice blessed."

2

2nd March 1916

Hubert and Annie's second argument occurred nearly five years into their marriage, towards the end of the hard 'turnip' winter of 1916.

The country had been at war for over eighteen months. Printing had been classified as a reserved occupation, although not in the same category as miners, ship builders, farmers and fishermen, and so Hubert was exempted from service. Even if this had not been the case, his poor eyesight – he'd worn glasses since he was a boy – would have rendered him unfit for duty. But following the calamities of Ypres and Loos, which saw British losses in 1915 exceed two hundred and eighty-five thousand, with more than twice that number wounded so badly that they would not be returning to the war at the Front any time soon, if at all, the Recruiting Officers were becoming less fussy in who they turned down, and the Government had just passed the Military Service Act, requiring compulsory conscription for all able-bodied men between the ages of eighteen and forty-one not engaged in what were deemed essential services at home. Printing no longer appeared in this new revised list.

Annie happened to catch sight of a leaflet shortly after nine o'clock on Thursday 2nd March, from which she was unwrapping her weekly delivery of finny haddock from the Fish Man. She scraped the pieces of melting ice from the already creased and torn paper and, holding it delicately between the thumb and forefinger of her left hand, she rushed out of their house, across the street to the Printing Works, where Hubert had been working since seven in the morning.

Without a word, she held it up in front of him. Hubert peered at it carefully and slowly in that maddening way of his until Annie could stand it no longer.

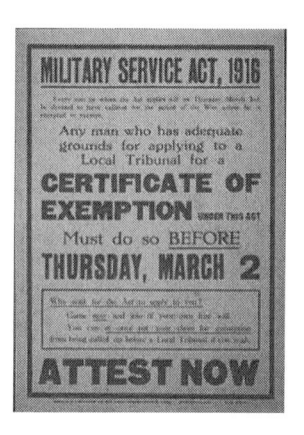

> **MILITARY SERVICE ACT, 1916**
>
> Any man who has adequate grounds for applying to a Local Tribunal for a
>
> **CERTIFICATE OF EXEMPTION** UNDER THIS ACT
>
> Must do so BEFORE
>
> **THURSDAY, MARCH 2**
>
> **ATTEST NOW**

"Well?" she demanded.

"Not now," he said, aware that the other workers were regarding them with amused curiosity.

"But look at the date," she began. "You've only got today."

"Let's talk about it at lunch time," he continued. His calmness only served to make Annie even crosser.

"Did you know about this," she asked, taking back the leaflet from him and waving it in front of his face, "and not tell me?"

"We've both of us known this day was bound to come," he said.

"Oh!" she cried. "You're impossible!"

And with that she turned on her heels and rushed out of the Works, screwing up the leaflet and flinging it to the floor as she did so. Hubert watched her go with a quiet shake of his head. He picked up the leaflet, carefully smoothed out its creases, folded it into four and put it in the front pocket of his overalls before quietly going back to the typesetting he was busy with before Annie had burst in.

As soon as she stepped outside, Annie paused to collect

herself. The deep rumble of the printing presses, which rolled incessantly night and day, and which had always before filled her with a sense of comfort and strength, their constant, earth-shaking vibrations providing a permanent backdrop to her days, so that at times she had found herself spontaneously dancing to the exciting cross-rhythms of the different machines, now seemed to strike a harsh and ominous note, like an unexploded mortar shell.

She returned the few yards to their house on Portugal Street, finished cleaning and preparing the fish that would serve for their lunch, her mind completely elsewhere. How had she allowed this to happen? How had she not foreseen what had clearly been inevitable? Outside a cold squall of rain had suddenly got up. Annie stirred herself, opened the front door and looked for George, their three-year old son, whom she'd left happily playing with the other children outside. She scanned the street up and down and quickly spotted him, contentedly poking a stick down a grid. He did not appear to have noticed the rain at all. Annie hurried towards him, scooped him up in a single, practised movement and carried him protesting back to the open front door. But George's complaints lasted no more than a moment. He was a happy child by nature and was soon distracted by a sheet of paper and some crayons.

Annie watched him become immediately absorbed, his tongue protruding from his mouth in studied concentration, a slight frown on his forehead, along with a steady stream of chatter as he un-self-consciously provided a running commentary on what he had begun to draw. Annie could always tell what his next craze or passion was going to be, for he would suddenly announce it by obsessively drawing it for several weeks until it was replaced by a new claimant upon his affections. Two months ago it had been birds – pigeons, starlings, thrushes; a month later it was vehicles – buses, trams and trains. Recently, hardly surprising, she supposed, he had begun to draw soldiers.

Annie continued to watch him, her mind a muddle, a tangled web of memories, which she now tried to unpick, like a ball of wool that had become knotted and snagged…

*

Three years earlier.

Just over two years after their double wedding George had been born.

George.

It was a difficult birth.

The labour was protracted and painful, accompanied by a fierce and wild thunderstorm, which appeared to be raging directly above their house on Portugal Street, just across the road from the Printing Works, drowning out Annie's shouts and cries, whose volume and frequency increased to such an alarming extent that the midwife felt obliged to send out Hubert into the driving rain to fetch Doctor Wilkes.

Hurriedly throwing his raincoat over his pyjamas, Hubert jumped onto his bicycle, which was parked in the narrow ginnel next to the house, and pedalled so furiously down the cobbled streets and alleyways that he crashed into a kerb, ending up in a sodden heap in a deep puddle in one of the gutters, where he attracted the attention of a local police constable, who tried to arrest him for being drunk and disorderly in possession of a bicycle, ignoring all of Hubert's shouted protestations of innocence.

"I'm sorry, Officer, but I just can't stop," he called out as he remounted his bicycle as quickly as he could. "My wife's having a baby!"

"Oh yes?" remarked the policeman sceptically as he removed a damp notebook from his breast pocket, unnecessarily licking his pencil as he prepared to write his report. "If I had a shilling for every time I've heard that excuse, I'd be a rich man."

But Hubert was gone.

By the time he returned home with the Doctor riding tandem on the cross-bar, the storm was at its height. A chimney pot crashed down from the house across the road from where they lived, landing just a few feet away from their front door, its shards puncturing the tyres on his bicycle.

Once inside, Dr Wilkes hurried upstairs to take over from the midwife, while Hubert paced anxiously back and forth, practically wearing a groove in the sitting room rug.

By morning the storm had blown itself out at last. Hubert, now dozing fitfully in the armchair by the hearth, watched the sun poke defiantly through the last dregs of dark cloud. At that precise moment he heard the unmistakeable cry of a new born baby catching at life.

George.

Hubert was only allowed the briefest of first glimpses for it was clear that Annie was exhausted. Her face, though managing the thinnest of smiles when Hubert sat beside her, was ashen.

Afterwards, downstairs, the Doctor's expression was suitably grave.

"Your wife has had the most difficult of times," he explained. "I believe she will recover but she will need several weeks to do so. Is there someone who can be here with her during that time?"

Hubert breathed deeply, replying that yes, he believed there was, and that he would see to it immediately.

"Good," sighed Dr Wilkes. It had been a long night for him too. "And another thing," he said, collecting his bag, "there's no easy way to say this so I'll just come right out with it."

Hubert looked up, attentive and concerned.

"It is highly inadvisable for your wife to have any more

children. She might not survive another delivery."

Hubert nodded seriously, confirming that he had understood.

"But you have a healthy baby boy, that's the main thing. Congratulations." He shook Hubert's hand warmly.

After Dr Wilkes had left at last, Hubert crept upstairs to his wife and son, both of whom were fast asleep. He watched over them, thinking who he might ask to be Annie's nurse and companion these next few weeks, until he too fell asleep beside them.

*

In the weeks leading up to their wedding, Annie had given little thought as to where they would be living. Hubert had assured her that she was not to worry about it and that he would see to everything. Which he did. When, a month before the two ceremonies were due to take place, he took her to the Printing Works for the first time, she had no idea that this initial tour of the shop floor, eulogising over each of the different machines and presses as he proudly introduced her to the typesetters, the paper cutters, the lithographers and photogravure artists, who all expressed their delight in meeting her, was merely the prelude to him showing the house he had secured for them.

As they stepped back out in the sunlight, Annie blinked, her eyes readjusting to the brightness after the crepuscular dusk of the Printing Works. Taking advantage of her temporary disorientation, Hubert stood behind her, covered her eyes with his hands and led her, giggling, across the street.

"I've got something to show you," he said.

When they had gone barely fifty yards, he stopped, took his hands away from her eyes and said, simply, "Here."

Annie looked about her, puzzled.

"Welcome to your new home," he added, a smile

spreading across his face. "Number twenty-five."

The surprise Annie felt quickly gave way to a feeling of disappointment. It was the end house of a long terrace, with a narrow entry at the side, nothing like the grand house Hubert lived in with his parents. But at least it was new. The Corporation had knocked down all the old back-to-backs a couple of years ago and were now in the process, in association with various independent builders, of putting up these brand new terraces. The front door opened directly onto the street, which was cobbled and empty. It was also directly opposite the Printing Works. It was not that different, from the outside, to the house she had grown up in and would still be living in until their wedding in a few weeks' time, except that it was newer. Yes, the neighbourhood was better, but only marginally. They were still right in the heart of industrial Manchester, having crossed the one and three quarter miles from Miles Platting into Ancoats. This was not what she'd been anticipating. Having by now visited Hubert's parents on a few occasions in their large house on Bignor Street, in leafy Cheetham Hill, with its large garden, she had, she supposed, been hoping for something similar. As if to underline her disappointment, a large rat scurried out of the ginnel beside the house and nosed its way along the street.

Hubert, sensing that his surprise was not meeting with quite the reaction he had hoped for, ushered Annie quickly across the street, away from the rat, taking out a key.

"I know it's not much, Annie, but it's a start, and it's ours. We could have stayed with my parents but I didn't think you'd want that – I know I wouldn't – and it's ever so convenient for the Works, I can pop home for lunch every day, and in any case it's only temporary. Once things settle a bit we can start looking for something better. I only want what's best for you, you know that, don't you…?"

Annie sensed his panic and, turning swiftly towards him,

she put a finger to his lips. "Shh..." she said softly. "It's perfect."

A relieved Hubert beamed.

"Let's take a look inside," said Annie. She took the key from Hubert and placed it into the lock. Placing his hand over hers, they turned the key together and slowly pushed open the door. A fresh, new coat of green paint would soon brighten it up, she thought, already beginning to imagine herself there. She turned back towards Hubert and grinned. "But don't think you can carry me over the threshold today. You'll have to be patient a few more weeks yet..."

They stepped inside. Although it was completely devoid of furniture, it had, she noticed, been recently decorated.

"Have you done this?" she asked.

He nodded.

"You've done a good job," she smiled.

"I'm glad you approve," he grinned back.

They walked about its empty space, mostly in silence, occasionally whispering to one another, for fear they might break the spell which seemed to have fallen over them since they had entered it. Stripped of all its furnishings, with no curtains at its windows or rugs upon its floors, just the bare boards, the house appeared to be waiting for them. Dust motes danced in pools of sunlight by the scrubbed hearth. "Look," they seemed to be saying, "here we are, waiting for you. When will you come and join us?" Soon, thought Annie, very soon. She imagined an armchair they would place there, where she might sit upon Hubert's lap by a warm fire in winter. She ran her fingers along the empty mantelpiece, where she would arrange a small carriage clock, flanked by a pair of Staffordshire flatback spaniels, two candlesticks, a photograph of herself and Hubert on their wedding day, of children perhaps. In the kitchen at the back she saw a row of cup hooks under a shelf and pictured the pans she would hang from them. Through the window she could see a small back yard. "We could paint that white," she said to Hubert, "and plant flowers and herbs, bulbs in pots in the spring…" Hubert smiled. "Tulips," he said. "Oh yes," replied Annie, seeing them there already. Back in the sitting room she thought she heard whispers coming from upstairs. The dust motes danced from tread to tread. "This way," they seemed to be saying. "Follow us." And they did. They crept up the narrow, steep, twisting staircase, noticing which of the steps creaked and which did not. "Here," the whispers seemed to be saying. "And here. Here you will be so happy. And here too." They followed the whispers into the larger of the two upstairs rooms. "This will be our bedroom," said Hubert. "We could put the bed here. What do you think? Can't you imagine it?" Annie took Hubert's hand and interlaced her fingers with his. "I don't need to imagine it," she said softly and drew him down to the floor beside her. "Are you sure about this?" he asked her. She nodded and smiled. "What difference does a single month make?"

After they had finished, Hubert lay asleep across her. She placed her hand carefully upon the back of his neck, which fitted exactly her palm, and felt her body gently rise and fall with the rhythm of his breathing.

The whisperers looked down upon them. "Yes," said one of them. "They will be happy here. Just as we hoped."

"Yes," said the other, "but they will leave. In no time at all, they will leave."

"As we all have to," said the first. "But part of them will remain, I think."

"Yes."

"To dance with us on the stairs."

Annie lay daydreaming, while Hubert slept.

The whispering stopped.

In the silence that followed she thought she heard a new sound, a different sound, a fluttering of tiny wing beats. At first she wondered if it was coming from inside her own body, but the more she listened, as it came and went, she began to locate its source. It seemed to be emanating from the smaller second upstairs room.

She removed her hand from the back of Hubert's neck and, as gently as she could, she eased herself out from underneath him. She smoothed down her skirt and crept barefoot along the wooden boards towards this second room. The fluttering was louder now. She inched open the door just sufficiently to allow herself to squeeze inside.

At first there appeared to be nothing. She noticed the window was wide open and she walked towards it, to close it. Her sudden movement at once alarmed the bird, which had been concealed in the shadow of a recessed corner, and which now began to fly around the room. It was a wren.

A wren so tiny that each time it alighted somewhere in the room – on a shelf, the window sill, the door jamb, the floor – Annie could barely see it. This continued for several minutes. The wren would take off, fly about the room, before perching somewhere new, almost as if it was marking out a territory, staking its claim upon the place. It was not, she realised, panicked or desperate to escape. Finally it landed on the floor, close to one of her feet, in a dappled pool of sunlight, where it seemed quite content to bask and bathe a moment. Very slowly Annie lowered herself to the floor and placed her open hand next to her foot. The wren bobbed its head up and down, as if deciding whether to hop into it or not. The two of them eyed each other intently. Then, without any further preamble, the wren suddenly hopped onto the palm of Annie's hand. She closed her other hand over it, very gently, and lifted it towards her face, so that she might look at it more closely. She could feel its body quivering against her fingers, like a pulse in her blood. She carried it over towards the open window and carefully placed it on the ledge. It did not leave at once. It continued to scrutinise her, moving its head swiftly from side to side, like a bus conductor inspecting a ticket to check if it was valid for this particular journey, before emitting a single, sharp chirp, almost like a scold, and then flying out of the window to land on a low branch in Portugal Street's only tree. Once there, it proceeded to serenade Annie with its entire repertoire of chirrups, chitters, rattles and trills. As if suddenly released from years of imprisonment within a dark, windowless cell, its song broke over the bricks and rooftops of the whole street in unconfined joy, before it flew away and out of sight.

Annie knew in that instant that she too would fly away from this house, that here was but the first step in her lifelong move away from the Tripe Colony, but that for now it would be perfect. She would make it so, and Hubert would delight in all the little personal touches she would bring to this, their first home together, but that for their next home, it would be she, not Hubert, who would find it, when the time was right, and present it to him as a surprise, before making him think that it had been his idea all the time.

"Annie…?" he called from the next room.

"I'm here," she answered, and he made his way, stumbling through the door, putting back on his glasses.

"I thought you'd gone," he said, a worried look upon his face.

"This will be the perfect room for a child," she said, looking back out of the window to where the wren had been. "I've just been picturing it."

The chorus of whispers grew to a crescendo all around them, looking down from the window to the street below, where the rat was busy excavating earth from around the base of the single tree.

*

When they finally moved in, four weeks later, the tree was in full bloom, its canopy a mass of tiny scarlet flowers. It was not a tree they either of them recognised, and further investigation (using the Encyclopaedia in Hubert's parents' house) revealed it was the *Euonymus Europaeus*, more commonly known as the spindle tree, for its hard wood was ideally suited for use in the cotton mills all around them. It was also, they quickly realised, not a tree which had been planted, but which had somehow arrived there, perhaps carried by the wind, or in the beak of some migrating bird, from Europe or the Middle East. She liked to think of it travelling across thousands of miles, such a tiny thing, such a fragile hope, and then landing here, by chance, in this built up street in the heart of a city, of its lying dormant in the thin soil, eroded and diminished by the years of pollution and waste, being covered over by gravel and cobbles, concrete and tarmac, then waking up, locked in its dark underground prison but refusing to be beaten, how it pushed its roots deeper into the earth, then strained upwards towards the light, breaking through the paving slabs, its raw power belying its humble, tender origins, before growing tall and defiant, spreading its hermaphroditic flowers, waiting for another bird to pick its berries and drop its seed elsewhere. Its Latin name, she learned, was from Euonyme, the Mother of the Furies, those goddesses of vengeance, personified curses, conceived as ghosts of the murdered and the dispossessed. Now, thought Annie, as she looked up at its blood red flowers glinting in the May morning sunlight, they had reclaimed their homeland, taken possession of the future, just as she would.

In her first few weeks and months in her new surroundings, released from the shackles of stirring the enormous tripe vats six steaming days a week, Annie walked. She explored every street, nook, cranny and corner of her new neighbourhood, familiarising herself with place names, landmarks, road signs and shop fronts, just as Hubert had done all those years before. She came to know every building, railway arch, warehouse and factory, cotton mill, church, chapel and school yard, drinking in the sounds of all the different nationalities, arriving like those migrating birds, to settle here, build new homes here, make again that which they had left behind, but newly wrought within the crucible of Manchester. She heard Urdu, Bengali, Hebrew and Turkish, the lilt of Irish and heart sore Portuguese, but more than any of these she heard Italian, its language dancing like fireworks all around her, its rise and fall a cadence to the traffic of the streets. Like the scarlet flowers on the spindle tree, Annie felt that she, too, was coming into leaf again, after so many years in the dark, rising before the sun, which never shone in the Tripe Colony, never pierced the smog and gloom, so that there she never lifted her eyes from the dark earth as she marched each day, body bent, head weighed down by the mountains of spoil tips at the end of each street. Here, less than two miles away, and still deep within the heart of the city's cauldron, yet there was colour – colour and music – which filled her with happiness. She heard barrel organs on every street corner playing Neapolitan love songs, she saw unfamiliar foods displayed in the windows of what she recognised, but could not yet pronounce, as *pasticceria* and *pastificio*. She was transported by the highly patterned, decorative tiles of the *terrazzo monocottora*, swept along by the fervour of the Whitsuntide Processions of the *Madonna del Rosario*, drawn with appalled fascination to the old women telling fortunes with caged birds, and like a child again over the discovery of the hand carts selling Italian ice cream.

But all of this, although it delighted her, she viewed from the outside, not knowing how she might penetrate this brave new world, until one day, standing outside Giorgio Punzo's *Paste Alimentari*, which rubbed shoulders alongside Carlo Tiani's Italian Deli, promising everything from *prosciutto*, *salami,* wine and olives, bread, cheese, biscuits and *pannetone*, to handmade Italian shawls, she felt a hand tap her lightly on her shoulder. When she turned around, a young woman of a similar age smiled and spoke to her.

"Would you like me to translate?" she said.

"Yes please," replied Annie. "I find it all so tempting but I don't know where to begin, and I'm nervous of saying the wrong thing."

"Follow me," said the Italian woman. "Let me show you. There's nothing to be nervous about. My name's Claudia, by the way."

"Pleased to meet you. I'm Annie."

Claudia guided Annie through this first foray, making sure her innocence was not exploited, and soon they looked out for each other in the streets and squares. They would meet on Saturday mornings, when Claudia would show Annie the way to get the pick of the best fruit and vegetables on the market stalls, and soon Hubert was being introduced to a whole new cuisine, one which was met with initially cautious but subsequently unbridled enthusiasm.

"It makes a change from tripe," he joked, after his first attempt at eating spaghetti.

"It certainly does," agreed a very happy Annie.

As the weeks passed, Claudia and Annie became firm friends. They could only meet on Saturdays because of Claudia's work the rest of the week.

"What do you do?" asked Annie one time, expecting, she supposed, that the answer would be in one of the many mills or factories in the area, so she was somewhat taken aback by Claudia's response.

"I'm a laboratory technician," she said, "in the Science Department of Manchester University."

Annie's eyes widened in surprise. Claudia smiled. "I know. I can hardly believe it myself. I've my old teacher at school to thank. It was she who got me the position."

"I loved school," sighed Annie, somewhat wistfully. "But I had to leave to help out at home."

Claudia nodded, understanding. "My parents died," she said.

"Oh," replied Annie. "I'm sorry."

Claudia shook her head. "They were happy. They came over here from Campania in southern Italy to make a better life, not just for themselves, but for their children."

"When was this?"

"1887. My brother – Matteo – he had been born the year before."

"So you were born here?"

"*Si.* I am a Mancunian. Just like you!"

They laughed together warmly.

"And so when my teacher at school – Miss Leslie – came round to see my parents when I was thirteen, urging them to consider allowing me to transfer to the Grammar School and study science, my father agreed at once. '*Qualunque cosa sia meglio*. We only want what is best *per nostra ragazza dolce, nostra cucciola*'. And so I went…"

Claudia broke off and looked away.

"What's the matter?" asked Annie.

"It's just that I'm so grateful to them, but sad that they're not here now to see what a difference their sacrifice has made for me."

Annie took both of Claudia's hands in her own and squeezed them.

"*Grazie.*" She wiped her eyes with the back of one of her hands. "It is also a big responsibility. I don't want to let them down."

"I'm sure you won't," said Annie. "What is it that you do at the university?"

"I work with Miss Leslie, who works with Professor Rutherford. A great man. He is trying to split the atom."

Annie shook her head. "I'm sorry," she said. "I don't

really know what that means."

"Nobody does," said Claudia, becoming immediately more animated. "That's what's so exciting. But still he tries."

"Can you explain it to me in a way I might understand?"

Claudia regarded Annie, this woman whom she'd known only a few weeks, but who was becoming a new and special friend to her. "I will try," she said. "Have you seen the statue of John Dalton in Piccadilly?"

Annie frowned. "Is he the one who looks like a Quaker?"

"Yes," said Claudia.

"My husband attends Meetings, and I sometimes go with him."

"Really? What are they like? I've often wondered."

"You should ask my husband. I… I find them… difficult."

"In what way difficult?"

"My husband finds the silence calming, relaxing. It slows him down, he says, and helps him to think about things in a new way. But I…"

"Yes?"

"I… I don't like it. I get frightened. Once somebody feels the spirit move them and starts to speak, I prefer it. I can concentrate on what's being said, listen to it, roll it around my head and think about it, whether I agree or disagree, but the silence, it feels like it might swallow me up and I would disappear, like when you empty water down a drain."

"You have a good way with words, and what you are saying chimes very well with the work I do. Before you tip that water out of the pan, think of what you cooked in it."

"What do you mean?"

"Have you noticed that when you are trying to melt something in hot water, different things take different lengths of time to dissolve, to 'disappear', as you say?"

Annie nods, trying to follow what Claudia is saying.

"This man in the statue in Piccadilly – John Dalton – he

noticed it too, just over a hundred years ago, and tried to understand why this was so. He carried out a series of tests in which he tried to absorb different gases in water, and he was able to measure that there were identifiable differences between the way oxygen, nitrogen and carbon dioxide reacted. Signor Dalton concluded from these observations that every element, therefore, must be made up of a different number of atoms, and that it was the number of atoms which would determine how quickly, or slowly, each element would take to be absorbed in water. Are you following me so far?"

"Yes, I think so."

"But these atoms are so tiny – not visible to the naked eye – that for many years people thought that nothing smaller could possibly exist. Then Professor Rutherford…

"The man you work for?"

"*Si*… well, his teacher, a Professor Thompson, he came up with the plum pudding theory.

"I like the sound of that."

"*Si*," laughed Claudia. "Less than ten years ago, he noticed that atoms seemed to behave unpredictably when electricity was passed through them, and so he wondered, what if there is something even smaller than the atom, hidden inside, that we haven't yet discovered?"

"Like the plums inside a pudding," interrupted Annie animatedly, "you don't know they're there because you can't see them, but when you dig into it with your spoon, there they lie."

"Exactly," said Claudia. "And that's why Professor Rutherford is trying to split the atom, to prove the plum pudding theory."

"It sounds so exciting."

"It is."

"And to think, it's all happening here, in Manchester, and you're at the heart of it."

"No, Annie. I'm right at the farthest edge of it, carrying

out tests and recording the results, that is all."

"All? I think it must be wonderful to have such a sense of purpose, to know that you're involved with something that might affect the future..."

"But you live in the present, in the here and now."

"Do I?"

"Yes. I've watched you, drinking everything in, so completely in the moment."

"With an eye to the future, though."

"In what way?"

" I suppose I see life as a series of stepping stones."

"And where do they take you, these stepping stones?"

"I don't know. Not very far, in terms of miles. I don't imagine I'll ever leave Manchester. Why would I?" Manchester was Annie's entire universe, filled with many different galaxies and constellations to which she might travel and not return. "I couldn't do something as brave as your parents did and leave for another country. But somewhere. Where there's more space to breathe. I'm not clever like you are, but I want a future that's brighter, for my children if I have any, so that they won't feel this same hunger to escape from their past. Like I feel."

Claudia let a few moments pass before she spoke again.

"There's another scientist who Professor Rutherford speaks of, who works in a similar field, a Swiss, by the name of Albert Einstein. About five years ago he presented an important paper which proved John Dalton's atomic theory once and for all. He spoke about how all the things we once thought of as fixed and true were maybe not so certain after all. Everything is relative, he said. Even time. He even made a joke about it. 'Put your hand on a hot stove for a minute,' he said, 'and it seems like an hour. But sit with a pretty girl for an hour and it seems like a minute'."

They laughed together and then fell silent once more.

"Do you have a young man?" asked Annie tentatively.

Claudia nodded, blushing.

"Tell me about him."

Claudia shook her head. "It's early days," she said. "His name is Marco. Because of our jobs we see each other only on Sundays, after church, and sometimes in an evening he will call round, but my brother is always there too, never leaving us alone, so we just sit there, the three of us, not speaking, until, after a few minutes, he gets up and says he has to go. I think I am understanding very well Einstein's joke, for the time between when we see each other seems to stretch into eternity, and then when we are together it just flies by like that," and she snapped her fingers to emphasise her point.

"Will you still carry on with your work if you get married?"

Claudia smiled. "I think we are getting ahead of ourselves here, but yes, I think I would. It is an important part of who I am."

Annie nodded, taking this in, thinking how light her own days had become since she had married and given up work at the Tripe Colony, not that she would want to go back to that, but meeting Claudia was beginning to expand her horizons, making her think that perhaps she needed occupation.

"And what if you then had children?" she continued.

"Ah well, then it might be more difficult," conceded Claudia, "but still, I would hope that it might be possible to find a practical arrangement."

"I could look after them for you," blurted Annie. "I love children. I hope I have lots."

Claudia laughed. "Like I said, we are getting ahead of ourselves, I think. Marco and I are not even engaged yet! Nor are we likely to be if Matteo never leaves us alone!"

The two friends linked arms as they continued to wander the streets of Ancoats. After a while, Annie stopped and said, "If you were not here beside me right now, I'd be completely lost. I've not been this way before, and I'm not sure I could find my way back."

"*Si*, is quite a maze, *non è vero*? But you'd soon find your way. Every quarter of an hour the bell in the church of St Alban's chimes. All you'd need to do is just follow the sound."

Annie nodded. "We need things like that to secure us, don't we? To anchor us, tether us so that we don't just float away for ever. That's what worries me about the silences in the Quaker Meetings."

"Did you ever read the Greek myths in school?"

"Oh yes. I used to enjoy those. Like Daphne turning herself into a tree to escape from Apollo."

"Do you remember the story of Ariadne?"

Annie shook her head. "I don't think so, no. Remind me."

"Ariadne was the daughter of King Minos of Crete, who kept a beast that was half man, half bull in the centre of a labyrinth."

"The Minotaur."

"Yes. It was Ariadne's job to feed the beast and so, over time, she had come to learn every possible route in and out of the labyrinth. When Theseus, a Greek prince, came to visit Crete, Ariadne fell in love with him, but her father, King Minos, would not agree to the match unless Theseues went into the labyrinth and killed the Minotaur. No one who had entered the labyrinth, apart from Ariadne herself, had ever escaped alive, and so, in order to help him, Ariadne first made sure the beast had been fed, so that he would be sleepy and slow, and then she gave Theseus a ball of wool, which she instructed him to unravel behind him as he made his way to the centre, so that, after he had killed the Minotaur, he would be able to find his way out again. Which is exactly what happened."

"Yes, I remember it now."

"Sometimes it's our job to kill the beast, but sometimes

it's our job to make sure we don't get lost."

Just at the moment, the bells of St Alban's began to chime.

"There we are," said Claudia, smiling. "Can you hear them? Now you can find your way."

Annie led Claudia towards the sound. "Yes," she said, as they entered a more familiar street. "I know where I am now."

They continued to walk together, stopping occasionally to look at something which had caught their eye.

"If I have a daughter," said Annie, "I might call her Ariadne." Her eyes briefly took on a faraway look. "What about you?"

Claudia shook her head. "Not me. I would name her Giulia. After my mother."

"My mother's called Gertrude," said Annie. "Gert for short. She doesn't even like it herself, so I'm sure she wouldn't want to wish it on her granddaughter."

They both laughed, completely at ease in one another's company, as if they'd been friends for years.

"Father Francis," said Claudia, "the priest at the church, he thinks that the work I am doing – or rather, the work Professor Rutherford is doing – is an insult to God."

"I don't understand. You're pushing the boundaries of what we know. That has to be a good thing, surely?"

"Not according to Father Francis. He believes that only God can know the truth of everything. Just like he believes in the great mystery of the Eucharist, where Jesus is quite literally present in communion, that it is His body we eat in the bread and His blood we drink in the wine."

"Don't you believe that?"

"No more than you do. Non-Catholics regard the Host as a symbol of Christ, not the actuality."

"It's always felt to me more that we were celebrating the resurrection…"

"... as opposed to the crucifixion, *si*. So Father Francis believes that science is an affront to faith, and tantamount to heresy."

"Oh."

"He still had electric lights installed in the church, instead of candles, though." Claudia laughed mirthlessly.

" *'Thou canst not see my face, for there shall no man see me and live'.*"

Claudia looked across to Annie, surprised.

"Exodus. We had to learn great chunks of the Bible by heart at Sunday School," she said.

"And it's true. We'll never know all that there is to know. There'll always be something else. Just as it seems now that there's something smaller than the atom. But I do worry all the same. When Professor Rutherford does finally split the atom – and there's no doubt he will, if not this year, then next, or the one after that – it's what we then do with that capability that matters. From my own calculations on the fringes of this work, and from the conversations I've had with Miss Leslie, splitting the atom will release an energy of such force and power, of a magnitude nobody has ever experienced before, that, if used well, it could bring untold benefits for the good of all, but if used unwisely, it could threaten the very existence of the planet and destroy us all."

Annie felt a shiver right through her body as she listened, not unlike the panic and emptiness which she feared might swallow her up during those interminable silences in the Friends Meeting Room on Mount Street.

"Then I begin to think maybe Father Francis is right, that we shouldn't meddle in such things, that we could all be vapourised and vanish in a heartbeat, but then I think it is only natural for us to look at the world around us, and then look even deeper into space, and continue to ask ourselves these questions: why, how, what if...? We humans are filled with curiosity, are we not? When Prometheus discovered fire, it was, we are told, an act of theft from the gods, yet still this doesn't stop us, does it, of gazing in wonder at the sheer mystery of it all, while at the same time trying to fathom what lies at the core of that mystery, or of dreaming of what is waiting for us beyond the next horizon, or round the next corner? We may just be tiny specks, but we're not invisible, and we won't disappear, not entirely, so don't worry, Annie, the next time you go with your husband to a Quaker Meeting. Let your thoughts fill the silence and let them take you wherever you want to go."

Annie nodded her thanks.

Claudia continued. "My teacher – Miss Leslie – worked in Paris with the great Marie Curie. That was why Professor Rutherford invited her to join him here in Manchester. He wanted to know more about their experiments with radiation. It was Miss Leslie who calculated how long it takes for different elements, or even different atoms, to decay when subjected to radiation, and Professor Rutherford has developed a set of theories and principles arising from these calculations. He calls it half life. The time it takes for things to reduce to half of their initial value. And then half of that. And then half of that again, and so on and so on. For some atoms this is just a few seconds, while for others it might be as long as thousands of years. But the point is, however small a quantity is left, it never disappears completely. You can always keep dividing something in half, on and on, right until the end of time. And I find that a comforting thought…"

Annie said nothing. In truth she had not understood a half of what Claudia had been saying to her, but something about the natural, ordinary way she spoke about such things, mixed in with talk of Marco and her brother, of listening out for the church bells to avoid getting lost, as they walked through the labyrinth of narrow streets and alleyways of what, for now at least, was her home, made her feel that she too did not walk alone, fearing that her footsteps made no sound, and that she could leave her own mark on the earth.

They made their goodbyes and took their separate ways. Annie lengthened her stride and quickened her pace, ducking under an arch into a courtyard she did not recognise, confident that she'd find her way home soon enough, where she thought she would surprise Hubert with one of his favourites for dessert – plum pudding.

*

If Saturdays were set aside for the sights and sounds of Little Italy with Claudia, Sundays for Annie were all about family.

She and Hubert operated a four-weekly cycle. Once a month they returned to Hulme Hall Lane, where they attended Sunday service with Annie's parents, sister and brothers and afterwards went back to Corelli Street for lunch. The following Sunday they might go to the service at Central Hall on Oldham Street, the nearest chapel to where they now lived – if they could find a space, that is. Built on the site of the original place of worship established by John Wesley himself in 1781, this proved so popular that not everyone who tried to get in could be accommodated, and so services were sometimes held in the Free Trade Hall, where thousands of people would attend each week, until the Neo-Baroque Albert Street Mission was built, complete with its horseshoe-shaped first floor gallery, where Annie used to like to sit, if they attended a service there instead of at Oldham Street, so that she could look down on all of the people below, its sloping floor, coloured glass roof lights, fine terracotta detailing around the doors and windows, with glazed tiles constructed by Claudia's brother Matteo and friends at Quiligotti & Stefanutti, the Ceramics firm, after which Annie would hurry back to prepare a return lunch for her family.

When Mr and Mrs Warburton first visited them there, they wanted to inspect every inch of it. Annie's mother clucked with pleasure at the newness of the kitchen, while her father ran his hand and eye along the recently re-pointed outside side wall with silent approval. "Ay, lad," he said to Hubert, lighting up his pipe, "tha's done well for tha' self."

On the third Sunday Annie and Hubert accompanied Hubert's parents to his old family chapel on Eggington Street, followed by a lunch of roast beef with all the trimmings at Bignor Street, presided over supremely by Mrs Wright, while Mr Wright would invite Hubert to carve the joint.

On the fourth and final Sunday of the cycle, Hubert would go alone to the Friends Meeting House on Mount Street, while Annie stayed at home, nervously preparing a meal for Hubert's parents. She felt she needed the whole morning to do this, so as to be as little flustered as possible, and so Hubert did not mind that she ceased to accompany him to the Meetings. Or, if he did mind, he did not say. Once, Annie decided to ring the changes and serve her parents-in-law an Italian meal of meat balls cooked in a traditional sauce, using a recipe given to her by Claudia. Although Mr and Mrs Wright complimented her politely, commenting on the unusualness and novelty of the occasion, Annie could tell that they did not really like it, and so she did not repeat the exercise, saving all of her Italian experiments for week nights, when it was just herself and Hubert, who quickly became an enthusiastic convert. And then the whole cycle would start again.

Although this meant that weekends were now fixed in the regularity of their routines, the week days, after the initial novelty of no longer rising before dawn to go off to Pendlebury's to work in the tripe factory had worn off, felt long and empty by comparison. She was a diligent housewife. Every room was always spotless and immaculately tidy. She made curtains for all the windows. She planted shrubs and flowers in pots for the back yard. She made sure that Hubert's clothes were always freshly laundered, ironed, repaired and darned. But this still left acres of time to be filled in. She needed employment, but she recognised that Hubert's pride would be hurt if she suggested a part time job.

She took to visiting the Printing Works in the afternoons. Perhaps, she wondered idly, there might be something useful she might do there? Hubert, sensing her frustration and remembering her artistic flair in designing the decorations for the Japanese-themed Spring Fête at Hulme Hall Lane the previous year, asked his Uncle Gordon, his father's older, retired brother, (the 'G' in F.G. Wright & Son), who liked to help out in the Printing Works most afternoons, to show Annie the processes involved with photogravure, a technique they were deploying with increasing regularity, as demand for high quality images to be incorporated into what they printed was rising year on year. Exceeding both of their hopes, Annie took to it immediately, demonstrating an instant grasp of the techniques required and revealing a genuine talent and flair for the work.

"Tell me about it," asked Claudia on one of their Saturday mornings together, shopping for food from the street markets. "Leave nothing out."

Annie was pleased for once to have something she could share with her friend, which she knew more about, and Claudia was equally content just to listen and learn.

"Photogravure," she began, "is a way of reproducing photographs and then printing them. It involves a process with an Italian name."

Claudia looked away from the tomatoes she was examining inquiringly towards her friend.

"*Intaglio*," said Annie.

"*Ah si*," said Claudia, her face brightening, "some kind of engraving?"

"Exactly. Hubert purchased the equipment from a firm in Altrincham, so that we're now able to produce full colour designs for the first time."

"How does it work?"

"I don't understand it fully. When I see photographs being developed, it always seems like a kind of magic the way the image just appears before your eyes when it does."

Claudia nodded in agreement.

"When a positive film has been made from the original negative, this is then coated with a light sensitive gelatine onto a copper plate under a layer of cold water, which is squeezed into place and the excess water wiped clear. Then it's placed into a bath of piping hot water to remove the paper and any unexposed gelatine before the etching begins. This is done by passing the plate through a series of trays filled with acid, which cuts wells onto the plate of differing depths to hold the ink. The depth of each well determines the varying degrees of light and shade, tone and colour. Once this is complete, the plate is cleaned and dried and is then ready to print. This is where I come in. I apply a thick, oily printing ink to the whole surface, using a small sponge. Then I remove the excess with a piece of muslin, making sure that the ink goes where it's meant to, in each of the etched wells. Once this is done, the plate is then attached to the printing press."

"It sounds wonderful. I'd love to see it some time."

"Oh I'm sure that can be arranged. Hubert is there every Saturday, supervising the latest print runs of whatever job we happen to be working on. Maybe we could go next week. I'll ask, shall I?"

"I get the feeling," said Claudia after a pause, "that you're not telling me everything?"

Annie blushed. "Although I began by doing what I've just described, applying the ink to the final plate, Hubert asked me if I might instead supervise the whole process."

"Really? Congratulations."

"He says I have a real eye for detail."

"I'm sure you do."

Annie shrugged. "I just know what looks right, and how each part of the process can affect the way it turns out. I don't really understand it, but I seem to have a feel for it. So – I go in two afternoons a week just to keep a check on things."

Claudia smiled. "And how do the men who work the machines take to having a woman supervising them?"

"I'm the boss's wife," said Annie, "what can they say?"

They both laughed.

"I don't think they mind really. Everybody there just wants to do the best that they can. They adore Hubert and would fly to the moon if he asked them to."

"I'd like to meet him."

"Yes. You must. I'll ask him this evening."

They walked on in silence for a while.

"Do you think we will one day?" asked Annie. "Fly to the moon?"

"I'm certain of it," said Claudia. "But maybe not in our lifetimes."

"I wonder what it would be like? To look down from so high? How would we appear to them?"

"They wouldn't see us, obviously," said Claudia, "but they'd see the things we've done, the things we've left behind."

"Like what?"

"I imagine at night they'd see a whole chain of electric light, fanning out like some giant spider's web, criss-crossing the earth."

"And what would they think, I wonder, about those of us still floundering around in the dark?"

"I expect they'd look even closer there. Like when you are etching those copper plates to make sure the ink goes everywhere it's needed."

" *'The people that walked in darkness have seen a great light. They that dwell in the land of the shadow of death, upon them hath the light shined'*."

"One of your Sunday School quotes?" asked Claudia, smiling.

Annie nodded. "Isaiah 9, verse 2."

Claudia linked her arm through Annie's. "Come on," she said. "Let's treat ourselves to an ice cream."

They enjoyed their wafers like giggling school girls on a trip to the sea side. As they wiped their sticky hands and mouths afterwards, Annie said, "I've been thinking. Watching the photogravure at the Works has given me an idea. I reckon I could do something similar, on a much smaller scale, for myself at home."

"What do you mean?"

"I could make collages on bits of old board, a mix of drawing, painting, carving, with objects stuck on, broken pottery, gravel, wool, sandpaper, anything I could find, and then, using some ink from the Works – I'm sure Hubert would let me – I could print them onto paper and frame them as pictures to hang on the walls, or give as presents."

"That's a marvellous idea. What will be your first subject?"

Annie needed less than a second to respond. "The spindle tree in our street. I'd use bits of its bark, flowers, berries, leaves. Maybe I'll make four, one for each season?"

"*Perfetto*," declared Claudia.

Thus Annie's time was parcelled up.

In addition to the two afternoons each week she spent supervising the photogravure process at the Works – or, to be more accurate, rotogravure, for Hubert used a curved copper plate, as opposed to a flat bed, which allowed for faster, larger, more continuous print runs – Annie spent another two in the company of her mother-in-law, whom she could never address as "Evelyn", or "Mother", but only as "Mrs Wright", whereas she was always just plain Annie, to avoid any social confusion whenever the two women, each of them now Mrs Wright, were out together in company which, on these two afternoons a week, they invariably were, for Evelyn was busily involved in a variety of charities and committees, to which Annie was introduced and expected to join.

Much of this work arose out of Hubert's parents' long association with the Manchester and Salford Mission, which set up a range of homes and hostels for individuals in trouble, such as the Hostel on Cross Street, run by the Unitarians, where Evelyn, and now Annie too, would assist with the soup kitchens for the homeless one night each month. In addition there was the *Women's Home and Refuge* on Great Ancoats Street and the *Hammond House Preventative Home for Girls*, both of which had been started by the Methodists, as well as the more ecumenical *Manchester Christian Women's Temperance Association*, which was directly linked with the Police Courts Mission, operating as a forerunner to the Probation Service. Police Court Missionaries, as volunteers such as Evelyn and Frank, Hubert's father, were known, were increasingly becoming appointed by local magistrates to 'advise, assist and befriend' those unfortunate souls who had committed no crime other than being picked up by the police from the city's streets for various acts of inebriation and/or prostitution, frequently as a result of being homeless. *The Temperance Association*, of which Evelyn was Chair, was encouraging the courts to commit such offenders to reformatory homes and institutions, where they might receive help and succour, rather than prisons, where no such support was available, and from which they would be tipped back out onto the streets again, only in all probability to re-offend within weeks.

Twenty years earlier, when Evelyn had first joined the

Association, she had contributed, with her husband's help, to the writing of a penny pamphlet entitled *'Civilisation and the Drink Traffic: a plea for the Establishment of a Home for Inebriates'*, which argued: "If the powers of justices were extended to allow the commitment of 'habitual drunkards' for longer periods than the current utterly futile single month, (being the maximum permitted by the law as it stands), and commit to six months to institutions more appropriate to their needs, instead of six separate committals of one month, this would give sufferers more time to be supported in throwing off the desperate stupor of chronic drunkenness."

The pamphlet's tone struck a chord, and it was not long before public donations raised the sum of £700, sufficient to purchase a home at Ash Lodge on Halliwell Lane in Cheetham Hill, followed a few years later by a second house, 'The Grove', on Egerton Road in Fallowfield, where beds for more than twenty women in each at any given time were available. Both were within easy walking distance of the city centre, but, it was felt, far enough away to reduce temptation, and both were situated in desirable middle-class suburbs, noted for their beautiful tree-lined surroundings, staffed with skilful medical help.

Unlike the Magdalen Laundries, or some of the other establishments set up by different Christian churches, the emphasis in these homes was not punishment, but prevention and rehabilitation, so labels such as 'penitents' or 'inmates' were consciously and scrupulously avoided and, when circumstances prevailed which necessitated the incarceration of so-called offenders, the Police Courts Mission pushed for the provision of independent Matrons for female prisoners within the city's police stations.

"*Need not Creed*," was the rallying cry, and it was this which Evelyn was keen to impress upon Annie on the first of her regular weekly visits, shortly after she and Hubert were married.

Evelyn's time was divided evenly between site visits to the various establishments the Manchester and Salford Mission supported and the committee meetings which underpinned them. Annie felt much more comfortable in the actual centres, where she could talk directly to the women being helped there, than she did within the confines of the somewhat stiff, procedural formalities of the committees, but she was sensible enough to be aware that the activities carried out at the former would not be possible without the unseen work of the latter.

She was impressed and humbled in equal measure by her first visit to the *Women's Home and Refuge* on Great Ancoats Street. Donated as a gift by a Mr James Scarlett, it was, she was informed, a fine example of an Arts & Crafts building, designed by Manchester architect William Sharpe with vernacular revival detailing. Annie had not known what to expect before she stepped inside. She had, she supposed, imagined somewhere grim and cold, poorly lit with stone floors and large, impersonal dormitories, affording little if any privacy, with harsh, punitive factory conditions, more like a workhouse than a home. But as she was taken on a tour of the building, admiring its canted oriel windows with mullioned frames and leaded lights, up the wide staircases with square balusters and moulded handrails, past the plainly furnished bedrooms full of light from the seven dormer windows at the front, down to the glazed tiled coffee house, which provided alcohol-free opportunities for the girls and women to socialise, her opinions changed utterly. Within minutes she found herself helping to make coffee, chatting amiably with the residents, a mixture of short and long term, depending upon the perceived level of risk for each individual. She met orphans now too old for their orphanages, wives who were victims of domestic violence, servants escaping the too close attentions of their former male employers, as well as unwed mothers and prostitutes.

For Annie they seemed all too recognisable, having taken roads she too might have travelled down, had she not been lucky enough to have had the support of her family, however poor, the kinship of her chapel on Hulme Hall Lane, and the rare chance that had brought her and Hubert together in the first place. Annie did not ascribe to fate. She had always been sufficiently clear-eyed to realise that you make your own luck, and that if a chance for a better life comes along unexpectedly, you must do what you can to seize it, as she had done. But she wasn't so naïve that she didn't recognise a close-run thing when she saw one, and so she quickly shed any notions that hers was a visit from some kind of loftier plane, as it might have been perceived by some of the residents. Instead she rolled up her sleeves and joined them in whatever activity they were pursuing and talked to them as if she were living there too about their hopes and plans for the future.

Evelyn was quietly impressed by how at ease Annie had been with the women, especially the younger ones, not phased or judgmental about their language or more lurid accounts of their experiences which had led them to be there in the first place. Her down-to-earth, commonsense practicality would be an invaluable counter to Hubert's laudable, if at times rather airy, idealism. Annie, on the other hand, privately acknowledged that she had married into a certain privilege, albeit one which had been earned by dint of hard work, but that with such privilege came a certain responsibility, and she was determined this was something she would not shirk. At the same time, she also recognised that the economic and commercial success which came with that privilege brought with it further rewards, not the least of which was an entry into different social circles, and the opportunity for influence which followed that. Annie saw no reason to think why she could not straddle both worlds equally.

*

Hubert's father, Frank, was rarely present on these afternoons when Annie accompanied Mrs Wright on her charitable good works. Sometimes he would put in an appearance, after they had returned and were sitting in the lounge drinking tea from fragile blue and white china cups. Annie enjoyed the opportunity these sessions afforded her to examine at her leisure the *minutiae* of the Wrights' modest tastes, unassuming but evidently expensive, unpretentious but of unarguable quality. She admired in equal measure the upright piano with its selection of sheet music, a mixture of hymns, light classical arrangements, *lieder* and parlour songs, which, very occasionally, Evelyn would play after they had finished drinking tea and on which, one day, she promised she would give Annie lessons; the small octagonal mahogany occasional tables with their green leather surfaces, which could be placed alongside the various armchairs, each with their delicate lace antimacassars; the ornately carved monk's bench in which were stored various assorted embroidered linen tablecloths, the framed print of *Bubbles, A Child's World*, by Millais in a gilt oval above the fireplace, and the corner cupboard where the blue and white twelve-piece tea set was housed, complete with milk jug and sugar bowl, which were taken out for their use on each of these afternoons.

Frank, Annie learned, as the Managing Director of the company, was responsible for procuring the firm's contracts, while Hubert was in overall charge of the actual printing operations at the Works, an arrangement which appeared to suit them both equally, for their individual temperaments matched their separate roles perfectly. Annie detected a growing concern in Evelyn that Frank was working too hard – there had already been one minor health scare the previous winter – and that Hubert showed little or no inclination to learn this more strategic aspect to the business, remaining content to refine and improve the efficiency of the actual printing instead, always keen to install the latest innovations in equipment and technology – witness their recent investment in the locally built rotogravure press – and preferred to get his hands dirty in the Printing Works rather than press the flesh of council officers, company chairmen and factory owners, which was his father's daily round. Annie listened with silent attention to these unspecific voicings of anxiety from Evelyn, knowing that it was hoped she might pass these on to Hubert with the clear intention that this might in turn spur him on to delegate more of his tasks in the Printing Works to his more than capable team and begin to accompany his father on more of the business meetings, with a view to him taking these on completely once Frank decided to retire, which, Evelyn intimated, she hoped would be sooner, rather than later.

"It would be nice just to be able to spend more time together," she said. "Like we used to."

"How did you meet?" asked Annie, picking up a photograph of their wedding from the top of the piano. Evelyn's outfit was not white, but a greyish-green, Annie learned, "intended for subsequent use", added Evelyn, "which it most definitely got," she laughed. It was not in fact a dress, but a matching skirt and jacket, worn over a white lace blouse. Inside Annie quailed at how immodest and wasteful her own white dress must have seemed by comparison. Evelyn's was the model of restraint, a mixture of silk and cotton with silver beading on the lapels and skirt, which was long with just the merest suggestion of a vestigial bustle at the back. She carried a bouquet of seasonal tulips – "still my favourite flower," she declared. "Mine too," added Annie – while on her feet she wore a pair of dainty leather ankle boots, the same pair Annie had seen her wear on several occasions since, all these years later, including today.

"Buy quality," Evelyn said, when this was commented upon, "that's what Frank says. Otherwise it's false economy."

Annie listened and digested.

"We met," said Evelyn, with an almost girlish grin, "at the City Art Gallery on Mosley Street. It was the occasion of one of the Lady Mayoress's *Conversaziones*. Tickets cost two shillings, and so this was a very special treat, paid for by my father to celebrate my becoming twenty-one. There was a kind of indoor picnic, followed by dancing. The music, I remember, was provided by *The Band of Hope Ladies Temperance Orchestra*." She giggled again. "All very proper. I had no idea how to dance – I still don't – but when I saw this handsome young man walking across the floor with such purpose towards me, I thought: how can I possibly refuse such a debonair, good-looking man? You won't mention this to him, will you, Annie? We wouldn't want him to be getting a swollen head, would we? Anyway, as soon as he laid his hand upon my waist, I felt completely safe. I'd like to say we glided smoothly round the floor, but I don't believe we did. We staggered somehow, and I remember saying to him, 'I'm not very good at this, I'm afraid,' to which he replied, 'Of course you are. We're getting round, aren't we?'" Annie was reminded of how she had used the same phrase the first time she and Hubert had danced. "Well," continued Evelyn, "I suppose we've muddled along the best we can ever since. Like Frank said, we get round. But I do worry about him, how hard he works, how tired and pale he looks sometimes..."

Perhaps further words were spoken, after the conversation during one particular Sunday lunch in Portugal Street turned in this direction, only for Hubert blithely to start extolling the virtues of the new thermostatically controlled linotype machines, which ran off electricity, rather than the traditional gas pots they had been using up until now.

"As you know," explained Hubert to Frank over the washing up, a tradition Evelyn had suggested the first time she and Frank came to visit – "so that you two boys can talk business, while Annie and I discuss more important matters" – with undisguised enthusiasm, "with our current version we have to spend an inordinate amount of time skimming off the excess dross on the casting section of the machine to keep restoring the original strength and properties of the lead, tin and antimony alloy that we need to be able to keep printing without having to reset the type. The gas pots constantly have to be checked and manually adjusted to maintain the right temperature. With the electric version, this is thermostatically controlled, which means we can raise production levels to three hundred thousand impressions per slug."

"But how much is this going to cost us, Hubert?" countered Frank. "We only bought the Simplex five years ago."

"I thought that's what you'd say, so I've been in touch with the people in Altrincham, and they reckon they can convert our current version to electric for only…"

"I don't want to know," said Frank hastily, holding up the palm of his right hand, brandishing a willow pattern gravy boat. "I'm sure you've looked into it thoroughly."

"Yes, Father, I have," said Hubert, taking the gravy boat from him and drying it with the tea towel. "I believe the savings we make in time, the increased reliability, plus our ability to print more copies faster and to the same consistent high standard, will recoup the initial outlay in less than six months, and at the same time it will enable us to attract new customers who want larger print runs."

"Like who, for instance?"

"Like magazines and newsletters, and maybe smaller local papers."

Frank rubbed his chin. "Hmm. Maybe. But who's going to have to find these new customers, Hubert? Not you."

"I believe we've finished the washing up, Father. Thank you," said Hubert, avoiding Frank's questioning eye. "You go and join Annie and Mother, while I put the kettle on for some tea, shall I?"

The following week, when Annie walked up to the front door of the *Women's Refuge and Home* to meet Evelyn as usual, she was surprised to find it was Frank who was waiting for her.

"Mrs Wright is not feeling too well this afternoon," he said, raising his silver-topped cane to the brim of his hat in that customary, formal way he had. "She sends her apologies, and so you must make the best of me, her poor substitute, for today, I fear."

"I am sorry to hear that, Mr Wright. It is nothing serious, I hope?"

"No, my dear, only a cold, but she wishes to nip it in the bud, for she is, as you know, so very busy. Nor did she wish to risk breathing in too much of the smoke and fumes from the mills and factories she would pass on her way here."

"No, indeed not."

"We are so very fortunate to be now living in one of the more salubrious parts of the city. She will be herself again by and by, I have no doubt."

"I'm glad to hear it."

"Now, if you will permit me," said Frank, taking Annie's arm and guiding her away from the entrance of the *Women's Refuge and Home*, "this is not a place where men are always welcome, and I would not wish to make you feel uneasy in the most important work you do there, Annie, and so I wonder if you might grace me with your company this afternoon at one or two meetings of my own I must attend."

"Of course, Mr Wright, if that is what you'd wish. I'm sure I don't want to be in your way either. Not that you would have been in mine," she added hastily.

"Good," he said. "Our first appointment's at the Town Hall in Albert Square."

"Oh," said Annie, looking down at her clothes. "I'm not sure I'm dressed appropriately for there. I wear these clothes in case I'm needed for more physical work inside the Refuge, or if I'm asked to look after small children…"

"Don't worry," said Frank. "You look fine."

When they arrived in Albert Square, Frank paused by the Albert Memorial statue and directed Annie's gaze up towards the clock tower rising high above the rest of the building.

"That's the highest point in the city," said Frank, "currently."

"Currently?"

"I expect someone will build something taller one day. Manchester's is a restless spirit, don't you find? Always questing upwards."

It was just approaching two o'clock, and, as they stood together in the square, the bell tolled the hour.

"Great Abel," said Frank approvingly.

Annie knitted her eyebrows together into a question mark.

"Named after Abel Heywood."

Annie shook her head.

"A great bell for a great man. He's something of a hero for me. He was born in Prestwich, just a couple of miles north of where Mrs Wright and I now live, but moved to Manchester after his father died when he was two, where he lived in grinding poverty. He left school when he was nine to work in a warehouse for pungent dyes and chemicals, earning less than two shillings a week, some of which he used to attend the enormous Bennett Street Sunday School in a cellar the size of a cotton mill, as well as *The Mechanics' Institute* in Salford to carry on his learning, a fine example of the virtues of self-help. He was summarily dismissed by his employer for reading a pamphlet on the premises, and so he set up a Penny Reading Room in Manchester for others like himself. He began publishing and circulating a local version of *The Poor Man's Guardian*, but refused to pay the stamp duty, which was placed on all newspapers back then in order to suppress mass publishing of populist views, and was sent to prison for four months as a result. But he was determined to make newspapers available and affordable for the ordinary man and woman, and he eventually opened up a successful book selling business in premises on Oldham Street, where he used to print various papers and pamphlets in a room at the back, including *The Northern Star*."

What's that?" asked Annie.

"Was," corrected Frank. "R.I.P. Alas no more," he continued. "But for a time it was the main voice for the Chartists and their cries for political reform. Manchester would never have got the vote, had it not been for men like Abel Heywood."

"Some of us still don't have the vote," added Annie ruefully.

"No, lass," smiled Frank weakly. "But it won't be long now, I reckon, not if there's any justice in this world."

"Not too long, I hope."

"It was he who first inspired me to go into printing," he concluded.

"What happened to him?" Annie had never heard Frank be so expansive about anything before.

"Believe it or not, he first became an alderman on the Council, and then rose to become Mayor of Manchester. Not just once, but twice. The first time was at the height of the Cotton Famine, which near exhausted him, but he was persuaded to stand a second time more than ten years later, just in time to guide the building of the new Town Hall."

"What happened to the old one?"

"It's funny you should ask that. It was just round the corner from where we're standing now, at the junction of King Street with Cross Street."

"What was wrong with it?"

"Nothing. We just outgrew it, that's all. It was a grand building, with Ionic columns in the classical style. It became a lending library for a time, then a bank. Earlier this year, when Lloyd's took over, it became too small for them too, so they took down the façade to make more space."

"What a pity…"

"But they re-erected it over at Heaton Park. As a Colonnade by the Boating Lake. They had a Grand Opening there earlier this year, with brass bands and speeches. Hubert printed all of the posters for it. Mrs Wright and I were invited to attend. Hubert was too, of course, but it was a Saturday, and so I expect he was working."

"Yes," said Annie, beginning to appreciate a different drift floating beneath the surface of their conversation. "I expect he was."

The two of them continued to crane their necks looking up towards the graceful clock tower.

"And so they named the largest of the bells up there after the great man, the one that actually chimes the hours, Great Abe, and carved his initials in the brass. And just beneath, they engraved the lines *'Ring out the false, ring in the true'*."

"Tennyson," responded Annie automatically.

Frank turned to her, somewhat surprised.

"It was our school hymn," she said. "I loved school," she added wistfully. "The last time we sang it, I cried." She looked back up towards the clock and quietly began to sing, barely audible above the afternoon traffic.

"Ring out the old, ring in the new
Ring happy bells across the snow
The year is going, let him go
Ring out the false, ring in the true…"

"You have a charming voice," said Frank, smiling towards her. "You must sing at one of our Charity *soirées*. Mrs Wright will accompany you."

"I don't know about that. I'd be far too nervous."

"Nonsense. It's completely informal. We all have our different party turns to offer."

What was his, Annie wondered privately to herself?

As if reading her mind, he said, "I whistle." And they both laughed. "And sometimes I play the spoons. Come on," he said. "Time to go in."

He nimbly took the stone steps to the front entrance two at a time, where a livery-suited doorman greeted him with a warm "Good afternoon, Mr Wright", as if Frank was a regular, which Annie realised he surely was, to which he replied with an immediate "And a good afternoon to you too, Joseph. How's that boy of yours? Tell him I said 'hello', won't you?" Joseph held open the door for them both with a "Yes indeed, sir, I certainly will."

Until that moment, Annie had not known that anyone could enter the Town Hall whenever they wished. Certain chambers and committee rooms were out of bounds, but the majority of the building was open to the public.

"It's the People's Palace," said Frank proudly, "built just forty years ago out of public subscriptions and donations. Here," he added, leading Annie down a corridor to their left, "we still have a few minutes. Let me show you something."

Soon they were walking through the Great Sculpture Hall, filled with the busts of remarkable men, all of them born in or around Manchester, all of whom had contributed not only to significant improvements for the lot of the common man or woman locally, but nationally too. They passed the Anti-Corn Law reformers Cobden and Bright, the Salford brewer James Joule, who studied the nature of heat, set out the first law of thermodynamics, and who had a unit of energy named after him, and then John Dalton.

"Oh," said Annie, stopping in front of him. "I know a little about this one. My friend Claudia told me about him."

"Is she the one working at the university to help split the atom?"

"Yes," said Annie and then laughed. "She would say that she's only a lab assistant, more like a clerk than a scientist."

Frank shook his head. "She's part of a team, that's what counts. *'Behold also the ships which, though they be so great and are driven of fierce winds, yet are they turned about with a very small helm'.*"

"James, chapter 3," said Annie, smiling. "I must remember that the next time I see her."

"Hubert too has a great deal to thank Mr Dalton for."

"Really? Why?"

"You know that he's colour blind, I presume."

Annie nodded. "It was one of the first things he told me about himself."

"It was John Dalton who first properly researched it. It's passed on from one generation to the next. Hubert's me to thank for it, I'm afraid."

Annie stopped, as if the thought was new to her. "Does this mean that any children of ours will also have it?"

"Not necessarily. It's a fifty-fifty chance, I understand, and it doesn't affect us a great deal. The lenses on our glasses have a particular tint, which, though we neither of us can truly distinguish between red and green, helps us to learn and recognise the difference. It doesn't seem to stop us printing things in the correct colour, does it?"

"Not a bit," said Annie, smiling.

"Now," said Frank, "we take this staircase. Here, on the landing, this is what I wanted to show you."

They were just outside the entrance to the Great Hall, and Frank was pointing with his cane to the mosaic tiles on the floor at their feet, which depicted a pattern of bees and flowers.

"Do you know what type of flowers these are?" he asked. Annie shook her head.

"Cotton."

"Yes, of course. I should've guessed."

"The wealth of Manchester's built on it. But it doesn't do to keep all of one's eggs in just one basket, does it?"

"I'm not sure about that. So long as you watch it carefully and take special care not to drop it. And one basket's easier to carry than lots, I'd say."

"But what if someone comes along and wrenches that basket from you? If you've got a few others squirreled away somewhere, at least you won't lose everything."

"I remember our teacher at school telling us that squirrels forget where they bury most of their nuts."

"But we're not squirrels, are we? Not if we've learned to read and write and do arithmetic. Then we can keep tabs on all our baskets."

Annie narrowed her eyes. "What's all this about, Mr Wright?"

Frank smiled. "You're a smart girl, Annie. I saw it the day Hubert first introduced you to us. That's why I've brought you here with me this afternoon. Fifty years ago we depended on America for more than eighty percent of Manchester's total cotton trade. When the Civil War started there, our decision not to support the slave-owning southern states – which was the right and proper thing to do – meant that we lost all that business and brought about the Cotton Famine. I'm over-simplifying, but you get my drift? When the war ended, we got some of that trade back, though nothing like what it had been before, but the famine ended. And why? Well, partly because we found other markets – in India mainly – and though they're doing quite well just at the moment, they won't last for ever. It's simply Murphy's Law. Whatever can go wrong, will go wrong. Eventually."

"That's a gloomy way to live."

"It's realistic. Expect the worst, but hope for the best."

"That sounds like a contradiction. How can you hope for the best if you always expect the worst?"

Frank pointed to the other mosaic tile of the bee.

"Work?" asked Annie.

"What else is there? If the cotton fails again, then everything else suffers too. We have to try to be as prepared as we can be, and in the meantime make sure we're stocked up with provisions."

"Seven years of plenty for the seven years of famine."

"Exactly so. Seventy years ago the city was granted an official coat of arms. Look – there it is above the door there."

Annie followed the direction of Frank's cane, which he now pointed towards the entrance to the Great Hall.

"I suppose I must have seen it before, but I've never really stopped to think about it."

"Every part of it has a meaning. The red shield with the gold stripes is taken from the Lords of Manchester who ruled here six hundred years ago when it was just a small market town and was first granted a charter to hold an annual fair on what's now St Ann's Square. Either side of the shield are an antelope and a lion, taken from the arms of King Henry IV, with the red rose of Lancashire on each of their shoulders. The lion represents courage and the antelope peace. Beneath their feet is the city's motto, *Concilio et Labore*, *'by counsel and labour'*, or, as some people prefer to translate it, *'to gain wisdom we must work hard'*. Above the shield is a ship in full sail, a reference to the city's growing trade with the rest of the world, and right at the top of everything is the most famous part, a globe…"

"… covered with bees," interrupted Annie excitedly.

"A hive of industry," added Frank, smiling. "Have you ever seen a bumble bee's nest?" he asked.

Annie shook her head. "I've seen hives, but never a nest."

"The queen makes them. She finds a hole in the ground,

at the base of a tree, or in the foot of a wall, or sometimes she just burrows into the earth. She might take over one previously occupied by a mouse or a shrew, which has been abandoned. Once she's found one, she crawls inside and lays her eggs, which she covers with wax made from the pollen she's eaten. After a few days the eggs hatch into little wriggling grubs, which eat the pollen and nectar the queen has gathered for them."

"It's hard to imagine those grubs grow into bees themselves."

"But they do, and all too quickly. Hundreds of them. Most of them workers, a few of them drones, and one or two destined to be the next queens."

"Is it true that after the drones have mated with the new queens they die?"

Frank nodded. "They've done their job. They've made it possible for the species to survive."

"It hardly seems fair."

"What is it Paul said to the Thessalonians?"

Annie shook her head. "I can't remember."

" *'And that ye study to be quiet, and to do your own business, and to work with your own hands… that ye may walk honestly toward them that are without, and that ye may have lack of nothing'.*"

Annie stood among the mosaic bees, imagining she could hear their low hum among the newly opened, creamy yellow cotton flowers.

"Come on," said Frank. "Time for our meeting. I'll tell you what it's all about on our way down."

Annie found herself standing by a polished mahogany door, which led to a small committee room close to the Ante Room beside the Mayor's Parlour. She had not followed Frank inside, presuming that she would merely wait outside until he had concluded whatever business had brought him there, but Frank signalled for her to follow. Surprised, she took a deep breath and stepped inside.

The room was carpeted and, as the door was closed behind her, she became immediately aware in the change of acoustic, which, after the echoing footfalls along the stone corridors outside, now enveloped her in a deep hush. The walls were oak panelled and lined with portraits of various be-whiskered gentlemen, whom she took to be former mayors of the city. A long, highly polished refectory table sat in the middle of the room, at one end of which sat three middle-aged men in dark suits, who rose as one upon seeing Annie come in. They were all of them smoking and they hastily stubbed out their cigarettes as she approached them. Annie smiled. Her father-in-law had already wrong-footed them with her presence.

"Good afternoon, gentlemen," said Frank. "May I present my daughter-in-law, Mrs Annie Wright?"

"By all means."

"Good afternoon."

"You are most welcome."

"A most pleasant surprise."

"An unexpected diversion."

"Please. Be seated."

"Annie," continued Frank, "this is Alderman Hardcastle, Councillor Grandage and Mr Flitcroft, who is Clerk to the Council."

Annie graciously inclined her head while they flustered around her. A chair was pulled back, and, once she had sat down, they all followed suit, their eyes collectively feasting upon her. An amused Frank remained standing momentarily longer as he watched them falling over themselves for her attention.

"Should we order tea, do you think?" wondered one.

"And biscuits?" added a second.

"Or how about cake?" enthused a third.

"No, thank you, gentlemen," replied Annie, seeing at once what was expected of her. "My father-in-law has not long since had lunch, and he has important business to discuss with you. We are well aware that you are all busy men and we would not wish to detain you any longer than is necessary."

"Quite so, Annie," said Frank. "My sentiments exactly. Shall we proceed, gentlemen?" He sat down and Annie was sure that, as he did so, he winked in her direction. "First of all, thank you for agreeing to see me today. You've read my proposal?" he asked, referring to some papers that were spread before them on the table.

"We have, Frank," said Alderman Hardcastle. "A most interesting proposition. Well argued and fully costed."

"Ay," butted in Councillor Grandage, "it mebbe well costed but it's not cheap neither."

"Remind me again of the amount," said Mr Flitcroft, "for the sake of the minutes."

"It's all in the papers there," said Frank.

Mr Flitcroft quickly perused them, then whistled. "You're right, Grandage. Not cheap at all."

"But good quality always costs, gentlemen," said Hardcastle, "and we can't have the Corporation associated with anything shoddy, can we now?"

"That's all very well," put in Grandage, "but how are we going to pay for it? We're right in the middle of The Great Unrest."

A worried Hardcastle turned towards Frank. "Well?"

"Times are difficult just now, especially on the world stage, where we in Manchester have always been such successful operators."

"If you'd come with this two years ago," interrupted Grandage, "we might've been able to look more favourably on it. Britain was leading the way on trade, but the rest of the world's caught us up. We've seen prices go up, wages come down, workers laid off."

"I'm fully aware of the current economic situation, Mr Grandage, which is precisely why I've come to you with this proposal today."

"Tha's lost me there, lad," said Grandage again, shaking his head, "tha'd best explain. Be quick, mind, for we haven't got all day." He sat back in his chair, as if his mind was already made up.

Frank calmly folded his hands together and looked out over his glasses at the three men, rather like a patient school master before a class of slow and reluctant pupils.

"We live in a time," he said at last, "of ever increasing speed. The Machine Age," he continued, "the Age of Speed. We can all remember, when we were boys, that the fastest any of us could go was the speed of the fastest horse or the quickest ship. Now we have trains and motor cars. Aeroplanes are flying across the channel. People are hungry for information. They see what's going on around them, not just here in Manchester but across Europe and the World, and they want answers. Why are our wages going down when prices are going up? And what are our politicians doing about it? Especially our local ones? Now I know very well, gentlemen, that you and your fellow councillors, aldermen and other officers all do the very best you can to make better lives for all our citizens, rich or poor, young or old. You've piped in fresh water from Westmorland. You've dug sewers. You've cleaned up some of the waste from the rivers. You've lit more streets. More houses and businesses now have access to gas and electricity. There are more buses and trams year on year. You've made railways and canals. You've built hospitals, schools and cemeteries. You've knocked down old houses and put up new ones. You provide a police service and a fire brigade. And people need to know about this. What I'm proposing is for F.G. Wright & Son to carry out all of the

Council's printing needs for the next three years, after which we can all meet again to review it. I'm talking about supplying you with everything – from letterheads, note paper, minutes and agendas, to newsletters, reports and information sheets, as well as individual posters for all your specific events through the year – public meetings, lunch time concerts, Tulip Sundays, brass bands in public parks – plus health warnings, planning requests and eviction notices. So that the public will always recognise whenever they see a notice or a letter that it's come from the Corporation, and that you'll be able to keep the public informed of everything you're doing."

"All our meetings are open to the public."

"But how many come? How many can?"

"If they're interested, they come."

"But what I'm proposing is a way of engaging with more and more people, so that they might feel that it's worth their while turning up, or writing letters, because their voices will have a better chance of being heard."

"This is all very well, Frank," said a still unconvinced Grandage, "but it sounds to me like you're encouraging sedition."

"No, Clarence. What I'm saying is the opposite, that you risk sedition if you *don't* keep the people informed and invite them to take part in the great debates of our time."

Frank sat back, and for the first time Annie could see just what this was costing her father-in-law emotionally. A lot was riding on this meeting. Not just a massive boost for the business, but that this was something he ardently believed in.

"You've convinced me," said Alderman Hardcastle. "Frank's right. The world's changing, and we've not just got to respond, we've got to take the bull by the horns, lead by example, otherwise we risk being left behind, becoming obsolete."

"I'm already obsolete, Warren. A dyed-in-the-wool

dinosaur."

"Stuck-in-the-mud, more like, Clarence," said the Alderman.

" *'All is flux. Nothing stays still'*," said Mr Flitcroft, suddenly. It was the first time he had spoken up since the meeting proper had started, and everyone turned towards him. He blushed. "Heraclitus," he stammered, somewhat apologetically. "Of Ephesus." The others continued to stare. "As quoted in Plato. His philosophy that change is central to the meaning of the universe... Everything moves... We cannot step twice into the same river..."

It was Councillor Grandage who broke the silence first. "Well, Mr Flitcroft," he said, "we don't all have the advantages of your classical education, but nothing's going to persuade me to step into the River Medlock once, never mind twice, till it's all been cleaned up, which we intend to do, provided that the money we need to do it isn't diverted into some kind of daft, hare-brained scheme like this one, Frank, begging your pardon."

"But mightn't a conversation with the people who live and work along the banks of our rivers be the best way to start going about cleaning them up? With respect, they will know better than any of us what needs to be done first. That way, you'll be saving both time and money. And pollution's only one of dozens of topics that people would want to talk to you about."

"How do you know?"

"That's just it. I don't. What I'm suggesting is a way of finding out more accurately what the people's priorities are."

"I'll tell you what the people's priorities are – a fair day's wage for a fair day's work, enough money to put a roof over their heads and food on their table."

"With respect, Clarence, those are matters for the national government, not the city council. What the Corporation does is provide services that all of us need – hospitals, schools, roads, transport, healthy air, clean water, parks and libraries, safe streets, better houses – and who better to tell you how best to deliver those things than the people themselves, in a series of big conservations?"

"Or picnics?" chipped in Annie. Everyone looked at her. She had surprised herself. She had not intended to speak, but the thought just popped out before she could stop herself.

"Yes, Mrs Wright?" said Alderman Hardcastle in a kindly voice.

"Well, it's just that… people work hard… and when they get home – from the mine or the mill or the factory, or the tripe works like I had to – well… they're usually too tired to think about going out again, unless it's to the pub on the corner… they're certainly not going to feel like coming here, to the Town Hall, it's too… well, until today I thought you would only come here if you were in some sort of trouble… but a picnic, on a Sunday afternoon, everyone enjoys those, don't they? And we all of us live somewhere near a park, or a piece of open land, or a school playground, or a church hall, don't we? You could hold your big conversations there. Only if you call them a picnic, more people are likely to turn up and they'll be less tired and more open to say whatever it is that's on their mind. I'm sure that's what the women would say anyway…"

"Thank you, Mrs Wright," said Councillor Grandage, somewhat witheringly, already beginning to turn away from her, back towards the men at the table, "but it's not the women who cast their votes at the ballot box, is it?"

"No, Mr Grandage," replied Annie, smiling sweetly, "you are quite right of course. But who is it, do you think, who wields the most influence in persuading their husbands, fathers and brothers which way they might cast their votes?"

"Bravo, Mrs Wright," laughed Alderman Hardcastle. "She's got you there, Clarence."

"Hmmph," grunted Grandage, folding his arms across his

chest.

"I think a series of Big Picnics across the city is a splendid idea, Mrs Wright, and would be an excellent first step towards the kind of greater openness between the Corporation and the people that your proposal is advocating, Frank."

"And we could design and print all the posters for them, couldn't we?" said Annie quickly, looking towards her father-in-law.

Hardcastle chuckled once more. "Your daughter-in-law has a keen eye for business, I see, Frank?"

Frank smiled back, saying nothing.

"But when we do go along this road of yours, Frank…"

"*If*," interrupted Grandage sharply. "Nothing's been decided yet."

"Quite so, Clarence," sighed Hardcastle, "but if we do, we'll need to give some serious consideration to the design. Half the things that come through the post these days look like a dog's dinner. You can't tell where they're from."

"I quite agree," said Frank, "and so I've brought along some preliminary ideas." He proceeded to take from his brief case a folder with a few sketches containing examples of possible envelope and letter headings. Annie detected immediately Hubert's immaculate copper plate hand done with the finest of italic nibs and experienced a faint pang of disappointment that he had not shown any of them to her, or even discussed them with her, before giving them to his father.

"They must have dignity," said Hardcastle, "a certain amount of grace and elegance. They should be quietly understated, but they must have gravitas and be instantly recognisable."

"Precisely," agreed Frank, as he spread the drawings across the table. "I believe these to have all of those qualities."

Annie, who had not been directly shown any of the potential designs to view herself, took a sidelong glance at each of them as they were being passed around between the four men. After a while, as the men held up first this example, then that, as their preferred choice, quibbling over fonts and lay-out, she found she could restrain herself no longer.

"Excuse me," she coughed. "May I be allowed to say something?"

The others all stopped and looked at her once more, almost as if, for the time being at least, they had forgotten she was still in the room.

"Yes, of course, Mrs Wright."

"Thank you. It's just that... while the coat of arms is all very fine, I'm not sure that everybody understands it. I know *I* didn't, not until my father-in-law explained its meaning to me earlier this afternoon. But everybody recognises the Town Hall, with the Clock Tower and Great Abe..." The others looked at her appraisingly with raised eyebrows. "And as I understand it," she continued, "isn't the point of this whole exercise about visibility and recognition." The men nodded and murmured. "So how about..." She reached across to take a pencil from Frank. "...something like this?" Quickly and expertly she sketched an outline of the roof of the Town Hall in the top left hand corner of both the letter paper and the envelopes. She sat back and waited for their reaction.

"Well... yes..."

"If we put the coat of arms down at the bottom... like this..."

"... and placed 'Manchester Corporation' here, instead of there..."

"... that would be perfect."

They all turned back towards her. "Thank you, Annie," said Frank. "Your idea has made all the difference. Wouldn't you agree, gentlemen?"

"Hear, hear!"

There were further mutterings of approval, and the meeting seemed to be on the point of breaking up, when Mr Flitcroft spoke up once more in his thin, reedy voice.

"Without wishing to be the spectre at the feast, as Clerk to the Council, I do feel it incumbent upon me to point out that we haven't, for the purposes of the Minutes, actually agreed on anything. I need to have some kind of formal proposal to take back to the next Full Meeting of the Finance Committee, who will have to ratify whatever that might be…"

"Ay, Flitcroft," spoke Grandage, relishing his role as the Voice of Doom, "and there's no guarantee they'll approve."

"Nonsense, Clarence," said Alderman Hardcastle. "If we recommend something, they're bound to take it seriously."

"Mebbe so, mebbe not," replied Grandage lugubriously, with evident enjoyment. "It depends upon what we actually recommend."

"Then what do you propose?" asked Hardcastle, generously between pursed lips.

"Some kind of pilot," mused Grandage. "One of these Big Picnics and a trial period of three months for the stationery."

Alderman Hardcastle looked troubled. "Frank?"

"If I may, gentlemen? Might I point out that if, after three months, you decide to continue with the new stationery, or to abandon it in favour of what you have currently, or move on to something different altogether, that would be something of a false economy?"

"How so?" demanded Grandage with determined belligerence.

"Well, for one thing, once the linotype has been set up for printing, to dismantle it and then create new designs is going to be double the expense."

"And with the new machines my husband has installed, the Linotype Simplex," Annie said proudly, "we can produce more than three hundred thousand impressions before the type has to be checked for any re-casting, which is really good value for money, I'd say."

Still Councillor Grandage did not appear wholly satisfied.

"Agreed," he said at last, "so long as none of this puts even a farthing onto the rates."

"Of course it won't," said a relieved Hardcastle. "It's going to save us money in the long run."

"Very well, he conceded.

"So," said Alderman Hardcastle, indicating to Mr Flitcroft that he should write this down for the official Minutes, "subject to agreement by the Full Finance Committee, our proposal is that F.G. Wright & Son should undertake all of the Corporation's design and printing needs, for both internal and external use, all stationery, reports, papers, posters, leaflets and newsletters, and anything else deemed necessary by the Corporation in pursuit of its day to day needs for a period of three years, with a review to be carried out after twelve months."

His voice took on the finality of a judge pronouncing sentence with a gavel, and as soon as he had finished, the meeting broke up. Frank began collecting up his papers and putting them back in his brief case. Alderman Hardcastle went over to Annie and shook her hand.

"It's been a great pleasure to meet you, Mrs Wright. I do hope that you and your husband might join us for dinner at one of our functions in the future."

"Thank you, sir. I'm sure we'd be delighted," replied a somewhat breathless Annie.

Councillor Grandage slapped Frank on the back as he was leaving the room. "Congratulations, Frank. No hard feelings, eh? It's my job to ask tough questions. I'm sure you'll do a terrific job for us. You always do. I'd offer you a cigar," he said, "if I didn't know you don't indulge. You don't mind if I do, though, eh?" he added, lighting one up as he opened the door. "I say," he whispered, though not so quietly that Annie could not hear, "you've got a shrewd new recruit over there – brains as well as beauty!" Laughing, he made his way out of the room and along the corridor, until finally only Frank and Annie remained.

"Thank you, Annie," he said. "You were quite splendid. Just as I knew you'd be."

"Does this mean you've won the contract?"

Frank paused. "It doesn't do to count one's chickens," he said. "I've learned that the hard way. But the signs look promising."

"So what happens next?"

"Well – you heard what they said. They take it to their Finance Committee."

"Will you have to go along to that too?"

"No, thank heaven."

"Why do you say that?"

"You know what committees are like. A team of bell ringers all pulling on different ropes and never finding the right notes. There'll be those who are against it because they're against anything that requires change. There'll be those who are against it because they didn't come up with the idea themselves. There'll be those who just like the sound of their own voices, and there'll be those who'll be wishing they were some place else. There'll be those who'll be worrying about someone who's sick, there'll be those who'll be wondering what's for their tea, and there'll be those who'll simply be wishing they were home."

Annie looked alarmed. "Won't there be anyone who's for it?"

"Don't worry, love," he said. "There'll be plenty of those too, and as Alderman Hardcastle's the Chair of the Committee, there'll be plenty who'll listen to what he says and agree with him."

"That's alright then."

"But mostly there'll be even more who'll take one look at

that drawing of the Town Hall you did and say to themselves, 'Now that's more like it. It's modern, and that's what we've always prided ourselves on being here in Manchester. Modern. One step ahead. And you showed 'em, Annie."

By now they had walked back along the corridors the way they had first come in and they found themselves just outside the large oak doors that led into the Great Hall.

"What's through there?" she asked.

"The Manchester Murals," said Frank. "Twelve giant paintings by Ford Madox Brown, or frescoes to be more precise, using the Gambier Perry process, each one depicting different scenes from the city's history."

"Oh," said Annie, her eyes lighting up, "I should like to see those."

Frank took his watch from his waistcoat pocket and frowned. "We've not much time," he said, "before I need to get back. I don't like to leave Evelyn too long if she isn't feeling on top form."

"No. Of course not," said Annie.

Frank registered the fleeting look of disappointment on Annie's face. "Maybe we've time to look at just one," he said. "Walk inside and go straight to the first one that catches your eye. We'll look at that one and come back another time to see the others. Agreed?"

"Agreed," she said, and she hurried through the great vaulted doorway, stopping immediately in front of one which showed a man, surrounded by cloth and tape measures, staring at what looked like the projection of the sun from a telescope onto a sheet of paper.

"Ah," said Frank, as he caught up with her. "An excellent choice."

"What is it?"

"*Crabtree Watching the Transit of Venus in 1639.*"

"And what's that in English please?"

Frank laughed. "William Crabtree was a draper – look,

you can see the bolts of material spilling out from a table onto the floor."

Annie nodded eagerly, studying the painting hard from very close up.

"He lived in Broughton, hardly any distance at all from where Mrs Wright and I now live. His good friend, Jeremiah Horrocks, a curate who lived in Preston, was an amateur astronomer, and he had calculated that Venus would pass between the sun and one of the larger planets on 4th December 1639. Horrocks asked Crabtree to watch for it and act as a confirming observer if it did indeed appear."

"And I'm assuming that it must have, given that this mural's been painted."

Frank nodded. "It was a cloudy day apparently, but just half an hour before sunset the clouds lifted and Crabtree was able to see it."

"What does it look like?"

"A bit like an eclipse of the moon, only much, much smaller, because Venus is so much further away. In just a few hours you can see what looks like a tiny black speck making its way across the face of the sun, and that's it – the transit of Venus."

"What's so special about it?"

"It's very rare, but – because of the work of Crabtree, who used it to make all kinds of other observations, like how big Venus is and how far away the Earth is from the sun – it's also very reliable. It's all to do with when the orbits of Venus and the Earth coincide. It appears twice in eight years, but then it won't appear again for a hundred and five years. Then, after another appearance eight years after that, it doesn't return for another hundred and twenty years. People have been observing it since ancient times. The Egyptians noticed it. So did the Greeks and the Babylonians, later the Chinese. But it was here in Manchester that it first began to be understood."

"When was it last seen?"

"Not that long ago actually. 1890."

"The year I was born," said Annie turning away from the mural. "I guess that means we'll not be seeing it again any time soon, will we?"

"Not in our lifetimes, that's for sure. 2012, or thereabouts."

"A hundred years from now." Annie breathed out a low whistle. "That sounds so far into the future, doesn't it? We might even be flying to Venus by then."

"Who knows? I expect Manchester will look very different by then."

"But I reckon this Town Hall will still be here and Great Abe will still be tolling the hours."

They stood in silence for a while, pondering time, each at different ends of the telescope.

"I was thinking," said Frank after a while.

"Yes?"

"What made you choose this mural? Out of all of the twelve, you came straight over to this one."

Annie paused, wondering whether or not to tell him. Why shouldn't she, she thought. "I nearly chose the one showing *The Trial of Wycliffe* – Hubert waxes all lyrical about it, you know, the birth of printing and all that?"

"Does he now?" said Frank, chuckling but clearly pleased.

"But then I saw the light coming through the window in Crabtree's attic, and it reminded me of when we could see Halley's Comet in the sky at night two years ago. Do you remember?"

"How could I forget?"

"That was the night Hubert proposed to me."

"Was it?" said Frank.

"Ay. He went down on his knees right there in our street next to our front door."

"How wonderful."

"Ay. It was."

Frank watched his daughter-in-law lost in remembering that time, and he tried to picture his son, normally so reserved, acting with such wild, unbridled spontaneity, but he found that he couldn't. He was pleased that Annie had shared this image with him.

"Thank you," he said.

She returned to the moment. "What for?"

"This afternoon. You were very brave to speak up the way you did. I had a feeling you could, though I wasn't sure you would, but I was hoping you might."

"Is that why you brought me along?"

"I had a hunch that you'd be interested in the business side of things."

"I'm interested in all of it," she said with sudden force and held Frank's gaze, so that it was he, not her, who looked away first, nodding and smiling.

"And that illustration you drew of the Town Hall…"

"You liked it? I mean, you weren't just saying so?"

"It's perfect. It's exactly what's needed to make the Corporation more in touch with the people, more in tune with the times. We'll definitely use it."

Manchester
Corporation

Annie couldn't help herself. She beamed.

Frank looked suddenly pale. Although the afternoon had, in the end, turned out possibly even better than he had hoped, it had taken a great deal out of him, she could see that now. He lowered himself down onto one of the chairs back in the corridor with the mosaic tiles of the bees and the flowers, and put his right hand to his chest. He was clearly in some discomfort.

"What is it?" asked Annie, suddenly alarmed.

Frank waved his left arm vaguely in the direction of his brief case. "Tablets," he managed to say at last, "in the side pocket."

Annie quickly found them and brought them across, together with a glass of water.

After he had taken two, his breathing began to calm and a little colour returned to his cheeks.

"Thank you," he said. "It's angina. I have to be careful not to over-exert myself."

"Let me help you home," said Annie. "We can get a tram from just outside that takes you almost directly to your door."

Frank shook his head. "I can manage. If you arrived home with me, Mrs Wright would only be worried."

"Then I shall simply say that I have come to see her, for you told me she was unwell, to see if there's anything I might do to help."

"No," insisted Frank. "It's very kind of you, but I can manage. I shall be perfectly fine in a minute or two."

Annie let him lean against her as they walked together slowly back towards the entrance of the Town Hall, where Joseph in his liveried suit wished them both a Good Evening". She then accompanied him to the tram stop, where they found another bench on which they could sit for longer. Frank gestured vaguely in the direction of the Town Hall.

"I don't want anyone from in there to see me like this. There can be no doubts that as a firm we're not up for the challenge of this new order. If we get it, that is."

This speech appeared to have exhausted him and he leant his back against the wooden slats of the bench.

"Just rest," said Annie, "till you've recovered your strength again. If anybody comes, I can tell them that it's me who's feeling tired. One of the advantages of being female," she added with a rueful smile.

He smiled weakly back.

She waited with him until the tram arrived and she had seen him safely aboard. She stood and waved till he disappeared from view.

The evening began to feel chilly. She pulled her scarf tightly round her throat. It was that hour of the day when dusk has started to descend, but it is still light enough to see. The street lights had not yet started to come on, though they soon would, casting their comforting orange glow as the smoky air danced around them, illuminating the many moths caught up in their shadow. Great Abe began to toll the hour, each heavy stroke sonorous in the twilight.

"Ring out the grief that saps the mind
For those that here we see no more
Ring out the feud of rich and poor
Ring in redress to all mankind..."

She walked purposefully through the city back towards Portugal Street, matching her steps to the rhythm of Tennyson's *In Memoriam,* her old Elementary School hymn. All the hundreds and thousands of strangers she shared this place with seemed to press in all around her. She had walked, for a brief hour, the corridors of power this day and witnessed just how the world operated, and now here she was again, thrust back in its midst, marching head bent into the wind, along the surface of the earth, feeling the mighty roar and rumble of its hidden workings rumbling beneath her feet.

"Ring out false pride in place and blood,
The civic slander and the spite
Ring in the love of truth and right
Ring in the common love of good..."

She raised her head. She felt a new determination course through her. Art and commerce. She would not be ground down. She would keep walking, and she would not stop until she had made her full transit.

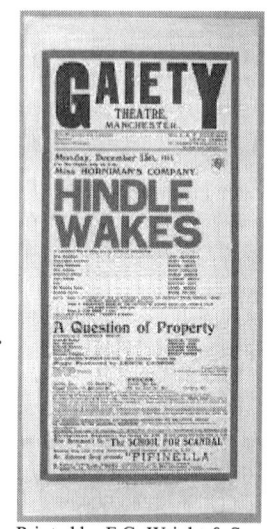

*

Printed by F.G. Wright & Son

Act One

The scene is the foyer of The Gaiety Theatre situated directly opposite the Free Trade Hall on Peter Street, Manchester. Originally known as The Comedy Theatre, it was designed by Salford born Alfred Derbyshire, a Quaker, who also designed the Friends Meeting House just behind the theatre on Mount Street.

It is 17th May 1912, a fine summer's evening. The theatre is presenting a new play, 'Hindle Wakes', by local playwright Stanley Houghton, starring Miss Edyth Goodall in the role of the feisty Miss Fanny Hawthorn, and a young Sybil Thorndike as the jilted fiancée, Miss Beatrice Farrar. Mr Houghton was born in Ashton-on-Mersey less than seven miles from The Gaiety Theatre, where he still lives and works as an assistant in his father's cotton mill. He is nervously pacing backstage, smoking a cigarette, ahead of this evening's opening performance, which is being presented by Miss Horniman's Company, the country's first ever permanent repertory company as part of a season celebrating what has come to be called 'The Manchester School of Dramatists', featuring the likes of Harold Brighouse and Allan Monkhouse, who have been championed by Miss Horniman as pioneers of the new trend of naturalism, which has been sweeping across the theatres of Europe during the past ten years. Mr Houghton hopes, if his play is a success this evening, to become a member of this much vaunted élite and devote himself full time to play writing, unaware that fate holds an altogether different outcome for his life's story, death from viral meningitis less than eighteen months later, aged only thirty-three.

Miss Horniman, the artistic visionary behind the company and owner of the theatre, has not yet arrived. She is currently to be found across the road, in the main lounge of The Midland Hotel, where she is doubtless holding court in her customary flamboyant manner. Granddaughter of John Horniman, founder of the world-famous tea company and later the esteemed philanthropist, Miss Horniman – or Anne Elizabeth Fredericka, to give her her full title – attended the Slade School of Art in London, before undertaking dashing cycling expeditions to the Swiss Alps. While in Europe she fell under the spell of the plays of Henrik Ibsen and first introduced these to British audiences, along with the early plays of George Bernard Shaw, William Butler Yeats and John Millington Synge at The Abbey Theatre in Dublin, which she ran successfully for several years. Always seeking new challenges, she next alighted upon Manchester, where she first began staging new and modern plays in the thousand-seater auditorium of The Midland Hotel, where she scandalised local society by smoking in public and wearing trousers. After many sell-out performances there, the opportunity arose for her to purchase The Gaiety from United Theatres for the princely sum of £25,000 in early 1908.

It is here, just four years later, where our drama is set.

The Stage Manager has just rung the half, and the lavishly decorated red and gilt foyer is already beginning to fill up with eager playgoers, meeting early for a pre-performance drink in the theatre bar. There is a buzz of anticipation at the prospect of another new, gritty play, typical of this new celebrated Manchester School, whose reputation has ensured another sold out first night.

Among those arriving early, and separately, are the WRIGHT family – Frank and Evelyn, their son Hubert and his wife, Annie, who look around admiringly at the décor. HUBERT and ANNIE enter first.

HUBERT:
  Well? What do you think?

ANNIE:
  I'm speechless.

HUBERT:
  That makes a change.

ANNIE:
> Ha, ha. I'm going to ignore that remark. Nothing's going to spoil this evening.

HUBERT:
> Happy Anniversary.

ANNIE: (*sotto voce*):
> I suppose it would be improper if I were to let you make love to me right this minute.

HUBERT:
> Especially as my parents have just arrived.

FRANK and EVELYN enter, looking around until they spot HUBERT and ANNIE to whom they wave excitedly.

FRANK:
> Sorry we're late. Evelyn kept changing her mind about what she should wear.

EVELYN:
> Don't listen to him, dear. I was ready hours ago. It was Frank who took an age. He simply wouldn't stop working.

HUBERT:
> Good evening, Mother. Father.

FRANK:
> Have you picked up the tickets yet?

HUBERT:
> No. I was waiting for you. I wasn't sure whose name they were in.

FRANK:
> Let's go and pick them up together then – there's quite a queue forming at the Box Office, I see – and leave these two ladies to gawp at all the fashions.

EVELYN:
> Really, Frank, the things you do say. I never gawp. And I'm sure Annie doesn't either, do you, dear?

ANNIE:
> This is my first ever trip to a theatre, don't forget. I feel like my eyes must be on stalks.

EVELYN:
> Then you have my permission to 'gawp' to your heart's content – although I think it is you that will be the centre of attention for everyone else tonight. You look positively radiant. That dress really suits you.

ANNIE:
> Thank you. Can I let you into a secret?

EVELYN:
> Please do.

ANNIE:
> It's the first dress I've ever bought. Everything else I've ever worn has either been passed down, mended or repaired, or, for special occasions, made, either by my mother, for when I was confirmed, or by me, for my wedding.

EVELYN:
> Oh yes, of course. You looked a picture that day, Annie. Happy Anniversary.

ANNIE:
Thank you.

EVELYN:
That shade of green suits you so well.

ANNIE:
Do you think so? It's not too…

EVELYN:
What?

ANNIE:
I was going to say 'revealing', but perhaps 'tight' is more accurate? I can hardly breathe.

EVELYN:
It's perfect. We ladies know what it means to suffer, do we not? Where did you get it?

ANNIE:
Kendal Milne's.

EVELYN:
I thought so.

ANNIE:
Hubert took me there last Saturday. He said I could choose whatever I wanted, and that I wasn't to look at the price tag.

EVELYN:
How generous. He takes after his father.

ANNIE:

> I'll tell him you said that. He'll be so pleased. How is Mr Wright?

EVELYN: (*looks at ANNIE sharply*):

> Fine. Why do you ask?

ANNIE:

> Oh, no reason. It's just that he appears to be working harder than ever.

EVELYN:

> He's looking to expand the business, that's all. It's a good time right now, he says, with lots of opportunities. He's securing more and more new contracts all the time. Like this one tonight with *The Gaiety* – and all the other theatres in Manchester now, I understand. And Hubert always does such a good job in terms of quality. Word gets around. My husband built this business up from nothing, Annie. He just wants to make sure that when he retires – which one day he'll have to, even if he doesn't want to accept the idea – he leaves it for you and Hubert in the best possible health.

ANNIE:

> Even at the risk to his own?

Pause.

EVELYN:

> Here they come now. Let's have no more words on this matter. We don't want to spoil the evening, do we? It's a special occasion. (*To FRANK*). Did you get the tickets?

FRANK:
All present and correct. Dress Circle.

EVELYN: (*looking around*):
Oh? Isn't that Mr and Mrs Young?

FRANK:
Ah, good. I was hoping we might run into one another this evening.

EVELYN:
Please, Frank. Not tonight. This is meant to be a celebration. Can't you leave work be just for once?

FRANK:
I'll not be more than a minute. One has to make the most of such chance encounters.

EVELYN:
Are you sure this was just chance? It sounded to me like you expected to see the Youngs this evening.

FRANK:
Not expected, Evelyn. Hoped. Will you come with me, Hubert?

HUBERT:
If you'd like me to.

FRANK:
I shan't be long. I'll just pay my respects, that's all. Hubert?

FRANK and HUBERT take their leave.

ANNIE:
Who are the Youngs?

EVELYN:
Mill owners. They own Beehive Mill on Jersey Street, and they've just put in a bid for the larger Victoria Mill on Lower Vickers Street – your old neck of the woods, Annie.

ANNIE: (*she nods*):
My father's sister, Jess, still works there.

EVELYN:
Oh Lord, Frank's bringing them over. Steady the Buffs.

FRANK and HUBERT return, accompanied by MR and MRS YOUNG, together with two younger people.

FRANK:
Mr Young, please allow me to introduce you to my wife, Mrs Evelyn Wright, and my daughter-in-law, Mrs Annie Wright.

MR YOUNG:
Delighted to meet you. My wife – Mrs Young. And this is our son – Cecil, and his fiancée, Miss Ruth Kaufman, who this very evening have announced their engagement.

EVELYN:
Congratulations. Then this evening is a double celebration, for today marks the first anniversary of Hubert and Annie.

MR YOUNG:
Well, well. Splendid. Perhaps you would care to join us

for champagne and oysters in *The Midland* afterwards.

EVELYN:
Well, that's most kind of you, I'm sure, but…

FRANK:
We'd be glad to.

MR YOUNG:
Excellent. Then you and I might have a chance to continue our conversation further, Frank. (*He looks around him at the assembled company with a self-satisfied smile*). Well, isn't this marvellous? Two young couples – one (*he gestures towards ANNIE and HUBERT*) who've just crossed the Rubicon, the other (*he turns towards CECIL and RUTH*) just about to.

MRS YOUNG:
Edward – honestly! You make marriage sound like some kind of military campaign. What are we to do, Mrs Wright?

EVELYN:
I think we should just leave them to play toy soldiers. Let's see about a programme, shall we, for tonight's performance?

MRS YOUNG:
A most sensible suggestion. (*They begin to move away*). I hear this new play might be about to raise a few eyebrows…

EVELYN:
Really? In what way…?

The party has naturally split into three groups. As EVELYN and MRS YOUNG leave to buy their programmes, FRANK and MR YOUNG move to one side, presumably to continue their business conversation, leaving HUBERT and EVELYN and CECIL and RUTH hovering together somewhat awkwardly.

ANNIE:
How did the two of you meet?

RUTH:
At church.

ANNIE: (*smiling*):
Hubert and I met at chapel.

HUBERT:
Where?

RUTH:
In Denton.

CECIL:
Before my family moved out to Whalley Range.

HUBERT: (*to RUTH*):
Is your father Kaufman Optics?

RUTH: (*brightly*):
Yes.

HUBERT:
We do your printing.

RUTH:
> Really?

CECIL:
> Wright's do everyone's printing.

ANNIE:
> Have you been to the theatre before?

RUTH:
> Twice. But not to *The Gaiety*. Both of them Shakespeare. *Much Ado About Nothing* at The Hippodrome…

CECIL:
> That sums it up perfectly – a great deal of to do about absolutely nothing at all…

RUTH: (*glares at CECIL*):
> … and The Tempest at *The Prince's*.

CECIL:
> That's more like it – shipwrecks, drunkards and monsters.

HUBERT:
> You're not a fan of Shakespeare, I take it?

CECIL:
> Not a fan of theatre full stop.

ANNIE:
> And yet you go quite often?

CECIL:
> My father believes it's good for me – improving for the mind.

RUTH:
> I agree with him. I'd love to come to every production here.

CECIL:
> And so you shall, my sweet, but please don't ask me to come with you.

RUTH:
> Take no notice of him, Mrs Wright...

ANNIE:
> Annie, please.

RUTH:
> Annie. It's all an act he likes to put on.

CECIL: (*looking round*):
> Then I must be in the right place.

RUTH:
> The last production you came to here you couldn't stop talking about for days afterwards.

CECIL:
> That's because it was so unimaginably dull.

RUTH:
> In that case, why bother to discuss it at all?

CECIL: (*spreading his hands wide*):
> I'm not.

HUBERT:
> What was the play called?

CECIL:
An Enemy of the People.

HUBERT:
Oh. I've not heard of it. It must have been before we started printing their publicity.

CECIL:
Well, it certainly made an enemy out of me.

ANNIE:
What was it about?

RUTH is about to explain but CECIL interrupts her.

CECIL:
A Doctor and his wife, who are driven out of a small town because of their controversial views. Whereas I would have driven them out simply because they were both so boring.

RUTH:
I think that we need the theatre today more than ever. We live in such complicated times, don't you think? Nothing's straightforward any more, is it? There are two sides at least to every argument, and what do we mean by morality these days? Who can truly say what's right or wrong?

CECIL:
You sound just like the Doctor's wife with her 'progressive' opinions.

RUTH:
If asking difficult questions is considered 'progressive',

then call me a blue stocking.

CECIL:
I shall call you whatever you desire me to, my love, whatever the colour of your stockings.

RUTH blushes but smiles.

A pause descends upon the four of them.

HUBERT:
What's tonight's play about? *Hindle Wakes?* Does anyone know?

CECIL:
The writer's father's a friend of my own father. They're both in the same business, and the writer went to the same school as me – not that I knew him, he was several years above me – but my brother said he could tell a good story, with plenty of jokes, so I have high hopes.

ANNIE:
I remember Wakes Weeks from when I worked at Pendlebury's before I got married. People got up to all kinds of shenanigans.

CECIL:
My high hopes have just got higher.

They all laugh as the bell goes to signal just five minutes remain before Curtain Up. FRANK, EVELYN, MR and MRS YOUNG all return.

MRS YOUNG:
I think we'd better take our seats. Perhaps we might

reconvene afterwards to compare notes?

They make their way towards the auditorium. Just before they separate, RUTH plucks ANNIE's elbow.

RUTH:
Do you not work now?

ANNIE:
Not paid work, no. But I help my husband in the Printing Works sometimes, and a couple of afternoons a week I do voluntary work at a Women's Refuge.

RUTH:
Oh. I should love to do something like that.

ANNIE:
It's an eye opener, that's for certain, and not for the faint-hearted.

RUTH:
You mustn't pay heed to Cecil. It's all an act, you know. Underneath he's very sweet. He cares about things deeply. He only adopts this pretence of not taking life seriously, that's all. He just needs to come out from under his father's shadow and find out who he is.

ANNIE:
That's what they all need to do.

The two women regard each other warmly.

ANNIE watches RUTH walk away as EVELYN rejoins her.

EVELYN:
> Are we ready?

ANNIE:
> Where's Hubert?

EVELYN:
> He's just coming. He's asking his father something.

They go in.

Act Two

The play is an undoubted hit, though not without its controversy. Miss Horniman and Mr Houghton are invited to join the cast on stage for the curtain calls, to the accompaniment of several resounding "Bravos", mixed with fewer, but equally voluble cries of "Shame". The author looks somewhat sheepish but Miss Horniman takes it all in her stride and sweeps through the auditorium trailing wreaths of silk scarves and cigarette smoke behind her as she makes her royal progress from there to the foyer and then seamlessly on to the lounge of The Midland Hotel where, among several dozen other theatregoers, are to be found the party of the WRIGHTS and the YOUNGS about to partake of their celebratory supper of champagne and oysters. HUBERT has gallantly suggested mimosa cocktails as an appropriate tipple, thereby successfully making it possible for the WRIGHTS to drink orange juice only, so as not to compromise their strict teetotalling temperance, while at the same time not appearing to be openly critical of those who prefer to imbibe, which they are not, for they are indeed true upholders of that other much written of Methodist trait, a modest desire not to draw any attention to themselves.

MR YOUNG:
> A toast. To the happy couples.

ALL:
> The happy couples.

MR YOUNG:
> Oh, to be young again, eh Frank?

FRANK:
> While knowing what we know now.

MR YOUNG:
> Ay.

RUTH:
> I don't know about that, Mr Young. It seemed to me that it was the young in the play we've just seen that showed the real wisdom, despite their lack of years.

CECIL:
> Please, Ruth, don't start.

RUTH:
> Why ever not? Surely the point of the play, whichever side you came down on, was to provoke discussion. Oughtn't we at least to devote a few minutes to that?

MRS YOUNG:
> This is meant to be an occasion to celebrate your engagement, dear.

RUTH:
> Then the play could not have been more timely, don't you think?

MRS YOUNG:
> I don't know quite what to think, dear, if I'm honest. It was certainly nothing like the last thing I saw at *The Gaiety*.

EVELYN:
> Me neither.

MRS YOUNG:
> Only it was still called *The Comedy* back then.

EVELYN:
> What was it you saw there?

MRS YOUNG is delighted to have the opportunity to turn the conversation away from what she considers might turn into something potentially awkward and leans closer to EVELYN.

MRS YOUNG:
> It was when Mr Pitt Hardacre still ran the theatre, and we took the boys to see a pantomime.

EVELYN:
> *Little Bo Peep?*

MRS YOUNG:
> That's right!

EVELYN:
> With Dolly Stormont.

MRS YOUNG:
> Did you see it too? We might have been there at the same time.

EVELYN:
> The auditorium's changed significantly then since then. Unless it's my memory. But I seem to recall that inside was all red and gold with carved Cupids and Cherubs.

MRS YOUNG: (*delightedly*):
> Yes. I remember.

EVELYN:
> It seems so plain now.

RUTH:
> But that's a good thing, isn't it?

Everyone turns to look at her.

RUTH: (*continuing*):
> I mean, now that the theatre's presenting much more serious plays, it's better not to be distracted, surely, by all of that unnecessary frippery.

MRS YOUNG:
> I'm sure you're right, my dear, but I for one could have done with some distracting from that horrid play. There – I've said it now.

RUTH:
> But why did you find it horrid?

MRS YOUNG:
> I should've thought that was obvious.

MR YOUNG:
> There, there, Mother, don't upset yourself.

RUTH:
I'm sorry you're upset, Mrs Young, but that only serves to underline just what a good play it was. I really admired the way Fanny exposed the hypocrisy of the Jeffcote family and refused to let them just sweep what had happened between herself and their son under the carpet.

MRS YOUNG:
Some things are best swept under the carpet. We all make mistakes but there's no call in parading them noisily in the street for all and sundry to see and hear, is there? Evelyn, can you come to my rescue here?

EVELYN:
I don't like the idea of airing one's dirty linen in public any more than you do, Margery.

MRS YOUNG:
Thank you.

EVELYN:
But...

MRS YOUNG:
There are no 'buts'.

EVELYN:
I do believe Ruth has a point. In the play Fanny never once threatened to speak of what had happened between herself and Christopher in public. She even turned down the chance of marrying him at the end.

MR YOUNG:
Now that's what I found so hard to make sense of. Here's a young lass...

RUTH:
Fanny...

MR YOUNG:
Ay – Fanny... who has the chance of really making something of herself at the end, by marrying someone from a better family, with money, a position, good standing in the community, yet she turns all that down. Why? For what?

RUTH:
Her integrity.

MR YOUNG:
Integrity doesn't put a roof over your head, though, does it? It doesn't put food on the table.

MRS YOUNG:
And this integrity you make so much of didn't stop her from going to bed with someone she wasn't married to, did it? I don't call that integrity. I call it disgusting.

ANNIE:
But what if Fanny had agreed to marry Christopher afterwards?

Everyone turns towards her, for up until this point it is almost as if they had forgotten the WRIGHTS were still there.

ANNIE:
Is that what upsets you so much?

MRS YOUNG:
I don't know what you mean. At least marriage would have made that disgusting thing that she did a bit more

respectable.

ANNIE:
But is it disgusting? If they truly loved one another?

EVELYN: (*shocked*):
Annie!

HUBERT looks towards ANNIE in undisguised discomfort.

ANNIE:
But Fanny didn't love Christopher, did she? She makes that abundantly clear at the end of the play. That's why she refuses to marry him when she has the chance. I agree with Ruth. Fanny does retain her integrity and Christopher's parents can breathe an enormous sigh of relief at the end precisely because they can trust her not to say anything.

MRS YOUNG:
Not that anyone would believe her word against theirs.

MR YOUNG:
And Christopher gets a lucky escape.

HUBERT:
What I don't understand is why Beatrice, Christopher's fiancée before the affair with Fanny happened, still agrees to marry him at the end. He gets to have his cake and eat it.

EVELYN:
To err is human, Hubert, but to forgive is divine.

RUTH:
> And it's more often in a woman's nature to forgive. Can you imagine if the situation was the other way round? If it was Beatrice who'd stayed overnight in a hotel with another man, and then Christopher had found out? Would he have been so forgiving? I think not. Remember Angel Clare and Tess. No, I think why this play is making people so upset or angry is that Fanny behaves exactly like a man, only with more honesty. "You're a man, and I was your little fancy," she says, and then: "Well, I'm a woman, and you were my little fancy." And though she admits that, in her words, they've "had a right good time together" and "enjoyed themselves proper", she couldn't ever marry him, she says, for "there's summat lacking".

FRANK:
> Love, I suppose.

RUTH:
> Exactly. I loved it when right at the end she declared her independence. "I'm a Lancashire lass," she said, "and I'm not without a trade at my fingertips. I shall earn enough brass to keep me going." I wanted to cheer when she said that.

MR YOUNG: (*smiling*):
> Well, Cecil, what do you reckon to this girl you're engaged to be wed to? She speaks her mind, I'll say that for her.

Everyone looks expectantly towards CECIL, wondering how he might respond.

CECIL:
> I think... I think that I'm the luckiest man who ever lived.

MR YOUNG:
Well said, son!

There is much applause and back-slapping and various exchanged looks passing between the different members of the party. Throughout it all CECIL and RUTH remain still, their eyes locked together. MR YOUNG pours CECIL another glass of champagne, who turns at last back towards his father, who shakes his hand. ANNIE leans across towards RUTH.

ANNIE:
I think you may be right about that young man of yours.

RUTH: (*noticing how, from the other side of the table, MRS YOUNG is regarding her with an expression that might almost be interpreted as hostile*):
I hope so.

FRANK taps the side of his glass with an unused oyster fork and calls for attention.

FRANK:
I think it's time for another toast. We've already raised our glasses to the health and happiness of the two young couples here with us this evening, one who are celebrating their first year of marriage together and the other declaring their intention to take that road the rest of us here this evening have been blessed to travel along these many years. If there's one thing this play has taught us tonight, whatever our views on its various merits and morals, it's that we're currently living in an age of great upheaval, with changes that at times threaten to shake the very earth we walk upon. For does not Peter encourage us in his First Epistle not to look upon the fire which has

come to test us as some strange, mysterious thing, but as something to rejoice in, for it doth prepare us for the coming of the Lord? Here in Manchester we are used to change. The foundations on which this great city is built have been forged by the fires of such change. Yet whenever change comes there are those who fear it, who resist it, because all of us find comfort in the things we know and find familiar. But the times we are living in now are changing faster than any that have preceded them. Or so it seems to me. Ships from all corners of the world arrive by canal right into the heart of our city, bringing people from every continent, with new ways of thinking, new ways of seeing and new ways of doing, from which we can all of us learn. Our printing presses roll non-stop, night and day, faster and faster, delivering information to all parts of the city, while your mills, Edward, use the most modern machines to produce mile upon mile of the best quality cloth to export right around the globe. Miners dig ever deeper under the ground to extract the coal that fires our factories and heats our homes, that makes electric power to light our streets. Miss Kaufman's father is grinding lenses which not only help me and my son to see this world of never-ending change we live in more clearly, but he is also manufacturing telescopes, which enable us to see the most distant stars in the galaxy, from where, if we could imagine ourselves looking back, what would we see of this little world? Not a great deal. But whatever spark of light might reach us out there in that universal dark, it might show us just what a precious stone it is that we inhabit, a jewel fashioned by the minds of men and women, who looked up from the earth, away from their usual daily grind, and watched, for example, an apple fall from a tree and asked themselves why, or how, or what if...? And so I ask you all this evening, to raise your glasses and drink a toast to change, to this city which has continuously embraced change and to young people, like Ruth and Cecil, Annie and Hubert, who have the courage to keep asking us older ones the difficult questions we'd rather not face. To change.

ALL:

(*raising their glasses, some more enthusiastically than others*): To change.

*

A more immediate change arrived for Annie when she learned a few months after the trip to *The Gaiety* that she was going to have a baby.

She was determined to carry on with all of her regular activities for as long as she possibly could. She continued to volunteer with Evelyn at the *Women's Refuge,* she increased, if anything, her rotogravure work for Hubert, she accompanied Frank on his meetings with potential new clients to develop possible new contracts – she knew for certain now, without ever having been told, that Frank saw her as the natural successor to this side of the business, rather than Hubert, whose heart lay in remaining hands on with the new machinery at the Printing Works – and she never missed a Saturday with Claudia.

She had always wanted children and still hoped for as many as possible, so she was delighted when she learned the news. The fact of *being* pregnant, however, proved more challenging than she had anticipated. Most of the time she felt ghastly. The morning sickness, which was terrible, lasted well beyond the first trimester, and Dr Wilkes confirmed *hyperemesis gravidarum*, for which he prescribed a cool lavender compress to be placed on her forehead with a warm one laid upon her belly. He recommended frequent cups of hot spearmint tea, suggested six small meals a day rather than the usual three larger ones and to suck on a piece of peeled ginger root between each, drink a few teaspoons of wheat germ dissolved in warm milk every hour until the nausea subsided, (which it never appeared to), and to put one table spoon of apple cider vinegar mixed with a table spoon of honey in cold water last thing at night. She craved bananas, which had become cheaper and more plentiful since the opening of the Ship Canal, along which vessels regularly brought them all the way from Madagascar, and which she ate as often as she could lay her hands on them, while Claudia would gently massage her with a soothing chamomile lotion her brother Matteo's mother-in-law swore by.

But inevitably, as the pregnancy progressed and the sickness failed to show any signs of stopping, she had no choice but to curtail all of her weekly commitments one by one and acquiesce to her growing need for rest. This also meant that she had to forego those other cultural pleasures that came with the increased success of F.G. Wright & Son and the growing network of connections which accompanied it. The visits to plays at the various theatres across the city they now did the publicity for, to orchestral concerts by the Hallé at The Free Trade Hall, to musical *soirées* given by the various charities they were associated with, the dinner dances, the social calls – one by one, each of these dropped away, until Annie found herself, from early 1913 onwards, a virtual prisoner at home.

With time suddenly on her hands, and Annie never having been one to sit idle, she wondered how she might occupy herself during all these empty hours she suddenly found herself presented with. It was Claudia who suggested the collagraphs.

"What are they?" asked Evelyn later on a visit to see how Annie was feeling.

"They're collages," said Annie. "What you do is glue bits and pieces of different materials – anything at all, bark, leaves, stones, bits of cloth – onto a board. Then, when the glue is dry, you varnish it so that you can then paint over it. It acts like a kind of printing plate. Once you've completed the board you press the paper on it, run a rolling pin over it, and there you have it."

"What?"

"Your finished print."

"I see. Very nice, dear. Now – what are we going to do about Hubert's tea?"

Annie began with a series of studies of the spindle tree outside their front window. If she positioned her chair in one particular place in the front room, she was able to track the way the light changed on it through the duration of a morning, an afternoon, or an early evening. She tried to capture it in all of its different moods, depending upon the season or weather, how the younger twigs were dark green and square, while the older stems became round, with a pale grey-brown bark, and the smoother wood below was more a greenish white. The leaves had short stalks and were small and oval, with toothed edges, which faded to orange-purple tints in late autumn. In May the tree produced yellow-green flowers, with four sepals and four petals of subtle, varying hues. The fruit, green berries in the early summer, turned bright pink in August, and split, revealing four seeds, each clad in a bright orange pulp. For just a few days, these attracted a wide range of small birds who feasted on the tree in flocks, stripping it bare before carrying off the seeds elsewhere. This was how, she presumed, the tree had arrived here in Portugal Street in the first place.

She made print after print of the tree, never quite capturing it to her satisfaction. Gradually she discovered that the less she attempted to create some kind of faithful reproduction of it, but instead tried to reflect its essence somehow, using the actual bark, twigs, leaves and berries of the tree as the raw materials for the collagraph, the more she succeeded. She asked Hubert to bring her books from the library in order to learn more about the different uses the tree had been put to over the ages, the folklore and superstitions attached to it, the better, she hoped, to understand it and so be more sensitive towards it as she continued to labour over print after print. She was delighted to discover that before the spinning wheel had been invented, all the woollen thread needed for cloth was spun by hand using the thin stems from the tree as spindles. This task was traditionally carried out by unmarried women, known as *spinsters*, who twirled short sticks in one hand. One end of each stick was hollowed out to fit a small stone inside it, which acted as a kind of rudder, around which the women, with their other hand, fed the loosely twisted wool from a hank, which the spindle then drew out into stronger, tighter thread. Spindle trees provided the smoothest wood for this task, kindest to the hands. Annie tried painting directly with a twig, or trailing wool that she'd twisted round the twig and dipped in paint to leave thin spidery trails.

The flowers, she learned, were simultaneously male and female, with both stamens and a pistil, self-sufficient hermaphrodites. If rubbed, they produced differently coloured dyes at different times of the year, all of which Annie incorporated into her experiments. The pulp of the fruit, if stewed, gave a shining hair rinse. Annie, having tried it, could vouch for this and, when she dried her hair, she allowed it to shower its drops onto the board where she prepared each print. If kept dry and powdered, the pulp was said to kill lice – thankfully she had no need to put that particular old wives' tale to the test – while the berries themselves were reputed to be a powerful emetic – no thank you, thought Annie!

While she was thus engaged, she became so totally

immersed in her efforts that she quite forgot the passage of time, and her sickness would subside. Eventually she managed to produce four she was moderately happy with, and these she persuaded Hubert to frame and hang in their living room.

Encouraged by this success, she created a single larger collagraph of tulips for their bedroom, which reminded her of their early courting days in Philips Park and, as her pregnancy continued, a series of interlocking, hexagonal hives of bees, for the baby when he or she arrived. Then, when Claudia announced at Easter that Marco had proposed and she had accepted, Annie devoted hours and hours to producing a collage made entirely of woollen thread, depicting a labyrinth.

"It's a reference to the myth of Ariadne," she said to Claudia, as she handed her the finished print. "Only instead of a maze, I decided to have a labyrinth. I'd thought they were the same thing. It was Hubert's father-in-law, Frank, who explained the difference to me."

"What is it?"

" 'A maze is a puzzle which might have more than one entrance or exit,' he'd said, 'with many different choices of paths you might take, some of them leading to dead ends. Its purpose is to trick you into getting lost. But a labyrinth has only a single path, which may be long and circuitous, but will eventually lead you to the centre, and then the same path will lead you back to the beginning'."

"You've got really good at these, Annie," said Claudia.

"Practice may not make perfect," she joked, "but at least I don't throw so many away now."

"It's beautiful. Thank you."

"A labyrinth is an ancient symbol related to wholeness," continued Annie. "That's what Mr Wright told me. It represents a journey into our own centre and then back again out into the world."

"Do you know what else it reminds me of?" said Claudia, holding it up against the window to the light.

"What?"

"How I imagine the inside of an atom, with all of its invisible particles orbiting around it."

Just then the baby kicked and turned in Annie's stomach. The two friends sat together side by side in the gathering dusk, their hands on Annie's belly, feeling a new life fluttering like a bird's wing under the skin. Outside the window a breeze rustled through the first spring leaves opening on the spindle tree.

*

THE TIMES

6th July 1913

A RIGHT ROYAL TOUR TO LANCASHIRE

Their Royal Highnesses King George V and his Queen Consort Mary of Teck will tomorrow begin a whirlwind tour of the County Palatine of Lancashire, where they will visit more than thirty towns and cities in only eight days, travelling in excess of two hundred and twenty miles.

They will begin their tour at Warrington, where they will arrive in the Royal Train at Bank Quay Station before transferring to a motorcade, which will transport them to Liverpool, Bootle, Wigan, Atherton, Newton-le-Willows, Leigh and St Helens (where they will visit the Pilkington's Glass Works), before venturing further north to Blackpool, by way of Ormskirk, Southport, Chorley and Preston (stopping off at the world famous Horrocks Mill), and then looping back through Blackburn, Burnley, Nelson, Colne, Accrington, Bacup, Bolton, Bury, Heywood,

Middleton, Rochdale and Oldham.

Their progress will conclude with a formal state visit to the cities of Manchester and Salford, where they will be conveyed by horse and carriage through the streets of both.

Against a backdrop of rising tension in Europe and the growing Suffragette crisis here at home, Their Sovereign Majesties have expressed that it is their most fervent wish to thank their loyal subjects in our nation's industrial heartland for being the engine and the powerhouse that will see us through these difficult challenges both now and in the times to come.

So three cheers for our energetic King George and Queen Mary as they embark upon what promises to be a most arduous but exhilarating tour of the Red Rose County, where they are certain to receive a most right royal welcome.

Accrington Observer & Times

12th July 1913

THOUSANDS CRAM TOWN CENTRE TO CELEBRATE ROYAL VISIT

More than twenty thousand people packed into Accrington's town centre to greet the first reigning monarchs ever to visit the town. Residents clambered on to the rooftops of the Market Hall, *The Commercial Hotel* and adjoining shops, houses, warehouses and walls to catch a glimpse of King George and Queen Mary with a sea of faces stretching as far as the eye could see.

The whole borough rejoiced and one of the many expressions of loyalty and jubilation was to be seen in the pretty decorations of heliotrope drapery adorning the Broad Oaks Works, which, we understand, the Queen was graciously heard to remark, were "a credit to the town". While visiting the Works, the King had a try at Calico printing, and his efforts were suitably first class.

Bacup Times

13th July 1913

TEA AT THE CO-OP FOR KING & QUEEN

Crowds lined the Rochdale Road in Bacup yesterday to welcome King George and Queen Mary to the Rossendale Valley. Despite pleas from Buckingham Palace for the town not to go to any trouble or expense for the royal visit, union flags were flying from every building and more than a hundred police officers were on hand to make sure the King's motor car would not be impeded.

Their Majesties were welcomed by Lord Derby, the Lord Lieutenant of Lancashire, and were entertained by the prize-winning Irwell Springs Brass Band under the baton of Mr Walter Nuttall, for whom the King had a special word of congratulations.

The royal party then proceeded to the local Co-op for a proper Lancashire cup of tea!

Northern Daily Telegraph

14th July 1913

KING LAYS FOUNDATION STONE FOR NEW CONCERT HALL

King George V graciously agreed to lay the foundation stone for the new concert hall to be built here in Blackburn, which will be known hereafter as King George's Hall and which will be able to accommodate audiences of up to three thousand five hundred to enjoy the highest quality music, opera and ballet, for what's good enough for London is surely good enough for Lancashire.

The King and Queen also visited the brand new Roe Lee Cotton Mill, where Their Majesties were able to witness at first hand the enterprise and skills which have made our county pre-eminent in textile manufacture across the world.

After watching a demonstration of the latest Jacquard looms, the King was presented with a monogrammed handkerchief, while his Consort, Queen Mary of Teck, received a miniature pair of wooden clogs, with which she was clearly delighted.

THE MANCHESTER COURIER

15th July 1913

ROYAL VISIT REACHES CLIMAX

The King and Queen's whistle stop tour of Lancashire concluded today with a formal state visit to Manchester and Salford.

The Royal Procession left Plymouth Grove in Rusholme and toured both Birchfields and Platt Fields Parks, where more than fifty thousand children, clearly enjoying the unexpected school holiday granted them by the Manchester Corporation, sang the National Anthem, which the King and Queen acknowledged with regal smiles and waves.

It was just twenty-five years ago, in 1888, that the King's elder brother, Prince Albert Victor, formally opened the parks. Had fate not intervened the following year, cruelly taking the

Prince from us through a severe bout of influenza, it might have been him returning to Manchester yesterday, for he, as the eldest son of the then Prince of Wales, would have inherited the crown upon King Edward's death. At the time of his death Prince Albert was engaged to Princess Mary, as she was then. It was during the period of mourning which followed that drew the present King and Queen together.

Long may they reign.

In Platt Fields the King reviewed a brigade of Army Reservists. Then, accompanied by a detachment of Life Guards, the open carriages took a salute at the Infirmary Flags, paused briefly at All Saints to acknowledge the enormous crowds thronging the streets, all dressed in their Sunday best and waving white handkerchiefs, before turning into Mount Street past *The Gaiety Theatre,* as they made their way towards the Town Hall, so much admired by the King's grandmother, Queen Victoria, where they alighted for a Civic Lunch.

And so this lightning tour of Lancashire by King George V and Queen Mary has come to an end. Covering more than two hundred and twenty miles and visiting more than thirty five towns and cities, our sovereign can have been left in no doubt of the devotion and loyalty of his northern subjects, nor of their vital importance in stoking the fires of the Empire's industry.

Long live King Cotton and Queen Coal and Long live King George and Queen Mary.

Two months after giving birth to George, Annie felt her strength and energy slowly start to return.

For the first few weeks it was simpler for her to move in with Hubert's parents while her body recovered. Evelyn was more than happy to look after her daughter-in-law, and Annie found the restful atmosphere of the house in Bignor Street to be exactly what she needed.

Fortunately for everyone George was an easy baby, contentedly sleeping between feeds and, after six weeks, delighting everyone who looked on him with a series of deliciously dimpled, gurgling smiles. But by that time Annie was eager to return home, feeling the need more and more each day to exert the kind of control over her and George's daily routines, which was not possible while she was a guest of Frank and Evelyn's. Even so, despite her many protestations that she was now fine, Hubert insisted, when she did return to Portugal Street, on a rota of women to drop by for a few hours each day to make sure that she did not over-exert herself. Annie's mother, who had now reduced to part-time hours at Pendlebury's, came two mornings a week, Evelyn continued to offer two mornings of her own, for she had grown fond of George and missed the new structure his constant needs had given to her days, Claudia was there each Saturday, Hubert was available on Sundays, and Annie assured everyone that she could manage perfectly well on her own for at least one day each week.

It was on one of these days with George by herself that Frank appeared. It was a beautiful, warm midsummer's day in June. The flowers on the spindle tree were in full bloom, and Annie had taken George outside for some fresh air in his pram. She had walked the mile and a half to Philip's Park, revelling in the return to energy brought on by the sunshine. She had pushed George along the entire length of the Avenue of Black Poplars, delighting in the way his pudgy fingers grasped like starfish at the flecks of light falling between the leaves of the trees, dappling the thin cotton sheet that covered him. By the time she returned to Portugal Street, he was fast asleep. Annie thought she might risk leaving him parked outside the front door, which she would leave open, while she began preparing Hubert's tea, but as she turned the corner, there was Frank, sitting on the step, his jacket over his arm, his shirt sleeves rolled up. Her first thought was that perhaps he was unwell again, but as soon as he saw her, he stood up and walked directly to greet her.

"There you are," he said. "I was just coming to speak to Hubert about the menus for the King and Queen's lunch at the Town Hall next week – you know we've been asked to design and print them…?"

"No. Hubert hasn't mentioned it."

"Didn't want to bother you, I suppose," he said, looking down on the still sleeping George. He paused, smiling a moment, before continuing. "Well, there was something I wanted to ask you first, so I thought I'd just wait half an hour on the off chance you'd soon be back. And here you are."

"I'm intrigued," she said. "Let's go in, I'll put the kettle on and you can tell me all about it over a cup of tea. We'll leave George outside till he wakes up. The air will do him good."

She made sure he was properly tucked in and then followed her father-in-law into the house. She paused briefly on the doorstep, listening to the deep, rumbling thrum of the printing presses turning through the day. She knew she must be getting ready to return to the life she'd established for herself before George was born. In the last few weeks since she'd been back, she'd not noticed that ever-present pounding rhythm emanating from the Printing Works across the street, all her thoughts instead focused on George's needs. But this afternoon she heard it, really heard it, and listened to it now with renewed pleasure. George slept on. He seemed not to notice it and Annie wondered if the sound of it somehow penetrated deep within his bones and brain, so that his body might somehow set its own pulse and heartbeat to be in tune with that of the machines.

She was roused from her reverie by Frank calling from

indoors.

"Where's that cup of tea then?"

When they were finally settled, Annie waited for Frank to come around to whatever it was that he needed to ask her. She knew now from experience that he would not be rushed.

"Well," he said at last, "the Corporation have got themselves into a right pickle."

"Oh," said Annie, smiling. "What about this time?"

"Over what to serve for the Royal Lunch next week."

"They're cutting it a bit fine, aren't they?" remarked Annie. "What's the problem?"

"They can't make their minds up, that's what the problem is, as usual. You've got Alderman Hardcastle on one side arguing that they've got to pull out all the stops, the pride of Manchester's at stake, to make sure they impress the King, and especially the Queen, who, apparently, has a reputation for being something of a gourmet, with Councillor Grandage on the other reminding members that the Palace has urged everyone on this visit not to go to too much trouble."

"For once I find myself agreeing with Councillor Grandage."

"Ay, lass, 'appen you're right, but you know what these Committees are like."

"They'll just have to take a vote on it then, won't they?"

"They did."

"And?"

"It was a draw."

"Oh." Annie began to giggle. She did her best to suppress it, but the more she tried, the worse it got, until in the end Frank joined in too, and the two of them sat helpless, with tears of laughter streaming down their faces.

"I'm sorry," she said, when they had finally caught their breath, "but it is a bit ridiculous, don't you think?"

"Ay, well – it's all very well you laughing about it, but Hubert's going to have to print all the menus and it'll be a bit of a rum do if, when it comes to the main course, it says, 'to be decided in Committee'!"

"So what are they going to do?"

"What they always do – prevaricate. They've formed a Special Sub-Committee, with just three members so they can't have another tie, to thrash it all out once and for all. I've told 'em we need to know by the end of the week at t' latest if we're to get the menus printed in time, so I'll be attending the meeting too to try and move 'em along a bit."

Annie waited. She knew that all of this had been by way of a preamble to what he'd really come to ask her.

So," he said, holding up his now empty cup, "I was wondering if you might have any ideas?"

"I thought you'd never ask," she laughed, and poured him a second cup.

"Well...?"

Annie thought in silence for a while. Then a slow, mischievous smile spread across her lips, an unmistakable twinkle in her eye.

"Tripe," she said.

Frank spluttered over his tea.

"I think," she continued, "we should give their Royal Highnesses tripe! It's local, it's cheap, it's what the common folk eat, but it can be got up in all kinds of fancy ways to satisfy even a gourmet like Queen Mary. I should've thought the Corporation Chef would enjoy the challenge of that."

"You know, Annie," said Frank, rising to his feet, "I think you may be right. By 'eck," he went on, warming to the idea still more, "that'd put t' cat among t' pigeons, and no mistake."

At exactly that moment, George woke up outside in his pram. On hearing the two grown-ups laughing inside the house, he decided he should join in too with a chortle of his own.

Manchester
Corporation

Royal Luncheon Menu

On the occasion of the State Visit to Manchester by His Royal Highness King George V and his Consort Queen Mary of Teck

Manchester Town Hall
Monday 14th July 1913

Soup
Manchester Particular
(boiled hock of ham with freshly grown celery)

Main
Honeycomb Tripe and Onions
(served with puréed fondant potatoes and peas)

Dessert
Manchester Italian Ice Cream

Printed by F.G. Wright & Son

In honour of the visit, the Council had declared the day a Public Holiday. This meant that Claudia had the day off from her work with Professor Rutherford at the University, so that when Annie received an invitation to attend the Royal Luncheon in the Town Hall Banqueting Hall, courtesy of her father-in-law, Claudia was able to volunteer her services to look after George for a couple of hours so that Annie might go.

When the lunch was over, the King and Queen formally received all of the guests, who paraded past them in single file, bowing or curtseying to each. The King ceremonially doffed his top hat to the gentlemen, as his Queen extended her elegantly gloved hand to each of the ladies in turn, before the state carriage, escorted once more by a detachment of the Household Cavalry Life Guards, safely delivered the Royal Party to London Road Station and their train back to the capital.

Annie basked in the glow of the late afternoon sunshine as she made her way back home afterwards. Her happiness, she felt, knew no bounds – a contented marriage, a successful husband and a healthy son, a profitable business, a growing number of influential friends and acquaintances, regular attendances at important functions, and now she had touched the hand of the Queen herself – so that when, just as she turned into Portugal Street, a small dark cloud briefly covered the sun, she paid it no heed. Instead she walked into the Printing Works to share her excitement with Hubert. She had to call his name three times before he could hear her above the constant roar of the rumbling machines.

*

When, just over a year later, war was declared, Hubert, like nearly all young men in Manchester, was swept along by the tide of patriotic fervour that persuaded him to try and enlist but, because of his colour blindness, his Daltonism, and generally poor eyesight, he was turned down. He was not overly disappointed. It was not in his nature to dwell on things beyond his control. He simply shrugged his shoulders, accepted the situation for what it was, and continued to carry on with things as before. Printing was a reserved occupation – not in the same front rank as mining or farming, but scheduled nevertheless – and F.G. Wright & Son were as busy as ever. The Government issued directive after directive, whole libraries, it seemed, of Public Information broadsheets, and Frank had managed to secure the contract to be the local printer and distributor for these. But as it dawned on the nation that the war would not in fact be over by Christmas, or indeed the Christmas after that, and as it entered its third weary year, with the country reeling from the shocking revelations of gas attacks at the Battle of Loos and the ensuing appalling casualties, with deaths running into the tens of thousands, Hubert's position as a young man not at the Front became increasingly difficult to defend. Especially for Annie, who, Hubert saw on more than one occasion, had to run the gauntlet of narrowed glances and insidious whispers. Or perhaps he was imagining this. Those too old for active service, who turned up uncomplaining for work each day, said nothing to his face, but every time he turned his back he sensed a growing sense of disapproval. The Printing Works was no longer the harmonious hive of industry it once had been. The ceaseless rolling of the printing presses had shifted from a soothing source of contentment to a gnawing, constant ache which churned unpleasantly in his stomach, and Hubert felt increasingly ill at ease. He found himself retreating to the Friends Meeting House on Mount Street more and more often, not just to attend meetings, but simply to sit in its silence, away from the bitter growl of the machines, and try to find solace there.

And so, on 2nd March 1916, when Annie waved that scrap of newspaper in front of him confirming the new Military Service Act, which now required all able-bodied men between the ages of eighteen and forty-one to be eligible for compulsory conscription, it was almost a relief. Now he would have to face up to his dilemmas once and for all. Nor did he think this time around his poor eyesight would absolve him from having to make a decision. The Army would not be so fussy on this occasion, he felt.

"Well?" she demanded.

"Not now," he said, aware that the other workers were regarding them with amused curiosity.

"But look at the date," she began. "You've only got today."

"Let's talk about it at lunch time," he continued. His calmness only served to make Annie even crosser.

"Did you know about this," she asked, taking back the leaflet from him and waving it in front of his face, "and not tell me?"

"We've both of us known this day was bound to come," he said.

"Oh!" she cried. "You're impossible!"

And with that she turned on her heels and rushed out of the Works, screwing up the leaflet and flinging it to the floor as she did so. Hubert watched her go with a quiet shake of his head. He picked up the leaflet, carefully smoothed out its creases, folded it into four and put it in the front pocket of his overalls before quietly going back to the typesetting he was busy with before Annie had burst in.

At lunch time he duly crossed the twenty yards from the Printing Works to their house, where he found Annie sitting calmly at the table waiting for him. The fish, which had been wrapped in the newspaper that had so enraged her earlier, was now cooked and sat on a plate with a tomato and some bread and butter. Annie, he noted, had no plate in front of her. She said nothing. This time she was waiting for him to begin. George was quietly crayoning on some paper on the floor. Even he seemed cowed by the atmosphere.

He put his hand on her shoulder, but she shrugged him off. He sighed, sat down and regarded the fish. Its cold eye stared back at him dolefully. With his usual meticulous precision he carefully dissected it, neatly peeling back the skin and eating the flesh off the bones, ensuring there was neither mess nor waste.

Annie waited.

When he had finished, he put down his knife and fork, wiped his mouth with the napkin Annie always laid out for him, then sat in silence while he composed his thoughts.

Eventually he spoke. "I've been thinking," he said.

"I should hope so," she snapped.

"The thing is, Annie, I just can't imagine bringing myself to the point where I could actually kill someone."

Annie looked up at him fearfully. She opened her mouth as if to answer him, but found that she could not speak, and so she shut it again.

"Do you think those German lads are any different from us? Haven't they got wives and sweethearts, mothers and children, just the same as we have? What gives me the right to go out there and try and kill some of them? I might as well take a bayonet to myself. Is that what you want, Annie?"

"What *I* want's got nothing to do with it, Hubert. The best outcome for me would be if they turned you down again. But we both know that's unlikely to happen this time, don't we? And even if it did, there'd be people who'd say we managed to pull a few strings, and then it'd be as bad as if you tried to excuse yourself, which is what you're thinking of doing, isn't it, Hubert?"

Hubert looked down, then back up again, so that his eyes met hers. "Yes," he whispered.

Annie wheeled away from the table, moaning. She lifted the pinny that was tied around her waist and buried her face in it. George stopped crayoning, picking up on his mother's distress and began to cry too. Hubert bent to pick him up but Annie snatched him away and lifted him onto her arm, from where he buried his face in her neck, crying even louder.

"Do you know what happens to 'conchies', Hubert?" she

spat out between trying to console George.

"I might go to prison," he said, "though I'm more likely to be put to work on a farm somewhere."

"In a camp," hissed Annie, "with barbed wire and armed guards."

"Probably," agreed Hubert, his voice barely audible.

"And d'you know what happens to conchies' wives?"

Hubert swallowed, dry mouthed.

"Well? Do you?" she repeated.

He nodded.

"Say it."

He shook his head.

"Say it."

"I can't."

"They tar and feather them, that's what."

"Not here. People know us here."

"Really? Have you forgotten already what happened to the Kaufmans after *The Lusitania* was sunk?"

"Please, Annie, don't. Not in front of George."

"But this is about George, Hubert. It's about me, it's about your parents, it's about what happens to the business, it's about what we leave behind us after we're gone. Don't you see? It's about much more than your conscience."

Hubert looked at his wife steadily. He'd never heard her talk like this before.

"Do you think I want you to be a soldier, Hubert? Do you think I want you to go out there and face all of that horror and risk never coming back? Of course I don't. That's the last thing I want. I want you to stay here, Hubert, with George and me, like you've always done. I want you to come home every day for your lunch. I want things to carry on as they have been doing. But they can't, can they? Not now. I wish the Government hadn't passed this new Military Service Act, just like I wish they'd never started this whole wretched war in the first place. But they have, and there's nothing any of us can do about either of those things."

"I'm not a coward, Annie, but I can't kill another human being, and that's all there is to it."

"But it's not all, is it. Nothing like all. I know you're not a coward, Hubert. You're a man of principle. That's why I love you. And I know it takes enormous courage to even think about having to stand up before a judge and declare that because of these principles you can't in good conscience allow yourself to go for a soldier. I'm also sure that you must have considered the terrible damage this would do for your reputation, and the reputation of the business, and that no doubt you think you're following some kind of higher call. To God, I suppose. '*Thou shalt not kill*', and all that. But don't you think it takes even greater courage to sacrifice those principles for the people you love, and who love you? George will be starting school next year. Do you want him to be taunted and bullied when he goes there? Because believe me, Hubert, he will be. Do you want white feathers to be posted through our letter box? Do you want slogans calling you a coward – and worse – to be daubed on the walls of the Works? Do you want, when this is all over, as one day it surely will be, for you to come home and find that no one will speak to you, no one will do business with you, that your parents, after all they've done for us, will be ostracised, so that we'd have to give up this house and then what? Where would we go? Back to the Tripe Colony? Because I won't do that, Hubert, I won't. Not after all we've done to make it this far. And isn't that, when all's said and done, what this war's supposed to be about? Fighting to preserve a way of life? Because that's what I'm prepared to do, Hubert, fight with every last ounce of strength I've got to make sure that everything we've worked so hard for doesn't get taken away from us. I'd do that for us, Hubert. For George. And for you. Won't you now try to do the same? For us?"

She stopped, exhausted. She'd talked herself to a

standstill. She sat down in an armchair, rocking a now inconsolable George back and forth.

Hubert looked down on the two of them, appalled. He waited until George began at last to quieten down.

But it was Annie who spoke again first, not him.

"I may not be clever, Hubert, but I'm not stupid either. Don't you think I've not known how this must have been running round and round inside your head? But while you've been wrestling with your conscience, I've been rooting out the facts."

"Annie..."

"Let me finish first. It seems to me that you've got a number of choices. I've been reading up on it. You could apply to join the Royal Army Medical Corps, which doesn't involve any fighting, just helping carry the wounded back to the field hospitals. I even went to Mount Street to talk to somebody there about it. Don't worry, Hubert. It wasn't anyone we know and I didn't mention any names. He said that Quakers have a range of options. They can simply decide to join up, like everyone else, on the grounds that this may in the end be the quickest way to bring the war to an end, and try their best not to behave or act in a cruel or unjust way, or they can take the other extreme and testify to a court that because of their religious convictions they believe all war to be inherently evil and refuse on moral grounds to take part in it in any way. But between these two extremes there are several middle ways. You might work for the Friends Emergency Committee, assisting enemy aliens resident in this country, people like the Kaufmans, whose father was interned. But that wouldn't help the situation as far as me and George are concerned, would it? You could volunteer for the Friends Ambulance Unit, which works with the Red Cross to support wounded soldiers when they're sent back home from the Front. But this is usually for men who are older than you, Hubert, and outside the scope of the new act. Or you could volunteer to help provide relief for ordinary people in France or Belgium who've been affected by the war. The man in Mount Street said that this typically involved working on the land or helping to rebuild things that have been destroyed by the shelling – houses mainly – you'd be good at something like that, Hubert…"

"Possibly…"

"But…" Annie paused. She stood up and approached Hubert until she was standing very close to him, George now quiet and still against her shoulder. She reached out a free hand and tenderly placed it against his cheek. "First you have to go along to the Town Hall to register, like the new act says everyone has to, and you have to do that today, Hubert, otherwise you'll miss the deadline. And after that, let's see, shall we? Who knows? Your eyesight might exempt you again, you never know. But go and register, and while you're about it, think on what I've said, love. Please."

Three months later, having offered himself for active service, and having once again been rejected, Hubert found himself behind the front lines at Verdun as part of a Field Ambulance Unit within the Royal Army Medical Corps, to which he had been unexpectedly assigned. The Field Ambulance Unit was responsible for establishing and operating a number of points along the casualty evacuation chain, from the Bearer Relay Posts, which were up to six hundred yards behind the Regimental Aid Posts in the front line, taking casualties away to what was referred to as an Advanced Dressing Station, or an ADS. It also provided a Walking Wounded Collecting Station, as well as various rest areas, which were in fact little more than hastily erected tents. When it was at full strength a Field Ambulance was composed of ten officers and two hundred and twenty-four men. It was divided into three sections. In turn, those sections had Stretcher Bearer and

Tented sub sections. Hubert had no wish to be considered for Officer status and served unassumingly as a stretcher bearer, trudging back and forward through the mud and debris, day after day, while the guns thundered and the shells rained.

Royal Army Medical Corps officers and men did not carry weapons or ammunition. In this way Hubert could assuage his conscientious objections to the war without having to proclaim them publicly, while, for Annie, his involvement in a recognised, highly valued and much needed army unit meant that her fears of a violent backlash against the family back home were at one stroke allayed.

Six weeks before his posting, Hubert slipped away quietly for training, not wanting any kind of fuss or send off. It was left to Annie and Frank to announce his departure to a tearful rest of the staff in the Works, who received the news with audible murmurs of sympathy, support, pride and approbation. It was a good thing that Hubert was not there to witness it, for it would have been more than he could bear.

Frank explained that they would be seeing a deal more of him than they had been used to and that his brother, Gordon, would be coming out of retirement to help out in a part time capacity. He knew the ropes and would soon slot back in. Several of the older workers remembered him well and smiled fondly. Gordon was nobody's fool.

"I'm sure you don't need me to remind you that the best thing all of us can do to support Hubert in his important work at the front – an action that he was under no obligation to undertake, but for which he volunteered gladly and willingly, eager to be able to play his part – is to make sure that we maintain a thriving business for him to return to."

Frank's remarks were met with prolonged and heartfelt applause. He then turned to Annie.

"It's particularly hard on Mrs Wright, of course, but she has asked me to say just how much she has appreciated all your words of kindness since her husband left to take up his post and that she thanks you from the bottom of her heart. She will be continuing in her present duties on the rotogravure printing when necessary, and in addition, she will be assisting me even more in my side of the business, in order to allow me to spend more time here in the Works, on those days when my brother is not here. Any questions? No? In that case, let's all get back to work. Thank you."

Annie walked back through the factory. The older workers came towards her, privately and individually, saying how they would remember Hubert in their prayers. Some of the women pressed her hand, with tears in their eyes. She passed between them, grateful that she could hold her head up high among them.

"That," said Frank, as they stepped outside into the cold morning, "must have been very difficult for you."

"It had to be done," said Annie.

Her face was stone. A bitter wind with a keen, raw edge rattled through the spindle tree on Portugal Street, shaking its leafless branches like dry bones. A hunched rat, clinging close to the side wall of the house, edged its way into the pale sunlight. Annie scooped up a handful of gravel, which she flung at it with an angry cry. The rat retreated back to the shadow.

3

15th June 1919

Hubert can hear an angel singing. He thinks he must be dreaming. Or dying. He looks up into a clear sky, the blue so brilliant it floors him. The grass is warm to his touch. There are wild flowers everywhere, as if someone has taken a handful of colours and scattered them carelessly, indiscriminately, an overturned box of paints. He becomes aware of three small figures a little way off from him, further down the slope of the hill. A man, a woman, a child. A family perhaps. It is the child who is singing. Hubert recognises the tune but the words are unfamiliar, French, and so it is as if he is listening to this song, one he has heard many times before with the other men, for the first time.

"Et quand ils nous demandent
Comme c'était dangereux
Nous ne leur dirons jamais
Nous ne leur dirons jamais…"

*

George is having to be quiet. Which he hates. Especially now since his Daddy's come home. He's got so much he wants to ask him. Are German soldiers really monsters who would eat children as soon as look at them? Did he drive a tank? Was he wounded? Did he see a zeppelin? But his Mummy says he's not to ask him anything at all. "He'll tell you in his own good time," she says. "When he's ready. And besides, I don't think he'll have that much to tell." Which can't be true. His Daddy's a hero. He's got medals. George knows this because he found them in a drawer in his Daddy's desk, the one he's not supposed to look in, so he'd put them back almost as soon as he'd seen them. "Have you been rooting?" his Mummy asks him afterwards. "No," he says back, too quickly, and he feels his cheeks go red. "Because if you have," she continues, pointing her forefinger towards him, "I'll know." (How does she always know?) "And then you'll be for it." George knows what that means. "Off to bed with no supper." And the worst punishment of all. "Your father will be so disappointed," she'll add, "if you've been saying things you shouldn't." And so George has to be quiet.

But that doesn't mean he can't watch. He may only be small, but he's brave. And being small has its advantages. "I can lie low," he thinks, "and if I keep very still, maybe I'll not get noticed. Maybe I might become invisible and disappear altogether…"

He decides he will be his father's shadow. He will haunt his footsteps. He will peep through keyholes. He will eavesdrop in doorways. He will drop bread crumbs behind him to make sure he doesn't get lost. He will hide behind lamp posts. He will search for clues – footprints in the mud, messages written in code (shopping lists and telephone numbers concealing who knows what secrets?) He will press his ear to the ground, listening for the approach of something coming, something big, from deep underground. Being a child has other advantages too. If anyone asks him what he's doing, he'll simply tell them he's playing a game. They'll be bound to believe him. And having to be quiet helps after all. It means he can keep what he discovers all to himself.

He follows his Daddy from room to room. Morning, noon and night. As soon as he wakes up, George pads downstairs in just his socks so as to make no noise, careful to avoid any step that might creak and give him away. On this particular morning, his Daddy is already in the back kitchen. He's sitting at the table. He doesn't move a muscle for what to George seems like hours. He just sits there, staring straight ahead. George wonders what he can be looking at. He follows the direction of his gaze, but there's nothing there as far as he can tell. George is sure his Daddy hasn't seen him either, watching him from the corner. In fact, he's certain that even if he stood right in front of him, his Daddy wouldn't notice him. He seems so far away.

Suddenly, without warning, he stands to attention and then heads straight for the back door, where he pauses and stands very still again for another long period of time, as if he's forgotten what it is he went there for. George has an idea. He lies his back flat against the kitchen wall and slides around the edges of the room, inch by inch, until he reaches just below where his Daddy is still standing. He silently manoeuvres himself into the tiniest of gaps that his Daddy has left between himself and the still shut back door. Then he stretches up his hand as slowly as he can, walking finger over finger, until he can just about reach the latch, which he flicks up so that he can delicately open the door with his foot. Once it is open, George thinks, maybe his Daddy will remember what it is he needed to check on outside. But as soon as he has managed to open it even the tiniest crack, his Daddy slams it shut again with a loud bang, almost trapping George's foot in it, and retreats quickly across the kitchen and out into the hall towards the front door, where he stops and stands rigid once again. This sudden darting movement, after all that stillness, frightens George, but he bites his bottom lip hard in order to be brave and not cry out. Taking a deep breath, he tiptoes out of the kitchen and curls himself up as tightly as he can into a ball on the lowest step of the stairs, from where he can see his Daddy, now with his face pressed close up to the letter box. His fingers, George notices, are drumming a rapid rhythm against the side of his trouser pockets. George wonders if this might be Morse code and watches intently, but if it is, he can't make it out. Suddenly his Daddy looks up, his neck so rigid that George can see the veins standing out. One of them is pulsing sharply.

"Five-nines!" his Daddy shouts out.

Is he asking me a question, George wonders? He's heard the older children chanting tables at school but he hasn't learned his yet, so he can't answer.

"Five-nines!" his Daddy shouts again, louder this time, and then ducks down quickly to the floor.

His Mummy calls anxiously from upstairs. "Hubert? Is that you? Hubert!"

George's Daddy sees him then. He puts a finger to his lips. That's clear as crystal, thinks George. Be quiet, it says. Don't move. His Daddy rises slowly to an upright position, his eyes transferring from George towards the top of the stairs, watching for George's Mummy to appear. Then, in a movement so fast George barely has time to register it, faster even than when a rat scurries away after someone has thrown a stone at it, his Daddy flings open the front door, leaps outside, slamming it shut behind him, just as his Mummy comes running down the stairs, almost tripping over him in her hurry.

"Where's he gone?" she's saying, her face pressed right up close to his. "What have you done? What have you been saying to him? Didn't I tell you not to pester him with your questions? Where's he gone?"

George, in an agony of slow motion, determined not to break his promise to either of his parents, says nothing. Instead he merely points with an almost comic solemnity towards the front door. But his Mummy is not following the direction of his outstretched finger. She is stooping down to the mat from where she lifts his Daddy's shoes, which she holds aloft like a discarded trophy, dangling them by their laces in distaste and disbelief.

*

Annie knows something is wrong the day Hubert returns

home. Has known before, even. From his letters. Not so much from their content – Hubert has always been the most circumspect of men, so she does not expect outpourings of emotion and is thus not disappointed not to receive any, nor is she surprised by the unchanging litany of his dutiful questions after her health, George's, his parents', before enquiring about the state of the business, needing to be reassured, she supposes, without ever being explicit, that the Printing Works is managing just fine without him, followed by occasional references to some of the other men ("decent chaps"), the wounded ("stoically uncomplaining"), and where, as far as rules and protocol permitted, in France he is stationed ("it must have been peaceful here before the shelling") – but from the nature of his handwriting. This is what disturbs her most. It is still the same immaculate copper plate she's come to recognise from him, but with each successive letter it grows tinier and tinier, until it has become almost microscopic, so that she needs to borrow one of the typesetter's loupes to be able to decipher it at all. It's as if he's disappearing right before her eyes.

She discusses this with Frank, shows him one of the letters. Frank peruses it, swiftly in case he might stumble across something too personal or intimate, then smiles lightly. "You know Hubert," he says, "and his fine margins. Waste not, want not. He's probably just erring on the safe side, in case he runs out of paper."

That would require him to have something to write first, she does not say, but thinks ruefully to herself.

She takes the letter back from her father-in-law and changes the subject, asking instead about the health of the business. She knows the answer already. The business is doing just fine, thank you very much. They should easily survive any slump that's bound to hit them once the war is over. She knows this because she's become more involved than ever, seeing new clients, earning new customers and contracts. The latest is to supply all the print material for Avro, the aviation company who, now they are supplying the country's fledgling air force with ever increasing numbers of bi-planes, have just opened new premises in nearby Newton Heath. Frank is looking tired, she thinks. She wonders if he has had any further recurrences of his angina. She feels certain he probably has and is looking forward to when Hubert comes home again and can take back more of the work Frank has had to pick up these last three years.

But now Hubert *is* home, and it's clear there's no way he can be relied upon for anything just yet. This morning's episode is ample demonstration of that and is just the latest in a whole string of similarly distressing incidents.

She turns back towards George. "You wait there," she commands, "and don't move a muscle till I get back." She flings open the front door and runs out of the house in search of her lost husband.

She finds him almost at once, less than fifty yards away, cowering at the base of the spindle tree down the road, whimpering. His hands cover his ears.

"Make them stop," he says desperately when she reaches him.

She puts a hand tentatively on his shoulder, frightened that the slightest touch might make him bolt once more. She eventually manages to enfold his body within her arms. It is quivering beneath her touch like a nervous, trapped bird.

"Make them stop," he says again.

"Make what stop?" she asks as gently as she can.

He points in the direction of the Works.

"The guns," he says. "Make them stop."

"Shh," she whispers, closing her eyes as a tear slides down her cheek. "There are no more guns," she says.

"But I can hear them," he shouts. "Why won't you believe me? Listen."

Annie allows herself to tune in to the constant dull roar of the printing presses, which she can feel, as much as hear, vibrating through her body. She remembers how, when she first came here, almost eight years ago now, she had thrilled to their ceaseless rhythm, which had made her want to dance. Now she has grown so accustomed to them she barely registers them. But this morning, feeling Hubert's shoulders trembling within her arms, she tries to make herself hear them anew, through his ears, but her imagination fails her. She simply has no knowledge of what he's been through. He never speaks of it, retreating instead deep within himself, where she cannot reach him.

"Come on," she says at last, and she lifts him carefully to his feet.

"Where are we going?" he asks plaintively.

"Away from the guns," she answers.

He sighs deeply. "Thank you," he says, and she feels some of the tension slipping away from his body.

When they finally reach their still open front door, she returns the shoes he has walked out of the house without back on the mat. "Let's put these on now, shall we?" she says. He nods numbly, standing there patiently while she kneels down in front of him to lift first one foot, then the other and place it inside each shoe, whose laces she then proceeds to tie.

George is still sitting on the bottom step of the stair, looking towards his parents anxiously, his thumb firmly lodged inside his mouth, a habit she thought he'd grown out of, but which has returned with a vengeance these last few weeks. This must be all so confusing for him, she knows, and she vows to be more patient with him than she has been of late. She gives him a cuddle. "You're a good boy," she says. "Go and get dressed. We're all going to Grandma's. Then how about we go over to see Auntie Claudia after that and see if she's got any ice cream in her cellar…?"

George doesn't need to be asked twice. He takes the stairs two at a time. Across the road the printing presses roll remorselessly on.

*

Evelyn opens the door to find Annie, Hubert and George standing there like three lost waifs. She quickly ushers them inside. One look at Annie's face is enough for her to realise that this is something of an emergency, and the tiniest glance at Hubert's shrunken figure propels her into immediate and swift action. Hubert is taken straight upstairs, into his old room before he left to get married, where the two women undress him, which he silently, passively, allows them to do.

"The bed's always made up," says Evelyn unnecessarily, "just in case any of you ever needed to stay over," before her voice trails away.

Evelyn tiptoes out of the room as soon as Hubert is lying down, leaving Annie a few moments of privacy with him. She goes downstairs to check on George, who is busily playing with one of his toys, a model bi-plane made from wood, which he is flying around the kitchen above his head, making a series of engine noises through closed lips.

"Would you like to help your Grandma make some biscuits?" she asks, tying an apron around her waist, immediately becoming busy.

George, instantly attracted by the thought of biscuits, puts down his toy and joins his Grandma, whom he adores, by the table. "Can I use the rolling pin?"

"Do you know," says Evelyn, as brightly as she can, "that's exactly what I hoped you say?"

An hour later, with biscuits baked and tea brewed, and George happily playing outside in the back garden with Tabitha, his Grandma's ginger cat, Evelyn and Annie at last have a chance to speak. Hubert remains fast asleep upstairs. Annie puts her undrunk cup of tea to one side and paces up and down the lounge, beneath the dreamy gaze of Bubbles above the fireplace, towards the piano, on top of which Evelyn keeps a gallery of framed family photographs. Annie pauses in front of them, surveys the passing of the years neatly arranged before her. First there are pictures of Evelyn and Frank as children. Then the two of them getting married. Then with Hubert as a baby. There's Hubert as a school boy, and there he is again at sixteen, on his first day at the Printing Works. Now she sees herself standing beside him, on the steps of the Hulme Hall Lane Chapel on their wedding day. Next, a posed family group of the five of them, for the occasion of George's christening, and finally one of Hubert in uniform, looking pale and serious. Annie has to turn away. She can see behind those eyes the struggle and compromise and betrayal she knows he went through, that she forced him through, in order to put on that uniform. And now it has come to this. She stops by the French windows leading out onto the back garden, where she can see George totally absorbed in his own private conversation, seemingly happily playing with his grandmother's ginger cat, and it breaks her heart.

Evelyn has never witnessed her daughter-in-law like this before. She appears to be completely unravelling before her eyes.

After a long pause, she tentatively breaks the silence with a small cough. "I have always found," she begins hesitantly, "that when one is faced with a somewhat intractable problem, the best thing to do is to keep busy. Work, my dear, is a great consolation. It gives us perspective, don't you find?"

Annie turns away from the window and looks directly at Evelyn, but as yet says nothing. She merely waits for what her mother-in-law might say next.

"How long has it been now since Hubert came home? Four, five months?"

Annie nods.

"And would you say his condition has become worse or

better in that time?"

Annie's eyes widen with incredulity. "You saw him this morning. How can you even ask such a question?"

"Yes, yes, I know. Most distressing. But maybe after a little rest, he'll be more himself again."

Annie has to bite her lip to prevent her from saying something she might later regret.

"What I mean is," Evelyn continues, "perhaps today's... episode... is just a blip. He's been working harder than ever since Christmas, almost as if..." She pauses.

"Yes?" says Annie violently, jerking her head in Evelyn's direction.

"... to make up for lost time. Perhaps we should have tried harder to persuade him to take things more slowly at first, to ease his way back in gradually, rather than fling himself back full time into the fray. But you know Hubert..." She laughs nervously.

"Today is not an isolated incident," says Annie and, with a certain angry finality, she sits back on the sofa, folding her arms and turning her face away from Evelyn.

"Oh," replies Evelyn, raising a hand to her mouth. "I hadn't realised." She sits beside Annie. "You should have spoken sooner."

"I tried to. Once before. With Frank."

"I see. He never mentioned it. What did he say?"

"The same as you actually. 'You know Hubert'..."

"I'm sorry." She reaches out a hand to take one of Annie's and squeezes it warmly, before delicately broaching her next question. "What are you going to do?"

Annie looks directly ahead. "I've already been to see Dr Wilkes. We neither of us used the words 'shell shock'..."

"I should hope not," said Evelyn, smartly removing her hand.

"... but we were both thinking it. In the end he recommended we do nothing. For the time being. 'Let nature take its course,' he said. 'Time is a great healer. Come and see me again in a few weeks if things don't get any better.' He advised more exercise, lots of fresh air, long walks, that sort of thing."

"Dr Wilkes was always very sensible."

"Yes, but… 'You know Hubert.' He just works."

"Yes. I know. Like father, like son."

"At this rate he'll work himself into an early grave. Or an asylum."

"Don't say such a thing, Annie. He's here now. You all are. And you're welcome to stay here for as long as you need. Until Hubert gets better. And he will get better, trust me. He needs a decent, proper rest, that's all, away from The Works."

"You're very kind," said Annie, softening a little. "He certainly can't go back to work just yet, that's for sure. The noise of the machines is really affecting his nerves. He can't sleep at night, they bother him so."

"That's settled then. You can all stay here. And it'll be nice to see more of George."

"Thank you. Which reminds me. Would you mind if George and I went out for a while? Only I promised him an ice cream. He's earned it. He's been such a good boy lately."

"He's always a good boy."

"Yes, he is," adds Annie, somewhat wistfully, watching him chase the cat around the garden.

"The two of you go. I'll be here when Hubert wakes up. I'll make him some onion soup. That's always been one of his favourites."

"Yes," replies Annie, regarding her mother-in-law curiously. "I know."

"It'll be like old times having Hubert back here."

Annie picks up her bag, puts on her jacket and goes out into the back garden to collect George.

"Come on," she says. "We're off to Auntie Claudia's

now. Time for that ice cream."

"Spiffing," he says, running up to join her, Tabitha immediately forgotten.

"Spiffing?" she laughs. "Where do you hear such words?"

"In the playground at school," he replies artlessly, putting his hand into hers. "Bye, Grandma."

As they walk back across town to Claudia's, an idea begins to form in Annie's mind. This will not do, she thinks. Hubert cannot be allowed to stay with his mother any longer than is absolutely necessary. But neither can he return to Portugal Street. That much is also clear. We must move, she decides. It's time to turn a new page.

*

Claudia is also looking at photographs. Her parents started an album as soon as they arrived in Manchester more than thirty years ago from Campania. There's the two of them standing on the cellar steps in Loom Street, their first home here, a damp, windowless dungeon that nevertheless seemed like a heaven on earth to them. Their poses are stiff, their expressions tremulous and grave. Matteo, her brother, is just two years old. He's encircled in his father's huge arms, no doubt to try and stop him from fidgeting. He was never able to keep still. He still can't, smiles Claudia. Always pitching in at one job or another. She herself is not there. Invisible. Though she might, by the time this photograph was taken, have begun to form inside her mother's belly. Claudia holds the picture close, trying to detect any signs she might already be present, a wriggling tadpole swimming in some amniotic sac. Is there anything in her mother's expression that might indicate she has begun to feel another life growing inside her, this first born in their new adopted country? But there's nothing Claudia can discern. Nothing apart from her mother's usual cautious retreat from scrutiny, from the camera's unflinching gaze…

Now a dozen years have passed. The photograph she looks at next shows a procession of young girls in white dresses, standing on the steps of St Alban's Church. Father Fratelli stands behind them, beaming. All the girls are aged eleven, or thereabouts. Some are smiling. One or two are waving at an unseen relative in the crowd of proud, admiring onlookers. All are aware that they are very much the centre of attention, for this is the occasion of their first communion. Claudia had been quite nervous, she recalls, worried that she might forget some of the responses she'd been learning and practising for weeks, but in the end she had remembered them all perfectly. She had caught sight of her mother in the congregation, sitting near the back as would have been her preference, not seeking to draw attention to herself, mouthing the words as Claudia spoke them aloud, then breathing out deeply when she had finished, tears of joy and relief threatening to spill down her cheeks. And afterwards, as the photographer was vainly trying to coral all the girls onto the church steps, Claudia remembers her mother fussing over the hem of her communion dress, the dress she had laboured long, sleepless nights over in the preceding weeks. But again Claudia cannot see herself in the photograph. She seems to be missing. What could have happened? She scans the faces of the other girls, many of whose names she's now forgotten, some she no longer recognises, but several who've grown into women she still sees regularly, in the markets on Saturdays, at Mass on Sundays, Bella, Francesca, Amanda, but as for herself, she's simply not there. Or – wait a minute – is that her? She brings the image closer towards her. Behind one of the girls who is waving to someone off camera is a figure that could be her, she thinks, the raised hand completely blocking her face…

Seven years later a third photograph captures a stage in a school hall, decked out for its Annual Speech Night and Prize Giving. There are flowers lining the front. A table is adorned with engraved cups and shields, next to another with assorted piles of neatly stacked hardback books. Claudia recognises her former teacher, Miss Leslie, she whose early evening visit to their house one day had persuaded Claudia's father to let her transfer to the Grammar School, who has returned to her *alma mater* to present the prizes and certificates. She remembers the Headmistress calling out her name in clear, dulcet tones. "And the Sybil May Leslie Award for the Most Special Scientific Achievement, presented this evening by Miss Leslie herself, goes to... Claudia Campanella..." Claudia can still remember the thrill of that moment, when she heard her name being called out and the generous applause which accompanied it. In her pleasure and haste she had almost stumbled up the steps on her way up to the stage to collect her prize. The photographer has clicked the shutter at precisely the wrong moment, just as Claudia has turned to shake Miss Leslie's hand and receive the book and certificate from her, so that now the photograph shows only the back of her head and her outstretched arm... She has the book still – *Principia Mathematica* by Sir Isaac Newton, which she fetches down from a shelf where she keeps all manner of souvenirs and mementoes and flicks it open. The certificate is still there on the fly-leaf, containing her name and the signatures of both Miss Leslie and the Headmistress. On the next is Newton's famous Foreword – "*at a round hole about one third of an inch broad, made in the shut of a window, I place a glass prism, whereby the beam of the sun's light, which comes in that hole, might be refracted upwards towards the opposite wall of the chamber, and there form a coloured image of the sun...*" – and elsewhere in the book she has underlined in pencil certain passages, which caught her imagination. Her eye rests on one of these now. "*I do not know what I may appear to the world, but to myself I seem to have been only like a child playing on the sea-shore, and diverting myself in now and then finding a smoother pebble or a prettier shell than ordinary, whilst the great ocean of truth lay all undiscovered before me…*" This had inspired her as a young woman. Now it only serves to remind her of just how thinly she's been stretched, how she feels herself being separated into fragments, tiny shards of a shell, never to become unified again…

There are no photographs of her wedding. It all had to be arranged so quickly to coincide with Marco's all fleeting leave from the Front, so it just wasn't possible. She knows that some were taken, by friends of the family, and that *Nonno* has them now, shut away in a drawer, for he cannot bear to look on them, they upset him so. Claudia thinks she should try and find a way of requesting one of them, that shows them both happy and smiling, which is how she remembers that day. All she has now is this brief snap lying in front of her on her lap, having fallen out of the album. Annie's Hubert had lent her his camera and shown her how to use it. "You can take just one picture," he had said, "so choose wisely." She tried unsuccessfully several times to get Marco to pose for it, but he wouldn't. "We have so little time together," he said, "to waste it on keeping still." But in the end she managed to catch him in an unguarded moment, smoking a cigarette in the dunes on the estuary of the River Dee, where he had driven them both in the borrowed automobile for that all too brief weekend. And she is looking at the photograph now. There he sits, hair ruffled, shirt unbuttoned, looking away to where the river joined the sea, the smoke of his cigarette framing his face in coiled wreaths. And there, falling across him slightly, is a shadow, *her* shadow, hands raised to her face, holding the camera, an obscure dark shape. She quickly replaces it in the album and turns the page…

Another leave. Nearly four years later. The last one. Marco is holding a three year old Giulia on his lap. He has been bouncing her up and down, and she is giddy and flushed. Claudia remembers asking Marco to stop so that the picture can be taken. They are in a photographer's studio – a gift paid for by Annie. When Claudia tries to join them in the posed group, Giulia protests loudly. She is such a Daddy's girl. She threatens to throw one of her spectacular tantrums, and the photographer, unable to coax or assuage her with dolls or balls, becomes impatient and anxious that they will overrun their allotted time, so that in the end Claudia relents, allowing Giulia to pose alone with her father, which is what she had wanted from the outset. "She's going to be a real heartbreaker when she grows up," Annie had observed on one of their occasional Saturday afternoons together, as Giulia proceeded to torment the life out of poor, patient, biddable George, who, like a puppy too eager to please, would fetch every stick Giulia might deign to throw his way and always jump up for more, tail wagging and eyes shining. "She already is," Claudia had replied. "She has Marco, Matteo and *Nonno* all wound around her little finger." Annie had laughed and said, "Never mind. There'll be other photos, when the boys come home..."

The next one, the final one in the album, does at last show Claudia. Taken just three months after news had reached them that Marco would not be coming home again. It is a serious affair. It must have been taken at Paulie's christening, but she can't think why, or by whom, or how she comes to have it here now. Matteo is there, back from the Front, safe but sombre. And *Nonno* too, looking like a deflated balloon, all the air punched out of him. They stand either side of her, framing her, while Giulia stands to one side, her dark eyes blazing, as if she blames her mother for her Daddy not returning home. Claudia, seated with a sleeping Paulie in her arms, looks out towards the camera, lost. Paulie – dear, gentle, affable Paulie – who slept like an angel, who can never do enough for her, who never saw his father...

Claudia studies the expression on her face in this, the only photograph to capture it. It is, she realises, even more absent than in all of the others where it doesn't appear. She turns away towards the framed callograph made for her by Annie and given to her as a wedding present, propped up on the chest of drawers beside the bed in which she now always sleeps alone. The labyrinth. Annie had been keen to point out, when she gave it to her, she recalls, the difference between a labyrinth and a maze. A maze is full of dead ends and blind alleys, while a labyrinth offers a single unified path to its centre and from there back out into the world again. Looking at it now, Claudia's eyes are drawn inexorably towards the vanishing point in the centre, the mystery at the heart of the atom, shrinking, shrinking, becoming ever smaller, until nothing remains, until it becomes, like her too, it seems, an ever-diminishing half life, invisible.

She picks up a letter that lies beside the picture, the one which arrived only this morning, which has prompted this regretful look back over her lost photographs, while Giulia is still at school and Paulie is having his afternoon nap. It is from the University.

Dept of Chemistry
Victoria University of Manchester
Oxford Road
Manchester

15th March 1919

Dear Mrs Locartelli,

Now that Professor Rutherford has left us to continue

his research at Cambridge, and in order to accommodate the officers and men recently returned from the War, we regret to inform you that there is no longer a suitable position for you here at the University.

We are sure that you will appreciate the change in circumstances, which has precipitated this decision, and we would like to take this opportunity of thanking you for all of your efforts during this difficult time in our nation's history.

Yours sincerely,

Dr D.S. Brooks
Msc, PhD

*

Hubert stands on the summit of Tandle Hill, ten miles north of Portugal Street, between Royton and Chadderton. He has no recollection of how he got there. It must be about noon, for the sun is almost directly overhead. It's a warm midsummer's day, and Hubert is perspiring from the effort of the climb. He's taken off his jacket, which he carries neatly folded over one arm. When he reaches the top, he looks around him at the three hundred and sixty degree panoramic view. He shades his eyes with his free hand and looks all the way across the plain to Manchester. Smoke is pouring up into the sky from the scores of factory chimneys laid out before him. From this height and distance the scene resembles a chequered tablecloth with row upon row of giant salt cellars. The earth appears to be smouldering after a great fire. It reminds Hubert of the fields of France, which once had been ploughed fields growing wheat or barley, now laid waste, the morning after a battle. Up here, on Tandle Hill, an old Celtic word for Beacon Hill, where fires were once lit in Saxon times, to warn of enemy marauders approaching, Hubert can now stand and survey the smoke and ruin below and feel a welcome detachment, escaping at last from the incessant noise of war, the pounding of the guns, the ghostly whine of shells, the earth shaking beneath him from their constant bombardment.

Today the sun beats down and Hubert contemplates the shifting landscape falling away from him, the city's ceaseless creep across the last few squares of unbuilt-on land, lava flows between the low stone walls that criss-cross the ground like crumbling bones. The city pours and tumbles over and between them like an army of rats scurrying and writhing in their determined foraging.

Away to the north rises the long, narrow ridge of Oldham Edge, stretching out towards the Pennines. This is a fine spot, thinks Hubert, sitting down on the grass, mopping his forehead with his handkerchief, on which Annie has embroidered his initials. A century before, almost to the day, crowds had mustered here with flags and banners, wearing wreaths of laurel in their hair, preparing to march to St Peter's Fields in Manchester to listen to Orator Hunt. He can picture them now, so full of hope on a warm summer's day not dissimilar to today, setting off with prayers and songs and such high spirits. Just as he can imagine the ancient peoples who once claimed this land as their own, looking out from here as he is doing now, scanning the horizon, for Roman legions clearing the earth of trees and laying their roads as they advanced, or, later, for Picts or Viking raiders from the north, appearing over the crest of the Edge like the apocalypse.

But not today. He takes a deep breath and stands up, filling his lungs with clean, fresh air. He looks back towards the city. He is filled with an immense feeling of pride for what this land of his birth has accomplished. Why then, he asks himself, is he running away from it now? Why does he no longer wish to plunge himself headlong back into the hurly burly of it all once again? He finds he has no answer, except to acknowledge that it is so.

*"When the hurly burly's done
When the battle's lost and won…"*

Three small figures are making their way slowly up the hill towards him.

*

REUTERS PRESS AGENCY – NEWSFLASH – 14TH JUNE 1919 – ALCOCK & BROWN TAKE OFF FROM LESTER'S FIELD NEWFOUNDLAND CANADA IN BID TO MAKE FIRST EVER TRANSATLANTIC FLIGHT – end bulletin - STOP

*

Hubert can hear an angel singing. He thinks he must be dreaming. Or dying. He looks up into a clear sky, the blue so brilliant it floors him. The grass is warm to his touch. There are wild flowers everywhere, as if someone has taken a handful of colours and scattered them carelessly, indiscriminately, an overturned box of paints. He becomes aware of three small figures a little way off from him, further down the slope of the hill. A man, a woman, a child. A family perhaps. It is the child who is singing. Hubert recognises the tune but the words are unfamiliar, French, and so it is as if he is listening to this song, one he has heard many times before with the other men, for the first time.

*"Et quand ils nous demandent
Comme c'était dangereux
Nous ne leur dirons jamais
Nous ne leur dirons jamais…"*

The woman, who is black, Hubert notices, her skin gleaming like polished coal, is unpacking a picnic. The man is a deep, warm chestnut. He is fashioning something with stiff brown paper and string. He works quickly with an easy focus. The girl, the angel of his imagination, is weaving a daisy chain while she sings, which she places round her head like a coronet.

When she has finished singing, the man calls her over to him.

"Chamomile," he says, and Hubert is unsure whether that is the girl's name, or that the man is pointing to one of the wild flowers.

She idly trails her fingers through the grass as she skips down the slope towards him.

"*Oui, Papa.*"

He is holding up a kite. This is what he has been making. In no time at all it is soaring into the sky. The man hands control of the string, which is wound around a piece of black iron which, Hubert notes with admiration, could almost have been forged especially for this function, to the girl who expertly lets out the string so that the kite flies higher and higher. He should bring George here, he thinks. They could fly a kite together too. Annie could make a picnic. Perhaps for his next birthday? When is that, he wonders? He can't remember. But Annie is sure to know…

Just then a pair of Avro 504's roar out of the sun. They appear to be diving down straight towards him. He throws himself to the ground, covering his head with his hands, but they bank away over the hill, heading out across the plain to Manchester. Hubert lets out a cry of pain or relief – he isn't sure which – as he stands to watch them disappear into the blue. Part of him wants to be up there with them, hurtling towards an unseen future, while part of him wants to stay exactly where he is, firmly rooted to the earth. Isn't that where he belongs after all? Isn't this the land he sacrificed his principles for to protect? The kite dances on the breeze left by the bi-planes' slipstream. The air hums like telegraph wires, buzzing with encrypted messages he can't yet decode. It sings of something coming.

*

Annie is standing in the kitchen of their new home putting away the tea towel after drying the breakfast dishes. They moved in a month ago and already things feel brighter than they have since Hubert first left to join the Royal Army Medical Corps. Each morning, after George has gone to school and Hubert has left for work, not the previous daily ordeal at the Printing Works, but driving around the city to meet new clients and develop new custom, a duty he has cautiously begun to share with Frank, Annie likes to walk around each room in turn, savouring the new furnishings, taking stock. There are so many windows in the house, so that it feels permanently flooded with light. She takes a deep pleasure in arranging things just so, the pictures on walls, the ornaments on mantelpiece, tables and sideboards, the fresh sheets in the linen cupboards, the newly hung curtains, which she has designed and made herself. This is a long way from the Tripe Colony, she reminds herself. She rolls the address round and round her tongue, relishing the sound and shape of it, its every syllable: Hirstwood, Daisy Bank Road, Victoria Park, Manchester. Every atom of it delights her.

Using the contacts she developed while supporting Frank over the past few years, she arranged the purchase entirely on her own initiative. The agent acting on behalf of the sellers was someone she had met at one of the many charity functions she now attended. "Yes," he had said when she raised the question of needing a house over dessert, "I think I may have just the property you are looking for. If you can move quickly," he added. "The quicker, the better" had been her reply. "In which case I might be able to offer the most favourable of terms," and he had knowingly tapped the side of his nose. "Do you know Victoria Park?" he asked. "A little," she answered. He withdrew a small newspaper cutting from the inside of his dinner jacket pocket, neatly folded in four, which he opened out and passed across to her. It was from *The Manchester Guardian.* Underlined was a phrase written by Neville Cardus about the particularly unique character of this sealed off suburb of the city. 'A sequestered purlieu,' he described it as. "I believe this will suit us perfectly," smiled Annie, as she handed the cutting back to him.

And so it does.

A sequestered purlieu.

Since agreeing the purchase, at a more than reasonable price, Annie has supervised every aspect of the move. "We shall not be selling the house on Portugal Street," she announced to Frank and Evelyn. We're promoting Harry Heath to Foreman at The Works, taking on many of the duties that Hubert had seen to before the War, and renting it to him and his young family." Frank immediately agreed to the plan, and his brother Gordon was brought back once more for a brief period to make sure that Harry Heath knew all that he needed to, while Frank gladly began to pass over more and more of his work to Hubert, privately reassuring himself with the knowledge that Annie would always be on hand to advise on any of the more tricky negotiations. Hubert, it was agreed, should not visit the Printing Works any more than he had to.

Hubert has been happy to let others make these decisions for him. He has an automobile now. "Not an indulgence," insists Annie, "but a necessity, now that you have to visit clients and customers right across the city." It is a Crossley Phaeton, manufactured in Manchester, in Gorton on Napier Street. He is immensely proud of it, as is George, and the two of them spend Sunday afternoons together cleaning and polishing every surface of it. George especially loves it when

Hubert lifts the bonnet and begins to induct him into the secret mysteries of the internal combustion engine.

"What's a Phaeton, Daddy?"

"It's from the Greek," explains Hubert. "Phaeton was the son of Helios…"

"Who's that?"

"The god of the sun. Phaeton borrowed one of the chariots of the sun and drove it too close to the earth."

"Did he crash?"

"He might have, if his Daddy hadn't stopped him in time."

"Does that mean I can borrow this car from you?"

Hubert laughs – a sound that Annie hasn't heard in a long while – and says, "Maybe, son. When you're older…"

George has settled in well to his new school and Hubert is beginning to seem a little better, with occasional glimpses of his old self again. He still has to be careful not to over-exert himself, but, looking round their new home each morning when she's by herself, this sequestered purlieu, Annie allows herself to breathe a little easier, and dares, once more, to imagine a future, and to hope.

*

Back on Tandle Hill a vice-like pain grips Hubert's chest. He drops to his knees. His mouth opens as if he is about to speak but no words come out. Only rasping, choking air trying to prise the hammer from his heart. He is aware of the young girl, with the coronet of daisies in her hair, standing over him, looking at him with wide-eyed curiosity, before she begins to sing once more.

"Et quand ils nous demandent
Et c'est certain vraiment qu'ils nous demandent
Pourquoi n'avons-nous pas encore la Croix du Guerre
Nous ne leur dirons jamais

Nous ne leur dirons jamais
En premier ligne c'est Dieu qui seul connaît..."

*

THE TIMES

16th June 1919

ALCOCK & BROWN COMPLETE HISTORIC FLIGHT

At precisely 8.40am yesterday the Manchester duo of pilot John Alcock and navigator Arthur Whitten Brown touched down their Vickers Vimy IV twin-engined bomber, powered by two Rolls Royce Eagle 360 hp engines, on the west coast of Ireland, making landfall in County Galway after a heroic, incident-packed sixteen hour flight to become the first to fly non-stop across the Atlantic and thereby claim the £10,000 prize.

The pair took off just after 1.45pm local time from Lester's Field in Newfoundland, Canada, and almost at once they faced the first of what were to prove several major challenges. The overloaded aircraft had difficulty taking off from the rough ground and barely cleared a nearby line of trees. At 3 o'clock their wind-driven electrical generator failed, depriving them of radio contact, their intercom and heating. At 5 o'clock they were forced to fly blind through thick fog. Navigator Brown was unable to use his sextant and they had not taken with them any gyroscopic instruments. Alcock twice lost control of the plane and almost crashed into the sea after one particularly spiralling nose dive.

Shortly after midnight they got their first glimpse of stars and Brown was at last able to make use of his sextant, through which he calculated that miraculously they were still on course. Their electric heating suits had failed, making them extremely cold in their open cockpit, but their coffee was laced with whiskey to compensate.

At 3am they flew into a large snowstorm. They were drenched by rain, their instruments froze, and the aeroplane was in danger of icing up and becoming unflyable. The carburettor did indeed ice up, forcing Brown to have to climb out onto the wings to clear the engines, a feat of extraordinary daring at a height of almost 12,000 feet.

They finally made landfall in County Galway at 8.40am not far from their intended landing place near Clifden, having been airborne for three minutes short of sixteen hours, with over fourteen and a half of these directly over the Atlantic. In total they covered a distance of 1,890 miles at an average speed of 115 mph. The aircraft was slightly damaged on landing, for Alcock mistook a bog for what he thought was a green field, but neither man was hurt. Brown told reporters on the scene that had the weather been kinder they could have flown directly to London.

In addition to the £10,000 prize, the heroic pair also received 1,000 guineas each from the Ardath Tobacco Company, and both are to be knighted by His Majesty King George V at Buckingham Palace in a few days time.

John Alcock was born in Basford House on Seymour Grove in Firswood, Manchester, while Arthur Whitten Brown, although born in Glasgow to American parents, moved to Manchester when he was just six years old. The aircraft, a Vickers Vimy IV, was constructed at the British Westinghouse factory on Trafford Park, which is also the current home of Rolls Royce, who provided the all important engines.

Another triumph for Great Britain and for Manchester, Cradle of the Industrial Revolution, now birthplace to the Age of Speed.

*

Gradually the facts become known.

Hubert climbs the steep path to the summit of Tandle Hill as a result of a chance conversation with Alliott Verdon Roe, Managing Director of A.V. Roe & Company, universally known as Avro, who had just moved to larger premises from Brownsfield Mill on Great Ancoats Street to Newton Heath, where the planes were manufactured, and where Hubert has gone to deliver a sample of leaflets, brochures and posters to advertise Avro's new range of products and services for approval before being printed back at the Works.

Mr Roe shows Hubert around the new assembly line where fuselages, undercarriages and fuel tanks, cockpits, wings and propellers are all being hand crafted and engineered in a series of large interconnecting hangars. Hubert is most impressed, as he always is, by the latest technological advances. He takes an enthusiastic interest in the design and construction of the instrument panels. They remind him, in their scientific precision and attention to detail, of the barometer he has recently purchased for their new house in Victoria Park, where he has hung it in the wide, welcoming entrance hall by the substantial front door, with its leaded lights and stained glass, through which the early morning sun streams in rainbow-coloured refractions. When he had tapped it first thing that morning, the gauge had indicated fine weather with a possibility of storms to come later.

He looks up now into a cloudless blue sky. He is recalling, as he inspects the instrument panel in a newly completed Avro 510, the smooth touch of the polished mahogany finish surrounding the barometer beneath his fingers, when he catches the tail end of what Mr Roe has been telling him.

"I'm glad you approve of our new premises, Hubert, but I have to say I've got my eye on somewhere else already. Not as a replacement, but as an addition. Over near Slattocks, midway between Chadderton and Royton. Not far from Tandle Hill."

Hubert looks up.

"Have you ever been out there?"

Hubert doesn't believe he has.

"Oh, you should. Wonderful spot. You can see for miles. A bit like being up in one of these beauties." And he runs his hand proprietorially along one of the bi-plane's wings. "I'm telling you, Hubert, from up there you can see the whole of Manchester laid out before you. Like a banquet, just waiting for you to pick up your knife and fork and tuck in."

" *'Then was Jesus led up of the Spirit into the wilderness to be tempted by the Devil'*," Hubert responds automatically.

"I beg your pardon, lad?"

" *'And he taketh him up into an exceeding high mountain, and sheweth him all the kingdoms of the world, and the glory of them; and saith unto him, All these things will I give thee, if thou shalt fall down and worship me'*…"

Mr Roe looks at Hubert anxiously. "Are you sure you're all right, lad?"

" *'Then saith Jesus unto him, Get thee hence, Satan'*…"

Hubert pauses, looking down at the ground. Mr Roe regards him strangely.

"Ay, well… There mebbe summat in that. But I'll tell you what else I see from up there, Hubert, and it's this. The future. Progress and speed, Hubert. Progress and speed. The future. There's nowt else. Time and tide, eh Hubert? Time and tide..."

Hubert drives away from Newton Heath in his Crossley Phaeton, completing the quote from Matthew's Gospel over and over in his head as he does so.

" *'Then the devil leaveth him, and, behold, angels came and ministered unto him'*..."

*

The first Annie learns of the incident is when the telephone she has just had installed rings in the hallway. It is a Doctor calling her, a name she does not recognise, from the Oldham Royal Infirmary.

"Is that Mrs Wright?"

"Yes?"

"Your husband," he says.

"What about him?" Annie grows cold all over.

"He's had a lucky escape."

"What do you mean?"

"Heart attack. Fortunately he was found and treated quickly. A family picnicking nearby. They came to his aid. But for their prompt action we might not have been able to get to him in time. He's not out of the woods yet, Mrs Wright, but I'm optimistic..."

Two hours later George is with Claudia, and Annie is by Hubert's bedside. She sits with him a long time. All through the night. Nurses come in regularly to check on him. Eventually, just as a weak sun pokes its way through the blanket of cloud, Hubert begins to wake.

When he opens his eyes, his first words are, "I saw an angel. I heard her singing to me..."

His fingers flutter beside him on the bed. Annie takes

them in her own hands as he drifts back into sleep.

*

Two years later, on a bright, unseasonably warm morning in October 1921, a large crowd has gathered on Tandle Hill to witness the unveiling of the Royton Memorial, a thirty foot high obelisk made of Portland stone, by the Earl of Derby, "in memory of those who gave their lives for the freedom and honour of their country". After a minute's silence the Chadderton & District Brass Band entertain the crowds with a medley of marches, hymns and patriotic songs, this same band who had accompanied those who marched to war seven years earlier, and to the Boer War fifteen years before that, and to St Peter's Fields more than a century ago. But the mood on this particular autumn afternoon is not sombre. It is more like a public holiday, a welcome break for those who have assembled there from the factories and mills and mines below, breathing in great lungfuls of the higher, thinner, cleaner air, as they look down upon the city where they toil.

As the brass band continues to play, the people scatter about the summit and slopes of the hill, laying out rugs for picnics, unwrapping bread and cheese, apples and ale. The atmosphere is festive. Here and there voices are raised to join in the choruses of the songs being played. Children run and tumble like gambolling lambs. Courting couples seek each other's waists or even risk a stolen kiss.

Among the crowds, just a few feet below the summit, is a small family group. Mother, father, son. The boy is hopping from foot to foot in unconcealed excitement as his father busies himself with something that, from a distance, is difficult to make out. Eventually he has finished. He holds out a kite to the boy, who runs as fast as he dares down the slope, while the father rapidly unwinds the string. At a signal from the father, the boy releases the kite and watches in sheer delight as it rises into the sky, dancing bravely on the breeze.

The father beckons the boy back to the summit, and he obligingly races back up to join him. As soon as he has reached him, the father hands over control of the kite to the boy who, with tongue protruding from the side of his mouth in studied concentration, lets out more and more of the string, until the kite is so high it is almost hard to make it out among all the other kites that are flying above the hill.

"Look, Mummy," cries the boy. "Ours is the highest one."

Annie catches Hubert's eye and they share a radiant smile together. George, his eye still fixed upon the kite, imagines himself up there, looking down on all of this, soaring higher and higher, until all below are merely dust motes, caught in the last of the day's sun, infinitesimally small, but teeming with untapped possibilities.

4

5th July 1930

George and Francis. Francis and George.

Their names are inextricably linked, although they have yet to meet. For more than ten years they will follow parallel paths – or perhaps tram tracks would be the more appropriate metaphor, criss-crossing the city they both inhabit, passing the same familiar landmarks, observing the changes that are taking place almost daily as Manchester continues to multiply and grow, while never alighting at the same stop at the same time. What are the odds, for two people who do not believe in fate, who are ardently self-determinist, who believe you make your own luck, control your own destiny, no matter what history throws at you, to find each other in a metropolis of nearly a million people and rising? Perhaps not so remote as we might think, once certain forces are in play...

> *"This is the tale of Thomas-à-Tattimus*
> *Who took two T's*
> *To tie two tups to two tall trees*
> *To frighten the terrible Thomas-à-Tattimus –*
> *How many T's are there in all that?"*

George used to love this tongue twister. As a child he'd ask his mother to repeat it over and over again, and then try to figure out the answer, which he never could. Annie, remembering her own puzzled frustration as a child herself, when her father had first taught her the rhyme, would grin. "Two," she'd say, "two. Work it out, George."

"But it can't be," he'd reply, going red in the face with the effort of trying.

"But it is," she'd say, then ruffle the top of his head.

When George finally worked it out for himself, he howled with frustration at having missed something so obvious. But it taught him something he never forgot – to look beyond the surface of things and find their true heart, usually something that would be staring him right in the face, but which he might have let extraneous forces distract him from seeing. He liked to pass this on to his students years later, when he was lecturing at *The Mechanics' Institute* in Salford, or in his own work as a photographer.

Two.

It would always come down to two.

But in 1919, when, aged six, George finally puzzles the riddle of Thomas-à-Tattimus for himself, this is all a long way into the future.

At the same time that Hubert first climbs Tandle Hill, Francis is completing his long walk back to Manchester from internment. He traces the route of the recently erected telegraph poles, marching across the land like giant soldiers, first close to the banks of the Manchester Ship Canal, where he endures that extraordinary, grisly encounter with Delphine and the decaying bodies of her dead parents, before branching east, where the line of the poles diverged, finally stopping in Denton, on the Hyde Road, outside the closed and boarded up premises of the late Friedrich Kaufman – optician, jeweller and engraver – beneath the sign of the rimless spectacles, whose blank, lidless eyes looked out towards the city.

Two years later, while George is flying a kite beneath the long, pointing finger of the shadow cast by Royton War Memorial, Francis is on a different hilltop, twelve miles across the city at Heaton Park. Just as a red-faced, smiling George is chattering nineteen to the dozen to his parents throughout the entire duration of their descent from the summit of Tandle Hill, scampering back and forth between them like a bouncy puppy, Francis is just beginning the long, slow climb through the ashlar sandstone archway of the Grand Lodge, which marks the entrance to the park, designed by Lewis Wyatt a century before for Sir Thomas Egerton, a close relation to the Earls of Ellesmere, by the Bridgwater Canal in Worsley. From there Francis walks along the main carriage drive towards the Hall with its Palladian columns of stuccoed brick, but turns aside instead past the Smithy Lodge, more commonly known by its nickname, the Pepperpot, because of its octagonal shape, along the line of the ha-ha below the Dower House, which formerly served as the Earl of Wilton's summer house, from which grazing cattle, aesthetically placed to please the eye, would once have been observed. Francis veers diagonally away from the recently constructed boating pool, at the edge of which stands the colonnaded façade of the old Town Hall from King Street, taken down and reassembled here brick by brick once the newer building in Albert Square had opened, towards the highest point in the park. Francis has his eye fixed upon the Greek Temple, a small rotunda of Etruscan columns, topped by a lantern, which was originally built as an observatory. Francis knows, because of his abiding interest in telescopes, that there used to be a fine example of one housed within it, specially commissioned from Dollond's of London, which cost the princely sum of £18. 5s. 0d, more than the annual salary of the Earl's under-butler at the time, but which has long since disappeared. Francis smiles. He now sells telescopes from his shop in Denton twice the quality and half the price of the Dollond, all of them made in Manchester, using lenses he himself has ground, such have been the advancements in manufacturing. But today he barely registers any of these landmarks. Today he has a different goal altogether.

He carries a large, heavy canvas bag upon his shoulder as

he struggles up the final steep slope that takes him to the summit of the park which, at just over three hundred feet, is also the highest point in Manchester. Below him now stretches the largest municipal park in all of Europe, more than six hundred acres, ringed by the tightly meshed circuitry of the city, surrounding him on all sides. It has been an unseasonably warm October day, and, by the time he reaches the top, he is perspiring and breathing hard. I really must do more exercise, he admonishes himself, but Francis is very much the night owl. He is rarely to be seen out of doors in the hours of daylight, electing instead to reside behind drawn curtains and shuttered windows, regarding the world from sequestered shadows through the prism of his jeweller's loupe, preferring to venture out into the world only after darkness has fallen. Consequently his skin has acquired an unattractive, nocturnal paleness, which now threatens to turn red and blotchy in the late afternoon sunlight. He feverishly scratches a raised up rash on the unprotected skin of his forearm, which flares in an orbit of angry circular pustules, like pockmarked moons around a denser planetary core. He wonders if he might be developing psoriasis. His eyes, unaccustomed to such brightness as he removes his spectacles to wipe them, are screwed tight and blinking rapidly. He really must take himself in hand.

I'm only twenty-four years old, he thinks, yet I look, and feel, almost twice that. He recalls a conversation he had less than a fortnight ago one evening at *The Reform Club* on Spring Gardens, which he has only recently joined…

A tall, confident-looking man, around twelve years older than himself, approached him briskly in the Reading Room.

"Have you finished with that paper?" he asked.

"Of course," replied Francis and passed it across to the still standing gentleman, who paused as he took the newspaper from him.

"Excuse me," he said, "but might I take a closer look at your arm?"

Francis frowned suspiciously.

"It's quite all right. I'm a doctor."

Francis relaxed and stretched out his arm towards him.

"Do you mind rolling up your sleeve?"

Francis duly obeyed.

The doctor examined his arm closely.

"I fear you may be presenting the beginnings of an outbreak of psoriatic plaques."

Francis widened his eyes in alarm. "Is that something I should be worried about?"

"Not necessarily. I believe we may have spotted it early. I'd need to take a closer look in my surgery first. Charles Trevelyan," he added, producing a card from his waistcoat pocket and handing it to Francis.

"Francis Hall," replied Francis, returning the gesture with a card of his own.

"Delighted to make your acquaintance. Optics, I see," he said, "a fascinating field."

"I think so," said Francis, rolling down his sleeve once more.

"We have much in common, I believe."

"Really? How so?"

"Both of us seeking beneath the surface of things, searching for signs the layman cannot see for himself. Your skin condition, for example. I should like to take a closer look at it through a microscope, for which you may well have ground the lenses."

"Yes," agreed Francis. "I see what you mean."

Charles seemed on the point of saying something further, when his attention was caught once more by the card Francis had given him. He seemed suddenly thunderstruck.

"I say, Trevelyan, are you quite all right? Here, take a seat next to mine," and he gently eased Charles into a deep red leather armchair. He summoned a passing waiter. "A brandy, please, as quick as you can."

"I do beg your pardon," said Charles after he had taken a deep sip from his glass. He held up Francis's card. "Your address is in Denton, I see?"

"That's correct."

"On Hyde Road?"

"Yes."

The Doctor took another long sip.

"There wouldn't happen to be a sign above the door featuring a large pair of spectacles, would there?"

Now it was Francis's turn to look surprised. "How did you know?"

Charles lay the card face down upon the table next to him. "I was a regular visitor there once, that is all. You must forgive me. Someone very close to me lived there."

Francis inclined his head in silent respect. He knew something of the story concerning his abode's previous occupants. "I never knew Miss Kaufman," he ventured carefully, "but I did once meet her father."

"Before he... went away?" enquired Charles.

Francis checked himself before he made his reply. He could not say he had seen Mr Kaufman in the Isle of Man, which was the truth, for that would reveal that he too had been interned there, and, since his return, that was a secret known only to himself and the strange young woman whose dead parents he had helped to bury by the side of the Ship Canal more than two years before, so he simply replied that Mr Kaufman had diagnosed an astigmatism for him before the War, when he was only a boy, and he removed his spectacles for added emphasis.

Charles nodded by way of response before finishing what remained of his brandy. It was clear to Francis that he was debating with himself whether to say more about his relationship with Miss Kaufman or not. In the end he appeared to decide that discretion was the better part of valour. He rose to his feet, offering his hand to Francis.

"Thank you," he said.

"For what?"

"For not prying too closely. I am grateful for that. And do come and see me at my clinic. Manchester Royal Infirmary. Oxford Road. We must get that rash of yours attended to." And with that he turned on his heel and strode swiftly from the room.

A fortnight later the two men were together again, this time in Dr Trevelyan's consulting rooms at the hospital.

"Yes," said Charles, drying his hands on a paper towel, "it is as I first thought. You have a mild case of psoriasis."

"Will it get worse?"

"It may. It's difficult to predict with any certainty. It may disappear for months, years even, but it will always be there, and could return at any moment, unless you follow my instructions."

"Which are…?"

"I advise you to follow a regimen of treatment advocated by a German physician, Dr Wilhelm Goekerman of Hanover."

Francis smiled inwardly at the thought of someone who shared an identity he had now renounced should be coming to his aid right now.

"He recommends," continued Charles, "a specialised form of heliotherapy. First of all, spend as much time as you can in direct sunlight. But if, as is the case with most of us, your opportunities for daily immersion are restricted by the need to work indoors, you should submit yourself to two hours of controlled artificial ultraviolet radiation here at the hospital."

"Under some kind of sun lamp?"

"Precisely so."

"How often?"

"Once a week for eight weeks, and then let us see what progress has been made. If all goes well, this need only be repeated at monthly, and then three monthly, intervals, until – who knows? – it may not be necessary again, unless the condition should for some reason recur once more."

"But the more time I can spend in natural sunlight, the less need I should have for the artificial variety?"

"That is the theory, yes."

"Theory?"

"It's still being tested. But early results are most encouraging."

Francis nodded. "Very well."

"Excellent. In addition you should apply coal tar ointment directly to the affected areas. Historically pine tar was used in this way, but recent studies have shown coal tar to be far more efficacious."

"And it's not as if we're short of the raw materials, are we?"

"Indeed. We have a ready supply from manufacturers in nearby Cadishead..."

Francis's mind drifts back to that chance meeting with Delphine by the Bob's Lane Ferry in Cadishead, and the acrid smell of smoke rising thickly from the funeral pyres...

Now, as the late afternoon sun starts to dip below the ridge of the hill at the top of Heaton Park, Francis sets to work. He lays the canvas bag he has carried all the way from Denton. The distance is less than ten miles but has required him to take three separate trains, the bag having been deemed too large to take on board a tram. First he had to travel just one stop on the Stalybridge train to Guide Bridge. From there he caught the stopping train from Leeds to London Road, followed by an arduous walk across the city down Piccadilly to Newton Street, left along Dale Street, right onto Oldham Street, left again at New Cross onto Swan Street, up Shude Hill, then down Withy Grove, across Corporation Street, into Todd Street and finally the Station Approach to Victoria, from where he was able to take the Bury train, alighting at Heaton Park itself. It has taken him the best part of the day, causing his psoriasis, which has been under control since he began the strict regimen of Herr Goekerman, under Dr Trevelyan's watchful supervision, to flare up again with the effort and anxiety of his task.

He takes out of the bag all of the various components he has brought with him and lays them methodically on the grass one by one: a long metal pole, a wooden mallet, a length of copper wire wound around a cardboard drum, a large tea chest, a pair of pliers, several small bobbins, a roll of adhesive tape and a number of stacking metal braziers.

When he has finished, he surveys them carefully, ticking each one with a specially sharpened pencil against a list he has taken from his jacket pocket. Yes. Everything is there. Nothing is missing. The bells in the nearby church of St Hilda's chime the hour. Francis checks the time on his own pocket watch. Six o'clock. He has just over an hour to ensure that everything is ready.

Seven miles away at Hirstwood, on Daisy Bank Road in Victoria Park, George is in his pyjamas and dressing gown eating pobs, pieces of bread in hot milk, which he has requested specially. It is not that he is ill. Far from it. But he is tired after the family day out flying the kite on Tandle Hill, although he won't admit it. Annie recognises the signs. He is an excitable boy and needs a quiet time before he goes upstairs to bed, otherwise she knows he will not sleep.

Hubert has brought out a box, which he had been saving for a wet Sunday afternoon, but this evening seems the perfect occasion, a perfect end to what has been a perfect day. He cannot remember feeling this well in years. The heart attack forced him to slow down, to pace himself, to savour each moment. Now that he no longer needs to spend such long hours in the Printing Works, now that he has satisfied himself that Harry Heath has proved more than just an able deputy, but a man, like himself, always on the look-out for the latest innovations, and now that he has become accustomed to this new pattern of working, he finds he enjoys meeting the clients, has grown into himself to be able to handle calmly what had previously been the rather unpalatable aspects of haggling over prices and quantities, with neither rancour nor aggression, no longer relying so much on Annie or his father to guide him through the delicate dance that accompanies all such negotiations, so that he is now more at ease in the Council Chambers, the Gentlemen's Clubs, the Masonic Lodges than he would ever have thought possible. He is pleasantly surprised to realise that he is well-liked, respected, not just for being his father's son, but for himself. The secret, he has learned, is not to be in too much of a hurry, to let the conversations unfold, like the waters of a brook tumbling over stones, with the possibility of their pursuing who knows how many different channels before eventually they join the broad stream on which he now sails almost serenely as it flows through the city, powered by commerce to be sure, steering that fine bottom line between profit and loss, but a vessel which still requires a crew to steer it, each with their own particular task, without any one of which the vessel might founder, with Hubert at the tiller, guiding it towards the confluence of a hand shake, a signature, a belief in that solemn bond which dictates that a man is only as good as his word, that the desire to do good in the world outweighs the drive to make more money than one actually needs, and that what counts in the end is what one might leave behind, a good name, a better future for George, and a knowledge that the journey has no destination, for in the end he will merely be passing the tiller into another's hands. F.G. Wright and Sons. It is a secret he has learned from his silent ruminations in the Meeting House on Mount Street, which he still attends weekly, and from Annie, whose burning drive and ambition, he now realises, is fuelled more by altruism than the promise of personal gain. He looks across at her now, as he fetches the box from the chest in his study where he has been keeping it for just such an evening as this. She still accompanies both himself and his father to occasional key meetings, though less so since they moved to this fine house she has transformed into such a comfortable home for the three of them, but more of her time is spent now in her charitable work, at the various women's refuges that have sprung up across the city and the many committees required to support them. She still sees Claudia whenever she can, and she still finds time to pursue her creative endeavours, the rotogravure, the collagraphs, and, like this evening, her more domestic crafts, the making of curtains, the embroidering of tablecloths and, tonight, the arranging of flowers. He watches her, head bent, forehead creased in silent concentration, eyes darting this way and that, as she picks and trims the different stems, and then pauses, rather like a kingfisher, beside that brook running over stones, poised and motionless as she considers the many choices that face her, before plunging a stem into the oasis as if spearing a minnow.

He lays the box on the table. George looks up from his pobs. He reads what it says on the lid and his eyes light up.

How To Build

Your Own

Crystal Radio Receiver

A crystal set radio receiver requires just a few components, which you will find inside this box.

The inductor – a length of wire wrapped around a cylinder

The capacitor – a separate coiled wire allowing you to tune the frequency of the radio waves being received

The crystal detector – a much finer wire, like a cat's whisker, held within the galena crystal, which affords reception of superior tonal quality

A pair of headphones – with which to hear the transmissions you receive

In addition, you will find a much longer length of wire for use as an external antenna, which you may decide to feed out of an upstairs window and attach to a nearby high point, such as a tree or telegraph pole.

Using the enclosed diagram create the necessary circuit and connect the various components.

Happy listening!

As the sky darkens, Heaton Park begins to empty. Many of its Saturday afternoon visitors have begun to leave, but many more than normal have stayed on, their curiosity piqued by Francis's methodical, painstaking, step-by-step construction taking place beside the Greek Temple at the park's highest point. But such an approach takes its time and Francis becomes aware of St Hilda's Church now tolling seven o'clock. He has less than half an hour if he is to be ready in time.

He begins to press-gang several of the hangers-on to help him.

"You," he says to one small boy playing with a ball, "hold this steady," handing him the long metal pole, around which he has attached the copper wire with the adhesive tape, "while you," to a woman pushing a pram with her sleeping infant oblivious inside, "take this length of wire," wrapping it round the handle of the pram, "to the end of the path over there."

Such is his sense of passion, together with the look of intense urgency in the pale eyes behind his round rimless spectacles, that nobody can refuse him, and soon the number of spectators has grown into quite a crowd, with more and more of them offering to help in whatever ways they can. A large, red-faced, beefy gentleman hoists Francis onto his shoulders so that he can reach the top of the metal pole with his mallet which, a few sturdy blows later, is securely driven into the ground. The small boy who had been holding the pole steady up until that moment now hurtles down the slope towards the pram, from which he detaches the copper wire and stretches it taut. On a signal from Francis, who has been ensuring the antenna is firmly attached to the pole, he stops at a point close by the Pepperpot. Francis then hurries to join the boy, taking the wire from him and connecting it to a small diode, before returning to the top of the hill once more, where he lays out a further length of cable from the radio mast, for that is what the metal pole has now become, to the tea chest, inside which is a small diaphragm he has made especially in his workshop behind the shop in Denton, which is then carried towards the Greek Temple by the large, red-faced beefy gentleman and placed inside, as an echo chamber to amplify even louder the sounds he hopes soon to be able to conjure from the air.

By the time Francis has completed his construction of the

giant radio receiver, close to a hundred people have gathered to witness his extraordinary behaviour. He checks his watch. Twenty-five past seven. It is almost completely dark. The sun has long ago set, but there is a full moon and a clear sky filled with stars arching overhead. An older couple, sitting on a bench, have become quite entranced by the hive of activity buzzing all around them and ask if they too might be able to help. Francis directs them towards the pile of stacked metal braziers, which he asks them to separate and place in two rows on either side of the taut, stretched copper wire, in order to keep people from tripping over it. During the preceding hour Francis has also recruited several of the spectators to collect armfuls of leaves and grasses from beneath the trees and fill these now unstacked metal braziers, which form a quarter mile long corridor linking the cat's whisker with the antenna, like the nave of a church. At a signal from Francis these are now set alight, forming a line of burning beacons from the Greek Temple right down as far as the entrance to Heaton Park Station on Whitaker Lane, just outside the entrance to the Park, opposite St Hilda's Church. When the railway line was first being constructed in 1879 between Manchester and Bury, the 1st Earl of Wilton would not allow it to, in his words, "disfigure the grounds", and so a compromise was reached whereby a tunnel was excavated beneath the park through which the trains would pass. As the crowds all wait, wondering what this strange young man will do next, a train passes through the entire seven hundred and thirteen yards of the tunnel. Everyone can feel the earth vibrate beneath them as it does so and can faintly hear its deep, low, rumbling thunder.

Francis waits until the train has gone and silence descends upon the Park. He wears a pair of headphones on his head and slowly, delicately, begins to tune the receiver, which he has placed on a wooden frame directly beneath the now stationary pram, inside which the baby still sleeps, blissfully unaware of the momentous event that is shortly about to take place. Francis's face is a mask of concentration, eyes closed, fixed, immobile, almost as if it has been cast in the same stone as the Greek Temple the long antenna now directly links him to. He strains every nerve and sinew to try and pick up the sounds he is searching for as he scans the airwaves minutely, by the tiniest of rotations on a dial, this way then that, through Paris, Luxembourg, Hilversum, Athlone, until suddenly he stops. The expression on his stone face imperceptibly shifts. Then, in a series of swift, sure movements, he opens his eyes, looks up at the stars wheeling above him in the night sky, clenches his fists, whips off the headphones, finds the extra cable which he connects to the converted tea chest speaker inside the Greek Temple and, with the aid of a triode vacuum tube amplifier, at once the Park is filled with sound. The air trembles with this music of the spheres. The crowd gasps as one, smiles broadly, applauds briefly, then instinctively suppresses itself, so that it can simply absorb and listen...

The strains of Beethoven sweep across them, enclosing the Park in a magical bubble of sound, soaring through the air, dancing across the night, rising and falling as the reception comes and goes, like waves breaking on a far off shore, while flecks of ember and ash hover in the air. It is the music for a little-known ballet he composed just before the *Eroica*, *The Creatures of Prometheus*, part of the programme of the *Last Night of the Proms* being conducted by Sir Henry Wood, beaming across the air waves to them live from *The Queen's Hall*, London.

Everyone listens, enraptured.

The older couple turn to one another in fond remembrance. The mother with the pram picks up her waking child whose crying is suspended by harp and flute, clarinet and bassoon, threaded between delicately plucked strings. The small boy, about to run after his ball, stops in mid-step, allowing the ball to roll unchased down the slope of the hill. The signalman at the station, his whistle half way to his lips, pauses to listen and does not blow, his green flag still unfurled by his side. A park keeper, prior to locking the gates, stands by a flower bed, where he has been raking up leaves ready for an autumn bonfire, and waits, heedless of the piled drifts now floating away on the night breeze, which, later, he will gather up once more while absent-mindedly humming the *adagio*. The whole life of the Park temporarily pauses, holding its breath, caught in a wrinkle of time, folding itself over everyone present, who, spellbound, do not move until the concert is ended, when they turn as one towards Francis, and this time the applause is loud and prolonged. Sheepishly he takes a small bow, then quickly begins to pack away his equipment, ready for the long journey back to Denton, which now he will not mind. He is exhilarated. The experiment has been a complete success.

The crowds melt away. The small boy chases after his ball. The young mother puts her baby back into her pram and continues walking along the path. The red-faced gentleman takes off his hat, mops his brow with a white handkerchief, puts his hat back on and waddles happily home. The older couple rise from the bench where they have been sitting and look out towards the city spread out below them, the smoke from a thousand coal fires rising into the sky, and the signalman at the station blows his whistle and waves his flag, so that the next train for Bury can enter the tunnel under the Park.

In combining three classical myths for his ballet – *Pygmalion,* who brings a statue to life, Orpheus, the god-like musician who charms the birds from out of the trees, and Prometheus himself, the bringer of fire – Beethoven was presenting an allegorical representation of man's place in the universe. "*Music should strike fire from a man,*" he wrote. "*It is the wine of a new procreation.*" Francis, striding back down the hill, his canvas bag now slung across his shoulder, feels a strong kinship with Prometheus, and smiles as he makes his way between the avenue of still burning beacons, sending sparks of flame up into the night sky. He has brought the outside world to this city where he lives, which he loves more than he can say. Next, he tells himself, he will broadcast Manchester to the rest of the world. Each step he takes brings him close, close, closer to his dreamt of destination.

"Time for bed now, George," says Annie, as the final strains of music fade away into the ether, to be replaced by the hiss and crackle of static, the multitude of voices jostling to make themselves heard, the thousand twangling instruments clamouring in all the tongues of the world.

"Do I have to?" moans George.

"Yes," says Annie firmly.

George looks pleadingly towards his father.

"Yes," says Hubert. "If your mother says so."

"And she does," says Annie, placing the finished flower arrangement on the window sill.

George reluctantly heaves himself up from the table, away from the crystal radio set, over which his eyes and hands have pored lovingly throughout the last hour.

"Up the dancers," says Hubert. "Clean your teeth and say your prayers."

Annie watches him go with a smile. She has observed the way he picked up the instructions for assembling the radio so intuitively, so expertly, his fingers nimbly manipulating the various fiddly components. Nine years old, she thinks. In two years he'll be eligible for a move away from his current elementary school, and at once her mind is whirring.

"What would you say to a move to Whalley Range?" she asks Hubert an hour later.

Hubert raises a puzzled eyebrow.

"It would be more convenient for George to get to Hulme's Grammar School from there. We could ask the Youngs about it."

"He has to pass the examination first," he says, "and that's a way off yet."

"I know," says Annie, putting her arms around her husband. "But it does no harm to plan, does it?"

As she kisses him, Hubert knows that in her mind it's already a done deal. He can see the flames of the idea flickering behind her eyes. Well, he thinks, so be it. Let the water run its course. The memory of Beethoven's Promethean ballet plays across his mind…

*

This is not the first time that music has come to Heaton Park unexpectedly. Elsie and Archie, the older couple sitting on the bench, recall the occasion twelve years before when they sat in this very spot, listening to the legendary Enrico Caruso…

Est. 1877

Prestwich & Heaton Park Guardian

20th September 1909

40,000 FLOCK TO PARK TO HEAR THE GREAT CARUSO

An estimated crowd of more than forty thousand people from right across Manchester and from all walks of life descended on Heaton Park yesterday to listen to the celebrated Italian tenor, Enrico Caruso. But not as you might imagine.

The week before Caruso had delighted a packed auditorium at the Free Trade Hall on Peter

Street with a mixed programme of operatic arias by Verdi and Puccini, together with popular Neapolitan love songs. Three thousand people paid extremely high prices for the privilege, with some tickets changing hands outside the venue at vastly inflated prices, such was the demand to hear the great man in person on his first, and possibly only, visit to the city. It is rumoured that one ticket actually fetched the princely sum of ten pounds!

The enterprising Mr William 'Billy' Grimshaw, known to all as 'The Gramophone King', secured permission to record the concert, and yesterday it was this recording he played to the delighted crowds in Heaton Park, where the ordinary working man or woman, unable to afford even one pound for a ticket, let alone ten, could now listen to the world famous tenor for free.

"This is a day I'll never forget," Miss Elsie Priest of Lower Broughton told our reporter. "I came here with my young man, Archie, who, after listening to Caruso singing *'O Sole Mio'*, went down on one knee and proposed to me right here in the Park."

Congratulations, Archie and Elsie, the soon-to-be Mr and Mrs Bishop! It is indeed a day that nobody who was there will ever forget. The 40,000-strong crowd remained as if spellbound, from the moment of Mr Grimshaw's arrival, carrying his state-of-the-art equipment on the back of a horse-drawn Prestwich Co-op milk cart, until the close of the programme which, it goes almost without saying, was enthusiastically enjoyed by all. News of the concert even reached Signor Caruso himself, at present a guest at *The Midland Hotel*, who sent a signed cartoon of himself with a letter of thanks to Mr Grimshaw as a token of his "most sincere appreciation".

So successful a venture has it been, *The Prestwich & Heaton Park Guardian* understands, that the Manchester Corporation has commissioned a series of further such events from Mr Grimshaw in parks right across the city. We believe that a programme of 38 concerts is being planned for next summer, with more than a quarter of a million people in total expected to attend, for which Mr Grimshaw is to be paid the modest fee of £1.15s per concert. That's what we call real Manchester Value for Money!

And so let us give three loud cheers for William 'Billy' Grimshaw, 'The Gramophone King', for making this all possible.

*

Mr William 'Billy' Grimshaw
The Gramophone King

in association with
Manchester Corporation

presents

THE GREAT CARUSO

in a series of
Sunday Afternoon Concerts
in parks across the city
April to September 1910

Alexandra Park   Birchfields Park
Boggart Hole Clough   Buile Hill
Colleyhurst Park   Debdale Park
Fletcher Moss Botanical Gardens
Fog Lane Park   Hough End   Ivy Green
Peel Park   Philips Park   Platt Fields

**Sunnybrow Park   Turn Moss
Whitworth Park**

**(with other sites to be confirmed
please see local press for details of dates and times)**

Printed by F.G. Wright & Son

*

"In nomine Patris et Filii et Spiritus Sancti."
"Amen."

Father Pappalardi can sense the eagerness in his congregation to leave the Church of St Alban's as quickly as possible and smiles. "They are like children," he thinks affectionately to himself, "so transparent."

Today, the third Sunday in May 1910, is the annual Whitsuntide Walk, the *Festa della Madonna del Rosario*, and he knows how everyone will be champing at the bit to get to the head of the procession, lining up behind the statue and the banners, the young girls excited in their white dresses carrying posies of spring flowers, the mothers fussing over them until the very last moment, the men laughing and shaking hands and raising glasses of red wine in a succession of toasts, the bands of the Boys Brigades tuning their instruments, before the whole Italian enclave, it seems, will make their way from the streets of Ancoats to Philips Park.

But today the excitement is heightened still further by the prospect of listening to *The Great Caruso* once they arrive there, for Billy Grimshaw, The Gramophone King, is scheduled to give one of his free Sunday afternoon concerts and the crowds are expected to descend in their thousands. The Council has even delayed their annual Tulip Sunday by one week to coincide, and so Father Pappalardi can afford to be indulgent towards his flock as they await his signal for them to be allowed to leave the church and make ready for the *Festa*. He is looking forward to it himself. Perhaps his former curate, Father Fracassi, now the priest in Failsworth, might also be there. They might even raise a glass or two together themselves.

Outside the church, on Fawcett Street, standing on the stepped bridge over the Rochdale Canal, is Claudia, alongside her parents, Maurizio and Giulia Magdalena, in order to obtain a good view of the procession once it sets off. Matteo, her brother, is not with them. He is with his friends, the Stefanutti brothers, with whom he works at their father's *terrazzo* tile factory. Up until two years ago, Claudia would have been taking part in the walk, her mother applying the last minute finishing touches to her new white dress, her last one, now folded away, wrapped in tissue paper for when (it is hoped, though not mentioned) it can be brought out for her own daughter in due course. But all that is in the future, undreamt of. Today she is just eighteen, about to finish her time at the Central Grammar School for Girls, where only last week she received the Special Science Prize, as a result of which, she learned in a letter received only the day before, she will progress to a position as a laboratory assistant at the Victoria University of Manchester on Oxford Road, as part of a team led by Professor Ernest Rutherford. Her proud parents have not stopped beaming since they heard the news and have been telling everyone they meet, which Claudia endures with a mixture of public embarrassment and private pleasure. Now it is Father Papardelli's turn.

"*Padre*," calls out Maurizio. "Have you heard? *Nostra figlia va all'università. Una scienziata molto granda.*"

"*Brava*, Maurizio."

"*Si. Grazie, Padre.*"

"*Papa*," hisses Claudia after Father Pappardelli has passed by, "please stop boasting about me. My position is a very humble one, the lowest possible rung on the ladder."

"*Si forse, Piccolina*. But you will climb, *verso alto*, right to the top."

"*Papa…*"

Claudia is spared any further embarrassment by the sudden and loud starting up of *O Sanctissima* by the band of *Gli Bersiglieri*. Claudia and her parents join the crowds following the procession, all singing as they walk.

"*O Sanctissima, O Piissima
Dulcis Virgo Maria
Quidquid optamus, per te sempamus
Ora, ora pro nobis…*"

"*O most holy, O most loving
Sweet Virgin Mary
Whatever we wish, we hope for through you
Pray, pray for us…*"

Four hours earlier.

Jabez, just turned nineteen, stands at the entrance to Philips Park next to his father, John, Head Keeper and Gardener for nine years now, since his own father, also called John, passed away on the same night as the old Queen. It had seemed fitting somehow, for Grandfather John had been born in 1837, the same year as Victoria had ascended to the throne, and so all of his own life's major landmarks had coincided with hers – Silver, Golden and Diamond Jubilees – until, like the Queen, he lost his appetite, began to look increasingly frail and thin, grew tired more quickly, and finally succumbed to a series of small strokes, dying early one morning, surrounded by his family. He had known only one monarch throughout his entire life, while Jabez is already onto his third, with the roguish King Bertie, Edward the Caresser, as the newspapers liked to call him, having died less than a fortnight ago. That had threatened to put a dampener on the whole of Tulip Sunday. There had been urgent last minute meetings convened by Mr Pettigrew of the Corporation's Committee for Public Walks, Gardens and Playgrounds, wondering whether, in the circumstances, it was appropriate to be unveiling a colourful floral display at a time of national mourning. The Lord Mayor himself had had to become involved, and it was he who finally decreed that they should proceed as planned, with a delay of a further week than initially advertised for propriety's sake. It would be a shame, as well as a waste of the public expenditure, after the months of planning and preparation involved, to abandon what was such an eagerly anticipated event in the city's calendar as Tulip Sunday had now become. It would be, the Lord Mayor had declared, with an air of respectful finality, what the late King would have wanted, he was certain. Bertie was always an admirer of a gay buttonhole. They would instruct the local Reddish Brass Band, whose turn it was this year to perform at the event, to play a stately version of the national anthem before the displays were formally declared open.

Jabez's father had breathed a huge sigh of relief when he learned of the Committee's decision. A lot of thought and work had gone into this year's display. When it was decided the previous autumn to hold a series of Billy Grimshaw's concerts in parks across the city during the following summer, John, who was a pal of Billy's, had let it be known, as subtly as he could, that he hoped the concert for Philips Park might be timed to coincide with Tulip Sunday, and he was delighted that this had proved possible. Knowing that there was bound to be a large Italian contingent from nearby Ancoats to listen to *The Great Caruso*, who was something of a national hero to them, John had concocted an overall design featuring the three colours of the Italian flag – green for the country's plains and hills, white for the snow-capped mountains of the Alps, and red for the blood spilled during the *Risorgimento*, not much more than half a century ago. Fortunately he had not shared this plan with Mr Pettigrew, who almost certainly would have frowned, knitted his brow, pursed his lips and muttered darkly about divided loyalties. John doubted now whether he would detect the homage when he cast his eye over the display later that morning, but the Italians most assuredly would, and would congratulate him afterwards. He had discussed his ideas with Jabez, who was proving a most able assistant. He was confident he would be able to hand over the care of the gardens to him when the time came, just as his own father had passed the responsibility onto him. It was Jabez who had suggested that, in places, they might incorporate some of the decorative Italian tiles made by both the Stefanutti and the Quigilotti Brothers, workers from both rival companies being known to Jabez, through his friendship with Marco Locartelli, with whom he shared a number of shifts down the pit at Bradford Colliery. John thought this an excellent idea and admired his son's forethought in avoiding favouritism and ensuring harmony. The *terrazzo* tiled features, placed sparingly and subtly at intervals throughout the garden, proved the perfect finishing touch to his Italian designs.

Jabez had listened with growing discomfort as his father had relayed the ongoing discussions being held by the Corporation's Committee, as they vacillated first this way, then that, in a near fever pitch of anxiety over what they continually referred to as "conflicting loyalties". Jabez was not sure how he felt about that particular thorny issue. Loyalty. Unlike his grandfather, who had admired Queen Victoria almost to the point of obsession, collecting the commemorative mugs, which took pride of place on the mantelpiece in their parlour, he felt no especial allegiance to any of the three monarchs who had already reigned during his short life. No doubt there'd be others later. Were you supposed to identify with the individual or the institution? He grimly recalled, as a nine year old boy, being carried on his grandfather's shoulders down into Piccadilly Gardens for the mass celebrations which greeted the Relief of Mafeking, of being frightened by the sheer size of the crowds, their noise and wild, unconstrained behavior – behaviour, he now understood, to have been influenced as much by alcohol as by patriotism – and afterwards the bitter words between his grandfather and father, who had been at work when the news broke and so had been unable to prevent his son from being exposed to potential risk and danger in the way that *he* had been, for where his grandfather was a loyal Victorian, his father, a regular reader of *The Manchester Guardian*, supported that paper's pro-Boer stance, condemning the British brutalities, particularly the rounding up of the native peoples into concentration camps, in which four thousand women and sixteen thousand children had died. He can still hear his father's voice today, more than ten years later, condemning the barbarism and cruelty. Could he be loyal to such things, if certain choices were demanded of him? He too had begun reading *The Manchester Guardian*, and articles hidden on the inside pages about the political manoeuvrings currently taking place between the various members of Queen Victoria's extended family elsewhere across Europe, in Germany and Russia, had not escaped his notice. If there was to be another war, would he be prepared to volunteer? Could he be loyal to a nationalistic cause? He didn't know. He didn't feel particularly British, if he ever considered the question at all. He would, he supposed, describe himself as a Mancunian first, but even that was too broad a category. He lived in the east of the city and knew that to be quite different from those other districts to the north and south, while over to the west, across the River Irwell, Salford was an altogether separate city, to which he rarely ventured. One thing he could define himself as with certainty was a supporter of Manchester City, whose fortunes he followed week in, week out, attending their home matches on Hyde Road as often as he could manage. Yet even this was not without its ambiguities. Until just a few months ago, before their move to Old Trafford, Manchester United had played in their old Bank Street stadium in Clayton, just the other side of where he is now standing with his father by the gates of Philips Park. Formed in Gorton as St Marks by two local vicars, the Reverends Connell and Beastow, as an outlet to curb violence among local young people, City had always been the miners' club, whereas United, despite being much more local to where Jabez lived, was the railwaymen's team. Nothing would have induced him to set foot in their ground, unless it was to watch City thrash them, and he smiles at the thought. Loyalty.

Now, he waits with his father who, checking his father's pocket watch, which he inherited from him when he died, and which will no doubt similarly pass down to Jabez in years to come, waits for the bells of St Jerome's to chime the hour of eight o'clock, before, with a flourish he evidently enjoys, opening the gates to the crowds already queuing up to get an early view of this year's Italian-themed tulip displays.

Four hours later Jabez hears another of the stirring marches being played by the Ancoats *Bersiglieri*, which heralds the arrival of the *Festa della Madonna del Rosario*, with its statues and banners, flags and pride, behind which walk the dozens of shiny young girls in their white dresses, carrying posies of white flowers plucked from the wayside, stitchwort, cow parsley, Jack-by-the-Hedge, followed by what seems like the whole of Manchester's Little Italy, hundreds and hundreds of them, comingling with the enormous crowds who have gathered in the park already, converging, indistinguishable one from the other, a carnival of brightly coloured rats trooping into Hamelin, Italian, German, British – Mancunian all.

"O suol beato
Ove sorridero
Volle il creato
Tu sei l'impero
Del armonia…"

"Oh blessed soil
Smiling fair welcome
From thy creation
All hail to thee
Thou realm of harmony…"

"Santa Lucia
Santa Lucia…"

Elsewhere in the park, along the Avenue of Black Poplars, Annie Warburton is walking out with Hubert Wright, her arm linked through his, as they do most Sunday afternoons, especially since their engagement, announced just two months before when Hubert had proposed beneath the trail of Halley's Comet. But this afternoon is different. Normally they have the park mostly to themselves and can easily slip away to somewhere secluded for a brief, undisturbed period of chaste canoodling. There will be no chance of that today. The crowds are too large and in any case all of their usual trysting spots are already taken, where, she notices blushingly, the courting couples are proceeding much further than she or Hubert ever do. She wonders if he has seen them too, but he appears not to have done. His eyes are elsewhere, scanning the enormous throng of people spread out across the entire park. He has his business face on, she thinks. He is trying to ascertain just what impact the posters he has produced in his father's printing works might have had on the attendance, and whether there may be people, influential people, he should seek out over towards the VIP tent, which is where his gaze has fallen.

Before he can say anything, she leans in towards him. "Very well. If you think you must. But I want to come with you."

"Of course," he replies. "I just wouldn't want you to be bored."

"I don't," she says, with a fierce expression on her face, "intend to be one of those wives who lingers in the background, who takes no interest in her husband's work."

"Like my mother?" says Hubert, his eyes glinting with a hint of mischief.

"I didn't say that," says Annie. "Marriage is a partnership," she adds with a steely resolve. "At least it should be."

"I agree. Come on. Let's get it over with. Then we can enjoy the rest of the day."

"Will the Lady Mayoress be there?" asks Annie, smiling.

"She might be," grins Hubert. "Why?"

"We'd best straighten that tie of yours then," she says, and afterwards adjusts her hat. "How do I look?"

"Perfect. But then I'm biased."

Annie playfully punches him on the arm as they make their way down one of the serpentine paths towards the VIP tent. While they are on their way, Annie notices a pair of elephants giving rides to the children and points them out to Hubert.

"From Belle Vue," he nods.

Annie notices a third elephant further down the slope, wading in one of the boating ponds, where he is being hosed down by his keeper. Gathered at the edge of the pond, in a wriggling squirm of delight, is a group of young boys, squealing with excitement, egging each other on to see who might be the first of them to be sprayed with water by the elephant. In that moment she has a premonition of the future, her future, hers and Hubert's, and a small boy, their son, in a similar knot of boys in ten years' time, hovering on the brink of life.

She links her arm once more through her fiancé's and together they walk towards it.

Over in the Park's Amphitheatre, William 'Billy' Grimshaw is busy setting up his equipment, eagerly watched by a growing crowd of curious onlookers, as well as those already arriving early to secure a good place for the concert, which is scheduled to begin in just over an hour's time. Among them is twelve-year old Francis Hall, still known then as Franz Halsinger, who is studying the self-styled Gramophone King like a hawk.

"There's no need to worry," calls out Mr Grimshaw. "The outdoor acoustics here in the Amphitheatre are the best in Manchester, and such is the strength and power of my speaker that you will be able to hear the music wherever you are in the Park. So please – enjoy yourselves, wander among the tulips, you've plenty of time before the concert begins."

Several of the crowd drift away, reassured, but many remain, determined to claim the best spot they can. Francis edges closer to the small stage on which Mr Grimshaw stands. He picks up a small business card from a pile near the front.

"William Grimshaw," he reads, "Bicycle and Gramophone Retailer, Prestwich."

Francis is delighted and places it in his pocket. He loves the idea of being a man of many parts, of diverse interests. Why restrict oneself to just one thing, he muses, as his father has done, and as he is already urging Francis to do likewise?

"Jack of all Trades, Master of None," declaims his father daily, like a creed. "Become an expert in something," he says. "Be the best in your field. Then you can be the leader of

227

that field."

His father's field is banking, but his passion is photography, in all its aspects. He has a string of shops across the city, selling cameras and all of their accompanying paraphernalia – tripods, enlargers, silver plated sheets of copper coated with light sensitive silver iodide, collodion and gelatine dry plates for the traditionalists, plus the more modern folding and box cameras, including the talk of the age, the sensational Kodak, incorporating all of the very latest Eastman innovations, such as celluloid film and mechanical shutters – as well as a number of prestigious studios where he can create specially commissioned portraits for the wealthy merchants of Manchester and their families.

Francis loves photography too, the almost mystical way in which an image will materialise out of apparently thin air in the red glow of the dark room. His father has already allowed him to experiment with different lenses, different lengths of exposure, different ways of composing an image. But that represents just one aspect of the modern world which, for Francis, is full of so many technical innovations, just waiting to be discovered and, if placed in the right hands, sensitive and artistic hands, such as those he already, at twelve years old, believes himself to be in possession of, exploited, so why this insistence on restricting oneself to a single field? He takes the business card from out of his pocket and looks at it once again. 'Bicycles and Gramophones'. An unlikely combination. One which flies right in the face of his father's thinking. Which perhaps explains Francis's fascination with the man behind the card. 'Bicycles and Gramophones'. One thing they have in common, thinks Francis, is the fact that they are both modern, of the moment, riding a wave with no clear sense of where either will take him, except that it will be somewhere new, as yet not even dreamed of, let alone invented. And it is that which fires Francis's imagination so strongly. To be right on the edge of things, the cutting edge, unafraid of failure, embracing risk and uncertainty, in a constant hurry. Hasn't Manchester always been the home of the new?

He watches the way Mr William 'Billy' Grimshaw sets up his gramophone equipment, aware that, as well as broadcasting these free open-air concerts of music, he has also recorded this music in the first place, and he hopes he might be able to find a way to speak to him about the types of microphone he has experimented with in order to obtain the most faithful sound reproduction. But for the present Mr Grimshaw is too busy wrestling with the most enormous speaker Francis – or anybody else in the Park, for that matter – has ever seen. It is shaped exactly like the horn to be found on all wind-up gramophones, not dissimilar, in fact, to the one Francis's parents have in their own home, where they listen to the latest recordings of Beethoven, Brahms, Schubert and Lizst, only many times larger. At a rough estimate, Francis reckons its diameter to be more than four feet across, certainly as wide as he is tall, and just at that moment the sheer weight and size of it threatens to defeat Mr Grimshaw, who is on the point of toppling from the stage, only for Francis to leap up and add his own hands to support it and prevent it from falling.

"Well, lad," pants a rather breathless Billy. "I reckon tha's saved the day."

"Is there anything else I can do to help, Mr Grimshaw?" asks Francis eagerly.

"Call me Billy, lad. Everyone does. First of all, tha' can bring that stand across from over there, while I hold this beast steady. Then tha' can help me lift it onto it. How about that for starters?"

"Yes, Mr Grimshaw – Billy."

Half an hour later, in return for all his efforts, Francis finds himself rewarded with a seat on the stage itself, next to the latest Edison Phonograph, which Billy has customised specially for outdoor performances.

"Here's the list of all the songs I'll be playing later this afternoon," says Billy. "All the records are in that case yonder. Can tha' make sure they're all in the correct order, then pass them to me one at a time as and when I need each one?"

Francis's grin is as broad as Philips Park's Central Carriageway.

Along that Carriageway, ranged at intervals of roughly fifty yards apart, stand the barrel organs, making a defiant last stand against what they know already will be the unstoppable advance of the gramophone. After the concert this afternoon, everyone will want one of the new machines, and it will not be long before the market is flooded with cheaper and cheaper models. And so today will be something of a last hurrah for the organ grinders of Manchester – the Marocca and Mancini families from Jersey Street, the Varetto and Rabino families from Blossom Street, and the Acaro and Gavioli families from Great Ancoats Street – with their monkeys and their dancing bears, the hurdy gurdy men, accordion and *zampogna* players from Lazio, their haunting, yearning bagpipes rolling across the Park, mixed in with the cacophony of a dozen different folk songs from Campania all being played at once on the different instruments – *La Monacella*, *Michelemmà*, *Ritornella della Lavendare del Vomero* and everyone's favourite, *Cicerenella*.

> "*Cicerenella tenea no ciardino,*
> *E l'adacquava coll'acqua e lo vino,*
> *Ma l'adacquava pò senza lancella...*
> *Chisto ciardino è de Cicerenella.*
> *Cicerenella mia si bona e bella...*"

*"Cicerenella, the gardener's daughter,
Spray'd her garden with wine and with water
Watered it well, though she hadn't a pail, ah!
This is the garden of Cicerenella
Cicerenella, darling, my bonny belle, ah…"*

*"Cicerenella teneva no gallo,
Tutta la nottence jeva a cavallo,
Essance jeva pò senza la sella...
Chisto è lo gallo de Cicerenella,
Cicerenella mia si bona e bella…"*

*"Cicerenella, she had an old rooster,
All night long on his back he would boost her,
Bareback she rode him, and rode him right well, ah!
This is the rooster of Cicerenella
Cicerenella, darling, my bonny belle, ah…"*

The crowds join in with each chorus, some dancing a *tarantella* as they do so, even the older, toothless women, who cackle and roar, as the red wine flows.

In between stand a whole host of fairground stalls and rides – rifle ranges, hoopla and tombola, the merry-go-rounds, boat swings and carousel horses. Claudia wanders freely and at ease amongst them in the warm afternoon sunshine, assailed on all sides by the sounds of street vendors hawking chestnuts, black beans, toy birds on sticks, balloons, while she watches her brother Matteo joking with his friends, the bear hugs, arm locks and play fights, which, it seems, young men must always greet each other with and indulge in, and although she shakes her head and sighs, because that is what is expected of her, inside she smiles, for she is as happy as they are to seize the day by the throat and not let it go until the last of the light has faded from the sky.

As the day proceeds, Claudia becomes increasingly aware

that she has a shadow. One of Matteo's young male friends is permanently at her side. Or rather, one or two paces behind. She can sense his eyes upon her back. Whenever she turns around, there he is, though looking away, as if his attention has been caught by something else. Eventually he will turn back and catch her eye, smile sheepishly and shrug his shoulders, as if to admit to being found out, his real intention (a chance to speak freely with her) unmasked. After this charade has been repeated a number of times, resembling more and more a game of Granny's Footsteps, she can take no more of it. She rolls up her sleeves and marches straight towards him, demanding to know what it is he wants from her. Inevitably, when faced with such directness, he is at once struck dumb.

"What's the matter?" she asks. "Cat got your tongue?"

He nods, saying nothing.

"I don't believe you," she adds and is just about to walk away, when the young man hurries to intercept her.

"It is not the cat," he says, somewhat foolishly.

"He speaks," says Claudia. "What, then?"

He frowns, uncertain what she means.

"If it's not the cat that's got your tongue, what has?"

He smiles. He senses an opening. "I am struck dumb by your beauty," he says.

Claudia rolls her eyes.

"No. Is true. At first I thought it was the sun blinding me, then I realise it is you."

"Now you're blind as well as dumb?"

"I don't hear such words."

"Deaf too?"

"I hear only music when you speak."

"Tone deaf."

Still smiling, he bursts into song.

"*La donna è mobile*

Qual piuma al vento
Muta d'accento…"

Claudia quickly interrupts him. " '*Woman is unstable? Like the feather in the wind, she changes*'? Is that meant to impress me? "

"You misunderstand me."

"Clearly."

"What I meant was, you are my muse, inspiring me to…"

"… to burst into song?"

"*Si.*"

"About how unstable I am and not to be trusted?"

"*Non.*"

"What then?" She begins to walk away, trying to suppress the smile forming across her lips.

"Wait. Let me start again."

She turns. "I think you'd better."

He holds out his hand. "*Buongiorno.* My name is…"

"Marco, I know."

"You know?"

"You're my brother's friend..."

"Matteo, *si.*"

"… though I can't think why."

"Hey – I could tell you things about your brother would make your toes curl."

"I'd rather you didn't."

He is still holding out his hand towards her. "Marco," he says again, bowing politely.

"Claudia," and, with a small mock curtsey, she extends her own hand in response, which Marco eagerly takes in his own.

"So cold," he announces, still keeping hold of her hand with one of his, while with the other he clutches his heart. "*Che gelida manina…*"

"Please don't start singing again."

" *'Your tiny hand is frozen'.*" He raises it to his lips to kiss it, but before he can do so, she snatches it away.

"Good things come to those who wait."

"The early bird catches the worm."

"But the second mouse gets the cheese."

"Whoa! I've not heard that one before."

"Perhaps because I made it up."

"What does it mean? What happened to the first mouse?"

"He was eaten by the cat."

"Ouch! What must I do?"

She leans towards him and whispers softly so that only he will hear her. "*Niente*. Just slow down, that's all. *Rallenta.*" Then she skips away and is lost in the crowd.

Marco rejoins his *compagni*, among whom is Jabez. Marco takes him to one side and presses him urgently. "Tell me. You have sisters. How do they like to be wooed?"

Jabez squirms in embarrassment. "*I* don't know, Marco. They're my sisters."

"You must know something. Tell me."

"Well," he thinks, scratching his head beneath his cap, "I think they'd like presents."

"Presents? What kind of presents?"

"I don't know. Chocolates, maybe? Flowers?"

"*Ah si, regali*. Excellent. Jabez, you are a genius," and he kisses his friend extravagantly on each cheek, before bounding off towards the fairground stalls. Shaking his head, Jabez wipes where his friend has kissed him with the back of his hand and rejoins the rest of his pals, whose attentions have turned elsewhere, in search of other pretty girls.

Marco is on a mission.

"*Regali,*" he mutters under his breath, "*regali,*" with every step he takes.

First he tries the coconut shy. His arm is strong and his

aim is true. In no time at all he has won himself a prize.

Claudia, mingling with the crowds and enjoying meeting up with other girl friends, is suddenly assailed by the sight of a coconut hurtling down towards her from higher up the slope. Dropping her bag, she manages to catch it just before it would have hit her. Her friends point up the hill, giggling. There, clearly very pleased with himself, stands Marco, who gives her a wink, a salute and a bow before heading back towards the stalls.

Next he tries his luck on the hoopla stall. His first two wooden rings teeter on the edge of a prize but fall away at the last moment. His final attempt has better luck, however, and perfectly encircles a jam jar filled with water, in which, swimming round and round in ever decreasing circles is a rather bemused goldfish. He collars Franco, one of his friend's kid brothers, tucks a cigarette behind his ear and points him in the direction of Claudia. Franco skitters down the hill, careful not to spill a drop of water from the jam jar, arriving just as Claudia steps onto one of the paths leading to the boating pond, where he presents her with the fish, before scuttling away. Claudia looks at the jam jar and shakes her head. It is difficult to say which is the more startled, Claudia or the fish. Her friends collapse on the grass in convulsions of laughter.

Over the next hour, Claudia is regularly regaled with further *regali* – a set of *Happy Families* playing cards from the tombola – with Master Soot the Collier's Son and Mistress Pill the Pothecary's Daughter placed on top – a green, white and red balloon filched from the back of the beer tent, a wooden bird from an American Indian selling homemade toys and trinkets, and finally a soldier doll from the rifle range.

Claudia plonks herself down on the grass, surrounded by all her trophies, outwardly disgruntled, but secretly delighted, as she arranges them all around her. Marco, surveying her from above, could not be happier, revelling in her discomfort, basking in the obvious pleasure she is taking from the puzzled looks of passers-by. He can contain himself no longer and he bounds down the slope to land by her side.

"Where have all these come from?" he asks in wide-eyed innocence.

"I wonder," she says, trying not to smile.

He picks up the two playing cards. "Who might these two disreputable figures be?"

"I can't begin to guess," she says again, biting her cheeks.

"Well – it's too late to wonder now. Look. The concert's about to begin."

As Claudia shifts her gaze towards the raised stage in the park's Amphitheatre, Marco leans in to steal a quick kiss on her cheek. She turns back at once to face him. Instead of the dark look he is expecting, or even a slapped face, which would still have been worth the risk, he sees only her bright eyes shining.

"Is that the best you can do?" she asks, teasingly.

He pulls her gently towards him.

At the last moment, she raises a finger to his lips. "As you say, it's too late to wonder now. I don't want to miss the concert."

They turn as one to face the stage. He is completely captivated by her.

With the confidence of a true showman, William 'Billy' Grimshaw keeps his audience waiting. As soon as a quarter of an hour has passed beyond the time he is scheduled to begin, and the audience of possibly even more than the forty thousand who had attended Heaton Park to hear the first of his concerts more than a year ago has reached a fever pitch of excitement mixed with rising impatience, he nonchalantly checks the fob watch hung from a chain in the waistcoat of his immaculate white tie and tails evening attire, pauses to twist the ends of his magnificent moustache, then climbs up onto the stage with his arms raised aloft. The crowd salutes him like a Roman emperor. All hail the conquering hero comes!

He waits for them to settle, then beckons to Francis to hand him the first of the seventy-eights. Francis is certain that his shaking hands must be visible to everyone present, but all eyes are on The Gramophone King as he places the record onto the turntable, which he energetically winds up, before delicately dropping the needle into the correct groove. A deep, expectant hush descends upon Philips Park.

He begins with a Neapolitan favourite, one which the crowd is sure to know, and as soon as they hear the familiar opening bars, a collective buzz of pleasure spreads among them – *Torna a Surriento* – and when Caruso begins to sing there is a spontaneous burst of applause. Soon many thousands of voices have begun to join in. They stand from opposite sides of the Amphitheatre and sing across to one another, as if remembering ancestral journeys along the Apennines, singing to their country, paying homage to their homeland.

Billy Grimshaw is not called *The Gramophone King* for nothing. He knows exactly how to work a crowd. Sensing the euphoria among the Italian members of the audience, he follows this up with another Neapolitan barnstormer – Luigi Denza's *Funiculi Funicula* – and the people go wild. Once again, many of them join in, this time complete with gestures, copied from photographs of *The Great Caruso* himself.

Time for something more classical now, he thinks, and he whispers urgently in Francis's ear. "Slight change of plan. Pass me the *Rigoletto*." Francis, quite unfazed, immediately complies. He is loving every moment of this. Caruso now launches into *Questa o Quello*. Immediately, all the women roll their eyes, while the men rub their hands and nod their approval. The women shake their heads, as if to say, "Fat chance," before, as one, they join together to sing the aria's final line:

"Non v'ha amor se non ve liberta..."
"There can be no love if there's no freedom..."

Billy's really hitting his stride now. It's as though the gramophone is a chariot and he is its driver, while the crowds in front of him are the horses, connected to him by invisible reins, which only he can control. All he needs to do is apply the lightest of pressure through his fingers and they will run wherever he leads them. A slight pull here, a gentle release there, and they will respond as one, straining at the bit to go further, run faster, than they ever dreamt possible. He follows the *Rigoletto* with another Verdi, *Di Quella Pira* from *Il Trovatore*. Then he throws in a quick Leoncavallo, *Mattinata*, as a kind of tease, before diving into what he knows they've all been waiting for, some full blown, heart-stopping Puccini – *Nessun Dorma* from Turandot, then *Che Gelida Manina* from *La Bohème*. When Caruso unleashes his full emotional range on this one, Marco dares to reach across and take Claudia's hand into his own again. It is no longer cold, he realises, but warm and soft. She does not pull away but responds to his touch by gently squeezing back.

Now Billy is winding up for his big finish, his grand finale. There can only be one contender. He has the audience in the palm of his hand as he permits himself a further indulgence of tossing the record into the air, allowing it to spin, like a planet in orbit around a star, glinting in the last of the light, catching it just as it might fall, then placing it onto the turntable with a deft, almost casual flourish, which causes the crowds to gasp at his audacity. He drops the needle onto the groove and, as the orchestra starts up, the people rise as one and cheer. It is, of course, that Leoncavallo masterpiece,

Vesti La Giubba from *I Pagliacci*. Tears course down forty thousand cheeks.

When the aria finishes, the crowd goes wild. The cheers and applause last a full five minutes. Billy knows he has to play them one more piece, and he raises his hands in a seemingly powerless shrug, almost as if he is reluctant to come back, but he has planned this moment all along. He holds out his right hand to the side and spreads open the palm. Into it Francis places the final record, and everyone sits back down on the grass. Something to calm them, thinks Billy, something to make them remember this evening for ever, to leave the park elevated from themselves, released, set free, something serene, something sublime. *E Lucevan Le Stelle* from *Tosca*.

Caruso begins quietly, almost caressing the words, the phrasing a miracle of heart felt tenderness, the timing perfect, as the first stars begin to appear in the sky. The air is filled with the sweet smell of tulips rising up from the earth.

*"Entrava ella fragrante
Mi cadea fra le braccia…"*

Marco places his arm around Claudia's waist.

Francis looks out at the thousands of people ranged before him. A sea of rapt, shining faces looks back. One by one they stand. Although their gaze is trained upon the giant horn speaker in the centre of the stage, from which this heavenly music mysteriously emanates, their eyes are elsewhere, reaching back to their own separate individual stories, of how they first came here, to this country, this city, how they crossed mountains, forded rivers, measured the plains and voyaged the oceans; how, since, they have dug canals, excavated coal, spun cotton; built railways, forged steel, driven machines; how they have laid cables, under the ground and high in the sky, printing newspapers, sending out messages, connecting the world. He watches Billy Grimshaw, *The Gramophone King*, basking in the glory of his own invention. He witnesses the hopes and dreams in the masses surrounding him, spellbound, caught in the mesh of electrically reproduced sound waves, and he sees a vision of the earth in constant, tumultuous upheaval, a world turned upside down, then made over again by music, and not just music, but all the arts, healing, transforming, reclaiming, and in this connection he sees as well his own future, a spark crackling in the darkness, illuminating a path he knows he must follow, harnessing the power of science to innovate, to bring the whole of human knowledge within the reach of everyone, the flick of a switch, the press of a button, the world at one's fingertips. He imagines a future where every single one of the thousands standing here before him in Philips Park, listening to Caruso singing from Tosca, will have a gramophone in their own homes, and a radio, and a telephone. They will each have their own cameras to record their memories, and he dreams of a day when cameras will reproduce not just still images, with stiff, posed figures staring anxiously into an unknown void, but moving pictures, capturing life as it happens, as it actually is, right now before his own eyes, which are recording images this very evening onto the back of his retina that will stay with him for ever, just as they will for the thousands of people now standing before him, faces shining with hope, resurrected by the vision of one man to imagine that a cylinder wrapped in tin foil with a very thin membranous diaphragm attached to a needle might capture these amplified vibrations and play them back as music, and for another man to dream up a way of connecting this record to a speaker large enough and powerful enough to relay it to a park full of more than forty thousand people, so that each and every one of them can hear it. Now it only needs a third man to find a way of picking up sound that is being broadcast somewhere else entirely and transmit it directly to people's front rooms. What if, Francis wonders, that third man is him? And if someone else does this before him, what's to stop him becoming involved anyway? Just as he has been today?

The aria approaches its end.

The crowd releases a single, collective sigh, like some giant unchained beast, which must be rounded up and taken back to its lair deep beneath the earth, where it will slumber till its time will come again, knowing it has been a part of something it will treasure for the rest of its life, something it has shared in, an unbroken line, an invisible current passing through every part of it, stretching back to the old country, reaching out towards new horizons, glimpsed possibilities, a gleam in the eye, caught like water, trickling through fingers.

Caruso sings the final lines.

"*E non ho amato mai tanto la vita, tanto la vita…*"

"*And I never before loved life so much, loved life so much…*"

Billy Grimshaw revels in the plaudits he milks from everyone. He collects his fee of £1.15s from Mr Pettigrew and returns to the stage to give Francis a shiny sixpence, a sixpence he will keep and not spend, and which, many years later, he will place alongside that other mounted sixpence, which he will discover on the mantelpiece of an otherwise empty room behind the shop he will buy on the Hyde Road in Denton, when he returns from the war, with its giant pair of rimless spectacles staring out across the city. Mr Pettigrew turns to Hubert and remarks, "I believe, thanks to your publicity, we may have topped the crowds of Heaton Park last year."

"I think the weather might have played a part," replies Hubert.

"Quite so," agrees Pettigrew. "Perfect weather, a glorious

floral display and unforgettable music."

John Chadwick begins the task of tidying the park before locking the gates, relieved that his colour-coordinated homage to Italy has not proved controversial.

As everyone prepares to leave, Caruso's voice still coursing through their veins, the serpentine paths echo to the chorus of *Ciaos* and *Buona Serras*.

"*Ci revidiamo a dopo.*"

"*A dopo, si.*"

Claudia tries to juggle with all her trophies, but no sooner has she picked up the coconut, than she has dropped the toy bird. She has the balloons looped around the wrist of one hand, with the soldier doll balanced on her shoulder, while with the other hand she has the string holding up the jam jar and goldfish wrapped around her index finger, with the other fingers trying to clasp hold of the playing cards. In the end Matteo has to come to her rescue. In the commotion and confusion, she loses sight of Marco. She looks around her but he is nowhere to be seen. Where can he be? With the thousands of people all heading for the exits at once, there's a risk that she will not find him, and that mithers her, for at the very least she wants to say goodnight. But Matteo seems not at all worried, and her parents are keen to be on their way.

In fact, Marco is at that very moment scurrying along the Avenue of Black Poplars with Jabez, who is leading him to a quieter corner of the Park, where he and his father grow the tulips in readiness for the displays. There, with Marco acting as look-out, he takes out his pen knife and proceeds to cut as many stems as he can in the shortest possible time, until a voice booms out.

"Jabez? Is that you?" It's John, his father.

"Coming, Father," he replies, then thrusts the dozen or so tulips he has just cut into Marco's arms, before heading off in the direction of his father's voice. "You owe me big time, Marco," he hisses over his shoulder as he makes his escape.

"Anything," replies a grateful Marco. "Anything at all. I won't forget."

"Nor will I," says Jabez, then he's gone.

Marco now scoots along the perimeter of the Park as fast as he can, trying to arrange the tulips into some kind of acceptable bouquet as he does so, arriving at the exit just in time to see Claudia and Matteo struggling through the gate.

"For you," he says, with a deep bow and flourish.

"Thank you," she says, laughing. "But how am I meant to carry them? Both mine and Matteo's hands are full already."

"*Si*. Is a problem," agrees Marco, rubbing his chin. "Luckily, I have a solution."

"You do?" replies Claudia, throwing an amused, sidelong glance towards her brother. "That *is* lucky. What do you have in mind?"

"I carry them for you. I walk with you back to your house. It's miles out of my way, I know, but I don't mind."

"My knight in shining armour," she says, and then walks on ahead to join her mother and father. Marco makes as if to follow her, but a look from Matteo stops him.

"We'll walk behind," says Matteo, "and you can tell me how you came by these fine flowers."

Marco laughs nervously and begins to whistle the final aria from Tosca.

"*E lucevan le stelle
Ed olezzava la terra…*"

The stars are shining, and the earth is scented…

When they eventually arrive home, just as St Alban's Church is tolling ten o'clock, and Marco has finally been sent on his way by Matteo, they are tired but happy. Claudia arranges the tulips in a vase and sets them on the dining table, watched by her mother, who taps her shoulder with a knowing smile, before putting away the rest of her bounty – the coconuts, playing cards, toy bird, soldier doll and patriotic balloons – while Matteo finds a bowl into which he can empty at last the grateful goldfish, gasping, from its tiny jam jar.

Maurizio lowers himself into the one armchair with a contented sigh.

"If I die this night, I am a happy man," he says.

"Don't talk such nonsense," scolds Giulia Magdalena, crossing herself.

"But is true," he continues. "To see my children grown and with good jobs, to come to England with nothing except dreams, and then to see those dreams come true, to find work and welcome here in Manchester, and finally to hear the Great Caruso singing songs from the old country here in our new home, what more can a man desire?" He says nothing about the possibility of grandchildren, although watching Claudia arrange those flowers, he thinks maybe they won't be too long in coming if that young man continues to press his attentions upon her so determinedly. He checks himself to make sure he has not actually voiced these thoughts out loud – he finds he does this more and more these days – then chuckles.

"*Per amor del cielo*," cries Giulia Magdalena. "Claudia, can you talk some sense into your father?"

"She's right, Papa," she says. "You shouldn't tempt fate."

But her words fall on deaf ears. Already he is sound asleep and snoring. Claudia and Matteo tiptoe quietly out of the room, leaving Giulia Magdalena to place a rug across her husband's knees. She tuts, smiling to herself, before placing a light kiss on his cheek and then going upstairs herself.

Once they are certain that their mother is asleep also, Matteo and Claudia slip quietly back outside to join *la granda passiegata* taking place the entire length of Great Ancoats Street. Spirits are still running high from the Caruso concert and people greet each other with extravagant hugs and embraces, almost as if they are all subconsciously aware that a great moment is passing.

On every corner the hurdy gurdies are playing – on Cotton, Loom and Jersey Streets, on Blossom, Radium and Naval Streets, on Bengal, Poland and Portugal Streets – as if their lives depended on it. It is their last hurrah, and it seems as though they know it. They have witnessed their demise in the coming of the gramophone. In five years time there will be half this number playing after the *Festa della Rosario*, and in ten, when the soldiers return home from war, there will be none.

But on this night they are everywhere. The air is filled with *Tarantellas, Saltarellos, Tresconettis* and *Marescos*. Claudia claps along in time as Matteo and his fiancée Constanzia whirl around the corner, and then, just as she hoped he would be, Marco is by her side. The hurdy gurdies strike up a *Furlana*, a courting dance, and Marco slips his arm around Claudia's waist. She leans her head against his shoulder. She pictures the unseen atoms dancing above them until the last of the twilight has faded from the sky.

The next morning, early, just as the day is beginning to get light, Giulia Magdalena comes back downstairs, expecting to discover Maurizio already up and about, but instead she finds him exactly where she left him, still asleep in the armchair. She is about to draw back the curtains when something makes her pause. She wonders what it is that is different. Then she realises. The quiet. Her husband is making no sound. She walks back towards him and knows at once.

His papery skin has lost its sheen. His hands and forehead are cold. His eyelids are closed and still. Across his thinly parted lips, from where no breath now comes, is a faint but happy smile.

Giulia Magdalena kneels by his side, says a silent prayer and then lays her head in his lap, where she will wait until, some time later, Claudia will find her.

With Maurizio gone, a part of Giulia Magdalena goes too, like a limb, or a vital organ, her heart itself, which, though it still beats, does so seemingly without purpose. Like someone who has lost an arm or leg, but who still feels pain where once it was, she cannot shake off the feeling that she is wandering in a dream, one from which she will wake up, to find Maurizio rising from his armchair to pour himself a glass of wine. She goes upstairs to fetch something but cannot remember what it is. She speaks only in Italian and then, after a few weeks, she barely speaks at all.

One afternoon she sits down in her husband's armchair and decides she will stay there. When Matteo comes home from work, this is where he finds her. He enfolds one of her gossamer thin hands in both of his and pats it urgently.

"*Mamma*," he says. "*Svegliati*. Wake up, *Mamma*."

A few minutes later, when Claudia arrives back from the University, he rushes towards her. "Sit with her," he demands, "while I go for the doctor."

Claudia places a hand on her brother's shoulder. "It's not a doctor she needs now," she says, as the last of the evening light is fading from the sky. "Fetch Father Pappalardi."

Two nights later there is a knock at the door. When Claudia opens it, she finds a soberly dressed, serious Marco standing on the step. He holds out a much more modest, restrained bunch of white tulips, which he offers to her.

"I am so very sorry for the loss of your mother," he says gravely. "She was a great woman, one of the rocks on which our community here was built, and the whole of Ancoats grieves for her."

Claudia thanks him and then asks if he would like to come inside.

"*Non, Signorina*. I do not wish to intrude at this difficult time for your family."

Claudia bows her head and thanks him a second time.

Matteo joins them on the doorstep. He and Marco shake hands, before Marco heads off down the street.

After he has gone, Matteo looks at the flowers, then turns to his sister. "He's a good man," he says.

"*Si loso*," says Claudia. "I know it."

Nearly nine years later, in a different house, where Claudia is on her hands and knees, furiously scrubbing the floors, in order to distract her from an even more raw grief, while the three year old Giulia and the six month old Paulie lie asleep upstairs, there is a second knock at the door. At first, in the noisy escaping of breath as she scrubs, she does not hear it, but the person knocking persists. When she hears it at last, she heaves herself up from the floor and wearily makes her way towards it.

"*Si?*" she says, not paying attention to the young man standing there in the uniform of The Manchester Regiment.

"Claudia?" he says. "It's me. Jabez. Don't you recognise me?"

Claudia wipes her hands on her apron, which she then unties and hangs on a nail behind the door, as she ushers him in. "*Scusa*. Please come in. I haven't spoken English in a few days. *Nonno* is through here," and she indicates the small front parlour. "But I must warn you. He may not remember you."

Jabez nods. He removes his army hat and looks for somewhere to place it. Claudia takes it from him and hangs it with her apron behind the front door.

"*Nonno*," says Claudia as they enter the room. "Here's Jabez come to see you. Marco's friend."

Signor Locartelli sees the uniform Jabez is wearing and is at once overcome. "Marco?" he asks, falteringly, in Italian. "Is it you? Have you come back to us?"

Jabez takes *Nonno's* hands in his and gently guides him back to his chair.

"Marco and I were in the same unit together," he says slowly, while Claudia translates his words into Italian. "We were together throughout the war..."

"*Erevamo insieme durante la guerre...*"

I was with him when he died..."

"*Ero con lui quando è morto...*"

"He suffered no pain..."

"*Non soffrivo...*"

"His final thoughts..."

"*Le sue ultimo parole furono...*"

"... were all of you. "

"... *tutto di te.*"

Marco's father squeezes his eyes as tightly shut as he can, but even this cannot prevent a tear escaping from each.

"Thank you," whispers Claudia, leading Jabez quietly out of the room and back into the hallway, where she takes down his army hat from the peg and hands it to him. Jabez places it back on his head and then takes from his inside pocket a rather creased and waterlogged envelope.

"Marco asked me to give you this if I made it through myself. I've tried to keep it dry but that's not always been possible. I hope the contents are not too damaged."

Claudia takes the envelope in her hands, reads her own name, even where the ink has run or faded, recognises her late husband's handwriting, and feels her throat tightening. She finds that she cannot speak. Jabez quietly salutes her, before marching back into the night.

Once outside and clear of the house, he pauses under a

street lamp to light himself a cigarette, which he draws on deeply. After a few moments, he begins to make his way back to his own family house, where now only his sisters live. He hears his footsteps echo loudly on the cobbles, reminding him with every step that he is still alive. His thoughts turn to the young woman he met at Philips Park Cemetery only yesterday – Mary – who he has an appointment to see again in three days' time. With each step he takes he feels he is walking towards a possible future.

Claudia waits until she can no longer hear his footsteps, then sits quietly at the foot of the stairs. She opens the envelope with agonising slowness, as carefully as she can, for fear she might tear it. In her trembling fingers it feels as fragile and delicate as a *fontanelle*, the soft membranous gap between the frontal and parietal bones in baby Paulie's skull, which pulse beneath her touch, which Marco's hands have never felt for themselves, nor ever shall.

When, finally, she opens the envelope, she finds a photograph. Marco must have arranged to have had it taken by one of those studio portraitists who accompanied the soldiers to the Front Line. The date on the back is just two days before he was killed. With it is a letter. "*Show this to Paulie,*" it begins, "*so that he will know his father when he comes home…*"

Claudia cannot bear to read any more.

At exactly the same moment, six year old George Wright is anxiously following his own father, whose behaviour is growing increasingly erratic, trying to keep silent and remain out of sight, as he pads barefoot around the house in Portugal Street, while a hundred and forty miles away, in the internment camp near Peel on the Isle of Man, Francis wonders, even now the War has ended, whether he will ever be allowed to return home. His long walk from Liverpool to

Manchester, tracing the march of telegraph poles to mark his solitary way, is still six months ahead of him.

*

In this modern age of speed and innovation, hardly a day passes without some new wonder.

On the same October night in 1921 that Francis is relaying Beethoven's *The Creatures of Prometheus* from *The Queen's Hall* in London to an awe-struck gathering of random passers by in Heaton Park, listened to by George on the crystal set radio receiver he has built with his father in their home in Hirstwood on Daisy Bank Road, Miss Esther Blundell is sitting in the audience at The Manchester Literary & Philosophical Society, the affectionately known Lit & Phil, at their headquarters on Deansgate, listening intently to a lecture being given by the Italian poet and activist, Filippo Tommaso Marinetti, founder of the Futurists and author of their radical manifesto, some of whose tenets, Esther feels, have found their time and strike a chord with many of those listening to him there that evening.

"Futurism," proclaims Marinetti, "is a celebration of speed. The motor car is our symbol. It is a thing of beauty, the perfect blend of art and engineering. Let us put our faith in the future," he continues, "in youth, in industry, when man and the machine are indistinguishable one from the other."

There is much murmuring at this and, Esther senses, tacit approval. She, too, can see the appeal in sweeping away the old order, of removing the barriers of rank and class and privilege once and for all, but something about his almost fanatical delivery unnerves her. Her neighbour, a woman she has not spoken to but has seen at previous meetings, raises her hand to ask a question.

"Signor Marinetti, I am sure we all agree with you that the future is important, but are you advocating the abandonment of everything that has gone before?"

"Unequivocally, yes. We want to demolish all museums, all libraries, blow them up, start afresh. Beginning with this building in which we are all so comfortably and complacently gathered this evening."

Unsurprisingly this remark causes a mass outcry. Even those who had lent his lecture a sympathetic ear until this point now rise as one to shout him down. But Marinetti is not a man to be cowed.

"Every level of society must be torn apart so that it can be rebuilt anew."

"I should have thought," counters the woman sitting on Esther's right, "that we have all experienced enough destruction to last us a life time."

A chorus of "Hear, hears" greets this remark.

"If," answers Marinetti, "you are referring to the recent so-called 'war to end all wars', I couldn't disagree with you more. War is a necessity for the health of the human spirit, a purification that allows for the growth of a new idealism."

At this, the normally polite Lit & Phil breaks into a mass of uncontrolled shouting, and a pale and trembling Chair of the Society vainly tries to establish order but is unable to do so. The meeting disperses without the usual vote of thanks for the evening's speaker, and Filippo Tommaso Marinetti remains on the platform, manicuring his waxed moustache, a wry, amused smile across his lips.

Afterwards, outside on Deansgate, Esther introduces herself to the woman who had asked the question which had sparked off the ensuing scenes of chaos and disorder.

"How do you do? I was most impressed by your courage in challenging our Futurist firebrand just now."

"I believe his bark is probably much worse than his bite."

"I would hope so."

The two young women laugh warmly.

"Esther Blundell."

"Delphine Fish."

"Until his final outburst, what did you make of him?"

"I'm not sure really. I thought much of his argument was at odds with itself."

"Yes. I thought so too. Although what he said about this being an age of speed struck a chord. Everyone does seem in such a great hurry these days."

"Making up for lost time, I imagine. The War was such a waste."

"Of lives and years, yes."

"Although I have a friend who is frequently impatient. Always wanting things done by yesterday."

"A friend?"

Delphine narrows her eyes. "What an astute young woman you are, Esther."

"I'm sorry. I've no wish to intrude."

"Not at all. He would like to be very much more than just a friend, I believe. But I am perfectly happy with the arrangement as it stands."

Esther nods, wondering what kind of arrangement that might be.

"I know what you're thinking," butts in Delphine. "But I'm not a tease, I assure you. I've made my feelings known to Charles – my friend – perfectly clear on more than one occasion, but…"

"But…?

"He prefers not to heed what I say, thinking to wear me down by a process of attrition."

"And will he, do you think, wear you down?"

Delphine pauses. "If I'm not always on my guard, he just might."

The two women laugh together once more.

"The thing is," continues Delphine, "Charles would have recognised in Signor Marinetti something of a kindred spirit. Why put off till tomorrow what you might do today? The notion of our living in an age of speed would appeal to him. He's a doctor and he's always seeking to bring in the latest discoveries in new treatments, new technologies, new drugs, and he rails against what he sees as the overly cautious approach of the hospital trustees – or the dinosaurs, as he so rudely refers to them as. His intentions are noble, but he does tend to regard his patients as guinea pigs, rather than individual human beings, each with their own set of unique, complex needs. He can't seem to grasp that not everyone will see things the way he does, and so he does have a tendency to go at life at a hundred miles an hour, like there's no tomorrow. Which can be rather exhilarating – hence my continuing forbearance of him." She smiles. "I'm sorry. I don't know what got me started on all of that."

"Perhaps he's simply trying to make up for lost time. I think the War has made all of us think like that at times. Perhaps he experienced a deep loss earlier in his life, perhaps he delayed over something, which turned out to have unfortunate consequences, and his current behaviour is some kind of atonement for it."

Delphine looks at Esther closely. "What a perceptive thing to say."

"Hardly. I'm the worst kind of amateur psychologist."

"But it's what I've wondered also, but if ever I try to ask him about his past, he tries to change the subject. And if I press him, he becomes tight-lipped, morose even."

"Best not to press him then."

"I agree. This age of speed will make daredevils of us all – impetuous hares, when it would profit us more to remember the tortoise."

"I'm sure you're right, but if I am to catch the last tram back home, I shall need to emulate the hare, or I shall miss it."

"Where is it you live?"

"Gorton."

"Then we can ride together, for the Gorton tram passes my road too."

They hitch up their skirts and sprint the last few yards to Princess Street, where they are just in time to leap aboard.

"Careful, ladies," calls the conductor. "Steady as you go. It's not a race, you know."

Esther and Delphine collapse into adjoining seats with a fit of the giggles.

"Was it something I said?" asks the conductor. "My missus is always laughing at me, though I never know what for…"

"Which stop do you get off at?" asks Esther.

"Just past the Infirmary."

"Is that where Charles works?"

Delphine nods.

"And what about you?" asks Esther again. "Where do you work?"

"Thank you for assuming that I do," says Delphine. "At the University. I used to be a teacher of deaf children. Now I teach teachers to be."

"That must be so rewarding."

"It can be. Frustrating too, at times. One of the things I try to emphasise to my current students is the importance of patience and perspective. What seems like nothing much at all to those of us blessed with good hearing can be a major achievement for a deaf child."

"One has to learn to measure progress differently, I imagine?"

"Precisely so."

"I wonder what our Signor Marinetti would make of this conversation."

"Oh, I rather think he wouldn't have time or tolerance for anything he might regard as imperfections, would you?"

"You're referring to eugenics?"

"I fear I am."

The two women shudder.

"And here's my stop," says Delphine, rousing herself once more. "I've very much enjoyed our conversation. We must do it again some time."

"I should like to."

"Really?"

"Yes. Very much."

Delphine pauses, as if debating with herself whether to say what is in her mind or not. "Let us take our cue from *Signor* Marinetti and be impetuous then. Can you be free a week on Sunday?"

"Yes. I think so. My father is something of an invalid, but with notice I may well be able to arrange something."

Delphine nods, taking this in. "Meet me in Platt Fields a week on Sunday then. Three o'clock. If you can, that is. I shall go anyway and understand if you don't make it. By the new statue of Abraham Lincoln. I'm reminded of something he once said. *'The best thing about the future…'* "

"Yes?"

"*… 'is that it comes one day at a time'.*"

And with a flurry she steps off the tram and into the night. Esther goes over their conversation and thinks how lucky that we should have been seated next to one another at this evening's lecture, and that I should have spoken to her on an impulse afterwards. A random, godless universe, governed entirely by chance and coincidence, need not be such a dark and sorrowful place after all, for do not shooting stars blaze there sometimes, however fleetingly?

And so, from time to time, Esther and Delphine arrange to meet each other, for conversation and a frank exchange of views. Just as Charles and Francis continue to run into one another at St James's, over billiards and brandy, to share their latest enthusiasm. Francis is not aware that Charles knows Delphine, whom Francis has not seen since that extraordinary meeting at Bob's Lane Ferry, but whom he has never forgotten, while Delphine has no notion that Esther once met Charles, briefly, at the funeral of Ruth, the shadow in his past he refuses to speak about, and it is only when Delphine shows her a photograph of him that Esther realises exactly who Charles is, but she decides, for the sake of some small vestige of belief she has that it would be better for *Charles*, when and if he is eventually ready, to recount that particular story, not *her*, to say nothing. We may be living in an age of speed, she reflects, whizzing around the circuit of life, but in the arena of personal relations, it is probably wisest to heed the advice of Mr Lincoln and let nature, and the future, take its course.

Speed.

Speed. Speed. Speed.

Francis is consumed by thoughts of it. Speed and distance.

Three and a half years ago, while he was still interned on the Isle of Man, time had hung so heavily. The seconds, minutes, hours passed with unbearable slowness, like drips of water in a cave, taking millennia to form into even the most minute of stalagmites. He felt as though his own feet were encased in rock. He would sometimes climb to the headland above the camp, turn his back on the harbour of Peel and the sea below him, and gaze instead across the island, towards Douglas, and the point of departure back to England, the promised land. Most days he could not see it, for it would be shrouded in mist or cloud. It was almost worse on those days when he did catch a brief, tantalising glimpse of the glittering Irish Sea, for although it was only twelve miles away, it might have been the moon, for all the chance he had of ever setting sail upon it.

Then, when he did finally make it back to England and decided to walk his way back to Manchester from Liverpool by following the path of telegraph poles marching across the land, that relatively short journey, less than thirty-five miles, took him the best part of three days. Now, he can send a message along the wires between those poles all the way to Glasgow in less than fifteen minutes, he can be connected by telephone to speak to a colleague there in just two, and last year he picked up music from the *Last Night of the Proms* in London directly as it was happening. It's all relative, he smiles to himself...

He recalls that momentous evening when he and Charles were fortunate enough to obtain the last two remaining seats to listen to the great man himself delivering his first ever lecture in the UK, right here in Manchester, in the neo-Gothic splendour of the University's Whitworth Hall, just three months before Francis's night time exploits in Heaton Park...

Dr Henry Miers, Vice Chancellor of the University and esteemed Professor of Crystallography, mounts the stage from where he addresses the audience of six hundred people seated in the body of the hall, in which there is already a palpable buzz of electricity crackling in the air. Professor Miers, caught up himself in the febrile atmosphere, can barely contain his own excitement at the prospect of this historic occasion.

PROF. MIERS:
Ladies and gentlemen, if I may crave your attention for just a moment...

The animated conversations in the hall die down at once.

PROF. MIERS:
I understand that our eminent speaker this evening has been slightly delayed.

A gasp of disappointment rises up from the audience like a squabbling of sparrows, desperate for every last crumb.

PROF. MIERS:
>Fear not. He is at this very moment making his way here from another, smaller building across the quadrangle with Professor Chaim Weizmann, whom many of you here know, where he has just been speaking to The Manchester Jewish Society about the prospect of the creation of a Hebrew University in Jerusalem. I am sure that...

At that moment the Professor is interrupted by an extremely tall, thin, elderly gentleman, in a black suit beneath a black academic gown, scurrying awkwardly up onto the platform. He resembles a rheumatic raven, the joints of his knees and ankles cracking loudly with each step he takes, to hand the Professor a note.

PROF. MIERS:
>Ah. Thank you.

He puts on a pair of half moon spectacles and hastily reads. He then folds the piece of paper, hands it back to the raven, removes his spectacles and, aware of the drama of the moment, with the whole of the audience leaning forward on the edges of their seats, wondering what he will next announce, holds the hall with the longest of pauses.

PROF. MIERS:
>Ladies and gentlemen, will you please give a warm Manchester welcome to our speaker this evening – Professor Albert Einstein.

The audience breaks out in immediate, enthusiastic and relieved applause, as a dusty, somewhat dishevelled man in his early fifties, wearing a well worn, rumpled cream linen jacket, shuffles his way to the podium. His greying hair stands out from his head, almost as if he has just received an electric shock, or come hot-footed from his laboratory after conducting an experiment that has gone wrong, involving a large explosion.

He shyly raises a hand to try and quell the applause, which continues to ring out across the Whitworth Hall, beaming benignly. Eventually there is silence. Professor Einstein takes out his own spectacles, which he polishes slowly, still smiling. He taps the microphone before him, to test that it is working. The noise it makes, reminiscent of a bittern's booming call, startles him and makes the audience laugh, their nervousness dissipating along with his own.

In the audience, towards the back, Francis leans across to Charles and whispers.

FRANCIS (*sotto voce*):
> That's a Western Electric Double Button Carbon. Top of the range. It was used by President Warren Harding in his Inaugural Address in Washington earlier this year.

CHARLES:
> And no doubt provided by you for this evening's occasion?

Francis spreads his hands with a smile. Charles returns the smile before another audience member sitting in front of them turns around with a fierce remonstration to them to "Hush!"

Finally Professor Einstein is ready. He holds a sheaf of papers in his right hand, from which he begins to read his lecture.

It is delivered entirely in German, but the audience follow him perfectly, spellbound, hanging onto every last syllable, What follows is a translation of part of this speech, as reproduced in the following day's edition of The Manchester Guardian, 26th July 1921.

EINSTEIN:

It is with exceeding humility that I stand before you today to talk about my scientific research. To have the degree of science bestowed on me by this famous university is a further honour of which I am unworthy. The foundation of the University of Manchester during the last century was laid down on the principles of freedom, the freedom to learn and pursue further knowledge without the restriction of religious belief. Without freedom I would not be here to talk to you today. Without freedom there would have been no Newton, no Faraday, no Maxwell and no Thompson – especially there would have been no Ernest Rutherford, a famous and most worthy son of Manchester and of science. It was here in Manchester, a mere ten years ago, that Rutherford deduced the wondrous structure of the atom. He laid before us the beauty of its simplicity and, at the same time, laid to rest the atom of another son of Manchester – John Dalton. My friend, Mr George Bernard Shaw, tells me that some men are famous because they are makers of empires, but their hands are stained with the blood of innocent men, women and children. Rutherford and Dalton – and Democritus – were makers of atoms, but their hands are unstained with the blood of any human being on earth. Democritus made an atom that lasted more than two thousand years. Dalton made an atom that lasted a hundred years. Rutherford has made a new atom, and I can't tell you how long that will last but, like Democritus and Dalton before him, Rutherford's name will go down in history, and be remembered for ever and, I might add, for ever in association with Manchester. It has been my fate, determined by the fortunes of pure chance, to work on several topics concerning the physical universe, and I hope you will have the patience this evening for me to describe some of them to you.

Einstein at this point screws up the first sheet of paper he has been reading from and tosses it over his shoulder. Different members of the audience turn to one another in some surprise at this unusual straying away from decorum. He regards them unconcerned.

EINSTEIN:
At least you now know that I am not going to repeat myself.

The tension of the previous moment is at once leavened and the hall is filled with laughter which gathers like a tidal bore rolling across the audience.

But I am afraid that I must start by talking about geometry, and for those of you who came here this evening to understand more about relativity, all I can say is: please remain seated, the doors have been locked. (*More laughter*). But before I discuss how relativity has changed geometry, it seems necessary to me to discuss first how the science of geometry itself must have arisen. Geometry has always had a very special relationship with physics, and the basis for the geometry we know today reached finality with the publication of Euclid's *'Elements'* nearly two thousand and two hundred years ago. No scientist has completed his or her education until this book, one of the most beautiful and influential works of science in the history of humankind, has been read. There is no time for me to read all of these Thirteen Elements to you tonight, but I must draw your attention to some of the ingredients crucial to the understanding of what the theory of relativity has done to geometry. The material out of which geometry grew must have consisted of isolated and empirical discoveries concerning geometric figures, such as the particular case of the theorem of Pythagoras....

In the audience Francis savours this particular phrase and runs it round his mouth.

FRANCIS: (*to himself*):
'Isolated and empirical discoveries...'

EINSTEIN: (*continuing*):
... that the square on the hypotenuse of a right-angled triangle must be equal to the sum of the squares on the other two sides. But how did this theorem arise? Surely, it was a consequence of human measurement? Someone must have walked three paces to the south, then four paces to the east, and found that they could return home by walking exactly five paces in a straight line. Three threes are nine, four fours are twelve, which, when added together, make twenty-five, or five fives.

He once again grins mischievously as he screws up another sheet of his lecture notes and tosses it over his shoulder to join the first one on the floor of the hall.

Less than one and a quarter miles away, in Daisy Bank Road, nine year old George is doing his maths homework, wishing that his teacher might have explained Pythagoras's theorem as simply and enjoyably as Professor Einstein just has…

EINSTEIN:
> But over time people forgot that these theorems grew out of empirical observation. They simply accepted that if Euclid said such and such was true for geometric measurements on land, then it must be true for all measurements, even the most abstract, in space. But this is not necessarily so. Let us go beyond Pythagoras for a moment. As a simple example, let us start a journey at the North Pole and travel about six thousand miles south until we reach the Equator. Now, we turn east and travel for another six thousand miles. We then turn north and, after six thousand miles, we arrive back at the North Pole. We have traced out a triangle that has three right angles, but for which Pythagoras's Theorem does not hold. Why? Because we have travelled on a curved surface. Curved space has a special effect. Here, in the north of England, you play a game that is played nowhere else on Earth, even in the south of your country, and it is called Crown Green Bowls. Imagine this game is being watched by a Little Green Man on Mars. He will observe the bowls travelling and curving away from the centre, no matter from where they are projected. The Green Man on Mars will conclude that some sort of force is acting on the bowl and pushing it away from the centre, but for anyone standing on Earth, they can see the reason why. The space is curved, and this is producing what appears to be an extra force. This is the essence of my General Theory of Relativity…

He screws up and tosses aside a third sheet of paper.

> … which I find to differ from the theory of Newton. Newton's theory predicts the bending of a ray of light as

it passes close to the sun. My theory predicts the same bending, but with an extra amount, caused by the curvature of space, because of the sun, and this extra amount has exactly the same size as the Newtonian portion, so the bending in my theory is twice that predicted by Newton. I confess to a feeling of extreme trepidation when Professor Arthur Stanley Eddington – another son of Manchester – led an expedition to the South Atlantic to observe the eclipse of 1919. This allowed my theory to be tested against the earlier models of Euclid and Newton, and also against exact measurements, and it is with extreme modesty that I now stand before you, knowing that it is *my* theory which appears to be correct. Thirty-five years ago, another famous son of Manchester, Professor J.J. Thompson, discovered the existence of the electron, for which he received the Nobel Prize. He used an apparatus called a Cloud Chamber, invented by C.T.R. Wilson – yet another famous son of Manchester – and laid the foundation for a new Physical Law, which states the equivalence of mass with energy. A hundred years earlier, another son of Manchester, Mr James Joule – *mein Gott*, how many famous sons can one city have?! – had proved, by careful, empirical measurement, the equivalence of energy and heat, sometimes referred to as work. It should have come as no surprise, for at that time new railways were being built right across Europe – here in Manchester you built the first one. The more coal one shoved into the engine, the hotter it got, and the faster it went. The connection between energy and motion could not have been clearer.

He looks around at the expectant faces of the audience, smiling, knowing he is about to embark upon the part of the speech that everyone has come to hear, but he has a further anecdote to tell them first, to make them wait just a little while longer.

Now, imagine, if you can, a person who is unfortunate enough to find himself in a lift, or elevator, which is falling freely under gravity. I have been told that in the Department of Physics here in this University people have been imagining this possibility for the past twenty years, but fortunately so far this has not happened and, in any case, I saw for myself today that the elevators are now brand new – phew! The person who is inside the lift does not know that he is falling. He is aware of the acceleration, but he doesn't know if it is caused by gravity or a motor. Now, without the assistance of some exceedingly painful equations, I am unable to carry this argument through in a mathematically rigorous sense, but I am already close to proving to you, I hope, that inertial mass and gravitational mass are one and the same thing. I now extend this argument to consider cases where a body is at rest, and the body emits radiation of some sort. I do not enquire in what form that radiation might be – it could be light, or X rays, or heat – but if the body has a certain mass before the radiation is emitted, and if the radiation has an energy – let us call it 'e' – then a very simple calculation, using only moderately uncomfortable equations, leads us to the inescapable conclusion that the mass of the body – 'm' – must be reduced by an amount equal to energy – 'e' – divided by the square of the velocity of light – 'c' – and thus I was led to this simple equation:

$e = mc^2$.

Professor Einstein leans forward and speaks his next sentence in a deep, hushed tone as if to underline its importance.

In essence my equation says that energy, when put equal to mass, multiplied by the square of the velocity of light, shows that a very small amount of mass can be converted into a very large amount of energy.

Your Professor Rutherford puts it another way. "The power of the atom is a mighty thing and equal to the power of a thousand horses." (*He shrugs*). And yet, it must be said, we do not yet know how to obtain or harness that power. But everything we know about the human race tells me that one day we will.

He tosses aside his final piece of paper, so that now he is surrounded by an orbit of screwed up balls, which roll around his ankles, like unstable atoms.

In conclusion I would like to recognise the honour of this degree you have bestowed upon me. It is an act of great-hearted liberalism in what are increasingly difficult political times. And I also appreciate the invitation to give you this lecture, which I regard not only as a gesture of good will and trust, but also a commendable endeavour in the sense that it is a renewal of the international fraternity of the educated.

Thank you.

*

Less than a year and a half after hearing the great man's lecture, Francis is a part of the team broadcasting live for the BBC directly from a converted warehouse in the Metropolitan Vickers Electrical Works in Trafford Park, Manchester, using the ornate water tower on the site as the transmitter for the newly created *Radio 2ZY*.

He is here now, as part of the BBC team, partly because

of his growing technical reputation, but also because of his business acumen. He has a nose for the main chance. Following the previous night's trial transmission from The Strand in London, this evening, Wednesday 15th November 1922, will see the first truly national live radio broadcast, and Francis, having supplied the Western Electric Button Carbon microphone for Professor Einstein's lecture in the Whitworth Hall, is the only stockist in Manchester to be selling the RCA Westinghouse, which he has imported from America, a newly developed vacuum tube receiver, which, he believes, especially if these early broadcasts from Trafford Park are a success, will rapidly replace the home made crystal sets used by most enthusiasts. The newly formed British Broadcasting Corporation, in association with General Electric and Guglielmo Marconi himself, who has been transmitting live entertainment as an experiment from his factory in Chelmsford since 1920, has decreed that members of the public must obtain a licence to be able to receive their programmes and has thus far issued only thirty thousand of them across the whole country at the somewhat prohibitive cost of ten shillings, but Francis is confident that both the ceiling on the number of licences issued will go up, while their cost to individual customers will come down, and, until a Manchester firm takes up the gauntlet of producing its own range of radio receivers to rival those of RCA Westinghouse, which he is certain will happen, he will sell the American model to those enthusiasts who, like him, want to be in at the beginning, to herald this new dawn.

At precisely 6pm, Mr Daniel Godfrey Jnr, the new station's manager, echoing exactly what Mr Arthur Burrows, the BBC Director of Programmes, had said the previous evening in their converted studio on The Strand, ushers in this new dawn with the following, somewhat modest words:

"Hello. This is *2ZY* calling, *2ZY*, transmitting to you on three hundred and seventy-five metres medium wave. Good evening…"

He then proceeds to read a short news bulletin – twice, in case listeners wished to take notes – followed by a weather forecast, and that is it. In less than fifteen minutes the historic first national radio broadcast is over. It has all been rather anti-climactic.

Over in Hirstwood, where George has had to sit quietly, listening to it after tea with his parents, there is a distinct air of disappointment. George isn't sure what he had been expecting, but surely more than this? Some music at the very least, possibly a story, maybe, even, a comedian telling jokes. George likes jokes. He collects them from the other children at school, and then torments his Mum and Dad with them when he gets home.

"What did one hat say to the other?"

"I don't know. What did one hat say to the other?"

"You stay here, I'll go on a head…"

Or…

"What did the sea say to the shore?"

"Nothing – it just waved…"

Or, his current favourite…

"What do you get when you drop a piano down a coal mine?"

"I don't know," says Annie wearily, having heard the joke already a hundred times.

"A flat miner…"

And George rolls on the rug in front of the fire in sheer delight like a beetle on its back, waving its legs in the air.

"Perhaps I should write to the broadcasters," he says a few moments later, "and offer to send in jokes to them…"

He likes this last joke even more since he began to learn the piano. Remembering Evelyn's front room in Bignor Street, Annie has installed a piano here in Daisy Bank Road.

One of the first things she does after settling in is to find George a recommended piano tutor. Mrs Sylvia Tiffin. George adores her, and she has his measure in no time at all. Unlike most children, George relishes practice, especially the scales which, Mrs Tiffin tells him, noting her pupil's love for tinkering, for taking things apart and then trying to put them back together again, are the nuts and bolts of playing the piano. George nods appreciatively and applies himself assiduously.

Francis, too, feels flat. After all of the build up, he'd been expecting... what? He's no longer sure. Something more momentous, something that more properly reflected the historic nature of the occasion, than the news and weather. Yes, he knows that this is what people want to hear, but not only that, surely? Even Marconi has been experimenting with light entertainment slots in his own privately funded pilot broadcasts. It's clear that Station Manager Dan Godfrey Jnr is experiencing the same kind of let-down.

"This won't do," he says afterwards, puffing furiously on his pipe.

But Francis has other fish to fry, other projects to pursue, other irons in the fire, to be too downcast for long. Six months in, the nightly broadcasts are now routinely incorporating music. Godfrey has formed what he calls "*The 2ZY Orchestra*", specifically to perform for the station. He has also instigated a choir and an opera company. As a result, a number of original works by British composers are given their first public airing, including Elgar's *The Dream of Gerontius, Enigma Variations* and Holst's *Planets Suite*. Gradually more and more listeners tune in. Francis sells more and more RCA Westinghouses. The BBC produces its first weekly copies of the Radio Times. F.G. Wright & Son print and distribute the copies for Manchester. In London John

Reith becomes the BBC's first General Manager and preaches a manifesto of radio as a medium for "educating and improving the masses", although, after initial reluctance, he does consent to the broadcasting of lunch time concerts by British dance bands from some of London's swankier hotels – Ambrose, Geraldo, Roy Fox, Carroll Gibbons – and this gives Francis an idea.

"Why don't we," he says to Dan Godfrey one night, "showcase the dance bands and singers to be found playing here in Manchester?"

Godfrey puffs even more furiously on his pipe. "Good idea," he says at last. "You track 'em, I'll transmit 'em."

From the moment he finally made it back to his adopted city and decided to change his name, to reinvent himself, from Franz Halsinger to Francis Hall, he has felt himself in a permanent hurry, as if he must somehow make up for lost time, those missing years of waste and neglect, when it seemed as though he was abandoned, forgotten, invisible. He has been in a race, with himself mostly, whether refining the grinding of ever more powerful lenses for his telescopes, or continuing to search for richer, more life-like reproductions of sound from the atmosphere, to probe deeper, travel further, penetrate the outer edges of the universe, to see and hear with greater clarity than ever before, to join in with the celestial conversations he encounters there, his attention straying wherever the sound waves take him, shining a pinprick of light into where, before, there was only darkness, restlessly striving for whatever might come next.

'Consider the end. Consider the consequences of your actions...'

These words run through Francis's mind as he heads out

of the makeshift studio at Metro-Vicks into a dark and wet November evening. They are inscribed on the inside of his cigarette case, a gift to him from his friend Charles. He attempts to light one now, sheltering from the wind on the corner of Fourth Avenue and Ashburton Road East, beneath the brick spire of St Anthony of Padua's Church, which is at that very moment tolling eight o'clock. He has to strike several matches, shielding their flame with his other hand, before one of them successfully catches. He turns up the collar of his overcoat, pulls his hat down over his ears and hunches his shoulders into the teeth of the rain. Needle-sharp it slants at an acute angle down to where it arrows into the greasy cobbles under his feet, following the hard, straight line of the shadow from a nearby street lamp, whose rusted upright stanchion forms the third side of this particular isosceles triangle, into which Francis now steps. The lamp, and its cohort of others strung along Trafford Park Road, where it overlooks the Manchester Ship Canal's final sluggish quarter mile before it reaches the Pomona Docks, illuminates the steady two-way procession of similarly belted-and-coated men and women leaning forward, heads down, making their slow, heavy-footed progress either towards or away from the densely packed brick-and-concrete, cement-and-asbestos forest of factories, which have sprung up and proliferated in the thirty years since the Canal was completed.

There are no footpaths here, only these cobbled roads, criss-crossed with rail and tram tracks, and the occasional deep pot hole, one of which Francis steps into now, unwarily, his eyes not looking where he is going, but instead regarding the scene as a whole, which reminds him, with its monochromes of murky browns and greys, shot through with just the slightest smudge of light here and there, revealing a sallow cheek, a bulbous nose, a pair of bloodshot eyes, of one of those remarkable miniature *pochades* by Pierre Adolphe

Valette, whose impressionist depictions of what he calls his "Manchester-scapes", Francis so admires. No larger than a postcard, these oil sketches on board, card, or whatever comes to hand, capture for Francis exactly what he experiences on his nocturnal ramblings, offering a brief candle into the darkness and shadows, to portray rare, precious, fleeting glimpses of unexpected beauty and unsung courage.

He extracts his foot gingerly from the pot hole, shaking as much of the excess water as he can from his trouser leg and shoe, but he is too late to prevent it from soaking the inside of his sock, which squelches coldly with each alternate step. He reaches the Swing Bridge just as it begins to open up to let through a large container vessel steaming its way from the Port of Manchester, back along the Canal, towards Liverpool, and from there to the world, laden with coal and cotton, iron and steel, tar and chemicals, raw materials to build and house, clothe and heat, all the peoples of the Empire, the Commonwealth. Francis, in the middle of at least a hundred other lost souls, stands in the centre of the bridge, suspended between one shore and the other, where the waters of the Canal merge with those of the River Irwell, dividing Salford from Manchester, watching the ship sail by, on which sailors of all nations can dimly be seen clambering from crate to crate, deck stacked upon deck. One of them hoists the familiar flag of the red oval, with the letters 'ML' in the centre, against a white background, on a pole beside the red and black striped funnel, signifying that this is a Manchester Liners ship, and around him several of the crowds corralled on the bridge raise a cheer. The sailor, hearing this, turns towards them, acknowledging them with a wave and a salute. Francis, caught up in the mood, despite the rain, raises his hat and waves back.

Moments like this, stories of the folk around him, standing as one as the bridge slowly glides back, these are what he wants the new radio to capture. How many of them, he wonders, listen to their play-it-safe broadcasts each evening. Hardly any, he thinks. And why would they? He turns his attention back towards the ship, already disappearing into the fog and the rain. He glimpses an antenna on one of the masts, for receiving telegraph communications, no doubt, in Morse code, warnings of storms or gales from the Meteorological Office. Why shouldn't they broadcast those shipping forecasts from the BBC? Anything, in fact, that was relevant or necessary for all kinds of people in all walks of life, or, he thinks, looking around him once more at the shuttered faces of his fellow bridge dwellers, all drawn into their own private worlds, something to divert, something to unify, something to lift their downcast eyes up and away from the ground?

The bridge reconnects to dry land with a jolt and all the pedestrians troop off silently and separately. Francis lingers a while longer. From this vantage point he can gaze down, through the metal cage of the bridge's outer structure, towards Pomona Docks. The whole of the Port of Manchester lies spread out below him, and it takes his breath away. Looking down upon this great leviathan from above, the cheek by jowl jostling of ship and tug, barge and scow, wagon and cart, crane and chute, swarmed over by this teeming, restless mass of humanity, Francis can see deep into the heart of the hive. From this height the bees tumble and writhe as a single entity, with no individual distinguishable one from another, all of them toiling towards a common purpose, to service the needs of the giant unseen queen, hidden from sight in the centre. He looks long and hard for her. As his eyes grow more accustomed to the scene, he begins to take note of certain details. The sparks of light from the welder's torch, radiating in a wide Catherine wheel arc, illuminate, just for an instant, a glimpse of her, her massive form convulsing as she gives birth to yet more slaves to feed her. But here and there, bubbling up from the groaning, heaving earth, he catches the strain of a different song, coming up for air, yearning, striving, for that one small piece of something it can call its own.

It is not unlike when he tries to tune his own receiver, to cast his net upon the vast emptiness of space, to capture strangers' voices, to summon music from the spheres, to somehow trawl through all the static and, from it, unscramble meaning. He believes it's something that everyone shares, this primal instinct we all of us have, to feel we are not alone, all of us wanting to be heard, to listen, to be a part of something, and connect, before we are sucked back down into that ever churning mud and slime.

Respice finem.

Consider the end.

Consider the consequences of one's actions.

Francis is thinking of another *Leviathan*. The one by Thomas Hobbes. Lent to him by Charles. Which Francis has been reading avidly.

"*Look upon what you would have, as the thing that directs all your thoughts in the way to attain it…*"

That has been his creed, one whose consequences he has not much considered. He is filled with a rush of doubt – he, who has been so certain all these years, driven by this need to make a name for himself and leave his mark upon the land – but now he wonders whether after all he hasn't merely been tinkering around the edges, fiddling while the city burns. Bread and circuses. That appears to be the sum total of his achievements thus far. There has to be more to it than this, surely? A news bulletin and a weather forecast?

He turns his attention back to thoughts of Hobbes. When Charles first lent him the copy he was immediately struck by the power of the image on the frontispiece, designed by Hobbes himself, which depicts the Leviathan as a gigantic, monstrous head made up entirely of writhing, tumbling human bodies. Not unlike the vision he has just witnessed in the Port of Manchester. When he first saw the image, his first, mistaken thought was that the bodies were rats, like the tangled knots of them he once saw pouring out of the sewers on one of his other night time ramblings, pursuing a common, unseen purpose, the instinct for escape, survival, resettlement. But he was wrong of course. These jumbled, falling figures are all contained, confined within the outlines and borders of a giant human form. The Leviathan. Built from the bodies of its citizens. A benign sovereign as its head. The Commonwealth. For Hobbes it is a metaphor for the perfect form of government. Humankind, he argues, is by definition materialist, acting entirely out of self-interest, inherently violent and awash with fear. It longs for peace but requires a form of strong, centralised government to bring this about. The Leviathan.

But Francis is troubled by this. He knows from his parents' Jewish traditions that "leviathan" is a word of Hebrew origins, meaning a monster, while in the Bible it is used to describe a sea creature rising from the deep and threatening to swallow the world. He can't get past these contradictions. In his conversations with Charles, he detects his friend's predilection for pronouncements of certainty, and he has at times envied that sense of surefootedness, with no room for caution or doubt. But as he reads more of Hobbes, he keeps tripping up.

"We need a strong hand at the tiller," argues Charles, "to guide us safely through the storms. There are too many damned committees in my opinion," he rails.

No doubt, smiles Francis at such moments, he is referring to the hospital, which never appears to move as quickly as Charles would like it to when it comes to implementing the latest innovations.

"I'd sweep the whole lot aside, if I had my way," he declares, usually after his second of third brandy, "knock the entire edifice down and start again."

Such immoderation usually occurs, Francis notes, if Charles has suffered a setback in his pursuit of Delphine, who seems to have his measure, which is more than can be said for myself, muses Francis, when lying awake at night, and picking up Hobbes once more. Why does he keep returning to it, he asks himself? Perhaps the answer lies partly in the notion of a common wealth, shared equally for the good of all? At first he hears only the echo of Charles in what he reads, raging against the chaos that must surely ensue without firm control.

"There is no place for Industry; because the fruit thereof is uncertain; and consequently no Culture of the Earth; no Navigation, nor use of the Commodities that may be imported by Sea; and the Life of Man solitary, poor, nasty, brutish and short..."

But then he reads on.

"For by Art is created that great Leviathan called a Commonwealth..."

By Art.

And this gives Francis renewed hope. Is not this what he is trying to achieve, in his own minor way, through his modest tinkering?

Respice finem.

Consider the end.

Consider the consequences of one's actions.

"That is to say, in all your actions, look upon what you would have, as the thing that directs all your thoughts, in the way to attain it..."

He recalls the cautionary words from Professor Einstein's lecture – isolated empiricism – and vows to try and live up to them, to be less impatient, both with himself and with others, as he plunges down the stone steps from the Swing Bridge into the vortex of wharves and basins below.

He crosses the footbridge over the Irwell via Woden

Street, from where he dives into the maze of back streets and alleyways, which allow him to detach himself from the main flow of human traffic, to cut through more quickly towards the city centre. He takes lesser known roads all named with a link to the history of the canals, Ellesmere Street, Worsley Street, Bridgwater Street and Egerton Road. Edging along a short, unculverted section of the River Medlock, he has now succeeded in losing most of the crowds completely, hardly surprisingly given the stink rising from the sluggish, clogged river bed below him. He skirts around the back of the Campfield Market Hall on Tonman Street, locked for the night, disturbing a family of rats rummaging their way through the scraps and leftovers of vegetable peelings trodden down into the mud by the day's trade. He winds his way past the edge of the old Roman fort at Castlefield, past a row of railway arches, beneath a grid of bridges carrying trains into the city from the south and the west. The yards behind are shut for the night. The coal cellars, smithies, brick works and tanneries lie in shadow, each arch now colonised by the nightly parade of prostitutes, marking out their territory, who, when they see that it's Francis, relax, bid him goodnight, ask for a light. He's well known to them, not as a customer – they know his interests lie elsewhere – but as a familiar sight, routinely pounding the pavements. He winds his way through to Ponchfield Square, behind John Street, where the first skirmishes of the Civil War took place, but which now house offices of solicitors and accountants, a short detour down Artillery Street, before emerging at last onto Deansgate, whose pavements are thick with pedestrians idly milling around the various public houses, all doing a brisk trade, *The Sawyer's Arms, The Old Nag's Head, The Briton's Protection*. Francis passes all of these. He turns down John Dalton Street, observes the queues already forming outside the Unitarian Chapel on the corner of Cross Street, the homeless, standing in the rain till the doors open for Bible Class and free soup. The men huddle together for warmth, repeatedly patting their arms around their backs to keep out the cold, trying to form as small a surface area as they can, so that as little rain as possible will fall upon them. They spit and curse, but then become as meek and biddable as lambs, as two women, one middle-aged, one younger, stand on the Chapel steps to invite them in – "Thank you, Mrs Wright," the men all say as they troop past, "God bless you," respectfully raising a finger to their foreheads – just as the deep, sonorous tones of Great Abel, in the Clock Tower of the Town Hall on the adjoining Albert Square, ring out over the city. Francis looks up at the clock. Half past eight. Starlings roost on the ledges of the city's civic buildings, sheltering from the rain, which continues to fall. Francis passes the Italian Palazzo that is *The Athenaeum* on the corner of Princess Street and Mosley Street, where a row of chandeliers shining through its nine long windowed façade beneath their rusticated quoins reveals men in dinner suits seated round a table with glasses of port, smoking cigars, animatedly gesturing. Francis wonders idly what they might be discussing, what great ideas they are debating, what great cultural decisions are being taken. Charles has proposed him as a member. Perhaps, in a few weeks time, he too might be sitting round that same table, inviting them to hold one of their meetings for a future live radio broadcast. He turns left into George Street, then right onto Charlotte Street, passing the Chinese laundries, before ducking into Pine Street, then squeezing along Chain Street, eventually arriving at the south-west corner of the recently laid out Piccadilly Gardens, from land cleared by the demolition of the old Infirmary. A young man asks if he might have a cigarette. Francis pauses, considers whether he might, flips open his cigarette case and offers him one, which the young man lights sulkily. The light of the match catches for a moment the inscription on the inside of the case. "*Consider the end. Consider the consequences of your actions."*

No, thinks, Francis. Not this evening. The rain is falling harder, He walks on.

As he reaches the far corner of the Gardens, just where they open out onto Portland Street, his attention is caught by a sound emanating from inside *The Queen's Hotel*, a few yards from where he is standing. A jazz band is playing, its rhythms syncopated and intoxicating. A woman begins to sing. At that moment the door opens and the sounds are suddenly louder. Francis hesitates. The man coming through the door notices him. It is the Head Porter, stepping outside for a breath of air and a sly smoke. He sees Francis havering.

"Would the young gentleman like to come inside out of the wet?" His accent is a thick Italian. On the lapel of his uniform, a deep crimson with gold épaulettes, is a small badge, declaring him to be *Luigi Locartelli, Queen's Hotel*. He gestures theatrically with his right hand, indicating the light and warmth and music to be found inside.

Francis climbs the flight of six stone steps towards the hotel door, then pauses once again, just as he is on the threshold.

"*Avanti*," invites Luigi.

Why not, thinks Francis, as he passes with a single step from one world into another, handing Luigi his completely sodden overcoat and hat.

"*Grazie,* Signor," smiles Luigi, putting out his cigarette, now all brisk and efficient. "You will not, I think, be disappointed…"

But Francis is no longer listening. Instead he is drawn by the music towards the crowded lounge. A young woman has just finished singing. The people applaud warmly. There is something of the cabal here, thinks Francis, an exclusive gathering for *aficionados* and *cognoscenti* only. Luigi shows him to a seat near the back, asks him what he would like to drink.

"What do you recommend?" asks Francis.

"A sazerac, Signor. Do you know it? "

Francis shakes his head.

"Three dashes of Peychaud's bitters, one and a half ounces of rye whiskey, a quarter of absinthe, and a sugar cube."

Francis nods and Luigi snaps his fingers towards the bartender.

The trumpeter from the band steps forward to the microphone. "Will you please show your appreciation once more for Manchester's best kept secret, Mademoiselle Chamomile Catch?"

"*Merci, tout le monde,*" whispers Cam, so quietly that Francis has to lean forward in his seat to hear what she is saying. "This next song I'm going to sing is one my *Maman* taught me. She first learned it as a child in Louisiana before she came to Manchester. It's a sad kind of love song. The singer, she says, 'I passed by your door. I called out, Hey, Beautiful? But nobody answered. *Oh-Yé-Yaille*, my heart is aching. When I looked inside, I saw a candle burning. *Oh-Yé-Yaille*, my heart is aching'. I hope you enjoy it."

She turns back towards the band and counts them in. "*Un, deux, un-deux-trois-quatre,*" then launches into the song with a voice so strong and sassy, Francis is hard put to believe it is the same woman who has just finished speaking so demurely. She has long, dark hair which hangs in thick, braided ropes. Tucked behind one ear she wears a large white feather to match her tightly fitting white dress, which sets off her honey-chocolate skin to perfection. To one side of the stage Francis notices a classily designed billboard on an easel, announcing *'Louis Mitchell's Jazz Kings, featuring Chamomile Catch'*. Over Cam's name is a drawing of a white egret in flight. As she sings, Francis's heart soars with her.

"J'ai passé devant ta porte
J'ai crié bye bye à la belle
Y'a personne qui m'a pas répondu
Oh-Yé-Yaille mon cœur fais mal

Moi j'm'ai mis à observer
Moi j'ai vue des lumières allumés
Y'a quelque chose qui m'disait j'devrais pleurer
Oh-Yé-Yaille mon cœur fais mal..."

As Cam takes her final bow, Francis recalls what Daniel Godfrey Jnr said to him barely three hours ago as he left the Metro-Vicks Studio.

"You track em, I'll transmit 'em."

Francis catches Luigi's eye.

"Same again?" he enquires.

Francis nods. "Yes, and whatever the lady's having. Please ask her if she will be so kind as to join me. I have a proposition for her, which may interest her," and he hands Luigi his card. Manchester's "best kept secret" might just about to be introduced to a much wider audience.

Mlle Chamomile Catch
Chanteuse
The Manchester Songbird

Printed by F.G. Wright & Son

*

Luigi has worked at *The Queen's Hotel* for twelve years. He's been Head Porter for the past seven. He feels part of the furniture, as much a part of the fixtures and fittings as the tank in one of the basement rooms where the live turtles are kept until they are needed for soup. Returning customers ask for him by name. He makes it a matter of pride to ensure that he knows the needs of each and every one of them before they have to ask: which of them requires a fine claret to be waiting for them when they arrive; who prefers to have their eiderdown turned back before they retire; at what time the gentleman in Room 201 will require his morning coffee; which newspapers are to be ordered; who is not to be disturbed before midday; which doors must not be opened, even after having knocked, until several seconds have elapsed to allow the Ambassador for Ecuador's 'guest' to have made herself scarce. Luigi runs the tightest of tight ships. He likes to keep the rest of the staff on their toes. Luigi will know who is occupying every single room at any given time without recourse to the hotel's guest register, and he requires his staff to know likewise. When he rings his bell on the counter at the front desk, he expects his bellhops to hop. Just as he had had to do when he first started, thirty-five years ago at *The Royal Pomona Palace Hotel*, which was blown up by the explosion at the nearby chemicals factory on his very first day.

He'd been lucky to survive, protected from the hailstorm of shattered glass by his Uncle Iacopo, who'd also survived, but who'd never been able to work again afterwards because of the injuries he sustained. Mr James Reilly, the hotel's owner, had put in a word for all his staff with his business contacts across the city, and Luigi soon found employment, again as a bellhop, at *The Seymour Hotel* in Stretford. But this was a shabby affair, mostly inhabited by long term residents, who resembled in Luigi's imagination macabre stuffed animals, covered in cobwebs, who mouldered away along with the faded carpets and threadbare curtains.

He quickly moved from there to *The Grosvenor*, a corner building a mere stone's throw away from Manchester Cathedral, alongside Victoria Bridge and the Irwell which, when its muddy waters rose in winter, frequently flooded the hotel's cellars. There he worked as a Night Porter – being close to Victoria and Exchange Stations, the hotel was convenient and popular with commercial travellers – and it was there Luigi learned the need for, and the art of, discretion, for these commercial travellers were frequently lonely, a fact not unknown to the painted girls who haunted the hotel lobby after darkness fell. Strictly speaking, Luigi was not meant to allow these nightly visitors admittance, but his guests would reward his ability to look the other way when required with generosity and gratitude.

But when an opportunity arose to join the staff at *The Midland*, the year the hotel opened in 1903, close to Central Station, on the site of an old house owned by a Mr Thomas Cooper, from a long-standing family of coach makers, with gardens that were famous for their strawberries, gooseberries, apples and flowers, he accepted with alacrity. It was by far the city's grandest establishment and reminded Luigi of the awe he had felt fifteen years before, on his first day at *The Royal Pomona Palace*. It was not a promotion – he was back to being just one of a team of porters, who manned the hotel twenty-fours a day, seven days a week – but he had the sense to recognise that his future career prospects could only be enhanced by the experience of working in such an internationally prestigious establishment.

Those were the early golden days of *The Midland*. It was Luigi who had served Messrs Rolls and Royce their coffee when they had met to dream up their first automobile together in the hotel's lounge the following year. It was in this lounge where Manchester's cotton traders would meet each week to make their deals with the city's wealthy mill owners over lunch, at what was nicknamed The Colony, and it was here where Miss Horniman would hold court when she first arrived from Dublin to set up the country's only permanent repertory theatre company. It was during those early years that Luigi discovered he had both the taste and talent for dealing with the particular peccadilloes of the city's growing Bohemian clique. Through them he came to learn that it was *The Queen's Hotel*, on the corner of Piccadilly and Portland Street, which served as the true epicentre for Manchester's artistic élite, and so, when he heard on the grapevine that the post of Deputy Head Porter was available, to the right kind of applicant, someone with not only the experience, but the requisite qualities of discretion, allied to a keen understanding of the especial needs of clients with more colourful tastes, more creative preferences to be catered for, he let it be known, discreetly, that he might be interested. An informal interview was arranged, an offer was made, and Luigi, after a period of due consideration, responded that yes, this was something he might be prepared to accept.

That was in 1912.

Five years later, when Alfonso, the incumbent Head Porter, who just happened to be a second cousin, passed away, Luigi was deemed ready to step into what were literally dead man's shoes. Since when he had not looked back.

He had missed the war, being, at forty-one in 1916, when The Military Service Act was passed, bringing in compulsory conscription, just too old. But the same was unfortunately not the case for his younger brother, Marco, who went to the Front as soon as war broke out, but who did not return, leaving behind a wife and two young children. Instead Luigi had been able to stay at *The Queen's* and establish his kingdom. In addition to attracting the underground artists, the hotel also served as a magnet for visiting dignitaries from across the world. As well as ambassadors, diplomats and sheiks, even princes were regular visitors, not to mention wealthy merchants and businessmen from all over Europe, drawn to Manchester, all of them wanting a taste of a fruit that might be forbidden in cities closer to heir homes.

And so *The Queen's Hotel* thrived, and Luigi along with it.

It was not that he made much money. Money did not interest him. His pleasure came from knowing that his clients – and Luigi preferred to think of them as *his* clients, rather than the hotel's – had everything they needed, and that he had anticipated these even before they had themselves. Nothing gave him greater pleasure than when a returning customer would bid him 'Good morning', ask for him by name, enquire after his wife and children, knowing that, when they reached their room, everything would be exactly as they wanted it to be, without them having to say a word.

He especially liked the hotel late at night, after the bars had closed, after the musicians had stopped playing, after those locals in the know, those non-residents who merely frequented the hotel to listen to the jazz, meet with their like-minded cronies, had left, and after the guests had all retired to their rooms, when he would patrol the corridors of every floor, walk up and down the wide staircases, running his hand with a deep, sensuous pleasure along the polished wood of the mahogany banisters, and pad silently through the hushed hallways, his silent, rubber-soled shoes sinking luxuriously into the deep pile carpets. It was at such times he felt as though the hotel belonged to him, that it was his domain, through which he could move silently, unseen, like a cat marking out his territory, his eyes aglow in its deeper shadows. He knew every inch of it and could have walked it all blindfold, his other senses minutely attuned to the slightest modification in atmosphere, which only he might detect, like tuning a radio station to pick up a previously undiscovered signal.

No – Luigi's wealth lay not in money, but in secrets, of which he had many, stored for safe keeping in the farthest recesses of his brain, like the safe deposit box that was locked behind his desk in the hotel's lobby, to which only he had the key.

*

On his second day at Hulme's Grammar School George is invited by Mr Vogts, his Anglo-German English master, to write a composition.

"I would like each of you to tell me something about yourself – who you are, where you live, what your hobbies are, what you might like to be when you leave school – so that I can get to know you just a little and learn how I might be of assistance."

Dutifully eager to please, George takes out the new maroon Sheaffer self-filling fountain pen bought for him from a shop in King Street as a present by his grandfather Frank for passing the entrance examination, and begins to write. He does not stop until the bell goes for the end of the lesson.

My name is George Wright. I am eleven years and four months old. I live at Number Twelve, Cromwell Avenue, Manley Park, Whalley Range, Manchester, Lancashire, England, Great Britain, Europe, The World. We have only just moved there. My mother wanted us to live near enough to the school so that I could walk to and from it every day. Manley Park is named after a large Hall that used to stand there. It was built for a Mr Samuel Mendel, who was known as The Merchant King of Manchester. Buffalo Bill once brought his Wild West Show there. I wish I could have seen it. But the house was pulled down in 1905 to make space for new houses, like the one I am living in now. I have only been living there a few weeks and so I haven't had a chance to explore much yet. I like exploring. I think that would be a very exciting thing to do when I am older. The other things I should like to do are, riding a motor cycle and becoming an artist. I love to draw and paint. I'm not very good yet but as my mother always says, "Practice makes perfect," and so I practise very hard. What I like to draw best are parts of the engine of my father's motor car. It's a Crossley Phaeton. Made here in Manchester. In Gorton. Every Sunday he strips it down. He takes out the spark plugs, wipes them clean with a rag, polishes them with something from a tin called Brasso, then carefully puts them back. Sometimes he lets me help him. I like using the spanner best. Father says, "I'm a natural." "But a natural what?" says Mother and she laughs. I think this is one of her jokes. I like jokes but I don't understand this one. When my father cleans the engine, he lays out all the pieces separately on his work bench and I try to draw them. I like the way things are made. I like to take them apart and then see how they all fit together again. "Nuts and bolts," says my piano teacher. Her name is Mrs Tiffin. She is very kind and I like her very much, but now that we have moved house, I may not be able to carry on with my lessons. "We shall have to wait and see," my mother says.

I am crossing my fingers that I can. In the meantime I will practise my scales on the piano in the front room of our new house. These are what Mrs Tiffin calls the nuts and bolts of the piano. I have lived in three houses now. The first one was quite small but I liked it. It was across the road from the Printing Works owned by my grandfather where my father went to work each day. But the noise of the machines was so loud, like bombs, it made him ill, so Mother said we had to move. He is better now. Our second house was much bigger. It was near the University on a road called Daisy Bank Road, but it didn't have a bank, and I never saw any daisies. There were rows of trees along each side. Father said it was more like an Avenue. When I was ten, I helped him to make a crystal radio set. We listened to music on it together. I drew lots of pictures of it. Now we have a proper radio. It's more modern, Mother says. It's called an RCA Westinghouse and we bought it from a shop in Denton. Mother says I am not to try to take this one apart because it cost a lot of money. But I would be very careful. I like the shop where we bought it. It has a large sign above it of a pair of giant spectacles with staring eyes that never close. I drew a picture of those after we got home. Mother says, "Why don't I draw pictures of things people would like to see?" "Like what?" I ask. "Oh, I don't know," she says, "flowers, trees, people, views…" I try to, but it's very hard. The thing is, when I look at a person, sitting on a bench or walking down a street, I can't help thinking about their skeletons, all of their bones and muscles, what we're all of us like under our skins. That's what I want to draw most, what's underneath everything, below the surface, the nuts and bolts of things, like Mrs Tiffin says. I suppose that's a bit like being an explorer too. Father says there are cameras in hospitals that can take photographs like that. They're called X rays. Perhaps cameras are better than pencils for showing what things are really like. It all depends, my father says, but when I ask him on what, he doesn't answer. He just says, "Try not to be in such a hurry all the time." But I like being in a hurry. That's why I want to ride a motor cycle when I'm older, as fast as I can.

At the bottom of the page Mr Vogts has written: "Thank you for such an interesting composition, George. Well done. I should very much like to see one of your drawings. Perhaps you could bring them along to school one day? Try to remember in future to use paragraphs."

*

On a Saturday morning, less than a fortnight before his thirteenth birthday, George comes downstairs to find a small envelope propped up against the tea pot on the kitchen table. On it he recognises his mother's handwriting spelling out his name, followed by the words, "Open me."

Not requiring a second invitation, George tears it open at once. From inside a small ticket flops out in front of him. Curious, George picks it up and reads.

Manchester Society of Modern Painters

INAUGURAL Exhibition
Blackfriars Street Gallery

featuring new work by

Iain Grant Karl Hagerdon Annie Swynnerton
L.S. Lowry
Margaret Nicholls Peter O'Brien Edgar Rowley Smart
Adolphe Valette

Private View 1st May 1926 at 6pm
Admit One

Printed by F.G. Wright & Son

Later that evening, George is hopping from one foot to the other in frustration as he and his father have to wait for his mother to be ready. Hubert merely sits in his armchair, patiently reading the latest book he has borrowed from the library on Lever's Row, *A Treatise on Cosmic Fire* by Alice Bailey.

"We're going to be late," wails George in increasing distress. "How can you keep reading like that?"

"You know your mother, George. She can't be hurried. She'll be ready when she's ready. I'm just making the best use of the time meanwhile." He smiles, holding up the book. "I knew the author. She used to live in Manchester, close to us in Bignor Street. That was before she went to America of course. She was Alice Bateman still then."

But George is not listening. He can't bear it a moment longer. He hurries into the hallway and calls upstairs.

"Mother?"

No answer.

George returns to the lounge, where Hubert is still

reading. "Actually, I think you'd find this interesting too. Not the book itself, it's quite heavy going, but what it's about."

George slumps down on the sofa as Hubert continues.

"Theosophy is a belief which places its faith in things which are unseen. A number of modern artists subscribe to it. They don't want to paint pictures that are familiar, or even life-like, preferring instead to try and show what's underneath what's right in front of us. I wonder if any of the painters in the exhibition tonight are theosophists."

"If we ever get there," sighs George.

Hubert chuckles quietly to himself.

"I hope not," says Annie as she walks into the room. "I like to be able to recognise what I'm looking at in a painting. Well? Are you two ready? What are we waiting for?"

"It's almost six already," moans George. "It'll all be over by the time we get there."

"Nonsense, George. These things always start after they say they're going to. It doesn't do to arrive early. We shall arrive fashionably late."

"Madam," says Hubert, offering his arm, "your carriage – or should I say, your Phaeton – awaits."

"Why thank you, sir," she replies, "but I believe I am already spoken for this evening. I have a prior arrangement with a young man celebrating an early birthday," and she links her own arm not through Hubert's, but George's.

"Mum," says George, embarrassed. "I hope you're not going to be like this all evening."

When, half an hour later, having parked the Phaeton on nearby St Mary's Gate, they climb the iron staircase to the Gallery on Blackfriars Street, Annie is proved right. The Private View has hardly begun and, although they are not the first to arrive, the rooms are still not full, and so there is plenty of space for them to view the paintings, before the main crowd shows up. Annie makes a beeline for the Margaret Nicholls, whose paintings depict a series of flowers in vases, from when they are newly picked, still glistening with dew, to the final ones when they are in a state of irreversible decay, petals drying and falling onto white linen tablecloths, where they slowly wither and curl, while Hubert meticulously studies the larger canvases of Rowley Smart, allotting the same amount of time to each, with their muted grey abstractions of industrial landscapes, bold geometric shapes and their absence of people.

George is immediately drawn towards Lowry, as indeed are most of the viewers. George gets as close to them as he can, his nose pressed as near to the canvases as he dares. His eyes dart across the surface, following the many different characters and stories he discovers there. At first glance all the people look the same, heads down, bodies bent forward, an anonymous mass of downtrodden humanity, dwarfed by the giant factory chimneys looming over them, belching smoke and fumes. But the closer he looks, the more he realises this is not the case. He begins to recognise different individuals, several of them turning up in separate paintings, people whom Lowry must see every day on his own travels across the city. A balloon seller, a man playing a barrel organ, children with a skipping rope, a mother pushing a pram, an older woman with a shawl wrapped tightly round her head, a dog barking, a drunk lurching unsteadily towards a lamp post, a policeman eyeing him closely, a man with a bowler hat and an umbrella lying on his back on the top of a low wall looking as though he is dreaming with a smile upon his face, and a disturbing figure in black, a woman without a face, her head covered in what might be a shroud.

George is completely absorbed, caught up in this ceaseless river of stories. Now, when he steps back from each painting, although the figures recede, subsumed within the overall impression of a crowded street, because he has looked more closely, he can still carry with him in his head the myriad of dramas all playing out simultaneously beneath what appear to be permanently heavy skies. Yet George does not find these pictures gloomy, as so many of the other spectators all around him appear to do. Sparks and splashes of colour ping out to him from within the overall tones of greys and browns, the red of a young woman's dress, the yellow of a tied balloon, the blue of the police constable's jacket.

"Such miserable paintings," he hears people say.

"I wouldn't want them on *my* wall."

"A child of five could do better."

"An insult to Manchester."

"The figures look more like matchsticks than real people."

George feels a light tap on his shoulder. He turns around and is surprised to see his English master from school, Mr Vogts.

"Well, George, do you agree with the general condemnation?"

"Oh no, sir. I think they're wonderful."

"Really? I'm surprised."

"Sir?"

"From what you wrote in your composition, I'd have thought they were not anatomical enough for you. Aren't you more interested in seeing beneath the surface of things?"

"Yes, sir, but…"

"Are these paintings anything more than superficial cartoons? The people in them don't even cast a shadow."

"I think so, sir, yes."

"Indeed? Explain them to me then, for their merits appear to have passed me by."

"Well, sir, let's start with those shadows, or lack of them. I think…"

"Yes…?"

"I think that the reason they cast no shadows is because Mr Lowry is wanting us to think we're all of us really small, that we don't matter that much, not even enough to leave a shadow behind us after we've gone. But that's only to begin with. Because when we look closer we see that we're not all the same at all, but that we're all of us different, unique, with our own story to tell. He makes us wonder just what those stories might be."

"I couldn't have put that better myself." This is not Mr Vogts speaking, but a different voice. George turns and finds himself staring at the waistcoat of a very tall man, so tall he has to look up to see his face, which has a large nose, small, round, recessed eyes beneath eyebrows that are so fair that at first George wonders if he has any at all, and a wide mouth which, although smiling just now, looks as though it is not normally accustomed to such an expression.

"Let me introduce you," says an amused Mr Vogts. "George, this is Mr Laurence Stephen Lowry. Mr Lowry, this is George Wright, a pupil of mine at Hulme's Grammar School."

"I'm very pleased to meet you, George," says Lowry, stooping down to shake his hand, which he pumps so vigorously George fears it might drop off. "Let's go where it's a little quieter, so that you and I can have a little talk." He leads George over to a corner of the gallery where there are fewer people, near one of Adolphe Valette's magnificent Manchester-scapes. "Now here's the real painter among us all. Taught me everything. At least he tried to. I can't say I've put all his teaching to much use yet."

George looks at the painting. "I think I prefer yours, Mr Lowry."

"Well – that's very kind of you to say so, my boy, but just look at the way he applies paint, suggesting so much with apparently so little."

"Where did you learn to be an artist, sir?"

"I'm still learning, George, and I doubt I shall ever stop. But if you mean, did I go to an art school? Then the answer is yes. *The Mechanics' Institute. The Royal Technical College* in Salford, to give it its proper title. Opposite Peel Park. And Monsieur Valette here," he indicates the painting beside them once more, "was one of my teachers."

George nods seriously. "I should like to be an artist one day."

Before he replies, Lowry regards the young boy looking up at him so eagerly. He knows he's probably going to remember whatever words come out of his mouth next for the rest of his life, especially if he's serious about becoming an artist, which Lowry believes he absolutely is. Best keep it simple then. "Let me give you three pieces of advice."

George's eyes are on stalks.

"First, whenever you possibly can, paint from life. Out in the streets, whatever the weather. Take a sketch book with you wherever you go, then, if you've got a spare five minutes, take it out and simply draw whatever you see, whatever's in front of you. You've got to breathe the same air, do you see?"

George nods, taking this all in.

"Second, be true to yourself, no matter what other folk around you might say. You can't please everyone, so don't even try. Just stay true to yourself."

"Yes, Mr Lowry."

"And third – and this is the most important piece of all, though you'll not think so after I've said it – find yourself a proper job."

"Isn't an artist a proper job, sir?"

"No, lad, it isn't. It should be, but most people have such high and mighty notions about beauty and art being above the everyday that, if you're not careful, you can become quite cut off from the world, so how can you then truthfully paint something you're no longer a part of? No, you've got to have a proper job, something that keeps your feet on the ground, keeps you connected to your fellow man."

"Do you have a proper job, Mr Lowry?"

"Ay, lad. I do. I'm a rent collector. I pound the same streets I grew up in as a boy. People know me. They trust me. That counts for something."

"Yes, sir. Thank you, sir."

Half an hour later, when the Gallery is so crowded that it is no longer possible to look at any of the paintings properly, Hubert finds George and suggests that, as soon as Annie has finished speaking with the person she is currently so earnestly engaged in conversation with, they should head home. George agrees. He is still going over in his mind the advice from Mr Lowry. He feels set on a path already and is quietly excited. What might be his own proper job, he wonders? A printer, like his father? Or something else not yet dreamed of?

In the melee he notices a young man juggling various pieces of electrical equipment – a microphone, an amplifier, a compressor, a turntable onto which he is placing a wax disc. George points him out to Hubert. "What's he doing?"

"Yes. I spoke to him earlier. He's interviewing some of the people here and recording them for broadcast later on *Radio 2ZY*."

"Will you be on the radio, Father?"

"I don't know, son. We'll have to tune in later to find out, won't we?"

George looks back. What he is drawn to even more than all the equipment the young man is setting up is his actual appearance. George doesn't think he has ever seen anyone quite like him before. His hair is so fair as to be almost white. His skin, too, is translucent, like a piece of paper when you hold it up to the light. His eyes are the palest blue George has ever seen, a kind of watery starlight.

Annie returns to them just at that moment. "Are we ready to go now?"

"I think so," says Hubert.

"George? Seen enough?"

George nods, still trying to observe the pale man discreetly.

"Well," says Annie, "this day just gets better and better. You'll never guess who I've just been talking to?"

George and Hubert turn towards her waiting.

"Only Monsieur Adolphe Valette himself." She indicates a thin man with a dark beard, coughing into a handkerchief. "He's retired from teaching now, but he still gives occasional private lessons…"

George's senses are suddenly on high alert. He looks in disbelief towards his mother.

"Yes, George. He's agreed to give you one lesson, to see if you show promise, and if you do, well – who knows…?"

George wants to fling his arms around her, but given the public space they still occupy in the crowded gallery, he merely whispers, as intently as he can, "Thank you, Mother."

Francis is trying to capture as many responses as he can from different members of the public to the exhibition, but his equipment, state of the art though it is, is still too cumbersome for the kind of *vox populi* he has imagined. Already his mind is turning to possible tweaks and adjustments, further modifications he might make so that next time…

He is pulled up from his day dreaming by the Anglo-German schoolmaster he has just finished interviewing, who is tugging gently at his sleeve.

"That's the boy," says Mr Vogts, pointing to George's receding back as he heads towards the exit. "His understanding of Lowry's painting, though obviously intuitive and naïve, showed remarkable insight."

Frances watches him finally disappear. "Too late, I'm afraid," he says to the schoolmaster. "This equipment is not as fleet of foot as I would like."

"No matter, says Mr Vogts. "There will be other chances, I'm sure."

George looks out of the car window as his father drives them home through the city centre, still musing on the words of advice from Mr Lowry. "A proper job, a proper job…"

Outside, as the car heads down Deansgate, before it will turn off into the Chorlton Road, George notices angry crowds of people, marching towards them, carrying placards and chanting. His father turns sharply left onto Peter Street instead to avoid them. There are even larger crowds massing in St Peter's Square, and Hubert has to weave his way carefully between them. Some of them slam their open hands angrily on the car's bonnet, or shake their fists at them through the windscreen, venting their fury at this symbol of wealth and privilege. Hubert and Annie stare, white-faced, beyond them, wishing themselves elsewhere, casting no shadows.

*

Thomas-à-Tattimus took two T's
To tie two tups to two tall trees
To frighten the terrible Thomas-à-Tattimus
How many T's are there in all that?

*

12 DAYS IN MAY

Screenplay for a Silent Film

1.

In white lettering against a black screen the following text scrolls up.

During The Great War the country's mining companies had been placed under government control. When the War ended the Miners' Federation pressed for complete nationalisation, calling for a national strike in February 1919. Following promises by Lloyd George's Coalition to hold a Royal Commission into the future of the coal industry, the strike was averted. The Commission recommended nationalization, but on 31st March 1921 the Government reneged on its agreement and handed back the mines to their owners. The very next day the miners were locked out, after refusing to accept immediately imposed harsher working conditions. Other unions promised to take action in support of the miners, but at the last minute called it off. After three months on strike the miners were forced to accept the owners' terms and return to work.

Four years later, in June 1925, faced with a declining economic outlook, the owners gave notice of their intention to reduce wages and increase hours from 31st July. On 10th July the General Council of the TUC met a delegation from the Miners' Federation and pledged their support, promising an embargo on the movement of coal anywhere in Great Britain should the miners be locked out. In the ensuing fortnight meetings between the owners, the miners and the TUC failed to reach an agreement, and at 4pm on 31st July Prime Minister

Stanley Baldwin announced to a tense House of Commons that the Government would subsidise the miners' shortfall until 1st May 1926. In the meantime a second Royal Commission would be set up to report on the future of the industry.

The following March the Commission produced its report. It came out against nationalisation. It recommended the withdrawal of the Government subsidy. And it endorsed the owners' decision to cut wages and increase hours.

On 30th April 1926 the coal owners locked out the miners.

2. EXT. WIDE ANGLED SHOT
Bradford Colliery in the East of Manchester.
Superimposed upon the scene are the words:

Day 1:
Saturday 1st May

The gates are padlocked. The yard is deserted. The pithead wheel is not turning. Police officers with Alsatian dogs patrol the perimeter. Rain is falling. A cold wind is blowing. In the distance children can be seen scavenging, with prams they push up against the mountains of undelivered coal, from which they take as many lumps as they can with their bare hands, before racing away as they are spotted by a police officer, who lets his dog off its leash to chase them.

3. CLOSE UP:
Notice on Fence.

```
By Order of The Association of
Mine Owners of Great Britain
```

```
Bradford Colliery is closed until
further notice
Or
Until such time as the Workers
recognise their Responsibilities
And
Accept the New Conditions of Hours
and Pay

  Signed: R. Tattershall, General Manager
```

The wind picks up and detaches the notice from the fence. The camera follows it as it blows up into the sky.

4. EXT. AERIAL SHOT:
The Colliery and its Environs.

The camera continues to follow the trajectory of the paper notice, rising up above the colliery and pulling back to reveal the grid of streets of terraced houses surrounding the pithead, until the notice begins to fall back towards the earth once more, where it lands on the cobbles of one of these streets and rolls up towards the open front door of one of the houses, where it finally comes to rest.

On the screen appear the words:

Melland Road, Gorton

A Funeral Director walks into the frame. He sees the notice brushing against the freshly donkey-stoned front step. He stoops to pick it up, briefly looks at it, then screws it up and places it in his trouser pocket, before removing his hat and heading indoors.

5. INT.
The Front Parlour of the Blundells' home.

The camera follows the Funeral Director inside the house, along the narrow hallway and then into the parlour. On top of the dining table lies an open coffin. Inside is the body of Walter Blundell. Ranged around it stand members of his family. At the head, looking down is Esther. She is not dressed in traditional funeral clothes. Instead she wears what she does every morning, simple, plain, working clothes, for she has been up since before dawn, cleaning the house and preparing everything that will be needed for the day. She is dry-eyed, stony-faced and angry.

On either side of the coffin stand Walter's sons, Esther's brothers – Harold, Frank and Jim. They are wearing their Sunday suits and look uncomfortable. HAROLD, his eyes, by contrast with his sister's, shining with tears, holds a brass cornet in his hands. He reaches down, as if about to place the cornet into the coffin, but is prevented from doing so by a sharp look from ESTHER. Instead he stands back, gripping the cornet hard between his fingers.

Around the edges of the room sit or stand the brothers' wives. Each is with a child or children, who fidget awkwardly. The youngest of them, a baby, picking up the sombre mood, begins to cry. The mother ineffectively tries to soothe her.

The FUNERAL DIRECTOR places the lid over the coffin. The screen goes dark.

Onto it are projected the words:

BLACK LUNG

6. EXT.
The Street.

Outside the rain is still falling. Despite this the street is lined with neighbours, who bow their heads as the funeral procession passes. The coffin has been placed onto a horse drawn wagon, with the words "*Co-operative Wholesale Services*" written on the side, behind which the family walks, with ESTHER at the head, defiant, alone, bare-headed. The rain runs down her face.

7. EXT.
The Procession.

The camera follows them as they make their way the mile from Melland Road to Gorton Cemetery, passing the entrance to Wembley Road, turning left onto Wayland Road, then right onto Shillingford Road, left towards the long haul of Fallowfield Loop, the crowds gradually thinning, before doubling back along the remains of the Nico Ditch, a high earthen bank, constructed as a fortification some time after the final Roman withdrawal from Manchester some fifteen hundred years before, at the end of which stand the imposing granite gateposts, flanking the Cemetery's wide wrought iron gates, which have been opened to let them through.

8. EXT.
The Cemetery.

The mourners stand around the gaping hole of the freshly dug grave, into which Walter's coffin is awkwardly lowered, hands slipping on the slimy ropes, wet from the rain. It is a family plot. Walter will be laid in the same earth as his wife, Alice, and his two sons, Arthur and Freddie, each of them lost in the War. ESTHER does not look down into it. Instead she turns away to face HAROLD, who raises the cornet to his lips, on which be begins to play a tune we cannot hear. A woman steps out of the group of mourners with an umbrella. It is Esther's friend, WINIFRED, who holds the umbrella over her. ESTHER allows herself to be led by her away from the grave.

The camera does a slow close up of the cornet, until all that can be seen is the dark hole at the centre of the horn, then blackness.

9. EXT.
May Day March, Ardwick Green

The camera emerges back out of the horn to reveal a different trumpet at the head of The Bradford Colliery Brass Band, leading out the Annual May Day March as it makes its way from Ardwick Green to Belle Vue, followed by a parade of Trade Union banners. The rain is still pouring.

Images of the march are intercut with the following caption:

Undeterred by the inclement Manchester weather, thousands of people carrying dripping banners and rain sodden umbrellas take to the streets to lend their support for the miners. Men and women in gleaming mackintoshes and wearing the red and yellow favours of the Labour Party walk shoulder to shoulder in dignity and solidarity, a splash of colour on this drab day.

10. EXT.
Belle Vue Pleasure Gardens

As the crowds march through the gates of Belle Vue Zoological and Pleasure Gardens to assemble in front of the Bandstand by The Kings Hall, close ups of their proud, determined singing faces are interspersed with separate close ups of lions roaring, tigers snarling, elephants trumpeting, a rhinoceros charging.

Onto the Bandstand steps Mr JOHN SUTTON to rousing

cheers from the marchers. He begins to make a speech. It is filled with flamboyant gestures. He spreads his arms wide. He thumps the lectern in front of him. He raises a finger and points it towards the heavens. He takes off his hat and bows before them. As he speaks, the camera moves round and behind him, looking out, from his point of view, at the sea of expectant voices below him, listening with rapt attention, hanging on his every word. The text of his speech is superimposed over these faces, scrolling upwards.

> *"You all know me. John Sutton, MP for Clayton, but before that I was a miner. There's many a face I recognise here before me today, men and boys I've stood alongside down t' Pit in years gone by, and I'm standing right beside you again today. I'm a simple man with a simple message. Those who are not with us are against us. And I urge the whole of Manchester to stand firm and strong in the coming fight..."*

The crowd applauds passionately. SUTTON continues.

> *"As I say, you all know me. A simple man with simple needs and simple pleasures. A fair day's pay for a fair day's work. And at the end of the day to go home to a roof over our heads, a fire in the grate, and food on the table, to go to church or chapel on Sundays, and listen to uplifting music. I'm reminded of such music today, as the rain falls – but are we downhearted?"*

No, cry the crowds.

> *"Are we daunted?"*

No, again the crowds cry.

"And will we be defeated?"

Another resounding 'No'.

"No indeed. And the heavens are telling us so…"

To further rapturous applause and the throwing of hats into the air, the added soundtrack on the film brings in the music of Haydn's *Oratorio: The Creation*, which the entire assembled crowds appear to be singing.

"The heavens are telling the Glory of God
The wonder of his work displays the firmament
Today that is coming, speaks it the day
The night that is gone, to following night…"

Silence. Blackness.

On the screen is written:

Day 2:
Sunday 2nd May 1926

11. MONTAGE:
Church Bells

A series of shots of Manchester church bells ringing dissolve into one another. The last of these is of the tower of the Church of St Lawrence in Denton. The camera pulls back to show the whole of Denton spread out below. The rain has stopped overnight, and a bright sun is shining, reflecting in the puddles of silent, empty streets.

12. CLOSE UP:
Blackbird in Flight

A blackbird alights in one of these puddles and shakes its feathers.

13. INT:
Winifred's Front Room

WINIFRED watches the blackbird through the half open window of her sitting room. She smiles. She breaks a crust from the piece of toast she is eating, which she tosses towards it, momentarily startling it before it pecks at it with its beak.

WINIFRED returns to the letter she is writing. VICTOR comes into the room. He is casually dressed in just a vest and trousers, the braces of which hang loose around his waist. He approaches WINIFRED and drops a kiss on the top of her head, looking over her shoulder as she continues to write.

14. CLOSE UP:
Letter from Winifred's POV

Dear Esther,

I am writing to offer you and your brothers our deepest sympathy for the loss of your father. I know how close the two of you were. I imagine you will be very busy in the coming days. There is always so much to sort out after a funeral. I remember from when my own mother died. But if you would like me to help in any way, you only have to ask. You have always been the strong one, but perhaps now I can be of some support for you, as you have always been for me in the past. I could easily come over in an evening after work. Victor has a big fight coming up and he will be training every night.

It is so quiet this morning. Nobody is out in the streets at all. It is as if we are all of us waiting to see what will happen when the strike begins officially tomorrow. As yet, we have not been called out at the Telephone Exchange and so I shall go in as normal tomorrow.

As I look out of my window writing this to you, I don't believe I have ever seen the skies so empty. The mill chimneys have ceased to smoke, and the pit wheels have ceased to turn. All over Denton, Openshaw and Gorton, Newton Heath, Clayton and Colleyhurst, the air grows clearer. The hills which ring the east of our city I can see with a rare sharpness.

Who knows what tomorrow will bring...?

Your friend,
Winifred

15. Cut To: INT.
Kitchen at Melland Road

ESTHER is furiously scrubbing the kitchen floor with a cloth on her hands and knees. She pauses to wring it out into the bucket beside her. With the back of a hand, she wipes away a stand of loose hair that has fallen across her face, which is streaked with dirt.

16. CLOSE UP:
Esther's eyes.

17. DISSOLVE to CLOSE UP:
Victor's eyes.

Both pairs of eyes have been staring intently into the camera, which now pulls back to:

18. INT.
Gymnasium at Ardwick Lads Club.

VICTOR is training. He is wearing a hooded robe, on the back of which, picked out in white thread, are the words, *"Vic 'The Volcano' Collins, North West Miners Champion"*. The gym is smoky. VICTOR is lit with a single overhead light. He goes through a series of exercises. First we see him skipping, his feet light and deft and quick. Next he is throwing punches at the large heavy bag, which swings in and out of the overhead light. Finally he is shadow boxing. The camera pans around him, until he is directly facing it, throwing fierce combinations of punches straight towards the viewer. With the last punch the screen blacks out.

On it is now written:

Day 3: Monday 3rd May 1926
First Official Day of the Strike

19. EXT.
London Road Station.

A small crowd of people gather outside the station entrance, where a sign reads:

> **NO TRAINS WILL BE RUNNING FROM THIS STATION TODAY.**

20. Cut to: EXT.
Victoria Station.

… where there are similar scenes, and:

21. Cut to: EXT.
Central Station.

Police officers are turning back frustrated passengers. There are signs declaring:

> **ALL TRAINS CANCELLED UNTIL FURTHER NOTICE.**

22. INT.
Manchester Telephone Exchange.

Inside, women wearing headphones are busy putting through telephone calls, removing and replacing cables rapidly. There is an air of great urgency in the room. Among the women is WINIFRED. She is speaking to an incoming caller.

CAPTION:
"Good morning, Caller. How may I help you?"

23. CLOSE UP:
A pair of male lips speaking into a telephone.

CAPTION:
"This is Lord Harding in London, speaking on behalf of Admiral Jellicoe for the Organisation of the Maintenance of Supplies. I wish to speak to Sir Robert Peacock, Chief Constable for Manchester."

24. CLOSE UP:
Winifred.

Winifred's eyes widening. She transfers more cables as she successfully puts through the call.

CAPTION:
"Is that the Chief Constable's office? I have an urgent call from Whitehall."

25. CLOSE UP:
Winifred.

WINIFRED surreptitiously, looking over her shoulder first to make sure she is not being observed, delicately inserts a cable so that she might listen in on this highly confidential conversation.

As she does so, we see the male lips from before speaking into one telephone superimposed above her to the right, while to her left we see the back of the Chief Constable, silhouetted against the light as he looks out over the city from his first floor office window, listening on another telephone.

WINIFRED, listening, her face registering the shock of what she is hearing, takes out a piece of paper from the drawer in the desk just in front of her, and makes notes.

26. EXT.
Albert Square.

Outside the Town Hall, a group of passers-by gathers around an official board at the bottom of the steps leading up towards its entrance, where a Corporation Official, is posting a notice.

VOLUNTEERS REQUIRED

TO ENSURE ESSENTIAL FOOD SUPPLIES AND OTHER SERVICES ARE MAINTAINED.

PLEASE APPLY WITHIN.

Just at that moment several hundred Police Officers march out of the Town Hall to form a protective cordon around the whole of the Square. The clock in the Town Hall tower shows 11 o'clock.

27. CLOSE UP:
Town Hall Clock.

28. DISSOLVE: to CLOSE UP:
Clock in Telephone Exchange, showing 11.30.

29. CLOSE UP:
Winifred's face.

WINIFRED is anxiously looking up towards the clock.

30. CLOSE UP:
Telephone Exchange Clock, which now shows 12 o'clock.

31. DISSOLVE:
Back to Town Hall Clock, now at 12.30.

32. EXT.
Albert Square.

The Police Officers are busily directing people and traffic away from the actual Square.

33. Cut to: EXT.
Piccadilly Gardens.

More Police Officers are in evidence. They have closed the Gardens off to the public.

34. CLOSE UP:
Winifred's face, still looking anxiously towards the Telephone Exchange clock.

35. Cut to: CLOCK,
which now shows the time to be one minute before 1 o'clock.

As the hands on the clock tip over to one o'clock, cut to:

36. CLOSE UP:
Electric Bell on a wall.

Although we do not hear it, we see the bell as it rings.

37. INT.
The switchboard at the Telephone Exchange.

All the girls push away from their work stations. Some put on coats and hats and head for the exit, while others take out a packed lunch and gather together at a table set aside for the purpose, routinely chattering. WINIFRED hurries outside as quickly as she can.

38. EXT.
Withy Grove.

The camera follows WINIFRED as she leaves the Telephone Exchange on the corner of Market Street, down which she now runs as fast as she can, weaving in and out of startled pedestrians, over into Corporation Street, and then into Withy Grove. The glass pane on the outer door of one of the larger buildings there announces:

"The Manchester Guardian".

Looking over her shoulder, WINIFRED quickly runs inside. The camera follows her up the narrow staircase into:

39. INT.
News Room of The Manchester Guardian.

WINIFRED thrusts the piece of paper on which she earlier wrote down what she had overheard of the telephone conversation that took place between Lord Harding and Sir Robert Peacock in front of one of the journalists. After the quickest of glances the Journalist rushes towards the Editor's Office, knocking and entering simultaneously. WINIFRED follows him in.

The Editor lays the piece of paper down upon his desk in disbelief and looks towards WINIFRED, who nods breathlessly. The EDITOR picks it up once more, re-reads it, more slowly this time, and frowns. He turns away, looking out of his office window, one arm behind his back, the other feverishly smoking his cigarette.

40. CLOSE UP:
The Piece of Paper

In WINIFRED's hurriedly scribbled scrawl, the following key points can just be deciphered:

Admiral Jellicoe – Organisation for the Maintenance of Supplies

Non-political (!)

150 fleets of private lorries placed on standby

Corporation on High Alert to keep supplies moving

100,000 "volunteers" from middle classes already signed up

> *TUC no plans at all – not even a Ways & Means Committee*

41. Cut back to: INT.
Editor's Office

The EDITOR turns back towards WINIFRED.

CAPTION:
Can you corroborate this?

Winifred sadly shakes her head. The EDITOR shrugs, puts out his cigarette and turns back towards the window. WINIFRED leaves. The JOURNALIST tears up the piece of paper.

42. EXT.
Withy Grove.

A rapid tracking shot transports the viewer along Withy Grove from outside the offices of *The Manchester Guardian* to those of *The Manchester Evening News*.

43. MONTAGE:

We see a quick succession of shots showing a newspaper being set up ready for printing. Type is set. The presses are rolled. A long sheet of newsprint is torn off and checked. Approval is given. The newspapers are printed. All the various processes are shown, until finally they are transported via a series of conveyor belts, from where they are lifted by hand and tied into bundles of fifty by string. These are then passed in a relay from the print room to the waiting trucks outside, which drive away, dropping off the bundles directly onto the streets, where newsboys pick them up and begin selling them. The front page spins like a Catherine wheel, eventually coming to rest upon the headline:

KEEP CALM AND CARRY ON.

44. EXT. Street Corner, Manchester Cathedral in Background.

A NEWS VENDOR is urging people to *"Read All About It!"* as various passers by drop a coin into his tin and pick up a copy of *The Manchester Evening News*. One CITY GENT, with bowler hat and rolled up umbrella, opens it up to read inside. The front page is displayed to the camera.

> *The security of the Constitution having been threatened by the illegal strike, the duty of every right-minded citizen lies plain before him. The Englishman, who never will be slave to Kings or Conquerors, will neither submit to the rule of a minority who seek to usurp the powers of government. The Government must be allowed to govern and the Rule of Law must apply to all.*

45. INT.
Tram

On the top deck of a crowded tram, WINIFRED is reading this article over the shoulder of the passenger sitting next to her. She sighs and shakes her head.

46. INT.
Melland Road, Gorton.

ESTHER picks up the same front page of *The Manchester Evening News* and very deliberately scrunches it up into a tight ball, which she throws onto the grate in the hearth in the back kitchen of her flat in Melland Road. She takes a match from a box close by, strikes it, sets the flame to the newspaper and watches it catch alight with a certain grim pleasure.

47. INT.
BBC Recording Studio, Metropolitan Vickers, Trafford Park.

DAN GODFREY JNR is preparing to read the nightly news. FRANCIS is making sure the microphone is all set up. At a signal from someone inside the Control Booth, FRANCIS counts down from five to one with his fingers, then points towards GODFREY, who checks the sheaf of papers in front of him, looks up towards the microphone and begins to speak.

CAPTION: (scrolls in front of his face as he reads)

And finally, in an atmosphere of rising tension in Manchester throughout the day, news has just reached us that the City's Tramwaymen will be holding a mass meeting at midnight in the Co-operative Hall on Downing Street in Oldham to decide whether to come out in favour of the miners. More than five thousand workers are expected to attend...

48. INT.
Lounge of The Wright Family, Manley Park

Annie, Hubert and George are sitting in their lounge, listening to the News on their RCA Westinghouse radio. ANNIE is bent over a flower arrangement she is in the middle of. HUBERT is fixing something electrical. GEORGE is drawing. On hearing the news, HUBERT and ANNIE look at each other in growing concern. GEORGE observes this.

49. INT.
Co-operative Hall, Oldham

The hall is packed to the rafters. The men, all wearing their Manchester Tramways Company uniforms, stand shoulder to shoulder beneath just a few naked light bulbs suspended from the ceiling, which cast dusty shadows. On a raised platform at one end the Union Convener is speaking passionately. By his side is a blackboard on an easel. Chalked up on it are two columns:

```
Motion: To Support The Miners As
Part of The General Strike

Those     in      Those
Favour            Against
```

The CONVENER points towards the column requesting those in favour. All the hands in the hall shoot up as one. The scene fades.

On the black screen appear the words:

Day 4: Tuesday 4th May 1926

50. AERIAL SHOT:
Manchester City Centre

The camera looks down on the city. It is morning. The Town Hall clock shows 7.00am. The streets are deserted.

51. CLOSE UP:
Great Abe, the Clock Tower Bell, strikes.

52. MONTAGE:

On each strike of the bell, we cut to a different part of the city – a railway station, a tram stop, a normally busy cross roads, a prominent landmark, such as the statue of Queen Victoria in Piccadilly, the Albert Memorial in Albert Square, *The Midland Hotel*. Everywhere is quiet. Nothing is moving. There are no people anywhere. Only litter, which rolls across the streets, starlings wheeling above the rooftops, a pigeon landing on the head of Queen Victoria, who does not look amused.

The screen goes to black.

Day 5:
Wednesday 5th May 1926

53. The screen remains black.

In white lettering the following text scrolls up:

The strike now reaches the breakfast tables of everyone across the city when the TUC, making what proves to be a catastrophic strategic error of judgment, decide to call out the printers and shut down all the national and local newspapers. In this one single ill-judged act they rob themselves of any form of reliable outlet through which their message can reach the man and woman in the street...

54. EXT.
Offices of *The Manchester Guardian*, Withy Grove.

A worker is posting up a notice on the inside of the windows of the offices before leaving the building, padlocking the door behind him. A small crowd gathers outside to read it.

MANCHESTER GUARDIAN REGRETS TUC DECISION

The decision of the Trades Union Congress to call out the printers and to silence the press seems to us a singular misguided policy, and we cannot believe it will be maintained. To put the press out of action gives a most dangerous power to the Government which, by its control of broadcasting, will enjoy a complete monopoly in its distribution of news and opinion. Is this what the TUC truly desires?

Among the small crowd is FRANCIS. He reads the notice with growing concern. Then an idea appears to strike him and he hurries away down the street with great purpose. The iris on the camera picks him out in a circle which gradually diminishes to just a dot as the scene fades.

Day 6:
Thursday 6th May 1926

55. EXT.
Piccadilly. The evening rush hour.

Piccadilly is crammed with people, jostling and pushing one another, as they try to make their way home after work in the chaos of a city without public transport. Taxis are charging higher and higher prices. Arguments break out between the drivers and their passengers. There is gridlock as motor cars, motor cycles, bicycles and horse-drawn vehicles all attempt to make for any kind of gap in the traffic that might appear. Market stalls are knocked over. Police officers try to keep order.

Among the crowd is WINIFRED. She is trying to battle the tide of people. She makes it to a spot further down Portland Street, where things are a little calmer. A huddle of young women office workers are waiting in a line. They each wear a red ribbon pinned to their coats. WINIFRED points to one of them.

CAPTION:
"What do the ribbons mean?"

56. EXT.
Portland Street.

The young women smile and show off their ribbons.

CAPTION:
"It means we're city girls looking for a lift home. We want to keep working but it's hard without the trains or trams."

Disgusted, WINIFRED walks away from them, determined to walk the five miles back to Denton. As she does so, she accidentally bumps into FRANCIS, walking in the opposite direction, back towards Piccadilly. It is three years before they will properly meet. They each apologise to the other and continue on their separate ways.

57. EXT.
Piccadilly Gardens.

FRANCIS battles his way through the crowds into Piccadilly Gardens, where finally he emerges, almost as if he has been squeezed out of a tube of toothpaste. Once there, he brushes himself down and tries to gather his wits. Hundreds of people are there. Some are sitting on benches but most are standing, waiting until things might calm down a little and they can then begin to make their various ways back home without having to endure the current crush. The sky is beginning to grow dark. Suddenly there is a great commotion. People begin pointing to the rooftop above Lewis's Department Store, where a light is flickering. FRANCIS pushes his way through several people to try and obtain a closer look.

58. EXT.
The Mutagraph.

The flickering light on the rooftop above Lewis's coalesces into a series of projected images from a Mutagraph, a powerful projector, which is being operated from a vantage point on top of one of the nearby bus shelters. The images depict what have now become familiar sights to the people of Manchester in these past few days – the empty railway stations, the closed tram depots with all the trams standing idle and empty, the chaotic crowds across the city. Over these images is superimposed the following text:

> **This is The Manchester Emergency Echo, now being published abroad and flown into the country by the latest Avro 510's built right here in Manchester.**
>
> **Don't pay attention to wild stories of public disorder, rioting, outrages and the like. Evil tongues are deliberately inventing these to try to scare you.**
>
> **Don't criticise the Government. They are doing the best they can**

> to deal with a difficult situation
> and they will do it better with
> your support and help.
>
> But do not denounce the strikers
> in violent terms. Many of them are
> patriotic Britons who have been
> dangerously misled into a foolish
> and desperate course of action,
> urged on by their reckless
> leaders.
>
> Above all, don't be frightened.
>
> **KEEP CALM AND CARRY ON.**

The message is greeted with a mixture of cheers and boos from the watching crowds. A few scuffles break out. Among those fighting can be seen VICTOR, who is preparing to take on all comers. The Police quickly move in to try and quell the situation. VICTOR punches one of the officers but is then overpowered by several others and roughly led away.

59. CLOSE UP:
Francis's face.

The camera looks down on FRANCIS, as if from the rooftop of Lewis's, where the images are still being projected. As it closes in on FRANCIS's face, we see reflections of these images glittering across the lenses of his spectacles, behind which his eyes are shining. He is oblivious to the fighting around him. Instead he looks enraptured, a Damascene transfiguration, uplifted by the power of technology to inspire such passion and emotion.

The screen fades to black.

Day 7:
Friday 7th May 1926

60. EXT.
Manchester Assizes, Great Ducie Street.

An establishing shot of the outside of the Manchester Assizes on Great Ducie Street in the Strangeways district of the city. Viewed from below, its massive Venetian Gothic architecture looms imposingly up towards the sky.

61. INT.
Manchester Assizes.

A MAGISTRATE is speaking from his bench. In the dock stands VICTOR, who stares defiantly back at the MAGISTRATE, who raps his gavel smartly once.

CAPTION:
"For serious affray, a breach of the peace and an assault upon a police officer, you are hereby sentenced to six months imprisonment with hard labour."

VICTOR is led away. From the Public Gallery, WINIFRED tries, but fails, to catch his eye.

62. EXT.
Portugal Street.

A black car pulls up outside The Printing Works of F.G. Wright & Son on Portugal Street. A crowd of small children gather curiously around it. A Chauffeur steps out and ineffectually tries to shoo them away, before opening the door for Mr JOHN SUTTON, MP, who, after looking round to see if he has been followed, goes inside.

63. INT.
F.G. Wright & Son.

Inside the Works, everyone is busy. SUTTON asks a question of HARRY HEATH, The Foreman, who points towards an office at the back. SUTTON thanks HARRY, pats him on the shoulder, then walks towards the office, knocks on the door and immediately heads inside, where HUBERT rises from his desk to greet him.

From HARRY's POV, we see the silhouettes of SUTTON and HUBERT earnestly discussing something. HARRY, wiping his hands on a rag, edges closer towards HUBERT's Back Office. He looks increasingly uneasy.

The door opens. HUBERT and SUTTON shake hands. SUTTON walks through the Machine Room, passes HARRY without acknowledging him, then outside into the street. HARRY watches him clear a path between the children who have returned to clamour around his motor car. We see the dust left behind as the motor car departs.

HUBERT claps his hands and calls the work force together and begins to speak to them.

CAPTION:
"There's an urgent need for a Strike Newspaper. We've been approached to see if we might help. I've said yes. I understand if this proves difficult for some of you. You must each make up your own minds…"

HUBERT is looking directly at HARRY, who puts down the rag he's been holding and sadly shakes his head.

CAPTION:
"I'm sorry, Mr Wright, but I'm a Union man. Printing

things that have got nothing to do with the strike was acceptable. But helping to bring out a newspaper, well... that's a different matter entirely. I can't see a way round that, I'm afraid. I'm leaving..."

HUBERT nods.

CAPTION:
"I understand, Harry. Does anyone else feel the same way?"

HUBERT looks around. One by one all the other men raise their hands. Slowly they each of them leave the Works, until HUBERT is left standing alone. Above his head The Printing Works clock shows the time. The camera slowly zooms in. It is just after 4 o'clock. The camera continues to zoom until the clock is out of focus.

Over the blank screen appear the words:

Day 8:
Saturday 8th May 1926

64. DISSOLVE:

The camera pulls back to reveal the clock once more. The hands go round and round showing the passing of several hours. It is now the evening of the following day.

65. INT.
F.G. Wright & Son

Inside The Printing Works it is dimly lit. There is an atmosphere of intense concentration, purpose and speed. The place is empty except for members of the WRIGHT family, who are all silently pulling together, each of them aware of their own specific task, which occupies them completely. No one is speaking.

HUBERT is working as the compositor, making up the type face. ANNIE is deciding on the design and lay-out, as well as working on the rotogravure machine to produce the images that will accompany the text. FRANK is working on the printing presses themselves, supervising the inking of the finished plates onto the paper, while EVELYN is stacking the folded newspapers – just four sheets per copy – into bundles, which GEORGE loads into a satchel he carries on his back. As soon as each batch is ready, he leaps aboard his bicycle and pedals off at top speed to deliver them to the agreed drop off points.

There is a real sense of camaraderie between them all. We watch them for a long time. After a while, when the last bundle has been stacked by EVELYN, they stop to drink mugs of tea poured from a thermos flask. ANNIE hands out sandwiches. They look at one another, still not speaking, a sense of shared satisfaction of a job well done. The clock shows half past nine.

66. EXT.
The Streets of Manchester.

GEORGE is cycling through a labyrinth of back streets – Poland Street, Radium Street, Bengal Street, across Great Ancoats Street, criss-crossing Brightwell Street, Oak Street, Cooperas Street, down Thomas Street onto Shude Hill, where he lets his bicycle coast before turning off into Hanover Street, Dantzic Street, Garden Street and Balloon Street, from where he makes a final dash up Todd Street towards Victoria Station Approach, where a lorry has been waiting for him. GEORGE tosses the final bundle to a MAN at the rear of the vehicle, who stows it inside alongside all of the rest. He knocks the side of the lorry hard twice with the flat of his hand and the driver pulls away. GEORGE wheels his bicycle around and immediately heads back in the direction from where he has come.

The MAN who has been loading the lorry has saved one of the copies for himself, which he now picks up to read.

67. CLOSE UP:
Newspaper from Man's POV.

The British Worker

> Let us be clear. The General Council of the TUC does NOT challenge the Constitution. It is not seeking to substitute the Government. Nor is it in any way desirous of undermining the UK Parliament. The Council's sole aim is to secure for the Miners a decent standard of living. We are not making war on the people. We are anxious that ordinary members of the public shall not be penalised for the unpatriotic conduct of the Mine Owners and the Government.
>
> Support the Miners.

68. EXT.
Hyde Road, Denton.

An establishing shot of Hyde Road, Denton, showing the giant pair of spectacles above *Hall & Singer's* Optics & Radios Shop.

69. INT.
Room above the shop.

FRANCIS is broadcasting via his own customised transmitter from the top of his house. He is tuning frequencies, setting up equipment, tweaking instruments, before finally speaking into a microphone.

70. ANIMATED MONTAGE

The camera pulls back from FRANCIS, out through the window of his makeshift studio, through one of the lenses of the giant spectacles, up into the night sky. An animation of radio signals, emanating in an ever-widening series of concentric circles radiates from the aerial on the rooftop of his house.

Superimposed onto this image is a series of different individuals tuning their own crystal radio sets in various attic rooms, wearing headphones, trying to receive the broadcast FRANCIS is transmitting. They revolve slowly around him in the centre of the screen.

Scrolling upwards over all of this are the following words:

"This is FH1 broadcasting from the City of Manchester to all the People of England. Support for the Miners remains solid. Strikers have manifested their determination and unity to the whole world. They have resolved that the attempt of the Mine Owners to starve three million men, women and children shall not succeed..."

71. INT.
Manley Park, Whalley Range.

The camera pulls further and further away from FRANCIS's shop in Denton, until the whole of the city is spread below, all of it contained within the animated pulse of the radio signal's concentric circles. It then descends towards a different street, in a different part of the city, to St Werburgh's Road, Manley Park, Whalley Range. It closes in on one particular house and flies through an open window into an upstairs bedroom. Inside GEORGE is listening intently to FRANCIS's message on his Crystal Radio Set through a pair of headphones. His face glows, caught in the fervour and excitement of the moment.

Day 9:
Sunday 9th May 1926

72. EXT.
Platt Fields, Rusholme.

The shot begins as a close up on the statue of Abraham Lincoln in the Park. The camera then pulls back to reveal ESTHER standing beneath it, clearly waiting for someone. She looks around her and then waves. DELPHINE enters the frame. The two women embrace warmly and then turn around to take in the scene.

Thousands of people have gathered there. The sun is shining. Everyone is in good spirits. A brass band is playing – The Bradford Colliery Brass Band. As ESTHER and DELPHINE approach it, ESTHER catches her brother HAROLD's eye. He is playing the cornet and, in between breaths, he nods towards them. The atmosphere is more like a picnic than a rally. There are many women and children there, handing out sandwiches and bottles of milk. Many of the men are reading copies of *The British Worker*, distributed in part the previous night by George, and discussing it animatedly.

ESTHER and DELPHINE make their way through the crowds towards a raised platform from where speeches are being delivered. A new speaker is announced to warm applause. HANNAH MITCHELL steps forward.

CAPTION:

Mrs Hannah Mitchell, Suffragist, Magistrate and Labour Party Member for Manchester City Council representing the Newton Heath Ward.

HANNAH gives a fiery, passionate speech, which the crowds respond to enthusiastically. ESTHER turns towards DELPHINE and says something to her. DELPHINE responds with surprise. ESTHER nods, then continues speaking. A flavour of their conversation is conveyed through the following, intercut with shots of HANNAH MITCHELL speaking, sections of the crowd listening, children playing. A SMALL GIRL is picking up handfuls of grass and throwing them idly at her baby brother.

CAPTIONS:

> ***Esther****: I met her once. Ten years ago. At Belle Vue.*
> ***Delphine****: Really? What did she say?*
> ***Esther****: She told me to stay true to myself.*
> ***Delphine****: Good advice.*
> ***Esther****: I was only sixteen, but she spoke to me as an adult.*
> ***Delphine****: Which you were.*
> ***Esther****: Hardly. But I think she recognised my idealism.*
> ***Delphine****: And encouraged it, clearly. It's important to hold onto it.*
> ***Esther****: But difficult.*

Delphine: Especially now. Charles says that if the Electrical Workers go out too, they will have to cancel operations at the hospital.
Esther: If it were me, I'd understand.
Delphine: But not everyone is you.
Esther: We're all of us, I think, at a kind of cross roads.

HANNAH MITCHELL finishes her speech. The crowds applaud. The Brass Band continues to play. People spread out across the Park, enjoying the sunshine.

The camera roves across the scene, returning once more to the statue of Abraham Lincoln. Sitting at the foot of it, cross legged, a pole strung with trapped moles by his side, is TOMMY THUNDER. ESTHER sees him and approaches him. He hands her a feather, then closes his eyes. As he does so, the screen snaps to black.

Day 10:
Monday 10th May 1926

73. EXT. Town Hall Steps, Albert Square. Morning.

The Lord Mayor, in full ceremonial regalia and wearing his chain of office, stands on the steps in front of the Town Hall. He is reading from a prepared speech. A few people have gathered around, while others, on their way to work, stop to listen.

CAPTION:
"I am here to assure you that, thanks to our careful contingency planning, food supplies continue to get through to the city, while all essential services are being

maintained. An army of volunteers has answered our call as patriotic citizens and several trains are now once again running each day."

74. EXT.
Platform 11, Exchange Station.

A train pulls into Platform 11 of Manchester's Exchange Station. The platform fills with steam which, as it clears, reveals a crowd of several dozen people. All are cheering, some encouragingly, others derisorily, as the train fails to stop where it should and continues on out of shot.

75. CLOSE UP:
Train Driver.

The train driver is a VICAR. He is mopping his face, which is streaked with soot, with a handkerchief. He is beaming. Then, when he realises he is not able to stop the train successfully, his expression changes to one of panic, as he tries to pull as hard as he can on the brakes.

76. EXT.
Platform 11, Exchange Station. (Reverse Angle).

Back on the platform, the waiting passengers have to chase the train to where it has finally come to a stop. TWO ENGINE DRIVERS, in uniform but evidently on strike, look at each other and tut, shaking their heads ruefully.

CAPTION:
   ***DRIVER 1**: It's a good job Platform 11 is the longest platform in Europe.*
   ***DRIVER 2**: Ay, any fool can start an engine, but it's when tha's learned to stop it we'll consider thee for t' Union.*

77. INT.
Warehouse at Sutcliffe's Flour Mill, Hulme.
A relay of men and women are passing sacks of flour in a great line towards the backs of a fleet of large lorries, loading them right up to the top.

78. CLOSE UP:
Female Volunteer Driver (at the wheel of one of the lorries)

There is a look of fear in her eyes. She grips the steering wheel tightly and swallows hard, before slowly engaging the gear and edging forward.

79. EXT.
Outside Yard of Sutcliffe's Flour Mill.

An angry crowd of protesters, held back by a cordon of Police Officers, is waiting to greet her as she pulls out into the yard. They are shouting angrily, their faces twisted with rage and fury. They break through the Police cordon and rush towards the lorry, which they begin to rock from side to side. The sacks of flour are taken from the back and tossed into the River Medlock, which crawls, dank and foetid, alongside. Some of the sacks burst open and strikers and the police hurl flour at one another until all are covered in white from head to toe.

80. EXT.
Pomona Docks, Salford.

In the midst of the mayhem at the Flour Mill, some of the strikers become aware of action taking place on the other side of the river, at the Royal Pomona Docks. They point and several of them storm across an iron bridge towards it. The camera follows them.

Soldiers are unloading a ship that has just docked. The Lord Mayor is shaking the hand of the Commanding Officer-in-Charge. A 2nd UNIT of SOLDIERS form a barrier to prevent the STRIKERS from disrupting this delivery of cargo. More fighting ensues.

81. MONTAGE:

The sign which said *"Day 10: Monday 10th May 1926"* turns round to become:

Day 11:
Tuesday 11th May 1926

This is immediately followed by a series of Newspaper Headlines spinning towards the camera, each becoming still long enough for us to read them, before being replaced by another.

"2000 Beds, Blankets & Pillows Arrive at Salford Docks To Support Volunteers."

"Hannah Mitchell Appeals for Strikers To Remain Calm."

"Keep Quiet! Stay At Home! Offer No Provocation!"

"Last Working Flour Mill In Manchester Joins Strike."

"Tramways Corporation Orders Strikers To Return To Work.
Failure To Do So Will Result In Dismissal."
"Electrical Unions Threaten To Cut Off Power If Tramway Workers Are Sacked."

"Ship Workers And Engineers Called Out."

"British Worker Doubles Distribution To 100,000."

"Too Little, Too Late?"

Superimposed over these headlines are further images of HUBERT, ANNIE, FRANK and EVELYN producing copies of the newspaper, and GEORGE cycling the city streets.

Day 12:
Wednesday 12th May 1926

82. EXT.
Tram Depot, Hyde Road.

A grey day in Manchester. A thick fog hangs over the city. Through the bandage of cloud a pale sun threatens to leach, but the gloom persists. Huge crowds line the streets all the way from the Tram Depot, along Hyde Road, marking the entire length of the route planned for the march, which is scheduled to begin at noon, until its final mustering point in Albert Square in front of the Town Hall, two and a half miles away.

The clock above the Tram Depot shows one minute before noon. As it ticks over to the hour, the procession, led by the Bradford Colliery Brass Band, heads out of the yard and onto Hyde Road. At the front is HAROLD, playing his cornet.

The band is followed by a representation of miners, more than a thousand of them, each wearing their lighted helmets and carrying their Davy Lamps before them, all made locally in Eccles, casting eerie, dancing shadows before them as they walk.

Then come the TRAMWAYMEN, five thousand of them in all, marching in step, in time to the music played by the Brass

Band. The front two carry a banner, which reads: *"No Surrender"*.

The crowds lining the streets applaud with deep and moving solemnity. They do not stop until the last of the six thousand men have passed before them. This takes almost an hour. When they have finally all left the Yard, the crowds fall in behind and follow them the rest of the way – around Ardwick Green, along Downing Street to London Road, left onto Whitworth Street, right onto Princess Street, before funnelling into Albert Square, by which time they have swelled to more than twenty thousand strong.

Among the throng are WINIFRED and ESTHER. They link arms as they follow the procession.

(Both are thinking back to another parade, ten years before, when crowds lined the city streets to cheer The Manchester Regiment on its way to France at the start of The Great War, Arthur – Esther's brother and Winifred's fiancé – among them. A different band played that day, a different tune, jauntier, full of hope, in marked contrast with this day's music, a march which is altogether more defiant. Back then, Winifred had been reminded of The Pied Piper of Hamelin, leading the marchers like rats, deep below the earth, never to return. Today her thoughts are with Victor, locked inside Strangeways Prison, who, but for his hot head and fierce temper, would have been marching at the front of this procession, carrying his miner's lamp. She will go and visit him at the weekend, she decides, and tell him all about today's spirit of '*No Surrender*', whatever the outcome. She understands that it is precisely his fierceness and temper that she loves, his sense of certainty, his refusal to yield. "Don't let the bastards grind you down," had been his last words to her before he was led away).

83. EXT.
Albert Square.

The Town Hall Clock shows 3 o'clock by the time the last of the procession has arrived in Albert Square. On a platform which has been erected in the centre of the square, a pale figure can just be seen putting up a microphone and connecting it to speakers. It is FRANCIS. When he has finished, MR JOHN SUTTON, MP climbs the stage and addresses the crowd. A pale sun tries to seep through the blanket of fog.

CAPTION:

> *"At this very hour the TUC is in session in Downing Street urging the Government to reject once and for all the recommendations of the Samuel Commission which, the Government says, are in any case not binding, and defend the miners against further victimisation. We expect news at any moment, and we wait with bated breath. While we wait, please give your full attention to The Manchester Songbird, Miss Chamomile Catch."*

CAM stands before the microphone and begins to sing, accompanied by HAROLD on his cornet, *The Ballad of The Black Lung*. She performs it with slow, raw, searing power and the crowds stand before her, completely enthralled. We hear the song in the added soundtrack. As she sings, the camera picks out various faces in the crowd listening intently to its unapologetic, uncompromising message, while cutting back to wide angled shots of the Square as a whole and back to CAM herself. The words scroll up the screen over each of these shots.

CAM:
He's had more hard luck than most men could stand
The mine was his first love but never his friend
He's lived a hard life and harder he'll die
Black lung's done got him, his time it is nigh

Black lung, black lung, you're just biding your time
Soon all of this suffering I'll leave behind
But I can't help but wonder what God had in mind
To send such a devil to claim this soul of mine

He went to the boss man but he closed the door
Well, it seems you're not wanted when you're sick and you're poor
You're not even covered in their medical plans
And your life it depends on the favours of man

Down in the poorhouse on starvation's plan
Where pride is a stranger and doomed is a man
His soul full of coal dust till his body's decayed
And everyone but black lung's done turned him away

In the background, while CAM has been singing, FRANCIS has received a message via telegraph, which he scribbles rapidly onto a piece of paper, then hands to SUTTON, who reads it disbelievingly. He appears to be asking FRANCIS whether he is certain he has transcribed it correctly. FRANCIS nods. SUTTON shakes his head. Reluctantly, he takes the microphone from CAM, who stands back perplexed, and speaks to the anxious, waiting crowd.

CAPTIONS:
"Following the Government's assertion that The Samuel Commission is not binding, the TUC has voted to call off the strike."

There is an instant reaction of shock and disbelief at this announcement.

> *"It has instructed all members to return to work."*

Shouts of *"Shame! Shame!"* can be seen to be issuing from thousands of lips.

> *"The Miners Federation has rejected this call."*

Cheers.

> *"But the TUC Executive is ordering everybody back."*

Boos.

> *"The Mine Owners, taking their cue from the Government that The Samuel Commission is a recommendation only, have decided to accept its recommendation and continue with the lock-out of the miners, unless they accept a reduction in wages and an increase in hours."*

"Never, never, never."
"No surrender! No surrender!"

The chanting continues as the ring of POLICE OFFICERS moves in threateningly in a ring around the angry crowds. SUTTON gestures for CAM to continue singing which, as she does so, gradually begins to calm the atmosphere down, until finally they are all listening with dignity and respect. Once again the words scroll up the screen. The camera lingers in a series of CLOSE UPS on different faces of individuals from within the crowd, including:

84. CAM singing.

> *"Black lung, black lung, oh your hand's icy cold*
> *As you reach for my life and torture my soul*
> *Cold as that water down in that dark cave*
> *Where I spent my life's blood a-diggin' my grave..."*

85. HANNAH MITCHELL listening.

86. WINIFRED, her head bowed.

87. FRANCIS, looking up from his equipment.

88. HUBERT, ANNIE and GEORGE, with arms around each other.

89. DELPHINE, closing her eyes.

90. HAROLD, lowering his cornet, and finally:

91. ESTHER, a single tear running down her cheek.

This is the first tear she has shed since the death of her father. The iris of the camera encircles her face and slowly closes to black, as CAM finishes the song.

> *Down at the graveyard the boss man he came*
> *With his bunch of white flowers, dear God, what a shame*
> *Take back those white flowers, don't you sing no sad songs*
> *The die has been cast now, a good man is gone...*

92. INT. Prison Cell, Strangeways.

The iris of the camera re-opens to reveal VICTOR, staring directly out towards us from behind the bars of his cell.

He begins to shadow box, throwing punches straight at the camera, which retreats further and further from him, until gradually he becomes merely a dot, then slowly disappears.

The End.

*

Four days later, as the bell in St Jerome's Church tolls eight o'clock, Jabez unlocks the gates at the Mill Street entrance to Philips Park to let the people in for the annual Tulip Sunday. A bright spring sun shines mockingly down, bouncing off the dew glistening on the newly opened leaves of the trees, the freshly mown grass and the tightly budded petals of the flowers.

There are far fewer people than normal. Jabez greets those who have made the effort to attend somewhat disconsolately, for his heart is not fully in it this year. The Parks & Gardens Committee has cancelled all the formal aspects of the day, and Jabez is grateful for that. There will be no official opening, no speeches, no cutting of a ribbon, no brass bands.

"Hardly appropriate," a rather gaunt-looking Mr Pettigrew had announced the day before, through thin, pursed lips, "in the circumstances." Jabez had sighed with relief. The appearance of the Lord Mayor, especially wearing his chain of office, would be bound to have provoked an angry reaction, and the thought of the fighting that would have inevitably ensued fills him with dread. The truth is, he may well not have been able to prevent himself from wading in too, and that would have done nobody any good, least of all Mary, who's not coming today. She's had another miscarriage, her third now, and is resting back at Garibaldi Street.

The sun continues to rise in the sky and, perhaps emboldened by its tempting warmth, the park slowly begins to fill up, families mostly, strolling along the various serpentine paths, setting up picnics on the grass. Jabez strolls among them, tipping his hat to those who know or recognise him.

Hubert and Annie Wright compliment him on the displays. "We need this colour," they say. Especially today."

"Thank you," replies Jabez, though he finds deep down he can't agree with them. When he'd first planned this year's display, last autumn, it had been such a wet summer, with the prospect of a really harsh winter, (which proved an underestimate, for January and February had been the coldest in more than a decade), he'd thought to dazzle visitors with the brightest colours he could imagine. But now, as he looks down over the Central Carriageway towards the Amphitheatre where the greatest concentration of tulips have been planted, he finds all these reds, golds, purples and oranges something of an affront, garish and insensitive. Next year, he thinks, I shall plant something altogether cooler, blues and greys and mauves, reflecting the different shades of the river perhaps, the boating lakes and bathing pools, the water running like a ribbon through the years, shifting, uncertain, a promise of more hopeful times to come. Yes. There might be something in that, and already he finds he's beginning to feel a little better.

He becomes aware of young George Wright's presence, hovering at his side, though not so young any more. He's all arms and legs these days, and his voice is not so predictable, on the cusp of breaking, lurching between a squeak and a growl.

"Excuse me, Mr Chadwick," he asks, "where are the elephants?"

Jabez smiles. "They're not coming this afternoon," he says. "Maybe next year, eh?"

The miners are locked out for six months. They maintain a vigil outside the gates of Bradford Colliery throughout that time, but spirits are low. Pockets of hungry men huddle in a desultory fashion around a permanently lit brazier, stoked with lumps of coal foraged during nightly raids over the wire fence from the stacked heaps piled there. The sight of women and children, begging on street corners, with a tin and a sign saying 'Support the Miners', becomes commonplace, almost to the point of rendering them invisible.

Finally, on Monday 15th November 1926 they accept the mine owners' unbending terms of reduced wages for extra hours and agree to end their strike.

THE TIMES

Tuesday 16th November 1926

CONFERENCE AGREES DETAILS OF BALFOUR DECLARATION

Last night leaders of nations attending this year's Imperial Conference of the British Empire issued the long-awaited *Balfour Declaration,* named after former Prime Minister Arthur, Earl of Balfour, now Lord President of the Imperial Council.

It declares the United Kingdom and the Dominions to be:

"... *autonomous communities within the British Empire, equal in status, in no way subordinate one to another in any aspect of domestic or external affairs, united by a common allegiance to the Crown, and freely associated as members of the British Commonwealth of Nations.*"

In other news, the last remaining pockets of resistant striking miners in Liverpool, Durham and Manchester will return to work today...

On the morning of 16th, when the pitmen make their way towards the colliery, converging as a single unit from all the different streets around, their boots striking up sparks on the shiny cobbles, slippery and wet from the rain that falls in windless stair rods, people line the pavements to honour them as they pass. Silent, unflinching, they stand as one, watching their husbands, fathers, brothers and sons marching, defiant and unbowed, towards the mine, whose steel gates open to receive them, an ever hungry mouth whose appetite is never sated. The families watch their loved ones disappear one by one as Harold, raising his cornet to his lips in the glistening rain, ushers them in with a mournful last lament, like rats lured into the cave under Hamelin's lonely mountain.

Esther is not among those standing in the rain. Nor is Winifred. Winifred is waiting by another set of gates, outside Strangeways Prison, from where Victor sheepishly shuffles out. He sees Winifred across the street and greets her with a nod and a shrug. She nods back, kisses him quickly, then links her arms through his and together they walk, not speaking, through the rain-soaked streets towards Park Place, where they can catch the first of the two trams they will need to get themselves back to Denton.

Esther meanwhile is sitting in the empty flat on Melland Road, where now she lives completely alone, mouldering among the memories and echoes of former years, reacting to each floorboard's creak or window pane's rattle, still half expecting one or all of her brothers to walk in through the back door. She has been darning the sleeve of her coat in the fading evening light. She sets aside the needle and thread and closes her eyes. She is exhausted. She resembles the seamstress in Richard Redgrave's portrait of the same name, painted to illustrate the lyrics of Thomas Hood's *The Song of the Shirt*, "*with eyelids heavy and red*".

Wearily she picks up a slim volume of poems by Wilfred Owen, flicks through the pages till she finds the one she's looking for, then settles in what was her father's armchair and reads:

> *"There was a whispering in my hearth,*
> *A sigh of the coal,*
> *Grown wistful of a former earth*
> *It might recall…*
>
> *But the coals were murmuring of their mine,*
> *And moans down there*
> *Of boys that slept wry sleep, and men*
> *Writhing for air.*
>
> *And I saw white bones in the cinder-shard,*
> *Bones without number,*
> *For many hearts with coal are charred*
> *And few remember.*
>
> *I thought of all who worked dark pits*
> *Of war, and died*
> *Digging the rock where Death reputes*
> *Peace lies indeed…"*

She shuts the book before she has finished the poem, closing her eyes and rubbing the bridge of her nose between the tips of her fingers. She thinks of Arthur and Freddie, and her father. She thinks of her three remaining brothers, Frank and Jim and Harold, all returning to those dark pits today. But mostly she thinks of herself.

This will not do, she tells herself. She is only thirty years old. Her life is not over, and she must stop regarding it as if it were. She rises to her feet, puts away the book and looks about the flat where she has lived since she was born. It's impractical for her now, too big, too painful, too expensive. This is a chapter which has closed, she realises, and that it is up to her to begin a new one.

She gathers her resolve, puts on her raincoat, picks up her umbrella by the back door and steps out into the yard behind.

She pauses.

She recalls her father playing his cornet the night her mother lost her last baby, a string of notes which hung in the sky like stars, tracing a line, back, back, back, to when Gorton was just fields and orchards, down through all the changes since, to that occasion, on that evening, right up until now, this morning, this moment. It carries me, she feels, sustains me, even today, when I am feeling particularly lost. I will endure.

She opens her umbrella and walks with renewed purpose towards the office of Sutton's, the Housing Association from whom she rents the flat, to enquire as to whether they might have something smaller, something more affordable, more suitable for a single woman of a certain age, about to open a new page in her life's story. She feels already a shift taking place, a metamorphosis, two Marys, being carried forward from Rossetti's sketch for her in *The Annunciation*, a figure cowering in a corner, to John Rogers Herbert's depiction of her during her *Flight into the Hill Country*, striding out with hope and vigour.

The rain begins to ease.

She lowers her umbrella.

After she has set in motion the first of the many actions she must undertake in order to effect the move from Melland Road to what is quaintly referred to as a smaller "widow's flat" on Darras Road, she stops off at the library in Levenshulme which, since its official opening in 1904, has long been her sanctuary, and settles herself to read the latest edition of *The Fabian Review*, smiling to herself at the disapproving glance she perceives is aimed in her direction by one of the librarians.

Tucked away on an inside page she comes across an

article about Queen Surayya of Afghanistan, and the radical social and educational reforms she has been trying to introduce there, particularly for young women, and a seed begins to grow inside her brain.

She thinks back to the seminal conversation she had with Hannah Mitchell when she was just sixteen, to the lectures she used to attend at The Manchester Lit & Phil, and the recent acquaintanceship she has struck up with Delphine Fish from the University. She will pick up these old threads again, she decides. She will feed and water her inner life. She will seek intellectual stimulation. She will root out Arthur's old bicycle and begin to broaden her horizons once more. She will return herself to life's thoroughfare. In short, she will get a job. Nothing too ambitious to begin with, just something that will make her financially independent and allow her sufficient time and energy for these other, more vital pursuits.

One step at a time, she thinks, and then let's see where the journey takes us. What might the next eighteen months bring…?

Cordelia Disinherited. John Rogers Herbert again. She sees herself standing on the threshold of a new independence, looking out, looking forward.

*

GREYHOUND
Racing Association Ltd.
BELLE VUE, MANCHESTER

OPENING MEETING

JULY 24TH, 1926
At 7.30 p.m.

SIX RACES

Printed by F.G. Wright & Son

It is the only occasion when George can ever remember his parents having an argument. It is, in fact, their third and final one.

Since his father's nervous breakdown after his return from the War, theirs has been a quiet household, and it remains so, even now he has made such a good recovery. The three of them tiptoe around one another, each accustomed to respecting the needs of the other two to be left undisturbed, Annie to her household chores, her creative pursuits, the flower arrangements, the collagraphs, her meticulous attention to the firm's accounts, which are entirely her domain, Hubert to his books, his motor car and his constant tinkering, and George to his drawing. They can go hours at a time without feeling the need to utter a word, while at other times, especially on jaunts or picnics, which have begun to play an increasing role on their Sunday afternoons, after Annie's Chapel and Hubert's Quaker Meetings, they can find themselves talking nineteen to the dozen, pointing out sights of interest, even singing, with the hood of the Crossley Phaeton rolled back, the wind in their hair, favourites from various operettas, *The Gypsy Baron, The Student Prince, Naughty Marietta*. Their current favourite is *Desert Song*, which they went to see at *The Hippodrome* the previous Christmas.

Now, on a Sunday afternoon in June, in an attempt to at least partly assuage their disappointment at what they believe has been the betrayal of the miners by a combination of the mine owners, the government and the other unions, not to mention the let-down they all feel after their intense efforts to print and distribute the thousands of copies of *The British Worker* had ultimately counted for nothing, Hubert has suggested a drive out to Lyme Park in Disley. It is only seventeen miles away and should take them less than an hour in the car, he says. "We could take a picnic."

"Which means, I suppose," says Annie, laughing, "that I'd better get a move on and make it, if we're ever going to get away in time. Come on, George. Give us a hand."

"Oh," says George, hoping he might not have to, "I thought Father might want help getting the car ready."

Annie and Hubert exchange a smile.

"Go and help your mother, George," winks Hubert. "I can manage the car."

Half an hour later they are speeding down Withington Road, into Mauldeth Road, and along Nell Lane.

"I like it round here," says Annie. "Can we take a short detour into Didsbury Village?"

"Uh-oh," says Hubert. "I can sense another move coming on."

"Don't be silly, Hubert. Not while George is still at Hulme's."

"I've got three more years at least," pipes George helpfully.

"Thank goodness," jokes Hubert. "A temporary reprieve."

After the detour to Didsbury has been completed, with Annie becoming quiet and thoughtful as they passed the grand houses on Wilmslow Road close to the Fletcher Moss Museum, they are back on the open road once more, driving through Cheadle, Bramhall, Poynton and Middlewood, singing their way through the score of *Desert Song*.

"Ho!
So we sing as we are riding
Ho!
It's a time you'd best be hiding
Low
It means the Riffs are abroad
Go
Before you've bitten the sword…"

George especially likes this song, accompanying the words with suitable actions, swinging his imaginary scimitar with great relish.

*"Over the ground
There comes a sound
It's the drum, drum, drum of hoof-beats in the sand
Quiver with fear
If you are near
Tis the Red Shadow's thunder in his following
band…"*

"I think I might be a Riff when I grow up," he declares.

Then, when the graceful Baroque lines of Lyme Hall heave into view, shimmering slightly in the afternoon's haze, Hubert switches to:

"*My desert is waiting
Dear, come here with me
I'm longing to teach you
Love's sweet melody…"*

George mimes being sick, which only encourages Annie to join in louder than ever.

"*Blue heaven and you and I
And sand kissing a moonlit sky
A desert breeze whispering a lullaby
Only stars above you
To say I love you…"*

"And here we are," announces Hubert.

"Thank goodness," says George. "Does that mean we can stop singing now?"

It is on the journey home when the argument starts.

They had had a golden day at Lyme, each of them enjoying different aspects of it. For Annie it had been the

Dutch Garden, with its orangery and fountains and the intoxicating aroma of so many roses. Having grown up surrounded by vats of boiling animal fat in the Tripe Colony of Miles Platting, it is always the scent of something which beguiles her first. For Hubert it had been the Caxton Missal, the only known nearly complete copy of the earliest edition of the Sarum Rite, containing details of the *Mass and Order of Service for the Use of Salisbury*, printed by William Caxton himself in 1487. "Four hundred and forty years ago," Hubert had exclaimed, gazing in wonder at the preserved freshness of the colours and the intricacies of the illustrations. While the highlights for George were The Cage and The Lantern, the former built first as a hunting lodge, later used as a lock-up for prisoners, the latter a belvedere, a folly with three storeys and a spire, from the top of which he could look out over the whole park and spot the herds of red and fallow deer roaming free. The entire landscape, with its historic associations with Henry V and The Black Prince, fires his imagination, conjuring scenes of Agincourt and Crécy, filling him with enormous pride, knowing that the city of his birth is not just the cradle of the industrial revolution, but has always been a mere heartbeat away from shaping the nation's destiny. Agincourt and Crécy. He scans the fields before him. The whole of Manchester must once have looked like this, he thinks, before the smoke stacks, cooling towers and factory chimneys he can just make out on the far horizon, began their inexorable advance. In his mind's eye he sees them as an outpost of horses, thundering towards him, like the Riffs in pursuit of the Red Shadow, a hailstorm of arrows, a volley of cannon fire, swallowed in an avalanche cloud of dust, an army of elephants on the move, unstoppable, invincible.

He carries this vision with him right through to their drive back home at the day's end, beneath a full strawberry moon. He likes this notion of a moon named by Native American Indians for a time of wild fruit ripening, and he remembers the man he saw at Tulip Sunday just last month, when he'd been wondering why there were no elephants this year, who wore a head dress of braided bird feathers, and whose eyes were like tunnels you might get lost in, while across the other side of the city, in his study at the top of the house with the sign of the giant spectacles, Francis stares through his telescope far across the night sky, losing himself in the rings of Saturn as the planet reaches full opposition. George can feel the surge of his father's car, the Crossley Phaeton, vibrating through him. Phaeton, Son of Helios, who one day stole the chariot pulled by horses of flame that drove the sun across the sky and lost control of it and was killed. George thrills at the thought of his father's motor car possessing the power of twenty-five to thirty horses, and longs for the time when he might be allowed to take control of the wheel himself.

It is while his thoughts are chasing after such intoxicating dreams that he becomes aware of the angry voices of his parents, raised in opposition, drowning out the sound of the Crossley engine. They rain into his consciousness with a sudden power, like noctilucent clouds emblazoned by the sun. What before was low and muffled is suddenly harsh and grating, releasing their hail of ice crystals like arrows from a bow.

"I simply don't understand, Annie, how you could make such a decision without at least discussing it with me first."

"I know you don't like to be bothered so much with the business side of things."

"But I'm always going to meetings with clients."

"After I've secured them in the first place. That's how it's worked for years now, Hubert. I seek out new customers, along with your father, and then you work out all the details and oversee the production."

"But that's not what's happened this time, is it? We've just driven past a poster that *we've* printed, which *I* knew nothing about."

Annie is silent.

"Well?"

"We needed this contract, Hubert. How do you think we'd afford the life we live if I didn't manage to win all this work for us?"

"We could live less extravagantly then."

"Really, Hubert? You'd be prepared to give up this car, would you? George's place at school? Our position in society? Because I wouldn't. We've worked so hard to get where we are. When I think of how far we've come from the Tripe Colony…"

"There's nothing to be ashamed of in where you grew up, Annie."

"I'm not ashamed. But that doesn't mean I'm not glad to have got away from it. I told you when I met you that that was my dream."

"So why didn't you talk to me first before going ahead with this latest notion of yours?"

Once again, Annie is silent.

"I'll tell you for why. Because you knew I'd be against it, didn't you?"

Still Annie says nothing.

"I'm right, aren't I?"

"Yes," says Annie quietly.

"I beg your pardon?"

"Yes! You're right. If that makes you feel any better."

"But it doesn't, Annie. It doesn't make me feel better at all. We're both of us Methodists…"

"… only when it suits you…"

"… Methodists, Annie, and we were brought up to believe gambling is wrong."

"For ourselves, not everyone else. *'Judge not that ye be not judged thyself'*."

"But by putting our name to all their publicity, we're

condoning it, aren't we? There's no other way to see it."

"It's business, Hubert. That's all. We're not telling people how to behave. We're just printing posters and tickets to let people know that greyhounds will be racing at Belle Vue if anyone should care to go and watch them."

"I should like to watch them," ventures George meekly, and then continues in a breathless rush. "I should like to very much. I believe they can reach speeds of forty-five miles per hour. That's almost as fast as this car, Father."

Hubert and Annie look at George, then at each other, and then smile. George senses the tension evaporating.

"Good idea," says Annie after a pause. "Why don't you take him, Hubert? I'm sure Major-General Anderson will let me have two tickets."

"Major-General Anderson?" asks Hubert.

"The Director of Racing," replies Annie.

George, sensing a truce in the air and the promise of treats, tentatively starts to sing:

"He is the very model of a modern Major-General
With information vegetable, animal and mineral..."

Smiling, Hubert and Annie join in, and the rest of their journey home is accompanied by song.

"He knows the kings of England and can quote the fights historical
From Marathon to Waterloo, in order categorical..."

Major-General Anderson is the first to admit that, when it comes to all things categorical, his knowledge is rather less than encyclopaedic, especially when it comes to greyhounds, but he knows a good business proposition when it is presented to him, as this particular one was by the American entrepreneur, Charles Munn, who was seeking to promote greyhound racing in Great Britain, having enjoyed a certain level of success with the sport on the other side of the pond. Through a mutual acquaintance, Brigadier Alfred Critchley, who was a leading figure in English field sports, the two of them were introduced to Sir William Gentle, a Lancastrian Justice of the Peace, who was aware that some suitable farmland was available for sale between Higher and Lower Catsknowle, which just happened to be adjacent to the Belle Vue Zoological and Pleasure Gardens. Between them they raised £22,000, £10,000 of which was in the form of a high interest loan, to purchase the land and, at the same time, they formed the National Greyhound Racing Association, thereby legitimising themselves at a stroke.

Henceforward, the very first greyhound race around an oval track in Britain takes place at Belle Vue on Saturday 26th July 1926. Thanks in part to the publicity provided by F.G. Wright & Son, nearly two thousand people attend to watch a dog called Mistley win over a distance of four hundred and forty yards, in a time of just twenty-five seconds, romping home by eight lengths at a starting price of 6/1.

Among those attending, as guests of Major-General Anderson, are Hubert and George.

Hubert finds the noise and press of people difficult to cope with. He has, over time, learned how to mitigate these, to prevent any repetition of the breakdown he experienced in his first months back from the Front, mostly through avoidance, but there are times, like tonight, when events can threaten to unravel him. The metallic rattling of the mechanical hare, as it's propelled around the outside of the track, its mock fur feathered by the rush of air, conjures the ever twitching barbed wire around the trenches, which at night would whistle on the wind, an eerie, ghostly lament reminding Hubert of the sound he'd once heard as a child of a hare screaming, like a baby crying, gasping for air, while the guttural, deep-throated roar of the crowds, as the traps are raised and the dogs fly out in hot pursuit, recall the men's primeval baying as they were ordered over the top. He has to measure his breathing in slow, regular amounts, to try and focus his gaze on just those objects immediately in front of him, to tune out all extraneous sounds, apart from when someone speaks to him. After a couple of races he is able to excuse himself, seek out refreshment from a small kiosk at the back of one of the stands, away from the general hullaballoo, and recover himself with a cup of strong, sweet tea.

The kiosk is a makeshift affair, he notices, more of a cart, with wheels and two protruding handles. Hubert falls into conversation with the proprietor, an Italian by the name of Matteo, who tells him the many advantages of having a business which is so portable, which you can quite literally wheel from one place to another, wherever there is a fair, or market, or sporting event. He is filling in, he tells Hubert, for the father-in-law of his sister, to whom the cart belongs, but who is not well enough these days to push it himself. He does not think he will come back here, though, he says, not unless they give him a better pitch, closer to the action, where more people will see him and buy from him. What is the name of your sister, asks Hubert, a faint bell ringing in a little used recess of his memory? Claudia, replies Matteo. Really, says Hubert. I did wonder. She's a good friend of my wife's. Annie, asks Matteo? Hubert nods and they shake hands warmly. *Un piccolo mondo*, laughs Matteo. Hubert raises his shoulders, spreading his hands, a puzzled look on his face. A small world, translates Matteo. And then they can say no more, for another huge roar erupts from the stands above them, followed by a shower of ripped up, discarded betting slips, falling in a gentle cascade all around them, like broken dreams. For a moment Hubert feels almost as if he is trapped inside a child's snow globe. He bends down to pick up one of the torn tickets and studies it minutely. Someone has printed these, he thinks...

George meanwhile finds the whole evening intoxicating. It streaks past him in a blur of colour, movement and speed. Especially speed. He knows he cannot place a bet. Nor does he want to. But he likes to pick out a greyhound to follow in each race. He hurries down to the front of the track where the dogs are paraded by their handlers, mostly young men hardly older than he is, wearing white coats and black bowlers. He had not realised there was such a variety of greyhound types – black, white, fawn, grey and, his own particular favourite, brindled. He studies how some are distracted by the noise of the crowds and pull on their leads, how some are intent solely on following a particular scent, noses low to the ground, while one or two hold their heads high and erect, looking disdainfully upon the scene as though they feel they really belong in some ancient Persian court, and that this whole spectacle is beneath their dignity. He is drawn to their litany of names and speculates on the stories behind each – Ross Regatta, Davyhulme Shilling, Beaded Jean, Demotic Mack, Danielli, Perdita. He is intrigued, too, by the way the specific colour of the small jacket each dog wears to signify which trap it will be placed in – red for one, blue for two, white for three, black for four, orange for five, and black and white stripes for six – interacts with the colour and demeanour of the dog, and the way the electric floodlights cast different shadows and tones. He tries to draw what he sees, but fails miserably. Everything is happening either too quickly or all at once, so that his eye does not know where to settle. Getting under the skin of things, finding the nuts and bolts as his piano teacher would call them, trying to see how something is constructed, has always lain at the heart of what he has tried to capture before, but now, when there are simply so many sights surrounding him, such a cornucopia of impressions, he doesn't know how to begin. He thinks back, a year ago, to the exhibition he had attended on Blackfriars Street, where he had met, and briefly spoken with Mr Lowry, and he tries to bring back just what it was about those paintings that had struck him so forcibly. Those were canvases, like here at the dog track, teeming with life, peopled with so many characters, creating, at a first deceptive glance, a sense of deadening uniformity, and yet, when examined more closely, each individual was rendered so deftly, so adroitly, as to give an indication of an entire life with only the minimum of brush strokes, a line here, a smudge of colour there. How had he managed that? What was it he had said to him? Paint from life – that's right – and breathe the same air. But faced with such a sensory overload, George feels a kind of paralysis stiffening his hand. He looks at his father, who seems to mirror his panic. Do you like it here, he says? George nods. What especially? George thinks for a moment, then says, the speed of everything. His father shakes his head ruefully. More of a grimace than a smile. Then try and draw that, he says. Don't worry so much about what a thing looks like, just capture the speed. If a greyhound flies past you in a blur in less than a few seconds, only draw for as long as you see it. He gets up when he's said that and says he just needs to stretch his legs for a minute, and that he'll be back again later. George watches him go, walking very slowly, placing one foot carefully in front of the other with deliberate slowness, almost shuffling. He realises his father doesn't like it here, is not enjoying himself one bit, is only staying for George's benefit, and immediately he feels guilty. He decides he will try to do exactly what his father has just advised, so he might show him his efforts when he comes back. The results surprise him. He focuses on the greyhounds. He may not be able to capture the architecture of their bodies, the skeletal musculature, the way sinew and bone, tissue and skin combine to manufacture that effortless grace, but he somehow finds a different set of nuts and bolts, a blurred sense of line and abstraction, a scribbled haze of heat and sweat, a vortex of speed. They are crude, raw, incomplete, but they have an energy about them, a restlessness that George finds appealing, an instantaneousness which he would like to explore further. He looks around him at the sea of faces registering all kinds of different emotions in the crowds against whom he now buffets and swims, and feels a cheek by jowl surge of affection, each of them with their own unique story to tell, stories he believes he might one day relate. He realises with a Damascene jolt that it is a camera he needs more than pencil or paint, but the kind of camera he's not sure even exists, not the one his father possesses, with its tripod and its black cloth and its individual plates and long exposure times, but one which allows him to take pictures as rapidly as blinking an eye. I wonder, he thinks, I wonder…

When his father returns, looking distinctly better, he shows him the lightning sketches, which meet with cautious approval. There's something in them, don't you think? Definitely worth exploring. Thanks, Dad, says George. So long as you've enjoyed yourself, says Hubert, that's the main thing. Yes, Dad. Yes. I have.

In spite of the evening's evident popularity, Munney, Critchley and Gentle are alarmed to discover that they have made a loss of more than £50 on this first meeting, but Major-General Anderson, as well as sensing when he is on to a good thing, is a military strategist and knows the benefits of playing a long game.

Sixteen thousand punters turn up the following week and, after the first three months, they are averaging that much every week. They pay back the initial loan, plus the interest, and shares in the new company rise from one shilling to a meteoric £37. 10s in no time at all, an increase in value of a staggering 750%, a fact not overlooked by Annie, who renegotiates an increase in the fee for the services of F.G. Wright & Son for the following calendar year.

Exactly two years later George experienced an even greater adrenalin rush of speed, when motor cycle enthusiast and telegraph operator Johnnie Hoskins from Wagga Wagga, Australia, decided to try his luck in England, and persuaded the promoter Eric Spence to hold the country's first ever dirt track racing event, or speedway, as it came to be called, on the same circuit where George had first watched greyhounds flying around it in pursuit of a mechanical hare.

It had everything the fifteen year old George could wish for – noise, motor cycles, excitement and speed. It seemed as though the public agreed with him, for within a year a new purpose-built stadium had been built, a quarter of a mile away down Hyde Road. The Belle Vue Aces were born, winning the Northern League at their very first attempt, before going on to win the National Championships on a never-to-be-equalled five successive occasions. George went every Friday night for the next six years, first as a runner, an eager fetcher and carrier, watcher and learner, gradually becoming a permanent and increasingly relied upon fixture in the pits, where his love of tinkering could be indulged to his heart's content. He could take a bike apart and put it back together again in less than five minutes, so stripped down and refined had these racing models become. With no brakes, relying entirely upon the rider's skill with the clutch, running solely on pure methanol instead of petrol, they could accelerate from nought to sixty in a matter of seconds. The real test of a rider's nerve lay in his ability to handle the machine's deceleration, each time it approached one of the four bends that constituted a single lap, the way the rider controlled the disconcerting skid of the back wheel, steering into it to hold the best line and avoid being overtaken as he pulled away along each straight. This was what marked out the true geniuses of the sport from the also-rans, the Frank Vareys, the Eric Langtons, with whom George soon became on familiar first name terms.

"Can you hear it, George?" they'd ask. "Something's not right. It sounds wrong." And George would know exactly what they meant. Success or failure, winning or losing, came down to the finest of fine gradations. Finding ways of shaving tenths of a second from each of the four laps which made up a single race in the less than half an hour a rider would have before embarking upon his next was what would make the difference, and for these miniscule adjustments, they looked increasingly to George.

"It's all about the timing," he'd say.

In a spark ignition internal combustion engine, the timing is relative to the position of the piston and the angle of the crankshaft, of the release of the spark in the chamber near the end of the compression stroke. Setting the optimum timing is crucial to the engine's performance. Sparks occurring too soon, or too late, can be responsible for excessive vibrations, which can affect the speed and handling or, in the worst case, lead to engine damage. Because the bikes used methanol instead of petrol, getting the timing right was even more problematic. Fuel, of whatever type, does not burn the instant the spark fires. Normally there is a slight delay. Reducing the length of that delay is crucial to a rider's ability to make the fastest of starts once the tapes are released. In speedway, as a rule, he who reaches the first bend first is usually the favourite to win the race. It takes an extraordinary skill to find the right line to complete an overtaking manoeuvre on the short straights before having to decelerate into the next bend. George's particular skills were in being able to ensure each engine's plugs were customised to release the spark at exactly the right moment and to maximise the amount, temperature and pressure of methanol required to fuel the bike, thereby rendering it lighter and swifter. He could diagnose within seconds any problem just by the sound an engine was making as it finished a race, and have it repaired and ready in time for the next.

Most of the technicians working in the pits relied upon a J.A.P Timing Wheel, produced by John Arthur Prestwich of Tottenham, which made the setting up of an engine a lot more straightforward.

George came up with a bespoke alternative, which he made himself, specifically designed to match the needs of Frank Varey and Eric Langton.

Nothing ever quite came close to the thrill of setting the timing of a motor cycle absolutely perfectly.

He loved every aspect of speedway – the Parade of Riders to herald the beginning of the meet; the blast of the siren announcing the two minute warm-up period before each race, when engines were gently simmered, like a pan of water coming up to boiling point but not quite reaching it; the guttural roar of the crowds as the tapes flew up for the start; the whine of the bikes as the riders strained every nerve and sinew to get the maximum speed and performance from them; the cascade of cinders flying up at each bend, showering the spectators with soot and grit; the raking of the track afterwards to smooth out the layers of shale and even out any pot holes that may have been created; the blur of bikes and riders as they crossed the finishing line and took the chequered flag – but what he loved most was simply being a part of it all, the satisfaction of solving a problem, of knowing that you mattered, that all those Sunday afternoons helping his father strip down the engine of his beloved Crossley Phaeton, had born fruit, and that, when it came down to it, the art of tinkering reigned supreme.

Timing is everything.

Not just for the tinkerer, but also for the businessman.

Francis likes to regard himself as being a bit of both. He is something of a butterfly. His attention is easily distracted. He has a habit of madly chasing after the latest new thing, only to drop it as soon as the next one comes along. He has a low boredom threshold. He is not a man who likes to persevere. For him, something must succeed at once, or not at all. To counter this, he knows he has a flair for spotting trends, before they've even become one, for sensing where there's a gap in the market and finding what's required to fill it. Above all, he is passionate about innovation, he is a champion of all things modern, and he sees Manchester as the natural birthplace of such discoveries and advancements, as it always has been. In industry, in science, in education, and the arts. He believes that everybody else shares this certainty with him, that all of us, he will say, to anyone who cares to listen, want to improve our lot in life. We all of us want better homes, better jobs, more money, more material comforts. We all of us want indoor plumbing, a telephone, a radio, to be in touch with the wider world, to be at the centre of things. That is what has guided him since he returned from the Isle of Man more than a decade ago, when he followed that line of telegraph poles marching across the land from Liverpool to Manchester, when he arrived in a place where nobody knew him, so that he might reinvent himself, start a new life, with a new name and a new set of dreams.

Francis, too, is aware of John Arthur Prestwich, who made his name initially as a manufacturer of scientific instruments, notably of condenser lens systems for microscopes, before collaborating with the electrical engineer Sebastian Pietro Innocenti de Ferranti and the inventor and photographer William Friese-Greene, who between them produced pioneering cinematography cameras and projectors, examples of which Francis has experimented with himself, and which he stocks in his shop beneath the sign of the giant spectacles.

G.F. Kaufman & Son, the sign had read. Optics, Jewellery, Engraving.

How things have changed since then. He has long since given up the optician work – although he still receives occasional enquiries – and nor any longer does he cut gems or precious stones, while he never even started with engraving. Optics, yes – he sells binoculars, telescopes, microscopes, many of them manufactured by Franks Ltd of Deansgate – and every type of camera, more and more of which he sells each year. More recently he has added radio receivers and gramophones to his stock and, as he predicted when he began to sell them before people even realised what they were, let alone that they wanted or needed them, the public's appetite for these has proved insatiable.

And yet...

His own appetite is far from sated. He constantly seeks out the new. We are living in an age of speed, he repeatedly says to his friend and doctor, Charles Trevelyan, when they meet to play chess at St James's. I agree with you, says Charles, which is why neither of us will ever be successful with this game. We're too impatient. Knight to Queen's Pawn Five, checkmate in three. He leans back, smugly satisfied with himself. I think not, my friend, grins Francis, you are forgetting my rook. There, cries Charles exasperatedly knocking several pieces off the board, my point exactly.

And yet…

For all his outward success, his circle of friends at *The Queen's* and his maverick role at the BBC, going over his accounts one evening at the beginning of the third week in May in 1929, he is disconcerted to realise that, in the words of his bank manager, he would appear to be living "in anticipation of some income". In other words, he's broke. Not only that, he's not sure where the money to pay his next set of bills is actually going to come from.

"It would seem," he confides later to Charles over a brandy, "that I am what is known in the jargon as 'asset rich' but 'cash poor'."

Charles inhales deeply from his cigar. "What you need," he says, a few moments later, "is a Passepartout."

"As in Phileas Fogg?"

"Exactly. Someone who can sort out your books, manage your invoices, put your accounts in order, deal with customers, organise your diary, answer the telephone, and – most important of all – tell you precisely where you should be going and what you should be doing at any given moment in the day, sort out your priorities for you, thereby allowing you the time and space to concentrate on what you do best, namely researching and developing the products."

"But where am I to find such a paragon?"

"Advertise, dear boy, advertise. In newspapers, shop windows, public buildings. Use your contacts."

Francis puts his head in his hands, defeated already by the prospect of all that this would entail.

"Believe me, it will be worth the effort. I speak from experience. Without Nurse McMaster I should be a gibbering wreck. But she ensures that all the tedious but necessary administration which accompanies every profession is dealt with first thing each morning, leaving me the rest of the day to carry out what I regard as my more important medical duties. Frankly, I don't think you have an option. You're in a pickle right now, you've admitted as much yourself. Do nothing and the situation can only get worse, but find yourself a Passepartout, allow him, or her, to set your affairs in order, and then you can return to doing what you do best."

"You make it all sound so simple."

Later that night, on one of his customary nightly perambulations, Francis can see the sense in his friend's advice. As a child, Francis had been an assiduous compiler of lists. One of his teachers, recognising this, had recommended he assist in the school library. There he had become drawn to the simple logic of its Dewey decimal classification system. He found beauty in order. He even wondered about becoming a taxonomist, for there was great pleasure and satisfaction to be found in the ordering of contents by their appropriate genus and species, while the imaginative possibilities offered by cross-referencing and indicative indexing seemed luxuriously limitless. This view was confirmed for him when he chanced upon an article in *The Library Journal*, a somewhat esoteric publication subscribed to by the school, in which the then little known Henry E. Bliss, Assistant Librarian for the New York City Library, advocated an alternative to the Dewey system based upon the principle of 'alternative location', whereby a book might be housed in more than one section, and where classification by subject became as a consequence a more fluid set of choices. This especially appealed to Francis, who was always keen to explore hitherto hidden links and unseen, or even unmade, connections. But gradually he came to realise that, whatever system for codified classification one might adopt, nothing could ever contain the total sum of human knowledge. While on the one hand he warmed to Bliss's methodology, being based almost entirely upon the eccentricities of his own personal, customised typewriter, leading to a highly idiosyncratic use of capital and lower-case letters, numbers and symbols combining a consistent, if seemingly random, accumulation of all the differently available typographical fonts at his disposal, at the same time he became increasingly aware that no taxonomy could ever be complete and, as such, he began to find them more and more unsatisfactory. He looked instead for new discoveries. He dreamed of everybody in possession of their own uniquely eccentric typewriter, on which, in their own bespoke, individual way, they might seek out connections across all manner of hitherto unimagined alternative locations, from where, at the touch of key, the information and knowledge requested might be instantaneously relayed, teleprinted automatically, directly to their Remington, their Gardner, or their Underwood.

Although he continued to derive comfort and pleasure from staring through his telescopes at the night sky, continually mapping the heavens, observing the traceable patterns of constellations, the fixed orbits of planets, what drew him to his unceasing quest for better quality lenses, with greater magnification and increased luminosity, was not so much to be able to see more clearly what he already knew existed, but to enable him, rather, to see further and deeper into the less charted, more distant reaches of the universe, in the hope that he might look upon something he had not seen before. Similarly, when he continued to refine his radio receivers and tune into as yet unheard frequencies, it was not merely that he wanted to transmit further – right around the world, or deep into space – but that he wanted to be heard, to make his mark upon the surface of things, for others to chance upon and find after he'd gone.

There should be no limits upon what a man or woman dreams, he thinks, as he pounds the city streets at midnight, no constraints upon our imaginations. Just as this city continues to expand and change, both accommodating and shaping the times, pushing its boundaries further and further outwards, so do our own horizons expand and, with them, our values, attitudes, morals and tolerances shift also.

He has reached Piccadilly Gardens. A young man under a street lamp asks him for a light, as young men seem so often to do. He feels his face flush. His collar seems suddenly tight and his hand tugs to loosen it. His psoriatic rash is particularly irksome on this evening. The young man is persistent. He asks again. When Francis obliges, he looks into his eyes as he inhales upon his now lit cigarette, to see if what he sees there might reflect these same restless imaginings. But he sees only smoke, clouding the expression on the young man's face, and Francis, as he routinely does, shakes his head and saunters, the air of disquiet hanging heavy on his shoulders, towards the shelter and relief of *The Queen's Hotel* just across the street, where the welcome is as warm, familiar and affirming as it always is.

"*Buona serra,* Signor Hall," says Luigi, as Francis hands him his hat and coat. "Your usual table?"

"*Si, Luigi. Come di solito. Grazie.*"

Inside Cam is already singing.

"*Once he dressed in silks and lace
And owned a Rolls Royce car
Now he seems quite out of place
Just like a fallen star…*"

She catches Francis's eye as he takes his seat, smiles broadly, then walks directly towards a pair of young women sitting at the next table to him, singing directly to one of them.

"*I'm not much to look at
Nothing to see*

*I'm just glad I'm living
And lucky to be
For I've got a woman
Who's crazy for me
She's funny that way…"*

Everyone smiles and applauds, understanding the codes. She then proceeds to sit on the empty seat next to Francis for her next song.

*"I was a humdrum person
Leading a life apart
When love flew in through my window-wide
And quickened my humdrum heart…"*

Francis takes out his cigarette case, which Cam flips open for him, puts a cigarette into his mouth, while Luigi is suddenly there at his side with a lighter, which Cam takes from him, flicks it and lights Francis's cigarette.

*"What is this thing called love?
This funny thing called love?
Just who can solve its mystery?
Why should it make a fool of me?
I saw you there one wonderful day
You took my heart and threw it away
That's why I ask the Lord up above
What is this thing called love…?"*

Cam takes Francis's cigarette from between his lips and inhales from it herself, before returning to the small stage opposite the bar to finish her act.

*

3rd April 1928

Dear Delphine,

I shall not be able to make our next appointment at The Lit & Phil, I'm afraid, as we had arranged. I almost wrote that 'something has come up', which would be true but irredeemably crass of me. Let me beat about the bush no longer. Reader, I am to be married!

I am as surprised to be writing this as no doubt you are to be reading it, for it is not something I ever imagined for myself. Since my mother died, when I was just thirteen years old, I have been more or less a full time carer, looking after my father and five brothers. I occasionally would think, at times of sheer exhaustion, that while I now possessed the skills expected of a wife in terms of running and managing a household on a restricted income, I had neither the time nor opportunity to meet any prospective beneficiary of such skills, even had I the inclination to find a husband which, I realised with perfect equanimity, that I did not.

What I never stopped to consider were those far more important aspects a marriage should contain, namely those appertaining to emotional, temperamental and intellectual companionship. I confess to you, Delphine, that I thought not at all about that other vital ingredient – sex. Oh, I received my fair share of wolf whistles from the men at the colliery during the time I was a pit brow girl there during the War, but recognised that this was merely 'pack' behaviour, each whistler only trying to impress his pals whenever they caught the scent of a young woman, rather than being directed explicitly towards me. At other times I had waltzed stiffly and awkwardly with a tongue-tied, embarrassed youth at one of the Gala Dances, but I don't honestly recall ever feeling lovelorn or unrequited in any way. I would vicariously experience the grand passions of Tess, Catherine or Anna and be swept along as I read them, but I never personally identified with them. Nor did I ever feel I was missing out in any way.

Once, perhaps, just as the War ended, when the telegram arrived informing us of Arthur's death, right in the last gasp of the fighting, I did experience a flicker of what I suppose might be connected with that mysterious 'otherness' which I had attributed to what a man and a woman in love might be expected to feel towards one another.

I was angry, furious at the futility and waste of it all, that such good and decent men as Arthur, and millions like him, should have been sacrificed – and for what? I snatched up his bicycle and pedalled recklessly into the night, heedless of where I was heading. The rain was bouncing off the streets and, to cut a long story short, I skidded in the wet, crashed and tumbled into quite a deep man hole, where water pipes were being repaired. It was obvious to me at once that I'd broken my leg and, try as I might, there seemed no way of hauling myself up and out of the trench, so I resigned myself to a long night, with little hope of attracting any passers-by for assistance, for only a fool like me would venture out on such a night.

About half an hour later, though, someone did pass by – a strange looking man with long, straggly hair beneath a wide-brimmed hat with feathers stuck in the head band. He had dark, chestnut brown skin and eyes like tunnels, which drew you so deeply into them that you saw fires burning inside them, across vast, unbroken plains stretching endlessly away. If this sounds fanciful to you, which I'm sure it must, I can only apologise and put it down to my heightened emotional state at the time – the loss of my brother, the pain from my fall – I believe I was quite delirious. The man leapt down into the trench beside me, where we found, of all things, a human thigh bone jutting out of the earth, which he used to fashion a splint and then tied it tightly to my broken leg. He told me his name was Tommy. Tommy Thunder. Such a curious name. I've never forgotten it. He then lifted me into his arms and carried me all the way back to my home, a distance of more than two miles. I seemed to weigh nothing to him, no more than one of those feathers slotted into the headband of his hat, and I leaned into him, feeling the rhythm of his breathing as he walked. He spoke little, nor I to him, we learned nothing about each other, and yet it was, up until recently, the most erotically charged moment of my life.

The private lives of married couples are a mystery to us all, I believe, no matter what Mr Freud might have us think to the contrary. I doubt any two are the same, the intimacies and intricacies shared between them known only to the couple themselves. I have no empirical evidence for this feeling, only what I witnessed between my mother and father, who were completely devoted to one another, which was evident for all to see. They met as children and had eyes for nobody else thereafter. When my mother died, the light went out of my father's eyes and it never returned, but this was only something I could observe, not truly understand, for romantic love was something I had simply not experienced for myself. In his final years, he would often confuse me with my mother, and this was because, I am certain of it, as he retreated further and further from the present back into the past, it was her face that he was seeing everywhere. Sometimes, too, the young women that my remaining brothers have married, would come and visit me, ostensibly so that I might see my latest niece or nephew, but often their real reason would be revealed, after the second cup of tea perhaps, which would be to hint, darkly and unspecifically, at some private trouble between them and Jim or Frank or Harold, as if somehow, because I had known them as boys, I might be able to offer insights into the type of man each had become. All I could do was offer sympathetic silence.

Then, when my father finally and mercifully died, I found myself alone in a flat that was far too large for my needs, and so I sought alternative accommodation from the Housing Trust. The allocation of a 'widow's flat' seemed a kind of mockery, an honest reflection of the reality of my situation, an acknowledgement that my sexual life was at an end, even before it had begun. And in all truthfulness I was quite accepting of this situation. Something one has never known is not something one can ever miss. I had a job – albeit not a particularly stimulating one, but in times such as these one is hardly in a position to complain. I had a modest, comfortable place in which to live. I had my books, my meetings, my small circle of friends and acquaintances, of which you had become a most valued member.

And then – quite unexpectedly and unlooked for – something happened. I met a young man. I encountered him on the steps outside the Bradford Colliery leading up from the Ashton Canal, where he was standing disconsolately in the rain, having suffered something of a personal humiliation during the recent visit of King Amanullah of Afghanistan. I too had experienced a minor disappointment – not so crushing as his – in the failure of Queen Surayya to accompany her husband to the mine, for I had hoped to speak with her, having been so impressed by her speech the day before at the Town Hall. The young man and I fell into talking. Something about his situation, along with the quiet and dignified way he was seeking to mask his hurt and rise above it, touched my heart. I found myself drawn into immediate, easy conversation with him, a conversation I wished to prolong, and so I acted in the most surprisingly forward manner. I invited him into my widow's flat, I encouraged him to take a bath, change into some dry clothes of my father's which I still had, cooked him some soup and even made up a bed for him on the couch!

That was a month ago, and a day has not gone by since then that we have not seen one another. I knew at once that I wanted to marry this man, and that he felt just as certain as I did, and so we are indeed to be married in just two weeks' time. If you are able to attend, Delphine, that would make me so happy.

His name is Hejaz Wahid – though the family uses the surname 'Ward', and he prefers the diminutive of 'Jaz'. He is the only son of Yasser – a mountain of a man who came over from the Yemen to help build the Manchester Ship Canal, where he works still – and Rose, who has become such a friend to me already. They live close to the Canal in Patricroft, where Jaz and I are to live too after we have married. Perhaps you might visit us there one day?

Now that I have made what appears to my brothers' wives to be an act of injudicious haste at best, or wanton folly at worst, I can sense their looks of pity boring into me as I turn my back to go to the kitchen here in my 'widow's flat' to make them a cup of tea when they visit. 'Desperate' is the word I am sure is springing to their lips as they whisper awkwardly to one another behind their gloved hands. But I say this: if you know in your heart that what you are doing is absolutely the right thing to do, what is to be gained by unnecessary delay, merely on the grounds of outdated notions of propriety? For most of my life I have been constrained by having to act for the needs of others. I do not resent this – please don't misunderstand me – but I have always subjugated my own desires. I have not felt so alive since before I was twenty, when I first met Hannah Mitchell and was inspired to take up the cause of the Suffragists, as I do now.

Your friend,
Esther

(Blundell – though not for much longer!)

*

5th April 1928

Dear Esther,

Congratulations! What wonderful news! I am so happy for you. Thank you for writing and sharing your thoughts and ideas with me in the way that you have. I shall miss the regular conversations we have recently begun to embark on since we have become such good friends, but I trust that we shall continue to correspond regularly once you are married and that we may carry on with the same frankness of discourse.

Now – it is I who have a surprise announcement to make to you.

I know the Wahid family – extremely well, too. My father helped to dig the Ship Canal. He was part of Yasser's team, who garnered quite a reputation for being one of the quickest gangs of all, and as such were sometimes singled out for special assignments. One of these was to build the Trafford Park Road Swing Bridge (having previously worked on the Barton Swing Bridge). While scoping out this new job, there was a terrible explosion in a chemical factory close to the Pomona Docks. Yasser was badly injured and it was my father who rescued him from the rubble.

Many years later, after both my parents died from the Spanish flu epidemic of 1919, Yasser came to my aid when I was in dire need of help. That's a long story for another time perhaps. But it was on that occasion that I met Jaz. He had just come back from the War and was about to start work as a draughtsman. He was extremely shy, I remember, and I thought perhaps he developed a little crush on me. I hope you don't mind my saying this? It was almost ten years ago now and anyway, nothing at all happened. He was too shy even to speak to me, but he was extremely kind, as the whole family were. They were there for me when I most needed them. I've not seen them in ages, although Rose and I do write to one another from time to time. Please give them my love, won't you?

And here's yet another coincidence. I have never hidden the fact that my father was an American Indian. He was brought to this country against his will as part of the Wild West Show at Belle Vue. After a few years there he and three others ran away. Their leader was none other than your knight in shining armour who rescued you from that rain filled trench when you broke your leg – Tommy Thunder. I didn't know him well, for they all split up shortly after I was born, when the land they had settled on near the River Irwell was sold to make way for the new Ship Canal.

That's where my father returned after the Canal was finished, to run a ferry across it for people to get to and from work. Mine was quite an unusual childhood, living by water, climbing trees, catching fish, skinning rabbits, and every few years Tommy Thunder would turn up and stay with us for a few days. He'd reverted to a more nomadic life again, taking seasonal work on farms and estates when and where he could find it, and sometimes this would bring him to our neck of the woods. He had a real gift with horses, I remember, and this took him to France during the War, after which I never saw him again. There was something about him, though, that was deeply compelling, once encountered, never forgotten, so I can completely understand the response he drew from you. But he was never the sort of man to settle down with a wife, I don't imagine, and so you are definitely better off with Jaz!

Just as I am perfectly content remaining single. I have my friendship with Charles, which suits me very well for the time being. I know that he wishes it were something more than what it is, but that kind of commitment is not something I am yet ready for. Or perhaps, unlike you, Esther, I have yet to meet that Mr Right!

Who was it who first coined that wonderful aphorism, 'Procrastination is the thief of time'? I believe it may have been the poet Edward Young in his 'Night Thoughts'. If there's one thing the War has taught us, surely it must be to gather those rosebuds while we may, before they wither on the stem. So I say pay no heed to any talk of injudicious haste. Carpe diem! To hell with propriety! I applaud your courage. Caution is the last resort of cowards.

I am so delighted by your news – thank you again for letting me know – and yes, I would very much like to attend the wedding if I possibly can. Please let me have the details of where and when as soon as you can, so that I am able to make the necessary arrangements.

*Your friend in return,
Delphine*

*

Back in *The Queen's Hotel* Cam is once again taking Francis's cigarette from between his lips. "Time to act," she says to her audience, though keeping her eyes fixed firmly on him, "no more of this endless – *qu'est-ce que tu dis?* – shilly-shally. What is it you say? *La procrastination – c'est le voleur de temps…*"

*"In olden days a glimpse of stocking
Was looked on as something shocking
Now Heaven knows
Anything goes…"*

The next day, having arranged to place the advertisement for his Passepartout in a range of prominent publications and strategic shop and office windows, Francis finds himself in the Gallery of the Town Hall in Albert Square, where he often repairs when he is seeking comfort or solace, to view once more *The Manchester Murals* by Ford Madox Brown. He finds a deep, quiet strength in standing in front of them, of viewing the arc of their historic achievements, which have cumulatively contributed to this city which he loves, becoming the magnet and success that it is, and trying to find his own place within it. At different times he has found himself favouring different ones of the twelve murals. Today he is standing before the final one, depicting John Dalton collecting marsh fire gas, an action which led to his development of modern atomic theory.

Francis recalls the lecture he attended with Charles given by Professor Einstein five years previously. Sometimes, he thinks, it is the smallest things to which we must pay attention.

At first he thinks he is alone. But then he becomes aware of a shadow falling across the tiled floor. He hears a throat being cleared, a chair being scraped.

" *'By their works shall ye know them'*," a voice hoarsely says.

Francis turns and sees an elderly man sitting beneath one of the murals, the one of Humphrey Chetham's Dream, of the charity school for poor children.

"I beg your pardon. I hope I do not intrude?"

"This is a public building, is it not? For the enjoyment of all."

"Indeed. But I've no wish to disturb, if you were seeking solitude. I know that I come here for that purpose sometimes."

"Please." The older man indicates the empty chair next to where he is sitting. "Won't you join me? I find I'm rather tired this morning. I need to sit a little longer. But I should welcome the company."

Francis inclines his head and obliges the man by sitting beside him. "My name's Francis, by the way. Francis Hall." He produces his business card, which the older man studies, then smiles. "What is it?" asks Francis.

"The name at the bottom," replies the man, "where it says, *'Printed by F.G. Wright & Son'*. That's me," and he begins to laugh, 'Frank Wright'."

"Oh, I see. Yes. What a coincidence," and Francis chuckles too in response, but then Frank's laughter turns into a rasping, painful-sounding cough. "Should I fetch you some water?" inquires Francis, but Frank waves his question aside.

"Thank you, no. I shall be fine by and by."

And in a few moments he is. "So, Mr Hall, what is it that brings you to peruse *The Manchester Murals* this fine May morning?"

Francis smiles, pausing before answering. "I needed some perspective."

"Ah. About what? If you don't mind my asking...?"

"Not at all. I'm..." He considers how much he should tell this kind gentleman whom he has only just met.

"Yes?"

"Let's just say that I'm experiencing cash flow difficulties at this present time." He explains a little about his current circumstances.

"And what have you decided to do about this most unfortunate situation?"

Francis relates in part the advice given to him by Charles.

"That sounds an excellent suggestion your friend has made. It's not easy running a business."

Francis sighs, agreeing.

"As Mr Micawber so wisely puts it: *'Annual income twenty pounds, annual expenditure nineteen pounds, nineteen shillings and sixpence: result, happiness. Annual income twenty pounds, annual expenditure twenty pounds and sixpence: result, misery'*."

"Quite so," says Francis bleakly.

"May I ask you a personal question?" asks Frank. "You must tell me if I am being impertinent."

"Not at all."

"Are you married, Mr Hall?"

"No. I am not."

Frank nods. "Then it is doubly difficult for you. A business comes with social, as well as professional responsibilities, and I am most fortunate that my wife handles that side of things so expertly that I don't have to trouble myself even with thinking about them. Without her, I know I should struggle. And then I have my son."

"Will he take over from you when you retire?"

"He already has." He refers once more to the business card. " 'F.G. Wright *& Son'*. That's what the card says. He now takes care of most of the day-to-day matters. But..." Now it is Frank's turn to pause, to wonder how much to say to someone he has only just met.

"Yes?"

"My son is an idealist."

"A good thing, surely?"

"Yes, of course. But there's a time and a place. He can be so idealistic at times that his head is in the clouds. He's a tinkerer. He is never happier than when a problem arises with one of the printing presses and he can then apply himself wholly to fixing it and hopefully improving it. He would spend his every waking hour if he could in the sole pursuit of the perfect printing press." Frank chuckles at the thought.

"I think I can understand that," replies Francis.

"Yes. I thought perhaps you might. And that is why I say running a business alone is especially challenging. But fortunately my son has married a woman with an immensely practical head on her shoulders. She understands the more mundane matters of commerce, what our American cousins refer to so succinctly as 'the bottom line'. Nothing passes her by. Her books are meticulous, a thing of wonder, a beauty to behold. I trust her completely with ensuring that my business will thrive and prosper in her safe and capable hands when I do choose to retire, while my son will continue to refine and, yes, tinker, so that the quality of what we produce will keep on getting better and better. So you see, they make a fine partnership, and have, I believe, passed on the best traits of each of them to their own son, George."

"George?"

"A dreamer and a tinkerer like his father, but his head in the real world like his mother."

"You must be very proud of them."

"I've been lucky, Mr Hall, extremely lucky. We're not all of us blessed with finding our perfect partner."

Francis nods silently.

"And so," says Frank, "I hope this advice from your friend will at least lead you to the perfect *business* partner."

"It's not a partner I'm seeking so much, more a…" He pauses over the right word. "… a solution to my… temporary impecunious predicament!"

"Splendid," roars Frank. "Micawber could not have expressed it better."

He rises to his feet, a little unstably, and Francis takes his elbow to steady him.

"Let's take a turn around the murals together, shall we?" asks Frank, once he has regained his balance.

"By all means. Which is your favourite?"

"What a curious question. Once upon a time I would have answered that the two originally envisioned by Ford Madox Brown but never actually completed would have been the ones I'd have been proudest of."

"Which were those? I don't know of them."

"One depicting Peterloo and the other portraying the suffering during the Cotton Famine. The powers that be thought they were too controversial and so refused Brown permission. But I disagree. I believe that both would have shown Manchester at her best, the spirit of ordinary people refusing to be downtrodden, rising up, proud and defiant. That's a Manchester I recognise. Instead they opted for *'The Baptism of Edwin of Northumbria'*, which didn't in fact take place anywhere near here, and *'The Expulsion of The Danes'*, the authenticity of which is questionable to say the least." He shakes his head with a rueful smile. "How about you? Do you have a favourite?"

"There are two in particular that I find myself drawn to," replies Francis. "Being something of an amateur astronomer myself, I've always enjoyed *'Crabtree Watching the Transit of Venus'."*

Frank nods in agreement.

"But today I sought out John Dalton."

"...which indeed is *'the least of all seeds: but when it is grown, it is the greatest among herbs, and becometh a tree, so that the birds of the air come and lodge in the branches thereof...*"

Francis knits his brow.

"Matthew," explains Frank. "Chapter 13, verse 32."

"I see," says Francis, who hasn't looked at a bible since he left school, "although given the current parlous state of my business affairs, perhaps *'The Proclamation Regarding Weights & Measures'* would have been more apt."

Frank smiles.

"So, out of those murals that are here," continues Francis, with an expansive gesture of his arm, attempting to take in all of the murals in a single sweep, "can you point to a personal favourite?"

"That depends, I suppose, on the circumstances of the day, the context against which one happens to be looking at them, don't you agree?"

"Sir?"

"Take this morning, for example. Here you found me, sitting beneath *'Humphrey Chetham's Dream'*, which is the mural I came quite purposefully to look at, for I had just attended a committee meeting here at the Council Chamber to make the decision as to who will be the architect awarded the brief to design the new library for the city. They held an open competition, and the winner is a Mr Emanuel Vincent Harris – sadly not a Mancunian – but you should see his plans, Mr Hall. They quite take the breath away. His vision is for an enormous rotunda, not unlike the Pantheon of Rome – appropriate, don't you think, for the industrial heart of another empire? There'll be nothing like it anywhere else, and it will be another first for Manchester, the first and largest public library provided by a civic authority anywhere in the country, and it will be completely free, for everyone. And that's why I wanted to take a look at this mural. Humphrey Chetham would have recognised and welcomed this new gesture to enable everybody, no matter what their circumstances or background, to gain access to all of the world's knowledge. His dream is finally coming to pass. That's something, isn't it?"

This long speech has exhausted Frank and he is breathing heavily.

"Are you sure you don't want that glass of water, Sir?"

"Yes. Perhaps you're right. Would you mind?"

Francis has barely reached the doorway leading out of The Great Hall, when his attention is arrested by a sudden noise behind him. He turns to see Frank clutching his chest. He tries to speak, but only a contracted, painful, gurgling sound can escape his lips. Francis rushes towards him, just in time to catch him as he threatens to topple to the hard, unforgiving marble floor. With his free hand, Frank catches hold of the lapels of Francis's jacket and pulls him towards him. For the briefest of seconds their eyes lock. Frank appears about to speak, as if he has something of the utmost importance to impart to this new acquaintance whom he's barely met, and then the focus slips. The light leaves his eyes, a departing tide which carries him away. The colour drains from his face and, it seems to Francis holding him in his arms, in the air around them both, becoming grey, an upturned pewter bowl, in which he can detect no reflection, not of himself, or of this decent, hard working man, who should have died surrounded by those who loved him, not here, with a stranger, on this cold marble floor, where Francis now lays him gently, among the mosaics of cotton flowers and worker bees.

He has spent too much of the past decade with his eye fixed to a telescope, searching among the cold and pitiless stars for objects he can never touch or see, like he is touching and seeing this man before him, or listening, through headphones with eyes clenched tight, the better to shut out all extraneous distraction, in order to pick out distant voices through the static's tinnitus and, in so doing, he has somehow missed what people closest to him have been saying. He has looked at life, he realises, as though it were a taxonomy, a stuffed owl housed beneath a bell jar, through which he might appreciate its fearful symmetry, but never feel the rush of air created by its silent swoop, whose passage might have caused the prickling of his skin, or the hairs on the back of his neck to stand up like an electrical charge, almost as if he has been, like Crabtree, watching for the transit of Venus, knowing that its next appearance will not occur for at least another seventy-five years, yet staying indoors just the same, his eye glued to his telescope, fixed upon the night sky, just in case, while all around him life teems, from which he knowingly excludes himself.

He resolves there and then to stop being a bystander, a recorder of other people's voices, other people's experiences, and begin instead to garner his own, and acquire a voice with which to articulate them. He needs, he now sees, more clearly than he has before, his Passepartout, his master key, quite literally to go everywhere, to unlock those hitherto sequestered rooms, to dispel doubt and shadow, and let the light back in.

Before this good, kind man's body is taken from him and administered to by the now steady arrival of doctors, priests, council workers and officials, before telephone calls are put through and telegrams sent, before funeral arrangements are made and invitations issued, and obituaries posted in newspapers, Francis leans across and, as gently as he is able, places a kiss upon his forehead.

Ten days later Francis is sitting as inconspicuously as he can at the back of the Albert Hall on Peter Street, the Methodists' eclectically grand Mission Hall for Manchester. Designed by William James Morley of Bradford, and built by J. Gerrard & Sons of Swinton in a mixture of Baroque and Neo-Gothic styles, it regularly seats more than two thousand, two hundred and fifty souls for Sunday morning services. Today, this last Thursday in May 1929, there must be almost twice that number, thinks Francis, for the funeral of Frank Wright, this man he had met just the once, but whose impact on him has been so transformative. The horseshoe-shaped Upper Gallery has also been opened up and it, too, is full, while there must be scores of people standing, with dozens more waiting outside to pay their respect to someone who had touched so many lives.

While he waits for the service to begin, Francis, who has never been in the Albert Hall before, takes in its surprisingly decorative flourishes, its ebullient floral decoration in the plaster work, the minutely detailed terracotta tiles around each of the windows, the slightly raked floor, and the coloured glass roof lights, through which at this moment the sun is streaming, refracting into reds and greens and golds, dappling the heads and shoulders of the mourners and adding a strangely medieval quality to the scene. Adolphe Valette would have rendered all this so subtly, thinks Francis, in muted tones, each shaft of light from above picking out the principal players in the scene, and then scolds himself for allowing his mind to stray in such an undisciplined fashion, at a time when his thoughts should all be with the family, feeling sympathy for their loss, which he tries to do, although this is difficult when he does not know them. He sees them, or who he assumes to be them, far away to the front of the Hall, in the row of seats reserved for them, arriving last, behind the coffin, which has been carried in by four of the undertaker's men, two of them old hands, their neatly trimmed moustaches now beginning to show tinges of grey, followed by two younger apprentices, red-faced boys, their cheeks scrubbed and shining, uncomfortable in their unaccustomed black suits and polished shoes, all of them slow-marching in step, the coffin perched expertly on their inside shoulders, their outside, free hands holding their bowler hats, which they will put back on their heads the moment they step back outside of the Hall, the older men covering their balding pates in a bid to keep their few remaining, errant wisps of hair under control, the boys to place upon their slicked back Brilliantined hair, from which a recalcitrant, wayward curl on each refuses to conform.

Francis transfers his gaze back to the family and tries to establish who is who. First comes the widow, plainly attired, a long black coat, in spite of the day's heat, a simple small felt hat, no veil, her face shriven. She is supported by a younger woman, more fashionable but also modest, an elegant black chemise dress of *crêpe de chine*, a black linen cloche, adorned with a black band and a black sewn-in rose. This must be the daughter-in-law, thinks Francis, the one with the unerring eye for business, the kind he hopes perhaps to find for his own assistant, though none of those who have so far applied have been remotely suitable. The two women are followed by three men – the first, older, tall, with more than a passing resemblance to Frank, the brother perhaps, speculates Francis, the 'G' of F.G. Wright & Son; he is followed by the son, the idealist and the tinkerer, now, Francis can see, fidgeting with the cuff of his jacket, trying to brush off an unwanted thread, his wife, as if aware of his disquiet by osmosis, turns and, in a swift, impatient gesture, removes it in an instant; and, finally, the grandson, the one who combines the best traits of both his parents, it would seem, a tall, strapping youth, Francis notes, who pauses by the coffin, looking straight ahead of him with clear-eyed, yet undisguised sorrow, as if he cannot comprehend how this man, who has seemed to him immortal, should now simply be no more. Francis finds that he can hardly breathe. He is simply transfixed by his beauty, regarding him as he stands in the central nave of Albert Hall, with the refracted sunlight from the roof glass falling on his hair and shoulders, illuminating him like one of Botticelli's angels.

When the service ends, Francis wonders whether he should linger, introduce himself perhaps to Mrs Wright, explain how he was with her husband when he died, that his last words were all of her, his son, grandson and daughter-in-law, and how proud he was of his family and all that she particularly had done to support him over their years together, but he realises that he would be doing so more for himself than for her, and so in the end he decides not to. He slips away quietly, while the rest of the mourners prepare to transfer to the Town Hall, where the Banqueting Hall has been made available for them, since the numbers attending are so great, a testament to the high esteem in which Frank was held by the city of Manchester. Instead Francis makes his way in the warm May sunshine towards Princess Street, from where he can catch the tram back to Denton, to the shop, where he hopes the morning post will have delivered fresh enquiries from would-be applicants for the post of his Passepartout.

Back outside the Albert Hall, the mourners are slowly making their way down Mount Street towards the Town Hall. Hubert and George have gone on ahead to make sure all is ready, while Evelyn once again leans on her daughter-in-law's arm for support. She is exhausted already, but the day has barely begun. This reception will be the greatest trial of all, but it must be borne, for all these people have turned up out of respect for her Frank, and she steels herself to be ready to accept their condolences.

On the Town Hall steps a middle-aged man in council livery holds open the door for her and raises his hat.

"Pardon me, ma'am," he stammers, "but I just want you to know how very sorry my wife and I are for your loss. Mr Wright was always so very kind towards us."

"Thank you," replies Evelyn, then stops. "It's Joseph, isn't it?"

"Yes, ma'am."

"Yes. My husband often spoke of you. How is that boy of yours?"

"He's well, ma'am, thank you, ma'am. The doctors say he's making fine progress. He's walking practically unaided these days."

"I'm very glad to hear it, Joseph. Please remember me to your wife, won't you?"

"Thank you, ma'am."

Annie regards her mother-in-law with sheer, disbelieving admiration, that, even at a time like this, she can summon up the strength to say exactly the right words to someone she has never before met. The two women enter the inner cool of the Town Hall, where George is looking out for them.

"This way," he says. "Everything's ready."

As they make their way towards the Banqueting Hall, Annie marvels at the stoicism of her mother-in-law. "What's the matter with Joseph's son?" she asks her.

"He was born with a club foot. Frank arranged for a doctor he knows at the Infirmary to take a look at it. The earlier the treatment, the better chance there is of a recovery."

There it is, thinks Annie, the spiderweb of contacts, the links in the chain that connects us all, if only we know how to forge it. You scratch my back, I'll scratch yours. Except that with Frank it was never like that at all. His motives were never self-seeking, always altruistic. Perhaps that's why, whenever he dropped a pebble into the stream, the ripples which spread outwards would also return back to him.

She looks now towards Hubert, nervously standing at the entrance to the Banqueting Hall, waiting to greet each of the guests in turn as they arrive. This must be purgatory for him, she knows, but he will not shirk from it, aware that it would be too much for his mother who, Annie can feel, is struggling, leaning more heavily on her arm.

"Let's sit down, shall we?" she says to her. "Look – George has organised a table for us. Hubert will do the honours at the door."

"Yes," says Evelyn, "he'll do the right thing. He's always been a good son."

And a good husband and father too, thinks Annie, looking back towards him, as he shakes hands now with the triumvirate of Alderman Hardcastle, Councillor Grandage and Clerk Flitcroft, but he is not his father's copy. He will not step comfortably into Frank's shoes, not when it comes to this necessary business of council committees, chambers of commerce, the deals done over the dinner table. Frank recognised this too, of course, which was why he brought her along with him so frequently to those tedious meetings, where she quickly learned the rules of the game, the coded phrases, the listening out for those things not said, the patience to wait until the official agenda items had been covered and then collar the right man – it was always a man – in the corridors outside. She will have to do a lot more of that now, she realises, but wonders if, without Frank's reassuring presence alongside, these men will take her seriously.

Well, she thinks, we'll find out soon enough, for here comes the triumvirate now.

"My deepest condolences, Mrs Wright. Annie," says the first.

"An irreplaceable loss," says the second.

"But look at the turn out today. That shows the esteem in which he was held by all," says the third.

Evelyn inclines her head in silent acknowledgement.

"Now then, Annie," says the first, "if I might have a word?" It is Alderman Hardcastle. "This business of the Library," he says.

"Yes," says Annie, "a project extremely close to my father-in-law's heart. My husband's too."

"Ay," continues the Alderman, "quite so." He pulls at his collar uncomfortably.

"The thing is," interrupts Grandage, "we're one short now on t' Committee, and we wondered if Hubert might like to stand in for his father?"

Annie has been expecting this. "He'd be honoured, gentlemen, but you will understand, I'm sure, if he takes a little time before deciding. There's simply so much to do now that my father-in-law has…"

"Yes, of course," butts in Hardcastle. "Hardly the most delicate of moments to be so insistent, Grandage."

"Mebbe not, Hardcastle," replies Grandage, "but the world moves on. Time and tide, *tempus fugit* and all that."

"Really, Grandage, you go too far. Have you no sensitivity?"

"It's quite all right, Alderman Hardcastle. Councillor Grandage is bluff, but he is not unfeeling. I quite understand the need for continuity and a smooth transition. I'm certain my father-in-law would have."

"Indeed he would," affirms Grandage, his face flushed in embarrassment nevertheless.

"And I imagine, Mr Flitcroft, that to find a replacement not recommended by your colleagues here would be procedurally difficult and take a considerable amount of time?"

"Co-correct," stammers Flitcroft, "it most certainly would."

"And time," continues Annie, "as our good friend Councillor Grandage has already so adroitly pointed out, is of the essence."

"Correct again," replies Flitcroft.

"Then might I make a suggestion?"

"Please do," says Hardcastle, a slow smile spreading across his lips.

"I'm sure I speak on behalf of the whole family when I say how very much we appreciate the deep honour you do us all by offering a place on this important committee, one which was so close to my father-in-law's heart, to my husband, especially on this very sad day, when so many of Frank's friends and former colleagues have gathered here this morning to pay their respects to the great service he has given so selflessly throughout his life to this great city of ours. Given the additional burden that will now inevitably fall upon my husband's shoulders, as he not only recovers from the loss of such an irreplaceable figure in all of our lives – as well as being a man of great business acumen my father-in-law was, as we know, such a generous benefactor and a loving father – but my husband must also now take on the mantle of being the new head of F.G. Wright & Son. Given all of this, might I suggest that instead of asking my husband to take up his father's place on the Library Committee, you ask *me* instead? I put myself forward for your consideration most humbly, aware that I can be at best but a poor substitute for my father-in-law, but optimistic in the hope that he so very kindly took me under his wing for so many years, taking me to meetings with him, where my contributions have not, I hope, gone unnoticed by the three of you standing here before me now."

"Bravo, Annie," beams Hardcastle. "You quite take my breath away."

"That would certainly be expedient," says a relieved Flitcroft.

"Tha's a canny lass," concedes Grandage. "I'll look forward to crossing swords wi' thee again."

Annie watches them cross the room towards other

colleagues, shaking hands and helping themselves to the potted shrimp sandwiches being handed round on trays by invisible waitresses. She breathes deeply. Round one to me, she thinks, and scans the Banqueting Hall for Hubert, whom she eventually spots trapped in a corner by a phalanx of wives from *The Women's Temperance Association*. I must rescue him, she thinks.

Back in Denton, Francis is about to close the shop for the day, which has been busy. There have been many radio sales, with customers keen to hear the news of the day's historic first, truly universal plebiscite, a fiercely fought campaign, this so-called "flapper" election – a term Francis does not care for, though he can grudgingly admire the cheek of the copy editor who might first have coined it – which has seen the town decked out in all its finery like a carnival, with bunting strung between lamp posts across the High Street, and people openly wearing favours on their jackets and coats, a veritable garden of red, blue and yellow rosettes. When he went to vote himself, on his way back from the funeral, the sight of so many smiling women, excitedly queuing to place their cross beside their chosen candidate upon the ballot paper, before emerging from the polling booth triumphant and proud to be met by applause from their other female friends, was infectiously uplifting. Francis had felt the atmosphere to be more that of a celebration than a contest, for, whatever the outcome, the mere fact that all these women were voting at all was victory enough.

Francis had allowed himself to be swept along on this tide of euphoria, so at odds with the mood at the funeral in the Albert Hall Mission that morning, which had flowed through the town all day, was still flowing as those women now returning from work in their mills and factories, offices and sales rooms were alighting from trams and trains and omnibuses to place their votes before heading home to cook and serve supper for their husbands and families.

One such woman is Winifred, for whom casting her vote has felt akin to taking her first communion, or her first time with Victor. She wonders what his mood will be like when he arrives back home later tonight. If he arrives home, that is. It has been a momentous day for Victor too today – his son Joe's first day down the pit, and Victor has arranged to be on the same shift. He'll probably buy him a pint afterwards. She can just hear him. "Get this down thee, lad. A proper man's drink for a proper day's work. That'll put hairs on your chest…" She only hopes he won't be tempted to stay on afterwards, for a few more with his pals. "Hair of the dog, one for the road." But she pushes the thought aside. He has a fight in a fortnight's time, and he doesn't usually over-indulge when he's back in training.

Being able to vote has really boosted her spirits, especially after the day she's had at the Telephone Exchange. It gives her hope that change is possible, and she skips along the pavement, dancing up and down the kerb to avoid the market stalls which are beginning to pack up for the day, swinging her bag in a carefree, devil-may-care way, until she twirls slap-bang into the arms of a greengrocer, who hoists her spontaneously into the air before depositing her safely back on the pavement, at which point her hat falls from her head.

Laughing, catching her breath, she stoops to retrieve it. Straightening up, her eye is caught by a small notice in a shop window.

"Assistant Wanted. Apply Within."

She looks up. She is standing directly beneath the giant pair of spectacles, which jut out from the shop front, staring out across the city. Her mood alters immediately. She has not set foot inside these premises since the night Ruth died, twelve and a half years ago. But something about the synchronicity of the day's events, the conjunction of endings and beginnings, which signal to Winifred that the time has come for her too to make a change perhaps. Ruth died in part because of fear and prejudice. Her courage, in defying the morals and conventions, should not, thinks, Winifred, be allowed to die with her. She recognises that she also has ploughed her own furrow, living under the brush with a married man, and that that, too, has taken courage, but she has not exactly proclaimed it either. She has scurried along these streets she has lived in and walked through since being born with her head down, her hat pulled low over her brow, eyes fixed on the pavement, never looking up, not until today, till just now. All those years ago she had cowered in a doorway while the streets burned and the mobs rampaged, and this very shop before which she stands now, hovering on its threshold, her hand lingering, undecided, above the latch, had its windows smashed, its glass shattered, its contents looted and its inhabitants beaten. And what had she done? Nothing. And on that terrible night nine months later, when Ruth's baby struggled into the world feet first, it was Mary who'd taken control, not she. She had just stood there, helpless and frightened, just waiting to be told what to do. Yes, she's had her own share of heartache since, the horrors of the Hooley Hill Munitions Factory explosion, which somehow she miraculously survived, the death of Arthur, cruelly, just a week before the end of the War, but she'd known happiness too, ecstasy at times with Victor, despite the stomach-churning plummets into doubt and despair he has caused her also, so that living with him has been like riding the roller coasters at Belle Vue, and she holds on to this fact, this knowledge, that the one time in her life when she did act, spontaneously and decisively out of some deep primal instinct or need, it has made her feel more wholly alive than anything else she has hesitated over, weighed the pluses and minuses of, and deferred to her usual caution. And she has not regretted it, not once, not even on those occasions when Victor has been drunk, or not shown up, or disappeared for days on end, for she has known, utterly and irrevocably, that in those moments when they were together, she felt complete, and that he felt it too, even if he never said as much, and that she was living a life, a life that had come about because she had thrown caution to the wind and displayed courage. Not the kind of courage Ruth showed, but a courage of sorts nevertheless. Isn't it time, she thinks, to throw off this yoke of the past once and for all and seize the present again?

The fingers of her right hand, which still hover uncertainly above the handle of the door, close around it, press it down, and push it open.

A bell jingles as she crosses the threshold.

"I'm just closing," says a voice.

"I've come about the notice in the window," she replies. "Are you still needing an assistant?"

Afterwards, Francis can't quite work out what happened. It was more that she had interviewed him, as opposed to the other way round.

"What exactly is it you're looking for?" she asked. "The advert says 'assistant', but that could mean anything, couldn't it?"

"Well," he replied, already a little unnerved by her directness. Perhaps, if he was to regain the initiative, it was already time to bowl her his googly. "I'm looking for a Passepartout…"

Francis sat back rather smugly, looking pleased with himself, but Winifred knocked the ball straight past his head for six.

"And you'd be Phileas Fogg, I suppose?"

"You know the reference then?" he asked, somewhat deflated.

" *'Around The World In Eighty Days'*. Yes. I read it at school. But what does that mean in practice? What would I have to do?"

Francis could feel himself floundering. "Whatever it is that I need. A bit of this, a bit of that…"

"Sounds a bit vague, doesn't it?"

"Yes, it does rather."

"Well?"

"I need someone who can mind the shop…"

"Mind it?"

"… well, run it, I suppose, while I…"

"Yes?"

"… carry out my research, conduct my experiments…"

"I see. And what else?"

"Someone to deal with enquiries, see to the customers, answer the telephone, write letters, look over the books, keep records, go to the bank and the post office, answer the telephone…"

"You've already said that."

"Oh. Have I?"

"Yes."

"Oh. Well, it's difficult to put into words. I'm looking for a person who can anticipate my needs, solve a problem before it becomes one, get the business back on its feet. A Passepartout…"

"Sounds more like a dogsbody to me."

He'd dried up after that. Winifred said nothing, as if expecting he might respond or elaborate. He could feel his rash prickling.

"Well," he began again, "the problem is this. I believe I have good quality products to sell, things which the public may think are only a luxury at the moment, but that in time, and quite soon, I think, they will come to regard as things they cannot do without. I'm good at spotting what these things might be, but the initial investment is costly, while, to begin with, the returns are quite small, and in the meantime…"

"… you need something to keep things ticking along, to make sure there's a steady flow of money coming in. Enough to pay for a Passepartout?"

"Precisely. You understand me perfectly."

"Yes," said Winifred, eyeing him with a dry smile, "I believe I do."

Francis hesitated, as if understanding that the initiative now lay entirely with this unprepossessing but sparky young woman sitting opposite him with a hint of mischief in her eyes. She was, he realised, managing him already, and it brought him immediate and quite blissful relief.

"I used to know the Kaufmans," she said after a pause.

"Who?"

"The people who used to live here before you."

"Yes, of course."

"Mr Kaufman was a bit like you. You remind me of him in fact. He, too, was a bit of a dreamer. He liked to stargaze."

"So do I."

"And you've done well out of him, I can see," she said, looking round at the display of telescopes, binoculars, cameras and the racks of lenses arrayed on the shelves. "But it's not your bread and butter, is it?"

"No," replied Francis, shaking his head, "it isn't."

Winifred sat back in her chair. "What happened to the optician side of the business?" she asked.

"Oh that," said Francis carelessly. "I let it lapse."

"Why?"

"Well, it doesn't interest me, and besides I don't have the necessary qualifications."

"You could acquire them, though, couldn't you, if you had to?"

"Yes, but…"

"But what?"

"Like I said. It doesn't interest me." He removed his dark glasses and instinctively turned away to polish them furiously with his handkerchief, allowing Winifred the quickest of glimpses of his pale translucent eyes, the red tint of the iris, the almost white lashes, before hastily putting them back on, and at once Winifred understood.

"You could rent out a portion of the shop," she said.

Francis frowned. "I don't understand."

"People need opticians," she said, "and they keep needing them year on year. There's a constant demand. You're lucky. Nobody else has opened one up in the town while you've been running it down here, so you don't face any competition. Not yet. But wait too long and it's bound to come, then you'll have lost the initiative."

"Yes, I see. But what do you mean by renting?"

"Women's hairdressers do this sort of thing all the time. A salon is often too large for one person to manage herself, and so very often she'll rent out a chair, where another hairdresser can come in, with her own customers, who she collects payment from, in return for which she pays the owner of the salon a weekly fee."

"And you're suggesting I come to a similar arrangement with an optician here?"

"Bingo."

Francis stood up and began pacing the shop. "We could put up a partition here, which would provide both privacy and the capacity for dimming the lights when needed, without inconveniencing the rest of the shop." He rubbed his hands together. "What an excellent idea."

"There's plenty more where that came from."

"Really? Such as?"

"Don't let the optician you bring in use his own name. Make it part of what *Hall & Singer* offer, along with everything else. You can repaint the spectacles outside, arrange for a new sign to let the public know *Hall & Singer* are now also *bona fide* opticians. You'll be turning people away within weeks. Where is Mr Singer by the way?"

"Ah," said Francis, looking distinctly uncomfortable once more, "he's not here. He's more of a sleeping partner."

"He's not real, is he?" said Winifred, beginning to giggle.

"No," said Francis, joining in. "I made him up."

Their giggling grew louder.

"He can be the name we call the optician by," said Winifred, laughing. Francis enjoyed the way she slipped in the "we" so unconsciously.

"Yes," he said, "perfect. And this way we get a regular weekly income for hardly any outlay of our own."

"You've got it," cried Winifred. "By George, you've got it!"

After they had finished laughing, they sat down again, looking at one another across the desk.

"So," said Francis, considering.

"So," answered Winifred, watching.

"Will you be my Passepartout?" he said eventually.

"*Oui, Monsieur*," she said. "But how about we give it a month's trial, to see how we get along together first?"

"Agreed," he said. "When can you start?"

"Today's Thursday," she said. "How about next Monday?"

She thrust out her hand towards him to confirm their arrangement. She noticed at once the moment's hesitation from Francis, as he tried to cover the rash on his wrist with the cuff of his jacket, but then decided not to bother, to let her see anyway.

"Till next Monday then.

It is late afternoon in Bignor Street. After the ordeal of the reception at The Banqueting Hall had finally concluded, Hubert drove his mother, Annie and George back to the family home in Cheetham Hill, where other close friends and relatives had been invited for afternoon tea. Everyone spoke in respectful hushed tones, with the same over-compensating camaraderie which the unaccustomed proximity with people one would not normally choose to spend such extended periods of time with invariably elicits, an atmosphere northern funerals unfailingly bring with them.

"It's been a fine day for it."

"Ay."

"Not too hot."

"No."

"And at least the rain's held off."

"That's a mercy."

"It were a grand turn out."

"Ay."

"The flowers were lovely."

"They were that."

"Everyone's shut their curtains along the street, I see."

"Ay, they have."

"Even the Jewish families."

"Ay."

"Who'd've thought so many people'd've turned out, eh our Evelyn?"

"Who'd've thought it?"

In the end, Annie could stand it no longer. Seeing Evelyn's knuckles whiten as she gripped the arms of her chair, she put down the tray of tea she was carrying with a loud clatter on the drop-leaf dining table, which had been extended to its fullest length for the afternoon. Everybody stopped talking and turned towards her.

"Actually," she said, exasperatedly tucking a loose strand of hair behind her right ear, "I *would* have thought it. I'm not in the least surprised by the thousands of people who turned up to pay their respects to Frank. He was a giant of a man. Never one to blow his own trumpet, or sing his own praises, but everybody knows just what a contribution he's made to the lives of all those he came into contact with. He was a quiet man, a modest man, a plain speaking, clean living man, who leaves the world a better place than when he first came into it. But he wanted no fuss, no bother, he didn't do the things he did with any thought for the rewards they might bring, only because he felt they needed doing, that's all. Not long after Hubert and I were married, he took me to the Town Hall, where we've all of us been today, for the very first time. He walked me down the long corridor with all the statues of the local worthies in it, pointing out some of his heroes to me – Cobden, Bright, John Dalton. He was so full of wonder for what they'd achieved and so proud to be living in the same city that such men had prospered in, but I'll tell you what *I* think. *I* think they should put up a statue to *him*, not that they ever will of course, and not that it's something he'd ever have wanted for himself, but if anyone ever deserved the title of a Manchester Worthy, it's Frank Wright, and if he were here with us now, which in spirit and memory he always will be, he'd say he was only an ordinary man, that there were dozens and dozens just like him, each of them doing their bit, doing their best, trying not to draw attention to themselves, to make the world a better place, and leave their mark upon it. Well, if he's right, I'd say 'Build a statue to each and every one of them'. But I don't think he is right, not on this occasion, for they broke the mould when they made Frank Wright, and we'll not see his like again. So let's not talk to each other in these oh-so-polite tones, uttering all these meaningless platitudes, pretending that we aren't, each and every one of us, feeling a pain so sharp, here, deep inside of us, a pain that, though it might lessen as the years go by, will never fully heal, for it's left a big hole there, a Frank-sized hole, which somehow we're all going to have to try and fill in, by doing the best that we can to follow in his footsteps."

And with that, she had burst into tears and fled to the kitchen.

An embarrassed silence fell upon the room. After a few moments had passed, it was Evelyn who broke it first.

"Hubert," she said quietly, "go and see if Annie's all right."

"She will be," said Hubert. "She'd prefer to be on her own just now."

"Hubert," repeated Evelyn more firmly.

"Yes, Mother," he said, and then hurried towards the kitchen.

"And now," continued Evelyn, "I'm rather tired. If you don't mind, I think I might go and lie down."

The few remaining friends and relatives rose as one to take their leave, like a small flock of pigeons in Albert Square, fountaining into the air as someone raises a casual hand, alighting once more in ones and twos around Evelyn, their heads like tiny hammers pecking towards her, before making their departures, each with a put-upon, hobbled strut, taking a proffered sandwich or cake with them, reluctantly, as though really they were doing the household a favour.

Until eventually they had all gone, and Evelyn could let out the breath she felt she'd been holding in all day, and feel her body shudder with the first true paroxysms of grief.

Now it is evening. Evelyn has had a short nap. Annie has washed up and dried all the plates and cups and saucers, put away the tablecloths, folded down the drop-leaf table, and drawn back the curtains to let in the last of the light before it goes dark completely. Hubert has driven George back home to Manley Park – George has school tomorrow – and now the two women sit side by side on the sofa in the sitting room Annie has always admired. Millais' *A Child's World* hangs above the hearth. The child has a faraway look in his eyes, watching each bubble that he has blown expand and rise, a delicate, translucent egg for ever on the point of bursting, before it disappears. The piano in the opposite corner waits patiently to be played, its lid down, the music for Handel's *Largo* resting on the stand. The elegant, unadorned grandmother clock ticks reassuringly between them.

Neither of them speaks.

Outside starlings begin their nightly murmuration, swooping over the rooftops, before alighting on the sycamore trees in huge numbers in Bignor Park. A flower moon rises, mocking the two silent, grieving women, with its signal for a time of new beginnings, its pocked shadows and craters threatening to swallow them.

Evelyn squeezes her daughter-in-law's hand.

"Thank you," she says finally, her voice barely a whisper, "for what you said earlier."

Annie shakes her head.

"No," says Evelyn, "those words... they needed to be said."

Annie remains silent.

"Why don't you play?" she asks after a while, gesturing towards the piano.

"Yes," says Evelyn. "For Frank."

She goes over to the stool, opens the sheet music. She lifts up the lid and places her fingers over the keys, where they hover, suspended. When at last she begins, she plays falteringly, quietly, privately. The slow repeated chords on the left hand, like a pulse, a heartbeat, swell, their funeral march a reassuring measure beneath the tremulous ringing melody on the right hand, unfolding like the petals of a flower, resounding like a gentle peal of bells. Evelyn plays as the starlings roost and settle for the night, and one by one the stars come out.

When she has finished, she holds her fingers over the keys for a long time, before finally lifting them away and closing the lid.

"Death was different when I was a child."

"How do you mean?"

"Frank and I were born at the height of the Cotton Famine. By all accounts we were lucky to survive. Death was not so tidy then, not so respectable, not so parcelled up into neat portions. Now, it's become almost polite. We're screened off from its worst excesses. Doctors, then undertakers, see to all of that for us. But back then, Death stalked the streets. You passed bloated corpses floating in the rivers, you saw bodies being flung without care into communal pits. You lived in constant fear of him tapping you on the shoulder and dragging you off with him. Hunger gnawed at your belly like a wolf. The history books tell you that the last wolf in England was killed nearly three hundred years ago, but as a child I saw them every night here on the streets of Manchester, nosing through the cellars and under the arches. Once I saw one in our house, in the bedroom I shared with my sister. She was very ill that time, and the wolf was sniffing the air around her. I threw my shoe at it, and it went away. The next day my sister started to get better. And gradually we stopped seeing the wolves altogether. I don't know what happened to them. They just melted away like a morning mist. But sometimes, at nights, I'd hear them, howling at the moon, and I'd turn to Frank and ask him if he'd heard them too, but all he'd ever say was, 'Hush, love. Go back to sleep'. And now I can't stop wondering whether he just said that to make me feel better, or that really he'd heard them too. What do you think, Annie? Do you think he heard them in The Great Hall when that young man found him? Do you?"

"No," said Annie, "I don't. He might have heard Great Abe ringing in the clock tower, but if he did, he'd have smiled. He loved the sound of that bell, just as he loved *The Manchester Murals*. He often liked to sit and look at them."

"Did he? I didn't know…"

"He showed them to me the first time he took me with him to one of his meetings there."

"What was the name of that man who was with him when he…"

"Mr Hall, I think. From Denton."

"Do you think I should write to him, to thank him? I think I should."

"That would be kind, but leave it a few days, eh?"

Evelyn nods.

"He used to enjoy those times you went with him."

"What?"

"Frank."

"Oh. Did he? He never said."

"Yes. He'd tell me some of the things you'd said. So brave. Speaking out like that. I couldn't do that. I went once myself. In our early days together. I didn't care for it. I found the building so intimidating, all those dark corridors and stone staircases, I kept getting lost. Once I took a wrong turning and found myself coming to a dead end, a locked door. I called out but no one came. Then I heard this scrabbling from the other side of the door. It reminded me of that wolf that came sniffing for my sister…"

She shudders. Annie puts an arm around her. An awkwardness hangs in the air. The grandmother clock continues to tick between them.

"Now," says Evelyn, a few minutes later, "if you want to get back home, I'll be quite all right. Those boys will be wondering where you've got to."

"They can manage for one night," smiles Annie. "I can

stay as long as you need me to."

Evelyn pats Annie's hand by way of thanks.

"You know," ventures Annie hesitantly, "you can always come and live with us. We might be moving again next year, after George leaves school, but we'll always have room. If you'd like to. If you're lonely."

"Thanks, love, that's very kind of you, but no. I'm used to things here, and I can't imagine myself settling some place where Frank hadn't lived. I've such happy memories here. I'll not be lonely. But I'll come and visit sometimes, if I may."

"You must, and often. And we'll still see each other at the Mission, won't we?"

Evelyn nods. "Hubert was very lucky to find you, Annie."

"I'll tell him you said so," laughs Annie.

"You'll look after him, won't you," asks Evelyn, suddenly anxious.

"Always."

They remain quietly sitting, each in their own separate thoughts, about Frank and about Hubert, about each other and about George as the darkness closes in further around them, neither of them wanting to switch on a light. Evelyn remembers a young man walking towards her across a ballroom floor and asking her to dance, while Annie thinks back to when that young man's son went down on his knees as a comet blazed overhead. Now, for Evelyn, that man seems always to be walking away from her. He may be getting older, but he still walks as nimbly as he ever did, as if he can't wait for the next dance to begin. "I'm afraid I'm not very good at this," she had said, when he first placed his hand upon her waist. "Don't worry," he'd smiled. "We're getting round, aren't we?" And to her astonishment they were, and they continued to do so all along the years. But now he is walking away from her. She wants to call out to him to stop and wait for her. But it would seem that it's not time yet. She must wait a little longer yet, and this no longer troubles her, for she knows now that, when the time does come, he will turn around, hold out his hand, which she will take, and they will waltz away together again.

Annie is remembering a corridor, along which Frank is walking, just a step or two ahead of her. It is the Great Hall of Statues in Manchester Town Hall. Frank is smiling towards her, beckoning her to look at each statue in turn while he tells her all about the person it depicts. But she doesn't hear his words, only sees his smiling face, gazing round in wonder and delight, saying, "We made this, all of us, together, and now it's your turn." Every statue that she passes has his face, and she knows his calm and reassuring presence will never leave her, so that when she next walks down that corridor, she will not be alone. At the end of it she sees a stained glass window, with light pouring through it. She runs towards it, determined to get closer to it, to be able to see what the different coloured panes of glass depict. Now she has it, a spindle tree, like the one in Portugal Street, but this one has grown so much taller and appears always to be in bloom. Underneath it, drawing in its shade, sits George, completely absorbed, and from its branches tumbles a thin unbroken yarn of thread, which she unspools, yard upon yard of it, mile upon mile, which she can unwind and tie one end of around Hubert's finger, the other around George's pencil, so they both might follow her and not get lost. But George is now in such a tearing hurry, clamouring for a motor cycle, which will only take him further from her, while Hubert seems to be getting slower and slower. She tries to keep pace with George yet, when she looks back, over her shoulder, sometimes she cannot see Hubert at all, and has to wait until he trundles into view, head bent, intent on winding up the yarn round and round his fingers, so that he can no longer move them and has to hold out his hands, helplessly, for Annie to untangle them. What she'd really like to do is snap it off between her teeth, so that she can hurry after George once more, but she knows that, were she to do this, Hubert would get lost completely, and it's her job now to keep this thread from breaking, somehow holding them all together in a single, continuous, unbroken line, except that it's no longer a thread of yarn, but the nerves inside her head, which are stretched as taut as piano wire, whose high pitched, vibrating hum will not let her rest.

At last, Evelyn rises from her chair.

"I think I'll go to bed," she says. "It's been a long day."

"I'll not be far behind you," says Annie. "Oh," she says, suddenly stopping short.

"What is it?"

"I forgot to vote."

*

Manchester Evening Chronicle

11th September 1929

WELCOME HOME, BOYS!

Not A Single Button Left Behind

The last British troops still stationed in Germany finally received their orders to stand down, nearly 11 years since hostilities in the Great War ceased and the Armistice was signed to bring an end to this war to end all wars.

Following the collapse of the Imperial German Army in 1918, troops from the victorious powers of Britain, France, Belgium and the United States have occupied the left bank of the River Rhine, as well as maintaining four bridgeheads along the right bank with a 20 mile radius around the cities of Cologne, Koblenz and Mainz, the whole area designated a demilitarised zone.

Four years ago the signing by all the major powers of the Locarno Treaties has led to the gradual withdrawal of these troops. The Americans had begun leaving as early as 1923, with the French and Belgians following suit shortly afterwards, until this final contingent of British soldiers departed yesterday.

Members of The Manchester Regiment landed in Dover, weary but content to be back on home soil once more. With a cheery wave to the thousands of civilians lining the docks to greet them back to Blighty, the boys in khaki put on a splendid show of patriotic duty as they marched ashore.

"All in a day's work," was the modest reply any of them would give to waiting reporters keen to hear how they thought their mission had gone.

Their Commander in Chief, General Sir William Thwaites KCB KCMG, was more forthcoming. "Our mission on the Rhineland was a simple one – to preserve the rule of law and prevent Germany from rearming, as she is forbidden to do under the terms of the Treaty of Versailles. But now our job is finished. We leave Cologne having done our bit to win the peace, just as a decade earlier many of these same chaps helped to win the War. When I was a boy my mother used to impress upon me always to leave a place better than you find it. I am proud to report that we left no stone unturned during our time on the Rhineland, and we leave not a single button behind."

So give three hearty cheers for the brave soldiers of The Manchester Regiment to whom we all say, "Welcome home, Boys!"

Victor spits into the gutter as he finishes reading this article. He screws up the newspaper and keeps it tightly balled up in his clenched fist.

"What a load of bollocks," he thinks as he lights up a cigarette. He doesn't follow politics all that closely but any fool can see that this is all a con, a cost-cutting exercise, dressed up to look like some major diplomatic triumph. The truth is, thinks Victor as he pounds the pavements, the Rhineland's more of a problem to the French and the Belgians than it's ever been to us, so we're getting out as quickly as we decently can.

He might have been one of them, he thinks ruefully. He was offered the chance to stay on in 1918, and he has to admit he was tempted, but some sense of duty pulled him back, his sister Doreen's voice ringing in his ear probably, about making sure he did the decent thing.

The decent thing. Is that what he's been doing these past years? He's damned lucky to have fetched up with Winifred, he knows that, but a part of him can't help feeling bitter that, without her, he wouldn't be managing half as well as he does.

Now he wonders what those returning men will find when they finally make it back to Manchester. There'll be no place for them in the Army any more, and there's not much other work to be found. The pits are taking on a few more again now, though mostly it's piece work. That suits him well enough, especially as Joe's on full time, and Winifred has her new well-paid job. It means he can concentrate more on his training. He's a fight coming up in a fortnight. Otherwise, he thinks, he might have stood a few of his pals returning home a drink or two, like the old days, in *The Bull's Head* at Ardwick, outside whose doors he is standing right now. Someone walks out. As the door is held open, he briefly hears the sound of laughter and music from inside, and sees the inviting, smoky orange glow of light from the vault, but then the door is shut, and he's left standing outside on the pavement. He stubs the last of his cigarette beneath the worn out sole of his shoe, tosses the screwed up newspaper into the air and kicks it into the street. Shoving his hands furiously into his jacket pockets, he storms across the road to the gymnasium, where he can take out his anger on the punch bag.

The boys of the Upper School of Hulme's Grammar tear into the classroom on this, the first day back after the summer holidays, on 12th September 1929, the start of their last year before they all depart for their separate journeys come the following June. The air is thick with banter, the easy camaraderie that has been built up over five years, and George, arriving at the very last moment as has become his habit, wonders if he will keep in touch with any of them after they leave. He is the only one of them who is going on to study Art, hopefully at *The Mechanics' Institute* in Pendleton, and proud of it, to which he has applied, where the celebrated painter Mr Lowry is now an occasional tutor. Most of his peers are intending to be doctors or solicitors or partners in their fathers' business enterprises, which is what George expects he will do also, although no pressure is being brought to bear upon him in this matter by either of his parents, both of whom are proud of his artistic leanings, but he remains conscious of those few words of advice Mr Lowry imparted to him at the inaugural exhibition of *The Manchester School of Modern Painters* he attended four and a half years ago – "get yourself a proper job," – words which George has never forgotten and which he has taken seriously to heart, and so, although he derives a certain inner satisfaction that he is regarded by his classmates as something of an oddity – not only bound for Art School, but also a devotee of the greyhound and speedway tracks – he has already privately decided that he will combine his studies at *The Institute* with learning a trade – sign writing is what he has in mind – as well as helping out at the Printing Works whenever time allows, which, following the death of his grandfather earlier in the year, he expects to be quite frequent, for his father, he has noticed, has become visibly slower and greyer in the weeks and months since.

The classroom door opens, the boys as one scrape back their chairs and get to their feet. An immediate silence descends upon them as Mr Vogts walks in.

"Good morning, boys."

"Good morning, sir."

"Please be seated."

A further scraping of chairs and shuffling of bottoms on seats ensues. Mr Vogts, they notice, is brandishing a newspaper in his right hand.

"I trust you have enjoyed your summer holidays?"

"Yes, sir. Thank you, sir."

"Normally, on a morning such as this, your first day back, especially as this is the start of your final year with us here at Hulme's, I like to make a little speech – about the importance of examinations coming up, the need for hard work, one last push, all that sort of thing, and how, when you leave us, the world is your oyster, to make of it what you will, hoping that you will find at least some of the things we have tried to teach you during your time with us may prove useful in your future careers, whatever they may be, even as budding artists, Mr Wright…"

Polite laughter greets this expected remark.

"However, this year I find I am at something of a loss for words. You may be glad at that prospect, but not, perhaps, when I tell you my reasons."

The boys turn to one another with puzzled looks. This is not at all what they had been expecting. A pep talk, yes, but this feels like the prelude to some dire apocalyptic warning.

"This," he says, holding up the newspaper, "is yesterday's *Evening Chronicle.* I wonder how many of you might already have read it?"

Several hands are nervously raised.

"Ah. Then perhaps one of you might be kind enough to enlighten those who haven't as to the contents of the front page." He holds it up before the class so that they might all see the headline. "Thank you, Mr Ridgeway," he says, pointing to a boy sitting near the front with his hand eagerly raised, whose ears stick out rather prominently on either side of his well-scrubbed red face, his freckled nose somewhat painfully peeling from exposure to too much rare sun.

"It's about the evacuation of the Rhineland, sir."

"And what else?"

"The last British forces are coming home."

"And what else?"

"Er…" Young Mr Ridgeway is beginning to falter, the redness of his cheeks now spreading to the back of his neck, before a new thought saves him from further embarrassment. "Many of those forces are from The Manchester Regiment, my Uncle Colin among them."

"Thank you, Mr Ridgeway, and I am sure that your Uncle Colin will be as pleased to be coming home as no doubt your family will be to see him returning safely at last."

"Yes, sir. Thank you, sir."

"This is all correct, but there is something else, which Mr Ridgeway has not mentioned – not that he can be blamed in any way, for this fact is also conveniently excluded from yesterday's *Evening Chronicle*. Might anyone be willing to hazard a guess as to what that might be?"

A long, uncomfortable silence follows. The boys try to look anywhere but at Mr Vogts, for fear his eye might chance upon them. Eventually George raises his hand.

"Ah, I was hoping you might come to our aid, Mr Wright. Well?"

"If the men coming back are being stood down from their regiment, which they probably are, what kind of jobs will be waiting for them? They've still not taken all the miners back round here, and it's been three years now since the General

Strike."

"Indeed. You are most perspicacious, Mr Wright, as always. Some of you boys will remember, I'm sure, the eloquent defence of the miners given by Mr Wright in the School Debating Society."

"He lost, though, didn't he, sir? Heavily, I seem to recall." This from Deryck Marshall, the class clown, who smirks over his shoulder at George, who turns away with a frown.

"Thank you, Mr Marshall. What a remarkable memory you have. If only you could apply that talent when it comes to Clause Analysis."

Some of the class laugh nervously. The smirk drains from Deryck Marshall's face.

"I suppose it depends upon one's definition of 'lost'," continues Mr Vogts. "I believe the motion *'This House Believes That The Actions Of The Mine Owners During The General Strike Were Justified'* was carried by fifty-seven votes to nineteen, a very clear majority, indicating more than three to one in favour of it. However, as you would also no doubt recall, if you were a regular attender at our school debates, before each session, before the speakers have entered the room even, I conduct a separate poll. I ask pupils to vote for or against the motion before they have heard any of the arguments, based on their pre-conceived opinions, and then compare this result with the actual one when the debate has concluded. Before the debate in question, only three people felt they were against the motion, but after hearing Mr Wright's arguments, that figure rose to nineteen. With such evidence, one could argue that Mr Wright in fact won the debate, for he changed more minds..."

George secretly glows inside when he hears this. He wonders why Mr Vogts has never mentioned this to him before – after the debate he'd felt mortified and humiliated, hot with self-righteous indignation – and why he has chosen this particular moment to divulge it at all.

"But we digress," he continues. "While it is true that the newspaper makes no mention of the current unemployment crisis facing the country, and therefore the almost certain likelihood that few of these returning soldiers will be able to find work immediately, there is an even more significant oversight, which is causing me even greater concern."

The class is now all ears and leans forward, almost as one, from their seats.

"This summer I returned to Germany as I have done these past five years and what I witnessed there this year disturbed me greatly. I am talking about the slow but steady rise in popularity of the so-called National Socialists Party. General Ludendorff, though widely ridiculed as a buffoon, still commands respect and attention among large sections of the general public, and his more outlandish views, attacking Jews and Catholics, are gaining ground, now being voiced by younger, more extreme, more ambitious and, in my view, very much more dangerous followers such as Joseph Goebbels and that Austrian upstart, Adolph Hitler. They do not report these matters in our newspapers here, for they do not see them for what they represent, a genuine threat to the future security not only of Germany, as it tries to get its industries working again, but of all of Europe. For once I find myself agreeing with Winston Churchill – something I thought would be absolutely impossible after his disgraceful opposition to women's suffrage – that this hasty withdrawal of British, French and Belgian troops from the Rhineland could lead, if we are not vigilant, to Germany rearming and marching back in to claim what these National Socialists believe is their birthright."

Mr Vogts has by this stage worked himself up into a state of near frenzy and has to turn his face away from the boys, who look at one another in some alarm.

"Are you all right, sir?" asks one.

"Shall I fetch you a glass of water, sir?" asks another.

"No. Thank you, boys. I shall be fine. Just give me a moment."

After a while, Deryck Marshall raises his hand.

"Yes, Mr Marshall?"

"Excuse me for asking, sir, but seeing as how you were born in Germany, I'd have thought you'd be glad to hear all this talk about German rearmament, sir."

"Really? Then in that case you are even more stupid than I thought."

Marshall reddens.

"Yes, I was born in Germany, but I moved here to Manchester with my parents when I was still a schoolboy. Younger than you are. If you are implying by your remarks that I might have divided loyalties, then that I would concede. I see no profit in millions of young men, hardly older than you are now, losing their lives because of the vanity and obstinacy of very much older men on both sides. And I worry today that, barely eleven years since the end of what was meant to be the war to end all wars, there may well be, ten or eleven years from now, another war, which, I hardly need point out, would be bound to involve some, if not all, of you sitting here this morning." He pauses, then turns to a boy sitting near the classroom door. "Mr Randall, I think I will take you up on your offer of a glass of water, if it is not too much trouble?"

"Of course, sir," replies Randall, a popular, gentle giant of a boy, who in his hurry towards the corridor, knocks over his chair, then, in his efforts to retrieve it, tips up his desk.

"Sorry, sir, I'll be as quick as I can, sir."

"Normally," says Mr Vogts, seemingly unaware of the clatter and commotion, "on this, the first morning of a new term, marking the start of the Upper School's final year, I like to speak of the future, to wish you well in whatever your chosen profession might be, to counsel diligence, to reassure you that, although you may not achieve your ambitions as quickly as you might wish, with patience and perseverance, you will find your place, and navigate your way through what I fervently hope will be a successful career for each and every one of you, a happy, healthy life, during which you may come to find that at least some of what I and my colleagues here at Hulme's have tried to teach you over the years will be of some service to you."

At this point Randall returns with the glass of water.

Mr Vogts thanks him and drinks.

"But instead, this year," he continues, gradually regaining his composure, "in the light of what is not reported in yesterday's *Evening Chronicle*, my advice is of an altogether different order." He puts down the empty glass on his desk and looks directly at the boys. "In the words of Horace, from his first Book of Odes, '*Carpe diem*'. Who can tell me what that means?"

"Seize the day," the boys reply in unison.

"Precisely. Seize the day. And so I say to you this morning to ignore all of my previous exhortations to not be always in such a hurry. From this day forward I urge you to *run* in the corridors, run as if your life depended upon it, which in a way it does. No longer consider patience a virtue. No longer be content with simply trying to play yourself in and see off the new ball. Instead, apply yourselves to scoring that century before lunch. Emulate the hare, not the tortoise, for yes, life is a race, so there's no time to take a nap part way through. And, as this is meant to be an English Literature class, and not a lesson in Modern Politics, I believe an extract from the Cavalier poet, Robert Herrick's *'To Make Much of Time'* might be in order, don't you?"

"Yes, sir," they chorus in response.

"Mr Wright, will you read us the first two verses please?"

"Yes, sir," says George, as he opens his copy of *The Oxford Book of English Verse*, edited by Sir Arthur Quiller-

Couch, and then begins to read aloud.

> *"Gather ye rosebuds while ye may,*
> *Old Time is still a-flying;*
>
> *And this same flower that smiles today*
> *To-morrow will be dying.*
>
> *The glorious lamp of heaven, the sun,*
> *The higher he's a-getting,*
> *The sooner will his race be run,*
> *And nearer he's to setting…"*

Exactly eight months later, on 11th May 1930, George turns seventeen. A certain confluence of events combine to make this an even more significant day than it would otherwise have been. For it is on this day he will come into contact with the first of what will be the two great loves of his life.

Arriving at the breakfast table that morning, he finds two envelopes waiting for him, propped up against the tea pot. The first is a birthday card, from his parents, hand made by his mother, as she does every year, a callograph depicting the spindle tree from Portugal Street. He now has a whole set of these, which he keeps on the top shelf of his bookcase in his bedroom, which tether him to those days as a small child, when he had first begun to draw, with chalks, sitting under that tree, and which serve to remind him of a time and a place, the details of which are already beginning to lose their sharpness under each successive layer imposed upon them by each different house they move to. They have recently relocated to Didsbury, a large, newly built house on Lapwing Lane, close to the junction with Palatine Road, backing on to Albert Park. Since Easter these are landmarks he has had to learn on his new bicycle route the two miles between here and Hulme's. This is the fourth house he has now lived in, each one larger and grander than its predecessor, and he has enjoyed living in them all, though Portugal Street still remains his favourite. He wonders at this restlessness inside his mother, which compels her, just as she might be beginning to put down roots, to up sticks and move on, and marvels at her seemingly inexhaustible energy. She tells George and his father that this will be their final move, that she has always had her sights set on Didsbury, but George will believe that only when it happens. He and his father exchange a wry smile when she says this, and George wonders whether beneath his calm exterior his father really does feel such apparent equanimity at these frequent upheavals. He has his car, he tells George, and so it is of little consequence to him where they actually live, so long as your mother's happy, that's the main thing. I shall always be able to get to work. And to The Meeting House on Mount Street, where George knows his father attends as often as he possibly can these days.

He thanks his mother for the card, and she smiles, averting her gaze towards the second envelope. She is clearly anxious to learn what it contains. George opens it, reads, then can't prevent himself from emitting an audible exhalation of pure pleasure.

"What is it?" asks Annie.

"Here. Look." He passes her the letter.

" *'We are delighted to inform you',*" she reads, " *'that your application to become a student of Art at The Mechanics' Institute, Pendleton has been successful'.*" She leans across to George and hugs him with genuine delight. "Hubert, did you hear?" she says. "He's got in."

"I never doubted it for a moment," says Hubert. "Congratulations, son. And happy birthday."

George is filled with a deep sense that he is on the cusp of life as an independent adult, a life of entirely his own choosing, and he feels a heady mix of elation and good fortune.

Annie and Hubert exchange a look between them.

"I think," she ventures, "this would be the perfect moment for your present."

Hubert nods warmly.

"Come with me," she says playfully. She stands behind George and places her hands over his eyes. "No peeping." She directs him towards the back door, singing as they proceed.

"Happy Birthday to you
Happy Birthday to you
Happy Birthday, dear George
Happy Birthday to you…"

She removes her hands from his eyes. "Now," she says, "you can look."

George opens his eyes. There in the drive before him Hubert is standing by something draped with a tarpaulin, which, at a signal from Annie, he removes, rather like a conjuror with a cloth, to reveal… a brand new motor cycle.

George's eyes are on stalks. "Is that what I think it is?"

"The very same," replies a grinning Hubert. "A 1925 DOT Racer."

George approaches it with a deep reverence, hardly daring to touch it, until finally he allows his fingers to caress its dark red mudguards and frame.

"Where did you find it?" he whispers.

"Oh," smiles Hubert, "I've been keeping an eye out. We do their printing as you know, and when I was last at their factory on Ellesmere Street, Mr Sawyer called me to one side after we'd concluded our other business. 'Come round t' back,' he said. 'I've summat as might interest you.' And there it was."

"Do you like the colour?" asks Annie.

George nods his head. It feels like a religious ritual to him, and already he is imagining the weekly anointing with oil, the Brasso three-in-one, the genuflecting before its cross-shaped handlebars, the donning of leather gloves and cap, like vestments.

"Why's it called a DOT?" asks Annie.

" 'Devoid - Of - Trouble'," reply Hubert and George as one.

"Unlike you two then," laughs Annie.

But George is not listening. He sits astride the machine, in complete thrall to it. He knows he will never forget this moment, and he doesn't, not even when the DOT Racer gives way in time to the DOT RS, then the DOT Bradshaw, later the DOT Mancunian, and finally the DOT Villiers. It is a love affair that will last the rest of his life.

Less than half an hour later, George is executing wheelies round the school playground of Hulme's, much to the delight of the other boys, who crowd around him, like admiring acolytes.

"And what do you think you're doing?" asks a disconcerted Mr Vogts, fanning away the exhaust fumes with an exercise book. The acolytes retreat to the shadows.

"Seizing the day," smirks George.

"Oh really?"

"Emulating the hare."

"Indeed?"

"Leaving..." And he revs the engine loudly before pulling down his goggles and roaring away down Spring Bridge Road.

Mr Vogts wipes his eyes, although whether from dust or tears it is not possible to determine. An acolyte edges towards him and asks for his exercise book, which Mr Vogts obligingly flings towards him.

Over the next three months, between impulsively leaving school and starting his new life at *The Mechanics' Institute*, a pattern establishes itself for George, made possible for him by his refusal to be separated from the DOT Racer for any longer than is absolutely necessary. He has even been known to sleep alongside it in their garage on Lapwing Lane. The bike has become an extension of who he is, like an extra limb.

He returns to school on occasional days to take examinations, which he finds no longer concern him. He does little or no revision but, as is so often the case in such circumstances, he sails through them. For two days of each week, mindful of Mr Lowry's injunction on him "to get a proper job", he becomes apprenticed to a Mr Archie Rowe, a traditional sign writer operating out of an old workshop near Buile Hill Park, a location deliberately sought out by George for its proximity to *The Mechanics' Institute*, with whom he has confirmed he will attend courses on three days and two evenings. On two other evenings he continues his work at the Speedway, no longer sharing the greyhound track on Kirkmanshulme Lane, having moved to a purpose-built stadium on Hyde Road, still within the vicinity of Belle Vue. This leaves one day and two evenings for him to help out at the Printing Works, where his father is instructing him in the intricacies of the linotype and offset lithograph machines. More often he is required to deliver small completed jobs to customers. He attaches panniers to his DOT Racer and he soon becomes a familiar sight weaving his way through the back alleys and side streets of Ancoats and Ardwick, Beswick and Bradford, Clayton and Colleyhurst.

Archie Rowe proves an excellent teacher. "Watch and learn," he says. "Don't try owt that's fancy, just copy what I do, and tha' shan't go far wrong. Unless tha's got summat worth sayin', say nowt. Right, lad?"

"Yes, Mr Rowe."

"And that's enough o' that Mr Rowe malarkey. Everyone calls me Archie, an' I reckon that'll do for thee, youth, an' all."

George nods.

"Now then, have a go at this for starters." He lays out before him a sheet of paper with the familiar sentence *'The quick brown fox jumps over the lazy dog'* written on it. George remembers having to copy this when he was first learning to write, with a pen dipped into the inkwell on the top of his desk. "This sentence contains all the letters of the alphabet in it," he recalls his teacher informing them, a fierce termagant by the name of Miss Brown, who would routinely line the children up at the start of each day to administer a sharp rap over the knuckles with her ruler. "That is merely a warning," she would say. "Should anyone really misbehave, they will find the actual punishment meted out far worse, I can assure you." Fortunately, her bark was far worse than her bite, and George was never to experience anything more stringent than these daily raps on the knuckles. On the contrary, she was often quick to praise George's penmanship. He was one of very few children who did not leave a trail of ink blots across his hands or exercise book. Nor did she ever catch him in the act of tormenting poor Anita Jones, a timid girl who sat in the desk just in front of George, whose long pig-tails he would occasionally dip into those same inkwells if he ever finished an exercise ahead of the others, which he frequently did.

He suspected Archie Rowe to be cut from the same cloth, and so it proved. He showed George where the tins of paint were kept – "you only ever need these five – red, yellow, blue, white and black – they can give you all the colours you'll want" – where the brushes were kept – "sable and ox hair – make sure tha' keeps 'em clean, lad" – and proceeded to induct him into the mysteries of the mahl stick. "This," he said, "is the sign writer's greatest friend. It can be made up of anything – a thin metal rod, a piece of dowling, a copper pipe wi' a cork on one end – so long as it's light, and so long as it's true. Tha' dun't want owt snappin' or bendin' on thee, else tha'll be up salt creek wi'out a paddle."

"What's it for, Archie?"

"It's to keep thy 'and from shakin', that's what. A sign must be written straight an' true, clear an' bold. If tha' takes too long o'er a single letter, it shows. It comes out all uncertain. Canst tha' see?" And he demonstrates, by painting a slow, spidery letter 's', which dribbles down the board before petering out near the bottom. "Now then, youth, what does that look like? No – don't say owt, for I'll tell thee what it looks like. It looks like when tha's a kid an' tha's been tryin' to write tha' name while pissin' against a wall."

George splutters.

"Don't tell me tha' never tried it tha'self as a nipper. Tha'd be a rum sort of youth if tha' didn't."

George says nothing.

"Quite right, lad. Silence is a virtue. Now, with this mahl stick, tha' can grip it in tha' left palm, whilst holdin' t' pot o' paint twixt t' thumb an' t' forefinger, rest t' cork end against t' sign board to hold it still, then balance tha' right 'and on t' mahl stick to keep it steady, whilst tha' paints t' sign, using t' stick to help thee swing up high or reach down low in a single sure stroke. Like this, see?" And he would demonstrate with a deftness that took George's breath away. Like all great craftsmen, he made a difficult thing look simple.

George persevered. He did as he was bid. He watched and he learned. In a few weeks he was able to render '*The quick brown fox jumped over the lazy dog*' in block or italics, in a variety of fonts and in a range of sizes.

"Ay, lad. I reckon tha's gettin' summat like."

They are standing outside Archie's workshop, which is tucked behind a railway arch, with a low brick roof, which gets even lower as it stretches towards the gloomy back wall, where Archie keeps a stack of wood for boards. Across the yard from where they are standing, in a ramshackle huddle of buildings tucked up against the embankment, which carries trains out of Salford towards Wigan Wallgate via Walkden, is a smithy. From time to time George has seen a broad shouldered, stooping figure emerge from within, bare chested, his skin a deep chestnut colour, his eyes in shadow, his frame silhouetted against the red glow of the forge burning inside. He and Archie will occasionally nod in the other's direction, but as yet George has never heard them exchange even a word. The man crosses the yard now. and then disappears into one of the other buildings, which George takes to be the smith's cottage.

"Who *is* that?" he asks, before he has time to check himself.

Archie throws him a withering look. "Ask me no questions and I'll tell thee no lies."

Later, when George has finished for the day, he waits while Archie locks up and pretends to be tinkering with something on his DOT Racer until Archie has left. Then George creeps across the yard towards the smithy and peeps inside.

It takes him several moments for his eyes to adjust to the Stygian darkness of the forge after the bright late sun outside. He ventures further in, fascinated, as he is increasingly becoming, by the different specialist tools of any given trade. He walks past a bench laid out with hammers of different shapes and weights. A second bench is lined with row upon row of neatly arranged files and rasps. In the corner is a mountain of discarded nails. Hung on a wall are dozens of horse shoes. The sun is dipping lower in the evening sky. While George is wandering silently and reverently through the forge, shafts of light begin streaming through the slats in the far wall. Motes of dust, like tiny dancers, circle slowly in each one. Letting his eye roam, he chances upon an arrangement of iron sculptures hanging from a beam near the roof. At first he cannot make out what they are. Intrigued, he moves closer, until he is standing directly beneath them. The way the light catches them, they remind him of a flock of birds caught on a current of air, and then, the more he studies them, he realises that this is exactly what they are, three birds in flight, with long necks and deep, strong wings. He thinks they might be egrets, but he is not sure. His father will know. He must try to remember every detail of them. A barrel is standing close by. George drags it over and climbs on top of it in order to get an even closer look. The light from the sun is now catching them with greater clarity and sharpness, and George can make out that all three birds have been fashioned from literally hundreds of individual, uniquely-shaped feathers, each one of them separately cast in iron. It is one of the most remarkable things he has ever seen. He reaches up his hand, carefully, tentatively, wondering if he might dare to touch them. His fingers inch towards them, tantalisingly slowly. He stretches to his full height, raising himself onto the tips of his toes, trying to maintain an increasingly precarious balance. Just as he is about at last to touch them, a voice booms from the open doorway.

"Hey! You!"

Immediately George overbalances and falls from the barrel, knocking it over as he crashes to the ground with a painful thud. At the last second his fingers had brushed against the birds, and now they swing above him, swooping in and out of the light, their metal wings beating against one another.

The bare-chested man towers above him. "You," he commands, "stay where you are." A dog growls at George, guarding him so that he won't try to slip away. The man rights the barrel, leaps upon it with surprising grace and agility, reaches up and calms the clattering birds, until they are still and silent once more. When he is finally satisfied, he leaps down to the ground and picks up George by the lapels of his jacket in a single, sure and threatening movement, the dog shadowing his every move..

"Who are you?" he says again. "Why are you here?"

George can only stammer a mumbled apology.

Catch looks at him closely. "You're still only a boy," he says at last. "Go. Do not come back. Unless you have business here. *Do* you have business here?"

George shakes his head.

"Then go."

George picks up his cap and runs to the door.

But when he reaches it, he stops. Something makes him turn around. He looks back to the smith, then points towards the iron birds.

"Those?" he asks. "What are they?"

Catch, surprised by the young boy's sudden bravery, pauses, deciding whether or not to answer him, or throw one of the hammers at him, to send him on his way.

"Egrets," he says. He thinks of how these birds made their long journeys across the plains, across the ocean, thousands of miles, to this place, here, now.

"Why are there three of them?" asks this strange boy.

This is too complicated a question to answer. He shakes his head. "You go now," he says.

"Might I come another time and look at them again?"

Catch walks swiftly towards him. He stops, barely inches from the boy's face, which he scrutinises intently, then nods.

"Thank you," says George, who turns away, sits astride his DOT Racer, kicks the starter and roars off in the direction of the city, throwing up a shower of dust behind him. The dog chases after him. Catch waits until the dust has cleared and settled, until the boy on the bike's just a dot in the distance, then whistles to the dog.

"Quilt?"

The dog runs back to his master's side, and the two of them head inside.

In the twelve months since Winifred cajoled Francis into taking her on as his Passepartout, the fortunes of *Hall & Singer* have blossomed luxuriantly, like a tropical flower in a hot house. Everywhere Francis looks, he sees change. The lay-out of the shop has been completely transformed. Instead of the somewhat random juxtaposition of different items, which had been its hallmark previously, now the space is divided up into separate departments. Sometimes Francis misses the way things were –

"It was eclectic," he'll say to Winifred, when he can't lay his hands on a particular item, "but at least I knew where everything was."

"It was a jumble sale" she'll scold. "No wonder things kept getting lost."

– but on the whole he thanks his lucky stars that Winifred just happened to see his advert in the window, that she took a chance and decided to enquire, that he hadn't closed up for the night (another minute and he would have been gone), and that she had read *Around The World In Eighty Days* at school and happened to know what was meant by Passepartout. On such slender margins are futures decided. If only this, if only that…

He finds himself returning repeatedly to Robert Frost's poem *The Road Less Travelled*, which he had first come across while he was interned on the Isle of Man. There he had found it a bitter poem, mocking and cruel, but now he reads it quite differently – such are we hostages to circumstance, he reflects. Now, when he comes across the lines '*And both that morning equally lay / In leaves no step had trodden black*', he realises how the poem is deceptive and slippery. In masquerading as being a meditation about the vagaries of choice, he now believes it more to be a justification of impulse over conscious decision, for in the poem both roads are described as '*equally untravelled*', but Frost, through a process of retroactive narrative, turns what was nothing more than an intuitive act into a deliberate choice, thereby elevating that choice into something almost pre-ordained and inevitable. For hasn't he always taken the less obvious route, he reflects? Surely, he concludes, he is, both genetically and temperamentally, immanently predisposed towards a less frequented path? But however much Francis likes to believe there was a certain inevitability in his decision to take a chance on Winifred – "it was manifest destiny which brought you to my door," he intones. "No, Francis, it was luck," she replies – deep down he knows it was as much, if not more, *her* decision, *her* impulse, and that any attempt to try and impose meaning out of such random collision is fruitless. Yet at the same time it is impossible to argue with the evidence set out before him, as Winifred creates order out of what before was chaos. Architect of this intelligent design, she has taken him back to that golden prelapsarian time of his childhood, where such deep pleasures were to be found in the making of lists, the inventing of new classification categories, the developing of intricate and bespoke filing and indexing systems. What had become a universe of lost things has now been transformed, where a place exists for everything and everything has its place.

"God needed six days to create the world," she jokes, "and then a seventh for a well-earned rest. I've required a little longer than that to make sense out of all of this, and I'm still waiting for that well-earned rest."

"I've told you a thousand times," he says. "Take a holiday whenever you want to."

"Oh yes? And what kind of mess would I be coming back to afterwards? I may have managed to sort the shop out, Francis, but managing *you* is still very much a work-in-progress."

And of course she's right, he thinks. He looks around and sees the fruits of her labour in evidence everywhere. There's now not one, but two opticians using the partitioned space in one corner, each for three days of every week. As a consequence, Francis has been able to develop a new sideline in the latest ophthalmic instruments, for which there is a growing market. Through Charles he has even managed to offer a service for bespoke adjustments to these instruments for specialists working in The Royal Eye Hospital on Oxford Road, while through Charles's friend's contacts in the Audiology Department at the University, they now also offer basic hearing tests once a week. There's a whole section of the shop given over to radios, gramophones and even records. Through his involvement with the recording of The Manchester Children's Choir's rendition of *Nymphs & Shepherds* the previous year at the Free Trade Hall, he has become one of the few main outlets in the city where members of the public can purchase a copy of the disc. It has been, and remains, a consistent high seller. This leaves ample space for his growing collection of cameras, a few manufactured here in Manchester, at Billcliff's of Altrincham, alongside more modern, top-of-the-range items imported from Germany. Again, at Winifred's suggestion, Francis has turned over part of the shop's cellar to a dark room, where they can develop photographs for customers. Winifred describes somewhat wistfully how Mr Kaufman used to cut jewellery and carry out engravings in this cellar, and it is not long before these two services are reintroduced, again on a rental basis.

Even in these difficult economic times, business is booming. In her first few days Winifred uncovered a whole raft of unpaid invoices, stuffed and forgotten in a drawer, and she quickly instituted new simple accounts and book keeping systems, which even Francis could manage if pressed. There are now no more awkward letters from bank managers, and Francis no longer feels embarrassed when talking to Charles about the state of his affairs. But curiously, if ever Francis invites his friend to come and take a look at the way his premises have been transformed, there always seems to be a reason why Charles is unable to do so, and whenever Winifred's name is mentioned, he quickly steers the conversation towards a different topic.

And so, on the last Saturday in June 1930, Francis is feeling especially buoyant.

"We need cake," he declares.

Winifred raises a wry eyebrow. "Do we? What are we celebrating?"

"It is now exactly a year since your initial four week trial period here was made permanent. Just look around at the difference you have made. It's plain for all to see. Surely that alone is worth a reward? A Victoria Sponge, I think, don't you? Or Madeira cake? Or perhaps Madam would prefer macaroons? I do hope so, for I have a sudden insatiable yearning for one..." He takes a shilling from the till and holds it out towards her.

"You choose, Francis, only I need to stay here. I'm expecting a delivery of all the new stationery we ordered last week. Mr Wright telephoned this morning to say his son would be bringing them round this afternoon, and I want to be here when they arrive to check they are as we instructed."

Francis's ears prick up at the mention of the son. In the year since Frank Wright's funeral at Albert Hall, Francis has often thought about the grandson, how the light poured through the coloured glass in the rooftop skylight onto the young man's hair, illuminating him like an angel. That vision has returned to him frequently in dreams, in which the young man's clothes have disappeared and the light falls instead upon his shoulders and bare arms, glistening on the fine gold hairs on his chest and back, out of which grow feathered wings of purest white, where Francis sits and is lifted high into the night sky, from where the two of them soar across the city. He usually wakes up at that point feeling a mixture of disquiet and elation.

"Francis?" enquires Winifred, shaking him from his reverie. "Are you quite yourself today?"

"Absolutely. I'll put a girdle round about the Earth and be back with macaroons 'ere the leviathan can swim a league."

Winifred shakes her head, smiling. He is a man of such capricious moods, she thinks, and so volatile in the shifting of them from one to another, ecstatic at one moment, plumbing the depths of despair the next. Perhaps it's the artistic temperament, she wonders, but doubts if this is really the case, for she has seen these same violent swings in Victor's moods, so that she has become quite expert in reading the signs.

"When am I going to meet this new boss of yours?" Victor had asked her once, and Winifred, having anticipated this request, had her answer ready.

"Oh, I don't think he's your sort."

"And what sort might that be?"

But when they did eventually meet up, quite by chance one evening when Victor decided to drop by the shop on his way from the pit to the gym, they got along famously. Victor even persuaded Francis to come and watch him fight, an invitation he accepted with alacrity, and afterwards could not stop talking to Winifred about how the whole atmosphere of the boxing ring had thrilled him. He wondered if Victor might consent to giving a short interview for one of his slots with the BBC – the last of his *'Portraits of Manchester's Sporting Heroes'* (previously he'd covered Tommy Johnson of Manchester City, who'd scored a record of thirty-eight goals in a single season, followed, by way of balance, with Harry Rowley from United; Willie Stephenson, England's tallest jockey, who'd won last year's November Handicap at the Castle Irwell racecourse on a horse called Promptitude, and Jack Tyldesley, the Lancashire cricketer who once hit a six all the way from Old Trafford to London, with a little bit of help from a passing goods train) – and, much to Winifred's surprise, Victor had consented. Then, a few weeks later, when Francis suggested they might all go out for an evening together at *The Queen's Hotel*, she was sure that Victor would not be able to refrain from passing less than complimentary remarks about the nature of the clientele there, but again his reaction wrong-footed her. He was an instant hit, and afterwards, when she asked him about it, he simply said, "A person's private life should be exactly that – private." They'd been back several times since, and Francis now came to Victor's fights whenever he could.

Winifred is brought back to the present by the tinkling of the shop bell as the door is pushed open by a young man carrying a large box. He is wearing a leather jacket and cap, with goggles pushed up from his face. He grins broadly.

"Stationery for *Hall & Singer* from F.G. Wright & Son," he says and drops the box by the counter.

"Thank you. Just put them on here, would you please?" asks Winifred. "I'd like to check them before you go."

George nods and leans nonchalantly against the counter while Winifred takes out one of the letterheads.

Hall & Singer

For All Your Seeing & Hearing Needs

Ophthalmology, Audiology, Horology
Telescopes, Magnifying Glasses, Binoculars, Microscopes
Radios, Telephones, Gramophones, Cameras

137 Hyde Road, Denton
Telephone: Manchester 962

Printed by F.G. Wright & Son

"Yes," says Winifred. "This will do nicely. Please tell your father to expect a repeat order imminently."

"I was thinking," says George.

"Yes?"

"Your sign outside could do with a bit of sprucing up."

"Yes, it could."

"I could do that for you too. If you like. I do a bit of sign writing."

Winifred regards him thoughtfully.

At that moment Francis breezes back in. At first he does not notice George.

"Beware Greeks bearing gifts," he declares, holding the box of cakes before him. "for I am in no position to vouchsafe their quality, since Betty's Bakery is mysteriously closed today. I have therefore risked Mr Constantinos's stall on the corner, who offers us these – ratafia cakes, which, I am reliably informed, are macaroons laced with liqueur. Whose is the Trojan Horse outside?" he asks, nodding in the direction of the motor cycle. "Such a vibrant colour."

"That would be mine," says George amiably.

Francis looks directly at him. He is momentarily lost for words.

"Half day," adds George, shifting his position.

"I beg your pardon?" mumbles Francis.

"Saturday," continues George, oblivious of the effect he is having. "Half day closing. I did wonder whether you might be closed."

"We never close," jokes Winifred. "Francis, aren't you

going to offer our guest some cake? I'll go and put the kettle on."

"Ta," says George. "Don't mind if I do. Milk, no sugar."

Winifred retreats to the back room where they keep the kettle and the tea things. Looking back through to the shop she can see George tucking into his ratafia cake with unabashed relish.

"Mmn, delicious," he says, licking his fingers.

Observing him from this distance, she realises how impossibly heroic and glamorous he must seem to Francis, in his leather jacket and cap, leaning with such *insouciance* against the counter, so easy in his body. It is no wonder, she thinks, that Francis is uncharacteristically at a complete loss for words. Better rescue him, she thinks, as she carries through the tea tray.

But just as she returns, George's eye is caught by the display of cameras in the opposite corner. He makes a beeline for them. "These are beautiful," he says, running a hand appreciatively over the curves and lines of one of them.

"Yes," says Francis, "and expensive." He rearranges the camera so that it is now just as it was before George picked it up, a gesture George notices.

"Sorry," says George. "I should explain." His tone becomes altogether more serious. "I'm an Art student. Or about to be. Though I intend to keep working at the same time. For my Dad, and for Archie."

"Who's Archie?"

"A sign writer."

"Ah yes," interjects Winifred. "George was telling me about it while you were out procuring macaroons."

Francis throws Winifred a withering look. He turns his attention fully back to George. "What kind of artist do you hope to become?"

"That's just it," continues George. "Ever since I can remember, I've drawn. It's my way of making sense of what's around me. I like to look at what's beneath things, what makes something what it is, the guts and bones of it. But lately I've begun to see the world differently. I help out at the speedway track most weeks, adjusting the timing on the engines of the bikes, and it strikes me that everything's about timing."

Francis and Winifred regard each other briefly.

"And now," says George, "since I got my own bike, I ride across the city, zipping in and out of traffic and people, and I realise I want to capture all of it, the speed, the excitement, the way the light is always changing, how everything blurs into a single streak of different colours, but then just occasionally your eye fixes on a single object, a face in the crowd, an unguarded expression in the eyes, a chance meeting between friends, a child letting go of a balloon and watching it soar above the rooftops, a flock of pigeons lifting into the air, and I'm beginning to wonder if I can ever keep hold of all that by drawing. Mr Lowry does it, in some of his paintings, I think, but perhaps a photograph might do it better – no, not better, just differently, that's all. I want to take dozens of photographs every single day, hoping that maybe just one or two of them might capture just the tiniest fraction of all the amazing things my eye records in a single second. I'll still draw of course, and I want to get better at it, so that I know how to look at things more closely, more precisely. I think taking photographs will help me with that too…"

He stops, pausing for breath. He is, Winifred notes, blushing. The back of his neck is flushed a deep crimson.

"Sorry," he says at last. "I get carried away sometimes."

"Please," interrupts Francis, suddenly serious, "one should never apologise for one's passions. Here – let me show you some of the cameras we have in stock. A serious photographer needs a serious camera, and I'm sure we could come to an arrangement concerning payment, a student discount perhaps?"

Francis is back on surer ground now, about to draw from his vast reservoir of specialist technical knowledge – no one understands better than Francis the latest technical innovations in radios, lenses, scientific instruments and, above all else, cameras – so Winifred leaves the two of them together, while she goes to sort through the rest of the delivery from Wright's.

"It depends on what you're looking for," begins Francis. "We've all manner of Kodak Boxes of course – *the Brownie, the Rainbow, the Hawkeye*. Mr Eastman is bringing out new models every five minutes but, with the recent tariffs on imports from America, they're no longer the cheap option they once were. I've this *Thornton Pickard Ruby Reflex Quarter Plate SLR*, made locally by Houghtons & Butchers, for Billcliff's in Altrincham, first designed in 1924, but still more than serviceable, its self-capping shutter's a particularly nice feature. However…" he pauses, looking back at George, "having heard what you said earlier, if it's speed you're after, and the capacity to take lots of pictures in rapid succession, I'd recommend one of our more modern German models." He takes George to a separate cabinet. "These are our latest arrivals, all from Germany." He looks at George directly. "Nobody can match the Germans yet when it comes to cameras," he says, opening the cabinet reverently. "The precision of their engineering is unequalled," he adds with a somewhat theatrical sigh. "This, for example, is the *Certo Dollina*. A Schneider Kreuznach lens. 35 millimetre. Nickel plated, strut braced, capstan knob, scissor action. Viewfinder possibly on the small side. This, however," he says, taking out a different model, "the *Voightlander Brillant*, has a superb viewfinder. Styled as a Twin Lens Reflex, that is in fact a slight misnomer, for the top lens is for viewing only and cannot be focused independently." He puts this back on its shelf, then takes out another. "This is a fun camera," he says, smiling. "*The Billy-Clack.* Agfa's equivalent to Kodak's

Jiffy. Cleverly designed, easily and rapidly assembled, good value for money, cheap but cheerful. A built-in feature to increase contrast between sky and clouds, and – this may be of interest to you, George, in view of what you said – a feature called the 'sportsfinder', enabling you to keep the camera even stiller when taking pictures of moving objects. Only fixed focus, though," and he returns it to its shelf. "Now this is an interesting camera," he begins, taking down the next one, "an unusual hybrid, the *Zeiss Ikon Icarette*. Uses both roll film or traditional plates. It's fitted with a plate back for critical focus work. Delightfully smooth and precise. But," he says, shaking his head, "requires patience and can be a little fiddly. Whereas this," he continues, now almost lost in a world of his own, "the *Reflex Corelle*, though not as refined as the *Exakta*, which we'll come onto in a moment – here, hold this for me, will you?" he adds, handing George an as yet unidentified camera, " – has its own rather quirky charms. Made in Dresden. Of course." He holds it up admiringly. "Sometimes, you know, I wonder if anyone in Dresden does anything at all other than make perfect cameras. This is by Kochman. Gives you twelve frames per roll, as opposed to the standard eight, with a variety of speeds plus a delayed release, still its tensioning system can be a little troublesome. But this, the *Exakta*…" He brings his fingers to his lips and kisses them. "A masterpiece. Based on the Kodak VP – vest pocket, one of the earliest miniatures – it has added so many subtle extras. Variable delayed release, timed exposures up to twelve seconds, function dictating form in a most pleasing design. It really sets the benchmark." He sighs again. "But not for you, George," he says, replacing it on the shelf.

"Why not, if it's as good as you say it is?"

"For one thing it's too expensive, and for another, you have to work your way up to it. You need something simpler to start with, something that has all the basic features, is quick and easy to use, sits well in the hand."

"So which one do you recommend?"

"You are holding it, George."

George looks down at the camera Francis had asked him to mind for a moment. It does indeed sit well in the hand.

"Let me introduce you to the *Foth Derby*," he declares with a flourish. "A delightful German 127 roll film camera." He takes it back from George and begins to demonstrate its various features. "Folding viewfinder, with a lens in front and a backsight. Collapsing lens panel with small bellows behind. Folding mechanism, a scissor strut. The focal plane shutter comprises two horizontally running cloth curtains controlled by a mechanism so advanced, the like of which I've never seen before. The shutter release is extremely light and smooth, via this button on the front, do you see? Shutter cocking and film advance are two separate operations which, for the beginner, are ideal. The shutter setting dial – here – only indicates the correct speed once the shutter is cocked – like so. Frame numbers are identified by the classic red window – here." He hands the camera back to George, who turns it over in his fingers, raises it to his eye, weighs it in his hand. 'Well," says Francis, "what do you think?"

"I think," says George, grinning hugely, "that I'm glad I was persuaded to stay on for a biscuit." They both laugh. "It's perfect."

"Then it's yours," says Francis. "We'll throw in the first roll of film for free. Miss Holt, will you wrap this for the gentleman please?"

"I'd be delighted to, Mr Hall," replies Winifred. "Will the gentleman be paying cash of charging it to his account?"

George hesitates, caught up in their banter. "Well, I – er…"

"Settle up by the end of the month," says Francis.

"That's today," says Winifred.

George looks somewhat alarmed.

"By the end of next month then," says Francis. "Now, any

more for any more?" He holds out the tray of ratafia biscuits.

"I think I ought to be on my way," says George. "I have other deliveries to make. Which reminds me – might you be able to display one of these?" He takes out a poster from the inside of his leather jacket. "It's for an event next weekend at Barton Aerodrome. We've done the printing for it, but it's something my father's especially interested in."

Winifred takes the poster from him. "I'm sure we can," she says. "I'll place it in the window right now. Wait a minute…" She holds it out towards Francis. "Isn't this what you were telling me about the other week?"

Francis reads it aloud. " '*The Festival of Speed. Featuring the Annual King's Cup Air Race'*. What a coincidence. Yes, I'm going along with my BBC hat on. They've asked me to try and capture the essence and atmosphere of the day. What I like to refer to as my 'sound poems'. I do them from time to time."

"Then I must have heard some of them. We listen to the radio all the time at home."

Francis smiles. "I'd also been toying with the idea of experimenting with a new cine camera I'm thinking we might sell. It's called a *Kinamo*, designed by Emanuel Goldberg, one of Zeiss's employees in Dresden. He's just added a spring motor attachment, which makes it ideal for hand-held filming. The public don't know it yet, but pretty soon, if it's as good as I think it is, they're all going to want one, and I want to make sure we sell them first. The only trouble is…" he looks away sheepishly.

"Yes?" says George.

"I'm not sure how I'm going to get it there, what with having to carry all the sound recording equipment too."

"How big is it?"

"Not large. Let me show you." He brings it out from the back room.

"And the sound equipment?"

"There. In the glass cabinet."

George considers a moment.

"No problem," he says. "I can fit those into the panniers on my bike, and you can ride pillion. That is, if you don't mind travelling there by motor cycle?"

"I shall consider it an added bonus. An adventure. I hope you will not be riding any slower on my account?" he adds, unable to suppress a smile.

"Not in the least," quips George, "though some consideration may need to be taken for the equipment."

"Till next Saturday then," says Francis, holding out his hand.

George takes it and shakes it warmly. "Till next Saturday."

"Bring your *Foth Derby*."

"I will."

Francis stands at the doorway to the shop and watches George roar away on his DOT Racer, then turns to face Winifred with a look of yearning in his eyes.

"Now you listen to me, Francis Hall," she says, "he's only a boy."

"An Adonis," he sighs dreamily.

"He's seventeen."

"As were we all once."

She narrows her eyes and gives him an old fashioned look.

"Don't worry," he says. "I shall be as good as gold. I promise. Now, who's for another ratafia biscuit? Waste not, want not. Isn't that what you say?"

Barton Aerodrome
Saturday 5th July 1930 from 2pm

MANCHESTER FESTIVAL OF SPEED
featuring

THE KING'S CUP AIR RACE

**plus a
Spectacular Aerial Pageant
showcasing the
Avro 510 and Vickers Vimy
Manufactured in Manchester**

**Grass Track Motor Cycle Races
Grand Parade of Classic Automobiles
Rolls Royce Silver Ghosts & Crossley Phaetons**

**with music provided by
The Eccles Subscription Borough Brass Band**

Printed by F.G. Wright & Son

*

"Good afternoon, ladies and gentlemen, boys and girls, and welcome to Barton Aerodrome, home of Britain's first ever municipal airport, for this afternoon's Festival of Speed. I hope that you have been enjoying the marvellous music provided for us today by The Eccles Borough Subscription Brass Band, current North-West Champions, conducted by Mr James Dow, who have just been playing the famous Royal Air Force March Past, composed by Sir Henry Walford Davies in 1918 to commemorate their incalculable contribution to our final victory. Highly appropriate and wonderfully stirring. We'll be hearing more from them later.

"My name is John Leeming, founder of the world's first ever flying organisation, the Lancashire Aero Club, and it's my job this afternoon to introduce to you all of the various exciting events we've got planned. You'll find me in the Control Tower alongside the central runway, the highest point in the aerodrome, if any of you fancy taking a look at how they manage all of the comings and goings here.

"First up this afternoon we have the Grand Parade of

Classic Automobiles, which I know so many of you have been looking forward to as eagerly as I have, as they motor around the airfield, each of them carrying one of our very special honoured and distinguished guests and dignitaries, who have most kindly accepted our invitation to join us here today.

"Leading the parade is a magnificent Rolls Royce Phantom Cabriolet, the first of two Rolls we have for you this afternoon, and it is bringing Sir John Francis Granville Scrope Egerton, 4th Earl of Ellesmere. It was his generosity in gifting this land to the Manchester Corporation in the first place that enabled this aerodrome to be built. We thank you very much, Lord Egerton…"

A generous round of applause rings around the airfield.

"The Earl is followed by Sir Edward Stanley, 17th Earl of Derby and High Sheriff of Lancashire, being driven in our second classic Rolls, a 1921 Silver Ghost. As many of you know, I'm sure, Rolls Royce began here in Manchester, following that now legendary meeting between Mr Rolls and Mr Royce in The Midland Hotel in 1904, after which they began manufacturing these beauties here in the city. They've since relocated to Derby, and so perhaps His Highness the High Sheriff might be able to use his influence as Earl of that great town to persuade Messrs Rolls and Royce to return to their true home.

"Next to arrive, in another Manchester classic, the Crossley Phaeton, manufactured in Gorton, and kindly loaned to us this afternoon by Mr Hubert Wright of F.G. Wright & Son, is Mr John Bloom, Mayor of Salford, under whose jurisdiction the aerodrome officially sits…"

Annie, standing close to where the cars are passing, applauds loudly. She tries to catch Hubert's eye, but he is so intently concentrating, making sure he keeps to the correct speed and route, that he fails to notice her. She waves enthusiastically anyway, and then begins to look forward to the VIP's Tea in the Aerodrome's Club Lounge later in the afternoon, where she hopes she will be presented to the two Earls.

"And finally, in another Crossley, his own 1927 Tourer, a rich maroon with black trim, we are delighted to welcome back the former Lord Mayor of Manchester, Sir Robert Noton Barclay, who has kindly stepped in as substitute for the present incumbent, Mr George Frank Titt, who has succumbed to a last minute chest infection. Thank you, Sir Robert, and get well soon, George.

"For those of you interested in these magnificent automobiles – and I know there are many of you here this afternoon – there will be ample opportunity to experience them close up, as these four splendid vehicles will be on display at the far corner of the airfield – close to Antonelli's Ice Cream cart which, thanks to a combination of today's glorious weather and the presence of Miss Manchester Ice Creams, the delectable Miss Giulia Lockhart, is already doing brisk business – where they will be joined by a whole fleet of other classic cars, including Talbots, Sunbeams, Wolseley 10s and Vauxhall 30s, the Riley Brooklands and AC6, not to mention a Morris Cowley, all manner of Daimlers, Bentleys and Austins, including the Salamander Special complete with Dicky seat. Something for everyone, I'm sure you'll agree..."

Giulia is delighted at how the day is unfolding. It is her first official outing as *'Miss Manchester Ice Creams'*, a contest she won just three weeks before, at Chorlton-on-Medlock Town Hall on Cavendish Street, where she was crowned by the Lady Mayoress, who complimented her on how pretty she looked. Her photograph had been in the newspaper, '*wreathed in smiles*', as the caption had put it, which had been passed around her entire family. She had wanted it framed and hung over the fireplace at home, but her mother would not hear of it.

"You're getting too big for your boots as it is," she had said, "*troppo grande per gli stivali.*"

But then her Uncle Leonardo had sat her on his knee and pinched her cheeks and she had felt better. He was not really her uncle, just someone who'd arrived in Manchester the same time as her grandparents had. He'd only been little then, but he'd done well for himself over the years and was now the Manager at the new Antonelli ice cream headquarters next to the cricket ground at Old Trafford, the Progress Works, where Giulia now worked – not in the factory, as she was quick to correct anyone who asked, but a good job, in the office, with prospects. She'd seen Leonardo before, but not for some time, and he didn't recognise her when she first showed up for the interview.

"You were just a child when I last saw you," he said, "*una piccola ragazza.*"

"Well," she'd replied, "I'm not any more."

It was Leonardo's idea that she should call him '*Zio*' – 'Uncle', '*Zio Leo*' – "but not in the office," he'd added hastily.

"*Si,*" she had said, with a smile that stopped him in his tracks, "*capisco.*"

It was his idea for her to attend the Festival of Speed.

"I'll need a new dress," she had said, and he had duly obliged.

Now she rides in an open top saloon car, a Lagonda, waving to the crowds. Over her dress, a shimmering blue, covered with sequins that sparkle in the Salford sun, she wears a sash proclaiming her title, and on her head she wears a tiara. When she steps down from the car, a young man approaches her, offers his arm and asks for her autograph. This is just the beginning, she thinks.

"We now come to the main event of this afternoon's Festival of Speed – the King's Cup Air Race, which we are delighted to be co-hosting here at Barton, together with other airfields around the country, at Cardiff, Newcastle, Hull and London. For those of you not in the know, The King's Cup is the most sought after and prestigious trophy in air racing today. It was established by His Majesty King George V in 1922 as, in his words, 'an incentive to the development of light aircraft and engine design', and so it has proved. It attracts pilots from all over Britain and the Commonwealth, and today is no exception, with a record one hundred and one entrants, of which we understand there will be eighty-eight actual starters, including their Royal Highnesses Prince Edward and Prince George, who have each entered an aircraft of their own, a Hawker Tomtit and a DH Hawk Moth respectively, as well as last year's victor, Flight Lieutenant Richard Atcherley, who is this year swapping his Gloster Grebe for the brand new Seagrave Meteor.

"Each year the race covers a different course. This year it begins at London Air Park in Hanworth, near Hounslow. Pilots must then steer a course westwards, over the Bristol Channel, where they must over-fly Cardiff, before heading north to here, Barton, where each of them must land, carry out any necessary running repairs, refuel, and stop for a mandatory thirty minutes, then take off in a north-easterly direction towards Newcastle, from where they turn south-east, across the River Humber at Hull, then due south back to Hanworth again, where the race finishes. The aeroplanes take off at three minute intervals and each aircraft is individually timed. The winner is the pilot who completes the seven hundred and fifty-three mile circuit in the quickest time. Although we shan't witness the actual finish here, we

shall have a thrilling opportunity to watch each of the aeroplanes as they come in to land and to see the pilots first hand and at close quarters as they prepare for the second half of the race. We are also in direct communication with Hanworth via telegraph, and so I shall be able to announce the result within minutes of it happening. We have just heard, in fact, that last year's winner, Flight Lieutenant Atcherley, has already had to withdraw, having experienced difficulties with the starboard engine of his Seagrave Meteor when attempting to take off. We expect the first arrivals in about half an hour's time, so look to the skies, everyone, and watch for their appearance, like the swallows in spring.

"And now, to entertain us once more, The Eccles Borough Subscription Brass Band, under the expert leadership of their conductor, Mr James Dow, will give us an 'Oriental Rhapsody' by Granville Bantock, quite appropriate, wouldn't you agree, with those brave pilots flying towards us even now out of the east...?"

George will take two dozen photographs that afternoon with his newly acquired *Foth Derby*, but he deliberately saves the first for Francis. He watches him set up his sound equipment in a small tent, a complex process involving microphones, a waveguide – a cumbersome machine allowing Francis to control the recording of electromagnetic sound with minimal loss of quality – a specially adapted orthophonic Victrola, and a folded horn, for both recording and playing back sound. George, with his love of gadgets inherited from his father, is fascinated by the way Francis customises them all in order to fulfil specific tasks he requires of them.

He will, he has explained, be collecting sounds – the noise of the crowds, the music of the brass bands, the roar of the aircraft engines, the whirring of their propellers, as well as interviews with different individuals – directly onto a series of discs. Then, once he is back home in his studio, through a process of overdubbing, he will layer these sounds on top of each other to create what he calls his 'sound poems', capturing both the narrative and the atmosphere of the day, which will, he hopes, transport the listener to imagine that they were actually present. This will then be transmitted by the BBC during one of their nightly broadcasts. They moved from their temporary home in the makeshift studios of Metro-Vickers in Trafford Park three years ago to a purpose-built Central Control Room in Piccadilly Gardens, as well as converting a repertory theatre in Hulme to what has become known as *The BBC Radio Playhouse*. Francis will complete his work on this sound poem in the Control Room at Piccadilly.

With John Leeming having just announced the imminent arrival of the first aeroplanes from Hanworth, Francis is now busy positioning himself with his *Kinamo*, his experimental hand-held cine camera, with which he hopes to capture footage of all the aircraft and pilots as they land. He will then send this off to *Pathé* and *Movietone,* both of whom have expressed interest in inserting edited extracts of any footage he might obtain into the Newsreel Film depicting *The King's Cup* each aims to present in cinemas by the end of the month.

Looking at him now, through the viewfinder of his *Foth Derby*, George thinks Francis looks like a pioneer, recording as it happens the *Race of the Age*, portraying these daredevils of the skies as latter day Christopher Columbuses, Vasco de Gamas, Amerigo Vespuccis, which they are, conquering new worlds, pushing the boundaries of human endeavour to the absolute limit, at exactly this moment, on this very day, in this very spot, placing Manchester right at the heart of this new spirit of adventure, and then communicating it to the rest of the world.

George waits until he sees that Francis is ready, framing him so that he stands in the centre of the composition, then calls out.

"Francis – look this way."

Francis turns, frowning as he seeks out the voice who has called him, then smiling as his pale eyes pick out George.

George clicks the shutter and takes the photograph.

"My first one," he shouts, his voice raised above the general hubbub. "I wanted it to be of you. Here in the present, about to capture for all time a moment that has yet to take place, but that soon will be consigned to history, using technology that is not yet available. I shall call it *'Future Perfect'*."

"I don't know what you're talking about," Francis shouts back, smiling even more broadly.

"Ladies and gentlemen, I can just make out the first of our fliers heading towards us. For those of you with binoculars, train them to the south-east, towards the Ship Canal. Waggling her wings in a cheeky wave as she skims across the Barton Aqueduct, piloting an Avro 594 Avian III, it's none other than Winsome Winnie Brown, Aviatrix Extraordinaire, born right here in Manchester, and one of just four lady pilots in the race today. The bird she's flying was built in Woodford, just fifteen miles to the south of here as the crow flies, or as Winnie does, and what a beauty she is – the aircraft, I mean, although Winnie's been turning heads too wherever she goes on the air racing circuit. There's no finer aeroplane in my opinion than an Avro. You can land her on a sixpence if you have to. I should know, having landed one just like her on the top of Helvellyn a few years back. Come on, Winnie, show us what you're made of..."

The crowd, which police estimates put as high as thirty thousand, parts like the Red Sea as Miss Winifred Sawley Brown swoops out of the sky and lands her flimsy bi-plane onto the centre of the runway, like an arrow into a bullseye, a heron spearing a fish. She taxis towards the hangar, where hundreds of well wishers have broken through the roped off cordon and are already surging towards her.

Among this throng of excited supporters is George, *Foth Derby* camera at the ready. He weaves between the press of people converging around the aeroplane, the stewards and engineers, the VIPs and hoi polloi. He manages to click the shutter just as she leaps from the cockpit, goggles pushed up from her smoke-blackened face onto the top of her head, revealing a mask of white around her startled eyes like a lemur descending from the clouds. She stands with legs astride and arms akimbo, bold and confident in her loose-fitting, leather flying suit, every inch a winner.

From the far side of the field, Giulia watches, perplexed. Why should everyone be paying such attention to this woman dressed as a man? She can imagine how thrilling it must be to fly a plane, but surely not in such unflattering attire? She herself would never consent to be seen wearing such ill-fitting trousers. If she had to wear trousers at all, she would want them to be tight, to show off her shapely legs, like Ruth Elder in *Moran of the Marines*, Eileen Sedgwick in *The Diamond Queen* or, even better, Bebe Daniels in *One Wild Week*. Yes, that is how she would want to look. Not like this... what was her name again?

By now the sky is thick with aircraft, their dark silhouettes a siege of herons, circling overhead, snapping at each other's wing tips for land fall. They must radio the control tower to report their position, confirm their start time from Hanworth, before taking it in turns to land and refuel. Francis films as many of the pilots as he can, before returning to focus on Winnie, who is now preparing to take off for the second half of the race. With a wave to the crowds she climbs back up into the cockpit, pulls down her goggles determinedly over her face, accelerates down the runway before slowly lifting off, the lead heron, flying alone, swaying her wings, once, twice, from side to side, before catching the high thermals as she banks and tacks towards the north.

"And there she goes, off into the blue, carrying the hopes of Manchester with her, Miss Winifred Sawley Brown. As things stand, Winnie is in the lead by eleven minutes from Mr Alan S. Butler in a D.H. Moth, with Flight Lieutenant Henry Waghorn a further three minutes back in his Blackburn Bluebird, while another of our female aviators, Mrs Lois Butler, wife of Alan, is hot on the heels of the Lieutenant just half a minute behind in fourth in her D.H. Puss Moth. Meanwhile, I am hearing that one of the race favourites, Sir Geoffrey de Haviland, also in a Puss Moth, has been forced to retire here at Barton with plug trouble. Bad luck, Sir Geoffrey! Also taking no further part in the race this year are Miss Diana Guest, Captain Ian C. Maxwell, Flight Lieutenants F.B. Tomkins, co-pilots F.T. Barrett and L.G. Pope, and Mr E.G. Hordern. We hope you all have better fortune next year.

"But for this year the race now takes our intrepid pilots north to Newcastle before heading south over the Humber and along the east coast back to London, where they are expected later this evening. We'll still be here to relay the final results as soon as we hear it ourselves and so, until then, let's keep our fingers crossed for Plucky Winsome Winnie Brown from Woodford.

"Now, after all of that excitement, let's once again enjoy the delights of The Eccles Borough Subscription Brass Band who, having won this year's British Open at Belle Vue, will be going on to compete in next year's World Championship at Crystal Palace, and are now going to play for us 'A Moorside Suite' by Gustav Holst, most appropriate for our setting here along the marshes and moors of nearby Chat Moss..."

A couple of hours later, as Hubert is driving them home to Didsbury, Annie reflects on what has been a most successful afternoon.

She has been introduced to both the Lord Lieutenant and High Sheriff of Lancashire. She has drunk tea with them and their wives. She has made small talk. Not bad for a lass from the Tripe Colony, she thinks. More than that, she has managed to secure an appointment with the Lord Lieutenant's secretary in a fortnight's time to discuss a possible re-design and printing for all of their letterheads and envelopes. If she is successful in winning the order, about which she is feeling quietly confident, she wonders, since the Lord Lieutenant is the King's representative in the County, whether she and Hubert might be permitted to add 'By Royal Appointment' at the head of all of their own stationery. She decides not to share this news with Hubert just yet, but to savour it a little longer as they negotiate the evening traffic.

At around the same time that Annie is keeping her counsel close, Esther is cycling along the tops of the raised narrow embankments which criss-cross the mosses to the south-west of her new home in Patricroft, where she has been living happily for the last two years. She too is nursing a secret, one which has been revealed to her earlier that afternoon, while she and Hejaz, Yasser and Rose had been enjoying the spectacle of *The King's Cup Air Race* at Barton Aerodrome, just a stone's throw from their shared house in Stanley Road.

"What is the world coming to, Hejaz," Yasser had asked, shaking his head, "when a woman is the fastest pilot?"

"And why shouldn't she be?" Rose had answered, sending Yasser a look which he knows from experience it would be wise not to challenge.

"No reason at all," he declared. "I am just marvelling at how the world has changed. In my grandmother's day women were barely allowed to leave the house and now they are conquering the skies."

"There's an American aviatrix," said Esther, "called Harriet Quimby. She was the first woman to fly across the English Channel. When she was asked to comment on her achievement, she said she had found that it was easier to fly than it was to vote."

Rose had roared when she heard that, a bark of laughter that had turned suddenly into a fierce bout of coughing.

"You two boys go and enjoy yourselves playing with your toys," she finally managed to say, "and give us ladies some private time. The cars and motor cycles are over that way," and she pointed to the far corner of the field.

Scratching his head, Yasser allowed himself to be led away by Hejaz. "Women," he said. "A man might live a thousand lifetimes and still get no nearer to understanding them."

"No, *Babba*," said Jaz, steering Yasser by the elbow and smiling, "but what would we do without them?"

As soon as the men were out of earshot, Esther had turned to her mother-in-law, who had during these past two years quickly become her friend, "What's wrong?"

"I'm not sure," said Rose after a few moments. "Maybe nothing, but..."

"Yes?"

"The doctor does not like the sounds he is hearing in my chest. He wants me to go to the hospital to have one of these new X-rays, so they can look more deeply."

Esther nodded, listening, trying to take in what she'd just heard.

"Will you come with me?" asked Rose.

"Of course. They're wonderful things, these X-ray machines. I saw them while I was working as a VAD during the war. If there's something wrong, they'll find out what it is."

"And then what?"

Esther shrugged. "It's always best to know what one is dealing with, I think."

"Forewarned is forearmed?"

"Something like that."

"And it may be nothing."

"Let's hope."

The two women walked together in silence, not heeding the teeming, jostling crowds around them. Rose inserted her arm through Esther's.

After a while Rose said, "Please don't talk of this to Jaz just yet. He would only worry and feel he had to mention something to his father. I want to be the one to tell Yasser. If it turns out that there's something to tell."

Esther squeezed Rose's hand resting on her arm. The lump forming in her throat made it impossible for her to speak.

"And now," said Rose, "I think I should like to go back home. Let's go and find those two men of ours, shall we?"

They spotted Yasser and Hejaz admiring the Earl of Ellesmere's Rolls Royce Phantom Cabriolet. "There they are," said Rose, smiling fondly.

After they had finally reached home, Rose took off her shoes and put her feet up on the couch in the front room, while Esther made everyone tea, which Yasser solicitously poured. "I think I must be getting a cold," said Rose. "Why don't you tell me a story from when you were a boy, Yasser, back in the Yemen, and I can spirit myself away there, to hot desert winds, and then maybe I'll warm up a little."

Yasser lit a fire, even though it was July, and began to talk about the mountains of Southern Arabia, the mountains which Hejaz had been named after, and which Jaz always enjoyed hearing about too. Esther decided she would let them have some family time alone together and quietly crept from the room. She slipped down the hallway, out into the yard at the back of the house, where Arthur's bicycle, one of the very few things she had brought with her from her old life in Gorton, leant against a whitewashed brick wall. She tied the white *qurqash* Rose had given to her as a wedding gift around her head and led the bicycle through the gate at the back of the yard, into the cobbled alley, before setting off, with no clear sense of which direction she would ride, having left a hastily scribbled note on the kitchen table that she would be back in a couple of hours.

Now, having skirted the quietening aerodrome beside the overgrown banks of an old ox-bow bend of the Irwell, separated from the rest of the river by the cutting of the canal, she has headed off down the tracks which penetrate the heart of the mosses. Barton Moss, Irlam Moss, Chat Moss. Past Black Wood, along Twelve Yards Road, down Raspberry Lane, almost as far as Four Lane Ends, deeper and deeper into the watery wilderness of Chat Moss itself, much of its ditches dry and sluggish in the summer heat. She cycles through clouds of flies, but also of moths and butterflies, past clumps of arrowhead, bareroot and brooklime, crowfoot, starwort and fleabane, until she reaches the high bank of Cutnook Lane, a long straight levee raised some twenty feet above the marsh, which runs like an arrow north to south across the heart of the moss for almost two miles, where she stops for breath. She leans the bicycle against a low stunted hawthorn tree, its gnarled, spindly bark rough and cool to the touch. She sits in the minuscule shade afforded by the tree's branches, from where she can look out over the wide expanse of the moss. A few ramshackle huts and houses hunker low against the land, so completely overgrown that they are almost indistinguishable from it. *Last Retreat. Hephzibah. Ebenezer Farm. Hope Cottage.*

The only sounds she can hear are the constant drone of

insects and the rustle of the wind through the tall sedge grasses. Cock's Foot, Bearded Couch, Timothy and Windlestraw.

As she sits and listens, Esther becomes aware of a new sound, a soft, dry slithering. Out of the corner of her eye she glimpses a grass snake emerging from behind a clump of Creeping Bent grass to cross the levee in front of her towards the wetter marshes on the opposite side. Just as it is about to drop down into the oozing mud and water, a white heron dives down out of the sun and pounces. Esther feels the sudden wind rush of air as its folded wings swoop past her to land just a few yards away from her on the edge of the water. She can clearly see the snake struggling to escape the heron's razor sharp, twelve inch bill. It tries to coil itself around the bird's beak, while the heron shakes it violently from side to side. The longer she looks, she realises that the snake too is in the act of swallowing a fish as it tries to free itself from the heron's vice-like grip. Just at that moment she hears a gunshot crack the air from somewhere unseen out on the moss, presumably somebody shooting at the heron, she thinks, the unbroken chain of predator and prey. She can stand this no longer. She gets to her feet, claps her hands and shouts. The white heron, startled by her noise and movement, releases the snake, croaks harshly and lumberingly lifts back into the air. The snake, in falling back to the ground, is jolted, so that the fish leaps from its mouth and back into the water. The snake slides away to lick its wounds. There are no further gunshots.

Esther is breathing heavily. She doesn't believe she's ever witnessed the tooth and claw of nature quite so close up before. Nor, now she comes to think of it, does she think she has ever seen a white heron before. Perhaps it was another kind of bird altogether.

She goes to collect her bicycle. It's time she was getting back. She fails to notice a pair of water rats nosing unconcerned around the other side of the hawthorn tree. Just before she begins to pedal away, she looks along Cutnook Lane, its surface flickering in the heat haze rising up from the moss. She can see the white heron a little farther off, perched on one leg by the water's edge, like a stone statue, and then she hears, or thinks she hears, a new noise. She pauses, concentrates. Yes, it is unmistakable now. Another drone. Not of insects this time, but something louder, larger. And then she sees the source of it. Appearing over the brow of the levee, just over a mile away, a motor cycle, red and black, with two black riders, whose indistinct shapes shimmer and re-form before her eyes, comes roaring towards her. The white heron lifts again in clumsy flight.

Once all of the aeroplanes have taken off from Barton Aerodrome, Francis decides he has enough footage, in terms of both sound and film, and wonders whether they might leave soon. Crowds tend to worry him after a while. People start to notice his pale skin and hair. They point, then look away. Mostly he can cope with this, but today it has begun to bother him, as it frequently does when he is faced with large numbers of people, which is why he generally tries to avoid them, why he prefers to go out at night, rather than in the full glare of sunlight, which can, while being beneficial to his psoriasis, at the same time exacerbate it.

He looks around for George. Foolishly they have not arranged a rendezvous spot, nor a time even. The crowds close in on him. This is like searching for a needle in a haystack, he thinks. I'll never find him at this rate. The camera too, although possible to operate by hand, has become heavy from all of the shots he has taken of the aeroplanes as they landed and took off again, of his close-ups of dashing pilots and scurrying engineers, the excited faces of the spectators, the empty skies again after the planes have all departed.

He decides to head back to the tent where he had set up his sound equipment, which is being looked after by one of the stewards, thinking that eventually George will be bound to show up, but while he is making his way there, he spots him trying to take a photograph of *Miss Manchester Ice Creams*. From this distance away he can see exactly what is happening and smiles.

George has noticed the girl pouting sulkily. She has taken the tiara off her head and is turning it over distractedly in her hands, while a stray dog has wandered over towards her and is sniffing curiously around her ankles. The girl is extremely cross. She tries to swat the dog on its nose with the tiara. George wants to try and capture these contrasts, these juxtapositions of mood, adulation and rejection, beauty and the beast. But he is not yet skilled enough, or confident enough, to trust his instincts and take what he sees, immediately, without a second's doubt. Instead he hesitates, he vacillates between one angle and another, and the moment passes.

Meanwhile, the girl becomes aware of him. She at once assumes a theatrical pose. She replaces the tiara on her head, she flashes the most radiant of smiles, while desperately trying to shake off the dog, who is persistently pulling on the ankle strap of her shoe. George no longer really wants to take the photograph. He doesn't want his subjects to be aware of his presence and to pose for him like this. He would prefer his pictures to be candid, catching people off guard, unaware. But now he doesn't feel it would be fair to disappoint this desperate girl still steadfastly smiling for him. He duly obliges, then thanks her.

"Oh, you're welcome," she replies. Her smile continues to dazzle and the dog finally loses interest in her foot, which he releases in search of something new.

George catches sight of Francis, waves and makes his

way over to him.

"Might we go soon, do you think?" enquires Francis.

George notices how strained his new friend looks. "Now if you like. I'll go and fetch my bike and we can pack everything up."

An hour later they are ready to leave.

"Fancy a spin?" asks George. "I was talking to one of the organisers earlier, and he was telling me there are some long, straight, quiet roads that cut across Chat Moss, just the other side of the airfield, where you can really work up a bit of speed." He pats the side of the DOT Racer. "It'd be great to put her through her paces a bit. What do you think?"

Francis watches George fasten the strap of his leather cycling cap under his chin and is once again swept away by how handsome he looks, how fearless and strong. He feels himself being borne aloft by the same spirit of optimism and adventure.

"Yes," he says. "Let's."

As soon as they leave the aerodrome and turn off from the Liverpool Road onto Barton Moss Road, Francis begins to relax. The crowds feel far away now. The land opens out around them, wide flat vistas, big skies and a horizon which definitively proves to any old flat-earth doubters that the world is unquestionably round. Dragon flies hover by the edge of the marshes, above which they now glide along a high bank, then swoop and disappear. Swifts skim and dive before them, carving the air in a dark tracery of speed against the blue canvas of the sky. George opens up the throttle on his DOT Racer and allows their speed to increase, conscious of Francis tightening his grip around his waist as he does. Francis experiences the rush of air against his skin and through his hair. He has rarely felt this happy, or this free. He wants to stretch out his arms wide and high, and shout as loud as he can.

This is us. Now. Here. In this moment. Alive.

But all that comes out of his mouth is a wild, wordless, throated roar. George, caught up in the same exuberance, joins in with him, the two of them roaring their pleasure to the sky.

At the same moment, lifting from the moss in front of them, a few hundred yards away, a great white bird takes to the air. Its neck is retracted deep into its shoulders. Its wing beats are heavy and long. It is gaining height with exaggerated slowness. Its long bill points towards them like an arrow.

Time stretches.

George sees the bird too late. He ducks his head and brakes as hard as he dare. He has such little margin for manoeuvre along the narrow embankment, whose slides slope steeply down on either side, so that the egret smashes into them. Its wings become entangled with the still outstretched arms of Francis, knocking him off the back of the bike, which George finally manages to stop, the rear wheel skidding in a complete three hundred and sixty degrees, as he has seen happen so often at the speedway track, so that he knows what to do to bring it under control. When he turns his head, Francis is nowhere to be seen. The white egret, freed at last, is gradually gaining height, seemingly uninjured, his great wings lifting him into the air and away over the moss.

The silence which now descends seems deafening. George runs back to where the bird first hit them, desperately searching this way, then that, until he hears a low moan from below him. Peering over the edge of the embankment in the direction of the sound, he can see Francis, some twenty feet below him, having slid down the bank, lying at the edge of the marsh, his left leg twisted awkwardly underneath him. George slides down the slope until he is by Francis's side. There are cuts on his face and hands from where he has tried to fend off the bird, and George can see at once that his left leg is broken. Nevertheless he manages to raise a small smile.

"You certainly managed to put us through our paces," he says, his voice barely a whisper.

"Yes," says George. "She did pretty well, all things considered. It's you I'm worried about."

"I'll be all right," he says. "Just stay here with me."

Esther watches the collision between the motor cycle and the bird in wide-eyed disbelief. For a few moments she is almost too stunned to react at all. Then, suddenly, she is galvanised into action. She collects her bicycle from underneath the hawthorn tree and pedals towards where the accident occurred as quickly as she can.

The haze, which is still shimmering above the road, out of which the motor bike had first appeared like one of the four horsemen of the apocalypse from the *Book of Revelation*, makes distances seem deceptive, and it is further than it had first looked. Eventually she reaches the scene, lets her bicycle fall to the ground and rushes towards where she saw the two men disappear down the bank.

One of the men catches sight of her and is immediately waving his arms and shouting for help. She scrambles down towards him while he breathlessly begins to recount what has happened.

"Yes," she says, "I know. I saw it."

He's clearly in shock, for now that she's come he can't stop talking. He's saying something now about being miles from anywhere and not wanting to leave his friend but not being sure what he should do.

"Stop," she says. "Be quiet a second. Let me take a look at him."

The firmness in her tone silences him at once. We're lucky, he thinks, This woman knows what she's doing.

Esther checks the prostrate man quickly and efficiently.

She turns back to the other.

"What is your friend's name?" she says.

"Francis."

"And your own?"

"George."

"Good. Now listen, George. As you can probably see, Francis has broken his leg. I want you to do exactly what I say. Do you understand?"

He nods.

"Tell me you understand."

"Yes. I understand."

"Right. I want you to climb back up to the road and find a piece of wood, roughly the thickness of a broom handle and about the length of your arm. There's a hawthorn tree about a quarter of a mile further along. You should be able to get something like what we need from that. If you think your motor cycle's still working, use it, you'll be quicker. If not, you can use my bicycle. You'll find it lying close to yours. Do you understand?"

"Yes."

"Then go. Quickly."

Francis becomes aware of George running away from him up the embankment. "George, where are you going? Don't leave me."

"He's not leaving you, Francis. He's going to get a branch from a nearby tree, and I'm going to try and make a splint for your leg, which is broken. I'll stay with you here till he gets back. In the meantime I'm going to try and see to these cuts on your face and arms. My name's Esther, by the way."

Francis nods. "Thank you."

"Don't try to speak unless you have to, or if I ask you something specific. You've had a nasty shock and you need to concentrate on making your breathing as regular as you can. All right?"

He nods again and tries to do as instructed.

"Good," she says. "That's the way."

She looks around, her eyes darting quickly among the reeds and the grasses that lie around them, until finally she sees what she's been hoping to find, a small patch of yarrow, its upturned plates of tiny creamy-white flowers glinting in the early evening sun, and plucks them by the handful. She rubs them gently across Francis's cuts.

"There," she says. "That should help. We used to grow this in the grounds of Brock House where I worked as a nurse during the War. Staunchweed, they called it there, soldiers' woundwort. It should ease the pain and it'll stop any further bleeding. It also reduces the chance of any infection, so I'll keep applying fresh leaves until your friend gets back."

"George."

"George, yes. Now," she continues, "I want you to chew some of these as well."

"What are they?"

"Burdock," she says, plucking the broad spade-shaped leaves from a purple thistle-like plant. "Your rashes have flared up," she adds gently. "These will help calm them down a little."

"Thank you," he whispers hoarsely.

"You might not say that once you taste them," she says. "Be warned, they're very bitter, but I want you to try and chew them for as long as you can."

George returns. He slides down the embankment, holding several spurs of hawthorn he has managed to break off, which he thrusts towards Esther. She quickly inspects them, then selects one, which she measures against Francis's leg.

"Now," she says, turning to George, "I'm going to need you to take off your shirt, I'm afraid." George looks perplexed. "To tear into strips so I can secure the splint to the leg."

"Yes. I see. Of course." He begins to do as she has asked.

"Francis, before I attach the splint, we're going to have to straighten your leg." She sees the fear pass briefly across his face. "Yes, I'm afraid it is going to hurt, but only for a moment. Can you do it? Or would you prefer me to?"

Francis tries but then shakes his head. "I'll look at George to distract me," he says.

Esther smiles. "OK then. Here we go. After three: one, two…" But before she has said 'three' she swiftly pulls Francis's left leg from underneath him, so that it is lying straight. Francis shrieks and Esther sees George wince at the sound. "There," she says. "All done. Now I can see it much more easily. I wouldn't look if I were you, Francis. It looks worse than it is. George, pass me your shirt so that I can begin tearing it into strips, while you remove any rough edges from the branch." The tibia is protruding slightly through the skin of Francis's lower leg. "At least it's a clean break," she says. "That will make the healing that much quicker."

"Thank goodness you came along," says George. "You seem so…" he searches for the right word, "…accomplished."

Esther smiles thinly. As she talks, she fixes the splint to Francis's leg. "Actually, something very similar happened to me once. About twelve years ago. I'd just heard some very bad news and was cycling too fast in the rain. My wheel hit the kerb, buckled and I was thrown into a deep trench where some men had been doing some repairs. I tried to climb out but I couldn't. I remember thinking about that old story of Robert the Bruce watching the spider in the cave, trying time after time to make his way towards the top and failing, until eventually he succeeded. But there was no way I was getting out of there, and so I thought I might just have to wait it out all night, till the men returned the following morning, but I was lucky. Someone turned up, like I did, right out of the blue. He fixed a splint for me just like I'm doing for you right now, Francis." She leaves out the part about Tommy Thunder using a bone for the splint that Esther had found protruding from a corner of the trench. "There," she says. "All done. I should imagine that feels better already?"

Francis nods. He looks down at his leg. Esther, while tying the strips of cloth from George's shirt around Francis's leg, has also covered the part where the bone was most visible.

"Good. But that was the easy part, I'm afraid."

Francis and George look at her alarmed.

"You can't stay down here," she says. "We've got to somehow try and get you back up onto the road, where it's flat, and where you can more easily be seen. It'll be dark in a couple of hours, so what I'm proposing is this. Once we get you up there – and we'll work that out in a minute – I'm going to leave the two of you here and cycle back to where I live. It's not that far, and from there contact a doctor, while you, George, stay here with Francis."

George is now looking almost as pale as Francis. The two men nod in agreement.

"Right," says Esther. "How to get you up? We can't carry you, the slope's too steep. What I think's best is if you, George, stand behind Francis and take the weight from under both arms. I'm going to place a couple of these other branches you brought and place them under your thighs, Francis. We're going to use them like rollers. George will slide you up the slope a few inches at a time, while I make sure your injured leg is not in any way bumped or knocked. When the branches reach the backs of your knees, I will signal for George to stop, while I reposition them higher up once more, then we start again. It'll be slow going, but it's better than risking dropping you. Are you ready?"

They both nod once more.

"Very well. Away we go."

It takes them nearly half an hour to drag Francis up the embankment. At times the pain is almost unbearable for him.

Twice the branches slip from Esther's grasp and she has to scramble back down to the bottom to fetch them, while George has to take all of the weight of Francis's body alone. At another time he nearly loses his grip under Francis's arms and Francis slides back a couple of feet before George is able to catch hold of him properly again.

Eventually they make it, just as the sun is beginning to dip towards the horizon. A cool wind is picking up, rustling loudly through the grasses and reeds. Francis is shaking.

"You must try to keep him warm," warns Esther, quietly to George, so that Francis doesn't hear her. George lays his leather motor cycle jacket across Francis. "You must try and keep yourself warm too," she says. "Luckily it's July, but once the sun goes completely, it's going to be cold. Keep moving as much as you can. And try to make sure you keep Francis awake. We don't want him drifting off. I'll go now and try and raise some help. I'll be back as fast as I can."

"Wait," says Francis, his voice dry and rasping. "Follow the telegraph poles."

"What?"

"It'll be quicker, I promise. Follow the telegraph poles. Follow the wires that split out from them to the nearest house. There'll be a telephone there. They may let you use it."

"Yes," she says, getting onto her bicycle. "Good idea." She is just about to pedal away when she turns back to George. "Try and find a way of getting him to drink something. Just small sips, as often as he can. The water in the moss is probably brackish and sour, but it's better than nothing. Try a sip yourself first, just to be sure. If *you* can stand it, however unpleasant, then so can Francis." She places a hand on his shoulder, then cycles away.

George runs over to his DOT Racer, opens one of the panniers, where he finds an empty film canister, the last roll of film he used earlier today is still in the camera, then he runs to the nearest place where he can see water, brown and unappealing in the dusk, makes a cup of his hands and drinks. It's thick with sediment but he forces himself to swallow just a little of it. Yes, he thinks, it's just about endurable. He fills the canister, which he takes back to Francis, who is still shivering.

"Here," he says, "sip this."

"Do I have to?"

"Our Angel of Mercy says so."

"Then I suppose I must."

"I've just realised, I don't even know her name."

"We must ask her when she comes back."

"Yes. But first, we must get you warmer. Does it help if I rub your arms and shoulders through the jacket?" he asks. "Like this?"

Francis shudders briefly, but then nods. "Yes. Can you keep doing it?"

"For as long as you need me to."

After a while, Francis raises a hand. "That's better. You can stop for a while now. I suppose I should have another sip of that gritty cocktail you just served up."

George tips the canister again to Francis's lips.

"Just like Gin and It," he says, wincing, "only without the gin and too much 'it'."

"That was a good tip about the telegraph poles," says George. "I didn't take you for a boy scout."

"A long story," he says. "I'll tell you about it one day."

"Why not now?" says George. "No time like the present."

"I suppose you're right," says Francis, "and it might help pass the time between now and when our Angel returns."

And so Francis tells, in between sips of the brackish waters from Chat Moss, the whole story of how he was interned on the Isle of Man, the bitter, wasted years there, his determination to reinvent himself on his return, the epic walk from Liverpool to Manchester following the lines of telegraph poles, which marched across land not dissimilar to the one where he is lying this evening. He even tells George of his meeting with Delphine, the strange and terrible incident at Bob's Lane Ferry, the discovery of the dead bodies of her parents from the Spanish flu, the digging of their graves, the thick black smoke rising into the night sky following the burning of their shanty dwellings on the shores of the canal, to his final arrival beneath the sign of the giant spectacles, pitilessly looking back in the direction from where he had come, while from the other side they stared out sightlessly along the roads not yet taken.

George listens with growing incredulity. His own life story feels so pallid by comparison, but as he relates some of it, the two of them begin to realise just how closely their lives have intersected, how they have nearly collided on so many occasions at different times and at different points across the city. It is as if they have each been riding the same tram for years and years, but hopping on and off at different stops, vaguely aware of a conjoined spark crackling in the cables overhead, until this highly charged evening, when the air positively bristles with electricity between them.

But Francis is now beginning to drift in and out of consciousness. He is becoming increasingly less coherent. George starts to panic. He gently slaps his friend's cheeks. "Don't fall asleep now, love," he says.

Francis's eyelids flutter awake, a look of astonishment on his face.

George begins to intone in a hushed, lilting, sing-song voice.

"This is the tale of Thomas-à-Tattimus
Who took two T's
To tie two tups to two tall trees
To frighten the terrible Thomas-à-Tattimus
How many T's are there in all that...?"

Francis slips away once more and so George sings it again.

"This is the tale of Thomas-à-Tattimus
Who took two T's
To tie two tups to two tall trees
To frighten the terrible Thomas-à-Tattimus
How many T's are there in all that...?"

"How many, Francis? Answer me. How many T's are there in all that?"

"I don't know what you're talking about," mumbles Francis, his words increasingly slurred.

"How many T's?" George is shouting now at the top of his voice. "Answer me. How many?"

"Two," whispers Francis at last. "Two." His pale eyes open and focus.

"Yes," says George, "that's right. Two." He can feel tears sliding down his cheek, which he wipes with the back of his hand. "There's only ever been two."

"Only ever been two," echoes Francis, patting the back of George's hand.

They smile and hold each other closely.

A pair of gynandrous clouded yellow butterflies graze on the underside of buckthorn leaves in the last of the light.

Just as they do so, another, stronger light sweeps across the moss, catching them in its beam. George looks towards it, shielding his eyes with one hand, while lifting up Francis to a sitting position with his other. A loud klaxon horn blares out. It's an ambulance. It pulls up alongside them, spraying up bits of shale and gravel. The driver and an attendant leap out and fetch a stretcher from the back. They are followed by Esther, who hurries towards a dazed George and Francis.

"How is he?" she asks.

"You got here just in time."

The ambulancemen are now covering Francis with a blanket before lifting him gingerly onto the stretcher.

"I'll ride with him in the back," says Esther in a tone that brooks no disagreement. "You go on ahead on your motor cycle. I'll meet you there."

"Where are they taking him?"

"Hope Hospital, Salford," she calls back. "It's not far."

A hospital called 'Hope', he thinks, must be an omen. He looks back towards the back of the ambulance just as Esther is climbing inside.

"What's your name?" he cries. "How can we ever thank you?"

She turns towards him, her face in silhouette, haloed from behind by the lamp inside the van. Her head is covered with the white *qurqash*, which reaches down to her shoulders.

"Esther," she says, but her voice is carried away from him by the wind. "Esther," she says again.

To George, as she recedes away from him towards the distant vanishing point, it sounds instead like '*Ishtar…*'

*

Two months later Francis and George are sitting in the darkened stalls of *The Grosvenor* cinema in the All Saints district of Manchester. It is a favourite haunt of Francis's, but this is George's first visit. Francis, now expertly manoeuvring himself around on crutches, takes pleasure in pointing out the alternate green and cream faience and terracotta tiles above the entrance. To him it embodies the whole notion of cinemas as palaces of dreams, and there's nothing that can quite match the thrill of entering its plush velvet interior, with its carved Cupid columns and crystal chandeliers, equalled only perhaps by that frisson of sitting in a large darkened room full of strangers, brought together by the single purpose of allowing oneself to be drawn into whatever exotic worlds are being depicted up there on the silver screen.

Now, the two of them risk touching hands, brushing fingers in the dark, eyes glued to the dancing images before them, which they watch through coils of cigarette smoke caught in the flicker of the projector's beam of dusty light.

The film they have come to see is the year's *cause de scandale*, Josef von Sternberg's *The Blue Angel*. But first they must sit through a Pathé Newsreel. After the customary cock crow and stirring, martial music, the title which is thrown up onto the screen makes them audibly gasp, then burst into laughter.

"22 YEAR OLD GIRL WINS KING'S CUP."

"More like thirty-two," says Francis.

"She looks like my Great Aunt Maud," hisses George, and the two of them giggle again.

An older couple sitting in front of them turn around, frowning at them to be quiet.

Further text scrolls up the screen.

"Miss Winifred Brown beats 87 other competitors, including all our best speed pilots, in the 750 mile air race around Britain in a time of 7 hours and 20 minutes."

The film then proceeds to focus on The Prince of Wales's aircraft, a Tomtit, piloted by a smiling Squadron Leader David Don, who winks confidently for the camera before take-off. There are a few shots of aeroplanes taking off, and then a couple more of some of them landing at Barton, including one of Winnie leaping from her cockpit.

"You shot those," whispers George proudly.

"That I did," answers Francis.

The film then switches somewhat abruptly to the

presentation ceremony. Secretary of The Royal Aero Club, Commander Harold Perrin, is making a speech. Because the film is silent, it is not possible to know what he is saying. Commander Perrin, who has a reputation for being something of a raconteur, is evidently enjoying the occasion, for he speaks for what appears to be an inordinate length of time.

Poor Winnie keeps on thinking they are about to present her with the trophy and steps towards the Commander, only to be swatted aside, almost as though she were a troublesome insect, rather than the winner of the race. She is now wearing a floral print dress with a wide-brimmed hat trimmed with more flowers.

She actually looks rather like my mother, reflects George, at one of her Charity Garden Parties for Fallen Women, than the heroic aviatrix he remembers at Barton Aerodrome, stepping down from the wing of her bi-plane in her leather flying suit, cap and goggles, a costume that would not have been out of place in the main feature, which now follows.

The Blue Angel.

Francis and George both find its decadence delicious, its Berlin setting exotically glamorous, although, as sexy and sultry as Marlene Dietrich most certainly is, "she's no match for our Cam at *The Queen's*," says Francis afterwards, which is where they're headed next.

When their taxi arrives at the hotel ten minutes later, Luigi is waiting for them at the bottom of the stone steps leading up to the entrance.

"*Buona serra,* Signor Francis," he says, opening the door of the cab. "And you must be Signor George. *Benvenuto.*"

Francis declines Luigi's offer of help, insistent that he can manage the steps quite satisfactorily by himself, which he can. Once inside they head straight for the lounge, where Cam is due to begin her final set for the evening in a few minutes' time. Everybody is there to greet Francis on this, his first outing since the accident, about which they have all been so solicitous. Winifred waves, notices George, then wags her finger warningly back at Francis with a smile. Victor winks, raising his thumb. Charles is there too, immediately pumping him with questions about his treatment and recovery. He knows the surgeon at Hope (of course), who's been keeping him informed. "A good man," he says. "None finer. I wish he was part of our team at The Infirmary." But then another voice quells him. "Charles, that's quite enough. Let the boy at least sit down first." Francis looks round. He recognises this voice. It is Delphine, who he hadn't realised was the friend Charles has so often talked about. "Well," she says, shaking his hand, "when Charles first spoke of you, I wondered if it might just possibly be you. Still following telegraph poles?" she asks. "Not any more," he replies. "They brought me here," and he looks round to see where George might be.

Winifred, observing this exchange from across the lounge, sees Charles and freezes. She has not seen him since the night Ruth died. At the same moment he sees her. His countenance grows pale. He narrows his eyes and frowns. He furtively puts his finger to his lips and shakes his head. Winifred nods hers, once, then turns away. She will not spoil Francis's evening.

"Who was that?" asks Victor, lighting a cigarette.

"Nobody," replies Winifred.

"Champagne," announces Luigi, pouring glasses all round. "Compliments of *The Queen's*."

The band begins to play on the small stage and into the spotlight walks Cam.

"Mademoiselle Chamomile Catch," croons the trumpet player into the microphone, and everyone applauds. She waits for silence to fall then, looking straight at Francis, she starts to sing.

"*Falling in love again*
Never wanted to

What am I to do?
I can't help it

Love's always been my game
Play it how I may
I was made that way
I can't help it
Men cluster to me like moths around a flame
And if their wings burn, I know I'm not to blame

Falling in love again
Never wanted to
What am I to do?
I can't help it…"

5

25th September 1931

The rats are running.

Following nearly a fortnight of torrential rain, it has at last begun to let up. The rats abandon the rusty sewer pipe along the edge of the canal, which has been their home for several generations, and head in a mass across the slippery grey flagstones of Angel Meadow, slick with raw waste. They need to find the higher ground. As they writhe and tumble in and around, over and through one another, they pass under the easel of a tall man in a raincoat painting the scene in front of him. So engrossed is he in trying to capture the rectangles of light glistening in the pools of stagnant water, reflecting the park's railings, factory chimneys, and the tower of the church of St Michael's and All Angels, which is the focal point of his gaze, that he does not notice them, not even when they pass within inches of his black round-toed shoes planted heavily a yard apart. Standing a few feet behind him is a younger man, wearing a motor cycle riding jacket and leather cap, now sporting a neat moustache.

George is watching Mr. Lowry intently. He has been studying at *The Mechanics' Institute* for just over a year now and is beginning to find both his feet and his voice as an artist. Mr. Lowry has invited him to watch him paint. "*En plein air*, as the posh folk like to say," chunters Lowry, "or out in t' bloody muck, as I prefer to call it. There's no substitute for standing in the very spot you want to paint, lad," he continues, then repeats his oft-quoted mantra. "Breathe the same air."

George agrees. Authenticity is everything as far as he's concerned – of experience, of life and of art. He himself does see the column of rats running across Mr. Lowry's shoes and marvels at how the great man does not appear to be even the slightest bit aware of their presence. Instead he continues to peer intently at the scene in front of him. Some children have come out, now that the rain has eased, and are populating the park. A few boys kick a football, while three girls skip with a rope. A cat has climbed a tree and a boy in a school cap and wearing a belted gabardine that is too small for him is trying to coax it down. Another small girl is furiously playing at whip-and-top, her tongue protruding from the corner of her mouth with concentration, while yet another trundles by wearing a pair of outsized shoes pushing a toy pram. She is not looking where she is going and runs the pram into a kerb, so that it tips up and the doll that is inside it, serving as her baby, falls out. The head becomes detached and the little girl dumps herself down on the kerb, where she tries in vain to re-attach it. At the same time one of the boys kicks the football wildly. It lands inside the pram, which then begins to roll down the slope towards the canal. It is only saved from falling in at the last minute by the skilful intervention of one of the girls with the skipping rope, who lassoes the pram with it at the last second. The cat in the tree spits and hisses. It leaps beyond the reach of the boy with the cap before settling himself higher up on a different branch.

Lowry sees all of this and rapidly applies further smudges of colour in an attempt to capture as much of it as he can, before he flings down his brush in frustration.

"Too dark," he says to nobody in particular and then, remembering George, turns and says, "I'll come back another night to finish it off. There's enough here to be going on with." He adds in a couple of street lamps, which have just come on, roughly indicating the orange glow they cast. As usual, he adds no shadows.

He packs away his easel and paints just as the rain returns, even harder. The children scurry away to find some shelter, while the cat miaows pathetically for someone to rescue it.

The rats run with an even greater sense of urgency. They make their way towards the boarded up church on the far side of the park. Without a second's doubt or hesitation they funnel their way into one of the drainpipes running down the western wall and climb up it. Each of them knows that, if one of them should fall, they will risk being trampled on by the others following on behind, so they loop their tails together in ever tighter knots and allow themselves to be hauled up by the sheer unstoppable momentum of the colony's flight and migration. From the top of the drainpipe they drop down onto a narrow rafter, high above the central nave inside the unused church, and scuttle along it towards the bell tower. From there they can burrow under the insulation felt beneath the slate roof, where they can be safe and warm for the night.

George wheels his DOT Racer through the park, which acts as a short cut through to Swan Street, from where he'll be able to turn left at New Cross up onto Oldham Road, before turning off into Portugal Street, where he mostly spends his nights these days to be nearer to *The Mechanics' Institute* and to Archie's workshop in Buile Hill. He is ten minutes away from home at the most, but the rain is now coming down so hard he knows he will be completely drenched by the time he gets there.

He is also having to steer a careful path between the last of the stragglers from the mess of rats which have been roaming the park. Park, he thinks ruefully. It's what everyone calls it, but there's not a blade of grass anywhere, just grey, uneven flagstones which, it is rumoured, cover where once was an open pauper's grave. Thousands of bodies lie under these stones, they say. Sixty years ago, in the year of The Great Flood, so many were washed away that for weeks afterwards the rivers and canals were thick with bones, adding just one more layer of decay to the filth and rubbish that accumulated there.

There are no bones sticking up out of the Rochdale Canal these days, although it is not uncommon for bodies to be flung there still, for this remains one of the more dangerous haunts of the city. Angel Meadow. Until the 18th century anyone staring down on this spot would have seen fields of wild flowers, tree-lined lanes and the sweet smelling River Irk flowing freely alongside. It was this idyllic setting, people would say, which gave the place its name. More likely it was from the pasture field adjoining *The Angel*, a coaching inn, much frequented by drovers, who would set their cattle there to graze. In later years, after the cemetery was covered over, people thought the name was one of sorrow for all the babies and children who had died there during the worst excesses of the slums. More recently, it was widely assumed to refer to the many child prostitutes who were to be found soliciting there most nights.

On this night, however, such is the force of the rain, Angel Meadow is deserted. Or so George thinks at first. Then, imperceptibly, he becomes aware of a darker recumbent shape curled on top of the flagstones. He detects the slightest rise and fall in this shape, like the bellows in a blacksmith's forge, gently opening, then closing. The shape, he realises, is breathing. The last of the rats are running towards it. Noses to the ground, pursuing a trail from which they cannot be deflected, they run up and over it, completely disinterested in it. When the last of them has gone, George approaches the shape. His shadow, cast by the orange street lamps, of the kind that Mr. Lowry would never choose to paint, falls across it, at which point the shape becomes aware of his presence, tenses, and changes position. He sees a face emerge from it, streaked with mud, a thick clot of blood matted in a clump of hair. The lips part. The mouth speaks, more of a croak, hoarsely.

"Excuse me, Mister," it says. "Do you want any business?"

Then the eyes flutter and roll. The lids flicker and close. A drool of spit oozes from the corner of the mouth and begins to speckle the chin. Then, from deep within the hidden folds of the shape, a long, low moan is emitted, followed by a shudder of the body, and a hand shoots from inside a threadbare, rain-drenched rag that serves for a coat and grabs George's wrist. He lunges forward, so that his shadow moves away from the face, which is now fully lit by the uninterrupted beam of the street light. On the left cheek is a livid strawberry mark.

Hubert has found that he now talks to his father more frequently since he died than when he was alive. There is always a running commentary going on inside his head these days. "What do you think of this idea, Father?" he might hear himself ask or, more usually, "Do you think I have done the right thing, Father?"

His father rarely answers in these imaginary conversations, although sometimes Hubert senses an opinion which, just as when he was alive, would rarely be voiced directly, but instead hinted at obliquely, a question answered with another question, a view never imposed, though subtly suggested. But today his father has been uniquely unequivocal. "Yes," he has said, "go to Darwen. I wish I were coming with you."

And so Hubert has risen early and set off before Annie has even got up. Now he is driving through Whitefield, almost half way there. Soon he will pass through Bury, Tottington, Ramsbottom, Edenfield, Rawtenstall, Haslingden and finally into Darwen itself. He is following the route taken more than a century ago by the thousands of men and women who marched the twenty-five miles with sprigs of laurel in their hair to St Peter's Fields in Manchester to listen to Orator Hunt lead the campaign for the right to have representation in

Parliament, only he is travelling in the opposite direction, away from the city, the way those who survived the massacre that day would have taken afterwards, on their weary return home, bloodied, bowed, but never beaten.

He is filled with an almost irrational hope. He is driving to Darwen, near Blackburn in Lancashire to listen to one Mohandas Karamchand Gandhi address the workers at Greenfield Mill there, at the invitation of the mill owner, Mr Percy Davies, a renowned local Socialist and Quaker. It was through his contacts at the Friends' Meeting House in Mount Street that Hubert had been introduced to Mr Davies, who had been impressed by his seriousness.

"I'm not quite sure what Mr Gandhi is asking for," Hubert had said. "By encouraging his followers back in India to boycott the movement of British goods, especially textiles, he is causing great suffering to the cotton workers and their families here in Lancashire, the very sort of people who he might hope would support him in his struggle for independence."

"I couldn't agree more," Mr Davies had replied. "I see the effects every day in my mill, where we've been forced to put everyone on much shorter hours."

"I'm not sure what he can be hoping to achieve," continued Hubert, now genuinely fired up with the bit between his teeth. "I'm sure he must have read his history and know that here in Lancashire we suffered so badly in the last century by supporting Mr Lincoln against slavery in America, but at great personal cost to ourselves. Surely he cannot wish to inflict further misery on us again?"

"Why don't you ask him yourself?" said Mr Davies. "I've invited him to Darwen to come and see at first hand just what the impact of his boycott is having on the town, and blow me, if he hasn't accepted!"

"At least he won't be wanting the red carpet or any sort of special treatment," said Hubert, "not if what we read about him is true…"

"… which I'm sure it is. Come and join us, Hubert. Next Friday. We'd be delighted to have you along.

"Thank you, Percy. I will."

No mention was made of bringing Annie along too, although Hubert was certain that she would be equally welcome. But as the days passed he kept putting off speaking to her about it, fearful somehow that she might try and turn it into another business opportunity, which was the last thing he wanted – he ardently believed that Gandhi's cause in seeking Indian independence from Britain was a just one, and that here was a man who was a true hero of the age – and so he had said nothing to her, until it was too late, when he heard, with a huge, inward sigh of relief, that she had a Committee Meeting scheduled for later the same day.

Now, as he drives past the turning for Rivington Pike, midway between the towns of Adlington and Horwich, with its Jubilee Tower on the summit of Winter Hill, he feels exhilarated. He's reminded of another drive, a dozen years before, when he had passed Tandle Hill near Chadderton and climbed up its steep slope in the heat of the day, how he had heard what he mistook for an angel singing to him in French, and had then woken up, some time later, in a hospital. He looks at his watch. He has plenty of time. If he continues at this rate he will arrive in Darwen far too early. He pulls over into a grassy lay-by and stops the car. There are rain clouds massing above the hill, but he has his umbrella with him and a pair of stout shoes, and so he thinks, why not? He steps out of the car and begins to climb.

A well trodden network of footpaths leads to the crag at the summit, whose humped shape masks the shales and sandstones of the lower coal measures, which stretch beneath the great Lancashire plain all the way back to Manchester. First he passes through wild, overgrown terraced gardens. Planted with rhododendrons which have spread rampantly and out of control across the heathland, the paths in places are all but impassable. Hubert smiles at the thought of this invasive Indian species. Mr Gandhi might well feel at home here after all, he thinks. Eventually passing through them, he makes his way towards the top, or pointed eminence, which marks the summit, the pike of *hreofing*, close to which Hubert observes abandoned bell pits, narrow shafts sunk into the earth to extract the coal or iron ore found near the surface, which was winched up in small buckets. These unprotected pits are dotted everywhere and Hubert must take care to avoid turning his ankle over, or tumbling down into one.

A plaque mounted on the wall of the tower informs him that on a clear day he would be able to see right across the West Pennine Moor as far as the Isle of Man. No such luck today, as the sky darkens and a squally rain begins to fall. He can see very little in fact of what lies before him. He takes shelter in the dark entrance to the Tower. This was once a prominent beacon, he reads. It still is. Fires were lit here to warn of the Spanish Armada, to celebrate the coronation of King George, and to mark the end of the Great War.

Hubert checks his watch again. It appears to have stopped. He shakes it slightly and holds it to his ear. He listens to its reassuring, resumed tick. Time to get going again. He starts his way back down from the summit of Rivington Pike towards his car in the lay-by at the bottom. He keeps his umbrella up and his eyes down, checking where he puts each foot, in case he might stumble or fall. One step at a time. Let the day slowly unwind, he thinks.

Annie, too, would like to have heard Mr. Gandhi speak. But Hubert had asked her too late if she would like to accompany him, for she was already committed to a previous engagement. Even so, she'd been extremely tempted. For one reason, Hubert so rarely suggested anything these days. Since his father had died he had retreated deeper and deeper inside himself. He'd always been a quiet man, but lately he'd become positively Trappist. It was almost as if he viewed his life these days as a continuous, extended Quaker Meeting, cocooning himself in silence, not even speaking when the spirit moved him, which Annie was sure it must do sometimes.

More and more they lived quite separate lives. He still went happily to work, either to the Printing Works on Portugal Street where, since Harry Heath had left them at the height of the General Strike, he had had to resume some of his former duties there while George was being trained up, or to drive out to meetings with customers to discuss the details of their orders, orders which she, Annie, had probably laid the ground work for initially. He could have done much of this over the telephone, but his quiet, unassuming manner meant that he rarely concluded business satisfactorily with it, and in any case, he would say, face to face meetings were always more reliable barometers of the temperature of a given relationship, and she had to concede that in that he was probably correct. He was happier back at the Printing Works, though, where he could roll up his sleeves, get his hands dirty tinkering with the intricacies of the various machines. Their noise, which had so overwhelmed him after he came back from the War, no longer seemed to bother him quite so much, although she could always tell from the moment he stepped in through the door after a day's work if he had been spending too much of it wrestling with the presses, for his face would be pale, his brow creased and his skin clammy. Then, after a brief exchange of news about each other's day, he would retreat to his study to read, or go out into the garage to continue with the Sisyphean task of stripping down the engine of his car, cleaning all of its components, and then replacing each one meticulously, so that he might repeat the whole process the following day.

They no longer slept together, had not done so, in fact, for almost fifteen years now, not since Hubert had first left so torn and conscience-stricken for the Front. At first she accepted his reluctance with patience and understanding, but as more time passed and he continued to rebuff all attempts by her to resume what Dr Wilkes so coyly referred to as "marital relations", she could not help but feel an overwhelming sense of loss and rejection. She had learned to come to terms with the fact that she could have no more children, although this was something which continued to clutch her heart suddenly and unexpectedly at times, at which points she had to deflect such thoughts with unrelenting hard physical work, or risk giving in to bouts of painful, dry-eyed sobbing, but she had still hoped for a regular, if cautious, sex life. Now such hopes had long been extinguished. In their most recent move to their house on Lapwing Lane in Didsbury, she gave up all pretence and had twin beds installed. In many ways this was a relief, for now at least there was no risk of limbs accidentally brushing against one another if one of them turned over in the night, raising a frisson of possibility for her, or a flinching of tension for him. Hubert had made no kind of comment at all.

But Annie also wished to accompany Hubert to see Mr. Gandhi because she was interested in the man himself. Much had been made of his visit to Manchester, to speak to representatives of the Cotton Industry, and what that might mean for the future of the mills. Even more had been made about his appearance – 'the little brown man in the loin cloth', as some of the more populist newspapers so disparagingly described him. Even the so-called quality press, not to mention the BBC or the Pathé Newsreels, spoke of him in undisguised tones of patronising amusement. Gandhi himself seemed either not to notice or, if he did, simply let it wash over him. Annie suspected the latter. She felt certain that, behind those rimless spectacles, there twinkled the eyes of a consummate politician, relishing his refusal of the offer of an umbrella to protect him from the traditional welcome afforded to him by the Manchester rain, actively seeking out the fresh puddles to walk through in his open-toed sandals, as he hoisted a part of his *dhoti* over his arm, rather as a Roman might with his toga.

Hubert became uncharacteristically animated. "Of course India should be granted independence," he pronounced almost vehemently. "Colonialism, by its very nature, is inherently wrong."

But excellent for business, thought Annie instinctively, grateful that she had not voiced such thoughts out loud, although it might have been interesting if she had, to see whether Hubert would have quarrelled with her. Part of her would have welcomed that.

But she has been too well schooled by Frank. She knows when it is best to speak out and when it is prudent to bite one's tongue. "Play the long game," had always been his motto, and so now, on this Friday morning of the 25th of September 1931, having reluctantly declined Hubert's request the previous evening to drive with him to Darwen today where Mr Gandhi is due to address the workers from Greenfield Mill, she waits until she hears his car pull out of their carefully weeded drive on Lapwing Lane, gets up, pulls on her dressing gown, goes to the window, opens the curtains and watches him drive away. After a few moments, she turns aside. She has business of her own – their own – to attend to in Manchester Town Hall, and there is much to be done before then.

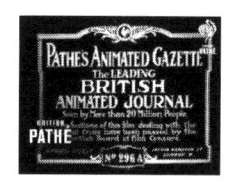

Jaunty Anglo-Indian music plays throughout.

CAPTION:
Gandhi is.... HERE!
The Indian Nationalist Leader, whose personality is intriguing the whole world, arrives.

The film shows a steam ship about to dock. Leaning from the rail, looking down, is Gandhi, flanked on either side by diplomats in blazers, linen trousers and ties.

VOICE OVER:
"Here he is at last – The Mystery Man of India – our first glimpse of him as 'The Rajputana' came alongside at Marseille.

Gandhi and his followers are now walking down the gangplank. Several of them are western women all dressed in white with veils over their heads.

"Here's the woman of whom you've probably all read but never before seen in a picture – Miss Madeleine Slade, the English daughter of an Admiral, who now prefers to be known simply as Mirabehn. She's one of Mr Gandhi's most devoted disciples. She's leading the way ashore now. There behind her is Mr Gandhi himself, dressed, just as he said he would be, in his loin cloth, even in the chilly climes of Europe. He's carrying with him his pots and pans, which he declared at customs.

Gandhi is standing on the steps of a French government building, surrounded by politicians and reporters.

"He was trotted around Marseille to several receptions and made one or two speeches, which rather frightened the French authorities but, when asked to speak into the film's microphone, he said, 'I think not.'

A ferry boat is crossing the Channel.

"And so we go on our way to England.

A busy port full of people.

"Well here we are at Folkestone, with the boat train pulled up alongside and, as Gandhi said, "It's proper English weather, pouring with rain and bitterly cold!" Miss Behn was the first ashore, attending to the luggage, seeing to the goat's milk et cetera. She was followed by Gandhi's son, and then came the little man himself, still scantily clad with an extremely wet blanket surrounding his tiny frame. I'm sure he must have been frozen. We were, in thick overcoats! He picked his way through the puddles along the quayside – he was wearing sandals, by the way – to the waiting motor car, for he'd decided he'd rather go up to London by road.

Gandhi climbs into the car.

"And he insisted on sitting in the front seat with the driver, saying he could see better that way, as he tucked himself in.

The car pulls away.

"So – off to London, whilst his followers make their way by the boat train.

London. Crowds line the street in the rain, holding

up umbrellas.

> *"In town, quite a lot of people had waited in the pouring rain outside the Friends' Meeting House on the Euston Road to see what the little man really looked like. But at first they were disappointed because he went in the back way.*

The crowds wait in puzzled silence until Gandhi appears among them.

> *"But shortly afterwards he left by the front way, and then they really did see quite a lot of him – even his knees!*

Gandhi walks through the cheering crowds, who can be heard shouting "Speech!" He modestly declines with a wave of his hand.

> *"No, he won't speak into the microphone.*

Gandhi is driven away once more and then is shown standing at a window of the Poplar Town Hall, waving to even larger crowds.

> *"And so to the East End, where he has requested to stay among everyday working folk, where we leave this bizarre little man for the time being, whose coming has caused so much comment, complete with loin cloth, spinning wheel and goat's milk, feeling sure that he cannot complain of his reception, or the publicity he has received, from which, we always understood, he shrank.*

The screen fades to black, then opens out once again to show a different setting – a cotton mill.

> *"Another day, another town. Mr Gandhi can now be seen*

standing on the steps of Greenfield Mill in Darwen, Lancashire, where he has been invited by the mill owner, Mr Percy Davies, also a Quaker, to see for himself the products manufactured there using cotton imported from India – that is, when Mr Gandhi's followers are not preventing such movement by their blockades at Bombay and other key Indian ports.

"There's ten-year old Gusta Green curtseying before the little man. She's almost as tall as he is already. I wonder what it is he's saying to her – perhaps what he plans to say at the upcoming conference with the government next week. Maybe Mr Ramsay Macdonald should telephone her to find out.

"And there's a Crossley Phaeton, waiting to drive Mr Gandhi away to the neat terraced cottages built by Mr Davies for his factory workers and their families, in one of which this little man in the loincloth will set up his own spinning wheel for the night."

The music swells briefly, then fades:

The End

As Hubert drives back to Didsbury later that evening, he goes over and over the events of the day. To think that Mr Gandhi had been a passenger in the front seat of his car. It had been the perfect opportunity for him to ask all of those questions he had so passionately articulated the week before to Percy, but when it came to it, his courage had failed him. Mr Gandhi was Percy's guest. It would not do to cross-examine him. Instead he drove him to his next destination at the Workers' Cottages in respectful silence, allowing the great man some time alone and undisturbed with his thoughts.

He was rewarded for his consideration with a single remark. As he stepped down from the car, Gandhi looked around him at the newly built homes for the mill workers, turned back to Hubert, thanked him and said, "The people here have taken me into their homes. They have treated me as one of their own. I shall never forget them. I understand their concerns. But they have no idea what poverty is."

He wonders if he will tell Annie this or not.

Annie sits all alone in the big house in Lapwing Lane.

Most nights George does not come home. He stays over at Portugal Street. Since he started at *The Mechanics' Institute*, she has seen him less and less. It's only to be expected, she tells herself, and she doesn't mind, not really.

Hubert is not yet back from his day out. She has no idea when to expect him. Perhaps he's been invited to stay on for supper. She doesn't begrudge him this, but would like at least for him to have let her know. They do, after all, have a telephone. And so she has put by some cold ham and lettuce for him in case he hasn't eaten.

She sits by the window of the lounge and switches on the table lamp, so that she has enough light to sew by. She resembles the women in several of William Kay Blacklock's paintings, head bent, occasionally frowning, a study in patience and absorption. *Lady Sewing by a Window.*

She has recently taken up embroidery, and she has embarked upon a modern sampler with which she plans to tell the story of their family. It takes the form of a map, a journey, with simple running stitch to link each of the different stopping off points along the way. At the bottom, near the middle, is the Tripe Colony, represented by the red UCP oval. Each of the four corners depicts one of the houses they have lived in – Portugal Street, Hirstwood, St Werburgh's Road and now Lapwing Lane – while right in the centre is the spindle tree. She is attempting to convey all four seasons simultaneously by using differently coloured threads and is quietly satisfied by the result so far. She's trying to incorporate motifs which reflect the interests of all three of them – a wooden printing block for Hubert, a motor cycle wheel for George – but has yet to decide on what to put in for herself. A spool of thread perhaps, like Ariadne's? She has stitched a border of tulips all around the edge, with each alternate flower being pollinated by a busy worker bee. Now she is contemplating a verse she might include, its words to weave in and out, around and through each of these images, but she has yet to decide which one.

As she sits and sews, wondering how it is that it should have come to this, all alone with the light fading, she is reminded of Luke, chapter 14, verse 28:

'For which of you, intending to build a tower, sitteth not down first, and counteth the cost, and whether you hath sufficient to finish it…?'

She frowns. This will not do, she tells herself. She snaps a piece of thread which has become snagged decisively with her teeth.

Something else is missing. There is a space above the spindle tree, in the centre, at the top, which needs filling.

She thinks back over the day…

When Frank first asked her to accompany him to a meeting at the Town Hall, he took her to The Great Hall and Picture Gallery, where he had shown her *The Manchester Murals* by Ford Madox Brown. She was greatly taken with them, as much by what they meant to him as the paintings themselves. It was a place he loved to visit time and again. Fitting, therefore, that this was where he should have died. Today, before her own meeting, she had deliberately arrived early, so that she might pay a visit there first, to sit in silent respect and remembrance. He liked to tell her the stories behind each one of the twelve murals. This was something he had done with Hubert when he was a child, and it had always felt like an additional link that stitched Annie closer to him.

This afternoon she had sat facing the one entitled *The Proclamation Regarding Weights & Measures.* It recorded the edict of 1556 requiring 'the burgesses and others in the town of Manchester' to 'send in all manner of weights and measures to be tried by their Majesties' standard'. Frank, when he first told Annie this story, had marvelled how more than three hundred and fifty years ago agreements had been reached to enable people all over the country to join in a common purpose of recognition. That if someone wanted to purchase a pound of apples in Nottingham, say, or Norwich, it would weigh the same as a pound of apples in Lincoln or Leicester, Preston or Perth. That five and a half yards is equal to one rod, pole or perch, whether a person measures that in Lancaster, Leeds, Halifax or Hull. And that the idea of standardising a system, so that trade might be conducted more fairly, on a level playing field, was first devised in Manchester. And that it was still in use today.

Weights and Measures...

Now she has it. Deuteronomy. '*That which was lost is found.*'

Yes, she thinks. That will do nicely. She will add a pair of kitchen scales to her embroidered sampler, to fill in that space above the spindle tree, and thread the text around it...

After she had been sitting in The Great Hall for several minutes, she felt sufficiently in balance to make her way along the labyrinth of corridors in the Town Hall towards Committee Room Number Four, where her meeting was to take place. When she arrived, the door was still open and she smiled at several faces she recognised. Alderman Hardcastle beckoned her over.

"Ah, Annie," he said warmly. "So pleased you could come. A cup of tea before we start?"

"Thank you, yes. That would be most fortifying."

"I must say, I'm looking forward to Mr Harris's presentation very much this afternoon."

Annie nodded that she was too.

This was a special sub-committee set up by the Corporation to keep tabs on the progress of the plans for the new Central Library which was to be built on St Peter's Square, with an adjoining passageway that would link it directly to the Town Hall. The architect, Mr Emanuel Vincent Harris, who had won the competition to design the library, was due to present his latest plans to the special Library Sub-Committee that afternoon.

Strictly speaking, Annie was not a member of the Committee, for she was not an elected member of the Council. But co-opting occasional outsiders with specific expertise or experience in the requisite fields of practice, or those who represented the needs of particular interest groups, or simply people with trusted local knowledge, or who were respected for their commercial or entrepreneurial success, was a common practice, and Annie, having been groomed by Frank, was here both as a member of several respected local charities and for her widely recognised business acumen. Not being a *bona fide* member of the Committee meant that, though she could not herself cast a vote when it came to making decisions, she could speak, and her opinion would be listened to by those who *could* vote.

Mr Flitcroft, as Clerk to the Council, nervously cleared his throat and called the meeting to order.

"*Venite incipere*," he declared.

"For God's sake, Flitcroft," interrupted a red-faced Councillor Grandage irascibly, "speak in English."

"Quite so, Councillor Grandage. Let us begin."

Emanuel Vincent Harris was introduced to the meeting. After thanking committee members for the opportunity, he proceeded to direct everyone's attention to the scale model of his proposed plans for the Library, which he revealed in the centre of the table around which they all sat, by removing the black cloth that had been covering it, with the dramatic flair of a magician at the Music Hall.

There was a gasp from several of the members. Some even broke out into spontaneous applause. Encouraged, Harris drew deeply on his cigar and began to speak.

"What you see before you," he said, "is a columned portico, conceived in the classical tradition, attached to a rotunda, a domed structure, which I have based loosely on The Pantheon in Rome. That has been my inspiration. You don't need me to tell you that, once it is built, this will be the largest library anywhere in Great Britain. It will also be the first ever to be wholly funded by a local authority, in a city which has always placed great pride in the importance of culture and learning. I wanted to match that ambition by designing a building that is both grand and beautiful, that says to all who look upon it, this is exactly the sort of thing which persuades one to believe in the perennial applicability of the classical canon."

This was greeted by a chorus of "Hear, hear!" and further prolonged applause, interspersed with murmurs of approval and appreciation.

Harris then took the committee through the details of the interior, not only the grand public areas, the marble staircases leading to different sections of the library, but also the more private, less glamorous, but still vital parts of the building, the offices and the mile upon mile of steel stacks, where books not on show on the shelves could be stored and from where they could be fetched for the more serious scholar.

"There is space," he declared "for two thousand reading

stations and two million books."

Like the showman he undoubtedly was, knowing that he had his audience in the palm of his hand, on the edge of their seats, he saved the best till last.

"And here," he said, "is the *pièce de résistance*." He paused, waiting until he was certain of their undivided attention, and then slowly removed the domed roof from the rotunda to reveal what lay inside. "This," he almost whispered, "is the interior of the Grand Reading Room."

The committee members sighed with pleasure, like children at a fireworks display, marvelling at the central circular desk with its ornate Italianate gilt clock above it, an island surrounded by a sea of marble, on which were arranged, like reefs, a series of polished mahogany desks, with an outer ring of high shelves cloistered behind more classical columns.

It was at this point that Annie intervened. She took a sip of tea from her cup, which she placed down carefully onto its saucer, cleared her throat and raised her gloved hand.

"Mr Flitcroft, might I be permitted to ask Mr Harris a question?"

"Of course, Mrs Wright."

The room fell silent.

"I'm sure I speak for everyone here," said Annie quietly, "by saying just how grateful we are to Mr Harris for his magnificent presentation to us all this afternoon."

"Hear, hear!"

"The effect of his design not only matches what we had hoped for, it surpasses it."

Harris bowed theatrically.

"One of our great aims with this library is that it shall be free, for all members of the public, regardless of age, gender, background or class, and that it should act as an inspiration for all to think that they can continue to strive, regardless of their status, to keep improving themselves. Speaking as I do, on behalf of some of the many charities who do such tireless work around the city to help those who are less fortunate than we are, sitting around this table this afternoon, admiring these wonderful plans, which I believe will deliver such a great public service to the people of Manchester, and raise our reputation as a generous, philanthropic city even higher, I would like to thank and praise Mr Harris for the splendour of his vision."

Following the applause which greeted these remarks, Mr Flitcroft lightly tapped the table with the palm of his left hand to bring the meeting back to order. "You said you had a question, Mrs Wright?"

"Yes, Mr Flitcroft, I do. I notice," she said, turning her attention to the exposed interior of the Reading Room, "that you have drawn two lines which run right around the perimeter wall just below the dome. Might I ask what these lines are for?"

"For a text," said Harris, "something which this Committee might decide is a suitable and uplifting message to the reader when he – or she," he amended swiftly, looking directly towards Annie, " – enters the room."

"Yes, I see," said Annie. "Thank you, Mr Harris. A most excellent suggestion."

Here she paused.

This was the moment she'd been waiting for. Details of the architect's plans had been privately circulated ahead of the meeting to the triumvirate's inner circle – Alderman Hardcastle, Councillor Grandage and Mr Flitcroft – and Hardcastle had described them to Annie in a telephone call between them the previous week.

Ever since that conversation Annie had been mulling over an idea. As she lay awake in her twin bed in the newly decorated bedroom of their house on Lapwing Lane, while Hubert, she presumed, slept quietly just a few feet away from her in his own separate bed, she recalled those early days between them when he had courted her, when they would take those Sunday afternoon walks together after Chapel, in Philips Park, whatever the weather, along the Avenue of Black Poplars, past the row upon row of tulips, lined up like crosses of remembrance, and she remembered one particular occasion, when he had spoken to her about a dream he had had, and his words had come back to her as vividly as the day he had first spoken them...

"And the centre of the ceiling was open to the sky, and the sun shone down through it, illuminating all who sat within. And in my dream, I was one of those sitting there. I looked up towards the sky, and as I did so, I was lifted upwards. I found that I was flying, high above the clouds, and once up there, I saw about me an even greater number of books, all the books that have ever been written in the world, and all the books that have yet to be written. They were as the stars in the firmament, countless and wonderful, stretching out into infinity, and they were all of them free. I simply had to reach my finger, up towards a star, touch it, and at once the contents of that book were delivered unto me. A great comet, a meteor shower of knowledge, raced across the heavens, leaving a trail of light behind it, for ever and ever, life everlasting. Amen..."

Lying awake that night, remembering these words, and the serene look of utter transformation on Hubert's face as he spoke them, filled her now with a great sorrow, a weight pressing on her heart, so that she found it difficult to breathe. She got out of bed and walked to the window. She looked out at the night sky, which was heavy and black. Not a star to be seen anywhere. But as she waited, there came a tiny break in the blanket of cloud, through which she glimpsed, briefly, the firmament beyond. A shooting star flared. Then the cloud regrouped and all was dark once more.

Annie returned to bed. An idea began to form, slowly. I wonder, she whispered to herself softly. I wonder...

Now, in Committee Room Number Four in Manchester Town Hall, that idea began to surface, to rise up and take shape, as Annie tentatively allowed it a voice.

"There is a quotation," she said, "from the Book of Proverbs, which members might like to consider."

Annie paused again, aware of everyone's eyes upon her. She took a further sip of tea, then continued.

"It is this." She opened her bag and took out a piece of paper onto which she had copied the words, which she now passed round for everyone to read. A silence fell on the room.

After a few moments, Harris stood up and spoke quietly. "May I keep this piece of paper?"

Annie nodded.

"With the Committee's permission," he continued, "I shall incorporate these words directly into my plans."

"All in favour?" said Hardcastle briskly.

"Ay," came the concerted response.

"Flitcroft?"

"Duly noted," said the Clerk...

"That," said Hardcastle afterwards to Annie, as the meeting broke up, "was masterly. Frank would have been extremely proud."

"Thank you," replied Annie, before collecting her things and quietly walking back along the corridor towards the main exit, passing the entrance to The Great Hall and Picture Gallery, where she paused to look one last time at *The Proclamation Regarding Weights & Measures*...

Now, back home at Lapwing Lane, sitting by the window, sewing, with the last of the evening light fading outside, she pushes the needle with her thimble firmly through the sampler.

Deuteronomy, chapter 22.
'That which was lost is found.'

In Angel Meadow the rain still falls. It runs in torrents down the slick, grey flagstones. The girl with the strawberry mark is gripping George's wrist.

At the same time she cowers from him, frightened and cautious, like the cat in the tree directly above her. With her other hand she pulls open the thin, threadbare rag which serves as an inadequate coat for her, then reaches towards George's belt. He stops her and brings her two hands together in front of her, in a mockery of prayer.

"What's the matter?" she says. "Ain't I pretty enough for you?" She turns her face away to one side so that the strawberry mark is in shadow.

George leans in closer to her.

"What's your name?" he asks her.

She freezes. The men as a rule don't bother to ask. "Lily," she says, as if only remembering it at that moment. "Lily Shilling." Then, recovering herself a little, she adds, "Shilling by name, if you're willing I'm game."

George closes his eyes. "Ssh…" he whispers. It's like he's stroking that wild cat up in the tree. He nervously removes some strands of hair from her face and smoothes her forehead. "Ssh…" he says again.

The girl blinks. The rain is falling hard upon her eyelids. This young man, barely older than she is, is looking at her with an expression she doesn't see so much these days. As if she might break. Like an egg. She is reminded of someone else who looked at her that way many years ago, when she was just a little girl, maybe six years old. She was in a park, with trees and flowers. It was warm and sunny, not like today. Someone blew a whistle and she remembers trying to carry an egg on a spoon, hurrying as carefully as she could.

Then a dog barked, and she dropped the egg, but a kind lady picked it up and put it back on the spoon. She looked at her as if she thought perhaps she wasn't real. Which sometimes is how she feels herself. She's used to being stared at.

When she was in the convent, the other girls would look at her all the time, pointing to the mark on her face. "What's that?" they'd say with a shudder of distaste. "It means she's special," Sister Clodagh would say if she overheard them. "God put that mark there so that everyone would know." Lily knows that Sister Clodagh was only trying to be kind – Sister Clodagh was always kind – but it didn't make things any easier for her. It just made the other girls resent her more. Until she got older, that is, when she'd learned how to take care of herself without Sister Clodagh's help.

"What are you staring at?" she'd say to any new girl who arrived. Then she'd grab the girl's wrist and yank her close to her face, pull back her hair so that the girl would be right up close to it. "Seen enough?" she'd snarl, and the new girls would all nod dumbly.

Afterwards, most stopped seeing it altogether. Some even developed a crush on her and would want to creep into her narrow bed after the lights went out and the Sisters had finished their nightly patrols. She'd let them do this, allow them to stroke her cheek, kiss it, there in the dark, then nod as they begged her to promise not to tell any of the others. That's one thing about her they can count on. She never breaks a promise. She doesn't make many, but once she does, she keeps it.

Now this boy is trying to ease her up onto her feet. She lets him do so. Maybe, she thinks, if I play along, he'll get careless. He'll let go of me and I can run off. But he doesn't let go. He's looking down at her bare feet. They're streaked with grime and dirt, flecked with dried blood where she's cut them.

"Where are your shoes?" he asks.

She looks at him pityingly, like he was born yesterday. "Oh," she says, "I must've mislaid them. I'll get my maid to fetch me a new pair. Where d'you think?" That was cruel, she thinks. He's only trying to be nice. But she's not used to nice, she doesn't know the rules.

"Would you like something to eat?" he says.

She looks at him sharply. She hasn't eaten in days, apart from some crusts of mouldy bread someone was throwing out for the birds by the canal. This is better, she thinks. She's on more familiar territory here. Barter and trade.

"What'd I 'ave to do?" she asks, eyeing him warily. Overhead she hears the cat purring.

"Nothing," he says. "I just thought you might be hungry."

She says nothing. He can see her weighing up the odds. Her eyes flick and dart about her. She's trying to work out what the catch might be.

"I live quite close," he says. "I can take you there if you like."

Her eyes stop darting now, their gaze entirely upon his. "But what if I don't like?" He shrugs, then looks away. She senses his grip relaxing on her wrist. Maybe her chance will come soon.

"Actually," he says, turning his attention back to her, "I've got a better idea."

She tenses. "What's that?" she says. Then, when he doesn't answer her right away, she adds, "Is this some kind of game? Am I supposed to guess, or what?"

"No." He smiles awkwardly.

The girl watches him curiously. He has a nice smile. "Well?"

"I was thinking of taking you back to my mother's…"

"Whoa! This is too weird." She begins to wriggle furiously, trying to break free of his grip. She lowers her head towards one of his hands, the one still tightly wrapped around her wrist, and bites as hard as she can. He yelps in pain, but still he doesn't let go.

"Listen a minute," he says. "My mother lives in a big house, in Didsbury. She has plenty of food, She has hot water, you can have a bath. There's a spare room with a comfortable bed and fresh sheets. She'd like to help you. I know she would."

"Why? She wouldn't want the likes of me going there and dirtying all her posh clean things. She'd take one look at me and just slam the door in my face."

"No, she wouldn't."

"Believe me, I know what I'm talking about."

"It's what she does. She's on all kinds of committees, she volunteers at hostels, she helps out at soup kitchens…"

"Takes in waifs and strays…?"

"Well…" George falters.

"No, I thought not. I've met her sort before."

"What sort is that?"

"The self-righteous bleeding-heart, good Samaritan sort, who hold garden parties with all their posh do-gooder friends to raise money for lost causes like me, fallen women, unwed mothers and the like, who sit in judgment with their cups of tea over whether I'm a suitable case for their charity to support, but who'd cross to t' other side o' t' street so as to avoid me."

"I'm not trying to avoid you."

"I wasn't talking about you."

"My mother's not like that."

"Like what?"

"Like those… people you describe."

"What *is* she like then?"

"Why don't you come with me and find out?"

The rain is now torrential. The girl is so wet her thin clothes cling to her body, whose outlines George can now see all too clearly in the orange glow of the street light. She shivers, sensing this. He looks away, embarrassed.

"Didsbury?" she asks.

"Yes."

"A big house?"

"Very big."

"A hot bath and a warm bed?"

"With fresh sheets."

"And food?"

"As much as you can eat."

"It's a long fucking way to Didsbury," she smiles. "How are we going to get there? You're not planning on carrying me, I hope?"

George points towards the railings on the edge of the square. The girl's eyes widen.

"Is that yours?"

He nods.

"I ain't never been on a motor bike before."

"That's not a motor bike," he grins. "That's a DOT Racer. Come on."

They hurry towards it. Just as they get there, she stops.

"Wait," she says, "I've forgotten something."

He looks at her, reluctant to let go of her wrist, now that he's got her so far.

"Please," she says, pitifully. "It's the only thing I've got that I can truly call mine."

He says nothing, considering, weighing up whether, if she bolts, he'd be able to catch her again, or even whether he should.

"I left it by that tree," she pleads. "I promise. If you let go of me, I'll come back."

"Why should I believe you?"

"Because I never break a promise."

They look at one another a long time. Slowly, he releases his grip on her wrist, finger by finger.

"Thank you," she says.

He watches her run back in the rain towards the tree

where he'd first found her, where the cat has now climbed down and is investigating a small bundle at its base. She shoos it away, picks up the bundle, then runs back towards him.

She holds it out for his inspection. It's the size of a large shoe box, wrapped in brown paper, which is becoming torn by the rain, then covered in cloth, which has been tied up with string.

"What is it?" he asks.

"It means all the world to me," she answers. "I thought I'd lost it."

And she remembers Sister Clodagh hugging her to her on the day she left St Bridget's, holding out the bundle towards her. "You mustn't be forgetting this," she was saying, wiping the tears from her eyes. And those annual garden fêtes held in the grounds at the back of the home in Audenshaw, Pound Days, where local people would be invited to donate a pound in cash or a pound weight in goods, such as food stuffs or other items, and how, on one occasion, Lily had put the bundle onto the scales, just to see how much it might weigh, what its equivalence might be – half a dozen packets of tea as it turned out, how did that equate to what her sole possession was worth to her – and that other day, years earlier in the park with all the tulips, where the kind woman with the dog, who'd put the egg she'd dropped back onto her spoon, knelt down to look at her, gently touching her shoulders, and Sister Clodagh's voice is saying happily, "That which was lost is found…"

George takes the bundle carefully from her and stows it in one of the panniers at the side of the bike.

"Now," he says, "climb up behind me, put your arms round my waist, and hold on tight."

"I bet you say that to all the girls," she laughs.

He kicks the starter and they roar off out of Angel Meadow towards the city centre, throwing up fountains of spray behind them, almost as if they were in a boat upon the sea, the water flecked with light and hope and new horizons.

Inside *The Queen's Hotel*, Francis looks anxiously at his watch. George was meant to be there half an hour ago. Ah well, he sighs, heading for the lounge, perhaps he's been delayed by Lowry, he thinks. He summons Luigi.

"If Signor George arrives," he says, "you'll tell him I'm here?"

"*Ovviamente, Signor.*"

At that very moment, unbeknown to either of them, George is speeding past the hotel entrance along the London Road, a pale translucent figure clinging to his back, casting no shadow.

Cam walks onto the stage. Her face is painted a ghostly white, with black eyebrows and crimson lips. Her thick, dark hair frames her head, which she turns in profile, tucks a stray curl behind an ear, to reveal a deep, finely etched blush of red on her left cheek

She lifts the microphone close to her mouth and starts to sing – a slow, gentle waltz, with a haunting, wistful chorus. The audience is spellbound.

"How do you measure a life
Beyond the investment of years
Daughter and mother and wife
Each with their suitcase of fears?

And how do you balance the worth
When the losses outnumber the gains
And the marks your feet make on the earth
Are washed away by the spring rains?

One bushel, two pecks
The balance and checks
Tournant en l'air, port de bras

Accepting our fates
In the measures and weights
En unités avoirdupois

And how can you count the true cost
Of everything you leave behind
Or retrieve all those things that were lost
Out of sight but yet not out of mind?

And how do you weigh in the scales
The minuses 'gainst every plus
When you step from the usual trails
To find a new journey for us?

So how to contain
Two links in a chain
Accroché dans la balançoire

Let's meet at the gates
In the measures and weights
Listé dans l'avoirdupois

So how do you measure a life
Beyond the investment of years?
Take heart from the storms and the strife
That nobody quite disappears

A cast in the colour of eyes
An expression that crosses the face
For no one completely dies
In all of us part of you stays

Eight furlongs one mile
The ghost of a smile
Not goodbye, but only au revoir

We'll end the debates
In the measures and weights
C'est la chanson de l'avoirdupois…"

When Annie hears the scrunch of wheels on the gravel drive, and sees a light pan across the curtains from outside, she assumes at first it must be Hubert returning from Darwen, but then she hears George's voice calling to her, loud and urgent from the mat in the hallway, just inside the front door.

She rushes through to see her son standing framed in the doorway, a silhouette with his back to the porch light behind him. In his arms he is carrying a young woman, wearing hardly any clothes, dripping with rain. He sits her down gently on the tall-backed, red upholstered arts and crafts hall chair, trying not to wake her. Annie switches on a low light, which softly illuminates the girl's pale face and hair. On her lap lies a small, wet cloth-covered bundle, which George delicately removes and places on the floor at her feet. As he does so, the string which is tied around it unravels, spooling out of her tightly closed fist, like a ball of thread.

Annie gasps involuntarily. The girl resembles Ariadne in the painting by George Frederick Watts. Annie takes the other end of the string and winds it around her own hand until the two have been joined.

The girl's eyelids flutter and open. "Where am I?" she asks.

"It's all right, dear," whispers Annie, kneeling by her side. "There's nothing to worry about any more. You're home."

*

Two years earlier.

Lily is having the dream of the nymphs and shepherds again, the one she first had on the night after the concert at the Free Trade Hall a fortnight before. She's been having it regularly ever since.

It usually begins with somebody brushing, or stroking, her hair. At first she thinks this is Sister Clodagh, but when she looks up into the mirror, it turns out not to be. Sometimes it is one of the women she remembers seeing from the top of the bus, looking down on Oxford Street, outside the theatres there, primped and powdered, with feather boas and high heeled shoes. Sometimes it is Jenny, on those nights she creeps into her bed, who strokes Lily's hair for comfort. At other times it is a woman whose face she cannot see, just a pair of black eyes and a hard, thin crimson mouth, who scrapes Lily's hair back and winds it tightly onto the top of her head, before applying rouge on her right cheek, to match the strawberry mark upon the left in a gaudy, clown-like way, so that she resembles a porcelain doll.

Then the shepherds come. First, singly; then, in twos and threes; finally, in gangs...

Earlier in the year, the girls at St Bridget's were taken on a trip to the City Art Gallery. There had been much excitement, for trips out were extremely rare. Once a year they were taken by train to the seaside, a treat they all looked forward to, even the Sisters. The sight of some of them raising their habits to paddle barefoot in the icy waters of the Irish Sea before retreating, shrieking and giggling, was a source of much mirth to the girls. They once went to the Museum, Lily remembers, and another time to Belle Vue Zoo. But the trip to the Art Gallery caused a certain dissent among the Sisters, who were clearly divided over the wisdom of exposing their charges to the morally corrupting influence of some of the paintings that were bound to be on display. Some of the Trustees of Trafalgar House, however, were proud of Manchester's cultural and artistic heritage and pressed upon the Sisters that coming into close proximity with the city's unparalleled art collection would provide important educational enlightenment, and that it would be a sin, moreover, to deny the girls access.

Unsurprisingly, Sister Mary Frances of the Five Wounds was in the former camp. "If we must go to such dens of sin and iniquity," she had said, "then let us at the very least devise an itinerary that ensures our girls do not see anything with the potential to disgust or deprave. '*Watch and pray that ye enter not into temptation*'," she had argued, " '*for the spirit is willing, but the flesh is weak*'." She scanned the refectory with her hooded eyes, daring anyone to challenge her. It was Sister Clodagh who smilingly picked up the gauntlet.

"Then let us, in the words of St Paul to the Ephesians, '*put on the whole armour of the Lord, that we may be able to stand against the Devil and all his wiles*'."

"I'm sure we all agree with Sister Clodagh," replied Sister Mary Frances of the Five Wounds begrudgingly.

"Excuse me, Sister, but I hadn't quite finished." Sister Clodagh had stood up. She stretched the palm of her right hand towards Sister Mary Frances to quell any further interruption. "Doesn't St Paul then go on to say, '*For we wrestle not against flesh and blood, but against principalities, against powers, against the rulers of darkness in this world, against spiritual wickedness in high places*'?"

A loud silence fell upon the refectory. The girls all stopped eating, looking towards Sister Mary Frances of the Five Wounds, whose opinion they'd never before seen crossed, wondering how she would respond. They did not have long to wait and they were not disappointed. Her hooded eyes narrowed to little more than a slit. Her lips widened into the nearest approximation to a smile that they were capable of, the muscles around her mouth almost cracking, like stone that has been hardened by centuries of ice and frost suddenly splitting when exposed to the sun for the first time. It was a most unpleasant, disturbing sight.

"We must all thank Sister Clodagh, I believe, for standing before us today in her breastplate of righteousness, her loins girt with truth. Oh yes, Sister, I know my Letter to the Ephesians. Are your feet shod in preparation for the battles to come? Do you carry the shield of faith, '*wherewith ye shall be able to quench all the fiery darts of the wicked*'? Do you '*wear the helmet of salvation*' and '*wield the sword of the Spirit, which is the true word of God*'? Are you ready to fight off the enemy at the gates?"

The girls, as one, turned their heads back to Sister Clodagh to see what, if anything, she might say in response to such a withering attack.

" '*Be not forgetful to entertain strangers; for thereby some have entertained angels unawares*'. Come along, girls. It's time for your next lesson…"

Lily had occasion to remember this exchange the following week, standing in front of painting after painting in the Manchester City Gallery, wondering what all the fuss had been about. There was plenty of naked flesh on display to be sure, but after the giggles and titters which greeted their first sight of Rodin's *The Age of Bronze*, standing in the entrance foyer, with its full frontal male nude, which they were very swiftly marched past by the red-faced Sisters, they had soon ceased to notice and concentrated instead on those paintings which caught their imagination through the stories they depicted, the secrets they contained…

She stands before *The Hireling Shepherd* by William Holman Hunt.

"That's a pretty picture," says Jenny, who scarcely leaves Lily's side.

"Do you think so? Why?"

"I like the trees and the fields and all the bright colours. I like the way the girl just leans back towards the shepherd as he puts his arm around her. I like the little baa-lamb on her lap."

Lily smiles at Jenny as she skips away towards a different picture, in a different part of the gallery, leaving Lily temporarily alone. She looks back at Holman Hunt's painting, peers at it closer, and frowns. She has quite a different reaction to it from Jenny. She finds the colours too bright, too hectic, almost garish. They remind her of how she feels when she has a fever. And there's something about the way the shepherd looms over the girl that Lily finds uncomfortable. His eyes are not upon her face, but look down, over her shoulder, down the front of her blouse. He puts his arm around her shoulder like he owns her, the way a person might be drawn to something shiny near the ground and then scoop to pick it up, which it appears is exactly what he has done, for in his left hand he is holding a moth, a death's head hawk moth, as if he is offering it up to the girl as a gift. She doesn't appear to have seen it. Or, if she has, she's taking no notice of it. Nor is she looking at him either. Instead her gaze is directed outwards, looking straight towards the painter, or the viewer, with an expression Lily can't fathom. Is she playing hard to get? Is she indifferent? Is she so accustomed to the young man's advances that she is no longer excited by them? Is she bored? She's not in any way resisting them, but neither is she enjoying them. Are they just something she's simply come to expect? Or is her apparent passivity more a languor, suggestive of a slow pleasure to come under the day's warm sun. Meanwhile, she ignores the baby lamb on her lap, allows it to feed on green apples, which are poisonous to sheep. Apples. Lily thinks of Eve in the Garden of Eden with the snake offering her one. Every day in the chapel at St Bridget's the girls would look at a stained glass window depicting this scene, and every day Sister Mary Frances of the Five Wounds would remind them that they are all Daughters of Eve and must be punished for her sins, which is why each month God curses them, so that they might remember and atone.

A young married couple now stand by Lily, looking at Hunt's painting. Immediately the man begins to pontificate about it, while the woman listens in respectful silence.

"Note the title," he says, fastidiously curling the ends of his moustache, "*The Hireling Shepherd*. A here-today-gone-tomorrow sort of fellow, not one to stick around, not to be trusted therefore. His interests lie altogether elsewhere, if the direction of his gaze is anything to go by. The sheep behind him graze untended on marshy ground, causing foot rot, the '*foul contagion*' in *Lycidas*, what?" He smiles at this reference. The woman sighs and looks towards Lily with a kind of indulgent shrug of the shoulders, before returning her husband's smile fondly. "Lambs of course are symbols for Christ," he continues, "but this one here's a sickly sort of chap, covered in a cloth despite the heat. I expect the painter is referring to the schisms in the Anglican Church. The rift between the so-called Evangelical and High Church parties in Britain at the time was enough to shake one's faith in the truth or existence of religion at all." He allows himself an indulgent chuckle. "Of course, that was Ruskin's view and there's no evidence that Hunt was aware of that at the time, but it makes one wonder, does it not, my dear?"

"Yes, dear, it certainly does. Is that what the moth is a reference to?"

"Why, what a clever poppet you are! But on further consideration I think not. The moth is merely a symbol of human mortality, the fate which awaits us all, salvation from which can only be achieved through Faith. Look at the apples, my dear. They are far too prominently placed in the painting's foreground for their appearance not to assume the greatest significance. Eden. Eve. Temptation and Fall. If the apples allude to the Fall, then the lamb is the Lamb of Redemption, and it is a sickly lamb, because it is in danger of being neglected. By succumbing to the temptations offered to her by the shepherd, it is her own chance of redemption that the girl is risking. Come. There's a Millais in the next gallery I particularly want to show you."

The woman links her arm back through her husband's as they turn to leave. Lily is forced to take a step backwards. The man sees her for the first time. He looks at her as if assessing an inventory, weighing up the assets against the liabilities, running his eyes over her as he might a set of figures on a balance sheet, the focus of his interest not dissimilar to that of the hireling shepherd in the painting behind him.

The woman now stares at Lily coldly.

"I believe it is this way, my dear," she says, steering him firmly in the opposite direction.

And sometimes the shepherds come in gangs.

Lily hovers at the entrance to an adjoining room in the gallery until she's sure that the married couple have left it. Once they've gone she steps across its threshold. Immediately opposite is the painting by Millais to which the husband must have been referring. *Lorenzo and Isabella.* Underneath it, on a small, glass-topped table, a typed sheet of paper kept under the glass informs her that the subject of the painting is taken from the Keats poem *Isabella, or The Pot of Basil*. Lily's not read it, but the sheet of paper tells her that Isabella was engaged to marry Lorenzo, a young man employed by her brothers, who are all merchants in the family business. When they find out about the romance, they plot to murder him, so that they can then marry their sister off to a wealthy nobleman they want to do business with. The painting shows Lorenzo, a pale and nervous young man, offering a cut slice of blood orange to Isabella at a dining table, around which sit all of her brothers.

But even before she has read about the story, Lily has found the painting deeply unsettling. It disturbs her greatly just to glance at it, and yet she finds that she cannot wrest her eyes away from it. There are all manner of tiny details which cause her shoulders to tense, her stomach to knot.

Just at that moment Sister Clodagh bustles in, all hot and bothered. "There you are," she exclaims. "I've been looking all over for you. Sister Mary Frances says it's time we were heading back, and it's my job to round up the waifs and strays. Come along."

"Is that what I am?" asks Lily. "A waif and stray?"

"You will be," says Sister Clodagh, "if we leave you behind."

Lily turns back to the painting. Her face screws up again immediately.

"Isabella," reads Sister Clodagh. "Now that's a very sad story. But that's all it is, Lily, a story, and one that happened far too long ago for you to be worrying your own head about." She instantly covers her mouth with her hand.

"What?" asks Lily.

"A slip of the tongue, that's all."

"Tell me."

Sister Clodagh looks at her sharply.

"Please."

"Lily Shilling, you're like a dog with a bone, I swear to God. You never ask a question without at least another half dozen following on close behind. But God knows I love you for it."

"You mentioned a slip of the tongue?"

"Indeed I did, child."

"Something to do with not worrying my head...?"

"Oh dear. Very well. But don't say I didn't warn you." Sister Clodagh mops her face before continuing. "Isabella, you see, found Lorenzo's body, after her brothers had killed the poor boy."

"Ugh!"

"So she cut off his head and hid it at the bottom of a pot of basil."

"Yuk!"

"Now you see why I didn't want to be telling you."

Lily is looking even more closely at the painting. "Knowing that makes the picture even more horrible."

"Horrible, yes, but beautifully painted. You can make out every last detail."

"That's what I mean," says Lily. "Look. Isabella's the only woman in the picture. All the others are men, and they're all looking at her. And it's not just that, it's the way they're looking at her, like they want to... I don't know, it's too disgusting to even think about it, let alone say it, especially if they're all her brothers."

She continues to scrutinise it, her eyes as close to the canvas as she can bear to bring them. The men are all dressed in such rich, lurid colours, while Isabella is pale and grey, as if they don't really see her, not her, who she really is, as if she were invisible and might just disappear right in front of them, which is perhaps what they're all wishing for.

Lily studies the brother sitting opposite Isabella, the way he's thrusting out his right leg straight towards her, pointing it directly between her thighs, the meaning behind it all too plain, an expression of such hate in his eyes. His hands violently squeeze a nutcracker, whose unmistakably shaped shadow falls from between his own legs across the white linen tablecloth, where a pewter salt cellar has been tipped over, spilling its contents. Isabella herself appears not to notice these things, though the tension in her body suggests she is aware of the febrile atmosphere, her eyes fixed instead on the offering by the nervous Lorenzo sitting beside her of the slice of blood orange.

Sister Clodagh takes Lily's wrist firmly in her hand. "And you, young lady," she says, not unkindly, but determinedly pulling her away from the painting, "have far too much imagination, far more than is good for you. Come along."

They hurry through room after room, passing painting after painting, until they all begin to merge into one, becoming a blur, all the Daphnes and Ophelias, Prosperpinas and Eurydices, Heros and Echos, Evadnes and Didos, Calypsos and Cassiopoeias, Lucretias and Ladies of Shallot, all drowning, descending into the underworld, becoming entombed in the bark of trees, or chained to a rock in the ocean, hurling themselves on their husbands' funeral pyres, hanged, impaled on swords, or daggers, or simply fading away, until there is nothing left but a shadow, a ghost in a mirror, the sound of a distant voice, so that Lily's eyes cloud over with tears.

"What on earth's the matter?" says Sister Clodagh when she realises. She catches her breath, lets go of Lily's wrist and wipes her face with her sleeve.

"Are there no happy endings?" asks Lily helplessly.

Sister Clodagh hands across her handkerchief to allow Lily to blow her nose and looks at this troubled child, whom she has known and looked after every day for fourteen and a half years, since she was just four days old, who will be leaving St Bridget's next week and who, it now dawns on her, she might never see again. What kind of answer can she possibly give to such a question?

"God loves you," she says in the end, "and that's a happy ending."

"But God also punishes," says another voice from just below them. Sister Mary Frances of the Five Wounds is climbing the stairs towards them with ice cold fury. She takes hold of Lily's ear firmly in her hand and hurries her back down to where the other girls are waiting. "He especially punishes those who are tardy," she adds, this last word accompanied by a sharp slap to the side of Lily's head. "He also punishes those who are selfish," she continues, administering a second slap for emphasis, "who think only of themselves," (slap), "who think nothing," (slap), "of keeping everyone else waiting." (Slap).

"Sister Mary Frances," says Sister Clodagh, "it's my fault, for it was I who delayed her."

"You are too kind hearted, Sister," smiles Sister Mary Frances. "You always think the best of the girls and they take advantage of you for that. They need a firmer hand. They must be taught discipline. Rules are rules, and there can be no exceptions." She turns back viciously to Lily. "See how you exploit the Sister's kindness. You need to be brought down a peg or two from the quite unwarranted high opinion you have of yourself, Miss Shilling." She scoffs derisively. "What a ridiculous name." She glances briefly back in the direction of Sister Clodagh. "Who could possibly have given it to you?" Sister Clodagh blushes, appears about to speak, but Sister Mary Frances of the Five Wounds ploughs on through, continuing to aim her invective at Lily like the arrows fired into Saint Sebastian. "There will be no supper for you this evening, young lady. You shall go at once to the Chapel the moment we arrive back at Trafalgar House, where you will say a hundred *Hail Marys* and then pray to St Teresa of Avila for the blessed gift of humility until I send for you. You would do well to ponder one of her many wise aphorisms. Like this one from *The Interior Castle*, a castle you have yet to even lay the foundations for inside yourself. '*If we turn from self toward God, our understanding will grow, and will be more ready to embrace all that is good*'." She brings herself so close to Lily that their heads are almost butting. She spits the words directly into Lily's face. Her eyes are filled with hate. " '*If we never rise above the slough of our own miseries, we do ourselves, and others, a great disservice*'." She leans back from Lily, stands up straight and tall once more, turns on her heels and marches towards the double doors at the entrance to the Gallery, swinging them wide as she passes through them. "Come, girls," she commands. "Let us all sing Psalm Number Twenty-Three to give us strength and fortitude for our journey back to St Bridget's."

The girls dutifully obey. Sister Clodagh squeezes Lily's hand surreptitiously, before joining Sister Mary Frances of the Five Wounds at the head of the crocodile. Jenny slips immediately and silently into the space she has vacated and entwines her own fingers in Lily's.

"*The Lord's my shepherd I'll not want*
He makes me down to lie
In pastures green he feedeth me
The quiet waters by…"

"Verse Three," barks Sister Mary.

"*Yea, though I walk in Death's dark vale*
Yet will I fear no ill
For Thou art with me, and Thy Rod
And staff me comfort still…"

And so Lily dreams.
Nymphs and shepherds.
Sometimes they come singly, sometimes in twos and threes, sometimes in gangs.
But always she is alone.

On her last night, after the lights have been turned out, all the other girls gather round her bed to say their farewells and wish her luck for the following day, as is the custom at St Bridget's. The Sisters know these rituals take place and tend to turn a deaf ear, but the way Sister Mary Frances of the Five Wounds has been acting lately, the girls are taking extra care this night not to make too much noise, in case they bring her wrath upon them. They whisper their goodbyes and press into Lily's hands the tiny presents they have made for her – a drawing, a poem, a shiny pebble, a speckled shard of egg shell – which Lily places carefully underneath her bed, wrapped in a piece of cloth, which she will take with her when she walks through the big front door of Trafalgar House for the last time and steps out into the world alone.

Normally, whenever a girl reaches her fourteenth birthday, there follows a period of intense speculation concerning where she will be placed when she leaves six months later. Some are found work in cotton mills, or chemical factories, the Tripe Colony, or as cleaners, or laundry girls. Luckier ones might become waitresses, or maids in one of the big houses nearby. If there are no situations vacant at the time a girl is ready to leave, they are transferred to one of the city's hostels for young women, as a temporary holding measure. Rumours have reached St Bridget's that many of these hostels are terrible places, indistinguishable from workhouses, with punishing regimes and endless drudgery, sucking all hope out of those who reside there, however briefly, before they are eventually tipped out onto the streets to fend for themselves.

But nothing appears to have been arranged for Lily. She has heard no news, not even an inkling, of where she is to go when she leaves. Evidently no position has been found for her. She presumes, therefore, it will be to one of these hostels that she'll be sent the following morning.

"I wonder what it's like," says one of the girls dreamily.

"I can't imagine not waking up here in St Bridget's," says

another.

"I can't wait to get out," says a third. "You'll not see me for dust."

"You say that now," says the first, "but just wait till it's your turn. I bet you'll feel different then."

Just then, Pearl, who's been put on guard duty at the door to watch out for any of the Sisters, as she always is because otherwise she would talk too much and risk them being disturbed much sooner, bounds back in, urging them to be quiet.

"Sister Mary Frances of the Five Wounds," she hisses.

At once all the girls scurry like mice across the dormitory floor back to their own beds. Only Jenny stays with Lily, slipping between the sheets next to her, hugging her close, trying not to breathe.

"Promise you'll come back for me."

"I promise."

Sister Mary Frances flings open the door and marches directly towards Lily's bed. She unceremoniously pulls back the sheet, shining her torch directly down upon the two girls. Her eyes flicker infinitesimally with shock, before their expression changes to an unpleasant mix of smiling disgust. Jenny, momentarily dazed at being discovered, stares back like a deer caught in the headlights, then bolts for the corridor and the sanctuary of darkness beyond. Sister Mary Frances watches her go without a word, then shines her torch directly into Lily's eyes, who raises a hand to shield them from its glare.

"There's been a slight change in plan," she says, fiercely grabbing that hand and dragging Lily from her bed across the dormitory, out into the corridor and down towards the main front door. Folded on a chair are a set of clothes. "These are yours, freshly laundered in readiness for your departure. Get dressed at once."

Lily obeys. She is shivering. "What's happening?" she

manages to say at last. "Where am I going?"

"Ask no questions, and you'll be told no lies."

Sister Mary Frances of the Five Wounds watches Lily dress with increasing impatience. "Hurry, child. Time and tide wait for no man. Or woman."

She is interrupted by a loud single knock on the front door. Lily is so startled she involuntarily shrieks. Sister Mary Frances presses her fingers to her lips. "Silence," she says. "Go to the bathroom. Wash your face. Comb your hair. Then report back here. Understood?"

Lily nods several times.

"Go."

Lily hurries back along the corridor as Sister Mary Frances of the Five Wounds pulls back the bolts on the heavy front door. She creaks it open and a tall, well-dressed gentleman steps in from outside, removing his hat as he does so, which he places on a small stand positioned by the door for the purpose.

"Good evening, Mr Godwit."

"Sister."

"You are punctual to the second, Mr Godwit."

"Punctuality is the soul of business. I insist on it in my employees. It would be hypocritical of me to behave otherwise myself."

"You set an admirable example, Mr Godwit."

"Is the girl ready?"

"She is. Shall I fetch her to you now?"

The gentleman nods.

Sister Mary Frances hurries to the bathroom where Lily is waiting for her.

"You're late," she hisses. "I told you to return to me directly."

"You were speaking to the gentleman, Sister. I didn't like to interrupt you."

"You've always got an answer ready, haven't you,

Missy? Come along."

As they reach the corridor Sister Mary Frances places her hand in the small of Lily's back and propels her firmly towards the front door, where Mr Godwit is waiting.

"This is the girl, sir."

Godwit approaches her. He looks at her directly without a word, walks around her as if appraising a filly before a race until, having completed a single circuit of her, he finally speaks.

"What's your name, child?"

"Lily, sir. Lily Shilling."

"Has Sister Mary Frances informed you of what your duties might be?"

Lily looks to Sister Mary then back to Mr Godwit. "No, sir," she stammers. "She hasn't."

Mr Godwit tuts.

"I thought that would be better coming from you, sir," says Sister Mary Frances, reddening.

"My dear girl," says Mr Godwit, looking back to Lily with more kindness. "No wonder you look so frightened. Being woken up in the middle of the night and told nothing. I have a business in the city which often keeps me working late, hence my arrival at this inconvenient hour. We have a vacancy for a maid. Your predecessor had to leave us suddenly, in most regrettable circumstances. I don't think I need to say more. And so I thought I would turn to St Bridget's – a former associate of my late father's was once a trustee here – where I might procure a girl of more reliable morals."

"You can depend upon that, Mr Godwit. All our girls are good here. They can recite their catechism, creed and commandments. Lily is no exception."

"Quite. And as for the lateness of the hour, Lily, the explanation is a simple one. We have an important dinner tomorrow evening, and I need you to start first thing in the morning. I shall be heading into Manchester early and so I wanted to see you settled first, introduce you to Mrs Baines, our housekeeper, so that she can explain your duties to you and you can begin at once. Is everything now clear to you?"

"Yes, sir," replies Lily.

"You'll be on a month's trial. Mrs Baines will lay out all the details to you. You're not afraid of hard work, I trust?"

"No, sir."

"Good girl. Well – let's see how we get on, shall we?"

"I'll do my best, sir."

Mr Godwit nods. "Now – I expect you still have one or two things to do to be ready, collect your things and such like. I'll wait in the car outside. Come out when you're ready."

Lily bobs a curtsey as Mr Godwit closes the front door behind him.

As soon as she is sure he's out of earshot, Sister Mary Frances swoops down on Lily and grabs her by the elbow. "You're extremely lucky," she hisses. "You don't deserve a position as good as this. It's only because Mr Godwit needed someone immediately, and there's no one else of the right age ready to leave apart from you. Otherwise, you'd be the last person I'd be recommending. I hope you understand that."

Lily smiles. For once, she realises, she has the upper hand. "Yes, Sister" she says. "I think I do."

The two look at one another. For a moment Lily thinks Sister Mary Frances might strike her, but just at that moment, a voice begins to sing. It is very faint at first, but unmistakable. It seems to be coming from the Chapel at the far end of the corridor. The voice begins to grow in confidence and volume, and soon the whole of St Bridget's reverberates to its sound.

Sister Mary Frances of the Five Wounds releases her grip on Lily's elbow. "What the Devil...?" She runs down the corridor to investigate, her habit rising behind her like a black crow.

Still the voice continues to sing. Lily recognises it at once. Only Jenny has such a voice, such purity of tone, such clear phrasing, as if she never needs to take a breath, but simply lets the notes pour out of her, as innocent as a thrush at evening singing simply for the sheer joy of it, but also a bell ringing a warning.

"Remember not, Lord, our offences
Nor the offences of our forefathers
Neither take thou vengeance of our sins
But spare us, good Lord..."

Lily listens, transported. She would like to go to the Chapel herself and watch Jenny as she sings. She imagines the light falling on her hair and shoulders from the stained glass windows. But she is brought back to the present by an urgent tapping on her shoulder. She spins round. It is Sister Clodagh.

"Shh," she whispers. "We've not long. Oh – will you listen to that girl sing? She's the voice of an angel. She came to me directly after you were woken up. It was her idea to distract Sister Mary Frances, so that I could come and see you before you go. I promise you, Lily, I had no idea about any of it. I've been on at Sister Mary Frances for weeks now, saying we had to find a place for you, but she only smiled and said that it was all in hand. It all seems very wrong to me, you being smuggled away like a thief in the night."

"He seems a very kind gentleman," says Lily.

"I hope to God you're right. Anyway, you'll write to me, I hope?"

"If I can."

"Good girl. Now..." Sister Clodagh holds out a small bundle wrapped in cloth and string. "I couldn't let you be leaving us without this."

"What is it?"

"Don't open it now, you haven't time. Hide it under your coat when Sister Mary Frances comes back. She'd only take it from you."

"I don't understand."

"It's what you came with. The day you arrived. The young woman who brought you, who'd been a friend of your poor mother, God rest her soul, she gave it to me and said that it was a gift, made especially for you by your grandfather…"

Lily holds the bundle, trying to imagine what it might contain with her fingers. She looks back towards Sister Clodagh, who pulls her towards her, holding her as tightly as she can.

The singing continues.

"Spare thy people, whom thou hast redeem'd
With thy most precious blood,
And be not angry with us for ever.
Spare us, good Lord…"

The notes wrap around them, then stop abruptly. Sister Mary of the Five Wounds swoops back towards them down the corridor, talons ready to pounce.

Sister Clodagh has retreated into an alcove.

"Go," screams Sister Mary Frances to Lily. "You mustn't keep Mr Godwit waiting." She flings open the front door and pushes Lily blindly into the night. The headlights on Mr Godwit's car are suddenly switched to full beam, dazzling her as she stumbles towards its opening door, while the door to Trafalgar House behind her slams heavily shut.

They drive the two miles from Audenshaw to Mr Godwit's

home in Dukinfield in complete silence. After a little over ten minutes the car pulls into a wide drive. The headlights sweep across a large double-fronted Georgian house.

"A humble abode, but mine own," says Mr Godwit. "Welcome to Globe Lane. My retreat and resting place. I try to keep this corner as a haven against the tempest outside. I cross its threshold to shut the world away, yet while I am here, it is all the world to me. Let's go in without delay. I see Mrs Baines has anticipated us already and is waiting to greet us."

Lily notices a rather stout, middle-aged woman, her grey hair tied back in a neat bun, standing in the doorway. She hangs an apron on a peg in the hall and then strides purposefully towards Lily.

"You must be the new girl."

"Yes, ma'am. Lily."

"Well then, Lily, let me help you with your things."

"She has nothing, Mrs Baines," says Mr Godwit, passing them in the hall. "Just what she stands up in, and that bundle she will not let out of her sight."

"Never mind," says Mrs Baines. "We'll soon sort you out. I expect there are still some things of Laura's here."

"Laura?"

"The girl before you. She was about your size to begin with."

Lily yawns widely.

"You must be exhausted, poor dear. What Mr Godwit thinks he's doing by dragging you from your bed half way through the night, the Lord alone knows. Follow me upstairs. I'll show you your room. The bed's made up. I imagine all you'll want to do is crawl right into it and get back to sleep. We've an early start tomorrow if we're to get everything ready in time for Mr Godwit's supper party. But don't worry about that now. Someone will wake you and fetch you and show you where everything is in the morning." They have now reached the top of the stairs. "Here we are," she says and pushes open the door. "It's all been cleaned and tidied since Laura left, but if you should come across anything that we might have missed, just hand it in to me and I'll make sure she gets it."

"Where's Laura gone?" asks Lily.

"Somewhere where people don't know her, so there'll be no pointing, or finger wagging, or whispering behind her back."

"Will she be coming back?"

Mrs Baines stops her bustling. "No, dear," she says with a certain finality. "She won't." She looks down with warmth at Lily, who has wandered over to the window, where she stares out into the darkness.

"Which direction is St Bridget's?" she asks suddenly.

"I'm not entirely sure," replies Mrs Baines. "That way, I think," she says indicating west. "Why?"

"I just want to picture where I've come from before I close my eyes."

Mrs Baines smiles. "I'll say goodnight now. See you in the morning. Sleep well. Pleasant dreams."

When Mrs Baines has gone, Lily sits on the bed and looks around her. It's only small, but it's hers. A room of her own. At least for now. It feels strange already to contemplate falling asleep without the accompanying sounds of forty other girls, their breathing nightly synchronising into a unified, gentle rise and fall, like the companionable ticking of clocks.

She will explore every inch of it tomorrow, she thinks, when it is light. Now she places the bundle on her lap and looks down at it. What could it be, she wonders? A gift from her grandfather, handed down to her mother, then saved for her by her mother's friend. These three shadowy figures from her earliest beginnings, beyond memory, beyond imagining. She pictures again the woman in the park with the tulips, who had picked up her dropped egg and placed it back on her spoon. Might she be the friend of her mother who Sister Clodagh spoke of earlier? She can't properly recall what she looked like. She just has an impression of a smiling face framed by curly hair, with dimpled cheeks and shining eyes, but she can conjure up no further details. She wonders if she'd recognise her again if she saw her by chance in the street. She'd like to think she would but she's not at all sure.

She unties the string and carefully removes the outer cloth. Underneath, the bundle is further wrapped in brown paper, which has become faded and creased over time. It's very thin in places and Lily has to take extra care not to tear it. Once she has removed this, she finds she is holding a cardboard box with a lid, slightly larger than a shoe box. She deliberately slows herself down, takes a deep breath, and then gently lifts the lid. Her eyes widen. Inside is a carved wooden boat. A yacht. When she takes it out, she sees that the mast can lift up and be slotted into a small hole on the polished deck. She smoothes the creases out of the sail between her fingers, then holds it up to the light. On the side of the hull, written in spidery yellow letters, as if the hand which painted them had belonged to an older person – her grandfather perhaps – is a single word:

'*T-u-l-i-p*...'

Lily feels the hairs on the back of her neck and all along her arms tingle.

Tulip.

She looks at it a long time.

Finally, she places it on a shelf above the small fireplace in the wall opposite her bed, from where she will always be able to see it whenever she comes into the room.

She undresses, climbs into bed, a bed so soft compared to the hard cots of St Bridget's that she feels she will sink into it, certain she will fall asleep within seconds, for she is so tired.

But she doesn't. She lies awake all night, trying to remember every single thing she can about her time at St Bridget's, the only life she's known, so that she will never forget any of it, all the girls from all the years, all the Sisters, especially Sister Clodagh, and Jenny. Sad, beautiful Jenny, whose voice had soared from the Chapel and saved her this evening, had allowed Sister Clodagh to come and say goodbye and give her the Tulip yacht, which spoke to her from a different time, from before she was born, from where she had begun. Jenny, whose bony body she misses, whose thin arms she wishes were wrapped around her right now, whose fingers were stroking her hair, instead of her own. She summons up her voice one last time.

"Remember not, Lord, our offences…
But spare us…"

It is only when the first grey streaks of light begin to feather the sky outside her window that she finally falls asleep, only to be woken, seemingly instantly, by a sharp knocking on her door, and the bustling figure of Mrs Baines carrying a tray, calling out, "Rise and shine, young lady. Chop, chop. Best foot forward. Goodness me, is that the time? Half-past six already! The day'll be gone."

*

Six months pass.

Mr Godwit holds his supper parties fortnightly on Fridays. They begin promptly at seven with dinner, followed by cards and drinking. Frequently there is music, occasionally supplied by a special guest, more usually a series of impromptu songs from Gilbert & Sullivan, operettas, and the music hall, with Mr Godwit himself providing the piano accompaniment.

Lily soon learns that these can turn quite raucous and will usually last well into the early hours of Saturday morning. Her job is mainly to wash the dishes after each course, although one evening, six months after she had first arrived, she is requested to bring in the coffee. A silence falls on the room as she enters.

"This is Lily," announces a benignly tipsy Mr Godwit to his friends gathered in the smoking room, where they have all repaired for coffee. "Our latest addition to Globe Lane."

Lily is aware, even through the thick fug of the cigar smoke, of all the men's eyes upon her, a few whispered comments.

"Would you like me to pour, sir?" she asks after she has placed the tray on a table.

"Thank you, Lily. We can manage."

"Will there be anything else, sir?"

The fraction of a pause.

"No. That will be all. Good night. Tell Mrs Baines she needn't wait up."

"Yes, sir. Thank you, sir."

Lily closes the door behind her and takes a deep breath. She hears the rising murmur of the men's voices as she climbs the staircase to her small room at the top of the house.

And that is how things continued for several weeks. Lily would take in the coffee at around ten o'clock. The gentlemen would suspend whatever conversation they were engaged in as she entered, watch her carry in the tray, then resume their remarks as soon as she left them. The only change to this routine was that now Mr Godwit would ask her to stay and pour the coffee. At first she was quite nervous about this. Her hand would shake and once or twice she would overfill a cup, whose contents would splash down into the saucer. At such times Mr Godwit would enfold her hand in his to steady the jug, and she would be aware of how the other gentlemen would notice this, but say nothing. On the second occasion she was asked to pour, however, she was prepared. Her hand did not shake and so there was no cause for Mr Godwit to take hold of it.

Gradually she began to recognise some of the faces of the more regular guests and put names to them. The identities of the attendees would vary, but there were two, Lily noted, who were ever present. These, she discovered, were Mr Snipe and Mr Crake.

"Birds of a feather," says Mr Snipe to her one Friday evening as she is pouring his cup.

"I beg your pardon, sir?"

"Godwit, Snipe and Crake. We sound like the most disreputable firm of solicitors, don't we, Lily?"

"I wouldn't like to say, sir."

"That's quite enough, Snipe," says Mr Godwit, a warning tone in his voice.

"Always dipping our beaks in the chaff."

"Ignore him, Lily. He's drunk."

"No more than you, Godwit. No more than anyone." He lurches to one side. He tries to steady himself by grasping the back of a chair, but he only succeeds in knocking it over and spilling his coffee over the Persian rug.

"I'll get a cloth," says Lily, and she hurries towards the door.

"Leave it," commands Godwit. "Let it wait till morning."

"Begging your pardon, sir, it will be much harder to remove the stain if I don't do it right away."

Godwit pauses. He regards Lily curiously. "Very well."

She returns with a bowl of warm, soapy water mixed with a few drops of vinegar and two white cloths. With one she sponges the stain with the mixture, while with the other, which she keeps dry, she blots where she has just wiped, until the stain begins to clear.

"Thank you, Lily. But this is not part of your duties. It

was not at all your fault that the incident occurred. We can see how you are going about removing the offending marks. I'm sure we can take it from here."

"It's no trouble, sir."

"Good night, Lily," says Godwit more firmly.

Lily immediately stops what she is doing and leaves at once. As soon as she is out of the room, she can hear raised voices and harsh words passing between Mr Godwit and Mr Snipe, with Mr Crake having to come between them. She then hears footsteps approaching the door. Not wishing to appear as though she were lingering in order to eavesdrop, she begins to run upstairs, only for Mr Godwit's voice to call her to a halt.

"Lily," he says. "Please come back down. There's nothing to be frightened of."

Lily obediently returns to the foot of the stairs, where she stands in front of Mr Godwit, her hands joined together in front of her, her eyes cast downwards.

Mr Godwin tilts her chin with his hand, so that she is looking up directly into his face. Lily experiences an unmistakable jolt pass through her.

"Take no notice of Snipe," he says softly. "He's a damn fool. At the next supper party, I'd like you to join us earlier please. Do you play cards?"

"Not really, sir. It was not the kind of thing the Sisters encouraged at St Bridget's."

Mr Godwit laughs. "No, I imagine not."

Lily smiles back.

"Then we'll have to teach you."

"Yes, sir."

"Off to bed then. Good night."

"Good night, sir."

She is aware of him watching her as she skips back up the stairs.

"The name of the game," says Crake a fortnight later, "is *Flinch*."

"Boo!" says Snipe, rapping his hand on the table directly in front of her.

"Don't be an ass, Snipe," says Godwit, joining them at the table.

"I think Lily's going to prove a natural," remarks Crake as he deals out the cards. "You will note, gentlemen, that she never 'flinched' a muscle at Snipe's clumsy attempts to make her."

"Who's for another brandy?" asks Snipe, ignoring their jibes.

"Not you," says Godwit. "You've had quite enough already."

"What a spoilsport you are, Godwit. You'll be turning these gatherings of ours into temperance meetings before we know it. Lily, my dear, what's your preferred tipple?"

"That's enough, Snipe," says Godwit. He looks at Lily, who is sitting patiently at the table, her hands meekly folded on her lap. His expression softens. "Perhaps some Madeira then. A thimble full only, mind."

Lily takes her first sip of alcohol – apart from the minuscule watered down drop that was permitted as part of Holy Communion at St Bridget's – while Crake explains the rules of the game.

"*Flinch* is based on a much older game called *Spite and Malice*, which gives you an indication perhaps that this is not a game for the squeamish. It's based on stock piling. The object of the game is to get rid of all your cards before your opponents do. Everybody's trying to do the same. The way you do it is by collecting as many sets as you possibly can, and the way you do this is to take from your opponents. Then, when you get a set, you simply dispose of it, by placing it on the table, face down, as if you never wanted it in the first place. You literally have all the cards, while everyone else has the leftovers. Are you following me so far?"

"I think so," says Lily, taking another sip of the fortified wine.

"We use a special pack. A hundred and fifty cards, ten sets each numbered from one to fifteen. These are the sets you're trying to collect." Crake then begins to deal. "First I deal each player ten cards, face down. This is your 'Flinch' pile. Next I deal everyone five cards. These are your 'Hand' cards, which means you get to pick them up and look at them, but no one else is allowed to see them. Finally, I deal the rest of the cards out evenly between everyone. These are kept face down and are your 'Reserve' pile." Crake deals out all the cards at a rapid speed, explaining the rules simultaneously. "How you play is like this: turn over the top card of your 'Flinch' pile. If it's a 1, you place it face down in the middle of the table." Lily turns hers over. "OK. That's not a 1, so you place that face up, so that we can all see it. It's a 7. Fine. That might come in useful later. Now the rest of us take our turn to repeat the same process." The game continues. Lily watches with earnest concentration. Crake continues to explain. "Now – it's your turn again. Turn over the next top card in your 'Flinch' pile. If it's a 2, excellent. If it's not, never mind. Look in your 'Hand' pile. Have you got a 1? Yes? Then you must play that. If you hadn't had a 1, or a 2, then you'd have to pick a card from your 'Reserve' pile and add it to your 'Hand' pile. As the game progresses, we all get to find out where each other's strengths and weaknesses lie – unless you're very skilled at concealing those – and we try to force our opponents, by the cards we choose to play from our 'Hand' piles, to have to keep picking up more and more cards from their 'Reserve' pile, while we keep completing the sets, in order from 1 to 15. Got it?"

"Yes," cries Lily, completing a set of 1s.

"I warned you, gentlemen. This girl's a natural."

"And she seems to have finished her wine," observes Snipe, waving the bottle of Madeira across the table, looking directly at Godwit, who nods, so that Snipe is immediately by Lily's side, pouring her another glass.

The game proceeds in an enjoyably competitive manner for the next half hour. Lily becomes more and more adept – and more and more excited – until eventually she places down her final card in triumph.

"Bravo!" shout Godwit, Snipe and Crake in unison.

"Beginner's luck," says Lily, her cheeks flushed with the wine.

"Nonsense," says Crake.

"There's no such thing," adds Snipe.

"And now some coffee, I think. Lily, would you mind?"

When she returns with the tray, Godwit has placed a record on his Garrard Grafanola, a gramophone of which he is extremely proud. Lily is under strict instructions to dust and polish this item daily. 'Purchased from *Hall & Singer*, Denton,' says the discreet sign on the back of the machine. It's a kind of music Lily has never heard before, harsh and metallic, the melodies determinedly unsentimental, but somehow haunting.

"What is it?" she asks as she pours the coffees.

"Don't get him started," says Crake.

"Or we'll have to listen to it all night," adds Snipe.

"You've heard of music of the spheres?" says Godwit, drawing deeply on his lit cigar. "Well, this is music for the modern age, the machine age, the age of the metropolis."

Snipe and Crake groan.

"But what is it?" asks Lily again.

Godwit holds up the record sleeve. "This," he says proudly, "is a special English language recording of *The Threepenny Opera* by Bertolt Brecht and Kurt Weill, imported direct from Berlin. That chap from *Hall & Singer* arranged it all perfectly. He has the most remarkable eye –

and ear – for whatever is the coming thing…"

"Queer as a bandicoot of course," interjects Snipe.

Crake laughs but is stopped at once by a look from Godwit. "Listen," he urges, holding up his right hand…

He closes his eyes while the next song begins, mouthing the words in sync with the singer, a woman, conjuring an atmosphere of smoky shadows, drawn blinds, uncertain identities. Snipe and Crake observe him with an amused expression on their faces. Lily, not seeing any of this, listens closely to the words.

"I once used to think in my innocent youth
(And I once was as innocent as you)
That someone some day
Might come my way
And then I should know what to do
And if he'd got money and he seemed a nice chap
And his workday shirts were as white as snow
And if he knew how to treat a girl with respect…"

Lily is jolted from her reverie, as Crake and Snipe stand either side of Godwit, put their arms around his shoulders, and join in with the final line in high falsetto voices.

"I'd have to tell him, 'No'…"

Lily watches as the three of them collapse, laughing, to the sofa. The collective force of their fall causes the gramophone to jump, and they proceed to pull her down between them. She finds that she is laughing too as the needle sticks on the record, replaying the last line over and over, again and again, but she does not hear it.

"I think someone's had enough excitement for one day," whispers Crake in her ear.

"I think someone's had just a little too much wine,"

whispers Snipe in the other.

"Time for bed, I think," says Godwit, scooping her up in his arms.

He carries her up the stairs to the top of the house, pushes open the door to her room with his foot, then gently lays her down on her bed.

"Good night, Lily," he says to her. She is already asleep. He smoothes a loose strand of hair away from her face. "Sweet dreams."

The next morning Lily wakes on top of the bed, still in her clothes. Her head aches. She has little memory of the previous evening, except for a game of cards, a strange song and a lot of laughter. She looks down at her creased skirt. She does not believe anything untoward has happened.

She becomes aware of hushed voices outside her door. It is Mr Godwit and Mrs Baines. They appear to be arguing.

"I know it's late," says Mr Godwit, "and that she should have been down and dressed an hour ago attending to her chores, but that is my fault, not hers. We kept her up late at our supper party last night."

"You know my opinion on that, sir," replies Mrs Baines. "She's too young."

"I assure you that nothing at all untoward took place," he says.

Lily listens – that word again. Untoward.

"I should hope not," says Mrs Baines. "But I've still got a house to run, and I need Lily to assist me. Otherwise you might just have to fend for yourself for dinner this evening."

"Don't trouble yourself over that. I shan't be home till late tonight. I'm dining out."

"I see."

Lily is fully awake now. She can picture Mrs Baines' pursed lips at this moment.

"Any other instructions, sir?" she asks.

"Yes," says Mr Godwit. "One."

"And what is that?"

"I'd like you to take Lily to be fitted for a new dress." Lily's eyes widen on the other side of the door. "She needs something more suitable for social gatherings, I think. Wouldn't you agree, Mrs Baines?"

"Whatever you say, sir. But...?

"Yes, Mrs Baines?"

"Why go to unnecessary expense? I'm sure we could get one of Laura's altered to fit Miss Lily."

'Miss', now, is it, thinks Lily?

"I've told you before. Laura was a fool. I don't want Lily to be tarnished by any association with her."

"But she already is, sir."

"In what way? Tell me."

"She's sleeping in her room for one thing."

"That's quite different. I asked for all traces of Laura's presence there to be removed."

"And so they were, sir."

"Then why have you kept her dresses?"

"Waste not, want not, sir. Money doesn't grow on trees. Even for you."

Lily hardly dares breathe.

"Whose clothes do you think she's been wearing up till now?"

Eventually Mr Godwit speaks. "I trust I can leave matters to you, Mrs Baines."

"Yes, sir."

"In that case, I must leave for the office."

Lily hears his footsteps retreating down the stairs. Then she hears the front door in the hall slam shut. Mrs Baines and Lily let out their breath simultaneously. Mrs Baines then knocks sharply on Lily's door.

"Quickly now, Lily. I know you're awake. We've a busy

day ahead of us."

The house in Globe Lane was originally built in the eighteenth century, though it had been much altered in the hundred and fifty years which followed. It was once a farm, with many acres of land surrounding it. Mary Moffat had lived there as a girl, before she went to Africa. There was a picture of her on the wall in the hallway, next to a long case clock.

"Who's that?" Lily had asked on her very first day, and Mrs Baines had explained. Mary Moffat, she had said. Don't you know who Mary Moffat was? When Lily shook her head, Mrs Baines had tutted, but not crossly, as Sister Mary Frances of the Five Wounds would have, just a gentle shake of the head, as if to say, what do they teach them in schools these days?

"Mary Moffat," she went on, "moved to Africa with her parents, who were missionaries. There she met and married…" She paused for effect, wanting to be sure she had Lily's full attention.

"Who? Who did she marry?"

"Only the most famous man in the world at that time, that's who," pronounced Mrs Baines with a degree of proprietorial relish. "The explorer David Livingstone."

"So Mary Moffat became Mary Livingstone?" asked Lily, wanting to be sure she had understood.

"Correct."

"And she lived in this very house?"

"Ay, that she did. Till she was about your age."

Lily beamed. She looked back at the portrait of Mary Moffat and thought about all the times she must have stood in this actual spot, where the long case clock now ticked so sonorously, how often she must have run up and down the same stairs Lily now stands at the foot of. How brave it must have been to have left all of this behind, all that was familiar, the only home she'd ever known, for somewhere so unimaginably far away as Africa. The dark continent. On those rare occasions when the Sisters had taken them into the city, Lily had marvelled when they ever saw someone with skin of a different colour. It made her realise what a strange and wonderful world she inhabited, and that all of it appeared to be drawn to Manchester like a magnet. How small her own world had seemed to her then, the narrow, enclosed surroundings of St Bridget's. Now she had taken a step into something larger, but this was still as nothing when compared to the journey undertaken by the girl whose face stared back at Lily from its portrait hanging on the wall of this house on Globe Lane.

In more recent times, much of the land had been sold off, for factories and the homes for the people who worked in them, but the house still had plenty of space around it. There were many pastures green remaining, in which to make down and lie, holding back the onward creep of those dark Satanic mills.

In addition to Mrs Baines, there was a gardener, and a boy to help him, a cook – Mrs Cloudsdale – who didn't live in but who came each day early on her bicycle, who, when introduced to Lily for the first time, had taken one look at her and said, "So this is the new one, is it?" And now Lily. And presumably, before Lily, there was Laura.

"How long was Laura here?" Lily asks Mrs Baines later that morning, while they are polishing brasses.

"Too long," says Mrs Baines.

"And who was here before her?"

Mrs Baines eyes Lily sharply. "You ask a lot of questions."

"I know," says Lily cheerfully. "That's what the Sisters at St Bridget's used to say."

"They were not wrong," says Mrs Baines, repressing a

smile.

"How else do you find out anything?" asks Lily.

Mrs Baines grips Lily's shoulders.

"By keeping your eyes and ears open, but your mouth shut," she says forcibly. "And by keeping your wits about you." She taps the side of Lily's temple gently with her forefinger. "Remember this."

Two hours later Lily is standing in the rarely used lounge at Globe Lane being measured for a new dress. The dressmaker – a Miss Tyler – is tall, thin, elegant and brisk. The material which has been chosen is a luxurious dove-grey silk, and Miss Tyler is in the process of draping it around Lily, taking pins from her thin, angular mouth to experiment with different ways in which the bias might be cut. After almost an hour, during which time Lily has not spoken a word, Miss Tyler is satisfied. She packs away the material, pins and tape measure, then makes a lightning sketch with a blue pencil, which she shows, not to Lily, but to Mrs Baines.

"I'm thinking something along these lines."

Mrs Baines studies it for a while. "You don't think it might be just a little too sophisticated? The girl's very young still."

Miss Tyler gives Lily a further cursory look. "She can carry it, I think," she says, coolly appraising her. "She's fairly tall, she has that angular look which is all the rage right now. I assume the dress is to be worn for elegant social occasions? Dinners, soirées, parties?"

Mrs Baines sighs. "Yes, though Mr Godwit prefers to entertain here at home mostly."

"And why shouldn't he? It's a wonderful house for a dinner party. Yes, I am sure this design will not disappoint him."

"Might..." asks Lily nervously, "might I see it?"

Miss Tyler looks at Mrs Baines, who nods. She holds out the drawing carelessly at arm's length, allowing Lily the briefest of glimpses. She is aware of a scooped back, diaphanous silk, a flowing skirt, before it is promptly snatched away again.

"Thank you," she says, hoarsely.

Miss Tyler turns back and looks at Lily as though for the first time. She takes a couple of steps towards her, scrutinising her closely. She blows smoke from the cigarette that hangs from her immaculately lipsticked lips casually from the corner.

"You're very lucky," she says. "I hope you realise that. Many young girls would give anything to wear something like this. Especially with your facial disadvantage. I expect he feels sorry for you. Still, they can do wonders with make-up these days, can't they? I could help you if you like?" She glances irritably at her watch, then turns away from Lily as though she has simply tossed away what was for a moment a vaguely interesting notion in a fashion magazine, which she has now decided to discard. "And now, if you'll excuse me, Mrs Baines, I have two more clients to see this afternoon. I'll have this made up for you by the end of the week. I assume you'd prefer delivery?" Mrs Baines nods again. "There'll be an additional charge of course."

"That shan't be a problem. Charge it to Mr Godwit's account."

The following Friday Lily is wearing the dress for the first time. It fits her like a second skin. So closely does it follow the contours of her body that she cannot wear underclothes beneath it. Its touch is cool and sensual. No expense has been spared with the amount of material needed to create its elegant, floor length bias cut. Its flared hem sweeps around her as she moves, caressing the floor beneath her feet, on which she has placed grey satin ball slippers, which have also been purchased for her, to match the colour of the dress, whose modest neck line follows the contours of her shoulders to reveal a bare back and cinched in waist. The arms too are bare and a pair of long grey gloves has been provided, which she now pulls on, almost deliciously. She looks in the small mirror on a stand on the chest of drawers beside her bed and touches the mark on her left cheek. She recalls the stinging words of Miss Tyler and wonders whether she should somehow try and disguise it. In the end she thinks not. She would only apply the make-up inexpertly. Instead she decides she will experiment, for the first time, with a little lipstick. Mrs Baines has said that she believes there is some in the top drawer of the chest, next to where some sewing things are kept. Lily rarely opens this drawer. She pulls it out now and gently rummages around until, near the back, she finds what she's been looking for. The lipstick's shade is a pale pink, one which will go well with her dress, she thinks. Her hands are trembling slightly as she tries to trace the curved bow of her lips. After a couple of false starts she gets the hang of it and manages a passable job. She presses a tissue to her mouth, which she then lays beside the mirror. The reflected palimpsest of her own lips pouts back at her disconcertingly and she screws it up quickly, tossing it towards the waste basket in the corner. She misses, and the pink lips reconstitute themselves as the scrunched up tissue opens like a damaged flower.

There is a knock on her door. Mrs Baines walks in, carrying something small in her hands, which Lily can't quite see.

"Mr Godwit would like you to wear these," she says, and she holds up before her, like offerings, a pair of ear rings and a necklace.

Lily takes them and holds them to the light, where they sparkle and dance.

"Did these belong to Laura?" she asks eventually.

"Don't ask," says Mrs Baines. "Here – let me help you put them on."

When she has finished, she stands back to regard her. "You'll do," she says grimly.

Lily, looking in the mirror, hears Sister Clodagh and Sister Mary Frances of the Five Wounds, perched on each bare shoulder, speaking into her ears, like the Good and Bad Angels.

"Don't you look a picture?" exclaims Sister Clodagh.

"Whore of Babylon," retorts Sister Mary Frances.

"The guests will be arriving shortly," says Mrs Baines. "I'll call you when it's time to come down."

After Mrs Baines has gone, Lily re-applies her lipstick one last time. She goes to put it back in the top right hand drawer of the chest but finds she cannot properly shut it. Something appears to be stuck at the back. She jiggles the drawer from side to side until eventually she can remove it altogether. As she does, something falls out from behind it.

Lily picks it up. It's a sheaf of folded paper, with minute hand writing scrawled across both sides, which look like they might be entries in a diary. She brings it closer to her so she can read it. It's Laura's – she knows it at once – it must be.

Mrs Baines calls up from downstairs. Lily puts the papers at the back of the chest and replaces the drawer, before preparing to make her entrance. She will read it later, when there will be no chance of being discovered.

The supper party that night is different from the more regular, informal gatherings she has grown used to. There are eight guests – Mr Crake and Mr Snipe and six others – and all of them are men.

As she enters the smoking room, she is greeted by spontaneous applause. One by one the men come up to her and introduce themselves. "*Enchanté*," they say, or words to that effect. "At your service." "Delighted to meet you at last." "I've heard so much about you." "But reports fail to do justice to the reality." Then each of them kisses her gloved hand. One of them offers her a cigarette, which five others rush to light for her. "Champagne," announces Snipe, and Lily finds herself giggling as the bubbles fly up her nose. "Music," declares Godwit, placing a record on the Garrard Grafanola, and the room is filled with the romantic strains of Strauss waltzes.

A moment later he is at her side, demanding the first dance. As they waltz around the room, he whispers in her, "How do you like your first party?"

"Very much, sir," she replies.

"The necklace looks particularly fine," he adds, and allows himself the luxury of stroking it, his fingers lingering upon her throat.

"I say, Godwit old chap," interrupts Crake. "This is hardly the action of a generous host, keeping our pretty guest all to yourself."

"Hear, hear!" the others call out in unison.

"Forgive me, gentlemen. You are of course quite right. I was momentarily dazzled."

"Share and share alike," says Snipe.

"Birds of a feather," adds Crake.

Godwit turns the volume of the music up as high as it will go. Waltzes give way to polkas, and one by one the gentlemen take it in turns to sweep Lily in their arms and dance her round the furniture. Such is the noise that they fail to hear Mrs Baines announce that "Dinner is served" so that she has to repeat this several times, finally resorting to lifting the needle off the record in the middle of the music. She gives the gentlemen reproving looks, saving her sternest stare for Mr Godwit himself.

"I thought you said this was to be a respectable evening.

You are not at your Club tonight, sir."

"Duly noted, Mrs B. From now on you will find us the epitome of dignity and decorum."

"I'm glad to hear it, sir."

Mrs Baines takes Lily to one side. "You look quite hot already, my dear. Try to pace yourself. You don't wish to spoil your dress now, do you? A lady never perspires."

Lily bites the inside of her cheeks to stop herself laughing. "Of course not, Mrs Baines. I shall try to remember."

They all transfer to the dining room, which is a kaleidoscope of polished surfaces, sparkling crystal, dancing light, reflection upon reflection, in the mirror above the fireplace, where a log fire burns and crackles in the hearth, the different glasses, the shining cutlery and place settings, all of which Lily is familiar with, having washed and dried and buffed and polished them so many times, but she has never seen them glitter quite like this before.

Mrs Baines has hired in another girl from Dukinfield to help her serve the many courses and clear away the plates and dishes in between each. This would normally have been Lily's job, and she watches how the local girl steals surreptitious glances at her from time to time, wishing their positions could be reversed.

Mock turtle soup is followed by Dover sole, with braised pigeon breast for the main course and syllabub for dessert, each accompanied by a different wine. Lily has never seen so much food in all her life and finds she is only able to manage a morsel of each dish. If this is noted, it is commented upon by no one, almost as if it is expected that a young lady will eat with modesty and restraint – unlike the gentlemen, who devour with relish everything that is placed before them. Similarly she manages to make her first glass of wine – a rather delicate white which, she learns, is a *Chenin Blanc* – last her all evening. Once again nobody tries to force any more upon her, not even Snipe.

Lily is entranced. She wants to be sure to stay completely sober, so that she will be able to remember this evening with absolute clarity afterwards, savouring every moment of it.

Godwit sits at the head of the long table and places Lily at the opposite end, facing him. The other eight gentlemen are lined up in fours along each side. This means that Lily is able to observe everyone at all times. She can hear snippets of all their different conversations, and her position means that she cannot be hogged by a single guest. On the contrary, each of them takes turns to engage her in all manner of small talk. She is, she realises, being flirted with, a situation she finds most agreeable. It is flattering to find herself the focus of attention, the epicentre of the room.

It is after the dessert when the mood begins to alter. Mrs Baines is instructed to bring in a bowl of fruit and then dismissed for the evening. She looks across anxiously towards Lily before she leaves, but Lily is too busy responding to some *plaisanterie* being whispered in her ear by the gentleman on her right to notice her.

The bowl contains a mixture of plums and cherries. Lily has never tasted either before. She removes her gloves in order that she does not stain them and hangs them over the back of her chair. She selects a cherry, then another, then another, placing each stone upon the rim of her plate.

"Are you trying to predict your future?" asks Crake, observing the pile of cherry stones mounting up before her.

Lily looks back at him blankly.

"You do not know the rhyme then?" he continues.

She shakes her head.

"Then we must enlighten her, gentlemen."

They all lean across the table to examine her plate. One by one they pick up a stone, chanting in turn.

"Tinker…"

"Tailor…"

"Soldier..."

"Sailor..."

"Rich man..."

"Rich girl, surely?" corrects Crake, laughing.

"Rich girl..."

"Poor girl..."

"Beggar girl..."

"Oh!" remarks Crake. "Your last one. Surely not...?"

"I shouldn't worry," says Snipe, his words slurring as usual. "You shan't have cause to beg while under the protection of this roof, shall she, Godwit?"

Godwit says nothing.

"No more cherries then," says Crake, steering them away from any possible awkwardness. "Try a plum instead, Lily."

He holds out the dish of purple fruit towards her. The lights have been lowered since finishing dessert. The intensity of the mirrored reflections in each glass and on the blades of each knife has sharpened. Her ear rings and necklace glint and sparkle. She is conscious of the glow from the flames in the hearth flickering against her bare back and along her arms. The plums, which must have been rinsed one final time before being brought in by Mrs Baines, are beaded with water, each separate drop glistening on the flesh of the fruit. Lily reaches forward and picks one. She rolls it gently between the palms of her hands.

She is acutely conscious of all the gentlemen's eyes upon her.

One of them runs his fingers up and down the stem of his champagne glass. Another offers her a fruit knife, the dark shadow of its shape stretching towards her from his hand along the white linen tablecloth. The rest lean their bodies forward.

The painting of *Isabella* by Millais suddenly swims before her eyes. She feels her skin grow suddenly hotter and she wonders if she might faint. She raises the plum to her lips. Its smell revives her. She opens her mouth and bites.

The sweetness of the taste hits her at once. She bites again, and again. The juice runs down her mouth towards her throat. One of the gentlemen knocks over a tall pewter cruet containing sugar, which spills onto the cloth. The others rush to her side, offering napkins. She takes one and wipes the stickiness from her face.

Godwit rises to his feet. "It would be customary at this point in the evening, for one of the ladies to get to her feet and invite the other female guests to withdraw and leave the gentlemen to their cigars and brandy. But as you are the only lady here this evening, Lily, in whose honour we hold our feast tonight, may we ask you instead to join us as we retire?"

"Thank you, sir," she replies. "I shall be delighted."

The gentlemen rise, chairs are scraped back, Godwit offers his arm to Lily, which she graciously accepts, and together they lead the exodus from the dining room into the smoking room.

The febrile atmosphere from the dining room dissipates. The gentlemen lounge around on sofas and in armchairs, listening to the latest jazz from the Clarence Williams Blue Five on Godwit's Garrard Grafanola, with Louis Armstrong on the trumpet and Sidney Bechet on saxophone. *Coal Cart Blues* and *Snake Bite Blues*. Snipe persuades Lily to join him in a cake walk, and soon the whole party is dancing. Afterwards, when the music becomes less hectic, as Sippie Wallace serenades them with *Trouble Wherever I Roam* and *Baby I Can't Use You No More*, Mr Godwit takes Lily in his arms and dances close and slow with her. Crake and Snipe watch them from the edges of the room.

The evening quietens. Lily circulates. She pours the gentlemen their drinks. She lights their cigars.

As the long case clock in the hallway chimes eleven o'clock, Godwit requests coffee. Lily immediately makes to move towards the kitchen.

"No, Lily," he says, placing his hand upon her arm. "This is your night. There'll be no servant's chores for you tonight." A look passes between them. "Snipe – do you think you're sober enough to manage coffee for us all?"

"Your wish is my command, old chap," he replies, before proceeding to fall flat on his face. This is the cue for the rest of the gentlemen to get to their feet.

"Don't bother with coffee tonight," says Crake. "Let's get this drunken reprobate a taxi home. Give me a hand, someone."

They haul Snipe to his feet and carry him out into the hall. They then all make their farewells, each one of them coming in turn to Lily to kiss her hand and bid her goodnight. "Not goodbye," they say, "but *au revoir.*"

"*Merci, monsieur,*" she answers coyly, until at last they have all departed and it is just the two of them left alone.

Godwit puts his arms around her and sighs deeply. "I thought they'd never leave," he says.

Lily knows what will happen next, has known, she thinks, since she first put on the dress that evening, that there will be a time when it will be just the two of them.

"Oh Lily," he says, "I want you so badly."

He presses his mouth firmly against hers. His moustache is ticklish and she smiles. Her lips part slightly, and it is all the encouragement he needs. He pushes his tongue between them until it makes contact with hers. His hands slide up and down her bare back, pulling her tiny body hard against him. This is the first time Lily has been kissed. Perhaps it is the occasion, perhaps it is the combination of the wine and the music, perhaps it is something about Mr Godwit himself, she doesn't know. But what she does know is that she is enjoying it. She likes the way their tongues explore each other's mouths. She likes the strength of his arms around her and the movement of his hands across her body. One of them has found its way to her breast. He slips it inside her dress and squeezes.

"Oh Lily," he says again.

He scoops her in his arms, not unlike that time before, when she had fallen asleep after playing cards, and begins to carry her upstairs. But this time she is not asleep. Nor does she flinch.

When they reach her room, he stands her on her feet and the two of them face each other in the darkness. Gradually her eyes accustom to the shard of moonlight that falls across the narrow bed. He places his hands on her shoulders and gently eases her arms out of the straps of her dress. Then he slowly unties the small bow at the back, so that the dress falls from her completely. He helps her to step out of it and looks at her. The moon silvers every skin cell of her body.

She lies back on the bed while he hurries out of his own clothes, removing cuff links, collar, bow tie, untying shoe laces, unbuttoning shirt and trousers, until finally he is ready. He greedily covers every inch of her with his mouth. He brings the fingers of his left hand to Lily's lips, which she sucks until they are completely moist, before he places them between her legs, inserting one, then two inside her, sliding them up and down, at first slowly, before gradually pushing them faster and deeper until he hears her moan.

"Are you all right?" he asks her.

Lily nods, her eyes closed.

When he enters her, it hurts, and she does flinch this time. She grips his arms and involuntarily tries to push him away from her. He pauses, and the two of them look at one another for several seconds. He lifts a hand to the strawberry mark on her left cheek. Gently he strokes it. Little by little her body relaxes. He continues to move against her, gradually finding a rhythm, which Lily tries to match with her own, but she can't keep pace with him for long, as he begins to move faster and faster, harder and harder, the bed thudding beneath them. She begins to feel him start to shudder, as he hastily withdraws, spilling all over her belly and thighs, before rolling away from her onto his side.

He remains there for some time, breathing heavily, saying nothing. Lily lies completely still. After a few minutes, he stands up from the bed and begins to get dressed. She watches him, the same actions she witnessed earlier now being carried out in reverse, with the same meticulousness. When he has finished, he picks up Lily's dress, smoothes away any creases, loops the shoulder straps of it over the wooden peg attached to the back of her door, and then looks down on her. His face is in shadow, so that Lily cannot read the expression on it as he speaks.

"Goodnight, Lily," he says. "This has been an evening to remember."

She is up the next morning before it is light. She goes downstairs and begins to clear away the debris and detritus of the dining room. The dirty plates and dishes, the smeared cutlery, the cherry stones. She looks down at the stained linen table cloth and thinks, this should have been dealt with last night, now it will be far more difficult to remove.

She stands at the sink in the kitchen washing up, when Mrs Baines arrives, evidently astonished to find Lily already up and doing.

"Is everything all right?" she says, taking off her coat and tying on her apron. "Was the evening a success?"

Lily nods.

Neither of them is really sure which question has been asked and which has been answered.

In the following weeks and months a pattern establishes itself. The supper parties revert to their more usual format of just Godwit, Snipe and Crake – the three birds of a feather, as they like to term themselves – with occasional additions. Lily does not join them until it's time to bring in the coffee, after which she will remain in the smoking room to play cards, or dance, until the last guest has finally left. Then she and Godwit will have sex. Repeatedly. Sometimes in the smoking room, sometimes on the dining room table with the mirror above the fireplace capturing their conjoined limbs in multiple reflections, sometimes on the stairs, once in Mr Godwit's study, once, even, in his own bedroom, but mostly these couplings take place in Lily's narrow, creaking bed at the top of the house.

It no longer hurts her, but she is aware that she does not appear to derive the same intensity from the act that Mr Godwit does, whose eyes squeeze tight shut at the moment of climax, when he emits a strangled sound more like an animal experiencing pain than pleasure. He never tries to force her. He respects her when it's the time of her monthly period. Then they sit downstairs and he plays the piano for her.

On one particular evening he proceeds to sing to her *Die Forelle* by Schubert. *The Trout*. Lily sits on the piano stool beside him, their thighs pressed close together. His face appears transformed by the music. Like the statue to St Anthony back in the Chapel of St Bridget's, the patron saint of missing things, beatifically smiling, when he has found what he thought was lost.

"*In a bright stream
A moody trout
Passed by in haste
Like an arrow
I stood there at the bank
And watched in blissful calm
The frisky fish's bath
In this clear stream…*"

He caresses the keys far more gently than he ever touches me, thinks Lily, watching him so totally absorbed in his playing, in his recounting of this tale of the frisky trout. Is that how he sees me, she wonders? Frisky? Has my behaviour become so transparent, that he can look at me, as though through water, and see me swimming in such unguarded nakedness?

> *"A fisher with his fishing rod*
> *Stood at the bank*
> *And watched with cold blood*
> *How the fish moved.*
> *I thought that as long as*
> *The water was bright, nothing could happen,*
> *He would not catch the fish*
> *With his fishing rod…"*

But I'm caught already, thinks Lily. He has reeled me in as surely as that fisherman. Cold bloodedly. She remembers how once, on a rare occasion when she was allowed outdoors at Globe Lane, she wandered down the garden towards a distant hedge, where there was a small stream, little more than a brook, an unnamed tributary of the River Tame, flowing alongside. The young boy who helped the gardener had caught a small trout, which he'd put in a tin bucket filled with water by his side. When Lily reached him, he grinned and plucked the fish out of the bucket, holding it out towards her, thrashing and wriggling, then deposited it onto her lap. Startled, she had stepped away from him in revulsion, flapping her hands like a fish herself. Mistaking her reaction, he picked up a stone and smashed it on the fish's head, repeatedly, until it stopped breathing and lay there inert on the grass, its cold unblinking eye staring up at her.

But Mr Godwit's eyes are closed, caught up in the music, to which he has given himself completely, the sequences of notes running lightly like water over stones.

> *"But soon the time was too long*
> *For this thief. He treacherously*
> *Made the stream murky*
> *And before I realized it*
> *His fishing rod stirred*
> *The fish flounced on it*
> *And with agitated blood*
> *I look down at the one who is deceived…"*

He pauses to glance at Lily, who has been following the musical notes on the manuscript, those indecipherable tadpoles swimming across the page, which she feels reverberate through her, connected to them by her proximity to him, transmitting from ivory to bone, slipping under her skin, swimming up inside her.

"There is another verse," he whispers, looking directly at her now. "It was once thought lost, but has recently resurfaced. I wonder whether to sing it to you or not."

"As you wish, sir," answers Lily softly. "I am enjoying the music very much."

"Very well then. Perhaps I shall."

He picks up the phrasing of the piece and once more closes his eyes. He sings from memory, for these words do not appear on the music.

> *"You who tarry by the golden spring*
> *Of secure youth*
> *Think still of the trout*
> *If you see danger, hurry by…"*

Godwit continues to play without singing, until he reaches the final line.

"Or else, too late, you'll bleed…"

He finishes playing. His fingers hang suspended above the keys. He opens his eyes, turns towards Lily and gently caresses her throat. She shivers.

She can't pretend she's not a willing participant, but she knows she wouldn't miss it if his hunger abated. She realises only too well the precariousness of her situation. She is only here under sufferance. Her duties as a maid are minimal. She is entirely dependent upon her ability to keep pleasing Mr Godwit for her continuing permission to remain there. It must be clear to the entire household what her role there truly is, though no one ever speaks of it, except Mrs Baines sometimes, obliquely, to notice when Lily has washed out her sanitary rags, expressing evident relief at the sight of them. What Sister Mary Frances of the Five Wounds always referred to as the Curse of Eve has become a source of blessing now to Lily, and she thanks God each time the blood appears, welcoming the cramping in her stomach with gratitude and relief. She sometimes thinks about leaving, but how would she engineer it? And where would she go? At the same time she enjoys being the centre of attention, the frequent treats, the petting and pampering, the nice clothes, the sense of power she has at times over him. She also knows, deep down, that the situation can only be a temporary one. Change is bound to happen eventually.

She takes hold of his hand, where it lies upon her throat and places it back upon the piano keyboard.

"Play me something lighter, can't you? Something to make me smile," she asks.

"Funny you should mention that," he says with a mischievous look in his eyes. "I've been thinking of what you might sing for our Christmas supper party."

"Sing? Me?"

"And why not? I do happen to know that you have sung

for a record at the Free Trade Hall."

"Along with about two hundred others."

"Your voice has already been heard by thousands of people up and down the land. How can you deny our small company?"

"You're teasing me."

Godwit strikes up on the piano, singing at the same time. '*Nymphs and shepherds, come away, come and play…*"

"I'm not singing that!"

"No. I'm not suggesting you should."

"What then?"

"A little tongue twister, something to make everyone smile." And he proceeds to teach her a short comic song, which she soon has by heart. "Perfect," he declares. "You'll be the toast of the town. Now, not a word to anyone till the party. Let this be our little secret."

A smiling Lily nods.

Christmas comes soon enough. Lily's second Christmas at Globe Lane. She has always enjoyed this time of year. At St Bridget's there had been a tree, and candles in the Chapel, and carols. The girls would make each other simple cards and gifts – a drawing, a painted pebble, a pressed flower.

At Globe Lane preparations are in full swing. Lily helps Mrs Baines decorate a huge tree in the hallway. She dragoons the three birds of a feather at one of the supper parties to make paper chains and lanterns, and then fetches a pair of stepladders, on which she climbs to hang them. Each of the three gentlemen takes it upon himself to solicitously place his hands upon her hips to steady her. There are delicious smells emanating daily from the kitchen as Mrs Cloudsdale prepares fresh oranges with cloves, mulls wine, bakes mince pies, brews fresh coffee. Excitement is high. Lily learns that Mr Godwit is especially generous when it comes to buying

Christmas presents for his staff. She wonders what her own gift might be.

On the last Friday before Christmas, Lily wonders whether there might be another larger gathering, as there was the previous year, when she wore the dove grey dress for the first time, but no. It is just to be Godwit, Snipe and Crake as usual. Lily is disappointed. She had hoped for a little more glitter and sparkle.

When Mr Snipe and Mr Crake arrive, it is immediately apparent that they have already been drinking. Their faces are flushed and their spirits are high. Snipe attempts to kiss Mrs Baines beneath a sprig of mistletoe he is carrying. She bats him away, red-faced and smiling, before taking her leave. Crake bows extravagantly before Lily.

"You are the angel from the top of the tree," he declares, "come down to bring glory to us mere mortals here below." Lily rolls her eyes. "I say, Godwit, we could stage our own Nativity, couldn't we? Lily here, having welcomed us as the Angel, can now be the Virgin Mary of course, while you, Snipe and I can be Shepherds, come to worship at her feet." He gets down clumsily onto his knees, dragging Godwit and Snipe along with him. "Then we can be the Three Wise Men – though not so very wise in your case, Snipe." And he begins to sing, leading the others in a procession around the room.

"We three kings of Orient are
One on a bus and one in a car
One on a scooter
Blowing his hooter
Following yonder star…"

"Oh Crake," says Godwit, "do stop being an ass."

"You're right," says Crake. "I am an ass. Lily, you can pretend to be Mary again and ride on my back to Bethlehem."

He gets down on all fours, looking up hopefully towards Lily, who rolls her eyes once more, shakes her head, but sits herself upon his back anyway. Crake brays triumphantly, causing Lily to leap away from him.

"Presents," she demands. "If you're the Three Kings, I demand my gifts, brought to me from afar!"

"Your wish is our command," says Snipe obligingly. "Gold, frankincense and myrrh."

"I bring frankincense," says Crake, picking himself back up from the floor and handing Lily a small bottle of perfume.

"I bring myrrh," declares Snipe, going down on one knee, holding out some honey and almond body lotion towards Lily. Just as Lily is about to accept it, he snatches it back and whispers *sotto voce*, though not so quietly that the others can't hear, "Promise me first to let me rub it onto you."

Lily tuts and takes it from him.

Godwit drags him roughly by the shoulder and leads him away.

"Godwit of course," says Snipe undeterred, "brings gold. Obviously."

Lily's eyes lock with Godwit's briefly before they each look away.

"Let's repair to the smoking room, shall we, where, if I'm not mistaken, Mrs Cloudsdale has left some hot mulled wine waiting for us?"

"Now you're talking," says Crake.

"*Ding dong merrily on high*," sings Snipe, following him.

Lily and Godwit are momentarily left alone.

"Here," he whispers, and picks a small box from the Christmas tree, which he places in her hands. "Open it."

She looks at him. "I've nothing for you," she says.

"Let's see how the evening unfolds, shall we?" he says, smiling.

Lily unwraps the box and lifts the lid. Inside indeed is gold. She takes it out and holds it up to the light.

"I saw it in the window at Hancock's in King Street," says Godwit, "and immediately thought of you."

It's a bracelet, a solid gold snake, with a double coil.

"Let me put it on for you," he says.

She holds out her arm, while he slips it over her wrist.

"Perfect," he says, and kisses it.

When they join Crake and Snipe in the smoking room, they find them hopping about with bird masks on their faces, like demented creatures from the Caucus Race in *Alice's Adventures in Wonderland*. "Prizes," they cry. "Prizes, prizes!"

They place a third mask on Godwit's face, then tie a piece of cloth tightly round Lily's eyes.

"Blind Man's Buff!" they chant, spinning her around.

They retreat to the corners of the room and sing in a quiet, slow, menacing tone.

"If you go down to the woods today
You're in for a big surprise
If you go down to the woods today
You'll hardly believe your eyes…"

Lily, giggling nervously, with arms stretched out in front of her, staggers about the room, trying to catch one of them. Still they sing.

"For every bear that ever there was
Will soon be there for certain because
Today's the day the Teddy Bears have their picnic…"

Snipe catches hold of Lily's wrist and pulls her down onto his knee. "Guess who I am," he growls, removing his mask. Lily feels forward with her fingers. Snipe guides them to his face.

"Oh," she shrieks, "I'd recognise that nose anywhere –

Mr Snipe!" And she pulls off her blindfold.

"My best feature," he sighs theatrically.

"What's my prize?" she says brightly.

"A kiss from your captive," says Snipe.

"Very well," says Lily, and Snipe makes an instant lunge for her, but Lily is too quick. She turns her right cheek towards him, pointing to it with her finger. Disappointed, Snipe obliges with a chaste peck, before replacing his bird mask.

"Again," he commands.

"No," replies Godwit. "I'm bored with this game. Let's have a song instead. Come here," he says to Lily, sitting himself at the piano stool and directing her to stand beside him. "Gentlemen, do you remember when you first had the good fortune to meet Lily?"

"Like it was yesterday," says Crake.

"What was she doing?" asks Godwit, beginning to play a few introductory chords while he speaks. "Can you recall?"

"She was serving us coffee. Isn't that right, Snipe?"

"The best cup of coffee I ever tasted," Snipe agrees, "served by these fair hands," and he tries to take them in his. Lily pulls them smartly away and playfully raps his knuckles. Crake and Godwit laugh.

"You're being very naughty, Mr Snipe," says Lily, teasing, "and unless you promise to be a good boy, I shan't sing to you after all."

"Oh, I'll be good, Lily, I promise," he says, sitting down cross-legged at her feet upon the floor. "As good as gold," he adds, eyeing her bracelet.

"I'm glad to hear it. Mr Godwit and I have been practising this for weeks."

Godwit has by now completed the introduction. He counts Lily in. "One-two-three-four..." And Lily launches into the song, laughing.

"All I want is a proper cup of coffee
Made in a proper copper coffee pot
I may be off my dot
But I want a proper coffee in a proper copper pot
Iron coffee pots and tin coffee pots
They're no use to me
If I can't have a proper cup of coffee
In a proper copper coffee pot
I'll have a cup of tea…"

As soon as she finishes, the three gentlemen burst into spontaneous applause, complete with whistles and cheers. Lily looks around the room and beams. Godwit pulls her down onto his lap while remaining seated at the piano stool. As he does so, she suddenly stops short. A memory from that visit to the City Art Gallery flashes through her…

She and Pearl are standing before a painting. *The Awakening Conscience* by William Holman Hunt. Pearl is gaily prattling as she always is, saying how she'd like to have a dress one day like the woman in the painting is wearing, and live in a big house like that, so richly furnished, and be able to sit on the lap of such a handsome, smiling gentleman. Lily lets her chatter on, not wanting to cloud her happiness by pointing out some of the painting's less comfortable aspects. The woman, Lily notices, is not wearing a wedding ring, yet her expensive clothes suggest she is in some way being kept. The word 'mistress' hovers at the edge of Lily's consciousness. The woman appears to be on the point of rising up from the gentleman's lap. The expression on her face seems stricken with the realisation of what she has become. Amid the sumptuous furnishings of the room, the polished rosewood piano, the gilded cushions, the highly decorative curtains, the contemporary carpet design, a ball of wool is unravelling, and under the round table a cat is devouring a dead bird.

Pearl skips away after a while, bored, in search of new stimulation, but Lily lingers longer before it, wondering what might have happened next in the story being depicted. Did the woman find the courage to leave? Or did she perhaps really love the handsome man at the piano and decide to carry on with the arrangement? Was the gentleman married? Or, if he was free, might he in the end come to realise he cannot be without her and ask her to marry him? No. She realises that that is not the way such stories usually end. More likely, if she did not leave herself, he would grow tired of her, and cast her off like last year's glove.

Sister Mary Frances of the Five Wounds swoops in beside her. She takes in the entire scenario of the painting in a single glance.

"Let this be a warning to you, Lily Shilling, not to succumb to the temptations of the flesh. They will only lead to eternal fire and damnation. Come along, child, and don't dawdle…"

Now, in Globe Lane, this all comes flooding back to her. She looks at herself, sitting on Mr Godwit's cat-like lap at the piano, pinned in his arms like a caged bird. The room spins around her…

"Bravo!" the gentlemen still cry. Snipe waltzes back in bearing a tray balancing cups and saucers, cream jug and sugar bowl, singing. "*Have a proper cup of coffee from a proper copper coffee pot.*" He is looking extremely pleased with himself.

"Let's have another game first," announces Crake. "A new one."

He then proceeds to tie the cloth around Lily's eyes again.

"I thought you said it was a different game?"

"It is," he says. "You'll see."

"But how?" asks Lily, "if you blindfold me once more?"

"A-ha," says Snipe, wagging his finger at Crake, "she has you there."

"Very well." He unties the cloth. "Crake and Godwit, form an arch in the centre of the room, while I place a chair here and another there on either side of Lily. She and I then have to walk in a circle around the chairs, passing under the arch each time. When the music stops, whoever is caught inside the arch is the loser…"

"… or winner," chips in Snipe, "depending upon the prize."

"Quite so. Now – are you ready?" asks Crake.

"Ready," says Lily.

Snipe and Godwit begin to sing as Lily and Crake eye each other warily, then scamper around the room, passing under the arch as cautiously as they can.

"Oranges and lemons
Say the bells of St Clement's
You owe me five farthings
Say the bells of St Martin's
When will you pay me
Say the bells of Old Bailey
When I grow rich
Say the bells of Shoreditch
When will that be
Say the bells of Stepney
I do not know
Says the Great Bell of Bow…"

Lily and Crake are now darting in and out of the arch faster and faster, while Snipe and Godwit speed up the tempo of their singing as it nears its climax.

"Here comes a candle to light you to bed
Here comes a chopper to chop – off – your – head!"

On the word "head" Godwit and Snipe bring down their arms from the arch to capture Lily. Godwit holds her tightly while she squeals with laughter. Snipe takes the blindfold and binds her wrists with it behind her back. They then lead her towards Crake as if to the scaffold.

All three solemnly put back on their bird masks.

Birds of a feather, recalls Lily with a rush of fear.

The air feels suddenly cold. She tries to picture herself some place else but finds she cannot.

Godwit takes the cloth from off her wrists and ties it round her eyes.

"Prizes... prizes... prizes," chant the three men together.

Lily feels the golden snake coil tightly around her arm. Drops of perfume are sprinkled onto her face and neck. Somebody's fingers roughly rub the honey and almond lotion into her skin, while somebody else pulls down her chin to force open her mouth. They then proceed to take it in turns to dip their beaks.

Squawk, squawk.

Gobble, gobble.

When Lily comes round, she has no idea how much time has passed, or how long she has been left lying there. She has not been carried back upstairs on this occasion, simply abandoned, when the party games were over.

She's cold. The fire in the grate has gone out. The lights have all been switched off, and she gropes her way along the floor towards the door. She takes hold of the handle and tries to use it to help her to stand. Every part of her aches. It takes every ounce of effort she can muster just to heave herself upright. She leans her back against the door frame while she tries to steady her breathing. After a minute or so, she feels strong enough to face the stairs. She goes out into the hall, closing the door to the smoking room behind her, trying to make not the slightest sound. She listens to the house in Globe Lane, whose creaks and groans have become so familiar to her during these last eighteen months. She hears the slow, measured tick of the long case clock in the hall, which she passes now. Tick, tock. Tick, tock. How many other footsteps have tried to match their tread to the clock's unceasing rhythm before her? She has watched Mr Godwit on Sunday evenings take out the key from inside the case, insert it into the centre of the clock's face, as though bent upon a mission to submit it to his will, wind it forcefully several times, check it against his own watch, which he takes from his waistcoat pocket, satisfying himself that the two timepieces are in agreement with one another, before striding back to his study. On one occasion he had beckoned Lily over to him, placed her hand tightly within his so that they might wind the large key together, then held his watch up to her ear, so that she might hear its inner workings spin and whir. Then he had passed one hand over it with a flourish, like a magician, and made it disappear, leaving Lily staring wide-eyed as he left her, with only the slow, heavy tick of the long case clock for company. Like now. How she wishes she too could make time disappear so conveniently, wipe the last year from her memory, as though none of these things had happened.

The portrait of Mary Moffat looks out towards her from its shadowed recess next to the clock in the entrance hall. Lily approaches it, tries to get her own eyes as close to Mary's as she can to see what she might see there. Who knows what sights they've witnessed here down the years? The countless comings and goings. Is it really possible to be in two places at one time? As I tried to be this evening? As you are, she whispers, away in Africa, yet still here on this wall? Dead for more than half a century but still alive in this painting? Is that what the expression on your face is trying to convey? Had you already decided to leave when you were sitting before the artist? Have you watched many young girls like me arrive and then creep away again some time later?

Laura, thinks Lily. It has been months since she first discovered those diary entries hidden at the back of the chest of drawers in her room at the top of the house. Why has she not thought to look at them since? Because, she knows all too bitterly now, she has been acting out some fairy-tale. Nursery rhymes and parlour games. *Blind Man's Buff, Oranges and Lemons. Alice in Wonderland.* Packs of cards secretly marked, dealt by Teddy Bears and Birds of Prey. *Beggar My Neighbour, Flinch.*

She drags herself painfully up the stairs, pausing every few steps, until at last she reaches her tiny room at the top of the house, though even there, she knows, she is not safe, for it is not her room, nothing at all in this house is hers, not her clothes, not her time, not even her thoughts, which she has allowed herself to offer up to others, to shape and influence and own.

What was it that the dressmaker, Miss Tyler, had said to her? "You're very lucky." Yes. That was it. "Many girls would give anything to have what you have…"

She reaches into the back of the chest of drawers, finds where the folded pieces of paper have been hidden away, takes them out, switches on the lamp beside her bed, wraps herself in a blanket and begins to read.

To the girl who comes after me – read and be warned...

I come 'ere to Globe Lane the day afore yesterday from the workhouse in Tintwistle, where I was born. It were called The Stocks and it were a mean place. I were glad to be fetched out...

Mrs Baines is very kind. She is the housekeeper. She lets me get up late. Till I get settled, she says. Then I'll 'ave to work like everyone else. I 'ave new clothes – a serge blue skirt, white shirt, maroon cardigan. They belonged to t' girl afore me. She must've been bigger 'n me, cos they're all too long an' too wide. I've 'ad to alter 'em. A good thing they taught you to sew at The Stocks, Mrs Baines says, and she gives me more clothes to mend. These are the master's – Mr Godwit's – so I 'ave to be careful. I'm to sew on new buttons. After, Mrs Baines says the master were pleased...

Today I got some new boots. The ones the girl afore me wore she din't leave behind, and I din't 'ave any of me own. I'm dead pleased wi' 'em. They look nice. Mrs Baines says I've to polish 'em every day, an' I mean to...

I've not seen t' master yet. But I've heard 'im. 'E 'olds what Mrs Baines calls 'Supper Parties' on Friday nights. 'Im an' 'is friends play t' piano in t' smoking room an' sing. Music Hall songs. Rude ones, I think, from t' way they all laugh after. I like the piano. I ain't never seen one before. In The Stocks we 'ad a 'armonium, but we weren't allowed anywhere near it. It's my job to polish the piano. Sometimes, if I think no one's about, I let my fingers run up an' down it. I like the sound it makes...

Mrs Baines is all in a flap today. It's what she calls "a special occasion". Mr Godwit's invited a whole lot o' people for dinner. Not just his usual pals. But posh folk from miles around. What Mrs Baines refers to as "big pots". I don't think she likes 'em much. They go puttin' on their airs an' graces, she says, but they're no better 'n you or I, Laura. I like it when she uses me proper name. In t' workhouse, they just used to shout "You", an' since I come here everyone calls me "Laur". I don't mind it much. But I prefer me full name. Laura. I 'ave a dim picture in me mind of me mother singin' it to me on 'er lap. But I don't know if this is true or not, or if I just made it up, summat I wish 'ud 'appened, but might not 'ave. Like a fairy story… Anyway, it were all 'ands to t' pump to get the 'ouse ready in t' time. I 'ad to polish all t' knives an' t' forks an' that. "Be careful wi' 'em," said Mrs Baines, "they're silver." And then later, "Don't dawdle," as I tried to see me reflection in one o' t' spoons. I din't recognise meself...

Everyone's gone now and the 'ouse is quiet, except for t' tickin' o' that big clock in th' hallway. I like the sound it makes, slow and steady, like a kind old man sittin' in t' corner of a room, tappin' 'is pipe on a chair, then rockin' back an' to. I've 'eard folk mention Old Father Time, an' this is who I think of when I 'ear that clock a-tickin' downstairs. It lulls me to sleep sometimes. But tonight I couldn't get off at all, so I thought I'd go an' take a closer look at it, for I don't 'ave time during t' day. I slipped me cardie over me nightie and crept down, tryin' not to step on any o' t' stairs that creak. I were just lookin' at t'clock – it 'as a sun wi' a smilin' face on in t' middle – when I 'eard someone cough behind me. I turned round an' it were Mr Godwit. I could've died. "Beg pardon, sir," I said, bobbin' up an' down, then tried to dash away. But before I'd reached t' bottom step, he called me back. "You're the new girl, aren't you?" he said, and stepped towards me. 'E switched on one o' t' lights, then said, "Let's get a proper look at you." I pulled me cardie tight across me chest. "Laura, isn't it?" "Yes, sir." "And what are you doing up and out of bed at this hour?" "I couldn't sleep, sir." "I sympathise. I have nights like that too sometimes." He looked at me full in t' face, till I looked down. 'E 'ad a key in 'is 'and. 'E saw me lookin' at it an' said, "It's one of my duties. To wind the old clock." I stood there, not knowing what to do. I started to shiver. "You'd best go back to bed, Laura," he said. "You'll catch cold. And we wouldn't want that, would we?" I bobbed another curtsey. "No, sir. Yes, sir. Good night, sir." Then I scarpered upstairs as fast as I could...

A few days later, Mrs Baines asked to see me. She looked right cross. I worried what I'd done wrong. "I understand you were wandering about the house the other night, after all the guests had gone home?" "Yes, Miss. Sorry, Miss. I couldn't sleep." She sighed an' looked away. She din't speak then for a long time. I began to wonder if she'd forgot about me an' if I should just go. But she 'adn't gi' me leave, so I waited. I could feel meself start to blush. It were as if I knew what she were goin' to say next. "It appears Mr Godwit has taken a shine to you, Laura. He's asked if you might serve him and his friends their coffee at their next Supper Party this Friday. Well? What's the matter? Cat got your tongue?" "Sorry, Miss. No, Miss. I'm sure I'm very grateful." She looked at me, and 'er eyes narrowed. Then she tutted an' shook 'er 'ead. "You're nothing but skin and bone. I can't think what he…" She put both 'er 'ands on me shoulders to straighten me shirt. "You'll need a new blouse," she said, "and a smart pinafore to wear over it, and a little cap." She were examinin' me like she were a magpie wi' 'er sharp eyes an' pinchin' fingers, lookin' for summat shiny to pounce on. "I expect you can manage with the skirt, and the boots are hardly worn in yet..."

An' that were 'ow it started...

I were ever so nervous come Friday night. I were feared I might spill t' coffee an' make a fool of meself. But it all passed off like clockwork. Mr Godwit introduced me to two other gentlemen – Mr Snipe and Mr Crake –

who each bowed to me in turn, like they was in a play or summat. I din't know what I were supposed to do, so I just curtseyed. Mr Godwit told me to take no notice of 'em, an' that I were to come back in 'alf an 'our to fetch th' empty cups. When next day Mrs Baines asked me how it'd gone, I told her what'd 'appened, an' I could see she were relieved. "Yes," she said, "Mr Snipe and Mr Crake do seem quite silly sometimes. Try to ignore them if you can..."

It were 'ard to ignore 'em, though...

Next thing I know I'm not just servin' coffee. I'm to stay an' light their cigars. Then they're wantin' to dance wi' me. I tell 'em I don't know 'ow, but that don't stop 'em askin'. An' we sing songs, an' we play games, an' they sit me on their knee, an' they feed me sweets on a spoon, an' I can see me reflection in it, an' in t' champagne glass they make me drink from, an' everything looks all twisted an' out o' shape, an' I can't seem to recognise anythin', an' I can see t' flames from t' fire flickerin' in their eyes, an' they're right up close, an' yet it all seems far away, like I'm so tiny I might slip through a crack in t' floor...

I wake up, an' I'm lying on t' top of t' bed. I 'ave no recollection of 'ow I got 'ere. Someone must've carried me. The room's spinning. I drag me head up from t' pillow and look down. Me clothes 'ave all been disarranged. I 'ear t' clock in the 'allway downstairs. Tick, tock. Tick, tock. An' I fall asleep...

'E comes up most nights now...

I don't like it. I don't like it. I want to tell 'im to stop, but 'ow can I? 'E'd send me away. I don't want to go back to t' workhouse. I'd rather this than that...

This mornin' I were sick on t' back step, just outside t' kitchen. I couldn't help it. I'm sick all t' time these days. Mrs Baines saw me. She knows...

I've 'ad to let out the skirt to 'ow it was when I first come 'ere. Soon even that won't be enough to stop me showin'. Is that what 'appened to t'other girl, I wonder? Where did she go? Where did they tek 'er...?

I 'ave to run away. There's nowt else for it. Last night I 'eard Mr Godwit an' Mrs Baines arguin' downstairs. Mr Godwit started shoutin'. "Don't go blaming me for your own failings," Mrs Baines shouted back. "May I remind you," said Mr Godwit, "who it is that pays your wages?" His voice were like ice. "And your sick son's hospital bills?" I 'adn't known about that. Mrs Baines never said. It explains a lot. ..

So I'm going. Tonight. I've no idea where. But I'll find somewhere. I'm going to

Leave this diary at t' back of t' wardrobe, hopin' that whoever comes after me'll find it, read it an' not make t' same mistakes I 'ave. It's gone quiet now downstairs. I can 'ear th'old clock ticking away. Tick, tock. Tick, tock. But time an' tide waits for no one. Goodbye...

Lily puts down the diary, rubs her eyes. She hears the long case clock in the hall below strike the hour. One, two, three, four.

Four o'clock.

She knows she must leave Globe Lane. Right now. This minute. She can put it off not a moment longer. She must not allow herself even the slightest room for hesitation, or else her resolve might weaken.

She pours the cold water from the jug by her bed into the basin and washes herself rapidly and roughly, trying to scrub away all trace of the night's events from her mouth and body. She finds the clothes she arrived in from St Bridget's and quickly puts them on. She will leave how she came, taking nothing that was not hers before. She looks at the dove grey dress that Miss Tyler had made for her looped on the peg behind the door. It's not a dress at all, she decides, but a costume for a play, a part she knows she must never play again. It hangs there like a skin that's been shed, let someone else wear it now. She carefully puts Laura's diary to the back of the chest of drawers where she first found it. Maybe another girl – and already she knows for certain that there'll be another as surely as day follows night – will find it sooner than Lily did.

Last of all she picks up the wooden yacht made for her by her grandfather, packs it away in its tissue and shoe box, wraps it in its brown paper and string, before adding its final covering of cloth, and holds it close to her.

She's ready.

She creeps down the stairs as the long case clock chimes the half hour, tiptoes past the portrait of Mary Moffat, whose eyes still refuse to yield their secrets, until she reaches the front door. Taking a deep breath she opens it, steps deliberately and purposefully outside, feels the sharp December frost on her face, sees it glinting on the gold bracelet, the coiled snake, still clinging to her arm which, in her haste, she has forgotten to take off. She studies it. This could be worth a lot of money, she thinks, several weeks of food at least, but she cannot bear the prospect of it clinging to her skin a moment longer. She pulls it off defiantly and flings it behind her into the hall, where it rattles and hisses on the tiled floor. She slams the front door shut, not caring who can hear her now, and runs.

*

Lily runs.

The gravel scritters and scrunches under her feet as she hurtles down the gravel drive of Globe Lane and out towards the road. In the eighteen months since she first arrived, she has never been out of the house, apart from to hang the washing at the back, or that one time she wandered down towards the brook, where the gardener's boy smashed the trout's gasping mouth with a stone. If ever anything was needed from the shops, it was either delivered, or Mrs Baines would go to fetch it. Once, when Lily offered to do this, she was told no, another time maybe, later. But that time never came. She never even accompanied Mrs Baines, never mind going out alone. And so, as she runs now into the dark of this December night in 1930, she has no idea where she should go.

She reaches the end of the drive. Left or right. She remembers on her very first night asking Mrs Baines which way lay Audenshaw, so she could picture St Bridget's, and she was told west. Now, she sets her face to the east, where the first streaks of light are beginning to poke through the black, and runs towards them, particles of change constantly in motion, randomly colliding. She has never before, she realises, until this very moment, made a decision for herself. At St Bridget's each day was carefully prescribed, like the order of service for the mass, fixed and unchanging. At Globe Lane her duties were selected for her, a pre-ordained sequence of acts, like a play already written, with set scenes and allocated lines. Now, as she runs towards the eastern sky, she is acting out her own choices, acutely conscious that other, alternative versions of herself are existing in parallel somewhere. What if she'd not read Laura's diary? What if, when she'd opened the front door, she'd decided not to step out after all? What if she'd headed west instead of east?

Winter. Night. A hard frost glinting. Stars arching clear and sharp. Black ink sky. Breath freezing in statues.

A narrow brick lane cuts between backs of houses, cheese-slicing the dark, a fixed point on the horizon she runs towards, footsteps pecking the stone, a beat too late. She pauses. Her shadow halts a nanosecond later, almost as if one of the other selves which split away from her is now following her, curious. The cold blurs her eyes. The image shifts. Double vision replicates in a tear of ice, focus pulled out and in, slipped frame mirroring, twisted reflection in a spoon, time-warped worm hole. Cross-over from the meeting point, this horizon shape-shifter walks to meet her, catches at her frozen breath, then is sucked back within. Curiouser and curiouser.

Ten minutes later she is forced to reconsider. She reaches a fence topped with barbed wire guarding a building site. '*Private Property*,' a sign screams out. '*Danger*,' shrieks another. '*Keep Out*,' commands a third. '*Unprotected Mine Shafts*,' warns a fourth.

Just as she's contemplating whether or not to scale the fence, a light from a torch is shone directly into her eyes. A security guard is running towards her, accompanied by a ferocious-looking dog, who barks and growls at her warningly.

"Oi!" shouts the officer. "Can't you read?"

Lily, paralysed by the light in her eyes, says nothing.

"You're only a child," he says, as he gets closer to her, his tone softening. "What are you doing out at this time of night?"

Lily still can't think what to say.

"Are you in some sort of trouble?" he asks, looking at her as he might an injured bird, not wanting to alarm her, in case she might flap against the fence and break a wing.

"What's in there?" she manages to say at last. "Why can't you let me in?"

"It's dangerous, that's why."

"I'm not frightened," she says.

"That's as may be, but this is where the old Astley Pit used to be. It was reckoned to be the deepest mine in the world when it was first sunk. Hundreds and hundreds of feet, it were. It's shut now, of course. Has been nigh on thirty years now. But since they started building here, they keep stumbling across more and more unmarked shafts. You could fall down one of them as easy as winking. Especially when it's as late as this."

Lily imagines the possibility, falling endlessly in the dark, rolling over and over, until she finally lands with a thud. Like Alice. Except that she knows it would not be like Alice. And even if it were, she wouldn't want that either. She's had more than enough pools of tears, of prizes and caucus races and 'drink me' and 'off with her head' to last her a lifetime, a lifetime she doesn't want to cut short.

"Sorry," she manages to say at last. "I'm just a little lost, that's all. What lies that way?" And she points diagonally away from the fence towards where a cold full moon glitters low in the sky.

"Er... let me think," says the security officer, scratching his head. "The Audenshaw Reservoirs, I think" he says.

"Thank you," she says and instantly darts off in that direction.

"Though what you want to go there for I can't begin to imagine. It's ever so late."

Lily runs.

She hears the man calling after her, the dog barking. She has a vague impression of a pale white rabbit with tiny pink eyes, blinking rapidly in the light of his own torch, evidently as startled by their encounter as *she* was.

The light in the sky continues to grow. Lily hardly meets a soul on the roads she runs down. She is following as straight a line as she can, so whenever she reaches a junction, or a fork in the road, she takes whichever path appears to be keeping her on course towards the distant moon. At St Bridget's the girls used to try and frighten each other by describing what they thought they saw in the craters of the moon. A witch, a hare, an old man, a black cat. On the way home from when she, Jenny and Pearl had been singing in the Manchester Children's Choir at the Free Trade Hall, Pearl became convinced that the moon was following her and started to panic. "Look," she had cried, "first it was between those two houses, now it's between these two. Why doesn't it stay in one place?"

Lily had tried to explain to her that it was simply because it was so big that it appeared to be everywhere at once.

"But it looks so small up there in the sky," wailed Pearl. "I don't understand. What will it do when it catches me?"

Lily had stopped walking then and bent down so that she was the same size that Pearl was. "The moon is nothing to be afraid of," she said. "It's lighting our way back home for us. Let's stand and look at it head on and imagine what it might be like up there."

Pearl slipped her hand into Lily's as they both looked up. "Is it really made of green cheese?" she asked.

"What do you think?" asked Lily back.

Pearl shook her head, smiling. "No, that would be silly. I think it looks lonely. Perhaps that's why she's following me?"

Lily smiled. Jenny took Pearl's other hand and quietly began to sing.

"Oh the moon shines bright on Charlie Chaplin…"

Then Lily joined in with the second line.

"His boots are cracking…"

Reassured, Pearl felt able to join in on the next.

"For want of blacking…"

All three then marched in step as one towards the front door of Trafalgar House.

*"And his baggy trousers will need mending
Before we send him
To the Dardanelles…"*

Remembering this helps Lily to quicken her pace as she chases the moon down a dozen unknown streets, ducking into back alleys, skirting factories and sewage farms, dodging the early morning trams, until the man in the moon puts down the lantern he's been carrying on his back, the witch folds her skirts across it, the black cat curls up beside them, the hare closes its milky eyes, and the last vestiges of them disappear, just as she climbs a short steep embankment up to the edge of the Audenshaw Reservoirs.

There are three of them stretching out ahead of her, covering more than two hundred and fifty acres. They were constructed by John Frederick Bateman fifty years before as part of the massive Longdendale Chain of seven reservoirs linked by the River Etherow to bring fresh water to Manchester and Salford from the hills of Derbyshire. Standing on the embankment Lily begins to feel what a cold day this is going to be, already is. The ground beneath her feet is hard with frost. The sky is iron, the water glass. A thin crust of ice is forming on the surface. Black moorhens are trapped in the shallows by the stiff, brittle reeds at the shoreline, poking through the ice like broken spears. A wind has started to pick up. It knifes the air.

Lily looks along the straight edge of the embankment. Nearly five yards wide and more than five feet above the water, it arrows away from her. It's the Nico Ditch, built so long ago that nobody is quite sure when. Some say it was a boundary marker between the kingdoms of Mercia and Northumbria. Others that it was built as a defensive fortification to keep out the Vikings. Legend has it that it was dug in a single night by the people of Manchester, with each man allotted a given span, which he was required to pile up with earth equal to his own height, and that a great battle took place there, which had given the nearby towns of Gorton and Reddish their names, from "Gore Town" and "Red Ditch".

But there is no red today, only the steel monochromes of earth and sky, ice and fog. No clash of sword on shield, only the lost cries of lone birds and hungry ghosts. A grey heron lifts from the far bank, slow and heavy. Its wide wings plough the still air. Its needle eyes scour the surface for fish, trapped beneath the skin of ice. Cautiously it comes in to land, its splayed, plate-like feet skitter and slide. Regaining its equilibrium it raises its beak like a missile. Beneath the ice the fish swim by believing they are safe. The heron takes aim, fires. The ice cracks and splinters with the impact. Its beak spears an unwary trout, scoops it up, swallows it, whole and wriggling.

On the far side of the reservoir, Lily watches this.

A rust-coated dredger slowly steams towards her, looming out of the mist. It carves its way through the ice, shovelling it into deep, piled pockets.

The heron is trapped. It beats its wings in a futile effort to break free its slowly sinking legs. It throws back its head and emits a long, protracted cry for help, a hoarse croaking rattle, a painful, rasping underwater gurgle, which is drowned out by the sound of the dredger's horn booming through the fog, grey mass heavy with regret, hanging. Out on the ice the creature cries, clanking chains scraping the deck, splintering hull stuck fast as in a frozen sea on the edge of the known world, howling, seeking its lost twin.

Lily looks away, sees herself reflected in the surface of the water, pitted steel wire, binding her wrists, lashed to the masthead, plunging, butchered bird around her neck, which stares back, accusing, the voice inside her skull, dredged up from the reservoir floor, from where all the smaller fish rise to the surface, their mouths gaping, as they press against the ice, like Pearl and Jenny, and all the girls at St Bridget's, singing in the chapel.

Promise you'll come back for me.

The shattering ice cracks. The heron breaks free.

Lily watches it fly to the far bank. They face each other on opposite sides, Lily's hand raised in recognition, or farewell. Till next time.

The ship's horn sounds.

Lily runs.

By eight she has left the reservoirs behind. She plunges into Denton Wood, where her feet crunch on the dry, frozen bones of fledgling birds and her face is scratched by thicket and thorn, but still the Nico Ditch holds her in its grasp. Holt Wood, Cringle Fields, Ladybarn. Debdale, Ryder Brow, Crowcroft. Through Levenshulme and Rusholme to Fallowfield. Sometimes it disappears altogether, dug up, cut through, built over, but still she feels her steps directed by the imprint of its old forgotten route, her feet pursuing the ancient highway, even when it's lost from sight, passing beneath the Thirlmere Aqueduct, paved over by Matthews Lane, then Old Hall Lane, before spilling out near Platt Fields.

Where the ditch has become a road.

Lily runs headlong into the city. It slaps her full in the face, the morning in full swing. Vans and lorries are delivering goods. Cars and buses clog the streets. People swarm, heads down, bodies bent, to offices and factories, cursing Lily, who runs against the tidal flow, as if she means to part the Red Sea. She steals an apple from a market stall, leaving angry voices skriking in her wake. She pauses briefly to catch her breath outside a draper's, where shop assistants put up Christmas lights and decorations. She watches in awed fascination a store front mannequin being undressed, its stiff, pink lifeless limbs being twisted and detached as its shape is reconfigured, hobbled and deformed to fit the latest fashion, its blank, featureless face staring out unblinkingly at Lily.

Dropping the apple core into the gutter, she sets off once more. She has no idea of where she is, or where she's going. Something will tell her, she thinks, when it is time to stop. The Nico Ditch will fade and dwindle, peter out or disappear completely, and then, perhaps, she'll know.

It has brought her to the thunderous roar of Wilmslow Road. She waits for what seems several minutes vainly seeking a gap in the endless traffic so that she might cross it, but every time she dares to place a foot upon the road, the angry blares of motor horns send her scurrying back. She becomes aware of a dark-skinned man wearing a red and gold tasselled hat upon his head waiting beside her. He is sucking on a hookah pipe, wreathed in smoke, hot liquid bubbling in a glass bowl. He stands by the edge of the road, where he waits patiently, while Lily keeps trying to dart across, each time losing her nerve.

"It's impossible," she shouts.

The dark-skinned man smiles. "Keep your temper," he says, so softly she barely hears him. "Look." He points to a pair of rats huddled against the lee of the pavement below them. "Watch, then follow." The rats raise their snouts to scent the air. With fatalistic determination they launch themselves into the centre of the road. "Now," says the dark-skinned man with the hookah pipe. He takes Lily's hand and, looking straight ahead, he follows the rats with unhurried slowness, never once breaking his stride. The cars and buses honk their horns like angry geese. Cyclists ring their bells. Drivers shout and curse, but nevertheless they brake, or swerve to avoid them, and Lily reaches the other side unscathed. She looks around to thank the dark-skinned man smoking the hookah, but he has already gone, a coil of vapour lost among the crowds thronging the pavement, a caterpillar patiently inching away. The rats, Lily notices, have already plunged into Platt Fields, where she follows them.

Standing in the shadow of a statue of a large bearded man, wearing a tall stove-pipe hat, she tries to work out which way she should go next. The Park is a labyrinth of footpaths criss-crossing the grass, heading off towards trees, leading to a bowling green, tennis courts, a pavilion. A boating lake, a museum, an old Hall. A chapel, an amphitheatre, a maze. The Nico Ditch threads its way between them.

Lily runs.

But before she has gone far, she catches her foot in a

rabbit hole. She trips and falls, rolling down a muddy slope, until she collides with a bench, where an old woman is feeding crusts of mouldy bread to a gossip of pigeons. She has a greasy piece of cotton tied around her head like a turban.

"Look what the wind blew in," she says, as Lily picks herself up and brushes herself down. She checks she still has the cloth bundle safely with her. She does. She has not let go of it once. She hopes that nothing's been broken. She rubs her head. She's beginning to feel distinctly unsteady. The old woman feeding the pigeons takes her arm.

"You'd best sit down," she says. "Every path has its puddle."

"Thank you."

"And the moral of that is, learn to walk before you run."

"But I…"

"Great haste makes great waste. Grasp all, lose all."

"Yes, I suppose, but…"

"But me no buts. Where there's a will, there's a way. Cut your coat according to your cloth."

Lily nods. She touches her head again, winces.

"No use crying over spilled milk. What's your name?"

Lily opens her mouth as if to answer, then shuts it again.

The old woman tuts. "A tree is known by its fruit, my dear."

Lily looks down. She feels that if she is not careful she might start to cry.

"Empty vessels make the most noise," says the old woman, shaking out the last remaining crumbs of bread in front of the pigeons. "And the moral of that is, still waters run deep. A bad penny always turns up. Grasp the nettle. Strike while the iron's hot." She starts to rummage through the pockets of her voluminous coat and finally pulls out from one of them a rather grubby looking handkerchief, which she passes across to Lily.

"Oh… thank you, but I…"

"Never look a gift horse in the mouth."

Lily reluctantly takes the handkerchief and dabs it to the bruise on her head.

The old woman produces a small tin which, when she opens it, contains pepper. She picks up a few grains, rubs them between her fingers, and raises them towards her nose, whereupon she sneezes loudly.

"Bless you," says Lily.

"*Gesundheit*," replies the old woman. "There's nothing like a good sneeze for clearing out the system. It's almost as good as crying." She eyes Lily keenly. " *'It opens the lungs, it washes the countenance, exercises the eyes, and softens the temper. So cry away'*."

"I'm lost," Lily is eventually able to say.

"Home is where the heart is," says the old woman. "And the moral of that is, we never miss the water till the well runs dry." She holds out her hand to the side. Lily wonders if she is meant to take it. "Handkerchief," declares the old woman.

"Yes, of course," says Lily, handing it back. "Thank you."

"Ah well, tide and time wait for no one. The early bird catches the worm." She gathers her many bags around her, heaves herself up and starts to waddle away, before half-turning back to Lily. "I used to be a Duchess, you know," she says, tapping the side of her nose with a crooked, stained finger. "And the moral of that is, never count your chickens. Still – you know what they say? A bird in hand is better than none." She smiles, disconcertingly revealing blackened stumps. She hobbles away, tunelessly croaking.

" '*The woods are lovely dark and deep*
But I have promises to keep
And miles to go before I sleep
And miles to go before I sleep…' "

Lily watches her go. The pigeons peck and scratch about her feet, hoping for more scraps. Lily shakes her head. "I could do with some food myself," she says to them.

On the far side of the park she sees a café, with a few desultory tables empty outside, and makes her way down to it. She's feeling less dizzy now, but decides to walk rather than run. It's open, but she has no money, so she heads towards a dustbin at the back, where she hopes there might be some of the morning's leftovers already deposited.

As she raises the lid, recoiling from the stench of rotting meat and vegetables, a voice stops her. At first she thinks it might be the proprietor about to call the police, but when she turns, she sees it is a tramp, wearing a threadbare, patched coat with a battered top hat.

"No room," says the Top Hat. "Ours," and he flings out a hand to indicate two accomplices, lurking behind him, one a very tall, unshaven man, with long hands and large ears, a forest of hair sticking out of each of them, the other a very small man, crouching on the ground, with his head resting on his knees, his hands over his head, who appears to be comatose.

"No room," shouts Top Hat again.

Lily replaces the dustbin lid and starts to hurry away from them.

"Wait." He produces a small hip flask from a flap beneath one of his coat's many patches. "Care to join us for some…" he pauses, shaking the flask enticingly from side to side… "tea?" he asks.

"No, thank you," says Lily.

"I thought you'd never ask," says Large Ears. The two men begin wrestling for it, knocking each other to the ground. Top Hat drops the hip flask, which is snatched up by Comatose. In one sure lightning quick motion, he unscrews the cap, drinks the contents in a single draught, screws the cap back onto the flask, which he then hurls high into the air, while the other two are still fighting, and resumes his original dormant position.

"I'm sorry," says Lily, catching the flask as it falls. "I've not got time…"

"Time," remarks Top Hat bitterly, having pinned down Large Ears, who flails at him helplessly with flapping fists. He lifts his head and spits. "If you knew time like I do," he adds, "you wouldn't be so cavalier about saying you hadn't got any. You'd hold onto it for dear life." His eye lights on the hip flask. He thrusts out a hand. Lily drops it into the waiting palm. He grasps it greedily. When he realises it's empty, he howls like a dog in pain. "I see your game," he snarls, staggering back to his feet and lurching towards Lily.

Lily runs.

She leaves Top Hat, Long Ears and Comatose cursing in her wake. "No room," she hears them cry. "No time."

She picks up the outline of the Nico Ditch once more beneath the grass. It leads her to the Platt Brook, past a small brake of trees, where a gap in the railings, just wide enough for her to squeeze through, beckons invitingly. She pushes through a leg, then an arm, but just as she is trying to manoeuvre her shoulders through, her head becomes caught. She twists, she turns. She tries to prise the railings further apart. She squeezes herself into the smallest shape she can to see if she might wriggle her way back to where she started. But all to no avail. The more she tries, the more hopeless the situation seems. She is completely stuck. Her head protrudes from the railings as if she'd been placed in the stocks.

A voice calls to her from somewhere above her, a child's voice. Lily looks up. A little girl is perched in the fork of a branch on one of the trees in the brake. From Lily's cramped position the girl appears to be upside down, suspended.

"You're in a bit of a mess, aren't you?" says the child's mouth, which appears to have been separated from the rest of its head.

Lily says nothing.

"You're trying too hard," purrs the child. "You'll get through eventually."

"You mean if I stay here long enough? I'll get so thin that it won't be a problem any more?"

The floating mouth smiles. The child reaches down and plucks it, returning it to her face, where it stretches wider and wider.

Lily tries to move her head slightly. She finds that the little girl is right. The smaller the movements, the greater her success.

"Can you tell me the way from here?" she asks.

"That depends on where you want to get to," says the child.

"I don't really care," says Lily, gradually freeing herself, inch by inch.

"Then it doesn't much matter which way you go, does it?" says the child.

"So long as I get somewhere…"

"Oh, you're sure to do that," says the child again, "if you keep running for long enough…"

With a final shrug of her left shoulder, Lily manages to squeeze her head through the gap.

"Thank you," she says. But the little girl has vanished, leaving only the echo of her smile hanging in the air.

Lily runs.

She follows the course of the Platt Brook as it dribbles away into Hough Moss. A mist hovers above it. It creeps towards her like a living thing. It swirls and gathers round her legs, making it difficult for her to decide where to place her feet. But as the day tips into afternoon, the sun has still not managed to worm its way through the carapace of cloud, an impenetrable pall, so that the earth remains solid, an ankle-wrenching, bone-breaking, hard-rutted grid, as unyielding as granite, the frozen ground a razor of splintered glass.

She picks her way across the dead marsh.

The Nico Ditch has disappeared. Some say this is where it ended, a thousand years before, a last skull-splitting axe on the edge of the city. Others claim it limped on another mile or two, the final drops of blood a sticky ooze staining the land brown towards the Urmston Meadows by the River Mersey.

In the distance Lily sees a dark tower, its clenched fist punching up towards the fallen sky. Crows fly from it as she approaches, circling overhead, cawing, nails in a rusty tin. A grove of obelisks, needle sharp, stab the air. Ivy-clad gravestones rise up through the mist leaning precariously, drunkards ready to fall. Some are surrounded by nine inch high spiked railings, a mace of black filed teeth, ready to snap at unwary ankles. Forgive us our trespasses and those who trespass against us. Some are completely overgrown, neglected, forgotten, the lichen eating away the leprous stone. But some are watched over by statues, winged marble angels, guarding, protecting, beckoning.

Lily stops.

After seven miles hard running Lily has reached the Great Southern Cemetery of Manchester, the largest burial ground in Europe, more than two hundred acres of bones picked clean by half a century of worms. She stumbles towards the tallest of the angels just as the last of what little light there has been this grey steel day is leaching away. She hears a low whimpering, not ten yards distant. Dimly through the mist she makes out an old, retired soldier, wrapping his arms around himself and rocking back and forth. She walks nervously towards him. A wound of medals ribbons his chest.

"I'm not who once I was," he says. His hands tremble. He tries to clutch a scarf to this throat. "I lost myself somewhere. I can't remember now." He coughs. Once he starts, he can't stop. His body wracks, convulses. Lily puts a hand upon his shoulder. Finally he stops. Beads of blood speckle his chin. He is silent a long time. The frost hardens on the moss. In the distance a dog barks. The old soldier begins his rhythmic rocking once again. He speaks in time to it, the words barely audible.

> " *'What matters it how far we go?' his scaly friend replied.*
> *'There is another shore, you know, upon the other side.*
> *The farther off from England, the nearer is to France.*
> *Then turn not pale, beloved snail, but come and join the dance...'* "

A heron lifts slowly in the air. Lily turns to watch it. She hears its wing beats hum. She wonders if it might possibly be the same one she saw earlier, at the start of this day that has been like no other, coming back to check on her. It circles overhead before flying in a wide arc across the moon. Its silhouette diminishes, then disappears. Lily turns back to the old soldier, but he too has gone. She thinks she catches a last glimpse of him shuffling off into the dark, but she isn't sure. She can't be certain that half of what she's seen today's been real or not. She's not eaten in nearly thirty-six hours, so she could be hallucinating. She wonders how many different versions of herself have split off from her in that time.

She walks the last few yards towards the marble angel. She rests her head upon its weathered feet, looking up at its child's stone face staring out across the city, hands clasped in prayer, wings outstretched.

The December moon climbs the sky. Lily holds her cloth bundle tightly to her, closes her eyes and waits for sleep. She fancies she hears Jenny singing to her again, just as she did when she first made her escape that morning from Globe Lane, singing about the moon, but a different song this time, a carol she remembers from St Bridget's.

*'The moon shines bright and the stars give a light
A little before the day
Our Lord, our God, He looked on us
And he bid us awake and pray*

*Awake, awake, good people all
Awake and you shall hear
Our Lord, our God died on the Cross
For us he loved so dear*

*And for the saving of our souls
Christ died upon the Cross
We ne'er shall do for Jesus Christ
What He has done for us…'*

The cold seeps into Lily's bones. She curls herself up into as tight a ball as she can. Sleep, when it comes, is fitful, a plague of fevered dreams. She is slipping down a hole into the earth. Her fingers scratch and scrabble at the soil but she can gain no traction. She tumbles over and over in free fall, deep underground. She feels the thud of marching feet pounding beneath her, the rumble of great machines tunnelling through rock, mile upon mile of trenches, shored up with bones of the dead, who rise up to dig again the bank of the Nico Ditch.

She jolts awake. Her hair and eyelashes are thick with frost. The angel looks down upon her, haloed by the moon. Jenny's voice is singing, far, far away.

*'For the life of man is but a span
And cut down in its flower
He's here today, tomorrow gone
The creature of an hour…'*

A few feet away from her something stirs. In a nest of

broken twigs and leaf mould, concealed behind the ivy wrapped around the base of the stone angel, a rat is suckling its young. A dozen squirming pups, two weeks old, coil and climb around each other. Their eyes have just unsealed, their ear canals unblocked. In two more weeks they'll be weaned. In two after that they'll be ready to have babies themselves. The mother is likely to be pregnant again too by then. Three weeks after that she'll be giving birth to her next litter. And so the year will turn. All of them ready to run. But for now, under the cold full December moon, they huddle close, burrow deep within their nest of mulch and mould.

Lily watches them till her own eyes droop and close once more. A weight drops from her shoulders. She feels safe. Mr Godwit will not be coming for her tonight.

'My song is done and I must be gone
And stay no longer here
God bless you all, both great and small
And send you a joyful new year…'

*

Three months later.

Lily is sitting on the steps of a different statue. Oliver Cromwell. Between the Cathedral Green and Exchange Station. It's her first stopping point each morning. Like stations of the Cross. She learned early on that there are others with a claim to each spot on her route, so she has to be careful to stick to her allotted time. These were dictated by a man she'd met the first day she arrived. He was covered from head to toe in old newspapers. He spent much of his time patrolling the railway platforms for discarded editions, which he would attach to various parts of him.

"What's your name?" he demanded.

Lily hadn't answered.

"Where are you headed?"

"I'm not sure," she said.

"A person ought to know which way she's gong," he said, "even if she doesn't know who she is." He paused briefly in his collecting and looked her up and down. "Oliver Cromwell," he said. "From eight till nine."

Lily reads the plaque beneath the statue.

"Oliver Cromwell, 1599 – 1658
The Gift of Elizabeth Salisbury Heywood
To the People of Manchester, August 1875."

Lily wonders who this Elizabeth Salisbury Heywood was and why, if she wanted to donate a gift to the people of the city, she had chosen this. Presumably it had cost a lot of money, money which might have been put to more obvious uses. Lily doesn't know a great deal about Oliver Cromwell, only what the Sisters at St Bridget's had told her. In their opinion he was the Devil Incarnate, who chopped off the King's head and, what was even worse, banned the Pope. He'd abolished Christmas too, yet here he was, right outside Manchester's Cathedral.

It's a good spot. Lots of people pass it by. She places a tin by her feet and waits. It isn't long before a few pennies begin to be tossed in. She also has to contend with a good deal of abuse as well. She shuts her ears to those remarks. But she can't avoid the gobs of spit that land on her from time to time. Mostly, though, she's invisible. Just another grey pigeon perched about the statue.

The prophecy of the cherry stones at Globe Lane has come to pass. Poor girl. Beggar girl.

Her next port of call is St Ann's Square and the statue to Richard Cobden. Other than his name, there is no further information on the plinth about him at all. Lily positions herself directly underneath him. He stands, she thinks, as if he is in the middle of delivering a speech to all the people in the square. His left hand is tucked inside his waistcoat. His right hand is raised, with his forefinger outstretched, as if emphasising a particular point. Lily wonders what he might be speaking about.

She reaches St Ann's Square just before eleven. Since finishing her stint by Oliver Cromwell, she has used a couple of her pennies to buy some bread and maybe an apple. A few of the stallholders recognise her now and tell her to come back later, just before they close up for the day, when there might be some leftovers to be handed out. She won't just be on her own then. There'll be dozens of others like her, dogs scrabbling for scraps. But one or two of the market traders might keep something back just for her, if she's lucky. Some of the others, though, just tell her to clear off, else they'll call the police.

At first she had to share Richard Cobden with a flower seller, an older woman, who'd resented Lily's presence.

"Find yourself another spot," she'd said. "I've been selling flowers here for years. People know me. They won't want your sort lowering the tone."

Lily had watched her then, setting out her stall with all the different varieties of flowers she had for sale, talking to them all the while, as if each one had its own particular character, respectfully to the roses, decidedly to the dahlias, carefully to the carnations and soothingly to the sweet Williams. "They have to know their place," she said, with a knowing look at Lily, who nodded and began to move away. The flower seller relented. "Oh to be sure, there's room enough for all of us, and I've been thinking for a while of shifting a little closer to the Cotton Exchange, so as to attract the gentlemen as they step outside after a morning's trading. Won't you help me with the cart?"

"I'm named after a flower," Lily confided.

"Are you indeed?" said the flower seller.

"Yes, it's…"

"Now don't tell me. Let me see if I can guess." She looked back at the thin, grimy-looking girl standing before her. There was something sad about her disposition, with the air of funerals about her. "It wouldn't be Lily now, would it?"

The girl beamed. Her whole face lit up, including that strange mark on her cheek.

"How did you know?"

The flower seller laughed. "Let's just say after all these years I've got the nose for it."

And so Lily found herself in sole possession of the Cobden statue between eleven o'clock and noon each day. It was the flower seller – "Call me Daisy, dear, everybody does" – who'd told her little snippets of information about the man raising his finger above them on the plinth.

"He was a great reformer," she said. "He got rid of the Corn Laws and championed the rights of poor folk like us."

"You mean things could be even worse?" said Lily, as she put down her tin at the base of the statue.

"Just thank your lucky stars you weren't around a hundred years ago." She plucked a lily that had a broken stem from one of the bunches on her stall and placed it into Lily's hair. "There," she said, "people might look more kindly on you with that tucked behind your ear."

"Thank you."

Daisy moved her hands around Lily's head. "You've got a most interesting skull," she said, pressing and prodding further. "My grandmother used to claim she could tell a person's fortune by the shape of their head. *He* used to go in for that too, they say," she added, indicating Cobden. "Phrenol-o-gy."

"So what does the future hold in store for me?" asked Lily.

Daisy quickly pulled her hands away. "I really couldn't say," she said brusquely. "I don't have the gift."

"Will I get a lot of pennies in my tin today?"

"Let's hope we both do."

The clock in St Ann's Church at the far end of the square strikes eleven, and out pour the gentlemen traders from Manchester's Royal Cotton Exchange, flushed with the morning's business. Many head straight for Daisy's stall to refresh their button holes or, if they've been especially lucky, to buy a whole bouquet for their wives or mistresses. Daisy always knows. "Roses for the mistress," she says with a wink, "'mums for the missus."

Some of them then drop a few coins from their change into Lily's tin. Most of them hardly give her a second glance. At times, in the past few weeks, Lily has wondered whether she might see Mr Godwit, doing business about the city, but she no longer worries about this. She doubts now whether he would even recognise her, her appearance has declined so much in the interim. Her clothes are threadbare, torn and filthy. Her hair is lank and greasy, lying flat against her head. Her skin is encrusted with dirt. Her legs and arms are bruised. There are blue welts on her shins. Her gums are sore and bleeding.

Lily looks around. The paving stones around the square remind her of a chessboard. She says as much to Daisy, who agrees, adding, "If that be so, I reckon we're just pawns, stuck here on the bottom row. But if we're lucky, and keep our heads down, then we might just make it to the other side."

"Then what will we be?" asks Lily.

"Maybe queens, you never know," replies Daisy, laughing. "But I think we might need the help of a knight or two to get us there, don't you? And they're a bit thin on the ground."

The clock strikes noon, and Lily picks up her tin and starts to make her way to her next pitch. As she bends down, a shadow falls across her – or rather two identical shadows.

She looks up. Two young men, twins, are grinning at her. Everything about them is exactly the same. The clothes that they wear, the expressions on their faces. Their movements mirror each other precisely. When one starts to speak, the other will finish his sentence. Their synchronicity is uncanny, disturbing.

Lily looks from one to the other of them. There's nothing to tell them apart, except for the tattoos they each sport above their left collar bones. One says '*Spider*', the other says '*Web*'.

"Won't you come into my parlour…"

"… says the spider to the fly?"

"Tis the prettiest little parlour…

"… that you ever did espy."

"The way into my parlour…"

" … is up a winding stair…"

"… and I've a many curious things…"

"… to show you when you're there."

Behind their backs, unseen by them, Daisy is making a cutting gesture with her finger across her throat and shaking her head.

Lily says nothing. She picks up her tin and cloth bundle and tries to walk away. The Twins dodge either side of Cobden's statue to intercept her.

"What's your…"

"… hurry, girlie?"

"We're just…"

"… being friendly."

"Don't you know…"

"… it's rude to walk away?"

Spider grabs her chin with his left hand, while Web strokes beneath it with his right forefinger.

"You know – you're…"

"… not a bad looker…"

"… beneath all this muck."

"I reckon…"

"… you'd scrub up pretty well."

"You could do…"

"… quite well for yourself – "

" – if you know what's good for you…"

"… and you do what you're told…"

"…if you know what I mean."

Lily knows exactly what they mean. The Twins step away from her, sneering. In unison they rub the thumbs and forefingers of their hands together, as if delicately disposing of a piece of worthless dirt beneath their fingernails, caught as a result of coming into direct contact with Lily's none too clean skin. They place their right foot in front of their left and perform a perfect pirouette, before heading on their way, with a final remark tossed over their shoulders.

"See you…"

"… but I wouldn't want to be you."

Spider takes a football rattle from the inside of his jacket pocket, which he whirls menacingly in the air – a bird scarer. Starlings rise from the rooftops, screeching. Web snatches it from him and whirls it twice more. Spider grabs it back, flicking Web's face with the back of his hand. Web head butts his brother in return. Laughing and snarling, the two of them disappear round the corner into St Mary's Gate, performing a series of elegant *cabrioles*.

A sudden squall of rain forces Lily to take temporary shelter in the Barton Arcade close by, a glittering palace of glass and cast iron, with mosaic tiled floors beneath domes and balustrades, but she is quickly and angrily moved on. Head down, she scurries into Old Bank Street, cuts through Back Pool Fold into Cross Street via Cheapside. She passes the Unitarian Mission, which will not be opening its doors for several hours yet – although Lily has yet to sample the delights of its soup kitchen, a legend among the city's street dwellers, for it only ever appears to cater for men. She debates with herself whether to make a short detour into Mulberry Street, where some afternoons she does good business underneath the statue to Our Lady of Manchester, outside the entrance to The Hidden Gem, but because of the rain decides against it. Instead she crosses Pall Mall into Norfolk Street, skirts the edge of the 'L' shaped Spring Gardens, pausing briefly outside the entrance to Parr's Bank to hold out her tin to a number of well dressed gentlemen disgorging through its revolving doors to be rewarded with a threepenny bit, skips, with spirits lifted, the length of Phoenix and Marble Streets, before spilling out of those narrow, lightless canyons onto the corner of Mosley Street, alongside Lewis's Department Store, from where she crosses over into the sunken gardens of Piccadilly, her last pitch of the day, John Cassidy's *Adrift*.

It is more modern than the other statues she has sat beneath today. Installed in 1907, it depicts a family in bronze, clinging to a raft in a stormy sea. The central figure is a half-naked man, holding a sheet aloft in his raised right hand, calling for help. Arranged around him are the figures of his wife and three children. His wife is leaning over to kiss their infant son. To the left, is the daughter, her raised arm held in her father's left hand. At the rear is the prone figure of a youth, the elder son, clutching his breast. Parts of the raft are visible in the waves which make up the base. Of all the statues in Manchester Lily has begged beside, this is her favourite. She loves its sense of adventure. The bronze waves seem as though they will crash over her too as she leans against them. She identifies strongly with the figure of the daughter, desperately clinging to her father. She admires the heroic self-sacrifice of the mother, bending over her baby to protect it from the storm. From time to time during her short life, she has occasionally speculated about her own parents. She knows nothing whatsoever about them, except for one detail, which Sister Clodagh let slip once – that her mother had been very brave and had died giving birth to her. That was all, but it was enough to fire Lily's imagination. She looks back up at the statue and thinks, "I would like to have been part of a family like this, holding onto each other in the face of such hostile adversity." It's like a story book, or a film perhaps, which she's never seen, but stops from time to time to lose herself in the giant posters outside the cinemas on Oxford Street and Deansgate. She likes to think they will be rescued.

As she also likes to think that maybe one day she will be too.

The lights begin to come on in Piccadilly, the signal for the starlings to begin their nightly murmuration, and for the arrival in the Gardens of the drunkards and the addicts, the dealers and the pimps, the mollies and the toms. Lily leaves as quickly as she can. She makes her way towards the Queen Victoria statue by Onslow Ford. In a recess at the back is the carved bronze figure of *Maternity*, meant to represent how the queen was the mother of the nation, scooping up lost children, but to Lily it always looks as though this is something people would prefer not to think about. Queen Victoria has turned her back upon the figure, staring away from Piccadilly, in the opposite direction. The expression on her face is unequivocally not amused, although this could be on account of the pigeon perched upon her head, shitting blithely down upon her. High above, hardly visible from the pavement below, St George fights the Dragon.

A voice wheezes behind her. "Tricky customers, dragons. Many's the time I've tilted my lance at their like."

Lily turns round to see an old man with long white hair and a drooping moustache. "Sorry?"

"No indeed, it is I who should be sorry, for we have not been properly introduced." He takes off his hat and bows low. "A true and perfect gentle knight," he says.

Lily, somewhat nonplussed, bobs a curtsey.

He leans in closely to her, his breath smelling of stale pipe tobacco. " *'Beware the Jabberwock'*," he whispers, "for they are all around us, in all shapes and sizes, all manner of disguises. Why," he adds with a chuckle, pulling himself back up to his full height again, "I might even be one myself," and he taps the side of his veined and pitted bulbous nose with his finger and winks. " *'One two, one two! And through and through, the vorpal blade went snicker-snack'.*" He draws an imaginary sword and brandishes it in the air, before pursuing further unseen dragons back into the sunken garden.

Lily hurries away towards the far corner of Piccadilly, close to where it meets Portland Street, and stops at the entrance to *The Queen's Hotel*. Lights have just come on inside, the glittering crystal chandeliers, and she can see some of the guests in the lounge enjoying an early evening drink beside an inviting coal fire glowing in the ornate hearth. She takes a couple of steps to try and get a closer look, when the door man shouts at her angrily.

"*Vattene da qui*," he cries. She doesn't understand the words, but his accompanying gestures make the meaning abundantly clear. She is not welcome there. "*O ti butto fuori da solo.*" Or he'll throw her out himself.

She is just beginning to leave, when another voice stops her, a woman's voice, remonstrating with the first. "*Fais pas ça,* Luigi."

The doorman tips his hat to the woman. "*Scusa,* Signorina Catch," and retreats back inside the hotel.

Cam approaches Lily, who stands on the pavement, quivering. "Don't be frightened," she says. "Would you like something to eat? Something warm to drink perhaps too?"

Lily pauses, not sure how to respond. What will she need to do in return, if she says yes? She waits. The woman looks at her. Lily has a chance to take in her exotic appearance, the patterned shawl, the gypsy skirt, the high heeled shoes, the rings on every finger.

"*Alors*," she says, smiling. "*Je ne vais pas te mordre.* I'm not going to bite you."

Lily nods. Cam puts a hand on her shoulder.

"*Attends ici.*"

Lily watches the woman go back up the steps of the hotel and engage in a fractious conversation once more with the doorman. He is clearly not at all happy that Cam wants to help this filthy street girl, whose mere presence will be a discouragement to potential customers. Lily feels embarrassed that she is causing this nice, kind woman such difficulties. Without a word, she runs off in the opposite direction. She hears a voice calling after her, but she doesn't stop until she reaches Market Street, where she can lose herself in the evening crowds.

Lily heads off down Tib Street, past all the stalls selling animals, a cacophony of caged birds, hundreds of them screeching and squawking, desperately flapping their lice-infested wings against the metal bars. She clamps her hands over her ears to shut out the din, cuts down Carpenter's Lane onto Oak Street as far as Foundry Lane, where she turns left till she reaches the narrow brick alley of Eagle Street, from where she can join New George Street to take her up to Shude Hill, whose booksellers continue to trade well after dark. Lily likes the look and feel of books and loiters a while among them. There were no books at St Bridget's, only bibles, and Mr Godwit kept his own collection in bookcases that were locked. One of the stallholders shouts at her to move on, suspecting her of being about to steal one. She plunges down from Shude Hill into Riga Street, and from there into Hanover Street, which takes her the last few yards towards her final turning, Dantzic Street and her journey's end, the railway arches at the back of Victoria Station, overlooking the stagnant, foul smelling ditch of the River Irk.

This is where she has made her home, though that is not a

name she uses. It's a shelter of sorts. The walls are blackened with soot and grime, but the ground is relatively dry. It protects her from the worst of the rain, which has come on hard again. When she had her moment of epiphany at Globe Lane, sitting on Mr Godwit's knee, his arms trapping her inside their span as surely as any of those bird cages on Tib Street, when she had seen herself reflected in the mirror like the young woman in Holman Hunt's painting of *The Awakening Conscience*, she had known then that she must eventually free herself from that cage if her wings were not to become permanently clipped, her feet tethered and hobbled, but she had little thought of where she might next alight in her migration. She could not have imagined this dark and dingy railway arch, with only a colony of rats for company. She takes out the last of the loaf that she bought in the morning, which she has saved for this moment, so that she might share the last few crumbs with them, break bread with them, as she looks out towards the north of the darkening city, from where danger has so often threatened, from the Picts through to the Danes, against whom the Nico Ditch was dug, along whose banks Lily has run, until she has fetched up here, cold and hungry by the clogged, rank stench of the Irk. She resembles the woman in a quite different painting now, the forlorn figure in the final image of Augustus Leopold Egg's triptych *Past & Present*, gazing in longing up at the moon, before it is covered once more by cloud.

*

Another three months pass…

The Twins snatched Lily a week later, having staked her out for days. They swooped out of a bloodshot northern sky, late one night from Red Bank, as she was sidling up Dantzic Street.

"Fancy meeting you here. What a…"

"... nice surprise."

"Isn't this..."

"... cosy?"

"Red sky at night..."

"... shepherds' delight."

They held a filthy handkerchief tightly over her face. It smelled vaguely of liquorice. Before she passed out, she had a vivid flashback of riding on the top deck of a bus on her way home from the Children's Choir recording of *Nymphs & Shepherds*, of looking down onto Oxford Street below, already thronging with the painted ladies of the town. She'd learned since that there were basically three types of prostitute – those who dressed well, who plied their trade quite openly outside the theatres and hotels, who probably had their own scented apartment somewhere in the city; then there were those who dressed less well, who had a squalid single room somewhere, possibly with a baby in a curtained off alcove, where they might take those customers whose tastes did not tend towards *al fresco* pleasures, and finally there were those who lived on the streets, making their nightly round of railway arches, alleyways and patches of waste ground. Some of these girls worked for themselves, though not many. Most were the property of people like the Twins.

When she came to, she was lying on a threadbare sofa in a top floor flat in an old Victorian building somewhere in the city. She had no idea where. There was a faded rug on the floor, which consisted of unpolished, bare boards. There was a small skylight above her, through which high clouds scudded across a chalky blue sky. Particles of dust danced in flickering columns of sunlight. One of the Twins was carrying a basin of hot water, from which vapours of steam rose up to smear the glass, while the other was standing over her, smoking.

" 'Ello, 'ello, 'ello..."

"Back in the land of the living, are we?"

Lily tried to stand up, but she was still feeling woozy, and immediately she fell back onto the sofa. Spider put down the basin of water on the floor in front of her, while Web blew smoke into her face.

"Slowly, slowly…"

"… catchee monkey."

"Life is just…"

"… a bowl of cherries."

"It's time we had…"

"… a little chat."

"So many things to talk about…"

"Ships…"

"… and shoes…"

"… and sealing wax…"

"… and cabbages…"

"… and kings."

The Twins giggled mirthlessly.

"But first you need…"

"… a bit of a wash."

"How long has it been…"

"… since you last had a good scrubbing?"

"Take off your things."

"You 'eard what 'e said."

"Take off your things."

"Every…"

"… last…"

"… stitch…"

"Or else…"

"… we'll take 'em off for you."

Lily slowly undressed, till she stood, shivering, before them, futilely trying to cover herself with her hands.

The Twins smirked and began to wash her. One lifted an arm, while the other rubbed her hard with a scouring brush. They then proceeded to work their way round the whole of her body – other arm, legs, front and back, face and neck, finally hair – in a way that suggested they'd done this many times before. When they'd finished, Spider carried out the basin, the filthy, scum-thick water threatening to slop over its sides, while Web flung her a towel and told her to dry herself quickly. When Spider returned, the two of them looked her appraisingly up and down.

"At least now we can…"

"… see what she looks like."

"There's not much to her, though, is there? She's…"

"… all skin and bone."

They sniggered.

"Lie down…"

"… over there, on the rug."

"The thing is, we've got our…"

"… customers to consider."

"So we have to…"

"… sample the product…"

"… test the wares…"

"… vouchsafe the quality…"

"… guarantee the goods…"

A drool of saliva hung from both their lips.

Once they'd each taken their turn, they stood up and left the room. She heard their footsteps clattering down the stairs and, far below, a heavy door slam shut, followed by the sound of a key turning in a lock, and the rapid whirring of their bird scarer rattle. Lily lay immobile on the rug, watching the light drain from the sky, till it grew completely dark, and the motes of dust stopped dancing.

The next day she was out on the streets.

Some nights, after she'd finished, and they'd come to collect the money from her, they'd let her go back to the room at the top of what had once been an old sewing mill, in a building adjoining a Ragged School and Working Girls Home, on Charter Street, an irony the Twins relished with delight, just a stone's throw from Angel Meadow, where Lily did her business, so that she might have another wash, if she'd started to smell particularly bad, but mostly they didn't bother. They left her instead to shift for herself, huddling in the locked doorway of the Church of St Michael's & All Angels.

Lily learns from the other girls the rules of the game – the dos and don'ts, the whys and wherefores, the way the transaction works, what to offer to do and what not to, how to spot the Jabberwocks, the jaws that bite and claws that catch, and give them a wide berth – and before too long it becomes routine, a habit that she wears like a second skin, the crust of dirt that serves as an extra layer. She learns the language of the trade, the business, and begins to stockpile each experience, not unlike the collecting of sets in the card game she played at Globe Lane, except that now she flinches all the time. Every sound sets her teeth on edge – footsteps walking behind her in a back alley, coins jingling in the pockets of men as they hawk and haggle, the brakes of trains hissing and screeching as they thunder overhead – along with the smaller sounds – a match flaring as someone strikes it, a child running a stick along some railings, a penny rolling down a gutter, then spinning precariously, caught in a glint of lamplight reflected from a puddle, before tumbling down a grid, the distant plop echoing each insistent drip from the roof of a railway tunnel, a baby crying needing to be fed, a lone rat squeaking. Sometimes she hears these sounds from far away, as in a dream, so that if somebody is speaking to her, she can't tell what they're saying, their words muffled and mangled all at once, while at other times they bang inside her head so loud she feels her ears will burst. And so she pulls each customer towards her, lets him grind himself against her, harder and harder, faster and faster, so that he'll come quickly, groaning like a chained beast in pain, that it will soon be over, and she can shove him from her, watch him limp away, while the next one in the queue steps forward.

Lily tries to take her mind somewhere else, a different place, a different time. She conjures up a spring day, in a park, surrounded by tulips. She's six years old. She's taking part in an egg and spoon race. She balances her egg with great care upon her spoon. The other girls charge ahead of her, but they keep dropping their egg and have to go back to the beginning and start again, while she maintains a slow but steady, even pace. She can see the finishing line in the distance. If she can only keep her egg from dropping, she will be all right. But then a dog barks, a happy, friendly bark, and Lily turns around. In doing so, she drops her egg. But it lands in the soft grass and doesn't break. A kind lady with a warm smile picks it up and puts it back on her spoon again. Lily sets off once more towards the finish, but the line's receding further and further into the distance. The trick, she now understands, is to not lose sight of it altogether. But afterwards, after the last customer for the night has spat into her face, or tried to smash her head against the brick wall, she catches sight of her reflection in a puddle of slime on the edge of Angel Meadow. The person she sees there is nothing but a shattered mosaic of shards of broken egg shell.

"*All the King's horses and all the King's men,*" she sings quietly to herself. She bends down to retrieve her cloth bundle with the wooden yacht wrapped inside. Somehow or other she knows she must try and find a way of putting herself back together.

Three more months pass.

    The Twins have now abandoned her.

    "The trouble is, you ain't..."

    "... pulling your weight no more."

    "And we've a..."

"… business to run. We ain't…"
"… a charity."
"So…"
"So…"

They each look at the other and then, in unison, turn back to her and say, "Ta-ta. No 'ard feelings…"

One of them takes out the rattle, the bird scarer, and flails it in the air, whooping. The other tries to snatch it from him, and they chase each other out of Angel Meadow.

Lily loses track of time. She no longer knows for certain whether it's day or night. The other girls give up on her. She talks to herself, to people she seems to see around her, jabbing her fingers at invisible shapes in the air. She clutches her cloth bundle tightly to her, wrapped inside her coat, the coat she wore on the night she first left St Bridget's, unrecognisable now, encrusted with dried blood and shit. It's the only article of clothing she has left. Underneath it, she's naked, no longer even bothering to fasten it up or keep herself hidden. In her fancy she's still gripping onto the spoon, trying to balance the egg, but her feet appear to be stuck in the earth, sinking slowly in the mud.

The rain is bouncing off the slick flagstones of the Angel Meadow now. She tries to run but slips, hitting her head on a paving slab. She feels the blood running down her forehead and rubs it into her hair. In the far corner she sees a man standing in front of an easel, painting. The church bells of St Michael's & All Angels begin to peal. She's aware of a long line of rats running across her as she lies there, and she thinks she hears someone singing. It sounds like Jenny. She tries to summon up her face, but she no longer can. Jenny, with her voice like an angel's. She's sure she must be imagining it. She feels herself slipping down a rabbit hole, but the memory of the voice keeps pulling her back.

"Oh the moon shines bright on Charlie Chaplin…"

And then she hears another voice, a young man's, asking her name. Nobody asks who she is any more. She becomes aware of children playing in the park. A small girl in outsized shoes pushing a pram. Some boys kicking a football. A cat in a tree.

"Lily Shilling," she says.

The young man picks her up in his arms. Like the knight in shining armour she and Daisy used to joke about. Only instead of a horse, he has a motor cycle. She has her arms looped around his waist and the whole of Manchester is speeding past her in a blur, like the sparks from a giant Catherine wheel.

The Sisters once took all the girls to Belle Vue to watch the fireworks. This was before Sister Mary Frances of the Five Wounds arrived, so Lily must have been very young. All treats of that sort were stopped as soon as Sister Mary Frances came. When Lily had complained and said that it was a shame not to be able to see the Catherine wheels again, Sister Mary Frances had lowered herself to Lily's eye level and hissed at her. "Do you know why those fireworks are so called?" she asked, her eyes ablaze with fury.

"No, Sister."

"They're named after Saint Catherine of Alexandria, a young girl from Egypt, who the pagan Roman emperor Maxentius lusted after and wanted to marry. When she refused, declaring that she had dedicated her virginity to Jesus Christ Our Saviour, he tortured her on a spiked wheel, but still she would not give up her vow of chastity. The wheel thereafter became known as St Catherine's wheel, and it's a wicked thing indeed to be wanting to take pleasure over her suffering by turning her into so trivial a thing as a firework. Let that be a lesson to you, Lily Shilling, and say a prayer every night to St Catherine that she might inspire you to dedicate your own life to Jesus, just as she did."

"Yes, Sister."

She feels that spike slicing through her now as the young man's motor cycle tears down London Road, through Ardwick Green, onto Hyde Road. They roar past Belle Vue, where the nightly fireworks display is in full swing, before heading off down Mount Road.

Lily keeps slipping in and out of consciousness. She remembers asking the young man where they are going.

"Didsbury," he tells her.

"That's a long fucking way," she remembers saying, before her eyes close again.

Another time he asks her if she's coming back.

"I promise," she says.

"Why should I believe you?" he says.

"Because," says Lily, "I never break a promise."

And now she thinks she knows who that promise was made to.

When she flung the coiled snake bracelet behind her at Globe Lane, when she first turned left instead of right outside the front door, when she randomly pointed over her shoulder in the direction of Audenshaw Reservoirs and followed the course of the Nico Ditch, when she got stuck in the railings in Platt Fields and finally managed to free herself, when she chose to go on instead of turn back, when she ran away from the woman with the gypsy skirt outside *The Queen's Hotel*, when she flinched at the sound of the Twins' bird scarer rattle, when she finally lay down on the flagstones of Angel Meadow in the pouring rain, her fingers scraping the slime from the paving slabs as though she were clinging to the edge of a raft, like the daughter in the family of John Cassidy's statue in the sunken gardens of Piccadilly, she has been cast adrift, cutting away separate versions of herself, one after the other, until all that was left of her was this bare husk, catapulted through the night on the back of a motor cycle, all the different particles of her coalescing like stars, like the glittering shards of an egg shell being slowly put back together again. The speed at which they're travelling, through the Manchester night, peels back her skin so that, for an instant, she sees all these other Lilys riding alongside her, until, when the young man decelerates on the gravel drive of a large house, skidding the motor cycle round in a complete three hundred and sixty degree circle, all of them are forced back into her with the impact of their stopping. She swallows, ingests them all. She is whole again, herself again. She knows she has made it at last to the other side of the chessboard. She is leaving behind that looking glass world, where things seemed back to front and upside down. She feels the sensation of falling, which has been churning inside her for as long as she can remember, begin to slow down and finally come to a stop with a gentle bump. The young man picks her up out of the rabbit hole, lifts her in his arms, and carries her through a door opening into a sunlit meadow. She remembers Sister Clodagh struggling to answer her question in the art gallery about when there might be a happy ending. "God loves you," she had said. "God loves you."

Lily is drifting away again now. She feels herself floating high in the air, looking down upon herself. The young man and a woman – his mother perhaps? – have laid her body down to rest upon a chair and are bending over her. Am I dying, she thinks? Is this the happy ending Sister Clodagh meant? The woman is holding a ball of wool in her hands, which she attaches to the string around my cloth bundle, joining them together. It is like a jolt of electricity, forcing me back down to re-enter my body. I feel myself waking up. I feel all those other Lilys tearing at my throat, desperate to be heard. I open my mouth and let them all begin to shout at once.

Now that they've started, they cannot be stopped.

The woman takes me in her arms. She holds me to her closely. She tells me to cry as much as I want to, that everything will be fine now, that no one will hurt me again.

"You're home," she says.

Outside, in the dark, the rats stop running.

*

Across the city, in the bar of *The Queen's Hotel*, Cam is singing her final number for the night.

"Good evening, ladies and gentlemen. *Guten abend, Meine Damen und Herren. Bon soir, Mesdames et Messieurs. Buona serra, Signore e Signori.*"

She lights herself a cigarette while the band begin to play the introduction.

"This is a little song for those among you who may have been... disappointed in love."

A wry chuckle greets this remark. Cam draws deeply on her cigarette.

"It's by Bertolt Brecht, with music by Hanns Eisler. It reminds us that we're not commodities." She inhales. "Nor are we goods. Nor are we chattels." She inhales again. "The moon shines down on all of us equally, and though her stare might seem pitiless and cold, it reminds us that she only has a hold on us if we allow her to. We should not flinch from looking straight back up at her, directly in the eye, and say to her..." She leans into the microphone and whispers. "Fuck you." The audience laughs and applauds, several of them saying "Fuck you" back. Cam smiles. "The tide that goes out today comes in again tomorrow..." The piano player waits for her to begin, his fingers poised suspended above the keys. She turns to him, draws again from her cigarette, then sings.

"At seventeen I went to market
The market where what's sold is love
They told me it was good experience
Much was bad, God knows
But that's the way it goes
Even so I found it rather rough

615

(spoken*: After all, I am still human – you know?)*

God be praised it all will soon be over
Love and sorrow and the heartache and fear
Where are the tears of yesterday evening?
Where are the snows of yesteryear?

Even though the passing summers
Simplify the trade of love
Let you take increasing numbers
Though your feelings may
Slowly fade away
Unless you hand them out too generously

*(*spoken*: After all, stocks don't last for ever – do they?)*

Study as you may that market
Haggle as you also may
Making money out of pleasure
Easy – that it ain't
Still I've no complaint
But it don't prevent you getting old

*(*spoken*: After all, you don't stay sixteen for ever – do you?)*

God be praised it all will soon be over
Love and sorrow and the heartache and fear
Where are the tears of yesterday evening?
Where are the snows of yesteryear…?

*

George comes down early the next morning to find both his parents already up, sitting in the breakfast room.

"How is she?" he asks.

"Still sleeping," says Annie. She looks exhausted. She has been up all night. After Lily had arrived, Annie ran her a bath, while George carried her upstairs. He'd left them then and gone to his own room, leaving the door ajar in case he was needed later. When Annie helped Lily step into the bath, she'd been too shocked to speak. Her body was covered in bruises, with even darker welts between her thighs. When Annie had, as gently as she possibly could, finally managed to clean away the weeks and months of encrusted grime and dirt, she was appalled to realise just how thin the girl was, her ribs plainly visible, poking through her skin. The warmth of the water eventually began to calm her, so that she was no longer convulsed by those deep sobs, and the shuddering that wracked her body began at last to subside. Annie did not dare leave her for a second, though, for she kept threatening to drift away, and Annie was worried she might drown. Finally she managed to persuade her to stand and climb out of the bath. She wrapped her in several towels and gently dried her, holding her close and hugging her, until at last she was quiet and calm. That was when she'd had to call for George one last time, to lift her up and carry her into the spare room, where Annie had made up a bed for her, with clean fresh linen sheets. She managed with difficulty to slip her into a night dress, for by this time Lily was deeply asleep, and then she had sat beside her in a chair throughout the night, not wanting her to wake up frightened and alone in a strange place. She had woken up at five, threatened to panic, her limbs thrashing a little, before gradually recalling at least a little of what had happened the night before.

"Where's the young man on the motor bike?" she'd asked sleepily. "My knight in shining armour..." And then she had drifted off back to sleep again. Annie thought it would be safe to leave her while she saw to Hubert's breakfast.

"One of your waifs and strays?" enquires Hubert over a piece of toast.

Annie's lips purse tightly. "Yes," she replies. "But this one's different."

"Aren't they always?"

"Yes. But this one's ill. Very ill."

"Hadn't you best call for Dr Wilkes then?"

"I think she needs to go to a hospital, and I'm sure that's what Dr Wilkes would say too if he saw her."

George intervenes. "Francis has a good friend at the Infirmary. A Doctor Trevelyan. Do you want me to call him?"

"Would you?" says Annie. "I'll go and see if she's awake again yet." She goes to the door that leads into the hall and then turns back to Hubert.

"We'll need you to take her in the car…"

Hubert nods.

"Mr Gandhi says that poverty is the worst form of violence."

"Does he?"

"And that here in Manchester we have no idea what real poverty is."

"So what does that mean? That we're supposed to simply walk away on the other side and ignore the likes of that girl upstairs, because… well – it's not real poverty? I don't think your Mr Gandhi would say that if he'd seen the state she was in when our George brought her home last night."

"You can't save the whole world, Annie," says Hubert wearily.

"She's only a child," says Annie, coming back to Hubert now and sitting beside him at the table. "What if she'd been our daughter?"

The two of them sit facing each other in silence a long while. George retreats to a corner to pour himself another tea.

"Last night," says Hubert eventually, "I drove Mr Gandhi to where he was staying for the night. It was a short drive, only about fifteen minutes. Mostly we sat in silence and I began to berate myself for having this rare moment alone with someone who the whole world admires, and I couldn't think of a single thing to say to him. What a waste of an opportunity, I thought. But I couldn't bring myself to, in case I should disturb him, or he might think what I had to say was trivial and foolish. In the end, as I was opening the door to let him out, he turned to thank me and said, 'You may never know what results come of your actions, but if you do nothing, there will be no results'." He takes off his glasses and wipes them with his handkerchief. "I don't have your capacity for action, Annie," he continues. "I think I might have had once, but not any more. I look at you, and it's like hanging onto the coat tails of a hurricane. I trail behind in your wake, not knowing where we might land, except…"

"Except what?"

"Somehow we always do."

"I'm just trying to do what I think's best. I know I'm impatient, and I get myself worked up over things, but sometimes I reckon if you think too much about everything beforehand, weighing up this and balancing that, you end up not doing anything at all."

"Yes. I know."

"So you have to take risks sometimes, that's all I'm saying, and you might fall flat on your face, but if you act with a good heart, then there's bound to be some good that comes out of it all."

"And this girl upstairs – is she a risk?"

"No question. I know nothing about her. Not even her name."

"Lily, I think," says George, rejoining them.

"But she's an even greater risk if we do nothing."

Hubert nods. "I'll go and get the car."

Annie takes his hand. "Thank you," she says. Then she goes back into the hall, runs up the stairs and calls out softly, "Lily? Are you awake?"

*

**Manchester Infirmary
Upper Brook Street Entrance
Ward C**

Date: 26th September 1931

Patient's Notes

Name: Shilling, Lily: Miss
Male/<u>Female</u>   <u>Single</u>/Married

Age: 16 years, 9 months
Height: 4ft 11ins
Weight: 5 stones, 12 pounds

Examined by: Nurse Iris McMaster
Doctor in charge: Dr Charles Trevelyan

History:
Miss Shilling was brought into hospital suffering multiple lesions – see below. She was in considerable pain, disorientated and confused, drifting in and out of consciousness. She was accompanied by a Mrs H. Wright, whose son had found the patient lying on the ground the previous night and had brought her home to his mother, who had given the patient a bath and a bed for the night, before bringing her into hospital this morning. She does not know the patient and so she is unable to provide an accurate history. It is not known whether the patient is normally in good health, but the condition in which she arrived would tend to suggest that she has been homeless for some time. There is

therefore no knowledge of any pre-existing medical conditions. The patient has a distinguishing haemangioma on her left cheek.

Physical Examination:
Upon arrival the patient was examined by Nurse McMaster before being referred to Dr Trevelyan for a more detailed diagnosis. She had sustained serious injuries to her arms, legs, back and ribs, consistent with having been the regular recipient of systematic beatings, and of routine rough handling, as indicated by the many examples of severe contusions, comprising haemorrhage in the tissues under the skin, as a result of blows and squeezing, which have been repeated with sufficient force as to rupture the blood vessels but not pierce the skin. The patient has also suffered a number of abrasions to the head and face, resulting in the scraping away of several layers of skin. There do not appear to be any fractures. In normal circumstances one would expect these injuries should heal over time. The fact that they appear to have been cumulatively sustained over a period of many months and are proving slow to heal, however, is further cause for concern. In addition, the appearance of petechiae – small red spots beneath the surface of the skin – combined with the more blueish spots upon the patient's shins, together with clear evidence of anaemia, the patient's complaint of acute myalgia, including bone pain, bleeding in the gums, the loss of some teeth, notably the upper left biscupid and the lower

right pre-molar, the beginnings of pulmonary edema and respiratory difficulties, lead me to a diagnosis of early stage scurvy. This would be consistent with the patient having been homeless and living on the streets for several months, thereby having unreliable access to vitamin C and the advantages of a healthy, balanced diet. There has also been severe bruising to the inner thighs and vagina, consistent with repeated aggravated violation. Swabs from the vulva, introitus, labia majora, labia minora, cervix, perianal and rectal areas have been taken and sent for further analysis. Serious genital injury, including hymenal laceration, is evident. The patient is not pregnant. It is not possible, however, to predict at this stage whether she will be infertile in the future as a consequence of these injuries. Although over a period of time the patient is expected to make a good physical recovery, Dr Trevelyan remains deeply concerned over the potential longer term psychological effects of her current multiple conditions.

*

The scene is the Oak Room, the Clarion Café, Number 50A Market Street. The time a little after six o'clock. This is one of its quieter periods. The ladies out shopping, who stopped here earlier for afternoon tea, have now returned to their suburban villas to cook their husbands' suppers. The sitting for dinner in the café is not scheduled to begin serving for another half hour, but it does not get busy as a rule until after seven at the earliest. They are too far away from Oxford

Street to cater for the pre-theatre dinner crowd, and gentlemen who require a stiffening brandy after a hard day at the office before readying themselves to return to their wives in Withington, or Whalley Range, are more likely to go to one of the clubs on King Street, or John Dalton Street. It is rare, therefore, for there to be many customers in the Oak Room at this hour, and today is no exception. The waiters have cleared the tables and are taking it in turns to step out the back for a quiet cigarette before the evening rush begins.

On this particular day, Monday 28th September 1931, it is especially quiet. A couple sit in a corner, heads bent low towards each other, urgently whispering over a pair of untouched sherries. The woman is twisting her wedding finger anxiously. The gentleman is pulling at his collar nervously.

"He knows," says the woman. "I know he does. Now you'll have to tell your wife."

"But how can you be sure?" he replies agitatedly.

"You don't want to tell her, do you…?"

In the opposite corner, sitting in a window seat, another woman waits alone. She is checking her watch. She has a pot of Earl Grey tea before her, from which she pours herself a second cup. She checks her watch again. She stands up, she sits down. She stands up again, more decisively this time, fishes for her purse in her handbag, from which she takes a few coins, which she deposits on the saucer. She is just about to walk out when a breathless young man rushes in.

"Darling," he says, "I'm so sorry. I just couldn't get away." He takes her, briefly, in his arms.

"Never mind," she replies, smiling. "You're here now. Shall I pour you some tea?"

"I think I need something stronger. How about you?"

She nods excitedly. "All right. Why not?"
"Champagne," he calls out to the one waiter still on duty.
"Champagne?" says the young woman.
"We're celebrating."
"Oh!" She takes out her compact and quickly checks her appearance in its mirror, hastily repairing a smudge of lipstick.

Charles, who is sitting by himself smoking a cigarette over a black coffee, is beginning to wonder about his choice of meeting place. Everybody here appears to be on an illicit assignation, with a secret to hide. Perhaps that's more appropriate than he would care to admit to, he considers, given the circumstances. Ah well, it's too late to do anything about that now. Delphine will be here shortly. She is never late.

He has arrived here a little earlier, to compose himself, and prepare more precisely what it is he has to say – though in truth he has thought of little else all day, ever since he received confirmation of the news and requested this meeting with Delphine.

The bell in the tower of the neoclassical St Ann's Church just around the corner chimes the half hour and, as if to prove Charles's hypothesis, Delphine steps into the Oak Room in perfect synchronicity with the last peal. She looks about the rather empty café, letting her eyes adjust to the dark panelled interior, until they alight on Charles. She walks towards him with some urgency, brandishing a piece of paper in her gloved hand.

DELPHINE:
Well? You called, I came. But really, Charles, a telegram? This is uncharacteristically melodramatic of

you. Has someone died? Judging from your somewhat agitated demeanour, I assume not. And here, of all places – *The Oak Room* of *The Clarion Club* – renowned for the more tawdry or desperate of assignations, the clandestine trysting place *par excellence*.

CHARLES:
I *am* desperate.

DELPHINE:
You're not going to propose again, are you? I've told you already, Charles. I'm perfectly happy with the way things are between us. I enjoy your company. I like going to bed with you. But I also like my independence. I have neither need nor desire for marriage.

CHARLES:
It is not about marriage that I wish to speak.

DELPHINE:
Thank goodness for that. What then?

CHARLES:
A drink first? I know *I* could do with one.

DELPHINE:
Very well. Why not? A dry white wine please. Something from the Mosel if they have it.

The waiter materialises at their table.

WAITER:
Certainly, Madam. And for you, Sir?

CHARLES:
> Cognac.

Once their drinks have arrived, Delphine takes a long sip of hers, expresses her satisfaction with it, then leans back in her chair.

DELPHINE:
> So, Charles – what's this all about?

Charles picks up his cognac, which he drains in a single draught. He pauses, lights a cigarette, offers one to Delphine, who refuses, then inhales deeply, pondering how he is to begin.

CHARLES:
> I rehearsed a whole speech before you arrived, but now that you're here, I find myself at a complete loss for words.

DELPHINE (*smiling*):
> And that is not like you, Charles.

CHARLES:
> Please – don't tease. Not tonight.

DELPHINE:
> I'm sorry.

She leans forward and rests her hand gently on his which, she is anxious to note, is palpably shaking.

DELPHINE:
> Whatever's the matter, Charles?

Charles looks up at Delphine, then stubs out his cigarette, as if having made a decision.

CHARLES:
> You will remember me mentioning my fiancée to you shortly after you and I met?

DELPHINE:
> Ruth Kaufmann. Yes, of course.

CHARLES:
> I… er – did not in fact tell you the whole story.

DELPHINE:
> I thought as much at the time.

CHARLES:
> Am I really that transparent?

DELPHINE:
> No, Charles. But normally you are so very sure of yourself – please don't take that as a criticism, I admire you for it. On that occasion, however, I sensed you were holding something back.

CHARLES:
> And yet you did not press me for more?

DELPHINE:
> I had no right to. It was private, and anyway, it was before you and I met. I assumed you would tell me eventually, when you were ready.

CHARLES:
> I see.

DELPHINE:
And I assume that that time has come tonight?

CHARLES:
Yes. It has.

He pauses.

CHARLES:
Do you mind if I have another drink?

DELPHINE:
Of course not.

CHARLES:
Waiter – another cognac please.

WAITER:
Certainly, sir.

The waiter brings the drink and places it in front of Charles, who swirls the liquid in the glass, looking deeply into it. He takes a small sip, then begins once more to speak.

CHARLES:
I believe I told you that Ruth died. I did not, however, tell you the cause of her death, the circumstances leading up to it, or, more crucially, what happened as a consequence.

He takes another sip of the cognac, then stares into it, as if summoning up the memory of all that happened.

CHARLES:
I first met Ruth in the May of 1915. Just after the sinking of *The Lusitania*. You may recall that there were terrible

anti-German riots which took place all over the country as a result, including here in Manchester?

Delphine nods.

CHARLES:
Ruth was English, born in Denton. Her father was German, but came to England when he was only five years old. He built up a successful opticians' business in the town. The family was much loved and respected. Nevertheless, a mob is not a thing to be reasoned with. Their shop was looted, stones were thrown, windows smashed, the house set on fire. Mr Kaufmann was attacked. Ruth... Ruth was extraordinarily courageous. She stood up to the mob, tried to protect her father from them, but they...

Charles puts a hand to his forehead to shield his eyes. Delphine nods, knowing what is coming next. She waits for Charles to recover himself.

CHARLES:
They beat her. They broke her arm, several ribs. They tarred and feathered her. Then they raped her.

Delphine covers her mouth with her hand, for this is worse than she feared.

CHARLES:
I learned all this from her mother and from a girl who worked for them – Mary, a remarkable young woman, brave, loyal, resourceful – the next day when they brought her into hospital, where I examined her.

He takes another sip.

CHARLES:
Because of the extent of her injuries, she was obliged to stay in hospital for six weeks. Her father was interned on the Isle of Man and her mother went to stay with relatives south of the city. Mary came in to visit Ruth every day. When the time came for her to leave the hospital, she was determined to return home and try and carry on her father's business. 'I've done nothing wrong,' she kept saying.

DELPHINE:
She hadn't.

CHARLES:
No indeed. But the situation was complicated by the fact that she was pregnant, and that there was no way of identifying who the father of the child was. A few weeks later Mary came to see me again at the hospital, requesting if I might go and visit Ruth, advise her perhaps on possible courses of action she might consider.

DELPHINE:
A sensible suggestion.

CHARLES:
Yes.

He pauses, as if, in the act of recalling what happened next, he sees it all vividly in his mind's eye.

CHARLES:
The sun was shining. I bought her a bunch of yellow tulips on an impulse from a flower stall in the street outside where she lived. She was delighted with them. They were her favourite flowers, she said... I learned then

that she was already engaged to be married, to a young Captain in The King's Own Royals, who was serving in France. She had not informed him of all that had happened to her, only that she had been attacked. I gathered that his parents had already distanced themselves somewhat from her and had not once been to visit her while she was in hospital.

Delphine shakes her head in disbelief.

CHARLES:
She was adamant that she did not intend to have the pregnancy terminated. 'It is not the baby's fault,' she argued. But as to the practicalities of what exactly should be done next, she had no idea. The obvious option would have been for her to go away somewhere, have the baby where nobody knew her, then give it up for adoption. I could have arranged this for her, if that was what she wished, but...

DELPHINE:
Yes?

CHARLES:
I sensed that it wasn't.

DELPHINE:
She wanted to keep the child?

Charles nods.

DELPHINE:
I now see what you mean about how courageous she was.

CHARLES:
It was a foolish hope.

DELPHINE:
No, Charles. Naïve, certainly, but not foolish.

CHARLES:
We talked the whole afternoon. The sun was slanting across her face through the open window. I found myself falling in love with her...

DELPHINE:
Yes. I see that now.

CHARLES:
She decided that she must write to her fiancé and explain everything that had happened to her, including her decision to want to keep the baby. She would state that she would completely understand if he felt differently, and she would release him from all obligations, but she hoped he might feel the same as she did.

DELPHINE:
What happened? Did she write the letter?

CHARLES:
She did. But shortly afterwards, she learned that he had been killed – needlessly, it was implied – and his parents returned all of her letters back to her with not a single note. The War was a feverish time, filled with so many uncertainties, it made us all behave more recklessly, I believe. I concocted an outrageous plan. I asked her to marry me. I would arrange for the wedding to take place north of the city, in Whitefield, where neither of us was known. Mary had let out a dress that would disguise the

nature of Ruth's condition. I would also arrange for the lying-in and, after she had given birth, I agreed that I would raise the child as my own.

DELPHINE:
That was a good thing to do, Charles.

CHARLES:
I loved her.

DELPHINE:
It was brave and honourable.

CHARLES:
Please don't say that – you don't know what happened next.

He takes another sip of cognac. His hands are shaking.

DELPHINE:
Are you sure you want to tell me?

CHARLES:
I have to.

He composes himself, breathes deeply, then resumes his story.

CHARLES:
It was then that I discovered I'd overlooked something.

DELPHINE:
In your plan?

CHARLES:
> In Ruth.

DELPHINE:
> What do you mean?

CHARLES:
> While looking again at some X rays we took of her when she was in the hospital, I noticed a congenital heart defect. Minor but unmistakable.

DELPHINE:
> How could you have missed that?

CHARLES:
> Don't you think I haven't asked myself that a thousand times since? I missed it because I wasn't looking for it. It's as simple as that. We were checking for broken bones at the time, and the need to treat her injuries was paramount. I instructed Mary to keep Ruth to a strict regime of a healthy diet and plenty of bed rest, and no one could have done more than Mary to enforce it. But the baby came early. Mary did everything that she could to save the situation, her actions were nothing short of heroic, but she was thwarted at every turn. The local midwife was away on another call, her replacement, who lived far away, was rather too fond of her drink, there was a fog so thick that night that all public transport was stopped, so that it took Mary longer to alert me than it would otherwise have done, and when she did reach me, I was in theatre with another patient. When I finally did get to Ruth, it was too late. She had died literally minutes before I arrived…

There is a long pause. Charles covers his eyes with the back of his hand. Delphine watches him and waits. The reason Charles is telling her this now is slowly beginning to dawn on her. Finally she speaks.

DELPHINE:
   And the baby, Charles? What became of the baby?

He looks up. She deliberately holds his gaze and will not let him look away.

DELPHINE:
   The baby, Charles?

CHARLES:
   Do you think I might have another drink?

She places her hand on his arm just as he is about to call for the waiter.

DELPHINE:
   No, Charles. You've had quite enough already. The baby. What happened?

Charles inhales deeply.

CHARLES:
   She survived.

DELPHINE:
   She?

CHARLES:
   Yes. A girl. Lily.

DELPHINE:
   Lily?

CHARLES:
   Her mother's last wish. She was perfect. Apart from a...

He lifts a trembling hand up towards his left cheek. He is on the verge of tears.

CHARLES:
   ... a strawberry mark. Here.

DELPHINE:
   Go on.

CHARLES:
   I signed the death certificate – omitting any mention of the congenital heart condition...

DELPHINE:
   ... thereby exonerating yourself of any further blame or responsibility?

CHARLES:
   Yes – although that would have been a minor contributory factor at most.

DELPHINE:
   Even so, Charles...

CHARLES:
   It would have served no purpose to have included it...

DELPHINE:
   And you had your position at the hospital to consider?

Charles looks up sharply at Delphine, then pauses.

CHARLES:
Yes. So – I made the necessary funeral arrangements, and then…

DELPHINE:
Yes, Charles?

CHARLES:
I… I had to decide what to do about the baby.

DELPHINE:
About Lily?

CHARLES:
Yes. About Lily.

DELPHINE:
And what did you decide, Charles?

CHARLES (*angrily*):
I did what I considered the best and only thing I could do in the circumstances.

DELPHINE:
Which was…?

CHARLES:
I arranged for her to be brought up in an orphanage – which is what she was: an orphan.

There is a long pause, which Delphine finally breaks.

DELPHINE:
Where was this?

CHARLES:
Audenshaw. Trafalgar House, I believe it was called.

DELPHINE:
You believe?

CHARLES:
A former convent. Run by Catholic Sisters. It has an excellent reputation. I thought she would be... better off there.

DELPHINE:
And was she?

CHARLES:
What do you mean?

DELPHINE:
Better off there?

CHARLES:
I... well – I suppose so.

DELPHINE:
You suppose so? Didn't you visit her? Didn't you request regular reports on her welfare? I have considerable experience of Children's Institutions, Charles. I know how such places operate. They are obliged to produce annual reports on every child's progress – their health, their education, their behaviour. Well?

CHARLES:
> I... have no idea.

DELPHINE:
> You never enquired, did you? You never once went to visit her.

CHARLES: (*looking down*):
> No.

DELPHINE:
> Oh, Charles.

CHARLES:
> I was under no obligation to do anything at all. The child wasn't mine.

DELPHINE:
> But you've already said you were prepared to overlook that fact when you asked Ruth to marry you.

CHARLES:
> But now Ruth was dead. That altered everything.

DELPHINE:
> As Ruth herself said, that was not the baby's fault.

CHARLES:
> I could hardly have brought her up myself. I had my work at the hospital to consider.

DELPHINE:
> You could have made her your ward. And you could have engaged someone to look after her. I imagine, from what you have said of her, that Mary would have been more

than willing.

CHARLES: (*looking down once more*):
She was. But I had her reputation to consider too. People might have made assumptions.

DELPHINE:
What kind of assumptions? That the baby was hers?

CHARLES:
Yes, I suppose.

DELPHINE:
Surely that was her decision to make, not yours?

CHARLES:
I don't know what you mean.

DELPHINE:
Or were you afraid that people might also assume that the baby was yours?

CHARLES:
No!

DELPHINE:
I believe you did, Charles. As soon as Ruth died, you regarded Lily as an unwanted inconvenience, a potential encumbrance around your neck, a millstone, an embarrassment, a reminder of your own failure, a hindrance to any possible future advancement of your career?

CHARLES:
I was distraught. I had just lost the woman I was in love

with, who I had hoped to spend the rest of my life with.

DELPHINE:
And whose child could have helped you overcome that grief, who could have brought you joy, instead of…

CHARLES:
What?

DELPHINE:
Guilt, Charles. Guilt. Otherwise, why are you telling me all this? And why tonight? Something has happened, hasn't it, Charles, which has prompted this confession?

Another long silence ensues between them. Charles lights himself another cigarette. Once again, it is Delphine who speaks first.

DELPHINE:
Well? I'm right, aren't I?

Charles nods.

DELPHINE:
Then aren't you going to tell me? Isn't that why you asked me here in the first place? Why you sent the telegram?

Charles does not look at Delphine as he speaks. He loses himself in the coil of cigarette smoke, which wreathes around him.

CHARLES:
It was *déjà vu*. Nurse McMaster, the same nurse who had attended to Ruth, called me in to look at a young girl

who'd just been brought into the hospital. Barely sixteen years old, who somehow managed to look much younger and much older simultaneously. Such terrible things that had been done to her. Beatings, bruisings. Apparently I didn't see the worst of it. The woman who brought her in, whose son had found her on the streets, had given her a bath, cleaned up the dried blood matted in her hair, washed away the layers of dirt and grime, got rid of the smell. But she was still a pitiful sight. Inside she'd been completely broken. She lay there like a discarded doll.

He pauses, wafts away some of the cigarette smoke that has enveloped him, before continuing.

I finished my examination and was able to confirm that on top of everything else she had scurvy. What kind of society are we living in that allows a child to get scurvy in the middle of the twentieth century?

Delphine waits until she is sure that Charles has finished before speaking.

DELPHINE:
It was Lily, wasn't it?

Charles stubs out his cigarette and nods.

CHARLES:
It was Nurse McMaster who pointed out the name on her chart. The unusualness of it. Lily Shilling. That was when I knew. When I left her at the orphanage, the space on the birth certificate for the father's name had to be left blank – unknown. The Sister explained that in such circumstances they would supply the surname. For some reason she chose 'Shilling'. I can't think why. But it

stuck. I always remembered it. Over the weekend I went back to Trafalgar House – the first time since I'd left her there when she was just a few days old. I checked. I asked questions. It was a different Sister I spoke to. She answered me with great reluctance. Only when she learned that I'd been sending them a cheque each year did she agree to tell me anything. She confirmed that Lily had left the orphanage some two years before. That she was sent to a big house in Dukinfield to work as a maid there – she wouldn't tell me the name of it – but that she'd run away – it doesn't take a genius to guess why – and that they'd not heard of her since. I took my leave. She called after me as I walked away, saying she hoped I'd still continue to donate to them as generously as I always had.

DELPHINE:

And will you?

CHARLES:

Credit me with at least some integrity.

DELPHINE:

But that's what this all boils down to, doesn't it, Charles? A financial transaction? You shut away the poor girl out of sight, out of mind, in the hope that, over time, you'd forget all about her and carry on with the rest of your life, and you assuaged your conscience by paying for her upkeep while she was there. But you never once went to visit her, you never stopped to consider if she was being well treated, if she was happy, what she might like to be when the time came for her to leave the orphanage, and how you might help her to do that. You erased all traces of her existence until now, when the chickens have come home to roost, like a bank calling in a bad debt.

CHARLES:
> That's not true, Delphine. I thought of her often.

DELPHINE:
> But not often enough to actually go and find out how she was. You could have prevented this.

CHARLES:
> Don't you think I don't know that? Why else do you think I asked to meet you here this evening?

DELPHINE:
> Because you wanted me to forgive you. To say, 'Oh how dreadful, how sorry I am for all you've had to go through, but you did the best you could, nobody could have expected you to do more, I'll stand by you'. But I won't, Charles. I won't say or do any of those things, because I believe that what has happened to Lily could, and should, have been avoided, and that you are very much to blame.

Charles breaks down. He is sobbing quite volubly. The other customers in the Oak Room become aware of him, sending covert glances in his direction. Delphine looks determinedly away. She will not stretch out a hand to comfort him. She will wait until he composes himself. She is reminded of the painting 'Woman's Mission: Companion of Manhood' by George Elgar Hicks, which she once saw in a visiting exhibition from the Tate at the City Art Gallery, which depicts a respectable, middle class gentleman holding a black envelope, evidently bearing some bad news, which has caused him to yield to the power of his grief. He has risen from the breakfast table and is covering his eyes, which are silently shedding tears. His wife stands by his side, the 'companion of manhood', comforting him. Every detail of the painting confirms the woman's role as that of the ministering angel. She is attractive and well groomed, but serious, not at all frivolous. She is in every way the dutiful wife. She is clearly able to run a comfortable and efficient home. The table is neatly laid for breakfast. There are fresh flowers in a vase. Her concern is solely for her husband's welfare and well-being. No. Delphine will not play that role for Charles. Eventually he regains his self-control and looks up at her. The expression on his face is quite naked.

CHARLES:
What am I to do then?

Delphine considers her reply.

DELPHINE:
Do not think for a moment that you can somehow now come riding in to that poor girl's rescue like some knight on a charger straight out of a fairy tale. Life does not work like that. Lily doesn't know you, and you haven't earned the right to expect her to trust you. She will probably find it difficult ever to trust any man ever again after all she's been through. From what you say, it sounds like for once Lily has been lucky, in that the woman who brought her in to see you, who so kindly took her in, who washed and bathed her, might just be the sort of person she needs right now. I suggest you speak to her as a matter of urgency, ascertain if you can if she might be able to look after her, at least until Lily is better and stronger, and discussions can then be had as to where might be the best place for her to go next. Do not interfere, Charles, in any way that might only make the situation worse and put the girl at risk again. Do not make the same mistake twice. It is not money alone that will sort this situation out, but kindness and consistency. Someone needs to be there for her for the long term.

You've already demonstrated, Charles, that you are not such a person. I know that what you want is to be able to wave some kind of magic wand, so that everything will be better for Lily, and that all of your own past mistakes can be erased at the same time, so that you might somehow wipe the slate clean, start afresh with her, tell her who you are and who her mother was, but that would be catastrophic just now, especially coming from you. She would only wonder why it was that you were so quick to abandon her. No, Charles. If you want to redeem yourself, to atone for your calamitous errors of judgment, you must do so anonymously, in the background, expecting nothing whatsoever in return, except the knowledge that she is safe and perhaps has a second chance now, by speaking to the woman who brought her in…

CHARLES:
… Mrs Wright…

DELPHINE:
Mrs Wright, yes – and see if she might be persuaded to look after her, for as long as might be necessary, until something more permanent – and safe – can be arranged.

CHARLES:
Might you perhaps speak to Mrs Wright for me?

DELPHINE:
No, Charles. It must be you.

CHARLES:
Very well. I promise.

Delphine looks across at Charles, nods, satisfied that he will keep his word. She gets up and extends her hand.

DELPHINE:
>I shall go now, Charles. No – please don't get up, or try to accompany me. I don't believe I shall want to see you again for quite a while. I will write to you when – if – I am ready to do so. But I will shake your hand, Charles. I recognise that telling me all of this tonight has required great courage from you. I only wish you could have found that same courage when it was needed most. Goodnight.

She leaves. Charles looks about him. He is now the last customer in the Oak Room. The waiter is wanting to lock up for the night. Charles stands, taking in for the first time his surroundings, the dark panelling, which gives the room its name, this side room of The Clarion Club, through which he now exits, musing on the establishment's Socialist origins, named in association with Robert Blatchford's 'Clarion' newspaper founded in 1894, the decorations by Bernard Sleigh on the walls illustrating 'The King's Lesson' by William Morris. One particular pre-Raphaelite frieze catches his eye. It shows a baby, lost in a wood. A winged figure is kneeling beside it. Underneath, the caption reads: 'A maiden walking alone heareth a cry and, searching about, findeth a little child'.

*

Another six months pass.

Lily recovers. She stays with Annie and Hubert in Lapwing Lane. She has become the daughter Annie always wanted. But she has been very clear. "I don't want charity," she says. "If I'm to stay here, I want to earn my keep." Hubert nods approvingly. "Quite right," he says. Annie recognises something of herself from when she was Lily's age, desperate to escape from the Tripe Colony. "What can I do," asks Lily, "that can be of some help to you? I want to be useful." Annie says she'll think about it. And she does.

One afternoon she calls Lily into the lounge. "For a talk," she says. "I've been thinking. These days I'm pulled in all sorts of different directions. First of all," and she begins to number each of the separate items off with her fingers, "there's the business. The meetings at the Council. The work at the Central Methodist Hall on Oldham Street. The hostels. The various charities and committees. There's Hubert to see to, Evelyn to keep an eye on, George to look out for, the house to run. Then there's the Chapel – not just the local one on Parrs Wood Rd, but all the others we've attended and kept in touch with, Hulme Hall Lane, Eggington Street, Hirstwood, Manley Park – and I'd like to see more of my friends – I've not seen Claudia in ages – and… I've run out of fingers now… there's another thing I want to talk to you about…" Annie pauses, wondering how best to approach it.

"Yes?"

"St Bridget's."

"Oh." Lily looks down. She has no idea where all this is heading, but at the mention of St Bridget's she becomes anxious and begins scraping the palms of her hands together.

"It's all right, love. It's nothing for you to worry about. Come and sit next to me, here on the sofa."

Lily accedes, and Annie takes her hands in her own to stop Lily making herself sore.

"I don't want," says Annie, "any girl from that place ever to have to go through what you did, Lily, do you?"

Lily shakes her head vehemently.

"So I've been doing a bit of investigating."

Lily's eyes widen.

"How many girls do you reckon are there at any one time?"

Lily thinks. "Well," she says, "it would vary, but I'd say never more than forty."

"That's what I thought. And they take girls in right from when they were born, at all ages, up until they're fourteen?"

"And a half," says Lily. "They were always very particular about the half."

"Why's that?"

Lily shrugs. Annie smiles at her.

"And how many girls would you say leave each year, once they've reached fourteen and a half?"

"That depends. The ages are never evenly spread, but I'd say about half a dozen."

Annie nods. "Good. That should be manageable."

"What?"

"I've been talking to one or two ladies at Central Hall. I reckon we could take every single one of those girls, every year, and find places for them, according to what might suit them best, organise where they'd live, make sure they were well looked after, had some kind of job to begin with, and most of all were safe. We'd do that for each and every one of them for two years, and then see how they were getting along. It's just a drop in the ocean when you think just how many young girls across the city are forced to fend for themselves from such an early age, but it'd be summat. What do you think, eh Lily?"

Lily can barely believe what she's hearing. "Could you really do all that?"

"We could try."

Lily flings her arms around Annie, who lets a few moments go by before disentangling herself. "I'll take that as a 'yes' then?"

Lily nods.

"So – you can see, with that new venture to take care of, along with everything else, I'm going to have my hands full. I don't want to stop any of the things that I do – in fact, I want to do all of them more efficiently – and so what I need is an assistant, someone who can keep a diary for me, put in everything – and I mean everything – that needs to go in there, including things like 'telephone Claudia', or 'invite Evelyn round for Sunday tea', and then make sure I do them. Sometimes that person might have to be quite firm with me, and sometimes she might have to do some of the things I don't get round to herself. Might that position be something a certain Miss Shilling could be interested in?"

Annie smiles mischievously as she waits for the penny to drop.

"Are you serious?" asks Lily.

"I wouldn't be asking if I wasn't."

"And do you really think I can do it?"

"Again, I wouldn't be asking..."

"I'd love to," says Lily, leaping up off the sofa and rushing to the telephone in the hall, which she picks up and speaks into in a posh voice. "Good afternoon. This is Mrs Wright's personal assistant. How may I help you...? Yes of course, Madam. I'll make sure she knows right away." She puts down the phone and runs back to Annie. "You won't regret it, I promise you. I'm a quick learner, and I'm not afraid of hard work."

"Then we'll both be all right, won't we?"

Another month later Lily is walking down the driveway of Trafalgar House in Audenshaw towards St Bridget's with a hard knot inside her stomach. To the left of her is Annie, and to the right is another woman. When they reach the front step, Lily pauses, scraping the palms of her hands together. "I don't think I can do it, Mrs Wright," she whispers.

"Yes you can," says Annie, prising Lily's hands apart. "We've been through everything you need to say. We'll be right behind you if you need us."

Lily nods, takes a deep breath, then steps up to the large front door and pulls the bell, which she knows will ring at the far end of the corridor, where the Sisters have their refectory. After what seems an eternity, Lily hears footsteps approaching. As they get nearer, she is able to make out the familiar shape of a nun's habit looming towards her through the opaque glass panel in the centre of the door, which now opens. It is Sister Mary Frances of the Five Wounds, who looks down on Lily as if she has seen a ghost, before her expression quickly alters to one of someone who has just stepped on something unpleasant with her shoe, which she would like to scrape off.

"Well," she says, "you've got a nerve, standing there as though butter wouldn't melt. You're a wicked, wicked girl, who doesn't deserve all the prayers that have been said in her name, hoping that she's coming to no harm, but certain that she probably has. And now you stand there, as bold as brass. There's nothing for you here, Missy," and she at once begins to close the door upon her.

"Actually, Sister Mary Frances," says Lily, growing in confidence, "I rather think there is." She takes a determined step over the threshold. "I've come for Jenny."

Sister Mary Frances looks at Lily with utter astonishment. Then she begins to laugh, a disconcerting sound, not unlike a murderous raven croaking over a mouse it is about to disinter, and an even more unpleasant sight, her unusually prominent Adam's apple bobbing up and down like a chicken bone stuck on a piece of wire.

"Jenny's future is all in hand, I'll have you know. A situation has been arranged, which I am confident Jenny will be much more appreciative of than you ever were of yours."

Lily smiles politely. "Can you tell Jenny I've come to collect her please?"

"I shall do no such thing."

"Oh, I think you shall," says Lily.

"You don't seem to understand how these matters work, Lily. St Bridget's has an arrangement with *The Women's*

Temperance Association now, through a Mrs Wright, who has kindly agreed to find a suitable placement for Jenny. We are expecting her this very afternoon in fact."

"I know," says Lily.

"How can you possibly?"

"Because I instructed her," says Annie, suddenly stepping forward. "I am Mrs Wright, and Lily here is my assistant. You must be Sister Mary Frances of the Five Wounds, I take it. I've heard a great deal about you. Is Jenny ready? Please be so kind as to fetch her, will you? Thank you."

A stammering, nonplussed Sister Mary Frances swoops back down the corridor calling Jenny's name, but not without first casting a savage look in Lily's direction over her shoulder.

In a few moments Jenny is walking towards them, carrying a small suitcase which, when she sees Lily, she drops.

"You came back," she says.

"I said I would," whispers Lily. "I promised."

"And you never break a promise."

"I try not to."

"I thought something had happened."

"It did. I was ill. But I'm better now."

She picks up Jenny's suitcase and takes her by the hand. Together they walk through the door of St Bridget's and out into the sunlight.

"You must be Jenny?" says Annie. "Lily's told me so much about you."

"She has?"

"I have."

"Where are we going?" asks Jenny nervously.

The other woman now steps forward.

"Do you remember Miss Riall?" asks Annie. "She tells me you show great promise as a singer."

"That's true. I've never forgotten how well you sang for

the Manchester Children's Choir, and when Mrs Wright contacted me…"

"At my suggestion," adds Lily excitedly.

"… to see if I might help when the time came for you to leave here, I said I'd see what I could do."

Jenny looks towards Miss Gertrude Riall with a kind of tremulous hope.

Miss Riall continues. "I am now the vocal tutor at The Manchester School of Music on Great Ducie Street. I've arranged for you to have lessons there – three times a week to begin with, to see how you get on – and then we'll take things from there. If that is something you might be interested in pursuing?"

Jenny is beyond words. Eventually she manages to say, "Yes, Miss Riall. Thank you. That is something I should like very much."

"You'll stay with us for a couple of weeks," says Annie, "while you get your bearings, and then we'll sort out something more permanent."

"There is some residential accommodation for students at the school," says Miss Riall, "which might be a possibility."

"And we'll look into organising you a job for the times in the week when you're not studying," adds Annie. "But all in good time."

When they reach the corner, Jenny turns back to give St Bridget's one last look. In one of the top floor windows she catches sight of a whole row of faces watching her go, followed by a forest of waving hands. She lifts her arm and waves back once, before striding purposefully away.

Lily watches her, remembering the words of the old woman in Platt Fields who said she'd once been a Duchess the day she ran away from Globe Lane.

"The woods are lovely, dark and deep
But I have promises to keep

*And miles to go before I sleep
And miles to go before I sleep…"*

She only knows that, until the final page of a book has been turned, there's no way of knowing how the story will end.

6

24th April 1932

NOTICE

to the

Ramblers & Walkers of Manchester

RECLAIM THE RIGHT TO ROAM

with a

MASS TRESPASS OF KINDER SCOUT

Sunday 24th April 1932 at 2pm

Rendezvous at Hayfield Recreation Ground

Special Trains Running from Gorton

Printed by F.G. Wright & Son
By Royal Appointment

*

Daily Dispatch

25th April 1932

MASS TRESPASS ON KINDER SCOUT

Free Fight With Gamekeepers On Mountain

Ramblers Held Up By Police Cordon
Amazing Scenes in Moorland Village

Members of the British Workers Sports Federation Manchester Branch who took part in the Mass Trespass on Kinder Scout yesterday

Photo: George Wright

More than 400 ramblers from Manchester converged on the tiny moorland village of Hayfield in Derbyshire yesterday to take part in what organisers were describing as a 'Mass Trespass' to climb the 2000ft summit of Kinder Scout, crossing land owned by the Duke of Devonshire.

Setting off from the Recreation Ground near Bowdon Bridge the protesters were confronted by a number of police constables who had been brought in by Chief Superintendents Macdonald and Else to prevent the walkers from assembling there in contravention of local by-laws prohibiting such meetings, which were read out in full by Mr Herbert Bradshaw, Clerk of Hayfield Parish Council.

The walkers followed the Snake Path along the bank of William Clough as far as Nab Brow, cheerfully singing songs until, on the slopes below Sandy Heys, they met a group of gamekeepers, who had been instructed by the landowner to "Protect the grouse by whatever means are necessary". A scuffle ensued during which some of the ramblers turned the gamekeepers' sticks to effective use upon their original carriers.

Having achieved their objective of reaching the summit of Kinder Scout the trespassers returned to Hayfield in triumph. This triumph proved short-lived, however, as five of the marchers' leaders were arrested. These included Benny Rothman (aged 21 years), the chief organiser of the protest, who had been witnessed handing out hundreds of unauthorised leaflets beforehand, together with Julius Clyne, Harry Mendel, David Nussbaum and two others, whose names have not been released. They will appear next week at the Derby Assizes under a variety of charges.

So can this Mass Trespass be considered a success? Only time will tell if new laws are passed granting free access for all over England's green and pleasant land.

See Inside Pages for further details and images

Miss Delphine Fish, Mrs Esther Ward, Miss Winifred Holt & Mr Victor Collins approaching the summit of Kinder Scout

Photo: George Wright

*

Victor looks at the photograph over a late morning cup of tea. Winifred has cut it out of the newspaper and pinned it on the kitchen wall.

"Look at me," she'd said, "I'm famous!"

Victor smiles as he remembers it. He'd enjoyed the ramble far more than he'd expected to. He hadn't really wanted to go in the first place and had only agreed to please Winifred, which is something he likes to do, even if he never says so. When the gamekeepers had shown up with their sticks and tried to turn them all back, he was itching to be allowed to lay into them himself, but Winifred held him back.

"You've got your big fight with Len Johnson in a few weeks' time," she'd said. "You can't risk damaging your hands before then." And she was right of course. But the other lads on the march were well able to take care of themselves, as it turned out, and they'd soon sent those posh beggars scarpering with their tails between their legs.

He might go hiking again one day, he thinks. It was good to breathe some really fresh air in his lungs, get out of the city for a bit. He had certainly felt the benefit of it the next day in the gym.

He looks up at the clock on the kitchen wall. "I'd best be getting a move on," he thinks. Winifred was out with the lark this morning, and I need to put in a few hours hard graft at the gym again today. "I'm feeling good about this next fight," he had said to Winifred the night before. "This could be the big one."

He finishes his tea, rinses out the cup at the sink, puts on his jacket and cap, and sets off on the five mile walk from Denton to Ardwick, whistling one of the songs they'd sang up on Kinder Scout.

"I'm a rambler, I'm a rambler from Manchester Way
I get all my pleasure the hard moorland way
I may be a wage slave on Monday
But I am a free man on Sunday..."

As Winifred arrives at the shop on the Monday morning,

there is already a queue forming right along the High Street impatient for her to open.

Inside Francis is scurrying about with piles of gramophone records, which he keeps dropping in his agitation and excitement.

"You look as if you've been up all night," remarks Winifred, depositing her bag on a chair and helping him to pick them up.

"I have," he replies, somewhat ruefully.

"I hope it's been worth it," she says.

"Oh, it definitely has," he says. "Just look at all the people. We'll sell out in less than half an hour, I reckon."

They place the records on the counter.

"Ready?" asks Winifred.

"Ready," says Francis.

"Right then," adds Winifred, looking up at the clock above the door, "five, four, three, two, one and... action!"

She rolls up the blind, pulls back the lock and flings open the door. Immediately she is engulfed by the stampede of customers charging into the shop, every one of whom is desperate to get their hands on a copy of one of the records, which Francis has spent all night recording, then copying onto this first batch of a hundred, with the promise of more to come the next day. He'd first made a rough copy out on Kinder Scout, where the young folk singer had originally sung his ballad, penned especially for the occasion, as part of a recording of the whole trespass he'd been making for one of his Sound Essays for the BBC, which Francis did as often as a new subject came up which excited him. He'd then cleaned up the track in his own studio in the cellar of the shop as best as he could. He put a copy of it on now, as Winifred dealt with the shoppers one by one, until the only copy remaining was the one Francis was playing, so that in the end, that had to go too, requiring him to lift the stylus in the middle of the final chorus.

The Manchester Rambler

Photo by George Wright

sung by

Jimmy Miller

Recorded by Francis Hall

"The day was just ending and I was descending
Down Grinesbrook just by Upper Tor
When a voice cried 'Hey you!' in the way keepers do
He'd the worst face that ever I saw
The things that he said were unpleasant
In the teeth of his fury I said
Sooner than part from the mountains
I think I would rather be dead

He called me a louse and said 'Think of the grouse!'
Well, I thought but I still couldn't see
Why all Kinder Scout and the moors round about
Couldn't take both the poor grouse and me
He said, 'All this land is my master's'
At that I stood shaking my head
No man has the right to own mountains
Any more than the deep ocean bed

I'm a rambler, I'm a rambler from Manchester way
I get all my pleasure the hard moorland way
I may be a wage slave on Monday
But I am a free man on Sunday..."

Derby Assizes

**Extracts from Transcripts of the Case against Mr Bernard (Benny) Rothwell
5th May 1932, Mr Justice Acton presiding...**

Extract 1

CLERK OF THE COURT:

Mr Rothman, you are accused that on Sunday 24th April in the Year of Our Lord Nineteen Hundred and Thirty Two, you did wilfully trespass on private land owned by His Grace the Duke of Devonshire...

JUDGE (*rapping his gavel*):

No, no, no. This will never do. Trespass is not a criminal offence. It is a civil wrong. As Mr Justice MacKinnon has so wisely stated in a recent ruling at the Chester Assizes, the Act of Parliament, which made it an offence to trespass after having been warned not to do so, has long been repealed, thereby making the *'Trespassers Will Be Prosecuted'* signs quite literally unenforceable. Is the Defendant accused of any other offence?

PROSECUTING COUNCIL:

I do beg your pardon, my Lord. The Charge should read 'Unlawful Assembly'.

JUDGE: *(peering above the rim of his half moon spectacles)*:
Are you quite certain?

PROSECUTING COUNCIL: *(stammers in embarrassment)*:
Your Lordship is, as always, quite correct. 'Riotous Assembly'?

JUDGE *(rapping his gavel once more)*:
Proceed finally...

Extract 2

PROSECUTING COUNCIL:
Will the defendant please state his name for the record?

DEFENDANT:
Bernard Rothwell.

PROSECUTING COUNCIL:
And you are more usually referred to as 'Benny'? Is that correct?

DEFENDANT:
Yes, sir.

PROSECUTING COUNCIL:
For the Court can you state your age?

DEFENDANT:
I am twenty-one years old.

PROSECUTING COUNCIL:
And you admit to being one of the leaders of what the newspapers are referring to as the Mass Trespass of Kinder Scout?

DEFENDANT:
Yes, sir.

PROSECUTING COUNCIL:
Do you also admit to the charge of Riotous Assembly?

DEFENDANT:
I do not, sir.

PROSECUTING COUNCIL:
Can you please tell the court therefore your intentions in organising this unlawful gathering, if not to cause wilful disturbance and confrontation?

DEFENDANT:
We ramblers, after a hard week's work, in smoky towns and cities, go out rambling for relaxation and fresh air. And we find the finest rambling country is closed to us. Our request, or demand, for access to all peaks and uncultivated moorland is nothing unreasonable...

Extract 3

JUDGE (*summing up*):

The Defendants have asserted that they were in their opinion merely exercising what they believe is their natural right to roam freely over privately owned moorland, however uncultivated. Members of the Jury, you may very well disagree with this claim. If so, you will have to find them guilty. I am equally sure that you will not allow yourself to be prejudiced by the rather foreign-sounding names of some of the defendants – Clyne, Mendel, Nussbaum and Rothman...

Jury finds you guilty of the offence of
\y. I sentence you to four months
..... Take him down.

*

The Manchester Guardian

11th May 1932

FURY ERUPTS OVER ROTHMAN IMPRISONMENT

Thousands Trespass In Protest At Winnats Pass

In a direct response to the widely condemned imprisonment of Bernard 'Benny' Rothwell for his role in organising the Mass Trespass on Kinder Scout three weeks ago, more than ten thousand people converged on the small Derbyshire market town of Castleton yesterday to protest their right to roam freely over uncultivated land. In the face of such enormous crowds – more than twenty times the number who took part in the original Mass Trespass – the police could do nothing. The ramble passed off peacefully and no arrests were made.

Banners demanding the release of Mr Rothwell were carried and, after several speeches made at the summit of Winnats Pass, he was given three hearty cheers, followed by a rousing rendition of the song that appears to be on everybody's lips right now, *The Manchester Rambler*, written by Jimmy Miller, better known perhaps as Ewan

MacColl.

In its edition immediately after the first of these marches, this newspaper was openly critical of the marchers and their methods. However, *The Manchester Guardian* is never afraid to admit when it might have got something wrong, or to change its mind in the wake of overwhelming evidence.

The imprisonment of Mr Rothman is not only unjust but it reflects a worrying rise in what can only be described as anti-semitism among the British judiciary, and a growing hypocrisy in the way the police responds to legitimate political protest. The same system which convicts Mr Rothman also stood by while members of Oswald Mosley's Blackshirts threw Mr Rothman from a balcony near Crumpsall Library when protesting against a rally being held there by the British Union of Fascists, yet it was Mr Rothman who was arrested and bound over for twelve months, not the thugs who attacked him.

The Manchester Guardian believes it is time for a change in the law to allow members of the public the freedom to roam over common land and open countryside, to bring much needed balm and reparation to Manchester's hard working city dwellers.

*

Victor will not go on this second march. It will be too close to his fight with Len Johnson for him to be distracted even for a day in his final preparation and build up. Neither will Esther, for Rose will have another of her bad days, and will need someone with her the whole time. Nor will Delphine, for the following day will mark the start of her students' end of year examinations, and she must make herself available should any of them be faced with sudden, last minute panics.

Winifred will go, however. She will accompany Francis and George, helping to carry some of their equipment. Francis will be able to capture many more interviews from individuals as they hike over Winnats Pass, a series of audio snapshots to accompany George's photographic impressions.

Buoyed by his success in getting his first paid professional work, following the publication of two of his images in the previous edition of *The Daily Dispatch*, George will decide, with Francis's encouragement, to hold a small exhibition to coincide with the completion of his formal studies at *The Mechanics' Institute*. For the venue they will choose the same gallery on Blackfriars Road where, eight years before, George first saw the paintings of Lowry and Valette, and dared to imagine a future as an artist.

*

NUTS & BOLTS

An Exhibition of New Photography

by

GEORGE WRIGHT

Blackfriars Street Gallery

in association with
The Manchester Society of Modern Painters
&
The Mechanics' Institute, Pendleton

Private View 25th June 1932 at 6pm

ADMIT ONE

Printed by F.G. Wright & Son
By Royal Appointment

George Wright: Nuts & Bolts
Artist's Statement

Ever since being a small child I have been fascinated by how things work. I have always enjoyed taking things apart, seeing how they are made, then trying to put them back together again. When I was seven, I took piano lessons. My teacher – a Mrs Tiffin, whose photograph you will see in the exhibition – impressed upon me the importance of practising my scales. "They are the nuts and bolts of piano playing," she used to say, and I have never forgotten this phrase. I sadly never progressed very far with my piano playing, but that was not Mrs Tiffin's fault, it was entirely my own, for I found that I preferred playing scales to actually playing tunes. And so when I came to photography, what excited me immediately about it was the way the camera could reveal surprising insights about people and their situations – a spontaneous gesture, an unexpected smile, the whole history of someone revealed in an unguarded look in the eyes – the nuts and bolts of a person, what makes them tick. I was particularly drawn to the relationship different people have with the jobs that they do, and so for this exhibition I have chosen to present a series of portraits of men and women at work. I spent time talking to them first to try and get a sense of just how they viewed this relationship themselves and how they would like to be photographed doing it. Not everyone, of course, is fortunate enough to have work. The days of full employment are long gone, it seems. If indeed they ever existed. And even those of us who have been lucky enough to secure gainful employment quickly learn that the wages earned from such work frequently don't stretch far enough to accommodate all our needs – rent, food, clothes – so that many people feel the need to try and pick up extra bits and pieces – taking in sewing, doing some cleaning, a night shift at one place, a day job somewhere else. But it's what all of us want – a job that we can call our own. It's what defines us. And so, before taking each of these photographs, I asked each individual how they wanted to be represented, what they wanted the image to portray. Every one of them, without exception, wanted to show how much pride they took in their work, a job well done, which they could derive satisfaction and recognition from. I hope you can see that pride in all of these faces. My father, a printer, (whose photograph you will also see here), is a great admirer of Mahatma Gandhi, who stressed the importance of the respect wrought through a person's labour. "It is beneath human dignity," Gandhi said, "to lose one's individuality and become a mere cog in the machine." I have tried in these photographs to show that while at times we all of us feel we are nothing more than one of those cogs, one of those nuts and bolts, we are at the same time all of us individuals, with our own unique contribution to offer, and should be celebrated as such. I have a friend who has a cigarette case with the phrase *'Respice ad finem'* inscribed on the inside, which roughly translates as: 'Have a regard for the end'. Here, at the very start of my career, I hope I am laying down a blueprint for the rest of my working life, to have a regard for its end, to look after the nuts and bolts.

Catalogue
(all photographs taken with a Foth Derby)

1. Archie Rowe, Sign Writer
Taken through a window from inside a shop. Outside Archie can be seen, right hand leaning on a mahl stick, holding a paint brush in the act of writing a sign directly onto the glass. His eyes focus on the words he is writing, which partially cover the rest of his face.

2. Freddie Catch, Blacksmith
Shot from a low angle looking up, so that Catch is a towering figure, lit only by the red glow from the forge. Bare-chested, hammer raised ready, he strikes a heroic pose. Above his head is the iron sculpture of the three egrets flying across the moon.

3. Hubert Wright, Printer
Hubert is bent over a printing press inspecting the beds of type. Each of the islands of text represents a separate page, his face a study in patient concentration, his spectacles pushed up on top of his head.

4. Sylvia Tiffin, Piano Teacher
She is seated at the piano, next to her pupil, a child, whose face is in shadow focusing on playing scales. Mrs Tiffin is pointing to the manuscript, smiling, a metronome ticking beside her.

5. Delphine Fish, Audiologist
Delphine stands in a booth, conducting the Weber test, holding a tuning fork next to a young person's ear, who is sitting facing her, away from the camera. Behind Delphine on the wall is a poster which reads: 'Introducing the World's Most Advanced Auditory Evaluator', depicting a machine with switches, grilles and knobs, an exact model of which Delphine is working with as the photograph is taken, her eyes focused on one of the dials.

6. Heinrich Vogts, Schoolmaster
Taken from the back of a classroom, over the heads of school boys all listening attentively to Mr Vogts, who stands at the blackboard, a black gown over his patched jacket and corduroy trousers. He has just asked a question. One of the boys has raised his hand. Written on the board are the words: '*Onomatopoeia – the murmur of innumerable bees...*'

7. Victor Collins, Boxer
Alone in a boxing ring at night, beneath an arc light, he shadow boxes in silhouette.

8. Iris McMaster, Nurse
Standing beside a patient's bed, taking his pulse, her right hand holding his wrist, her left lifting the watch pinned to the front of her uniform, a window behind her illuminating her with an almost mystical sunlight.

9. Luigi Locartelli, Hotel Porter
Leaning across his polished mahogany desk in his full livery. He looks directly into the camera as if welcoming a new guest to *The Queen's Hotel*, whose name is lit up behind.

10. George Wright, Photographer
Self portrait. A close up of George's hands working with a spanner to tighten the nut on a wheel of his DOT Racer. A part of his face can be seen reflected in the highly polished gleaming chrome work.

Around the walls of the gallery are dozens more photographs – road menders, coal merchants, miners, milkmen, typists, cotton workers, ice cream vendors, greengrocers, railway porters, tanners, dyers; farriers and foundry men, fitters and firemen; French polishers, plumbers and plasterers, welders and window cleaners; women donkey stoning their door steps; seamstresses, laundresses, waitresses, car mechanics, tripe boilers, barbers and bargemen; bus conductors, electricians, lab technicians, engineers, milliners, shop girls, delivery boys, panel beaters, pattern cutters, rag and bone men, butchers, bakers and candlestick makers – representing every walk of life, so that the viewers find themselves surrounded on all sides, just as they are across the whole of Manchester, by the ceaseless activity of work, work, work, the convulsive upheaval of all this constant change, witnessed through the eyes of everyone George has photographed, these faces of the city. The gallery pulses with them. The air vibrates. The earth shakes.

Several of the people whose faces line the walls are there in the flesh, regarding themselves juxtaposed with others who are complete strangers, but who are now standing beside them, looking at each other through new eyes, the tanner and the typist, the milliner and miner.

Hubert and Annie bask in the glow of their son's success, while Lily welcomes each guest as they arrive, circulating with trays of drinks and refreshments.

Mrs Tiffin is there. "Nuts and bolts," she says to George, "I like that."

So too is Mr Vogts. "I enjoyed reading your Artist's Statement," he says, "although it seems you have still to master the correct use of paragraphs."

And so too is Delphine, with a couple of students in tow, to whom she signs as they walk around the exhibition.

Victor is not there. It is still too soon after his mauling by Len Johnson for him to venture out. "He will recover," says Winifred, "but it's going to take a long time. Months, the doctor thinks, before the internal bleeding heals and the bruising fades." She looks anxiously at her watch. "I can't stay long," she says. "This is the first time I've left him alone in an evening, and he frets if I'm away too long. It's a pity he can't be here. He'd love the photo of him shadow boxing. Congratulations, George." She kisses him on the cheek, then slips away.

Catch is not there, nor is Archie – "Tha'll not catch me poncin' about in one of them galleries," he'd said – "but I like the picture tha' took. P'raps we can 'ave a copy to 'ang in t'shed...?"

Cam arrives – late. She has agreed to sing before people start to leave. Francis records everything on his hand-held *Kinamo* cine-camera – "for our own private home movie," he whispers to George, "laid over with Cam's singing for the soundtrack." Francis helps her set up and, when she is ready, she steps up to the microphone.

"Good evening, everybody. I'm delighted to be here. My father is in one of the photographs. Over there," she says, pointing to the one of the blacksmith. "It captures him perfectly. I don't know how you managed to get him to agree to pose for it, George, but I'm so glad you did. Looking around at all these faces on the walls, we're reminded of just how many miles some of us have had to travel just to be here. My father had to cross an ocean. We all of us know just how hard won these freedoms have been – the right to work, the right to roam, the right to live in a place we can call home. In the photograph of my father, there's an iron sculpture hanging above his head, in the roof of the forge, which I remember him making. It shows three birds flying across the moon. The song I'm going to sing this evening reminds me of them, and I hope it strikes a chord with you too. So – if you're ready, George, I think we should start."

To everyone's surprise, especially Mrs Tiffin's, George sits at the piano in the corner of the room and strikes up a few chords, over which Cam begins to sing very gently.

> *"Oh I think I'll go where flamingos fly*
> *Where the sun hangs low in a ruby sky*
> *And the surf at night sings a lullaby*
> *Oh I've got to go where flamingos fly…"*

Cam works her magic as usual. The guests stand motionless and spellbound, all eyes fixed upon her, just as those of the figures in the portraits seem to be, so that all appear indistinguishable, held in silent rapture. Hubert is transported back to an afternoon on a hillside just to the north of the city, Tandle Hill, where a kite was flying, and a voice was singing in French above him, rescuing him, tethering him back to the earth. He experiences a sharp pain momentarily gripping his chest. Annie, standing beside him, senses the tension in his body, sees the most fleeting of winces pass across his face. She looks at him questioningly. He shakes his head, smiling, then gently squeezes her hand, which is linked through his arm.

"For flamingos fly where the storms all cease
Where the soft winds blow and the world's at peace
And it's there I know that my heart won't sigh
Yes I think I'll go where flamingos fly…"

7

17th July 1934

Hubert is sitting in the Friends' Meeting House on Mount Street. It's the middle of a weekday afternoon and he's quite alone. He finds himself drawn there more and more frequently, seeking that oasis of silence, which wraps itself around him so comfortingly.

He has time on his hands these days. The business is in good shape. George has got the Printing Works ticking over like clockwork. He knows each of the different machines as intimately as if they were his children, his ears minutely tuned to their own particular individual sounds, so that he can tell in a heartbeat if one is running out of sync, or if another needs oil, or another requires a sharp smack. The workers love it when he is there and never tire of telling Hubert what a good boy he is, that the place is in good hands, and that he, Hubert, might consider putting his feet up a bit more.

Annie continues to develop new clients. She has a flair for it, her antennae always alert for a new opportunity, a new direction they might pursue, just like a dog picking up a new scent and following it to its source. He has never been good at that part of the work. His father knew that, of course, which is why he allowed him to focus more on what he *was* good at, refining and improving their technical capabilities, and why, when he sensed Annie's natural talent for business, he encouraged it and allowed it to flourish, so that now she's a force to be reckoned with, respected and admired across the city, feared too by those who've dared to doubt her, rivals who've been made to rue such lack of faith to their lasting cost. She even managed to carve out a role for Hubert too, after Frank died, which has given him status and respect, but which has never overtaxed his strength, which since his breakdown after the War has never fully returned.

But even Annie seems these days to think they've reached their full capacity. With all the repeat requests that now keep coming in from their extensive portfolio of clients and customers, they've more than enough orders on their books, reaching out well into the future, so that she devotes more and more of her time now to her charities and committees, extending her sphere of philanthropic influence ever wider. Since Lily's arrival, whom Hubert adores, Annie has, if anything, redoubled her efforts, as if that union with her surrogate daughter has provided even greater incentive, as well as the energy to match it.

And so Hubert finds himself further and further from the centre of things, viewing the world from its periphery, rather like T.S. Eliot's *Prufrock*, which he's found himself re-reading of late. '*I am not Prince Hamlet*, he thinks, *nor was I ever meant to be. I'm growing old,* he realises with a wry smile. *I shall wear the bottoms of my trousers rolled...*'

He sits in the Friends' Meeting House, savouring the silence, examining the way the light pools through the windows, observing the dappled patterns it makes on the polished mahogany of the hard wooden benches, which are not comfortable, but which provide the necessary stimulus for quiet thought and contemplation.

He is only forty-five, but he feels much older. His hair is a silver grey. He has inherited his father's angina, for which he must take regular medication. He has a permanent cough. He tires easily and is frequently short of breath.

Encouraged by Dr Wilkes to take regular exercise, preferably in air that is fresher than that more commonly found in the centre of Manchester, he has taken to driving to local beauty spots for short walks. Lyme Park, Tatton, Dunham, Hollingworth Lake, Healey Dell. He has also, inspired by George, developed his own interest in photography. But unlike his son, whose exhibitions continue to throng with people from all walks of life, Hubert prefers to take photographs of views, hills and moors, woods and streams, so that he can look at these again afterwards and imagine himself back there, especially after a particularly trying day at work, an emotion recollected in tranquillity, to replenish himself in these wide, empty landscapes. Surrounded as he is the rest of the year by the noise of traffic and industry, the constant press of people, the pounding furnaces of steel works, the underground explosions from the mines, the twenty-four rolling of the printing machines, all of which remind him of the ceaseless barrage of the cannons at the Front, whose low, rumbling thunder has never fully left him, living in the shadow of factory chimneys, smoke stacks, cooling towers and spoil heaps, he falls into the solitude and silence of those moors and mountains like a Lethean embrace, seeking solace and reparation, a balm he also finds in music – Handel, Bach and especially Purcell – which he listens to nightly on the radio.

He knows he should really get up and return to work, but the silence of the Friends' Meeting House on Mount Street is seductive. Just a few moments longer, he decides. After all, it's not as if he'll be missed, will he?

Evelyn, on the other hand, feels she has been silent too long. Ever since Frank died, the house in Bignor Street has seemed so empty, too big just for her. She rattles around it, not knowing what to do with herself. She insists on sticking to her regular routines – breakfast at seven in the morning room, correspondence at her desk between eight and ten, a little bit of food shopping on Cheetham Hill Road, with the chance of bumping into neighbours and acquaintances, followed by a meagre lunch of boiled ham and bread and butter, or possibly some soup (she finds she has little appetite these days), then off to a committee meeting perhaps, or a visit to the Central

Methodist Hall on Oldham Street, or the library (although she finds it harder to concentrate now and frequently returns her books unread), before returning home for a cooked tea, which she eats alone in the dining room, sometimes listening to the radio, although she finds most of its content of decreasing interest for her, so frequently she turns it off part way through whatever happens to be on. Then, after she has washed the dishes, dried and put them away, she feels the weight of the evening, with all of its empty hours, hanging over her head like a heavy pall. When Frank was alive, there might have been a concert to attend, or a function to do with the Chapel or the Works, or they might have had friends round, or if not, they would have sat companionably together, chatting, reading, perhaps she might have had sewing to attend to, and the evening would have passed so quickly, so pleasantly, that it would feel almost a shame that it had to end, but then they would climb the stairs to bed together, where they would fall asleep each night, wrapped in each other's arms. Now, she has nobody to sew or mend for. Friends do not call round, for fear of intruding on her privacy, and once, when she did attend a concert, she received such pitying looks from people, who nodded politely but otherwise steered a wide berth around her, almost fearing her grief might be contagious. And so she sits alone, looking around at this home she and Frank had made together, all of its furnishings and ornaments now tainted with sorrow, and listens to the tick of the grandmother clock in the corner. What had once been such a solid, reassuring sound now appears to mock her with its unstoppable march, as if beating out the relentless rhythm to which she must match her own steps until she can join Frank in the adjoining plot at Manchester's Southern Cemetery, which has been ordered and paid for, and now lies waiting for her.

No. This will not do, she tells herself. Brought up on a strict regime of discipline and self-help, she knows she must snap out of this downward spiral she has found herself in, when the highlight of her week can be a conversation with the Fish Man when he delivers her finny haddock.

She still sees Annie and Hubert regularly – George less so these days, he seems to be so busy, flying off here, there and everywhere on that motor cycle of his. He keeps asking her if she'd like a ride on the back, but so far she's always said no. She wonders why. She may be nearly seventy, but she's still fit and spry. Perhaps the next time he asks her, she'll surprise him by saying yes. Hubert comes round most Sunday mornings to drive her back to Didsbury, their latest new house, on Lapwing Lane, which Evelyn always found rather daunting when she first used to go there, rather like a show house that you might see pictures of in a magazine, so that she was always rather afraid of disturbing anything. If she moved a cushion, for instance, on the new settee in the lounge, Annie would always surreptitiously try to replace it, after Evelyn had stood up, to exactly the same position it had occupied before.

But since Lily arrived, things have changed. Annie is more *laissez faire*, more easy going and relaxed, and Evelyn much prefers it that way. She could fling a cushion across the room now and Annie would probably just laugh. She laughs a lot these days, she notices, her eyes lighting on Lily with such love. And so, when Lily makes a suggestion one Sunday afternoon, Evelyn finds herself answering immediately, "Oh yes please, I think I should enjoy that very much…"

"Mrs Wright?" says Lily.

"Yes," reply Annie and Evelyn simultaneously.

The three of them laugh.

"Well – both of you actually," continues Lily. "In a month's time Pearl will be fourteen and a half, and ready to leave St Bridget's, won't she?"

"Yes," says Annie.

"And we've not sorted her out with a placement yet, have we?"

"No. We're still waiting to hear back from Miss Brooks."

"Is that Phillipa Brooks," asks Evelyn, "the milliner?"

"Yes."

"She's closing down, I hear. Getting married and moving to Preston. Mrs Telford was telling us at Central Hall last week. She'd been hoping to purchase a hat from her for her own daughter's wedding."

"That explains why we've not heard from her then," says Annie. "So, Lily, what's your idea?"

Lily pauses. "Well... I was wondering if you, Mrs Wright," she said, somewhat falteringly addressing herself to Evelyn, "mightn't like Pearl as a live-in companion?" She notices Annie's eyes widen in surprise and decides to carry on before she is interrupted, or loses her nerve. "Forgive me if I'm speaking out of turn, but it seems to me you must get quite lonely sometimes living all by yourself, especially in such a large house, which I'm sure requires an enormous amount of work to keep up, and you're such a busy person, with all of your various committees to attend to, and so I thought that if you had someone to help you with the cleaning and the shopping and the cooking and the washing, that would make things easier for you, and also you'd have someone to talk to in the evenings, and believe me, Pearl is a great talker, she's a real chatterbox, but she's very good, very well behaved and a really hard worker, you should see her scrubbing the refectory floor, she goes at it like billy-o, and it would be a really good start for her, and..."

"Lily, stop!" says Annie, laughing. "Give us all a chance to breathe – you've gone quite red in the face."

"Sorry, Mrs Wright."

"That's all right. There's nothing to apologise for. It's an interesting idea. But it must be up to you, Evelyn."

"Oh yes please, I think I should enjoy that very much."

"Perhaps you'd like to think it over for a few days?"

Lily looks from one Mrs Wright to the other, her head turning between them as if she's watching a game of tennis.

"No," says Evelyn. "Let's 'not let the grass grow', as Frank used to say. When did you say Pearl was leaving St Bridget's, Lily?"

"In a month's time."

"Good. That leaves me plenty of time to get everything ready for her. Perhaps I'll give her Hubert's old room. What do you think, Annie?"

"Well, he shan't be needing it, that's for sure."

"I've been meaning to give it a clear out for years. I don't know what's been stopping me. Sentiment, I suppose. This is just the boost I've been looking for. Thank you, Lily."

Lily beams and tucks into a second helping of rhubarb crumble.

Now, three months later, it's as if there's never been a time when Pearl hasn't been there.

Lily was right, Pearl *is* a chatterbox, she never stops talking from the moment she wakes up in the morning until she goes to sleep at night, but it's like having a bird inside the house, thinks Evelyn, fluttering from room to room, filling the air with song.

One evening, as Annie finds herself unexpectedly alone in the house on Lapwing Lane – Hubert has gone to another Quaker Meeting, Lily is visiting Jenny in her lodgings on Whitworth Street, and George is at the Speedway track – she is relishing the rare silence, when the telephone suddenly rings. So lost in her own thoughts had she been – what a turnaround in all their lives Lily's arrival had prompted – that its sonorous ringing had quite startled her.

"Yes," she says, picking up the receiver, "Didsbury 728, Mrs Wright speaking."

"Annie? It's Clarence Grandage here. I hope I'm not disturbing you?"

"Not at all, Councillor."

"Clarence, please. We're not in the Town Hall now, so I think we can dispense with the formalities. After all, how many years has it been since we started crossing swords in there?"

"More than I care to remember, Clarence. How can I help you?"

"It's not a question of help, more of information. I just thought you'd like to know that your proposal for the inscription around the domed ceiling of the new library has finally been formally approved at the Full Council meeting this evening. *Nem con.*"

"Oh, that's wonderful news, Clarence. Thank you for letting me know."

"Aye, well… I know it meant a lot to you."

"Yes, it does."

"It's still all pretty hush hush, though. The Council wants to keep what the words say a secret till the whole thing's unveiled on the day the Library's opened."

"Of course, Clarence. I shan't say a word. Do we have a date yet?"

"Aye, we do. 17th July. A Tuesday."

"That's less than four months away. Will everything be ready by then?"

"It'd better be. The King's agreed to come and open it."

"Really? How exciting. Have the Committee decided on who's going to paint the inscription up on the wall yet?"

"No, Annie, they haven't."

"Only I happen to know of an excellent sign writer…"

"Annie Wright, you never miss a trick, do you?"

"Well – would you like me to approach him?"

"I'll leave it in your capable hands – though I didn't authorise it."

"But you'll request a letter of confirmation from Mr Flitcroft?"

"It's already in the post, Annie."

The two of them chuckle down the telephone.

"Thank you very much, Councillor Grandage."

"Think nothing of it, Mrs Wright."

Annie stands in the hall and breathes a deep, long sigh. At last. A promise made is a promise kept, and now she will be able to keep hers, one she has made to no one but herself for fear of disappointing others, especially Hubert, for whom this promise has been made. She recalls her father warning her as a little girl, when she'd vowed that one day she'd leave the Tripe Colony. "Promises and pie crusts are made to be broken."

Well – she's broken plenty of pie crusts since that day, but no promises. Not yet. Though there are still miles to go before she sleeps.

She must speak to George first thing tomorrow. It's a Wednesday. He'll be at the Printing Works. She can feel her mouth widening into a smile. Just then the front door opens and Hubert walks in.

"Hello, love," he says. "You look like the cat who's got the cream."

"I am," she says. "How was your meeting?"

"Oh, you know. The usual. Quiet."

*

Giovanni Locartelli dozes in the warm May sunshine. He spends most of his days, once the clocks spring forward, sitting on an old wooden chair, which Paulie places on the pavement, just outside the front door, each day before he sets off for work. He's a good boy, is Paulie, thinks Giovanni. He always has time for his *Nonno*, though he's not such a boy these days, not since he started as an apprentice platelayer on the railway, working out of the Locomotive Depot at Newton Heath. No longer a scrawny kid, thinks Giovanni fondly, but a man, mature beyond his sixteen years, though still as amiable as ever he was, and a good boy for his *Mamma*. Where is she, wonders Giovanni? Will she bring me something to eat soon? But before he can go back inside the house and see if he can find her, he drifts off to sleep again.

He dreams, like he always does, that he's back in Italy, so that when he wakes up, a couple of hours later, he's confused, no longer sure where he is. He looks up and down this unfamiliar treeless street, with its cracked pavement and shiny cobbles, watching a few grey pigeons scrabbling in the dust at his feet. He shoos them away and then he hears a woman's voice, scolding him.

"*Paparino*, you've hardly touched your lunch. Let's see if we can manage a few mouthfuls, shall we?" Her face is familiar to him, but he can't quite place her. She's trying to feed him sliced *salsiccia* on a fork. Perhaps she's his mother?

"*Mamma*," he says. "*Ho freddo*."

"No wonder," she says, "you're sitting out here in only your vest. Let's put your shirt on, shall we?"

"*Si, Mamma.*"

Claudia sighs. Before she can manage to get one arm through the sleeve, Giovanni has fallen asleep again. She fetches a blanket from inside and lays it over him. At least it will keep him warm for a while, until it slides from him. He hardly recognises anyone these days, not her, not Matteo, not Giulia. Only Paulie, who adores him. Or Paul, as she must learn to call him now. Even though she changed their name from Locartelli to Lockhart nearly five years ago, she still struggles to anglicise his first name. Paul. Paul. That is what his new work mates call him, and so must she.

Last month she saw him walking with a young girl, an

English girl, Harriet, who is clearly taken with him. "Yes, Paul," she kept saying. "I agree, Paul." "Let's go there next weekend, Paul."

Claudia smiles, remembering. Paulie – Paul – had asked if he might bring someone back for tea one Saturday afternoon, and of course she'd agreed. She'd assumed it would be one of his new friends from the railway yard, and so she wasn't prepared for when she opened the door to find this self-possessed young girl standing there, with very pale skin and very clean fingernails.

"Excuse me," she had said, "is this where Paul Lockhart lives?" When Claudia had nodded, she'd continued, "That's a relief. I was worried I might have got the wrong address. You must be Mrs Lockhart then? Is Paul here? He asked me round for tea. I hope it's not inconvenient, only my mother said that if it was, if, for example, Paul had somehow forgotten to tell you, then I was to leave right away."

"No. It's fine. Come in. Paul did say he'd invited someone, he just didn't say who." Once the girl had come inside, Claudia called up, "Paulie, your... guest has arrived."

Paul took the stairs three at a time, bounding into the kitchen at the back, where Claudia had led her.

"Hi," he said, his face reddening.

"Hi," she replied, beaming.

After a few moments, when neither of them had spoken further, Claudia turned back to Paul and said, "Well? Aren't you going to introduce me?"

"I'm sorry," said the girl, immediately taking charge. "I'm Harriet. Harriet Chadwick."

"Pleased to meet you."

"Mutual, I'm sure."

"Er... would you like some lemonade? I've just finished making some."

"Maybe later, *Mamma*," Paul chipped in. "I thought we'd go for a walk before tea."

Harriet frowned at him. "I'd love some, Mrs Lockhart. We can go for a walk later, Paul."

Claudia fetched three glasses, removed the muslin cloth from the jug on the table, and poured for each of them.

Harriet drank hers in a single draught before wiping her mouth with the back of her hand. "Mmm. That was delicious."

"Would you like some more?" said an amused Claudia.

"I'd love some, but no thank you. There'd be none left for anyone else then, would there, and my mother said I was to be appreciative but not greedy."

"Maybe later then," said Claudia, replacing the muslin over the jug. "Where do you work?" she asked.

"I'm still at school," replied Harriet.

Claudia raised her eyebrows and looked at Paul sharply.

"Oh," said Harriet, catching the look, "I'm fifteen. Nearly sixteen. I go to the Grammar School on Kirkmanshulme Lane."

"Do you?" said Claudia, brightening. "So did I. A long time ago, of course. Do you enjoy it?"

"Very much."

"What do you want to do afterwards?"

"Train to be a teacher."

"Will you have to go away to do that? Or can you do it here in Manchester?"

"Here in Manchester. What did you do?"

"I was a scientist. At the university."

"That must have been exciting."

"Yes. It was…"

"You don't remember me, do you?" said Harriet, suddenly changing subject.

"I'm sorry, no. Should I?"

"You gave me an ice cream once. At Philips Park. But I was only little then. That's where we live now. In the Lodge. My dad's the Park Keeper. Your brother helped us move. He came round to our old house with his horse and cart, and we loaded everything we had onto the back, and then we walked behind him all the way to the park. Afterwards, he gave us rides on the horse. Bombola. Paul was there. He remembers. Don't you?"

Paul nodded, laughing at how unstoppable Harriet is, once she's in full flow.

"Chadwick," said Claudia. "Of course. I wasn't paying attention properly before when you said your name. Your father must be Jabez?"

"Yes," said Harriet. "The one and only."

"He was my husband's best friend," said Claudia. "In the army."

"Was he?" said Harriet, widening her eyes. "He's never said. Not even when I mentioned I was coming here today. But he never talks about the War."

"No," said Claudia. "It's best forgotten. And anyway, your father might not have realised. We've changed our name since then. My husband's name was Locartelli."

"I see. Yes, that would explain it. Why did you change your name? I'm sorry. It's not my business. My mother says I ask too many questions, but I can't help it. There's just so much to know."

"It's all right. There wasn't just one reason. In the end I thought, we're English now. Paul and Giulia were born here. I was born here. We should have an English name."

"Yes. I see. At least, I think I do. It's complicated, isn't it?"

"Things usually are," said Claudia. "Now – you two go out for your walk, while I make the tea. Is there anything you don't like, Harriet?"

"No," she said. "I like everything."

The evening is a continuing pleasure. Not even Giulia's

unexpected arrival, storming in like a hurricane, could dampen the mood for long.

She lived away from home during the week these days, with her Uncle Leonardo, her *Zio Leo*, as she liked to call him. She teased and tormented the poor man mercilessly. At first Claudia had been understandably concerned when Giulia had initially suggested the arrangement. She did not know this Leo. He was not in fact an uncle, more some kind of third cousin, twice removed, but because of his age, he seemed like an uncle. When Giulia first mentioned him, Claudia's immediate thoughts were that he might turn out to be some kind of lascivious Lothario, nor, she had to confess, would she have been surprised if he had been. Giulia's flirtacious behaviour would unquestionably attract such a man, and there was a part of her that thought it perhaps wouldn't be such a bad thing if she actually got her fingers slightly burned, nothing too serious of course, but a narrow escape might teach her a lesson, but as soon as she met Leonardo, she could tell at once that there was nothing to fear from him. He was a vain, perspiring, overweight, middle-aged man, completely under the thumb of his wife, who put up with his obsequious pampering of Giulia as yet one more entry in the account book she undoubtedly kept of things she might use to humiliate him. What was more, it was quite clear that Giulia was in complete control of the situation insofar as it affected her. She had allowed him to send her flowers, buy her chocolates, shower her with perfume merely in order to let him think he was somehow held in high regard in terms of her affection for him, so that she could then ask him for whatever favour she wanted, such as free bed and board at his home (where she was completely safe from any unwanted advances because his wife would watch him like a hawk), lifts to and from work in his brand new motor car, a series of promotions within the office, and the security of knowing that none of the other girls could complain about her to him, because he was *their* boss, but *her* uncle. They may have laughed at her behind her back, but what did she care, so long as he carried her bags, took her out to dinner occasionally, and opened doors for her, both literally and professionally? It was through *Zio Leo* that she'd been able to enter the *Miss Manchester Ice Creams* Contest, but it was her own talent that had enabled her to win it, and it was through *Zio Leo* that she'd been able to by-pass the factory floor at Antonelli's, where the wafers, cones and cornets were all graded, sorted and packed, to go straight into the office, but it was through her own ability that she'd since been able to rise so rapidly, so that now she was part of the Advertising Team, helping to write copy and come up with ideas for new designs and campaigns. She was on a fast track to higher things. Of that she was certain. She was eighteen now, beautiful and going places. By the time she was twenty-one they wouldn't see her for dust. She didn't know quite yet just where the next fork in the road would lead exactly, only that she'd know it when she saw it, and that it would be sooner, rather than later. Then it wouldn't be '*Arrivederci, Zio*', so much as '*Addio, Leo*'.

She still liked to come home most weekends, though, where she expected her mother to wait upon her every whim. She would lie on her bed, flicking through her magazines, while her painted fingernails dried. It came as quite a surprise when things did not quite work out like that. "If you want something to eat, you'll have what you're given, when you're given it, otherwise you'll have to cook for yourself, or go without," Claudia had said, after Claudia had come home the first weekend. "You're earning more than I do now, so you should think about contributing some of your wages for your upkeep."

"But I don't live here any more," Giulia had complained.

"Then what are you doing here now?"

"Visiting."

"In that case you can pay for two nights bed and board. If you treat this place like a hotel, then you should expect to be charged. Plus extra for meals."

Giulia had pouted and sulked and threatened to go where she felt more welcome, but in the end she had stayed, and she'd continued to come every weekend after that, leaving two half crowns on the kitchen table when she left early each Monday morning.

And so, when she'd arrived in a flurry and a foul temper that Saturday evening when Harriet first came to tea, her mood threatened to turn even more sour when she saw that another young female was invading her territory, but in the end Harriet's refusal to rise to any bait that Giulia might throw her way, her determinedly cheerful disposition and good humour managed to win her over.

"Actually, we've met before, though you probably don't remember me."

"No," said Giulia, "I don't."

"We were both in the Manchester Children's Choir that sang *'Nymphs & Shepherds'*. You got one of the boys to knock your elbow while you were drinking a glass of water beforehand, so that you had to take off your cardigan."

"I knew it," cried Claudia, "and you told me at the time it was an accident."

"Can you blame me?" laughed Giulia.

"Not really," giggled Harriet. "I'd have wanted to do the same but wouldn't have had the nerve."

In subsequent weeks Giulia secretly looked forward to the possibility of locking horns with her again. As the summer progressed, they became firm friends, and Claudia marvelled at the change in her wayward, recalcitrant daughter.

"How did someone as dumb as my brother come to meet such a doll as Harriet?" she asks her mother one night after Paulie had left to walk Harriet home.

"First of all, he's Paul now," replies Claudia. "Second,

he's not dumb, he never has been. He's good and kind and loyal. And third, don't call Harriet a doll. She's going to be a teacher one day, and a very fine one too."

Giulia is silent for a while, then says, "How come I don't get to meet anyone like that?"

Claudia stops what she was doing and looks at her daughter hard. "Because you're in too much of a rush. You try too hard. Boys might like Jean Harlow in the movies, but not in real life."

"No. They prefer Janet Gaynor. Like in *Daddy Long Legs*."

"If you say so, Giulia. I never get time to go to the cinema."

"Where she has to choose between an older man, who's secretly supported her, or a much younger suitor. Guess which one she chooses?"

"I've no idea. You tell me."

"The younger one, of course. He's much better looking."

"Maybe there's a lesson in there for you somewhere?"

But Giulia is having far too much fun to let such a remark stop her. "*Merely Mary Anne,* or *Tess of the Storm Country*." She's in her element now, striking various poses.

"I don't know what you're talking about," laughs Claudia, enjoying her daughter's antics.

"She always plays orphans, *Mamma*, or girls who are down on their luck, but she's plucky and brave and patient and loyal, and she always ends up marrying the handsome lead in the last reel, usually played by Charles Farrell, who's an absolute dreamboat."

"There you are then," says Claudia, putting the last of the dishes away. "Model yourself on *her* instead of the *femme fatale* – patient and loyal."

"Her hair's curlier than mine, though, that's the trouble. Look," and she thrusts a picture of her from one of her magazines in front of her mother, who bats it away impatiently.

Just then they are interrupted by Harriet running back in. "Silly me," she says, "I forgot my scarf."

"Here it is," says Giluia, tossing it to her. "Tell me, Harriet, which look should I adopt? Janet Gaynor or Jean Harlow?" And she poses beside a photograph of each, which she holds up alongside her face.

"Definitely Janet Gaynor," says Harriet.

"There," declares Claudia triumphantly, "you see?"

"But I'll never get my hair to look like that," moans Giulia.

"Of course you will," says Harriet encouragingly. "Tell you what – how about next Saturday I come round a bit earlier and I'll do it for you."

"Would you?"

"Yes. It'll be fun."

"Then I'll do yours."

"Oh, mine's a hopeless case," laughs Harriet, "a frizz and a fright. Quite beyond redemption."

"I like you as you are," says Paul from the doorway. "Nice and natural. Don't let my sister anywhere near you. She'll ruin you. Come on, or you'll be late. I don't want to be in trouble with your father."

"Goodness, you're right. Look at the time. We'll have to run all the way. See you next week. Thank you, Mrs Lockhart." And they are both gone in a flurry of coats and closing doors.

Giulia tosses her magazines onto the kitchen table and slumps in a chair.

"Nice and natural," she mutters.

Claudia looks at her from behind and shakes her head. She can almost see the dark cloud of gloom which Giulia has conjured hovering above her head. Where did this cuckoo in the nest spring from, she wonders, not for the first time? She decides to leave her to her black mood which, she thinks,

692

Giulia probably enjoys, and goes to look in on *Nonno*, who is dozing in an armchair in the front room, but restlessly so. His hands jab at something only he can see in front of him, his fingers clawing at invisible shapes. He wakes for a moment, sees Claudia kneeling beside him, and grips her wrist tightly. "Where's Marco?" he asks urgently. "Will you ask him to come down? There's something I have to tell him."

"He's not here, *Paparino*," she says gently.

"It's important. Get him to come right now."

"I'm sorry. He just can't."

Giovanni is becoming increasingly agitated. "You must tell him," he says, trying to rise from his chair.

"Tell him what, *Nonno*?"

"To hold on to that girl of his, the one who works at the university, *lei è un tesoro*."

A treasure. Claudia's eyes well up. Giovanni continues to shout for Marco, until finally he begins to settle.

"*Si, Paparino*," she whispers, smoothing his puckered brow with her cool fingers. His murmuring quietens. She watches his chest erratically rise and fall.

She moves to the table by the window, where she keeps her sewing machine now, draws the curtains, sits down and continues with the garment she is currently making, a white dress for a neighbour's daughter's first communion. The rhythmical tack-tack-tack of the machine seems to soothe Giovanni, whose breathing becomes deeper and more even.

In the last couple of years, as her father-in-law's condition has worsened, it has become impossible for Claudia to leave him for longer than a few minutes, and although Paul unhesitatingly tips out all of his wages onto the kitchen table each Friday evening, keeping nothing for himself, preferring instead for Claudia to allocate him an allowance for his own spending money, a task she does bitterly, always wishing she could give him more, it is still not quite enough for their needs, even with the extra five shillings Giulia has begun to contribute, and so Claudia has been forced to take in bits and pieces of sewing to make up the shortfall. Mostly it's simple repair jobs, letting down hems, cinching in waists, patching the elbows of jackets, sewing on buttons, embroidering collars. Nothing too fancy or difficult to begin with, but gradually, as more and more people have begun to hear about her, she has been asked to take on more challenging requests, like this communion dress that she's struggling with this evening. Although she's following a pattern, it is still quite complicated, and she keeps making mistakes, which require her to unpick much of what she's previously done to start again.

Much of this work she does at night, while sitting beside Giovanni, so that she can be there to attend to him whenever he needs her, which means that she gets little sleep herself. She is beyond tired most of the time, with dark shadows under her eyes, made even more so by the pallor of her cheeks, which are sunken and gaunt. If she ever catches sight of herself in the mirror, it's almost as though she is literally fading away, imperceptibly decreasing right before her eyes, the brightness of her diminishing one lumen at a time. She inhabits a permanently twilit world, Eurydice slipping back into the Underworld. She is reminded of her time at the University, working as part of Professor Rutherford's team, bombarding nitrogen atoms with a beam of alpha particles fired through a thin sheet of gold foil. Afterwards they would carry out experiments to measure their radioactive half life. Once an atom had been split it would become unstable and start to decay. They calculated that in the case of nitrogen the atom's half life was five thousand seven hundred and thirty years. It would then take the same amount of time again for half of the half that remained to decay, and so on *ad infinitum*. The atom in fact would never completely disintegrate, but simply diminish, endlessly halving itself, until it became all but impossible to detect. Since Marco died and Giovanni became ill, Claudia feels she has been living just such a half life, continually shrinking, until she has become invisible both to the world and herself.

But ever since Harriet began to pay her weekly Saturday visits, that sensation has started to reverse. She begins to see herself as Harriet sees her, measured in the scales of another's perception. Her physics training tells her that, technically speaking, reversing half life decay is impossible, but there are ways of transmuting isotopes so that they mimic the effects of such a reversal, were it actually possible, by pounding a nucleus with a proton. It's as if Harriet possesses the force of such a proton to affect the decline in the very heart of the nucleus that is Claudia.

Sometimes Harriet brings her brother Toby along – if her parents are both busy for the day – who fits in just as easily. He reminds Claudia of Paul, the same, amiable, easy-going nature. He hero-worships Paul and wants to know all about his work at the Engine Shed. Does he get to drive a steam train, he asks? No, smiles Paul indulgently, but I do get to lay down the tracks and split the rails to make the points, without which the trains couldn't run at all. Toby is suitably impressed and tells Paul about the wagons that run on tracks down the mines at Bradford Colliery, where his dad, Jabez, works still sometimes, though less often now that they live at the Lodge. Ay, says Paul, some of us lay those tracks too. Toby tells them he's going to be a miner when he leaves school next year. He says this quite cheerfully, and Claudia shudders at the idea of this bright, open child being enclosed hundreds of feet beneath the earth's surface. Aren't you frightened, she says? No, he says, shaking his head. I'm looking forward to it. Claudia pictures him in the cage ascending from far below, blinking in the sunlight as he steps back out into the upper air. Is that what she's beginning to do, she wonders?

One afternoon Harriet brings her sister Gracie with her.

"You don't mind, do you, Mrs L?"

She's taken to calling her this lately, which Claudia finds she likes.

"Of course not. Hello Gracie? Would you like some lemonade?"

"Yes please."

Gracie's in some kind of push chair, from which she adroitly unstraps herself, then climbs down onto the floor, where she can manoeuvre herself by a mixture of crawling and dragging with extraordinary speed.

"How old are you, Gracie?" asks Claudia.

"Nearly three," she says.

"She gets her first calliper then," says Harriet, "then we'll all have to watch out, won't we, Gracie?"

"Watch out," she says as she zooms between their legs and under the table.

"What's wrong with her?" whispers Giulia, retreating to the edge of the kitchen.

Harriet looks at her squarely in the eye. "Nothing is wrong with her. She was born with a mild case of *poliomyelitis*, that's all. Polio. One leg's weaker than the other, but once she gets the calliper, she'll be able to walk just fine."

"And run," Gracie calls out from under the table, "and climb trees, and ride a bike."

"Let's just see, shall we?" says Harriet, diving under the table to tickle her. "One step at a time."

Gracie wriggles with pleasure.

"What's your name?" she says, suddenly noticing Giulia for the first time.

"Er – Giulia."

"Come and play."

"Well, I – er…"

"Yes – come on, Giulia," laughs Harriet, "come and join us. There's plenty of room under here for all of us."

"Oh... all right." She gingerly gets down on all fours and crawls under the table where Gracie and Harriet are giggling.

"Can you do this?" asks Gracie.

"What?" says Giulia.

"Spin round on your bottom – like this. Wheee!"

"Er – no, I don't think I can."

"Try."

"Go on, Giulia," says Harriet, enjoying her new friend's discomfort. "Try."

"All right then – one, two, three." Then, rather self-consciously, she adds, "Wheee," after which she manages to complete, very timidly, one single spin.

"That wasn't very good, was it?" laughs Gracie. "But it was your first go. I expect you'll be better next time."

"Next time?" gulps Giulia.

"Yes. My mummy says you never know what you can do till you try."

"Your mummy sounds very clever."

"Yes. She is. I'm clever too, aren't I? Watch." And Gracie spins even faster.

"Now you're just showing off," says Harriet. "Look – Mrs L's poured your lemonade and given you a biscuit. You'd best come out from under there. I'll get a cloth to wash your hands."

Gracie obediently follows her sister out from under the table, then squirms and grimaces as Harriet rubs a flannel across her face and hands, blowing away the hair of her fringe from off her forehead with noisy relief when Harriet has finished.

After Harriet has left that evening – earlier than usual because of having to take Gracie back – Claudia and Giulia nevertheless look at each other, then collapse, flopping into chairs, giddy with near hysterical exhaustion.

Giulia has spent the day watching Gracie almost as if she were an alien species – or, to be more accurate, she has spent the day watching the way Harriet copes with her with such patience and pleasure, never losing her temper, always finding the right word at the right time. She knows that, if she were left alone with Gracie, she wouldn't last five minutes. When she confesses this to her mother, Claudia just shakes her head. "It's what you do," she says. "You don't have a choice. It's what being a mother means."

"I don't think I'm cut out for it then. Just a single afternoon and my nerves are shot to pieces."

"Oh Giulia, why do you always have to be so dramatic? Gracie was a delight."

"But she was so demanding."

"Not half so demanding as you were at that age."

"Well," she yawns, "I think I'm going to bed. Goodnight."

But when she lies down, she finds that she cannot sleep after all. The events of not just this day, but the last few months, roll around her thoughts and will not let her rest. Something is changing inside her. She knows this, but she can't quite put her finger on what it is, and this disturbs her. She no longer feels so sure about what she says or thinks any more. They've begun to notice at work too. "Where are you, Giulia?" they ask, when she doesn't answer a question. "Daydreaming again?" And whereas before, if that had happened, she would have been able to come back with an immediate cutting or witty riposte, these days she merely shrugs and apologises. When she first began coming back home for the weekends, it was to get away from *Zio Leo* for a couple of days, from his slavish, lap-dog devotion to her, which she was finding increasingly pathetic and distinctly unappealing, but now she begins looking forward to Friday evenings almost as soon as she arrives back at Antonelli's on a Monday morning, when she can get the bus from Old Trafford to Piccadilly just five minutes after finishing work at five o'clock, then run the final quarter mile to Ancoats and Little Italy. It's not just that Harriet has become her best friend, her closest confidante, she's her only friend, and that is giving her further pause for thought, as sleep continues to elude her.

Finally, at around midnight, she creeps downstairs to get a glass of water. Perhaps, she thinks, if her mother's still up, she'll try to put these jangly feelings into words. But the kitchen's in complete darkness. She can see a light's still on in the front room, though, spilling under the door. She opens it carefully, not wanting to disturb *Nonno*, who's snoring quietly in his chair, thinking she'll find her mother busily bent over her sewing machine. But when she steps fully into the room, she sees that her mother, too, is fast asleep, the dress she is finishing still on her lap, a needle dangling from her thumb and forefinger. She sits, completely motionless, like some ghostly waxwork suspended in the shadows, lit only by a street lamp from outside, filtering through the threadbare curtain, which has only been partially drawn. She is like the figure in Kuroda Seiki's painting *Woman Sewing*, eyes closed, hands suspended, barely breathing. As Giulia contemplates her, it is almost as if she is fading away right in front of her.

Giulia looks at her mother a long time.

After several minutes, she knows what she will do.

She creeps towards her, carefully removes the needle from between her mother's thumb and forefinger, desperate not to wake her, slides the unfinished dress from off her lap, and sits in the chair opposite. She looks at the pattern lying half open on the floor, lifts the material up to the light, and studies it minutely.

After another minute a slow smile spreads across her face.

She looks back at her mother, still unreachably asleep, reaches for the cotton and a pair of scissors, and then, with deliberate sureness, she begins.

A few hours later Claudia awakes with a jolt. She feels completely disorientated, and it takes her several seconds to realise where she is. She must have fallen asleep over her sewing again, she thinks. This is happening more and more often these days. She aches all over with stiffness and she rubs the top of her left shoulder with her right hand, rolls her head slowly from side to side, feeling every bone in her neck crack and separate. She's feeling cold too, and her mouth is dry. She stands to go and get herself a glass of water, and it is then that she sees it. The dress is completely finished. It hangs on the mannequin form that stands in the corner of the room. It falls perfectly. Claudia rubs her eyes. She has no memory of putting it there, or even of finishing it. She walks towards it. The dress is utterly different from the one she started. It bears no resemblance to the pattern she'd been following. She's fully awake now. She holds up the skirt of the dress and sees that it has been cut on the bias. This is a technique Claudia avoids if she possibly can, because it's so tricky. One false cut and the whole material could be wasted. But this has been perfectly executed to accentuate the line and curve of the body, causing it to drape softly and effortlessly. It's exquisite.

Claudia takes the dress from the form, rushes out of the room and heads upstairs. Giulia is lying, not under the covers, but on the top of her bed. She opens her eyes sleepily as Claudia comes in.

"*Buongiorno, Mamma.*"

Claudia holds up the dress. "Did you do this?"

Giulia's bottom lip begins to tremble. She sits up. "*Si, Mamma.*"

Claudia goes to the window, pulls back the curtain and lifts the dress to the light.

"*Sei arrabbiata, Mamma?* Are you angry with me?"

"*Non, Tesoro. È un miracolo.*"

The following Saturday Harriet is all agog when she learns from Claudia what Giulia has done.

"How did you know what to do?" she asks.

Giulia shrugs.

"Weren't you worried you'd make a mistake?"

Giulia shakes her head.

"I don't think anything makes you nervous, does it?"

Giulia smiles. "Your sister Gracie does."

Harriet laughs.

"Maybe all those hours I used to spend poring over fashion and film magazines," says Giulia, "weren't such a waste of time after all."

The Saturday after that Harriet arrives carrying a stack of leaflets.

"Look at this, Mrs L," she announces, tossing one onto the kitchen table.

"What is it?"

"A brochure for the Elizabeth Gaskell College on Hathersage Road in Ardwick. They do courses in Fashion Design. Maybe Giulia could enrol?"

"I don't think so, Harriet. She can't just give up her job, and anyway we couldn't afford it."

"Couldn't afford what, *Mamma*?" says Giulia, joining them.

"She wouldn't need to give up her job, Mrs L. They do what they call Continuation Classes. Once a week at Night School. Look, Giulia." She thrusts the brochure towards her.

She is grinning from ear to ear.

Giulia takes the brochure from Harriet and looks at it closely, then turns back to Claudia.

"I'd like to give this a try, *Mamma*."

"But how much does it cost?"

"Six shillings a week for a year. I can pay for that out of my wages."

Harriet looks from Giulia to Claudia and back again.

"Well," she says brightly, "it's such a nice day, Paul and I thought we'd go for a walk. Didn't we, Paul?"

"Did we?" says Paul, bemused.

Harriet glares at him. "Yes, Paul. We did."

"Oh, right. So we did. Come on then."

Once they have gone, Giulia and Claudia remain in silence alone together. Eventually Giulia says, "Harriet's right, *Mamma*. It is a nice day. Why don't you go out for a walk yourself? Maybe have a look round the market. You might meet up with some of the neighbours. I'll sit with *Nonno*."

"Are you sure?"

"*Si, Mamma*."

"Thank you. I'd enjoy that."

Claudia steps outside, savouring the warmth of the sun on her face. A pair of noisy sparrows skitters in the dust. One of them shakes its feathers luxuriously. Giulia watches her mother walk down Radium Street till she reaches the corner, where she turns and waves. Giulia heads back inside.

She goes into the front room, where *Nonno* is awake, stretching his arms. He looks at Giulia as she walks towards him and smiles.

"*Ciao, Nonno*," she says, sitting beside him.

He looks at her closely, then nods his head. "Ah, Claudia," he says. "I'm so glad you're here. I've been telling Marco all morning. 'You hold on to this girl, my boy. *Lei è un Tesoro*."

Giulia's eyes fill up. She looks away. "*Grazie, Nonno,*" she says.

*

In the two years since George has completed his studies at *The Mechanics' Institute*, his weeks have fallen into a regular routine. On three days he is to be found at the Printing Works on Portugal Street, deputising for his father. He enjoys getting his hands dirty with the various presses and machines, for which he has inherited from Hubert a natural affinity. This has earned him a warm respect from the rest of the work force, so that when it comes to the management and supervisory roles of his position, he finds himself comfortably growing into the role of 'boss' on those days that he is there.

For one day each week George concentrates solely on his photography, although barely a day goes by when he doesn't take at least one picture, something catching his eye as he zips across the city on his still trusted green DOT Racer with the red mud guards. Francis has set up a dark room for him in the cellar below the shop in Denton, and George has continued his documentation of the working men and women of Manchester, as well as, at Lily's urging, portraits of the various young girls being helped by his mother's committees, together with their stories. An exhibition featuring these poignant portraits is mounted in the Central Methodist Hall on Oldham Street, where it receives thoughtful reviews. George is quickly acquiring a reputation for the dignity and compassion of his photographs, a reputation he is keen to foster by honing further his eye for composition, for which he continues to attend drawing classes one evening a week at *The Institute*.

He still attends Belle Vue Speedway track on two other evenings per week, where his skills with setting the timing of the bikes' engines are widely sought. The remaining four evenings he divides between Francis and his family, though these days he rarely spends the night at Lapwing Lane, preferring instead the freedom and flexibility of Portugal Street in the centre of the city.

That leaves three days each week which find him still with Archie Rowe in Buile Hill. He's completed his apprenticeship as a sign writer and Archie now trusts him, albeit in a gruff, begrudging kind of way, which George has come to recognise as his way of offering tacit approval, with more and more demanding jobs. Archie's motto remains the same. "If tha's nowt to say, then don't say owt," which more accurately translates as never offering praise, but always being immediately forthcoming if, for any reason, he finds George's work does not come up to scratch. "Tha' closet seat," he'll rail, "tha' big girl's blouse, what dost tha' call this then, youth? I'll not be setting my name to that rubbish." But these comments issue from his tobacco-stained lips much less frequently these days, and so the two of them can mostly be found working side by side in companionable silence, punctured by the occasional, "Ay, that'll do, youth," or even, on one unforgettable red letter day, "Not bad, young 'un. In fact I'm minded to say 'reet gradely'."

It is something of a surprise therefore when George arrives one Monday morning at the beginning of April 1934 to find Archie already waiting to intercept him as he parks his DOT Racer in the yard outside his workshop. Catch's dog, Quilt, who has now become quite a friend of George, has loped across the yard from the forge to have his ears stroked and fondled, without which the day can't properly be said to have started, but Archie is thrusting a piece of paper right under George's nose.

"What dost tha' make o' this, lad?"

George reads it slowly and carefully twice, then looks back at Archie with eyebrows raised.

"Ay, that's what I thought, an' all."

Archie snatches it back and reads from it aloud.

FAO Mr A. Rowe, Sign Writer

The following order is issued by the Central Library Sub-Committee, which has been appointed to consider the most suitable situation for the creation of a new Reference Library in the Town Hall Extension Site with responsibility for the character of the building and for all fittings and fixtures required to meet with the agreed architectural designs as approved by the Corporation.

It is hereby resolved:
that the following order be placed – see below;
that the Town Clerk be instructed to prepare the necessary contract, and
that under the direction of the Lord Mayor the Corporate Seal be affixed thereto.

Particulars:
To carry out the required inscription around the domed ceiling of the Great Hall Reading Room of the new Central Reference Library

Amount Authorised:
According to the Schedule – a figure not exceeding £100, to include all materials

Signed: *A.A. Flitcroft*, Town Clerk
pp Alderman Joseph Binns, J.P., Lord Mayor

Manchester
Corporation

Archie scratches his head. "I don't understand it. It's not like we tendered for it. I know nowt about this Library, do you?"

"It's the large circular building in St Peter's Square," replies George, still fondling Quilt's ears.

"Ay, I reckon," says Archie, still frowning. "I've not seen it. I don't go into Manchester much."

"I think," says George somewhat diffidently, sending Quilt padding back towards the forge, "that my mother might have something to do with this. She's a co-opted member of the Committee that issued the order."

"So tha' knew all about this beforehand? Why didn't tha' say summat?"

"I didn't. My mother probably didn't like to say anything until it was all agreed. This is as much a surprise to me as it is to you."

"Well, I'm blowed."

"You're not cross then?"

"Cross? Tha' doesn't look a gift horse in t' mouth, dost tha', lad? An' a hundred pound is as much as I'd make in a half year. We'd best be tekkin' a look at yon library then, youth, an' see what we're lettin' ourselves in for. Is there room for me on t' back o' that bike o' yourn?"

Half an hour later they're standing in St Peter's Square looking up at the new library, still clad in scaffold. Archie shakes his head. "I see what tha' means about t' shape, lad. It's a rum 'un, and no mistake. It looks more like a gasometer than a library. Still, ours is not to reason why. Let's go inside and see this domed ceiling. I'm not sure I like the sound o' that either."

Once inside the scene resembles a great upturned ship, with the sound of hammers and saws, drills and machinery. Great arcs of flame fountain from the welders' torches, showering on plumbers, electricians, carpenters and stonemasons. They are directed up a newly finished marble staircase to the first floor, where they are shown into the Great Hall, which will be the library's Central Reading Room. In here, by contrast, all is calm and quiet. The major building work is finished and an army of decorators is painting the walls. Everyone speaks in hushed whispers, the reason for which soon becomes clear as Archie, recognising one of the painters, calls out his name. The echo bounces around the walls and returns to him at the same time as several other voices badger him to be quiet. Loud voices are of no use here, and George notices how many of the men are using a kind of mimed, sign language to communicate to each other whenever they need to shift a ladder or require a new paint brush. There's a kind of unified harmony to the work in here, which reminds George of a ballet. He itches to take out his camera and capture some of its orchestrated synchronicity, but that will have to wait. Archie, now standing in the very centre of the room, beckons George towards him, with an exaggerated, slow motion gesture. The choreography of the space is contagious, and already the two of them are part of it, adding their own individual movements to the overall pattern and frieze.

Archie gulps. "There's no way I can go all the way up there," he whispers, pointing to the domed ceiling where the inscription is to be placed. "It's all I can do to go up two storeys these days." And it's true. Frequently, George is the one these days to attach their signs, once they have been painted, onto the fascia boards of buildings, especially if they're on the second floor. Archie becomes wheezily breathless when climbing stairs and is becoming more and more shaky if required to ascend ladders. "How high dost tha' reckon it is? Sixty foot if it's an inch! Nay, lad, *tha'll* have to do it."

"But I'm not ready for such an important job."

"Tha'll 'ave to be, there's nowt else for it."

Archie's estimate turns out to be uncannily close. The ceiling is actually sixty-one feet in height, while the perimeter is three hundred and ninety-nine feet all round. The inscription that they are required to write is fifty-two words in length which, including spaces and punctuation points, adds up to two hundred and ninety-four characters in total, meaning that they must allocate a rectangle of one foot four inches by one foot for each one, allowing an additional two inches in height to compensate for the foreshortening effect caused by the writing having to be applied to a surface that slopes inwards at an angle of approximately thirty degrees.

They check and re-check their measurements and calculations. Archie then instructs and supervises George in a series of trial runs, letter by letter, on various surfaces back at the workshop, experimenting with different fonts and colours, until they settle on the *Wallau* font, designed a decade earlier by Rudolf Koch in Offenbach, Germany, in Antique Gold paint.

"The Germans produce beautiful fonts," enthuses Archie, in a way that reminds George of how Francis had waxed so lyrically about German makes of cameras. "Rudolf Koch started out in Hanau in a metal goods factory, where he also started to draw. He studied in Nuremburg an' was a great admirer o' William Morris an' th' Arts & Crafts Movement. He began to provide type faces for t' Klingspor Factory there, along wi' t' likes o' Paul Renner, Otto Beckmann an' Peter Behrens." George has never heard Archie give such a long speech before. His face has taken on an expression close to rapture. He goes to a desk at the back of the workshop and pulls out a book, in which there are several examples of Koch's work, both his lettering and some woodcut illustrations.

"Ay, lad," he concludes, "I reckon that the *Wallau*'s got the right kind of heft for this job, eh youth?"

George nods in agreement, revising his view of his normally bluff, taciturn employer.

Over the next few weeks, in between their other jobs, Archie and George continue to refine and practise their use of *Wallau*, gradually increasing in size, until George feels ready to take on the task *in situ*.

The foreman at the library negotiates with Archie for them to come in during the evenings after the other workers have left for the day. They need to be left undisturbed for the duration of the task, for if anyone were to distract George while he is working, or accidentally jolt his elbow in midstroke, the results would be catastrophic. He needs to allow his arm time and space to discover the rhythm and freedom necessary for the long, bold, uninterrupted brushwork that will be required to complete the inscription in such a way as to render it weightless, soaring free and unencumbered above the heads of those who look up to read it, like a coronet adorning the head, the crown of which is suffused with light falling through the glass in the ceiling's apex.

George climbs the labyrinth of scaffolding, ladders and platforms until he reaches the point where he is to begin, directly above the gilded clock atop what will be the central, circular information desk, within which the librarians will sit. Archie waits below, ready to offer advice and correction if necessary from below on the as yet unpolished floor, still covered with sheets to protect it until the final phase of the work is completed. He stands surrounded by the sixty-six marble columns which encircle the Great Hall, their mottled, golden colour dappling in the last rays of the sun slanting down upon them through the skylight in the dome above, a colour which will be picked out even more by the Antique Gold paint, the first tin of which George is about to dip his brush into and make his first mark with. He lights a candle, which he places on a platform just to his left above his head, which will illuminate the expanse of ceiling he is to begin. He recalls the descriptions by Vasari of Michelangelo embarking upon the Sistine Chapel, hoisted to a similar height on a precariously swinging cradle, which his Art History lecturer had read to him at *The Mechanics" Institute*. Not that what he is attempting comes anywhere close to such an enterprise, but it encourages him to think of it.

"'*Faith in oneself is the best and safest course*'." That was one of Michelangelo's. "'*It is necessary to keep one's compass in one's eyes and not in the hand, for the hands execute, but the eye judges*'." That was another.

He closes his eyes, takes a deep breath, picturing the whole inscription revealing itself letter by letter in his mind around the ceiling's span. They have done their calculations, they have measured lightly in pencil the upper and lower reaches of the imagined lines between which he will write.

"'*I saw the angel in the marble and carved until I set her free*'." That was a third.

He's ready.

He opens his eyes, dips the brush into the paint, steadies the mahl stick in his left hand, rests his right arm upon it, and begins.

The light outside fades. The glow of the candle flame intensifies. George works, and Archie watches, in perfect silence. Each can hear the breathing of the other.

The work will take them five nights. They have calculated that each letter will take George ten minutes. There are two hundred and forty words, which means the whole inscription will take forty hours to complete. Five nights of eight hours each.

They begin on Monday 9th July 1934, exactly one week and a day before the library is due to be officially opened by King George, so there's no margin for error. They must finish by Friday to allow the foreman and his team the weekend to take down all the scaffolding and give the whole interior a thorough cleaning in time for any last minute adjustments on the Monday to be ready for their Majesties on the Tuesday.

George completes the first letter. He looks down towards Archie, who nods. And so he proceeds, letter by letter, throughout the night, trying not to think of the enormity of the Great Hall's perimeter, concentrating instead only on keeping his painting hand flowing freely and evenly in long, measured strokes, making sure he is never tentative, but always bold. At the completion of each letter, he lowers both arms, shakes out the stiffness, rolls his shoulders back and forth, takes a swig of water, before calling out the next letter to Archie below, who responds by repeating it back to him, so there can be no room for error.

"W?"
"W – check."
"I?"
"I – check."
"S?"
"S – check."

At the end of each word, George will stand back as far as he dare on the flimsy scaffold, crane his neck and read it back to Archie.

"W-i-s-d-o-m…"
"W-i-s-d-o-m…"

At four in the morning, as the light from the sky begins to

seep through the round window in the centre of the dome, George puts down his brush and replaces the lid on the tin of paint. Forty-eight letters done. Another forty-eight tomorrow.

And so the week progresses.

Tuesday night, another forty-eight letters. Wednesday night, forty-eight more. Thursday night, a further forty-eight, until Friday night arrives, and the final forty-eight wait patiently to emerge upon the ceiling wall, floating like ghostly palimpsests from where they have been lying beneath the plaster, waiting to be born, angels about to be set free and take wing.

As the last full stop is painted, doubled with a final flourish by George into a colon, so that the reader, from wherever he or she may stand in the Great Hall, looking up, will quickly be able to orientate themselves as to where to begin, George lets out an audible sigh, which empties him. Archie, permitting himself to speak at last, is content with merely an "Ay, lad, tha's done it. I reckon Rudolf Koch himself could've done no better."

George feels suddenly overwhelmed with dizziness and has to steady himself against an upright scaffold, behind which, lying prostrate along one of the platforms, he spots a window pole. He slowly draws it along towards him, raises it up to the skylight in the dome above his head, where a new dawn is beginning to poke through, and pulls sharply on it. It opens to let in some much needed, welcome fresh air, which George drinks in deeply.

A few moments later, they both hear a fluttering against the glass. A tiny wren is perched on the roof outside, curiously looking down at them through the glass. It tips its head first one way, then another, before opening its beak, from which pours forth a glorious descending cascade of rapid notes, followed by a series of inquisitive churrs and chitters. Then, no longer able to contain his curiosity any longer, it dips under the skylight and begins to fly around the vast, empty chamber of the Great Hall, swooping through and between the scaffold towers, perching between the great marble columns, before finally alighting on top of the gilt clock, which delicately chimes the half hour. The wren, startled, trills back in response and then takes off for another skittish orbit of the domed ceiling, passing each of the painted letters in turn, until eventually it lands on the floor between Archie's feet.

With aching slowness, he lowers himself towards it and, with a sudden lunge, scoops it up in his huge ham hands. George joins him. Together the two men look down on the tiny trembling bird, fluttering against Archie's fingers like a pulse in the blood. He carries it carefully down the marble staircase towards the front door, where the men who are to take down the scaffolding have already started to arrive and are stamping their heavy boots on the stone steps. George puts his finger to his lips, and the men stand back like the parting of the Red Sea to let them pass. As soon as they are outside, Archie opens his hands and the wren flies away, landing a few yards ahead of them on the recently unveiled Cenotaph designed by Sir Edwin Lutyens in St Peter's Square, from where it eyes them dispassionately, its head bobbing up and down and from side to side.

George and Archie wait until it takes off again, and they can no longer see it, before returning inside the Library, where the men have already begun to take down the scaffolding in the Great Hall, revealing the full inscription unencumbered, as if shaking off its iron carapace. The letters glitter in the morning light, as if ready to take wing.

*

Manchester Evening News

Tuesday 17th July 1934

CITY GETS READY FOR ROYAL VISIT

Central Reference Library To Open Today

At 4 o'clock this afternoon the brand new Manchester Central Reference Library will be officially opened by their Majesties King George V and Queen Mary of Teck in what promises to be another spectacular royal occasion for our city.

It is now four years since former Prime Minister Ramsay MacDonald laid the foundation stone for this extraordinary building, which has been the focus of so much excitement and anticipation as city dwellers have watched its progress, mushrooming up into the sky, opposite another famous Manchester landmark, *The Midland Hotel.*

Becoming a popular fixture in the public's imagination before it has even been completed, the new library has already been affectionately nicknamed as the *Corporation Wedding Cake* and *St Peter's Gasometer*, in homage to its remarkable rotunda-like structure springing up in St Peter's Square. Designed by the illustrious architect Mr E. Vincent Harris to reflect the Pantheon in Rome, this neo-classical temple to culture, leisure and learning will be the largest library in Great Britain.

Last minute preparations have been carried out right around the clock to make sure that, when this particular wedding cake is unveiled, she looks her absolute best. Staff Librarian Isabel Wallman, (Miss), told us that she had been working "right up to the last minute" to get everything ready in time for their royal visitors.

"On Sunday evening I was busy with a pen knife in the Technical Library removing the brown wrapping paper from the brass handrails leading down to the Library Stacks, where the more than ten miles of books are stored. The rails gleamed so brightly as I gave them their final polish I could see my reflection in them."

Miss Wallman, together with the rest of the Library staff, will be issued with personal passes today so that they may stand in a privately cordoned off area from where they will be able to see more than just their reflections, but the entire royal party, as His Majesty will carry out the formal opening ceremony, at which, we are told, he will use a specially fashioned key made from Welsh gold, which afterwards will be on display in the Library for all to see.

Meanwhile, fine weather and cloudless blue skies are forecast for this afternoon, as thousands of excited and patriotic Mancunians are expected to line the streets to give their Majesties a right royal welcome. King George and Queen Mary will be escorted by Battalions from The Manchester Regiment, to whom a set of Ceremonial Drums will be presented in recognition of their loyal service to the Crown.

A special commemorative book, printed by F.G. Wright & Sons By Royal Appointment, will be available from all newsagents from tomorrow, containing photographs of the event, together with further interesting facts about this first ever Free Public Library to be erected wholly by a local authority. Yet another first for Manchester!

*

Noon, Tuesday 17th July 1934.

Mr Algernon Askerwith Flitcroft, Town Clerk to the Manchester Corporation, goes over the timings for the afternoon one last time with all of his staff. Today's events have been meticulously planned to the second, and yesterday's rehearsal had proceeded like clockwork. Of course, that rehearsal did not – could not – allow for the variables made possible by the whims and foibles of royal guests, who had the unfortunate habit of departing from the script at times, of irritatingly going off *piste*, so to speak, to hold unplanned for, impromptu conversations with members of the public, especially Queen Mary, who was noted for it, but Flitcroft was confident that he had created sufficient leeway within his schedule to accommodate such departures.

He reminds his staff that to be forewarned is to be forearmed. He throws in a quote from the Roman Stoic philosopher, Seneca the Younger, by way of additional motivation.

" *'Difficulties strengthen the mind as labour does the body'.*"

One or two members of his staff try – unsuccessfully – to conceal a smirk. They had privately wagered with one another on how long it would be before Flitcroft threw in one of his classical quotations, and he has not disappointed. Less than two minutes. He has a reputation for punctilious attention to detail that is second to none, a reputation from which he derives great personal and professional satisfaction, and today's visit by their Majesties King George and Queen Mary provides him with an unparalleled opportunity to attain yet greater heights.

He pictures in his mind's eye a saying by Heraclitus, whch he keeps always on his desk.

" *'Good character is not formed in a week, or indeed in a month, or even a year. It is created little by little, day by day, in barely measurable incremental increases. Protracted and patient effort is needed if one is to develop it at all'."*

He takes out his pocket watch, a modest brass Swiss-made fob purchased from Thomas Russell & Sons of Manchester by his father, which he inherited on his untimely death. On either side of the city's coat of arms just below the Roman numeral for twelve is inscribed in Latin *'Tempus fugit'*, and this has quite literally been his watchword throughout his working life. At school he had been a conscientious, rather than a gifted student, a distinction he readily acknowledged, earning his success by dint of hard, methodical study rather than being reliant on flair. The same systematic approach has served him equally well in his working life. He joined the Corporation's accounts team shortly after his twenty-first birthday, kept his head down, sought neither notice nor favour, but quickly garnered a reputation for assiduous reliability, a keen analytical mind and a meticulous sense of duty. These qualities were recognised and then rewarded, and gradually, little by little, as Heraclitus would have it, he began his rise up the professional ladder, eventually becoming Town Clerk just one year short of his fortieth birthday, a position he has held for twenty-five years. This afternoon's royal visit, with all its attendant paraphernalia, will be his crowning glory before he retires later in the year, a milestone he will approach with the same level-headed equanimity with which he has faced every new challenge. He will, he has decided, devote some of this newly accorded spare time to become more thoroughly versed in the writings of his favourite Latin poets and philosophers, particularly those Stoics whom he much admires.

" *'Happiness and freedom begin with one principle'*," wrote Epictetus, expressing a sentiment, by which he has tried to live much of his life. " *'Some things are within your control and some are not'*."

He shares this with his team as part of his closing

remarks. "Wise words," he adds, somewhat unnecessarily. He looks back at his watch. "We now have forty-five minutes before we need to make our way to our respective positions. I trust that each of you knows what your allotted task is to be this afternoon, and I am confident that you will fulfil that task to the best of your ability. Consequently I do not intend to say anything further. As Pythagoras has always urged us, '*Do not say a little in many words, but a great deal in a few*'. I suggest therefore that we all now retire for a light lunch and reconvene at our various stations at one o'clock. Good afternoon and good luck."

Polite applause greets these closing remarks as everyone disperses, some back to their offices, some, as Flitcroft has encouraged, to the Town Hall refectory. Flitcroft himself – Mr Algernon Askerwith, named alphabetically after each of his grandfathers – repairs to his office, where he retreats to a small cubicle at the back, while he changes into the formal frock coat, winged collar and top hat required for his afternoon with the King and Queen, for Flitcroft will be in attendance throughout the entire ceremony, ensuring that his meticulously laid plans for the day are carried out to the letter with the minimum of fuss. If he can remain more or less invisible from now until their Majesties leave Manchester for Liverpool early this evening (where tomorrow the King is due to open the Mersey Tunnel), he will have done his job well.

He scrutinises his appearance in the mirror in the recessed cubicle, satisfied that his appearance is suitably modest, with little or no danger of attracting any unwarranted attention. A small framed text hangs above his desk, which catches his eye now as he sits behind it to begin a frugal lunch of boiled ham, lettuce and a tomato, accompanied by a glass of water, which his secretary, Miss Higham, has left for him as requested. It is from Plato and it is his, Flitcroft's, own personal creed. It reads:

'Good actions give strength to ourselves and inspire good actions in others.'

He tucks a napkin into the front of his shirt as he fastidiously nibbles his tidy way through lunch, going over one final time the schedule for the afternoon, which he has learned by rote.

3.10pm

The Royal train arrives on time at its special platform at Victoria Station. At a nod from Flitcroft, the Earl of Derby will greet King George and Queen Mary and formally present to them Alderman George Binns, Lord Mayor of Manchester, his wife, Mrs Binns, the Lady Mayoress, and Sir John Maxwell, the Chief Constable of the city.

3.14pm

Flitcroft himself will usher the Lord Mayor and Lady Mayoress into the official black Corporation Daimler, bearing the city's insignia on its side door, to precede the Royal Procession along its designated route, in order to ensure that they arrive in good time to be ready to receive their Majesties on the steps of the Town Hall.

3.15pm

Flitcroft, looking over his shoulder, will be relieved to observe the Royal Procession getting underway. In the first car will be seated the Earl and Countess of Derby, the young Lord Stanley and his fiancée, Miss Ruth Primrose.

In the second car will be the King and Queen, accompanied by the Dowager Countess of Airlee, (the Queen's Lady-in-Waiting), and the Honourable Oliver Stanley M.C, M.A, Secretary of State for the Armed Forces.

Following in the third car will be Lady Stanley, the Earl of Sefton, and Major Archibald Hardynge C.R., C.V.O., M.C., Assistant Private Secretary to the Palace.

Bringing up the rear in the fourth car will be Captain Marcus Bullock, M.P. and Lieutenant-Colonel Reginald Harris Seymour, both Equerries-in-Waiting.

Flitcroft takes a sip of water.

The route, which has been carefully planned by him to ensure that the largest numbers of crowds can be accommodated safely, will take the procession down Hunts Bank, onto Victoria Street, along Market Street as far as Piccadilly, from where it will turn right down Portland Street, before turning right again at Princess Street, which will take them into Albert Square, where thousands more people will throng the pavements in order to get a glimpse of their sovereign and his consort, many scaling the various statues there: the reforming Bishop James Fraser; John Bright, promoter of free trade; Oliver Heywood, the banker and philanthropist, and the four time Prime Minister, William Ewart Gladstone. Even the monumental Albert Memorial will have people hanging from every corner of its edifice, from each of the Four Arts, Four Sciences, Four Continents and Four Seasons.

Flitcroft dabs the corners of his mouth with his napkin and permits himself a quiet smile at the thought of these 'outrages', with the police powerless to prevent them.

3.30pm

Upon arrival at the Town Hall the Royal Party will be presented by the Earl of Derby to Lieutenant-General Sir Willoughby Marchant St.George Kirke K.C.B., C.M.G., D.S.O., the Commanding Officer-in-Chief of the Supreme Western Command, and to Major-General Kenneth Gerald Buchanan C.B., C.M.G., D.S.O., Commander of the 42nd Division of the East Lancashire Territorial Army. Flitcroft rather enjoys this formal insistence by all military personnel that each of the various honours and titles bestowed on them are listed in full.

A Guard of Honour from the 2nd Battalion of The Manchester Regiment, under the command of Captain Charles Henry Keithley M.B.E., will be inspected by His Majesty the King, while the Band of the Battalion will play a stirring march. Flitcroft has requested *Lilliburlero*, which he has heard is a particular favourite of Queen Mary, who at the same time will carry out an inspection of an Attachment of the Territorial Army Nursing Division.

Flitcroft has a minor qualm concerning this section of the schedule, for it is extremely difficult to be precise with regard to timing. Both their Majesties are notorious for spontaneously entering into conversation with one or two individuals whilst carrying out such inspections.

As soon as is possible, therefore, The Lord Mayor, on behalf of the public subscribers, will then present to His Majesty the King, in his role as Colonel-in-Chief of The Manchester Regiment, two sets of silver drums for use by both the 1st and 2nd Battalions, which His Majesty will graciously accept.

All the invited guests, who have been assembled on the steps of the Town Hall during these inspections, will then be requested to make their way inside to their allotted seats within the Large Hall.

3.40pm (*or as close to this thereafter*)
The National Anthem will be played by The Baxendale's Works Band of Pollard Street, Manchester, runners up in the Belle Vue British Open of 1933. Flitcroft pauses, his fork poised above an about-to-be-speared slice of tomato. This will be his big moment. It is his duty as Town Clerk to read aloud the Lord Mayor's address, welcoming their Majesties to Manchester Town Hall. He reminds himself to make sure he sucks a menthol lozenge he has brought with him specially to ensure his throat will not become dry or hoarse, but remain sufficiently lubricated for him to be able to deliver this short

address without in any way drawing attention to himself. The King will afterwards declare himself pleased to reply thereto, after which he will be presented by Alderman Hardcastle to all current serving councillors and former Lord Mayors.

3.50pm
Flitcroft himself will then lead the assembled company behind the Mace out of the Large Hall back into Albert Square, along Lloyd Street and into Cooper Street, to the site of the Foundation Stone of the Town Hall Extension. The Band of The Manchester Regiment will accompany them during this short but necessary journey with a sprightly rendition of *Rose and the Laurel.*

3.53pm
Upon arrival in St Peter's Square His Majesty will be presented to the waiting Emanuel Vincent Harris, Chief Architect and Designer of the new Library, who will instruct the King in how to re-lay the Foundation Stone by means of an electrically controlled apparatus, with which Flitcroft fully expects His Majesty, well known for his fondness for gadgets, to be visibly delighted.

3.56pm
The procession will re-form and make its way round to the Portico, the Front Entrance to the Library, where the members of the Library Sub-Committee, both elected and co-opted, will be waiting to be presented to their Majesties, among them Councillor Grandage and Mrs Annie Wright, for whose permission to attend Flitcroft has been obliged – happily, he concedes – to waive strict protocol.

He puts down his knife and fork neatly on his now clean plate. He has a soft spot for Mrs Wright. Almost more than any other aspect of the afternoon's programme he is eagerly looking forward to what will be his first glimpse of the inscription she has proposed to encircle the domed ceiling of the Library's Great Hall rotunda. He takes another sip of water as he pulls his thoughts back to the schedule.

3.58pm

Mr Harris, the Architect, will then ask leave to introduce to Their Majesties representatives of the vast work force who have helped to construct the Library, including Mr John Arthur Strange, Director of William Moss & Sons, the Principal Contractors, Mr Alan Smith, Clerk of the Works, Mr Walter Bird, Chief Foreman, and a number of workmen, including Mr Archie Rowe, the Sign Writer.

This is another of those moments about which Flitcroft feels slightly anxious, for Queen Mary is almost certain to speak at some length to several individuals. He even imagines her sharing a joke with Mrs Wright! But there's no point worrying about things over which he can have no control. Royals will be Royals after all, and by the time the party will have reached this point, his role will almost be at an end.

4pm

Finally the Lord Mayor will be able to invite the King to open the doors, and he will present him with the special key of Welsh gold to do so. His Majesty will duly oblige, and the Grand Opening of the Doors will be accompanied by a fanfare of trumpets, after which the King will address the waiting crowds in St Peter's Square.

Flitcroft wonders what King George might say. Thankfully the King is not a lover of public speaking, so if he does choose to speak, it will not be for long. There had been some debate in Committee as to whether a microphone should be installed so that the enormous crowds they are anticipating in St Peter's Square will be able to hear him, but in the end, as Councillor Grandage had most sensibly, if characteristically bluntly, pointed out, that might be interpreted as presumptuous on the part of the Corporation, as if they expected His Majesty to deliver a speech, rather than offering to say a few words if he so chose.

If he does indeed decide to speak, this will be followed by a further fanfare, which will ring out over St Peter's Square, invoking even louder cheers from the thousands looking on.

Flitcroft imagines King George raising his hat to acknowledge their enthusiastic approbation, before making his way inside to inspect the Libraries, at which point Flitcroft will hand over the reins for the remainder of the programme to Alderman Hardcastle and slip quietly and unnoticed further into the background, the anticipation of which causes a narrow smile to cross his thin lips as he finishes the last morsel of lettuce recalcitrantly trying to evade the probing tines of his pewter fork…

Two months later, on Flitcroft's last day in the Town Hall before he takes his retirement, his final duty is to attend a meeting of the Finance & General Purposes Committee, at which, under Any Other Business, Alderman Hardcastle proposes a formal Vote of Thanks "for services rendered to the Council". Flitcroft records for the Minutes, in his immaculate copper-plate hand, the following:

'Resolved unanimously – that the Committee desires to express their heartfelt gratitude to Mr A.A. Flitcroft for the valuable services rendered by him as Town Clerk in the interests of the Corporation during the past five and twenty years and to record their sincere appreciation of his unwavering courtesy and propriety when attending to any and all matters arising'.

Flitcroft inclines his head to one side as the applause rings out. He is further surprised by the arrival of his secretary, Miss Higham, carrying a package wrapped in brown paper under her arm, which she gives to Alderman Hardcastle, who, before presenting it to Flitcroft, calls on all persons present to offer three rousing cheers.

Flitcroft, not accustomed to making public speeches himself, stammers a few words of thanks. He then opens the package to reveal a splendid mahogany wall clock, manufactured, like his own inherited fob watch, by Thomas Moss & Sons. Inscribed in the centre is the phrase: *Initium Novum*. A new beginning…

But all of this lies in the future. Flitcroft checks his father's watch on the third Tuesday in July 1934. One o'clock precisely. He pushes back the chair from his desk and rises to his feet. He takes the four strides he needs to reach the door to the outer office.

"Miss Higham," he calls. "It is time, I believe."

"Yes, Mr Flitcroft," she replies. "Good luck."

Flitcroft nods, then steps out into the corridor, which takes him along the avenue of busts and statues of Manchester Worthies, whose collective gaze falls upon him as he strides towards the main exit. He notices a speck of dust on his otherwise gleamingly polished shoes and stoops to flick it aside. He pauses as he does so to observe the mosaic of bees and cotton flowers in the tiled floor, before striding out into the July sunshine, where the crowds are already several thousand strong.

Among that crowd of several thousand is Francis, who has decided he will film the event and then conduct a small experiment involving the latest technical innovations in telegraphic broadcasting. Right now, with the Royal Procession expected in about an hour, he has installed himself on the second floor of *The Queen's Hotel* at the junction of Piccadilly with Portland Street. With Luigi's connivance he has been able to commandeer a landing close to a window, through which he is now training his *Kinamo* camera on the swelling crowds below him.

Manchester Corporation has declared the day a Public Holiday and most of the schools, mills, factories and shops have followed suit, thereby allowing as many of the city's official population of 142,000 people the opportunity to attend. The true figure, Francis knows, is much larger, for this does not include the adjoining towns of Salford, Stockport, Ashton, Bury, Rochdale, Oldham or several others currently not officially a part of the city, but who naturally fall within the greater conurbation, with much of their trade flowing into the centre far more quickly than the still sluggish Irwell, Medlock and Irk.

Despite the warm weather, many in the crowd, Francis notes, are dressed up in their Sunday best – jackets with collars and ties for the men, smart coats and hats for the women. They are kept back from encroaching too far onto the carriageways by the substantial presence of police constables, many on horseback, and lines of soldiers from The Manchester Regiment, who form a veritable human chain around the city. Nevertheless the mood is light and festive. A holiday spirit pervades indeed. It hardly seems credible that only eight years ago these same soldiers and police were being deployed to keep order during the General Strike, when the mood was far from festive.

Now, though, that all appears forgotten. Francis recalls other mass gatherings that Manchester has known – the ugly riots after the sinking of *The Lusitania*, not yet twenty years ago, which had forced his internment on the Isle of Man and four wasted years, and the joyous celebrations on Armistice Night, when people who, just three years before, had fought against one another so bitterly, then danced together in the fountains of Piccadilly Gardens. Francis was still locked up in Peel on that night, but he read about it in the newspapers and has seen photographs of it. He wonders whether he too might have been able to forgive so easily. Since his reinvention of himself, as Francis Hall from Franz Halsinger, he hardly considers his German heritage at all these days, although he still takes vicarious pride in the technical innovations of the engineers and designers in Berlin, Leipzig, Dresden and Frankfurt, who continue to produce such high quality cameras – like the *Kinamo* he is looking through this afternoon. Looking out over the crowds now covering every square inch of the city centre, cheering as yet another attachment of soldiers on horseback parades down Portland Street, he cannot help but think about that other infamous occasion when a Manchester Cavalry rode through the city's streets, slashing and slicing their way through the panicking crowds, who had gathered on a similarly festive summer afternoon a hundred and fifteen years before to listen to the speeches of men like Orator Hunt, urging Parliamentary Reform. "No taxation without representation," had been their rallying cry, until they were cut down by sabres flashing in the sunlight, the slaughter and mayhem reaching their height on St Peter's Fields, the exact same spot where the new Central Reference Library is to be opened later, where Francis will take himself after he has photographed the arrival of the procession. There seems thankfully no prospect of a repeat of the Peterloo Riots today. Francis finds such compliance vaguely surprising. There may now at last be universal suffrage, but unemployment is at an all time high. We may have the vote, he thinks, but where are the jobs?

"Penny for them, Francis..." It's Winifred who speaks. "You were miles away."

"Yes. Sorry. I was."

Francis too has closed his shop for the day and Winifred is here to assist him. She will carry and operate the sound recording equipment, while he concentrates on the camera. "Just get an overall sense of the atmosphere," he tells her. "The chance remark, the sounds of the horses, the cheers, the bands. But do try to capture what the King says when he declares the Library open."

"Yes, sir!" she replies with a mock salute.

"That's if he deigns to say anything at all."

"Oh, he will, won't he?" asks Winifred. "He wouldn't want to disappoint all these people, who've come specially to see him, would he?"

"Bread and circuses," says Francis.

"You sound like my friend Esther when you say things like that."

"You don't mention her so often these days."

"No, I don't get to see her like I used to, not since she got married and moved to Patricroft. She'd have had a thing or two to say about all this," she adds, gesturing to all the crowds below. Her mind casts back to the first time she had witnessed The Manchester Regiment, marching down Deansgate, then passing this very spot on their way to London Road Station and the Troop Train that would carry them all to France and to war, her fiancé Arthur among them. She shivers, in spite of the warmth. Thank goodness she had met Victor when she did. Although he too, like Esther, would have cocked a snook at all this.

"Where's Victor today?" asks Francis, as if reading her thoughts.

"He had to work," she says. "The pit didn't declare a holiday." He'll be deep underground somewhere, she thinks, possibly right below where they're standing, for the seams stretch for many miles. "He's only been back a few months, so he can't afford to turn shifts down."

"How is he?" asks Francis quietly.

"He's recovered pretty well, thanks. His injuries have all healed, more or less. He can breathe without it hurting him now, and he's getting stronger every week."

"Does he..." begins Francis tentatively, "... miss the boxing?"

"No," says Winifred simply. "I thought he would. But he doesn't. 'You've got to know when to quit,' he says. 'I were beaten fair and square by the better man'."

Both are silent for a few moments, each remembering the appalling drubbing Victor had received at the hands of Len Johnson, for each had been present on that terrible night. The dignity of the two men had stayed with Francis particularly, the magnanimity of Johnson in victory, the courage of Victor in defeat, the two of them embracing when the final bell sounded. That memory lasted far longer than the shambolic attempt by Oswald Mosley and his gang of Blackshirt thugs to hi-jack the Kings Hall afterwards, though he continues to cause trouble up and down the land, frequently protected by the same police constables who are holding back the peaceful, patriotic crowds below them now in Piccadilly...

Just then there is a sudden surge and shout from the crowds.

"Here they come!" cries Winifred.

"Steady the Buffs," says Francis, picking up the *Kinamo*.

"Look," says Winifred excitedly, "he looks just like he does on the new minted pennies, only more sun-tanned." The open top car passes below them, the King doffing his top hat to the cheering crowds who, as has become customary for welcoming visiting dignitaries, are all waving white handkerchiefs in the air.

Like an act of surrender, thinks Francis, but he does not say. Instead he whispers mischievously to Winifred, "I just love Queen Mary's toque hat. Is it my colour, do you think?"

Winifred playfully punches his arm.

"Hey," he says, "you'll knock the camera."

A few minutes later, as the royal motorcade heads down Portland Street, Francis and Winifred, having rapidly dismantled their equipment, are dashing down the second floor corridor of *The Queen's Hotel* towards the lift, which Luigi is holding for them. They emerge somewhat chaotically into the hotel foyer, Winifred dropping her bag, Francis tripping over a length of cable, and then proceed to duck and weave their way behind the main body of the crowd until they reach the junction with Charlotte Street, where they dodge under the police cordon and rush across to the other side of Portland Street, cut through George Street, into Nicholas Street, then out onto Mosley Street towards St Peter's Square. Once there, brandishing his BBC pass, Francis manages to manoeuvre their way through the crowds until they have obtained a prime spot right in front of the Portico steps at the entrance to the Library, with just enough time to set up their equipment once more as Mr E. Vincent Harris, the Chief Architect, is instructing the King in the mysteries of the electrically controlled apparatus which can re-lay the Foundation Stone. Francis is able to capture the expression of almost child-like delight on King George's face as he does so.

Winifred is now holding out the microphone in the direction of the Great Front Doors, where the King and Queen stand, waiting for the heralded fanfare of liveried trumpeters to finish, before stepping forward to address the crowds directly. Winifred looks over her shoulder back towards Francis, smirking. "See? I told you," she mouths.

"In this splendid building," announces the King in his customary deep gravelly voice, "which I now declare open, the largest library in this country provided by a local authority, the Corporation have ensured for the inhabitants of the city magnificent opportunities for further education and for the pleasant use of leisure."

A second fanfare follows as the King ceremonially turns the lock in the doors with the key of Welsh gold, then the Royal Party proceeds inside the Library.

A loud sigh of happiness issues from the crowd as they

now begin to disperse. The Band of The Manchester Regiment continues to play stirring marches to entertain them, but in less than half an hour the vast majority have gone, some dashing round to Albert Square to watch the King and Queen depart later, some to sample the delights of the various street vendors selling food on every corner, but many simply to head back home. Among this third category are Francis and Winifred, for Francis has many hours of work still to do before this day is over.

Sitting on the upper deck of a bus they catch from Princess Street, but unable to find seats next to one another, they each allow their separate thoughts to drift by them. Winifred, as she always does when riding a bus, remembers her time a decade and a half before when she was a conductress criss-crossing the ever expanding network of routes from one side of the city to the other, never ceasing to marvel at the constant, convulsive change she has witnessed down the years, while Francis by contrast looks to the future, not lamenting the upheaval which change inevitably brings in its wake, but embracing instead its uncertainty and unpredictability.

Back in his workshop behind the shop in Denton, Francis is running the film from the *Kinamo* through a miniature *Moviola*, which he has managed to borrow from the BBC. He quickly discards sections of it and within a couple of hours he has managed to splice together what he considers to be an effective patchwork of the afternoon's events. Next he runs through Winifred's sound recordings on a recently acquired *Blattnerphone*, a pioneering reel to reel recorder using steel tape, named after its Anglo-German inventor, Ludwig Blattner, who owned and managed a chain of cinemas across Manchester, including *The Grosvenor* in All Saints, where Francis and George had watched their first film together, *The*

Blue Angel. It enables him to cut an atmospheric sound montage of cheering crowds, marching bands, overheard comments and the faint but discernible voice of the King declaring the Library open.

Francis then plays back simultaneously the edited film and sound from the *Kimano* and the *Blattnerphone*, at the same time re-recording it onto 17.5 millimetre film containing its own magnetic sound strip along each frame. While this is still wet he scans the now complete sound film, using an old *Nipkow* disc that he has been able to acquire from the *BBC Radio Theatre* in Hulme, where all the talk currently is of John Logie Baird's experiments with live television broadcasting. Three years before, Baird had made and transmitted the first ever outdoor broadcast, of The Derby at Epsom, and there are rumours that the BBC will begin launching its own television programmes, as well as radio, in less than two years. Francis is thrilled by the possibilities he envisages emanating from this technical breakthrough, and he is keen to demonstrate that Manchester, too, can be part of such a scheme. Once his film has been successfully transferred onto the disc, he is then able to transmit it as a radio signal telegraphically the two hundred and eight miles to the London headquarters of the BBC in Portland Place, from where, just after midnight, he receives a reply confirming that his filmed record of the opening of Manchester Central Reference Library by His Majesty King George V has been received. In his mind's eye he sees the line of telegraph poles marching across the heart of England.

In the end the BBC begin transmitting live television programmes from Alexandra Palace in November 1936, but whereas radio broadcasting began in Manchester simultaneously with London, television programmes do not proceed to be made there until 1954, when the BBC leases the Dickenson Road studios and a national network of transmitters enables televisions to be watched all over the country. Francis will be one of the first Manchester, but that is twenty years into the f

Now, in the early hours of the mornin 18th July 1934, Francis is firmly ahead of the curve, so often been already, sure in his belief that what Manchester does today, the world will do tomorrow. As he starts to fall asleep, he dreams of what might be the first live event that will use television to unite the nation, not imagining that it will be another royal occasion, the coronation of the current King's granddaughter two decades from now, whose image will be beamed into living rooms right across the country, including his own, to which he will invite the entire High Street to come into his shop to watch it with him, when he will look back and smile at this day, twenty years before, his prescience and forward thinking having enabled him to make a film of King George V's visit to Manchester, which in the end was never seen.

He hand delivers the processed film in its can to the Central Reference Library the following week, where it lies on a shelf, forgotten and gathering dust, until eighty years later, when a researcher from the North West Film Archive stumbles across it while the Library is closed for a major refurbishment in 2010, digitises it and uploads it onto vimeo, where it can now be viewed from across the world at: https//www.archivesplus.org/history/the-building-and-opening-of-central-library/

The last image Francis remembers, before falling exhaustedly to sleep, is of the King opening the Front Doors at the top of the Portico Steps with the specially fashioned key of Welsh gold and then walking inside, the two great doors closing behind him.

Also walking inside, a few paces behind the King shortly after four o'clock on that Tuesday afternoon, are George and nie. As soon as the doors close behind them, a sudden informality falls upon the group. The King and Queen are whisked away upstairs to the second floor, to a Refreshment Room and a suite of private apartments that will normally be set aside for the use of the Chief Librarian, but whose first use will be to entertain their Majesties. Annie, along with the rest of the Library's Sub-Committee, has been invited to join them. George, who is present as a guest of Archie's, lingers downstairs. Just before she heads upstairs, Annie has time to mouth towards him, "Find your father," and then she is gone, swept along on the tide of acolytes in pursuit of what they hope might be an individual word with the King or Queen.

Such hopes are soon dashed, however, when, upon reaching the second floor Refreshment Room, the royal visitors are immediately ushered into the private apartments by their Equerries-in-Waiting. Later Alderman Hardcastle, one of a select few who manage to penetrate that inner circle, will inform Annie that the King made a bee line for a stiff whiskey and soda, which he declared "most welcome" and "much needed", while Queen Mary took tea from a brand new china service purchased especially for the occasion, never to be used again but locked away in one of the Town Hall cabinets. While sipping her tea and declining the offer of a slice of Madeira cake, she enquires of those sitting close by her whether there is to be a repeat of the menu from her last visit to the city, back in 1913 before the War, as part of their ten day tour of Lancashire, when she was served tripe for luncheon. The Chief Librarian shudders. "Your Majesty can rest assured there will be no repeat of that impropriety on this occasion," he declares. "Pity," she replies. "I had rather hoped there might be." Hardcastle chuckles broadly as he relates this to Annie afterwards, who smiles delightedly, for it had been her mischievous suggestion to serve their royal guests tripe back then.

It takes George some time to find his father. Hubert has

no desire whatever to be introduced to the King or Queen. He loiters away from the rest of the invited guests and their spouses in a far corner of the Entrance Hall, what he now learns is to be called the Shakespeare Hall, after the huge stained glass window above the great front doors. Donated by Mrs Rosa Grindon, Hubert reads, in memory of her late husband, Leo, the esteemed Manchester botanist, who, like George, had attended *The Mechanics' Institute* to learn his craft. Together with the calico printer Joseph Sidebotham, he founded *The Manchester Field Naturalists' Society* and donated a *herbarium* of 'every cultivated and wild plant to be found in Britain' to the city's Museum. He also collected every piece of botanical writing or drawing he could lay his hands on, including of the Manchester Moth. 'I desired to introduce,' he wrote, 'every bit of printed matter referring to the plants that might come in my way, with descriptions alike of the individual species and of the Natural Orders, their uses and other particulars. Seeing that Botany is wreathed with all kinds of poetical and other human associations, everything that would illustrate these also, I decided, should to go into the collection, including the various species of *Lepidoptera* which graze upon them,' such as the Manchester Moth, that 'singular black-bodied variety of the otherwise white-peppered moth, which had evolved a new skin enabling it to blend in with the city's soot-blackened buildings so successfully that it could safely bask upon them,' captured so exquisitely by the entomologist R.S. Edleston, whose delicate lacewing illustrations were featured in Grindon's *Hebarium*, which Hubert remembered seeing as a small boy when taken to the museum by his father, Frank. The moth's acquired ability to become invisible, to be absorbed into its surroundings so as not to draw attention to itself, is something which Hubert has thought about a lot in more recent years. He has, he realises, been attempting to emulate it, so that whenever, at a social function, like today's opening of the new library, he hears Annie calling to him in that exasperated but concerned tone she adopts so frequently these days – "Oh there you are, Hubert, so this is where you're hiding, I'd completely lost sight of you" – he can emerge from the shadows, eyes blinking, smiling in that self-effacing way of his. "Here I am, dear. I was just looking at…"

Like today, as his attention is once more distracted here in the Shakespeare Hall. He studies the intricacies of the window, the interplay of lead and light. It depicts a portrait of the playwright surrounded by scenes from several of his plays. Gradually, as the guests begin to disperse, Hubert has the Hall more or less to himself, allowing him the chance to enjoy its self-confident grandeur even more. There are two other stained glass windows, he notices, plus several heraldic decorations. On the ceiling are the coats of arms and crests of the Duchy of Lancaster, Lancashire County Council and the City of Manchester, while on the walls are those of Manchester Grammar School, Manchester University, The Manchester Regiment and Humphrey Chetham. The Library reminds him of a classical temple, but dedicated to learning, rather than any false idolatry. He doesn't know when he has been prouder to have been born a Mancunian. That a building as magnificent as this, with all its thousands of books, containing all the knowledge of the world, including more than thirty *incunabula*, books printed before 1500, some even associated with Guttenberg, should be bestowed upon everyone, regardless of birth or rank or class, free and open to all, is nothing short of miraculous. It reminds him of that dream he had once had as a young man, which he had shared with Annie while they had been courting, that quote from *The Tempest*, a scene from which can be seen now in the stained glass window above his head, which has always haunted him, how in dreaming, the clouds, he thought, would open and show riches ready to drop upon him, that when he waked he cried to dream again...

He pauses to rest on a landing half way up the left hand staircase, from where he can take in the whole vista, and he notices a small statue of white marble standing shyly close by, which charms him utterly. He studies the plaque beneath it. It is called *The Reading Girl*, and the sculptor is the Italian Giovanni Ciniselli, who died half a century before. It has been donated, he reads, by Daniel Adamson, the first Chairman of The Manchester Ship Canal Company. The book the girl is holding is blank. What is it that she might be reading, Hubert wonders, that so completely captivates her? Nobody knows for certain. Scholars have claimed it was a poem, called *The Angel's Story*, and that originally it was printed on paper and pasted onto the marble, but by the time she came to the Library, this had disappeared, and no one has been able to trace it since.

Hubert likes the idea of the poem having been printed on a specially measured and cut piece of paper. *The Angel's Story*. What might it have been, he asks himself? He thinks of Lily, and then of the girl whose voice he heard up on Tandle Hill fifteen years ago, and finally of the dream he had as a young man, the clarity of whose vision has been slipping away from him ever since, rather like the poem on *The Reading Girl's* book, washed away like printer's ink in the Manchester rain.

He stays there a long time, imagining what might have been written there, and decides that he rather likes the idea that it has been lost, so that each individual can fill in the blank space with his or her own selected text, a unique response which allows the viewer to be in conversation with the artist, completing the work for him, different every time, so that the sculpture remains timeless, constantly refreshing and renewing itself.

George eventually spots him there, a shy moth quietly retreating from the world, and joins him on the landing.

"Come along," he says gently. "Mother's expecting us on the first floor."

Hubert pulls a face.

"Don't worry," says George, smiling. "It's not another reception. Just something we'd both like you to see."

Hubert perks up at that and slowly rises to his feet, putting his hand to his chest as he does so.

"Are you all right?" asks George.

"I'm fine," says Hubert. "Just a bit out of breath, that's all. I could do with a bit more exercise if I'm honest."

They climb the stairs together to the first floor, where Annie is waiting for them.

"You're just in time," she says, grinning. "They're about ready to start."

"Who are?" says Hubert.

"Start what?" asks George.

Annie taps the side of her nose with the finger of her left hand. "You'll see," she says, a twinkle in her eye.

She leads them through the double doors into The Great Hall Reading Room, where a small crowd has already gathered – not the King and Queen and their entourage, but most of the other invited guests. Hubert stops in his tracks as he enters. The sheer height of the domed ceiling uplifts him, while its perfect circular symmetry suffuses him with a deep sense of calm. It appears to have affected everyone similarly, for all have fallen still, staring about themselves in silent wonder. Even George, having spent five long nights there, is impressed. Now that the clatter of scaffolding's been taken down, he can more fully appreciate the sense of space, which is viewed as the architect intended, from the ground looking up, as opposed to from the roof looking down. The inscription encircles the space, a slim, elegant coronet, modest and unadorned, an imprint on the skin, like a wreath of laurel leaves.

Standing in the centre of the round information desk,

beneath the gilded clock, in the heart of the hall, is Gertrude Riall, who has been asked by Annie to set the words of the inscription to music. Hubert catches sight of Lily, who is watching Annie carefully, waiting for the signal that everyone is ready. As soon as she receives it, she nods towards Miss Riall, who raises her baton to begin.

To Hubert it appears that Gertrude is standing in the hub of a mighty wheel, with each of the long, polished mahogany reading desks radiating from it like the spokes. On the far edge of each of these spokes stands a singer, all taught by Gertrude at the Manchester School of Music on Great Ducie Street. As one they begin a low, wordless humming, the sound soaring upwards towards the skylight in the apex of the roof, through which the late afternoon sun slants down, where it falls upon one of the singers, a young girl, all dressed in white, her hair hanging loose about her shoulders, who stands barefoot on top of one of the desks, directly opposite the double doors through which the people have all entered, where Hubert still stands.

It is Jenny.

She raises her right arm and points upwards towards the domed ceiling. Hubert follows the direction of her pointing finger until his eyes alight upon the antique gold inscription running around the perimeter. The gasp as he recognises it is almost audible, adding to the cascade of antiphonal voices echoing all around him.

Jenny sings.

Each word falls like a drop of water from above.

"Wisdom is the principal thing
Therefore get wisdom
And within all thy getting
Get understanding

*Exalt her
And she shall promote thee
She shall bring thee to honour
When thou dost embrace her*

*She shall give to thine head
An ornament of grace
A crown of glory
Shall she deliver to thee…"*

Hubert feels Annie's fingers interlace with his own. He remembers the night he proposed to her, the night when Halley's Comet trailed across the sky above them, and he shared with her this dream he had, of knowledge descending like riches upon the open, hungry mouths of everyone. Now, as these notes hang suspended in the air above and around him, their echoes decaying in a never-ending half life, like the dying embers of the last sparks in the comet's tail, still illuminating the air, never to be extinguished, he knows his dream has come to pass.

A gentle hand begins to squeeze his heart, clenching him tighter and tighter in its grip which, though it does not hurt him, will not let him go. The pain which slices through him is exquisite, a kite dancing on a hillside delicately cutting the air, which he knows he must release. He is lying on the cool marble floor looking up at the sun falling through the skylight. He sees Annie's face bending over him. Behind her head a tiny wren is fluttering, its wings gently beating against his now closed eyelids.

*

Just as Hubert had had two weddings, so he should have two funerals, thought Annie. Not the grand civic affair that she had organised for Frank, with more than three thousand people spilling out of the Albert Hall – Hubert would have hated that – but something quieter, simpler, more modest, and so she had decided on a mirror image of their wedding, with two small contrasting services at the same places, with the same two ministers officiating.

The first of these took place on a Thursday morning, ten days after Hubert had died, at The Friends' Meeting House on Mount Street, arranged for them by Mr Edward Judd – not strictly a minister, for Quakers do not believe in the need of any intermediary between themselves and their God – who had served as the Clerk for their wedding ceremony there some twenty-three years before. The only people present were herself, George, Lily, Evelyn and Pearl, plus Mr Judd, as well as a handful of Hubert's Quaker 'friends', whom Annie did not recognise. There was no service, no eulogy, just a period of reflective silence, with the mourners arranged on two sides of The Meeting Room, with its clear, unleaded windows and whitewashed walls.

"This is for you," thought Annie, looking dry eyed down upon Hubert's coffin, a plain, unpolished wooden box, which was placed on a table in the centre, unadorned except for a simple bunch of yellow tulips. "I've never felt comfortable in this place, but I know that it was always very important for you." After nearly half an hour one of the 'friends' stood up and said how he would always remember, and be grateful for, Hubert's many acts of kindness, of which he himself had been a beneficiary. "He never wanted a fuss," said the man. "That was certainly true," thought Annie and wondered privately what the particular kindness was that Hubert had performed for this man she did not know existed until this morning.

The second service took place the following day at Hulme Hall Lane Chapel on the edge of the Tripe Colony, where Annie had been a regular attender as a child, and where she and Hubert had continued to go whenever they could, even after they moved away to Victoria Park, then Whalley Range and now Didsbury. She managed to persuade the Reverend William Appleby to come out of retirement to conduct the ceremony. He'd be happy to, he said, then seeing the stricken look on Annie's face, swiftly revised this. Happy to be of service, he had meant of course. There were more people present for this than at The Meeting House the previous day – the same family members, a large contingent from the Printing Works, which was closed for the day out of respect, representatives from all of the various Committees each had belonged to, chapelgoers from across Manchester, as well as many of their regular customers, plus Alderman Hardcastle, Councillor Grandage and Mr Flitcroft from the Corporation, all of whom offered Annie and George their deepest condolences. "A fine man," remarked Alderman Hardcastle. "We'll not see his like again," agreed Councillor Grandage. "*Mors non est finis*," said Mr Flitcroft.

Picking up on this for part of the eulogy, Reverend Appleby agreed. "Death is not the end," he said, "and I know that Hubert would not want us to be sad today. He leaves behind him a legacy and an example that we can all of us aim to follow, though once again Hubert himself would dismiss such a notion. I'm sure that Annie won't mind me mentioning this, but earlier, when she first asked me to say a few words to you all this morning, we discussed the matter of Hubert's headstone. He's to be buried, as some of you may know already, later today at the Southern Cemetery, next to where his father lies. Annie wondered what words she might choose to place upon the headstone. She remembered a quote from *The Tempest* that she knew meant a lot to Hubert. 'We are such stuff as dreams are made on, and our little life is rounded with a sleep.' It's a beautiful sentiment, isn't it? I can see many of you nodding in agreement. Yes, it is. But what I said to Annie then, and what I say to you all here now, is this. Hubert's was not a little life, was it? No. Far from it. He touched us all, leaving each of us with our own particular special memory of him. I remember when I first met him – at a Bazaar to raise funds for our overseas missions, which Annie had organised with a Japanese theme. '*Cherry Blossoms*', it was called. Do you remember, Annie? You sang *Three Little Maids From School*, I recall." Affectionate laughter greeted this remark. Reverend Appleby smiled as he continued. "Somehow or other, Annie, you managed to persuade Hubert to sing too. He must have been very keen to win your favour, for as we all know Hubert was not normally someone to place himself in the spotlight, was he? No. But sing he did. *A Wandering Minstrel, I*. And so I suggested to Annie that the last line of that might be appropriate for his headstone. *'Dreamy lullaby'*. For that is what we hope he is now experiencing. But no. That wasn't right either. And then I remembered something else.

"When I was training to be a minister, more years ago now than I care to remember, I went on a walking tour with some friends to Devon. We planned our route around some of the outdoor places where John Wesley had preached – Okehampton, Torbay, Bampton – camping in between, until finally we came to Exeter. We were all of us especially keen to visit the old Mint Street Chapel there, which we did, and a very special place it was too, filled with the spirit of our illustrious founder. As we were coming away from there, we heard what sounded like a small bell ringing out across the city. It had a lovely sweet sound but, try as we might, we couldn't locate its source. Eventually we had to ask someone. 'Oh,' she said, 'that'll be St Pancras,' and she pointed us in the direction of the Guildhall. When we eventually stumbled upon it, it was no wonder we hadn't been able to find it ourselves, for it was the tiniest church any of us had ever seen. To give you a sense of just how small, there were six of us on that walking tour, and we could just about all fit into it at the same time. And it was very old too. The majority of it was built from coarse, local Heavitree stone around the thirteenth century, but the font is at least two hundred years older than that, and we were told that parts of the doorway were older still, most likely Saxon. You could sense the weight of all those years, and it was wonderful to think that Christians have been worshipping on that same spot for more than a thousand years. Now – we Methodists don't put much store by the notion of saints, do we, though we do respect the good deeds done by anyone, especially in the face of violent opposition? This tiny church in the heart of Exeter was dedicated to St Pancras who, legend has it, was a teenage boy killed by the Emperor Diocletian in 304AD. Well – whether that's true or not, we have no real way of knowing, but the courage that his story represents, that's something we can all of us understand. The church has no tower, but it does have a turret at the western end, and in there was the bell that we'd heard ringing out unseen across the city just a few moments before. We learned that this bell was medieval, more than five hundred years old, but still in full working order. On it, we were told, is a Latin inscription.

'*Quamvis sum parva*
tamen audior
ampla per arva…'

"Now, I wonder if our Classics scholar might translate that for us?" He gestured towards Mr Flitcroft, sitting on the back row.

"Well," replied Flitcroft, clearing his throat nervously and pulling at his collar, "I would say, '*I may be small, nevertheless I am heard over a wide distance*'." He then sat down to murmurs of appreciation all around him.

"Thank you. '*I may be small*'," repeated Reverend Appleby, " '*nevertheless I am heard over a wide distance.*' I don't know about the rest of you, but I reckon that's a pretty fair description of Hubert, don't you?"

Voices answering in agreement rippled around the congregation.

"And though his body may have left us, we're going to be hearing that bell of his ringing out across the city for many a year to come."

Councillor Grandage thumped the side of his pew rapidly five times with the flat of his hand in emphatic agreement with the Reverend Appleby's address, who looked up in his direction to nod his thanks.

"Let us pray."

After the prayers had all been said and the service had followed its more traditional liturgy of call and response, the Reverend finally brought the ceremony to a close.

"Before we leave today, we are to be treated to a musical item, which has been requested by Miss Lily Shilling who recently became the adopted daughter of Annie and Hubert, and who henceforward is to be known as Miss Lily Wright. It is to be sung by students from The Manchester School of Music under the direction of Miss Gertrude Riall, who will be able to introduce it to you far more eloquently than I. Miss Riall?"

Gertrude steps forward from where she has been sitting. She speaks quietly and nervously, so that the congregation has to lean forward to hear her.

"As most of you here will know already, Hubert died at the opening of Manchester Central Library, where the choir you are about to hear was singing at the time. Naturally we were all of us deeply distressed by what had happened, but Mrs Wright – Annie, as she insists I call her – said we were not to worry, for Hubert could not have been happier when he died. The music, she said, had, quite literally, transported him to another place. I have always felt that music has the power to do this, to take us outside of ourselves, and no music does this more profoundly in my opinion than that written for the human voice. It was Lily who wondered if we might be able to sing the anthem we are about to perform. She said that its composer was a particular favourite of Hubert's. I am sad to say that I never met Mr Wright. Having listened to the words of Reverend Appleby this morning, and having spoken to many of you as you arrived here, I am beginning to get a small indication of what a very special man he was. I wish I had met him, and I am honoured to have been asked to prepare this piece, which my students will shortly sing for you. It's a setting by Henry Purcell, of words taken from Sir Thomas Cranmer's Book of Common Prayer. *'Remember Not, Lord, Our Offences'.*"

On her signal the choir of fifteen students stands as one and walks to the front of the chapel, facing back towards the congregation, while she positions herself some feet further back in the centre of the aisle. Once she is satisfied they are all settled and that she has their complete attention, all eyes upon her, she raises her hands to bring them in. The first word, set as a simple block chord, hangs in the air, holding the congregation spellbound from the start. *'Remember.'*

"*Remember not, Lord, our offences*
Nor th' offences of our forefathers
Neither take thou vengeance of our sins
But spare us, good Lord…"

Lily, listening in the front row, is at once taken back to the night she left St Bridget's, when Jenny sang this tremblingly alone in the Convent Chapel in order to distract Sister Mary Frances of the Five Wounds for long enough to allow Sister Clodagh to give her the wooden boat made by her grandfather, which she has carried with her ever since, through the long nightmare of Globe Lane and Angel Meadow, the one connection she had with her lost, vanished family, before she was rescued by George, who sits beside her now, her adoptive older brother, her knight in shining armour, who rode with her on his charger to his home in Lapwing Lane, where she was taken in and cared for by this man she'd begun to regard like a father, who'd shared with her his love of words and music, so that this hymn by Purcell she'd at last been able to exorcise from its associations with her own unhappiness and hear it once again with the same fresh innocence and hope that she had experienced when she first heard Jenny sing it at St Bridget's.

Jenny is singing it today, too, but not alone. Instead she is subsumed within the harmony and counterpoint of the whole choir, singing in five full parts, in humble supplication, seeking solace and redemption, balm and reparation, for Hubert's damaged soul.

"Spare thy people, whom thou hast redeem'd
With thy most precious blood,
And be not angry with us for ever.
Spare us, good Lord…"

*

In the end Hubert's head stone bore no message other than his name, the year he was born, the year that he died, and the simple epithet, *'Son, Husband, Father, Printer'*.

"It's what he'd prefer," says George now, looking down upon it.

Annie nods. "I know," she says. "You're right. I just wish it were otherwise."

They stand in silence a few minutes longer, then George turns towards her. "I've decided what I shall do, Mother. I'll not try to step into Father's shoes, for I know that's not what he'd have wanted. 'You're your own man,' he'd have said. I'll give up the sign writing. I'll manage the Printing Works full time and, under your tutelage, Mother, I'll try and learn the other aspects of the business. But I'll still keep on with my photography, when time permits. I'll still go to Evening Classes at *The Mechanics' Institute*, and I'll drop down to just one night a week at the Speedway. I'll live at Portugal Street, if it's all right with you, for it'll be much more convenient for work, and for everything else I want to try to do, and I'll come round each Sunday to Lapwing Lane."

Annie squeezes his hand. "Thank you," she said. "As long as you don't give up the photography. Not now you're doing so well. Your father was so proud of you. And so am I. F.G. Wright *& Sons*," she says.

"& Sons," repeats George.

The following week, coming out of his freshly painted front door on Portugal Street, George finds himself singing *A Wandering Minstrel, I* from *The Mikado*.

"A thing of shreds and patches…"

He sets up his *Foth Derby* on its tripod and focuses it on the spindle tree just along the street, which is now thriving. Its roots have cracked the pavement, its canopy is more than twenty feet high and nearly as wide, its light green leaves, so shiny that they might have been waxed, are just beginning to turn orange, as if dipped in flame, and are smothered in epicene flowers of blood red.

George has decided that he will take a photograph of it every day for a year, documenting its changes through the seasons, beginning this morning, his first day as Manager at the Printing Works across the street.

As he looks through the viewfinder, a wren lands on one of the tree's slender branches. It bends gently beneath it, up and down, up and down, like a piece of muslin lying across a baby's mouth, rising and falling with each delicately exhaled breath. George waits until it is absolutely still, then presses the shutter.

He has begun.

Tulip continues in:
Volume 4: Return
(Ornaments of Grace, Book 5)

Dramatis Personae

(in order of appearance)

CAPITALS = Major Character; **Bold** = Significant Character;
Plain = appears once or twice

ANNIE WRIGHT, nee Warburton, husband of Hubert
HUBERT WRIGHT, a printer
Mr Samuel Warburton, Annie's father
Mrs Jessica Warburton, Annie's mother
FRANK WRIGHT, Hubert's father
EVELYN WRIGHT, Hubert's mother
Reverend William Lampton Appleby, Hulme Hall Methodist Chapel
Miss Agatha Aspinal, Chapel Organist
CLAUDIA LOCARTELLI, mother of Giulia and Paulie
GIULIA LOCARTELLI, Claudia's daughter
Paulie Locartelli, Claudia's son
Giovanni Locartelli, Claudia's father-in-law
Matteo Camapnella, Claudia's brother
MARCO LOCARTELLI, Claudia's husband
Jabez Chadwick, Head Gardener at Philips Park
Mary Chadwick, Jabez's wife
Harriet Chadwick, Jabez & Mary's daughter
Gracie Chadwick, Jabez & Mary's younger daughter
FRANCIS HALL, a sound recordist
GEORGE WRIGHT, Hubert & Annie's son
DELPHINE FISH, an audiologist
ESTHER WARD, now living in Patricroft
Harold Blundell, Esther's brother
Yasser Wahid, Esther's father-in-law
Jaz Wahid, Esther's husband
Rose Ward, Yasser's wife
CHARLES TREVELYAN, a surgeon at the Royal Infirmary
WINIFRED HOLT, a telegraphist

VICTOR COLLINS, a boxer and miner
Dr Wilkes, Annie's doctor
Albert Einstein
Joseph, doorman at Manchester Town Hall
Alderman Hardcastle
Councillor Clarence Grandage
Mr A.A. Flitcroft, Clerk of the Corporation
Stanley Houghton, playwright
Miss Anne Elizabeth Frederika Horniman, owner of The Gaiety Theatre
Alliot Verdon Roe, Managing Director of AVRO
Harry Heath, Hubert's deputy in the Printing Works
William 'Billy' Grimshaw, The Gramophone King
Father Pappalrdelli, St Alban's Church
Maurizio Campanella, Claudi's father
Giulia Magdalena Campanella, Claudia's mother
John Chadwick, Jabez's father
Filippo Tommaso Marinetti, founder of the Futurists
Dr Henry Miers, Vice Chancellor of Manchester University
Daniel Godfrey Jnr, Head of BBC in Manchester, 1922
Mrs Sylvia Tiffin, piano teacher
Mr Heinrich Vogts, George's English teacher at Hulme's GS
L.S. Lowry
Luigi Locartelli, Head Porter of Queen's Hotel
CHAMOMILE CATCH, a singer
Peter Ridgeway, classmate of George
Philip Rushton, classmate of George
David Randall, classmate of George
Archie Rowe, sign writer
Catch, a blacksmith
John Leeming, Lancashire Aero Club
Winnie Brown, aviatrix
M.K. Gandhi
Percy Davies, owner of Greenfield Mill, Darwen
LILY SHILLING, an orphan
Jenny, a friend of Lily
Pearl, another friend of Lily

Sister Clodah, a nun at St Bridget's
Sister Mary Frances of the Five Wounds, a nun
Mr Godwit, Globe Lane
Mrs Baines, Mr Godwit's housekeeper
Laura, Lily's predecessor at Globe Lane
Mr Snipe, Godwit's friend
Mr Crake, Godwit's friend
Miss Tyler, dressmaker
Myopic Security Guard, abandoned miner shaft
Man wearing fez with hookah pipe, Wilmslow Road
Duchess, an old woman feeding pigeons, Platt Fields
Top Hat, a tramp, Platt Fields
Long Ears, a tall man, Platt Fields
Comatose, small crouching man, Platt Fields
Smiling Girl in Tree, Platt Fields
Old Soldier with Medals, Southern Cemetery
Phoebe, flower seller St Ann's Square
The Twins, Spider & Web
Old Man with white hair and drooping moustache, Piccadilly
Gertrude Riall, a music teacher
Benny Rothman, leader of Mass Trespass
Mr Justice Acton, Derby Assizes
Prosecuting Council, Derby Assizes
Miss Isabel Wallman, Staff Librarian
Reverend William Appleby, Methodist Minister

The following are mentioned by name:

[Man in Friends Meeting House]
[Knocker Up on Nelson Street]
[Women walking to work in the Tripe Colony]
[The Lounge Ladies Orchestra, Vose & Sons, Wigan]
[Gordon Wright, Frank's father]
[Miss Letitia Dring, soubrette]
[John Wycliffe]
[John of Gaunt]

[The Lollards]
[Margaret Ness, school friend of Annie]
[Penny Williams, school friend of Annie]
[Ian Rogers, school friend of Annie]
[Michael Bell, school friend of Annie]
[Johannes Guttenberg]
[William Caxton]
[William Tyndale]
[Miles Coverdale]
[Platt Brothers, Oldham]
[Toyoda family, Kyushu]
[Mr Mather, Manager of Beehive Mill, Ancoats]
[Mr Eames, caretaker of Hulme Hall Chapel]
[Attenders at Hulme Hall Chapel Fête]
[Miss Gladys Hinckley, later Mrs Appleby]
[Two older ladies singing from The Mikado]
[Children dressed as Bumble Bees]
[Edward Judd, Clerk of Friends Meeting House, Mount Street]
[Clearness Committee]
[Oversight Committee]
[Jack Warburton, Annie's 11 year old brother]
[Congregation at Annie & Hubert's wedding]
[John Dalton]
[Professor Thompson, Professor Rutherford's teacher]
[Theseus]
[King Minos]
[Ariadne]
[Prometheus]
[Quigliotti & Stefanutti, tile makers]
[Mr James Scarlett, benefactor]
[Residents of Women's Refuge]
[Lady Mayoress, 1912]
[The Band of Hope Ladies Temperance Orchestra]
[Alderman Abel Heywood, Mayor of Manchester 1865]
[Joseph's sick child]
[Richard Cobden]
John Bright]
[James Joule]
[King Henry IV]
[Heraclitus]
[Plato]

[Jeremiah Horrocks]
[Alfred, Lord Tennyson]
[Sir Alfred Derbyshire, architect]
[Edyth Goodall, actress]
[Sybil Thorndyke, actress]
[Mr Houghton, Stanley's father]
[Harold Brighouse, playwright]
[Allan Monkhouse, playwright]
[Henrik Ibsen]
[George Bernard Shaw]
[W.B. Yeats]
[J.M. Synge]
[Stage Manager]
[Audience at The Gaiety]
[Mr Pitt Hardacre, manager of The Comedy Theatre]
[Dolly Stormont, music hall singer]
[Crowds in Accrington, Bacup, Blackburn, Rusholme to see King George & Queen Mary]
[Lord Derby, Lord Lieutenant of Lancashire]
[Walter Nuttall, conductor of Irwell Springs Brass Band]
[Prince Albert Victor, King George's late elder brother]
[Brigade of Army Reservists]
[Detachment of Life Guards]
[Corporation Chef]
[Staff of Wrights Printing Works]
[Tabitha, the ginger cat]
[Dr D.S. Brooks, Chemistry Dept, Manchester University]
[Orator Henry Hunt]
[Neville Cardus]
[John Alcock, trans-Atlantic pilot]
[Arthur Whitten Brown, navigator]
[Doctor at Oldham Royal Infirmary]
[Nurses at Oldham Royal Infirmary]
[Crowds at Royton Memorial]
[Chadderton & District Brass Band]
[Lewis Wyatt, designer of Heaton Park]
[Dollond's of London telescope makers]
[Waiter in The Reform Club, Spring Gardens]
[Wilhelm Goekerman, German physician]
[Saturday afternoon visitors to Heaton Park]
[Small boy with ball]

[Woman pushing a pram]
[Red beefy-faced gentleman]
[Sir Henry Wood]
[Elsie & Archie Bishop, old couple reminiscing in park]
[Signalman at Heaton Park Station]
[Park Keeper]
[Pygmalion]
[Orpheus]
[Enrico Caruso]
[Whit Walkers]
[Bands of the Italian Boys Brigades]
[Grandfather John Chadwick]
[Edward VII]
[Crowds in Philips Park for Caruso Concert]
[Courting Couples in Philips Park]
[Marocca & Mancini families from Jersey Street]
[Varetto & Rabino families from Blossom Street]
[Acaro & Gavioli families from Great Ancoats Street]
[Hurdy-Gurdy men]
[Zampgna players]
[Monkeys & Dancing Bears]
[Tarantella dancers]
[Street Vendors]
[Claudia's girl friends]
[Franco, Marco's friend's kid brother]
[Audience listening to Marinetti speak]
[Chair of the Manchester Lit & Phil]
[Tram Conductor]
[Abraham Lincoln]
[Professor Chaim Weizmann, Manchester Jewish Society]
Michael Faraday]
[Democritus]
[Euclid]
[Pythagoras]
[Professor Arthur Stanley Eddington]
[C.T.R. Wilson, physicist]
[Mr Arthur Burrows, Director of Programmes for BBC Radio]
[John Reith, BBC General Manager]
[Ambrose, Geraldo, Roy Fox, Carroll Gibbon, dance band leaders]
[Pierre Adolphe Valette]
[Sailors on board a Manchester Liners ship]

[Crowds on Trafford Park Road Swing Bridge]
[Thomas Hobbes]
[Prostitutes beneath railway arches around Castlefield]
[Pedestrians and pub-goers on Deansgate]
[Men outside Unitarian Chapel]
[Dinner-suited men inside The Athenaeum]
[Young man asking Francis for a light in Piccadilly Gardens]
[Louis Mitchell's Jazz Kings]
[Ambassador for Ecuador + Guest]
[Bellhops at The Quuen's Hotel]
[Thomas Cooper]
[Alfonso, Head Porter of The Queen's before Luigi]
[Samuel Mendel, Manchester merchant]
[Buffalo Bill]
[Iain Grant, artist]
[Karl Hagerdon, artist]
[Emanuel Levy, artist]
[Anne Swynnerton, artist]
[Margaret Nicholls, artist]
[Peter O'Brien, artist]
[Edgar Rowley Smart, artist]
[Alice Bailey, née Bateman, author]
[People attending Private View of inaugural exhibition of Manchester Society of Modern Painters]
[Angry crowds, St Peter's Square]
[R. Tattershall, Manager of Bradford Colliery 1926]
[Police officers patrolling locked colliery]
[Funeral Director]
[Mourners at Funeral]
[Bradford Colliery Brass Band]
[TUC Parade]
[Marchers in support of Miners]
[Crowds outside closed railway stations]
[Row of telephonists]
[Lord Harding]
[Admiral Jellicoe]
[Corporation Official, Town Hall]
[Police Officers, Albert Square]
[Journalist. Manchester Guardian]
[Sub-Editor, Manchester Guardian]
[News Vendor]

[Passengers on crowded tram]
[Union Convener, Manchester Tramways Co]
[Workers at Meeting]
[Office worker, Manchester Guardian]
[Small crowd, Withy Grove]
[Jostling crowds, Piccadilly Square]
[Women office workers standing at tram stop wearing ribbons]
[Police Officer punched by Victor]
[Magistrate, Manchester Assizes]
[Chauffeur for Mr John Sutton MP]
[Children on Portugal Street]
[Workers in Wright's Printing Works]
[Lorry Driver, Victoria Station Approach]
[Picnicking crowds, Platt Fields]
[Lord Mayor, 1926]
[Waiting passengers, Exchange Station]
[Vicar, driving steam train]
[Two striking Engine Drivers]
[Relay of people loading sacks of flour into lorries]
[Volunteer Female Lorry Driver]
[Protesters, Sutcliffe's Flour Mill]
[Police officers, Sutcliffe's Flour Mill]
[Soldiers, Pomona Docks]
[Marching Miners with Davy Lamps]
[Applauding crowds along route of march]
[Women and children begging on streets]
[Arthur, Earl Balfour]
[Disapproving Librarians, Levenshulme Library]
[Henry V]
[Black Prince]
[Major-General Anderson, Director Belle Vue Greyhound Track]
[Charles Munn, US entrepreneur]
[Brigadier Alfred Critchley]
[Sir William Gentle, JP]
[Crowds at Dog Track]
[Dog handlers]
[Johnnie Hoskins, Australian motor cycle enthusiast]
[Eric Spence, Speedway promoter]
[Frank Varey, speedway rider]
[Eric Langton, speedway rider]
[John Prestwich, motor cycle engineer]

[Sebastian Pietro Innocenti di Ferrante, engineer]
[William Friese-Green, inventor and photographer]
[Franks, instrument makers, Deansgate]
[Francis's Bank Manager]
[Henry E. Bliss, US Librarian]
[Sigmund Freud]
[Edward Young]
[Edwin of Northumbria]
[Humphrey Chetham]
[Mr Emanuel Vincent Harris, architect of Central Reference Library]
[William James Morley, designer of Albert Mission Hall]
[Mr J. Gerrard of Swinton, builder of Albert Mission]
[General Sir William Thwaites, Commander of The Manchester Regiment]
[Man leaving The Bull's Head]
[Peter Ridgeway's Uncle Colin]
[Joseph Goebbels]
[Adolph Hitler]
[Horace]
[Robert Merrick]
[Arthur Quiller-Couch]
[Mr Sawyer, manager of DOT motor cycle factory, Ellesmere Street]
[Miss Brown, George's teacher at Elementary School]
[Anita Jones, girl who sat in front of George at school]
[Robert Frost]
[Billcliff's, camera stockists, Altrincham]
[Tommy Johnson, Manchester City footballer]
[Harry Rowley, Manchester United footballer]
[Willie Stephenson, jockey]
[Jack Tyldesley, Lancashire cricketer]
[Betty's Bkaery]
[Mr Constantinos, confectioner]
[Mr Eastman of Kodak]
[Houghtons & Butchers, camera manufacturers, Manchester]
[Kochman, Dresdedn camera manufacturer]
[Emanuel Goldmann, designer of the Kinamo]
[Zeiss, maker of cine cameras, Dresden]
[Eccles Borough Subscription Brass Band]
[James Dow, conductor]
[Henry Walford Davies, composer]
[John Bloom, Mayor of Salford]

[Sir Robert Noton Barclay, former Lord Mayor of Manchester]
[George Frank Titt, unwell Lord Mayor]
[Zio Leo, Giulia's Uncle Leonardo]
[Prince Edward & Prince George]
[Flight Lieutenant Richard Atcherley, pilot]
[Granville Bantock, composer]
[Ruth Elder, film star]
[Ellen Sedgwick, film star]
[Bebe Daniels, film star]
[Alan Butler, pilot]
[Lois Butler, pilot]
[Sir Geoffrey de Haviland, pilot & aircraft designer]
[Diana Guest, pilot]
[Captain Ian C. Maxwell, pilot]
[Flight Lieutenant Tompkins, Barret & Pope, pilots]
[Mr E.G. Hordern, pilot]
[Gustav Holst]
[Harriet Quimby US aviatrix]
[Rose's doctor]
[Ambulancemen from Hope Hospital]
[Josef von Sternberg]
[Marlene Dietrich]
[Squadron Leader David Don]
[Commander Harold Perrin, secretary Royal Aero Club]
[Children playing in Angel Meadow]
[Miss Madeleine 'Mirabehn' Slade, follower of Gandhi]
[French politicians, Marseiile]
[Crowds waving to Gandhi]
[Gandhi's driver]
[Gusta Green, ten years old, presenting posy to Gandhi]
[Members of Corporation Library Sub-Committee]
[Girls at St Bridget's]
[Rodin]
[Married couple in Art Gallery]
[Keats]
[St Theresa of Avila]
{Bertolt Brecht]
[Kurt Weill]
[Mary Moffat, later Livingstone]
[Mary's parents]
[David Livingstone]

[Gardener at Globe Lane]
[Boy who helps gardener]
[Mrs Cloudsdale, Cook at Globe Lane]
[Dinner Guests, Globe Lane]
[Johann Strauss]
[Servant Girl, Globe Lane]
[Clarence Williams Blue Five}
[Louis Armstrong]
[Sidney Bechet]
[Sippie Wallace]
[Schubert]
[Hancock's jewellers on King Street]
[Laura's mother]
[Mrs Baines's sick son]
[John Frederick Bateman, engineer Audenshaw Reservoirs]
[Cyclists, drivers, Wilmslow Road]
[Elizabeth Saisbury Heywood, benefactress]
[Oliver Cromwell
[Commuters, Exchange Station]
[Cotton merchants, Royal Exchange]
[Phoebe's grandmother, a phrenologist]
[Well-dressed gentlemen coming out of banks]
[John Cassidy, sculptor]
[Drunkards, addicts, dealers, pimps, mollies, toms in Piccadilly Gardens]
[Onslow Ford, sculptor]
[Stallholders on Tib Street selling birds and animals]
[Booksellers, Shude Hill]
[Augustus Leopold Egg, painter]
[Prostitutes on Angel Meadow]
[Punters on Angel Meadow]
[St Catherine of Alexandria]
[Emperor Maxentius]
[Hanns Eisler]
[Ladies in the Oak Room after shopping]
[Waiters, Oak Room]
[Couple in corner of Oak Room]
[Woman waiting alone in Oak Room]
[Young man late for assignation]
[George Elgar Hicks]
[Bernard Sleigh, illustrator]

[William Morris]
[Ramblers on Kinder Scout
[Gamekeepers on Kinder Scout]
[Members of British Workers Sports Federation, Manchester branch]
[Police officers, Hayfield]
[Duke of Devonshire]
[Chief Superintendents Macdonald & Else]
[Mr Herbert Bradshaw, Clerk Hayfield Parish Council]
[Julius Clyne, accomplice of Rothman]
[Harry Mendel, accomplice of Rothman]
[David Nussbaum, accomplice of Rothman]
[Jimmy Miller, aka Ewan McColl]
[Mr Justice MacKinnon, Chester Assisez]
[Protesters at 2nd Mass Trespass]
[Men & Women featured in George's portraits]
[T.S. Eliot]
[Fish Man]
[Miss Brooks, milliner]
[Mrs Telford, Central Methodist Hall Committee Member]
[Zio Leo's wife]
[Office girls, Antonelli's]
[Jean Harlow]
[Janet Gaynor]
[Charles Farrell, screen actor]
[Kuroda Seikli, painter]
[Alderman Joseph Binns JP, Lord Mayor of Manchester 1943]
[Plumbers, welders, electricians, carpenters, stonemasons, decorators Central Reference Library]
[Rudolf Koch, designer of type fonts]
[Paul Renner, designer of type fonts]
[Otto Beckman, designer of type fonts]
[Peter Behrens, designer of type fonts]
[Vasari]
[Michaelangelo]
[Scaffolders]
[Sir Edwin Lutyens]
[Seneca the Younger]
[Epictetus]
[Miss Higham, A.A. Flitcroft's secretary]
[Plato]

[Alderman George Binns, Lord Mayor 1934]
[Lady Mayoress]
[Sir John Maxwell, Chief Constable]
[Lord Stanley]
[Miss Ruth Primrose, Lord Stanley's fiancée]
[Dowager Countess of Airlee]
[Honourable Oliver Stanley, Secreatry of State for Armed Forces]
[Lady Stanley]
[Earl of Sefton]
[Major Archibald Hradynge, Palace Private Secretary]
[Captain Marcus Bullock, Equerry-in-Waiting]
[Lieutenant-Colonel Reginald Harris Seymour, Equerry-in-Waiting]
[Bishop James Fraser]
[William Ewart Gladstone]
[Lietenant-General Sir Willoughby Marchant St George Kirke]
[Major-General Kenneth Gerald Buchanan]
[Captain Charles Henry Keithley]
[Attachment of Territorial Army Nursing Division]
[Mr John Arthur Strange, Director Wm Moss & Sons, Principal Contractors]
[Mr Alan Smith, Clerk of the Works]
[Mr Walter Bird, Chief Foreman]
[Thomas Moss & Sons, watchmakers]
[Crowds lining streets for Royal Visit]
[Ludwig Blattner, inventor of the Blattnerphone]
[John Logie Baird]
[Chief Librarian]
[Mrs Rosa Grindon, philanthropist]
[Leo Grindon, Manchester botanist]
[William Shakespeare]
[Giovanni Ciniselli, sculptor]
[Singers from the Manchester School of Music]
[Edward Judd, a Quaker]
[St Pancras]
[Emperor Diocletlan]
[Sir Thomas Cranmer]
[Henry Purcell]
[Thomas Shadwell]

Acknowledgements
(for *Ornaments of Grace* as a whole)

Writing is usually considered to be a solitary practice, but I have always found the act of creativity to be a collaborative one, and that has again been true for me in putting together the sequence of novels which comprise *Ornaments of Grace*. I have been fortunate to have been supported by so many people along the way, and I would like to take this opportunity of thanking them all, with apologies for any I may have unwittingly omitted.

First of all I would like to thank Ian Hopkinson, Larysa Bolton, Tony Lees and other staff members of Manchester's Central Reference Library, who could not have been more helpful and encouraging. That is where the original spark for the novels was lit and it has been such a treasure trove of fascinating information ever since. I would like to thank Jane Parry, the Neighbourhood Engagement & Delivery Officer for the Archives & Local History Dept of Manchester Library Services for her support in enabling me to use individual reproductions of the remarkable Manchester Murals by Ford Madox Brown, which can be viewed in the Great Hall of Manchester Town Hall. They are exceptional images and I recommend you going to see them if you are ever in the vicinity. I would also like to thank the staff of other libraries and museums in Manchester, namely the John Rylands Library, Manchester University Library, the Manchester Museum, the People's History Museum and also Salford's Working Class Movement Library, where Lynette Cawthra was especially helpful, as was Aude Nguyen Duc at The Manchester Literary & Philosophical Society, the much-loved Lit& Phil, the first and oldest such society anywhere in the world, 238 years young and still going strong.

In addition to these wonderful institutions, I have many individuals to thank also. Barbara Derbyshire from the Moravian Settlement in Fairfield has been particularly patient and generous with her time in telling me so much of the community's inspiring history. No less inspiring has been Lauren Murphy, founder of the Bradford Pit Project, which is a most moving collection of anecdotes, memories, reminiscences, artefacts and original art works dedicated to the lives of people connected with Bradford Colliery. You can find out more about their work at: www.bradfordpit.com. Martin Gittins freely shared some of his encyclopaedic knowledge of the part the River Irwell has played in Manchester's story, for which I have been especially grateful.

I should also like to thank John and Anne Horne for insights into historical medical practice; their daughter, Ella, for inducting me into the mysteries of chemical titration, which, if I have subsequently got it wrong, is my fault not hers; Tony Smith for his deep first hand understanding of spinning and weaving; Sarah Lawrie for inducting me so enthusiastically into the Manchester music scene of the 1980s, which happened just after I left the city so I missed it; Sylvia Tiffin for her previous research into Manchester's lost theatres, and Brian Hesketh for his specialist knowledge in a range of such diverse topics as hot air balloons, how to make a crystal radio set, old maps, the intricacies of a police constable's notebook and preparing reports for a coroner's inquest.

Throughout this intensive period of writing and research, I have been greatly buoyed up by the keen support and interest of many friends, most notably Theresa Beattie, Laïla Diallo, Viv Gordon, Phil King, Rowena Price, Gavin Stride, Chris Waters, and Irene Willis. Thank you to you all. In addition, Sue & Rob Yockney have been extraordinarily helpful in more ways than I can mention. Their advice on so many matters, both artistic and practical, has been beyond measure.

A number of individuals have very kindly – and bravely – offered to read early drafts of the novels: Bill Bailey, Rachel Burn, Lucy Cash, Chris & Julie Phillips. Their responses have been positive, constructive, illuminating and encouraging, particularly when highlighting those passages which needed closer attention from me, which I have tried my best to address. Thank you.

I would also like to pay a special tribute to my friend Andrew Pastor, who has endured months and months of fortnightly coffee sessions during which he has listened so keenly and with such forbearance to the various difficulties I may have been experiencing at the time. He invariably came up with the perfect comment or idea, which then enabled me to see more clearly a way out of whatever tangle I happened to have found myself in. He also suggested several avenues of further research I might undertake to navigate towards the next bend in one of the three rivers, all of which have been just what were needed. These books could not have finally seen the light of day without his irreplaceable input.

Finally I would like to thank my wife, Amanda, for her endless patience, encouragement and love. These books are dedicated to her and to our son, Tim.

Biography

Chris grew up in Manchester and currently lives in West Dorset, after brief periods in Nottinghamshire, Devon and Brighton. Over the years he has managed to reinvent himself several times – from florist's delivery van driver to Punch & Judy man, drama teacher, theatre director, community arts co-ordinator, creative producer, to his recent role as writer and dramaturg for choreographers and dance companies.

Between 2003 and 2009 Chris was Director of Dance and Theatre for *Take Art*, the arts development agency for Somerset, and between 2009 and 2013 he enjoyed two stints as Creative Producer with South East Dance leading on their Associate Artists programme, followed by a year similarly supporting South Asian dance artists for *Akademi* in London. From 2011 to 2017 he was Creative Producer for the Bonnie Bird Choreography Fund.

Chris has worked for many years as a writer and theatre director, most notably with New Perspectives in Nottinghamshire and Farnham Maltings in Surrey under the artistic direction of Gavin Stride, with whom Chris has been a frequent collaborator.

Directing credits include: three Community Plays for the Colway Theatre Trust – *The Western Women* (co-director with Ann Jellicoe), *Crackling Angels* (co-director with Jon Oram), and *The King's Shilling*; for New Perspectives – *It's A Wonderful Life* (co-director with Gavin Stride), *The Railway*

Children (both adapted by Mary Elliott Nelson); for Farnham Maltings – *The Titfield Thunderbolt, Miracle on 34th Street* and *How To Build A Rocket* (all co-directed with Gavin Stride); for Oxfordshire Touring Theatre Company – *Bowled A Googly* by Kevin Dyer; for Flax 303 – *The Rain Has Voices* by Shiona Morton, and for Strike A Light *I Am Joan* and *Prescribed*, both written by Viv Gordon and co-directed with Tom Roden, and *The Book of Jo* as dramaturg.

Theatre writing credits include: *Firestarter, Trying To Get Back Home, Heroes* – a trilogy of plays for young people in partnership with Nottinghamshire & Northamptonshire Fire Services; *You Are Harry Kipper & I Claim My Five Pounds, It's Not Just The Jewels, Bogus* and *One of Us* (the last co-written with Gavin Stride) all for New Perspectives; *The Birdman* for Blunderbus; for Farnham Maltings *How To Build A Rocket* (as assistant to Gavin Stride), and *Time to Remember* (an outdoor commemoration of the centenary of the first ever Two Minutes Silence); *When King Gogo Met The Chameleon* and *Africarmen* for Tavaziva Dance, and most recently *All the Ghosts Walk with Us* (conceived and performed with Laïla Diallo and Phil King) for ICIA, Bath University and Bristol Old Vic Ferment Festival, (2016-17); *Posting to Iraq* (performed by Sarah Lawrie with music by Tom Johnson for the inaugural Women & War Festival in London 2016), and *Tree House* (with music by Sarah Moody, which toured southern England in autumn 2016). In 2018 Chris was commissioned to write the text for *In Our Time*, a film to celebrate the 40th Anniversary of the opening of The Brewhouse Theatre in Taunton, Somerset.

Between 2016 and 2019 Chris collaborated with fellow poet Chris Waters and Jazz saxophonist Rob Yockney to develop two touring programmes of poetry, music, photography and film: *Home Movies* and *Que Pasa?*

Chris regularly works with choreographers and dance artists, offering dramaturgical support and business advice. These have included among others: Alex Whitley, All Play, Ankur Bahl, Antonia Grove, Anusha Subramanyam, Archana

Ballal, Ballet Boyz, Ben Duke, Ben Wright, Charlie Morrissey, Crystal Zillwood, Darkin Ensemble, Divya Kasturi, Dog Kennel Hill, f.a.b. the detonators, Fionn Barr Factory, Heather Walrond, Hetain Patel, Influx, Jane Mason, Joan Clevillé, Kali Chandrasegaram, Kamala Devam, Karla Shacklock, Khavita Kaur, Laïla Diallo, Lîla Dance, Lisa May Thomas, Liz Lea, Lost Dog, Lucy Cash, Luke Brown, Marisa Zanotti, Mark Bruce, Mean Feet Dance, Nicola Conibère, Niki McCretton, Nilima Devi, Pretty Good Girl, Probe, Rachael Mossom, Richard Chappell, Rosemary Lee, Sadhana Dance, Seeta Patel, Shane Shambhu, Shobana Jeyasingh, Showmi Das, State of Emergency, Stop Gap, Subathra Subramaniam, Tavaziva Dance, Tom Sapsford, Theo Clinkard, Urja Desai Thakore, Vidya Thirunarayan, Viv Gordon, Yael Flexer, Yorke Dance Project (including the Cohan Collective) and Zoielogic.

Chris is married to Amanda Fogg, a former dance practitioner working principally with people with Parkinson's.

Printed in Great Britain
by Amazon